KU-333-012

Testimony of Two Men

TAYLOR CALDWELL, an Englishwoman by birth, has lived in America since 1906 when her family emigrated to New York State. After many years of research, writing and discouragement her novel *Dynasty of Death* was published in 1938: an immediate bestseller, it launched her on a spectacularly successful writing career.

Since then she has published thirty-one more books – the most recent is *Ceremony of the Innocent* – with settings ranging from modern and nineteenth-century America back to the golden age of Athens and the legendary kingdom of Atlantis. Two of her most famous bestsellers, *Captains and the Kings* and *Testimony of Two Men*, have now been made into successful television series.

Available in Fontana by the same author

Captains and the Kings
The Wide House
Melissa
Dear and Glorious Physician
The Arm and the Darkness
Great Lion of God
The Beautiful is Vanished
Dynasty of Death
The Eagles Gather
The Final Hour
Let Love Come Last
The Romance of Atlantis
Tender Victory
There Was a Time
A Prologue to Love
This Side of Innocence
Glory and the Lightning

TAYLOR CALDWELL

Testimony of Two Men

It is also written in your law that the
testimony of two men is true. JOHN 8: 17

Collins
FONTANA BOOKS

First published in 1969 by William Collins Sons & Co Ltd
First issued in Fontana Books 1971
Second Impression January 1975
Third Impression September 1977
Fourth Impression November 1977

© Reback & Reback 1968

Made and printed in Great Britain by
William Collins Sons and Co Ltd Glasgow

All the characters in this book are fictitious
and any resemblance to actual persons,
living or dead, is purely coincidental.

CONDITIONS OF SALE
This book is sold subject to the condition
that it shall not, by way of trade or otherwise,
be lent, re-sold, hired out or otherwise circulated
without the publisher's prior consent in any form of
binding or cover other than that in which it is
published and without a similar condition
including this condition being imposed
on the subsequent purchaser

FOREWORD

I first heard this story of 'Jonathan Ferrier' when I was a little girl, and I heard it from our family physician.

The history of medicine has its martyrs as well as the history of religion. Though many know the Saints who died for them, by name, few know the names of the physicians who lived and fought for them, and who were as dedicated to humanity as the Saints themselves.

Few know the names of the men who brought asepsis to modern hospitals, and immunology, yet millions of us now living would not be alive now except for those men. Millions of diabetics are following healthy and productive lives because of insulin— but how many know the name of the man who saved them? Children are now in school who would have died except for the men who formulated vaccines for diphtheria and smallpox and poliomyelitis, but how many remember them?

Scores of these heroes suffered ignominy, exile, ridicule and dishonour to save us. Some were driven mad and to suicide. Yet, they persisted.

Among them was the man, always unknown to me, but whom I have named 'Jonathan Ferrier' in this book. If he seems somewhat excessive and bellicose, he was fighting for the lives of all of us who were born, as I was born, in the twentieth century. He was one of thousands, unwept, unhonoured and unsung, and remembered, perhaps, only by God.

TAYLOR CALDWELL

Dedicated with respect and admiration to the memories of those men who, like Jonathan Ferrier, suffered so much and fought so hard to bring us modern medicine's blessings.

CHAPTER 1

When young Robert Sylvester Morgan had occasion to write his mother he always made what he wryly called 'a first draft.' This was done on foolscap paper (he had been taught thrift) and then recopied on a better grade where he could use his elegant Spenserian—which he loathed—in a way to please his mother, and in words and phrases which would not startle her.

> 8th June, 1901
> Hambledon, Pennsylvania
> Quaker Hotel

'Dear Mama:

(He paused. Why in hell wouldn't she let him call her 'Mother'? 'Mama,' at his age, for God's sake!)

'You will be happy to know that matters have culminated successfully since I arrived here a week ago. Hambledon is a beautiful town of about twenty-five thousand people, not to be compared with Philadelphia, of course, but adequate and lively. It is situated on the river, quite broad near at hand, almost a bay, and studded, here and there, with pretty islands. Very picturesque.

'The people are pleasant and friendly and very civil. There is considerable industry but it is located near the fringes of the town so that the air is clear and fresh, an excellent thing for your arthritis and asthma. Though on the water, the atmosphere seems dry. There appears to be little poverty and the working-class is energetic. The better sections of the town are charming, with broad streets, fine old lawns, magnificent trees—elms, birches, oaks, pines, spruces—and houses which would be considered impressive even in Philadelphia. I have already selected four for your choice and approval, and will take you about to them when you arrive next week. Any of them would delight you. (Would they? Nothing delighted his mother very much. Perhaps he was being uncharitable, or even irritable. He had never felt this way towards his mother before. He paused to wonder, then shook his head, baffled.)

'Behind the town rises a whole ridge of mountains, inspiring at dawn. (He had seen the dawn only once this week and then

7

inadvertently, but his mother liked the mention of dawns.) The very best people live on the lower reaches of the mountains in splendid residences. As for hospitals, the most important things to me at this time, there is one great one, called The Friends', though it is not exactly Quakerish. It is partly town-supported. The other hospital is private and select and very expensive. To be on the staff is something to be coveted.

'Hambledon's hospitals serve not only the town but the villages and the farms outside, and have the best of reputations. In fact, the hospitals here would be admired even in Philadelphia or Boston or New York. Very modern. (He frowned at the last word; his mother could not bear anything 'modern.' But he let it remain.) I confess I was agreeably surprised. I have met a number of physicians and surgeons here, all enlightened men and all gentlemen with distinguished reputations. Three are regularly called into consultation in Philadelphia, Pittsburgh and even New York, for they are specialists in their field. One of them (he winced) is Dr Jonathan Ferrier, though you may find that hard to believe. But I have read his lectures and his articles in the organ of the American Medical Association, and I can assure you that he is greatly esteemed.'

He wrote faster now: 'It is my belief, based on constant association with Dr Ferrier, that he has been a much-maligned man, and that he was truly innocent of his wife's death. I need not recall to you that he was forced to demand a change of venue from Hambledon to Philadelphia in order to get a fair trial. But the Philadelphia newspapers were hardly more just than the newspapers in Hambledon. However, as you know, he was acquitted. He has had his licence to practise restored. But he is very embittered. He has talked little with me on the matter, but quite enough to arouse my own indignation. I can't blame him for his resolute decision not to practise in Hambledon any longer. He was once the most popular surgeon in the town, and his family is well-bred, established, wealthy and highly respected. Old settlers. (His mother loved old settlers.) But you will remember all this was aired in the newspapers. I have met his mother, a great lady though somewhat of an invalid. Mrs Ferrier is very anxious to meet you and make you welcome. (A rich lie, but certain to elate his mother.)

'Dr Ferrier is not certain of his future plans at this time, though he mentioned going abroad for some time. I imagine he will finally settle in New York. He had helped to build up both the hospitals, using his own money lavishly, and was very devoted to The Poor. (His mother approved of 'The Poor,' provided they never crossed her path except to furnish her with competent servants.) He feels that never again can he feel any friendliness for the people of the community, considering their hostility towards him after his young wife's death, their conviction of his guilt prior to his trial in Philadelphia and during it, and what he calls their "disappointment" when he was acquitted. He was shabbily treated. (Robert underlined this. His mother, herself, though never having met Dr Ferrier, had detested him upon reading the newspaper accounts and had been 'disappointed,' herself, upon the acquittal. She was still certain he was guilty.)

'Now the town feels very righteous when it accuses him of "deserting" his own people. Some are beginning to remember his devotion to them, the free wards he built, and the excellent nursing schools he insisted on establishing in the hospitals. They cannot understand, they claim, why he wishes to leave them! Is that not a commentary on human nature? I sometimes thought, when I was a child, that you were slightly rigorous concerning human nature, but now I know you were correct. (That ought to soften her!)

'There are still currents here.' (He stared at these words, pursing up his lips. Then he crossed them out. His mother couldn't endure 'currents' of any kind. She considered them impertinent and ill-bred and not to be countenanced at all. Gentlefolk never had 'currents' in their lives. All was serenity —if they were gentlefolk.) He substituted: 'Dr Ferrier's colleagues have tried to persuade him not to leave, but he is adamant. His mother is neutral on the subject. But his decision is very fortunate for me. We have come to an agreeably mutual decision on the price of his practice, etc. His offices, very large, very handsome, are near his house, where he lives with his mother, and are marvellously well appointed. He had a telephone extension from his offices to his residence, so that he could be called in an emergency, and respond without delay. He now refuses all petitions except from old patients who stood by him during his unfortunate trouble.

'One of the houses I have in mind for us is near those offices, so it will be most convenient for me when I set up practice here. Dr Ferrier has already introduced me to the most influential doctors and other citizens, and at the cost of modesty I must admit that they appeared to approve of

9

me and my credentials, though this will be my first practice. They were impressed that I interned at Johns Hopkins.

'The rent Dr Ferrier has asked me for the offices is most reasonable. I am sure you will be pleased. All in all, I feel extraordinarily lucky in obtaining this practice, though you would have preferred that I practise in Philadelphia. But when you see Hambledon, and breathe its delightful fresh air, and meet the ladies of the town, and understand my good fortune, you will feel reconciled. A young doctor in Philadelphia, in his first practice, has a miserable time—as I have discovered. Jealousy on the part of established doctors is not unknown in Philadelphia; they are very proud of their prerogatives. I did not meet with this attitude in Hambledon. They welcomed me, though they remain stiff with Dr Ferrier because of his decision to leave them. Their position seems to be, "We have forgiven you. Why can't you forgive us?" I find that very unreasonable. Do you not think so? (Of course, she wouldn't think so. She would consider it very magnanimous on the part of the other physicians and surgeons to 'forgive' Dr Ferrier for a crime he had not committed, and she would also consider his rejection of them as 'unpardonable.' What's wrong with me lately? young Dr Morgan asked of himself. I never had these thoughts of my mother before I came here; I was always the dutiful son, saying, 'Yes, Mama, you are quite right, Mama,' when I knew damn' well, in my heart, that the old girl was not only a prig but somewhat stupid, too, and pretentious.)

'I have already rented a fine rig with two spirited black horses. Dr Ferrier rarely uses any vehicles around the town, since his acquittal. He rides horseback, and has a wonderful stable of his own.'

The young man considered. Then he deleted these remarks about Dr Ferrier. His mother would be outraged at such a lack of 'gentility.' 'Mama,' he said aloud, 'you are an ass.' His own remark shocked him for a moment, then he grinned and straightened his young shoulders under the excellent broadcloth of his suit. After all, it was time for the old girl to remember that he was no longer a child and no longer dependent upon her.

He removed the big gold watch, which had belonged to his doctor father before his death, looked at it, saw that it was almost ten o'clock, and that Dr Ferrier was calling for him soon. He replaced the watch in his vest pocket and straightened

10

the heavy gold watch chain over his paunchless front. He concluded his letter with a flurry of affectionate remarks, then set out to recopy the edited paragraphs. Upon conclusion, it seemed to him a very priggish letter, itself, but just what his mother would expect. The unexpected, to her, was outrageous. Nothing unexpected occurred to the well-bred, certainly nothing dishevelled. Such a life, thought the young man, feeling exhilarated by his new objectivity. How he'd like to lure her into an obstetrical ward! Or a V.D. one, for instance, not that she'd ever heard of venereal disease and the surprising numbers of the 'gentry' who turned up there regularly! She had never heard of a D&C, he was sure. Ladies did not have uteri. Their children 'emerged' gracefully from undefined regions.

Robert lit a cigarette and relaxed, smiling thoughtfully through the window. It was a gorgeous June day, and the town was scented with its own roses and lilies and warm lawns. Sun poured down the green and purple mountains in an avalanche of sparkling light, and there was a feeling of vivacity in the air which was not present in plodding Philadelphia. He could see the river from where he sat in his hotel room on the fifth floor. It ran with colour, violet and green and shimmering blue, curving and broadening about the town. He saw the ferry-boat bustling across the water to the other side, and heard its tooting. He saw other busy river traffic. And there was that island called 'Heart's Ease.' Yes, it was heart-shaped, and the largest island in the broad river, but only a woman could think of such a sickening name. It lay quite deeply in the water, and Robert could see the tops of its many crowding trees and a glimpse of the grey granite walls that hedged it in almost completely.

Dr Ferrier's brother, Harald, and the latter's daughter, lived there all alone except for three servants. This was all young Robert knew of the island, except that Harald's dead wife's first husband had bought the island and had built what was called 'the castle' on it, because, on his honeymoon, he had become enamoured of the river and the island. He had never lived there himself. But his widow had lived there prior to her marriage to Harald, and then for the two short years she had survived after that marriage. Dr Ferrier had told Robert that much, but no more. He appeared reticent on the subject. He had mentioned that his brother had inherited a great fortune from his wife, or at least the huge income on it, for his life-

11

time so long as he lived on the island. The daughter had inherited only one hundred dollars a month pocket-money. However, if Harald should tire of the arrangement, and leave the island permanently, he would receive only fifty thousand dollars and the money, in trust, would revert to the daughter. Jennifer? Jenny? Something like that. If Harald married again he would receive only twenty-five thousand dollars as a 'wedding gift' from his first wife.

Mrs Ferrier's first husband had owned a tremendous steel mill in Pittsburgh, and oil wells in Titusville. Income from both continued to bloat the trust. Very, very nice. There had been no envy in Dr Ferrier's voice when he had given these facts to Robert. But his dark face had become sardonic, and closed, and Robert's curiosity, always very lively, was much stimulated. 'Your much older brother?' he had asked with pardonable avidity.

'No,' said Jonathan Ferrier, and had appeared amused. 'My younger brother. I'm thirty-five. Harald's thirty-three.'

'The child must be just a baby,' Robert had suggested.

Dr Ferrier had seemed even more amused. He had changed the subject. No, he was not envious of all that money. He was a rich man, himself, inherited as well as earned money. His mother had been a Farmington of Philadelphia, and everyone knew that the Farmingtons were immensely wealthy. It was rumoured that the Ferriers had come from France, or Belgium, over two hundred years ago and had always lived in this vicinity. Dr Ferrier owned three rich farms nearby, which he rented out.

'Never deprecate money,' Dr Ferrier had told Robert. 'Poverty is no crime, but the populace doesn't really believe that. You can be a saint with all the heroic virtues, but if you have no money you'll be despised.'

It was Dr Ferrier's wealth, the newspapers had more than hinted, which had procured his acquittal, for he had been able to 'buy' the very best lawyers in Philadelphia, a city noted for its lawyers.

Robert, in his hotel room, and waiting to be called by Dr Ferrier for another tour of the town, thought about the accusations and the trial, which had occupied the first pages in the Philadelphia papers for months. Dr Ferrier had been charged with performing a botched abortion on his young wife, Mavis, which had resulted in her death two days later. That had happened nearly a year ago. The defence had had to struggle for weeks to obtain an unprejudiced jury. Dr Ferrier had testified in his own defence. He had not been in Hambledon at the time of the alleged abortion, but in Pittsburgh, and he had witnesses. He had not even known that his wife was pregnant. She had never told him.

'We had been married over three years,' he had testified calmly. 'There were no children. My wife didn't want any. She had always had a delicate constitution.' He had hesitated here. 'Yes, I wanted children— No, I can't even hazard a guess at the name of the abortionist. My wife died of septicaemia, of course, as a result of the abortion. I am a surgeon. If I had performed the abortion myself, it wouldn't have been botched, I assure you!'

The witnesses called for the defence had been distinguished doctors and surgeons, themselves. They not only testified that Dr Ferrier, indeed, could not have performed such a gross operation. He was, in fact, operating in Pittsburgh on the two crucial days, under their very admiring eyes. Brain tumours. He had used the Broca method. He had been in Pittsburgh not only these two days but the day before and two days afterwards, to be certain that his patients were out of danger. Five days in all. Dr Ferrier had not appeared to be listening to those testifying in his defence. He sat 'like a stone,' said one newspaper, 'staring blackly into space,' occasionally passing his lean hand over his thick dark hair.

He had been acquitted. The jury, reluctantly, had had to believe the witnesses for the defence. There was no way around it. Still, the opinion remained that had Dr Ferrier not been a rich man, a very rich man, he would have been found guilty.

There were even some vile rumours—which did not appear in court—that Dr Ferrier had deliberately 'bungled' the operation so that his young wife, only twenty-four, would die. So he remained, in many eyes, a double murderer: the murderer of a young woman and his own unborn child, three months an embryo. Among the many so fiercely convinced was his wife's maternal uncle, Dr Martin Eaton, a much respected surgeon in Hambledon. This was strange to friends, for Dr Eaton had, before Mavis's death, been deeply fond of Dr Ferrier and had regarded him as a son, with pride and admiration. Mavis had been brought up from childhood by Dr Eaton and his wife, Flora, after her parents' death. They had finally adopted her, for they had no children of their own.

13

Dr Eaton, a tall stout man of sixty, had sat grimly in the courtroom all through those days, and had stared fixedly at Dr Ferrier with open hatred. When the jury had returned with their sullen verdict of 'Not Guilty,' Dr Eaton had stood up and had desperately shouted, 'No; no!' Then he had turned, staggered a little, and left the courtroom. He had returned to Hambledon that night and had suffered a stroke, from which he was still recovering. Hambledon sympathised with him with real compassion.

Someone knocked on the door. Dr Ferrier was waiting below for Dr Morgan.

To Robert's surprise Dr Ferrier was not on horseback as usual, but in a handsome phaeton drawn by two of his wonderful black horses, wild-looking beasts with white noses and untamed eyes. He smiled at Dr Ferrier's horses, then turned his face on the older man with sincere pleasure.

He'll do, thought Dr Ferrier, though he's still naïve, and he's a plodder. At any rate he's honest and competent, which is more than I can say for a lot of hacks in frock coats and striped trousers whom I know. A Mama's boy. I can make short work of that—I hope.

He said, 'Robert. I thought I'd call for you in my mother's phaeton.' He smiled bleakly at the younger man, who was only twenty-six and whose stocky build made him appear smaller than his nearly six feet of height. Robert had sandy-red hair, thick and glossy, a round and boyish face pinkly coloured, good wide blue eyes, a short and obstinate nose, a gentle mouth, a dimpled chin. He also had a small moustache, the colour of his hair, and big shoulders. His hands, too, were big and square, and so were his feet in their black and polished boots. The day was hot; he wore black broadcloth and a New York derby. His collar, of course, was high and stiff, which gave his florid colour an unfortunate enhancement, and his tie was black and fastened firmly with a pearl tie-pin.

To Robert's surprise the usually austere and correct Dr Ferrier was dressed as if for golfing, or for hunting or lawn bowling; his coat was a thin woollen plaid, his trousers light grey flannel, his shoes low. Yet his native air of hard elegance had not diminished for all his informal wardrobe. 'Get in,' he said with his usual quick and abrupt manner.

'I thought we'd forget the operating rooms and the hospitals to-day,' said Jonathan. He laughed briefly. 'Two diploma-mill

14

hacks in frock coats who have never heard of Pasteur and Lister. But full of dignity and presence. They are slicing and sawing and grinding away at a great rate this morning, and if any of their patients survive I'll be surprised. Only good luck and excellent constitutions kept their other patients alive after the general bloody slaughter.'

'Why do the hospitals keep them, then, Doctor?'

'How many times do I have to tell you to call me Jon? After all, I'm not old enough to be your father. Why do they keep the hacks? Well, one of them is the governor's cousin, and the other is Chief of Staff of the medical board at St Hilda's, our very fashionable private little hospital. Oil-well rich, on his wife's side; he bought his way in.' He chuckled with a dry and cynical sound. 'In fact, he is operating on his wife's sister; ovarian tumour. I diagnosed it as probably carcinoma before—' He paused. 'But affable Dr Hedler thought, and thinks, my diagnosis is ridiculous. He's possibly just finding it out, or even one of the interns is diffidently informing him, or even one of the nurses! He'd never know, by himself.'

Robert was horrified. 'And you say nothing—Jon?'

Jonathan gave him a brief hard stare. 'Why should I? Oh, a year or so ago I'd have kicked up a stink. But not now. Why should I? She chose Dr Hedler. He's very impressive, and ladies love that, and he speaks with the authority of the ignorant. Presence. It's true I'm still on the staff, and the board, but I've learned, recently, when to keep my mouth shut. I recommend that to you, too, young Robert. At least for a few years. I had a bad time, myself, when I was first practising and tried to introduce asepsis into the operating rooms, and white trousers and jackets for the surgeons, and lots of hand-washing and rubber gloves. If it hadn't been for my family's name—and money—they'd have thrown me out. My mother had promised a wing at St Hilda's. The hacks still wear their frock coats and striped trousers and wipe their scalpels in a lordly fashion on their sleeves, or the nurses' backsides, or whatever is handy. With a flourish. And they come, many of them, right from the dissection rooms. One's an obstetrician. He's delivering a baby this morning.' He laughed again. 'The lady will be very lucky indeed, not to die of puerperal fever.'

'And there's nothing you will—I mean, nothing you can do?'

'No. Would they listen to me, some of them, these days? No. I've heard it said that few would trust me to treat their dogs.'

After the trial, thought Robert.

'So,' said Jonathan Ferrier, 'that sort of thing convinced me to get out of here.'

'You haven't forgotten, though, that you'll stay and make the rounds with me, and be on hand in the operating rooms?'

'I gave you my promise, didn't I?' said Jonathan with impatience. 'I hope you'll like it here. I had ten applications, you know, for my practice. I interviewed them all. You were the last.'

Robert coloured with shy pleasure.

'Don't be too anxious to embrace this damn' town,' said Jonathan, as they rolled rapidly through the streets. 'We have a lot of new-rich here; oil people. Upstarts. We have a few authentic families, but not very many. Just an American town, just any town. Mostly populated by fools. Do you suffer fools gladly, Robert? I never could. That's where the Church and I differ. Violently.'

Robert could connect Jonathan Ferrier with many things, but not with any church. He was constantly discovering startling things about the other man, some of them disconcerting.

'You—belong to a church, Jon?'

Jonathan turned his head slightly and gave Robert his unpleasant stark grin. 'In a way. Why, does that surprise you? The Ferriers had a hard fence to climb over two hundred years ago, when they came to Pennsylvania. They were—are—what you people call Papists. Nominally, I'm a Catholic. But I haven't been to Mass for years. You see, once I was as downy-headed as you, Bob. My fellow man soon disillusioned me.'

Robert was becoming too warm in his heavy clothing. He unfastened his tie, and then his collar. He took off his coat. The sun was very hot; the soft shadow of trees and the dark caves they made of the streets were very refreshing. The houses were now more scattered. The scent of stone and vegetation filled the quiet and shining air. There was a great deal to be said in favour of small cities and villages, Robert thought. At least they smelled—honestly. He saw that they were approaching the river and that Jonathan had turned the phaeton towards the river road. He caught glimpses, between the houses and the trees, of that island which some fool of a woman had named 'Heart's Ease.' In fact, he saw the red-tiled roof of the castle clearly, brilliant in the sun, the walls hidden by trees and the granite enclosures.

Now they were not only on the river road but across the water and the island seemed only yards away.

'Let's move into this grove of birches,' Jon said, 'and look for birds,' and he grinned at Robert.

The grove of old birches was aromatic with sweet and pungent scents of earth and leaf and fecund ground. The warm sunlight did not penetrate here. The air was as cool as a fragrant cellar. There were large stands of wild flowers and mushrooms. Robert, the city man, was exhilarated. He breathed deeply and listened. Jonathan held his binoculars to his eyes and swung them about, searching the tops of trees and the sunlit branches. He held out the binoculars to Robert who put them to his eyes and directed them at the island.

The glasses brought the island so close that Robert felt he could reach out and touch it. He could see the granite enclosure clearly, and the white walls of the 'castle,' and the crowding masses of trees and the brilliance of flowers beyond them on lawns. The red roof of the building flashed scarlet in the sun.

A figure was climbing up the widest point, and Robert caught a glimpse of blue. The figure appeared young and lithe, climbing with ease and vigour. Then it reached the highest point, just behind the granite enclosure. Suddenly it was completely revealed. A tall young girl stood there, staring directly across at the grove of birches, and her face, whitely luminous, glowed in the sunlight like marble.

It was a beautiful face, exquisitely boned and delicately formed and strong. A great mass of curling black hair swung about it and fell to the shoulders and below, held back by a red ribbon. The nose was faintly aquiline. Robert noted this, but what demanded his acute attention were her eyes. They were intensely blue and large and dense with black lashes and arched with very dark brows. So extraordinary was the blue of the eyes that the sparkle of them seemed to fill her face, making it blaze.

They were full of passionate and unequivocal hatred, directed at the grove of trees. The hatred struck at Robert and made him drop the glasses.

'She sees us spying on her!' he exclaimed.

'Nonsense,' said Jonathan, taking the glasses and putting them to his eyes. 'That island is almost a mile out in the

17

water. She can't see that far.' He chuckled, as he studied the girl. 'Yes, she's staring at this grove, but she doesn't see us. She can't.' He gave the glasses back to Robert. 'Pretty wench, isn't she?'

Robert hesitated. He looked through the glasses again. The girl was still looking towards the grove. She was not only tall. She had a lovely figure, curved and graceful and slender. Her blue dress was simple, and open at the throat, the sleeves came half-way down her arms. She wore a coarse brown apron over her dress, like a servant or a girl who worked in the barns.

'I still think she sees us,' said Robert, with uneasiness. 'She's looking straight at me. And she doesn't like it at all.'

'No, she can't see us,' repeated Jonathan. 'She's just hating everybody, as usual.'

'Who is she, Doctor?'

'My niece. Technically.'

Robert turned to him, and stared. 'What did you say? Your niece? How could that be? The girl is twenty, or older. And your brother is younger than you!'

Jonathan was silent a moment. The fretted shadow of the birches trembled over his face, and it was bleak and hard. He finally said, 'Technically, I said. My brother, Harald, married her mother, a Mrs Peter Heger. She was twelve years older than my brother. And that's her daughter by her first husband. Jennifer. Or Jenny, as she's usually called.'

'She's living there? With your brother? All alone?' Robert blushed at his own words.

Jonathan grinned, and Robert again wondered whether he liked or disliked the older man. It was such an unpleasant grimace. Jonathan said, 'Ambiguous? Well. That's a nice word for it. The people in Hambledon don't think it's nice at all. However, there're servants there, too, three of them. And Jenny, apparently, doesn't give a damn what people say. Her father bought the island and built that silly house there, called the castle, in a fit of honeymoon preposterousness. He left all his fortune to his wife, who wasn't what you'd call very intelligent to begin with. And she left the income to my brother, as I told you before, so long as he spends seven months of the year on the island and considers it his home. If he gets tired of the arrangement, and wants to leave, he gets fifty thousand dollars outright and no more. But I told you. Then it falls into sweet Jenny's hands. She has a reason,

I suppose, to be outraged, her mother leaving her only one hundred dollars a month for her dainty little purse. And at the mercy of my brother for her living expenses. You can never tell what an infatuated woman will do with money, and Myrtle—foolish name, isn't it?—was infatuated with my brother. He's a natural roamer, and an artist, and didn't have a cent in the world when he caught Myrtle's attention.'

Jonathan paused. 'My father knew what he was doing. He divided his money between my mother and me, and left artistic Harald only a small, lifetime income, not enough for his exquisite tastes. He's a very bad artist, but thinks he's a genius, as all bad artists think themselves. He's elegant and "sensitive." I don't know much about art. I only know Harald stinks. He never sold a painting in his life, but he's been all over the world, at Dad's expense. I suppose Myrtle was a godsend to him. Anyway, he married her and they lived very happily for several years together until she died. I was her physician.'

'Why doesn't the girl leave?' asked Robert. 'It—it mustn't be nice for her.'

'What? On one hundred dollars a month, after she'd been brought up like a princess? Jenny's a shrewd piece. And that island was her home for years until Harald firmly took up residence on it. It was her father's. He died when she was quite young.'

'I don't suppose they like each other, your brother and—the girl?'

Jonathan laughed again. 'There's a rumour they like each other only too well! I despise both of them, sweet Jenny, and Harald. Not that I listen to gossip, which is plenty in the town. In a way, I suppose it's all right, their living in the castle. It should have been left to Jenny, anyway. The servants are there. Still—'

Robert put the glasses to his eyes once more. The girl was still directing her hatred at the grove of trees. Then, as Robert watched, she bent her head and descended back the way she had come and disappeared. He saw the white flash of her neck through the trees.

'I still think she saw us,' he said.

'No. Impossible. She was just hating Hambledon in general. She doesn't go into town very often. When she does, she often calls on my mother, technically her grandmother. They are great friends. But she leaves at once if I appear. I don't think she likes me.'

I wonder how many do? thought Robert, and was embarrassed.

'How about visiting the hermits?' asked Jonathan. 'They'll be your patients, you know. You might as well know them.'

'Oh,' said Robert. 'Perhaps not to-day.' He was again very uneasy.

'Why not to-day?' Jonathan was suddenly very brisk. 'They have three rowboats. One is always on this bank. Come on. Why are you rooted there?'

Robert did not know. He simply felt a reluctance to make the acquaintance of the ambiguous couple on the island. But Jonathan took his arm and firmly led him out of the grove. 'I go over there at least twice a week, just for the fun of it,' he said.

Carrying his thick coat on his arm, Robert followed Jonathan. For some reason he set his hard black hat firmly on his head. They reached the bank of the river and saw that a rowboat with oars was pulled up on the thick grass. 'Perhaps your brother isn't at home,' said Robert, hopefully.

'Now, where would he go? In Hambledon? How are you at rowing?'

But Jonathan took off his jacket and lifted the oars, after the two young men had pushed the boat down into the water. 'You can row back,' said Jonathan. 'It's wonderful exercise, and doctors need it. They get too fat in their pompousness.'

Robert settled down in the boat as Jonathan strongly thrust the oars into the water. He had a new suspicion that Jonathan had intended this visit from the first, and his uneasiness grew. He told himself that he was not accustomed to 'this kind' of people. All his life had been surrounded by those on whom one could depend, of whom one was sure. Good solid people, kind people, helpful, friendly people. Decorous, church-going people who always voted Republican and suspected 'Papists' and Jews and 'foreigners.' People who made Sunday calls and left cards and never swore or acted indiscreetly. People to whom adultery was only a word, and sin something persistently to be avoided. Women who were modest and not ambiguous, and never showed their ankles; men who wore frock coats on Sundays and carried canes and talked in modulated voices. I am certainly a long way from Philadelphia! thought young Robert Morgan.

He looked at the bare-headed Jonathan Ferrier. The Ferriers were 'different.' French, or Belgian? One never knew what 'that sort' would do next. They were unpredictable, and Jonathan Ferrier was more unpredictable than most. Sinister? Robert thought of that, as the hot sun glared in his eyes and the water threw back brilliant ripples of light. Probably sinister. Was it possible that he was really guilty of his wife's and child's murder after all? No, no. Of course not. A swell of water made the boat rock, and Robert clutched the sides quickly.

'Not seasick, I hope,' said Jonathan.

'No. But shouldn't we have called first to see if we'd be welcome?'

'They don't have a telephone. Myrtle could never stand telephones. She wanted the island to be very rustic.' Jonathan grinned. 'They have no gas, and no electricity. They have oil lamps and a barge delivers coal in the winter for that stupid pile of rock, and they burn nice apple-logs, very expensive, in the fireplaces. And once a week the servants bring in loads of groceries in the boats. If they didn't get high wages they wouldn't work there, I can tell you. It must cost a fortune for all that pretentiousness.'

The water lapped at the boat and the sun glittered on the water and Robert became hotter every moment. The island's wide indented prow was looming above him. He could smell the flowering earth and the trees and hear the silence above the voice of the river.

'Here we are,' said Jonathan. He caught a rope dangling from a pile, and tied up the boat swiftly. 'All right; we're anchored. You'll have to jump a couple of feet, though.' He jumped; his foot slipped on the damp brown earth, and he would have fallen back into the water had not Jonathan caught his arm.

'Steady, there,' said Jonathan. 'And here's the path. What? Putting on your coat? What for?'

The girl was standing on the climbing path. She looked down at them with an ugly expression on her beautiful face.

'What do you want?' she demanded. Her voice was lovely in spite of her brutal words.

Robert was acutely embarrassed. He looked angrily at Jonathan. But Jonathan was smiling up at the girl, and a more unpleasant smile Robert had never seen before.

'Why, Jenny,' he said in a coaxing voice, 'didn't you expect me, as usual? Jenny, dear, this is Dr Robert Morgan, who is taking up my practice. Bob, Jenny Heger, my niece. Miss Jenny Heger.'

The girl glared down at them in silence, her hands on her hips. She did not acknowledge the introduction, beyond giving Robert a contemptuous silence. Then she swung about and left them, climbing rapidly like a deer. Robert replaced his hat. He was angrier than ever. 'I don't think we're welcome,' he said.

'Oh, Jenny never welcomes anyone. Don't let it bother you. She probably rushed off to inform the cook that she has company for lunch.'

'Lunch? I don't think I want to stay.'

'But you must meet Harald, the genius with the paint brushes!' Jonathan seemed ingenuously surprised. However, Robert was mistrusting him more and more. 'Harald loves guests. He especially loves me. Come on. You have a tendency to grow roots wherever you stand. Don't mind Jenny, the rustic plough-girl. Badly brought up. That fool of a mother. If Jenny ever smiled, like a normal woman, the world would crack of the Apocalypse come down. Watch where you're walking. This path is very steep and perpetually wet. And full of roots. I nearly killed myself walking up it, when I got the dramatic light-signal from the roof one night. It's an arrangement I have. Isn't that kind of me, considering the bad manners of sweet Jenny?'

I don't like him at all, thought Robert with misery. He mocks everybody. He mocks everything. He mocks me, too. Robert began to climb. The shadow of many thick rare trees and shrubs crowded along the path, and it was much cooler and the scent of earth was dank and musky in the shade. Jonathan climbed easily as if the high path were a city pavement. He pointed out the trees and the shrubs.

Robert paused on the path to wipe his sweating face. He was again confused, and uncertain. Jonathan continued to climb. The shade was very deep where Jonathan stood high on the path. He was silent, but Robert could feel the bitter penetration of his dark eyes. He suddenly arrived into broad sunlight, clean and bright, and the dank scent was gone and the heavy odour of wet moss and slimy earth. He stood on level green grass, filled with warmth and ease. For a moment he did not see Jonathan Ferrier standing, waiting, at a little distance ahead. He saw the miniature castle at a distance on its lawns, with minute battlements and rounded towers and slit windows. A little *Schloss*, thought Robert. He saw a green house, its glass windows sparkling in the sun, and small buildings that housed tools. He saw massed trees and formal gardens and hedges and red-bricked walks and lily ponds and an old roofed well. There were spruces, too, and flowering shrubs, vivid with colour. The river flowed about the island, enclosing it. It was no longer mawkish to Robert. All it needed, he thought, was a moat and a drawbridge.

Enchanted, Robert walked slowly towards Jonathan. In silence they approached the castle. The walk that led to it was of slabs of white marble; three broad marble steps fanned to the bronze doors, and on each side crouched white stone lions, life-size. 'What do you think of it?' asked Jonathan.

'Beautiful,' said Robert. Jonathan gave up. 'A vulgar man's dream,' he said. 'At least, his dream of a dream.' But Robert did not hear this ill-tempered remark.

The bronze doors opened before they could reach them, and a tall young man in a crimson velvet morning-jacket walked easily down the marble steps to await them. Robert saw him in that clarified light of noon, long-headed, casual, smiling. He had a florid handsomeness, unusual in one so slight and young, and bright, ruddy hair, and excellent features, well-cut and candid. He came to them eagerly, as if they were the most welcome of guests, holding out his hands. Now Robert could see his eyes, brilliantly hazel and shining with good temper, and his gay smile. His whole air was frank and boyish and pleased.

'Jon!' he exclaimed. 'Jenny just told me.' He turned to Robert with that look of deep candour and open expectation. His voice was a lighter version of Jonathan's.

'My replacement,' said Jonathan. 'Robert Morgan. Young Bob.'

'Good! I've heard of Dr Morgan. How do you like our town?'

'I like it. I like it very much,' said Robert with a fervency that made Jonathan smile wryly. He shook hands with Harald Ferrier. This brother was not 'foreign,' nor odd nor secret. He was as transparent as sunlight and as warm. He made a man feel secure and welcome.

'I'm glad,' Harald said. 'I'm very glad. Bully, as Teddy Roosevelt would say. Well, come in, come in. You're both staying for lunch, aren't you?'

Though his voice resembled Jonathan's it lacked Jonathan's resonance, its undertone of hard grittiness. Robert, lulled by all this good-will, this tremendous kindliness and affability, hesitated. 'Well, I—' he said, and looked at Jonathan.

'We came for lunch,' said Jonathan. 'Don't I, usually?'

'Except when you come for dinner,' said Harald, laughing. He winked without reason at Robert, as if drawing him into a delicious conspiracy against his brother. 'We get a little bored here, without visitors. I'm a gregarious fella; love company. It seems such an effort for friends to row across that water. Effete.'

Robert murmured something. What nastiness had he been thinking of Harald Ferrier only a few minutes ago? He could not remember. But he was ashamed. There was such joyousness about Harald, such simplicity and humour.

They entered a square hall, all black and white marble squares, with four suits of armour arranged along the walnut walls. A dark wooden staircase rose from the hall to a landing with a stained glass window. The hall smelled of the ages, a faint but pleasurable mustiness, and Robert saw hanging banners in various colours, hinting of family standards.

'For God's sake, let's go out on the terrace, away from this fakery,' said Jonathan.

Harald laughed without offence. 'Everything is fake to Jon,' he said to Robert. 'But old Pete brought this entire hall from Germany, so what is fake about it? Nothing! And the whole castle is furnished in authentic furniture, brought from all over Europe. Sheraton. Chippendale. Spanish. Well, let's go on the terrace.' He had taken Robert's arm. 'Don't listen to Jon. He tries to sour life for everybody.'

'Not for everybody,' said Jonathan. 'But I'd love to make it a little sour for you.'

'Dear old Jon,' said Harald without resentment. 'This door, please, Dr Morgan.' He opened a large carved oaken door and a blaze of sunlight struck into the hall. Beyond it was a terrace of smooth grey stones and tubbed flowers, all surrounded by spruces. The white granite wall of the castle threw a sharp blue shadow on it all, and there was fine garden furniture waiting, rustic swings, rockers covered with chintz pillows, sofas in red and blue and yellow. Rattan tables held flowering jars and bowls. The lawns moved smoothly away from the terrace, down to the granite enclosure. The river lay beyond, and the farther shore and the mountains gave their own peace and tranquillity to the scene. Somewhere, unseen, a fountain tinkled, and there was a scent of wet stone and luxurious grass blowing over the terrace.

Robert sat down. Jonathan sat near him, his thin legs crossed, his profile to Robert as if he had forgotten him. Harald smiled at Robert amiably. 'A drink before lunch?' he suggested.

'Whisky and soda as usual for me,' said Jonathan, still staring absently at the river. Robert considered. His mother did not believe in strong liquor and he had known, even in college and at medical school and at Johns Hopkins, only beer and wine and sherry. He doubted, in this atmosphere, that any of them would be the proper thing. 'Sherry,' said Jonathan, as if reading his mind. Robert hated himself for the heat in his face. 'No,' he said. 'Thanks, just the same. I think I'd like whisky, too.'

'Good,' said Harald. He struck a bell on the table near his elbow. The sound was abrupt in that peaceful stillness. A moment later an elderly man in a white jacket came to the door. 'Three whiskies and soda, Albert,' said Harald, in his kind voice. 'Please.'

The old man smiled at him like a father. 'Surely, Mr Ferrier,' he said. 'At once.'

'And would you mind, Albert, asking Miss Heger to join us here. You could bring the sherry for her, too.'

'Whisky,' said Jonathan, still not turning his head.

'Oh, come now, Jon! Don't be disagreeable. Jenny doesn't drink whisky! She's a lady.'

Jonathan yawned. 'She usually drinks whisky, too. Don't put on for Bob!'

Harald still smiled, nodded to Albert. 'Four whiskies, then.' He hesitated. 'You'll be giving Dr Morgan a bad impression of us here, Jon.'

'He'll get worse, in town.' Jonathan spoke indifferently. He looked now at Robert. 'My mother drinks whisky, and likes it. And why not?'

Robert did not know what to say. He wished that Jonathan were less intolerable. But Harald was saying with enthusiasm, 'Hambledon is a splendid town, really! You'll enjoy it, Doctor. Nothing like Philadelphia, of course, but nicer in many ways—'

'Why, then, are you always scheming with lawyers to leave it?' asked Jonathan.

Harald leaned earnestly towards his brother. 'Now, Jon. You know that's not true. Isn't Hambledon my home? Didn't I always return to it when—'

'Dad's money began to run out, or he refused you any more.'

Harald laughed lightly. 'Oh, come on, Jon! This is Dr Morgan's first visit here and—'

'We mustn't give him a bad impression. Yes, I know. But do you expect he'll never hear about us in the town? There're hundreds of old biddies of both sexes who'll be only too anxious to tell him all about the Ferriers. Better if he hears it at first hand.'

'You make us sound disreputable, or something.'

'And that's what we are.'

Harald was silent. He continued to smile, however. The door opened and Jenny came out upon the terrace. She had removed her brown apron, but her blue cotton dress was stained here and there, carelessly, with earth, as if she had come fresh from the garden. Her expression was sullen and remote. She did not look at any of the men, and did not acknowledge them when they rose and greeted her. She moved quickly to a distant chair, sat down and folded her large white hands in her lap.

'I've ordered whisky and soda for you, Jenny,' said Harald in a very gentle voice, almost pleading. 'I'm glad you can join us.'

Albert returned with a silver tray, a bottle of soda water, and a bottle of whisky. The men began to watch him prepare the drinks, as if he fascinated them. The silent girl, apparently, was disturbing their peace of mind, though she did not even look at them. Albert took a glass to her and she accepted it in silence, not turning her head.

'Cheers,' said Harald, nodding amiably at Robert. 'And good health to you, Doctor, and may you be with us a very long time.'

'Thank you,' said Robert. He paused. 'And please call me Bob.' He smiled like a shy youth. 'No one does, in Philadelphia. I'd like to start it, in Hambledon.'

He was still vaguely disturbed at the sudden tension in the atmosphere. Then he saw that Jenny was looking at him, with the lack of interest of a statue. Her eyes stared into his, clouded and aloof. Yet Robert knew that she was studying him with hard thoroughness. He suddenly wanted her to like him, to

26

know him as harmless. He swallowed, made himself speak through a tight throat. 'Do you like gardening, Miss Heger?'

It was as if she either had not heard him or had no intention of replying to him. Then she shrugged and said in a dull tone, 'I just work in my father's rose gardens. He planted them, himself. But he never lived to see them flower.' Her face did not change, nor the indifference in her voice.

'Sad,' said Jonathan. Robert's mouth tightened. Did he have to mock everything so meanly, even a girl's grief for her dead father?

Jenny still looked only at Robert. 'Sad,' she repeated. 'He never even saw the house completed. He never lived a single day here.' She spoke without emotion.

Harald said, 'Jenny was only a little girl when her father died. They were very fond of each other. Then Myrtle, Jenny's mother, and Jenny, came to live here. It's a happy place.'

'A very happy place,' said Jonathan. 'Felicity. Charm. Sweetness. Enchantment.' He put his glass down with a thump. 'And sentimental.'

'Don't be insulting, Jon,' said Harald, with mildness. 'We like it, Jenny and I. It was old Pete's dream. It's unfortunate for him that he didn't live—'

'But fortunate for you,' said Jonathan.

Jonathan was indolently studying the water again, as if forgetting everyone on the terrace. Harald said to Robert, 'You mustn't mind his nasty remarks, Bob. He's always making them. There's nothing personal in them, I assure you.'

'Always personal,' said Jonathan. 'Come off it, Harald. I never insult anyone except intentionally.'

Harald, still determinedly smiling, said, 'How's Mother to-day?'

'Do you care? However, she's as well as possible.'

Jenny regarded her glass intently. 'Hasn't she improved? It's been a month since I last saw her. I thought she didn't look well.'

'Heart,' said Harald with sympathy to Robert. 'Not very serious, but disabling sometimes. That was the trouble with Myrtle, too. She had to take digitalis regularly.'

'I'm sorry,' said Robert, with a feeling of helplessness.

Jonathan replied to Jenny. 'She isn't very well. She's had a lot to bear.'

'Let's forget morbid things,' said Harald, rising. 'I hear the lunch bell.'

Harald pleasantly insisted on showing Robert part of the house after a lunch which had seemed disastrous to him. 'And don't forget your studio,' Jonathan suggested.

'The studio, by all means.' Harald was not perturbed. 'What a joker,' he said, with the utmost amiability. He took Robert's arm.

The vast drawing-room was in the tower wing, and it had been made oval accordingly. There was the breakfast-room, round and cheerful, with furniture in birch and maple, which Robert liked at once, and the morning-room all dark oak, and bright chintz, and the library, thin, narrow, long and gloomy, lined with books which obviously no one ever read, and whose leather covers had been chosen only for their colour-value. The leather furniture in black, dark blue and crimson, was ponderous and forbidding, and there was a dank and leathery smell here, as of disuse.

Robert was very weary not only of the castle, which did not seem to him to be as charming as at first, but of the wrangling brothers. There was an undertone in their objective insults which vaguely alarmed him, for though the overtone was light the one below was vicious. Harald, at least, was tolerant and had a sense of humour, Robert thought. It was Jonathan who was the most offensive, determined to be insulting and even crude.

'Now the studio!' said Jonathan, in a voice ringing with false enthusiasm. 'The heart of the castle, the real reason for its being!'

'Oh, shut up,' said Harald, smiling broadly. 'Bob wouldn't be interested in my daubs.' But Robert, who was liking him more and more in contrast to Jonathan, whom he was liking less and less, said, 'I don't know much about art—'

'But you know what you like,' said Jonathan with a straight face. Robert flushed. Harald took his arm again, as if in amused consolation. 'I tell you again, Bob, you mustn't listen to him. Just a rough, unpolished diamond, our dear Jon. Do you really want to see my studio? It's on the second floor with a good north light.'

He led the way up the dark staircase with its sombre window of stained glass. Here Robert was conscious of an odd feeling of oppression again. The narrow hall above was lined with heavy oaken doors, carved and cold, and the floor was covered with a narrow Oriental runner. Harald opened one door on a chill and sunless northern light, and they entered a large bare room, stacked with canvases, the curtainless big window looking out on the river. Some of the paintings were already hung on the walls; one large canvas was on an easel. The room smelled of paint and turpentine and wood and dust, and brackish water.

Robert saw at once that not a single painting was like anything he had seen before, for none contained anything recognisable. There were whirling whorls of violent colour, splashes of red with magenta and blue, black lines in geometric designs, twisting spirals in opposed hues, flat lengths of colour that led to no conclusions. He was bewildered.

'Look at this,' said Jonathan, drawing his attention to the wildest hung canvas of them all. Robert dubiously approached. There was something like a scarlet sun burning in the very centre, but the rays and crooked lines and whirls were violet, green, purple, pink, blue, black, yellow. On the left-hand upper corner there was a splotch of enameled white dotted with staring black.

'Magnificent, isn't it?' asked Jonathan, with an air of tremendous admiration.

'I'm not familiar with art, in this form,' said Robert, trying to find some meaning in this furious and incoherent mass. 'Just New York Metropolitan, I'm afraid.'

'You're provincial,' said Jonathan. 'Now, I'll tell you what this is. It's Harald's impression of the war, in which he wasn't engaged, he being in Paris at the time, while I was sweltering away in those damned Cuban jungles and getting malaria.'

'It does look like a jungle,' said Robert, who had never seen a jungle.

'It isn't a jungle,' said Harald, without annoyance. 'Jon's at it again. It's my impression of American towns.'

Surely he was joking, thought Robert. Then he saw that Harald wasn't joking at all.

'My impression of undercurrents,' said Harald, 'which imply vehemence and vindictiveness, burst of energy, a stagnant sun which rises and falls on nothing, half concealed animosities and prejudices, dirty little sins, avidity without an object—in short, almost any small American city.'

'You do,' said Jonathan, tilting his head as if to study the canvas more critically, 'give an impression of stench. Don't you think so, Bob?'

'I thought you liked Hambledon,' said Robert to Harald.

'Oh, I do. But that doesn't prevent me from seeing it clear and seeing it whole.'

'Oh,' said Robert. Jonathan burst out laughing.

'I won a prize for this, in New York,' said Harald, without animosity. 'I was offered five hundred dollars for it, but I like it too much to part with it.' He pointed to a red ribbon at the foot of the canvas. 'I'm proud of it.' He smiled in Jonathan's direction. 'Of course, provincials don't understand, but this is the coming art-form. You'll see.'

'I shouldn't wonder,' said Jonathan. 'This surely will be the age of the uneducated and mentally illiterate, and artists without art, and men who never learned the discipline of art, or even how to draw. It'll be the age when the colour-blind will be doing most of the painting.'

'Art must shock, not soothe,' said Harald, still good-tempered 'We've passed the age of complacency. And unthinking engagements in directionless activity.' He led the way down the dark staircase. They went out into the hot sunshine, and Robert felt relieved. He feared complexities and smothered hostilities. He had come here from Philadelphia and Johns Hopkins, believing he would encounter the utmost simplicity. But the conversation he had heard between these brothers had alarmed him. Small towns were not, as he thought, simple places filled with good hearts and uncomplex emotions, and bright with honest good-will.

Harald offered to conduct his guests down to the river and the boat, but Jonathan said, 'What? In those patent-leather shoes of yours? Don't soil them, pray.'

So Harald said his good-byes at the door of the castle and went inside.

'Amiable rascal, isn't he?' asked Jonathan, as he and Robert strolled down the brick path between the lawns.

'I think he's very kind,' said Robert with some stiffness.

'He is, he is. That he is,' said Jonathan. ' "Smile and smile, and be a villain".'

Robert had encountered no one who was less a villain than Harald, so he said nothing in reply to this malicious remark. They came upon Jenny, who had put on her brown apron again. She was busy at a rose-bed, her rough blue dress hanging over her upturned heels. Jonathan strolled on, but Robert hesitatingly remained behind. The girl ignored his presence.

Her hands were brown with warm earth, her knees sunken in soil.

'The roses are very beautiful,' said Robert. She turned her head slightly, a trowel in her hand. 'Thank you,' she said, sullenly. Her white forehead was wet with sweat, and her full lips were very red. Her loose hair was in a rich tangle down her back.

'I've enjoyed visiting you,' Robert went on. Now she frankly stared at him.

'Why?'

'Well. Everything is so charming.'

'Is it?' she asked, with abruptness, and went back to her cultivating.

Jonathan impatiently whistled to him and Robert started. He had been staring at Jenny's beautiful young body, and feeling that tingling again. 'Coming,' he called. Then he saw that Jenny's hands had stopped their vigorous movements and that she was gazing at Jonathan with that look of despair, or something else, that Robert had noticed before. Disturbed again, Robert went on and joined Jonathan.

Something was very strange here, he concluded. He did not like it.

Jenny Heger continued to cultivate her father's roses after the guests had left. But now there were tears on her cheeks, which she childishly wiped away with the backs of her hands, leaving smudges on her skin.

After a while she felt hands on her shoulders, and then fingers moving softly through her hair. She did not lift her head. She said, 'I warned you not to touch me. One of these days you'll make me kill you.'

'Sweet Jenny,' said Harald.

'Take your hands away from me!'

Harald stood up, sighing. 'I love you, Jenny. I want to marry you. What's so offensive about that?'

'I will really kill you,' said Jenny. She sat back on her heels and regarded him with hatred, her blue eyes one savage blaze.

'I will surely kill you,' she repeated. She looked at him with all the power of her strong young body and spirit, and after a moment he strolled off.

CHAPTER 2

The warm June weather had suddenly disappeared. Now the sky was grey and the air chill and damp. The mountains were lost in fog and moisture dripped from trees and shrubbery and eaves.

Jonathan Ferrier and his mother, Marjorie Ferrier, sat in the breakfast-room of their sturdy red-brick house with the white shutters and doors and trimmings of brass brightly shined. The casement windows were shut tightly, the blue draperies partly drawn, the gas chandelier lit in this early morning, and a brisk little fire rustling on the white-brick hearth. It was pleasant here and fragrant with potpourri and wax and coffee and burning wood.

Marjorie Ferrier, fifty-five years old, was tall and slender. She wore a well-fitting shirtwaist of white lawn and lace, the high neck boned, and a long black skirt of silk. Her tall pompadour was black, with ribbons of grey through it, and there were small pearls at her ears. In appearance, she greatly resembled her son, Jonathan, for her complexion was dark, her mouth austere, her nose sharp and somewhat long. But her eyes were brilliantly hazel, and large, like Harald's, with thick short lashes.

Mrs Ferrier was a handsome woman and only the faint pallor about her lips suggested that she was not in the best of health. She never spoke of illness or disability, for she was a lady. She rarely descended to the personal, for she was a woman of reticences. Neither of her sons knew her well at all, and Jonathan the least. It was her nature to preserve her privacy even from her children, and though she had never punished them, she had, in their childhood, only to give them a stern glance to quell them. In many ways they feared her. They did not know that she loved them dearly.

Marjorie gave Jonathan the jam-pot. 'Jon, dear, did I tell you that Jenny is having tea with me to-day?'

'Dear, sweet Jenny,' said Jonathan, and made an ugly grimace.

'Now, Jon. I do hope Harald will bring her. It's such a nasty day, and it's a long row across the river.'

'Darling Harald,' said Jonathan. 'How's the scandal running in the town lately?'

Marjorie was distressed. 'Isn't it horrible? Such evil-minded people.'

'You can't blame them, when it comes to our Harald.'

'Jon, I do wish you'd stop your everlasting sneering at your brother.'

He looked at her sharply. 'I forgot. He was always your pet, wasn't he?'

No, thought Marjorie, with deep sadness. You always were, dear. She said, 'Harald doesn't have a very strong character. I thought when he married, he'd choose a firm-minded girl, who would direct him and guide him. But he married Myrtle.'

'For her money.'

'Poor Myrtle. We mustn't vilify the dead.'

'Oh, certainly not. I wasn't vilifying Myrtle, Mother. I was vilifying Harald, if that's possible. A "firm-minded girl"? Like Jenny, for instance.'

His mother looked at him strangely. It seemed incredible to her that Jonathan was so blind. 'Jenny,' she said, in her gentlest voice, 'is a wonderful girl. I love her dearly. You are so harsh about her. You are quite wrong, and so is the town.'

'I know. An untouched lily. Never mind.' He stood up.

'Where are you going this unpleasant morning, dear?'

'To try to badger that old—, I mean, old Louis Hedler into accepting Bob Morgan on the staff of St Hilda's.' He paused. 'I couldn't induce you to part with twenty-five thousand dollars, could I, to match my own twenty-five thousand dollars, for a new nurses' wing?'

Marjorie raised her black brows. 'That's a large bribe,' she remarked. 'For a young man you hardly know.'

'But you'll remember that you were considering that—a year ago.' He looked at her, and they both remembered that Marjorie and he were going to give that to the expensive private hospital—until the trial.

'Yes,' said Marjorie.

'You'll let me mention that, then? They really need that wing, you know.'

Marjorie sighed. She played with the handle of the cup. Then she said, 'Nothing, I suppose, will change your mind, Jonathan?'

'Nothing.'

She said, 'I want you to know this, dear. If you want me, I'll go with you wherever you go.'

'And leave sweet Jenny and darling Harald? Mother!'

The pallor about her mouth increased. It was utterly beyond her training to reach out her hand impulsively, to take her son's, draw him to her and kiss him, and let him know how dear he was to her. So she remained silent. After a moment or two she said, 'Very well. I will keep the promise I made. But is it necessary?'

'Yes. That's why I brought the matter up. Old Hedler's too close to Martin Eaton. Even if Eaton is still recovering from his stroke and just learning to walk again.'

He'll never forget, thought Marjorie, and never forgive. He was always a relentless little boy. She said, 'How cruel of them. Jonathan, does Dr Morgan deserve the effort you are making in his behalf?'

'I think so. I hope so. By the way, his mother's arriving to-day. He never told me much about her, but I gather she's a vulgar, pretentious, arch sort of woman. Yet his father was a gentleman. I hope to be able to rescue Bob from her, eventually, and get him married off to the firm-minded character you were referring to. On the other hand, maybe he needs a soft girl to bring out his latent virility.'

He bent stiffly and kissed his mother's forehead, and she gave him a cool kiss on the cheek. She watched him go. There was a pain in her which did not rise from her heart. She thought of Mavis Eaton, Jonathan's dead wife. She had never liked Mavis, the vital, zesty, tantalising, laughing girl. Pretty blonde Mavis, so gleeful of voice, so alive and vivid, so stupid and cruel! How Jonathan had adored her. How strange it was for Jonathan, who was so perceptive, not to have known all about Mavis at once, even when she was a child. But men were peculiar when it came to women. The dullest woman could deceive the most intelligent man. Marjorie had subtly expressed her disapproval to Jonathan a thousand times before the wedding, but had aroused only his anger and indignation. She had attended the wedding, calm, serene, smiling, while she had cried inwardly and with foreboding. She had accepted Mavis in her house, after the honeymoon, and had behaved towards the girl with kindness and affection. It had been no use at all.

Marjorie shuddered. She dared not say a word. One word would bring disaster, and it must never be spoken.

'Well, now,' said Dr Hedler, 'the diploma-mill hack,' as Jonathan called him. 'That's a magnificent offer, my boy, really magnificent. So good of you and charming Marjorie. But she was always generous. I knew her in Philadelphia, you know, and her family.'

'Yes, I know,' said Jonathan. 'I'm sorry about your sister-in-law, by the way.'

The soft, fat, elderly face across from him changed. Dr Hedler sighed and said, 'Yes. Too bad. But there was no way of finding out that she had cancer before the operation. We could only sew her up, and lie to her.'

Jonathan had been regretting his remark, a brutal one; but now he knew that he was applying a little blackmail, and that he was dangerous to Dr Hedler. Good. For Dr Hedler knew that Jonathan had made the diagnosis of possible carcinoma over a year ago, and had been ignored, and among the more urbanely ridiculing had been Dr Hedler himself. Dr Hedler might be Chief of Staff at St Hilda's, but everyone was aware of his 'medical' background, especially the younger physicians, and everyone, even his enemies, knew that Dr. Ferrier was a famous surgeon and diagnostician, and that his diagnosis had been verified in the operating room. Yes, I'm a dangerous type, thought Jonathan, with pleasure.

They were sitting in the dignified but luxurious Chief of Staff's office, all panelled wood, heavy crimson velvet draperies, and dark mahogany furniture. It had begun to rain, a warm murmurous rain mysteriously full of promise. It ran down the tall windows in silvery rivulets.

'I have a feeling about cancer,' said Jonathan, very grave. 'About six people out of ten thousand die of it, in one form or another. That's comparatively few, compared with the other killers, such as diarrhoea and tuberculosis. And pneumonia and influenza and diphtheria. These are our present murderers, while cancer is rare in comparison. It won't always be that way. Twenty years ago one person in ten thousand died of it. In forty or fifty years? As we conquer one disease another takes its place. Balance of nature. But cancer is the foulest disease of all.'

'It will always be rare,' said Dr Hedler, with the indulgence of the experienced towards the more youthful and inexperienced. 'And it only affects the very old in most cases, though Georgia isn't old, I admit. However, she isn't very young either. Do you know that she's only the tenth case I have seen in all my long years of practice?'

I wouldn't doubt it for a moment, thought Jon, without charity. But he only nodded his head.

'I've heard of only one case of leukaemia,' said Dr Hedler.

'I've had about eight,' said Jonathan. 'I think that form of cancer is increasing, too.'

Dr Hedler smiled and shook his head. 'I doubt it. Well. Let us look again at young Dr Morgan's credentials. Um.' He put on his pince-nez. 'Interned at Johns Hopkins. That's very nice.' He sighed. 'I did take it up before with Martin Eaton, you know.'

'And he turned down his thumb.'

Dr Hedler was pained. 'Jon, he's a very reasonable man, and he did found St Hilda's, and it's his pride and joy. Gave a quarter of a million dollars—a huge sum! I showed him Dr Morgan's credentials. He, er, said the staff is filled.'

'Closed staff. Curse of hospitals,' said Jonathan, with contempt. 'We need all the physicians, and surgeons, we can get for Hambledon and the surrounding territory. Keep the newcomers out and off the staff, and we won't be able to meet the demand. And the hospitals we have will deteriorate.'

'We have to protect the income of the staff, Jon.'

'Protect the staff's income. Let the public be damned. Who said that? Was it old J. P. Morgan, or one of the Vanderbilts? It doesn't matter. The public deserves better treatment from its doctors and its hospitals. What're we here for, anyway?'

'We can't let the new young doctors enthusiastically fill up all our beds! They love that. Gives them a reputation. What of the people who really need beds?'

'We can always intrude our own judgement, if a boy gets too ambitious,' said Jonathan. 'Now, old Martin. He's acting out of spite, and you know it, Louis. I know the other members of the staff will go along with you, if you say so and give Bob Morgan your approval. Old Martin's been domineering you for years; we all know that. Show your independence.'

Dr Hedler turned dark red, but he controlled his fury. 'One of these days, my boy, your tongue will hang you.' He stopped abruptly. But Jonathan only grinned.

'It almost did, once,' he said. 'We're getting off the subject. Hambledon's growing; so is the whole territory around here. Industry moving in. The medical population has to grow, too, to keep up. Keep denying young doctors a place on the hospital staffs and they'll have to go somewhere else, and Hambledon's the loser. We're lucky to have a fellow like Bob Morgan applying. Let's get some fresh air in this town!'

He waited. Dr Hedler did not speak. 'Come on, Louis,' said Jonathan, with impatience. 'Old Martin will never be able to practise again, and you know it. If you go over his head, and you have the right to, as Chief of Staff, there'll be some indignant growling, and then it will be forgotten. Besides, I'm leaving, as you know damned well. Who are you privately considering to replace me?'

Before he could stop himself Dr Hedler said, 'Martin has someone in mind. He will finish his internship in December.'

'What hospital?'

But Dr Hedler merely shook his head. He looked again at the credentials. Jon said, 'Fifty thousand dollars. Where are you going to get that much so soon? Off the street?'

Dr Hedler silently stared down at the credentials. 'Look here,' said Jonathan, 'take Bob Morgan. Or I'll stay here on the staff and where will Martin's precious protégé be then? I'll tell you something: if I stay old Martin's going to blow out another cerebral artery. Not that that wouldn't be a good idea in the long run, or maybe even the short run. You'll be doing him a real favour, Louis, if you take my choice.'

'When you put it that way— Yes, I can see what you mean. Give me another opportunity to talk with him, Jon. And, as you said, fifty thousand dollars is a lot of money, and we need the nurses' wing practically at once.' Dr Hedler became genial. 'Let me thank you, Jon. And Marjorie.'

So it's all right, thought Jon. Blackmail, bribe, a chance for revenge. Who can resist all these? Not old Louis!

'No, no, no flowers,' said Robert Morgan to the hotel manager who had just brought in a vase of highly scented roses. 'My mother is sensitive to all flowers. But thank you, anyway.' He looked longingly at the roses. They reminded him of Jenny Heger. He added, 'I'd like them in my own room, though.'

He was in the best suite the modest hotel could offer.

'We'll be happy to welcome Mrs Morgan, Doctor,' said the hotel manager. 'Tell her, in my name, that the hotel services are hers to command.'

And she'll certainly command them, thought Robert, and was at once ashamed.

'You haven't found a suitable house yet, Doctor?'

'Not yet. But I have four in mind, and when my mother comes we'll choose among them.'

'We'll be sorry to lose you, Doctor.' The door closed after the manager. Robert returned to his own room. It seemed uncommonly small and bare to him, in the dull dusk of the rainy day. He looked at his watch. His mother would arrive at the station in one hour. He must look for a hack at once; they had a way of being invisible when it rained. He put on his hat—and his gloves—and went to the elevator. He had remembered to put his white silk handkerchief in his breast pocket and to wear the frock coat and striped trousers which his mother felt to be the only uniform for a doctor. He even took his cane with him.

Only an hour ago Jonathan Ferrier had had him called to the hotel telephone to tell him that he was practically certain that he, Bob Morgan, would be named to the staff of St Hilda's. And, very soon, to the staff of the Friends' Hospital. 'A matter of a few days,' said Jonathan. 'I thought you should know.'

'It's very kind of you,' said Robert.

You don't know how damned and expensively kind it was! thought Jonathan, a little annoyed that the young doctor should take it all so casually. He said, 'You're very lucky.'

Robert was puzzled. He said, 'Well, I was always told I was born under a lucky star! Hallo?' But Jonathan had hung up the receiver. Robert stared at the telephone. These small towns! Central was always disconnecting people. He did not think of that call as he went down the elevator. It had never occurred to him that he would not be accepted on the staff of the hospitals. It did not occur to him now. Robert found himself thinking of Jenny Heger again. It was odd that she came into his mind so regularly and that he could see her face so clearly. It was unpardonable of Jon Ferrier to bait her so cruelly and despise her so openly. Robert forgot all the gossip he had heard in Hambledon about Jenny and Harald Ferrier. He could only resent Jonathan.

Jonathan spent the dingy cool afternoon in his offices, in the long preparation for his departure from Hambledon forever.

His mother had built the premises for him as a gift when he had set up practice ten years ago. Like the house where he had been born, and his father and grandfather before him, it was built of red brick with white and brass trimmings, a single-story structure nearly three acres from the house. There was also a white picket fence between, with a gate that was usually locked. The offices consisted of a small but well-appointed pharmacy, where he concocted his own remedies and improved on those already available, a comfortable waiting-room, a consultation room, a small office for his bookkeeper-typist, a file room, and two examination rooms, also heated by gas. Marjorie had had electricity installed, though she disliked it for her own house, considering it too stark. There was a telephone directly connected with the house, and a public one.

He got up and strolled through the suite, restlessly. Everything was silent except for the dripping of the rain and gusts of late spring winds, and the small hiss of the gas fires. The suite already felt deserted and abandoned. Jon paused in the waiting-room. His patients would not gather here any longer; they would be young Bob's patients very shortly. He went into the room where his bookkeeper had sat; the typewriter was covered, the little desk and chair empty. The lady would return, she had promised, under 'the new doctor.' He slowly entered the pharmacy, and saw his jars and bottles and boxes of pills and powders and liquid, all bright and shining under the light, and also waiting. Then he went into the examination rooms, so well equipped with modern tables and white chairs and cabinets full of his precious instruments for minor operations and inspections.

At last he stood in the short hall with the doors and the silence about him. He stood there a long time, thinking. He still had to go over the files of his patients, with special notations for young Bob. The files of peoples lives, with all their ailments and their histories, their fears and their impending condemnations to death! He went into the file room and stared at the rank of green steel files, discreetly locked so that no one had access to them except himself. A man's life was his own.

Was it? In less than a few months his, Jonathan's, was no longer his own. It belonged to no one at all, even himself. He was already an exile. Very shortly, this beloved place would be rented to another and he would be forgotten. He would be—where? He shrugged. He did not know. His mother was not aware that he had been considering never practising again, but going abroad to live in quiet and solitude, perhaps in Cornwall, perhaps in Chartres, perhaps in serried and lonely Spain, perhaps in Berlin. There was no place for him in the world he had known; he was not only exiled, but he was self-exiled. He had never had an enormous affection for his fellow man, for he felt that overt affection was an insult to others and a condescension. He did not believe in 'warmth,' which was something you extended only to a beloved dog or cat, or, in private, to a wife or a husband or a dear child. But he had had compassion for all that lived, especially infants, young mothers and the fearful old. Pain and suffering were abhorrent to him. He found nothing 'noble' in agony, nothing to be offered up for the sake of others, nothing in the way of 'reparation,' as the clergy said. On this, too, he had parted company with the Church.

A young priest had said to him, 'Pain is God's punishment on our fallen race, since the sin of our First Parents.'

'And you don't believe in a whiff of ether or chloroform for a woman in childbirth, to relieve her pangs? Did you ever see a difficult birth, Father? Or a breech-presentation? Now, honestly, would you advise operations without anaesthetics?'

'Well, no, Jon. Of course I wouldn't. But woman was condemned to suffer in labour—'

'Maybe ordinary labour. I don't believe in much interference then, except during the last ten minutes or so; it could be dangerous to both mother and child.'

'Yes, Jon, I know. But your ferocious war on pain—which is exemplary—does seem a personal battle to you, a personal insult—'

'That's because I believe in the dignity of man.'

He no longer believed in it. He no longer cared what happened to his fellows, because of what they had inflicted on him, because of the derision and hatred even those he had so tirelessly helped had heaped on him.

The young priest had said, 'You must not desert humanity, Jon.'

He had replied, 'But humanity first deserted me. I don't care about their pain any longer, Father.'

'That is a sin against God. He made you a physician.'

'That's why I'm resigning!' He had grinned. But he was resigning because he had lost his compassion—he hoped.

He was thinking of this now. He felt anger against young Father McNulty, to whom life was very simple. Father McNulty 'loved' people. Oh, for God's sake! What was there to 'love'? Suddenly he thought of Jenny Heger, the trollop. He turned and went into his office again and sat down at his desk. Aimlessly, he began to clear out the drawers.

He found the small framed photograph of his dead wife, Mavis. He set it on the desk and stared at it. Beautiful Mavis, with the womanly breast, the tiny waist, the swelling hips, the rounded arms and thighs! He took the photograph carefully from the frame and tore it to bits and threw the fragments into his waste-basket. After a moment, he dropped the frame into it, also.

'I'm glad you're dead, Mavis,' he said. 'I often wanted to kill you.'

He opened another drawer and took a bottle of whisky and a glass from it, and began to drink.

Mrs James Morgan looked about the suite so anxiously prepared for her by her son. 'It really isn't very elegant,' she said in a discontented voice.

'Mama, it's the very best this town can offer. I know.'

She leaned on her two canes and gazed with deeper discontent at everything.

'It's not what I'm accustomed to, in the home.'

She turned to Robert. 'To-morrow,' she said, 'if I am a little better, we must look at the four homes you mentioned, my dear.'

He could not help himself. He said. 'You mean houses, Mama.'

She frowned. For some reason he was not now intimidated at her frowns. 'Homes, dear Robert.'

'Mama. A house in which one lives becomes a home to those who live there. But other people's houses are not "homes." You don't refer to other people's houses as "homes," only houses.' He took a deep breath. 'To call other people's houses "homes" is a vulgarism.'

'Indeed! Did you learn that silliness in this little town, which wouldn't fit in a corner of Philadelphia?'

'I'm learning a lot of things I never knew before—Mother. And Hambledon may be small, but it is alive.'

'How you have changed, Robert! In these few short days! I hope that horrible man, Dr Ferrier, don't corrupt you.'

' "Doesn't," is the word, Mother. "Don't" is plural, not singular.'

'Are you correcting my English now, Robert?' She was very agitated.

'Mother, you are among strangers, in Hambledon. In Philadelphia you had friends who overlooked your errors. Forgive me, but it is true.'

'My father was an intellectual minister! He didn't believe that ladies should be overburdened with learning, but he taught me, himself.'

'Mother, you needn't stay here, if you don't like it. You can always live in Philadelphia.'

'Leave you—to stay here, alone? Alone! Among corruptions? You must think I'm an unnatural mother! Robert, how could you have possibly believed that? My only child! Thrown to the heathen.'

I must be patient, thought Robert. She said, 'That murderer! And to think my only child has been influenced by him! It's criminal. He should be driven from the country.'

Robert sighed. 'He was acquitted, Mother.'

'We've come to a pretty pass, in this nation, when criminals can be loosed on the public again to continue their crimes.' She put her handkerchief to her dry eyes. 'I only know this, Robert. He will never enter the home so long as I am alive.'

'I don't think he'll come without an invitation. Mother, wouldn't you like to lie down before dinner?'

She was tempted not because she was really in pain but because bed had always been her retreat, and her revenge against her family. But Robert was 'strange.' She must know more of this mystery in order to defend herself. She said, 'I am too stimulated by that dreadful journey, and all the soot and the noise. It was my first experience in travelling. I didn't like it. Those vulgar people!'

'It was only four hours, Mother, and you travelled Pullman.'

'Four hours of sheer misery, Robert! You don't know what it means to be a delicate female.'

Thank God, thought Robert. 'Well, it's over now. We can make plans. The house nearest the offices is smaller than the others I looked at, but it's very comfortable. Four nice bedrooms, with a good view. And servants are cheaper than in Philadelphia. There's a nice garden and really pleasant lawns. The price is very reasonable, too. I think you'll like it.'

'Only four bedrooms? One for you, Robert, one for me, the other two for servants. Where shall our guests sleep?'

'We can build another bedroom on to the house. There is a lot of land.'

'Expensive! What do they want for the home?'

'Only ten thousand dollars.'

'Exorbitant! In this little country place!'

'It's in the best section. By the way, Mrs Ferrier has asked you to tea, to-morrow, if you feel well enough.' He added, 'She is considered the first lady of Hambledon, Mother.'

'I shouldn't dream— You said, "the first lady"? How could that be, with her son a murderer?'

'Mother, the judge and the jury decided he wasn't a murderer! Please remember that. If you call him a murderer, here, you can be sued for libel. Well, I must decline the invitation, then?'

'Oh, how my poor head aches! You confuse me, Robert. Decline? Did I say so? How you confuse me!'

'Suppose you think of it to-morrow? You'll know better, then, how you feel.'

'Sleeping in that bed, there.' Her thin high voice was full of self-pity. 'How can we be sure it don't have vermin—'

'Mother, it's very clean, I assure you. The word is "doesn't," not "don't".' Robert said, 'I've ordered a nice little dinner for us here in the suite, Mother.'

'I don't believe I can take anything, Robert, but a little cinnamon toast and hot lemon tea.'

'Very well. I'll cancel the order, and give your own, and I'll go down to the dining-room and have my dinner for myself. It would be wrong for me to nauseate you by having my big dinner upstairs.'

'Let you eat alone in a public dining-room? Robert!'

'I've been eating there almost every night, Mother, and I haven't been seduced yet.' Unfortunately, he added to himself.

'Robert! What shameless talk is this? No, I will sacrifice my natural revulsion. Order the dinner, Robert.'

'Only one order? For myself?'

She looked up at him sharply. She didn't like that easy tone, that indifferent tone, from a son ordinarily most solicitous. 'I will sacrifice myself,' she repeated. Robert, smiling under his red-gold moustache, rang for the double dinner. He then excused himself to wash in his own room. He hummed when he went down the corridor. Poor old girl. She was a terrible bore and prig, and, yes, vulgar.

The moment she was certain her son had left, Mrs Morgan briskly put aside her canes and moved smartly to the windows to look down on the town. The sidewalks were gleaming with moisture in the dusk. Umbrellas moved in a solid phalanx below, and the gaslights were lit, surrounded by auras of dull and streaming yellow in the rain. But the lamps were scattered, and it was very quiet. Horrid little town. Her Robert would soon tire of it, and then they'd return to civilisation, in Philadelphia. Well, she'd see. She'd have tea with that woman to-morrow and let her know that Mrs Morgan was condescending to her, she the mother of a murderer.

'I really cannot force myself to eat anything,' she complained to Robert when the table was laid in her suite and the savoury food set before her.

'Oh, that's too bad,' said Robert, taking up his soup spoon with enthusiasm. 'This is very tasty. Do try a sip.'

She ate a very hearty dinner, even more than Robert, and complained and sighed and murmured dolorously all through it. As a thrifty woman she deftly tucked two buttered rolls into her handkerchief for later nibbling. After all, she told herself, she slept badly. And waste was sinful. It had been paid for. It didn't do to encourage gorging in servants, who were allowed left-overs. 'Two dollars for this dinner, Robert? Do you think you are a millionaire?'

'An odious woman, really,' said Marjorie Ferrier to her son two days later. 'So affected. She spent most of tea-time preening and condescending and bragging genteelly and talking in what she doubtless considered a very "refined" way. How could such a nice gentlemanly boy like young Robert have such a mother?'

'And how could such a nice mother like you have such odious sons?' Jonathan asked her. 'It's all inheritance from distant ancestors.'

'My sons are not odious,' said Marjorie. 'Here, dear, do try this English marmalade. You aren't eating very well these days. What a wonderful morning! It's bright and warm again. I think I'll work in the rose garden. Where are you going now, Jon?'

'Taking young Galahad on the rounds, as usual. I want to be sure—'

'Of what, dear?'

'It doesn't matter. Nothing matters any longer.'

Oh, God, thought Marjorie, if only Mavis had never been born! If only Jon had never seen her! If only she had died at birth! But life, it seemed, was tragically made up of 'if onlys.'

She knew it was best for Jonathan to leave Hambledon

and never return, but her opinion was not based on his nor those who knew him. There were times when she felt she could not wait for him to go—for every day was a day of danger and impending terror, and pretence.

'Here we are,' Jonathan said to Robert. 'Jewel-like St Hilda's, as some lady once called it.'

They had arrived at the somewhat elaborate wrought-iron gates of the small hospital. Beyond were wide gravel drives and handsome lawns and elms and neat flower-beds and benches for convalescents. The hospital itself was of shining white-brick with red chimneys and blue-shuttered windows and even curtains against the glass of the expensive private rooms.

'Well, it looks as a hospital should look, and not a barracks,' said Robert. A man came running, as they drove up to the white steps, and caught the horse's bridle. The two doctors jumped to the ground and they entered the hospital through doors opened wide to the fresh breeze and the odour of growing things. It was cool and light inside, the inlaid linoleum polished on every one of its yellow squares, and the hall was lined with comfortable chairs and tables. A nurse at a desk looked up, saw Jonathan; her face closed. She said, 'Good morning, Dr Ferrier. And Dr Morgan.'

The hospital was four-stories high, and very hushed, the corridors, in spite of Jonathan's protest, richly carpeted. After all, he was told, the patients who could afford St Hilda's had delicate sensibilities and they could not endure clacking noise. 'And the hell with being sanitary,' Jonathan had told Robert. 'It's a wonder they didn't carpet the operating rooms, too, and the water closets. A lot of the more costly rooms do have rugs in them; there're still a lot of pompous quacks who don't believe in germs, or, if forced to look at them through microscopes murmur that they're "interesting little creatures".'

The very few patients whom he had recently accepted—and who had believed in him in the blackest of times—were on the second floor. So the two young men walked up the wide white-painted stairs, which wound up to the top in a graceful spiral.

Jonathan swung open a broad door into a big and comfortable room full of sun. His manner changed at once. 'Well, how are we this morning, Martha?'

A little girl, not more than ten, was listlessly lying on heaped pillows, her fair hair streaming about her shoulders.

Robert had not seen her before. Jonathan took up her chart from the white dresser, glanced over it swiftly, frowned. 'This is Martha Best,' he said to Robert. 'The daughter of one of my best friends, Howard Best, a lawyer. In fact, I'm her god-father. Aren't I, Martha?' His face had become gentle for all its darkness, and he went to the child and bent and kissed her cheek. She caught his hand, her blue eyes fixed anxiously on him.

'I can go home soon, can't I, Uncle Jon?'

'I hope so,' he said. 'Aren't you going to speak to Dr Morgan?'

The child eyed him shyly but did not speak. When he said, 'Hallo, Martha,' she bent her head and the golden hair fell like a curtain over her cheeks.

'Now, Martha, Dr Morgan is going to help me with you,' said Jonathan. 'He looks like a big red bear, doesn't he, but he doesn't bite little girls. Honestly.'

The child giggled convulsively, and peeped at Robert. Jonathan gave him the chart. 'Acute anaemia. Intractable fever of 102°. History of severe infection of throat, now reduced. Present slight infection of lungs and nose. Joint pains. Transient bleeding from mouth, bowels, kidneys and nose. Slight liver enlargement. Spleen perceptibly enlarged. Lymph nodes discernible. Pallor. Lassitude. Diagnosis of admitting physician, Dr Louis Hedler: Rheumatic fever with few signs of heart involvement. Family physician's diagnosis.' There was, as yet, no diagnosis recorded from Dr Jonathan Ferrier.

Robert laid down the chart. He looked searchingly at the little girl, at her ghostly colour, at the lack of pinkness in her lips, at the bluish hollows under her eyes. He thought of something. It sickened him. He had never seen a case—

Jonathan was watching him sharply. 'Martha has been slightly sick, so her parents told me yesterday. A little cold, they said. Then she became really sick, and they called me. She came in last night. Well?'

Robert went slowly to the little girl who was now staring at him inquisitively. He took her hand; it was chill and faintly tremulous. She let him examine her throat. He took out his stethoscope and listened to her heart. It was a little more rapid than in health, but there were no overt heart sounds. Her tongue was very pale, but her gums were congested.

'Well?' said Jonathan. His voice was curiously muffled.

'You've taken blood? There doesn't seem to be any reference to a blood-test on the chart. I—I'd like to see if there are any blast forms—and the leucocyte count.'

Jonathan sighed. 'Am I very sick?' said the little girl with anxiety. 'Uncle Louis said I had rheumatism. Am I going to be a cripple?'

'Uncle Louis,' Jonathan began, 'is an old—' He stopped. 'Of course, you aren't going to be a cripple, Martha. In fact, when this fever goes down a little you can get out of bed. And a little later, you can go home.'

A cheerful nurse came in, all rosy dimples and bounce, with a white cap on her high black pompadour. 'Good morning, Doctors!' she sang. 'We are doing very well this morning! We had a lovely little breakfast, too, and enjoyed it! Didn't we, Martha?'

'Yes, ma'am,' the child said with politeness.

'And such a pretty nightgown!' said the happy nurse, admiring the white silk embroidered garment Martha wore. 'Such a nice sleep in it.'

'Bob,' said Jonathan, 'this is one of Martha's private nurses, Mrs Chapman. Mrs Chapman, Dr Morgan, my replacement.'

'How nice,' said the pleasant woman, vaguely.

'Bring me a glass slide from the laboratory,' said Jonathan. 'And quickly, please.'

He sat down on the side of the bed and regarded the child with real tenderness. 'Martha, I'm going to prick your ear and take a little blood from you. It won't hurt much; just a little. You aren't going to make a fuss, are you?'

The child immediately looked frightened. Jonathan took one of her hands and held it warmly. 'I don't like to bleed, Uncle Jon,' she said. 'It makes me sick to look at it.'

'I won't let you see it, then. You just keep your eyes closed, and when I tell you to open them you won't see any blood at all.'

'And I don't have rheumatism?'

Jonathan looked at Robert, and the child looked at him. 'No,' said Robert. 'You don't have rheumatism, Martha.' There was a sudden hard silence in the room.

'What do I have, then?' asked Martha with the curiosity of childhood, and the importance.

'We have to look—at things—first,' said Robert, and felt sick.

'You mean it isn't bad at all?' she said in her chirping voice. She was a little disappointed.

'Be cheerful and optimistic at all times before the patient,' Robert had been sternly taught. 'Never indicate by tone or manner that the patient is gravely ill, or in a terminal condition.' He thought it nonsense, but had not so expressed himself to his teachers.

How did one say to a child, 'Darling, you are going to die'? Or did one say, 'Soon, dear, you'll be in Heaven with God'?

Please, God, he said in himself, let me be mistaken. After all, I've never seen a single case before. I could be wrong. Let me be wrong. He turned away and walked slowly to the window and looked outside and saw nothing. It was wrong for the young and lovely to die! They had a celebration to make to life. Life was not a joyous thing in itself—he knew that, for he was a doctor and had seen too much pain and death and had heard too many desolate cries. But it was like spring, in its infrequent periods, and a child had a right to spring. He heard the door open and shut and the bright voice of Mrs Chapman, bringing the slide.

'Now, Martha,' Jonathan was saying. 'Just close your eyes. You'll feel a little prick. Tell me, how is school?'

'I don't like it, Uncle— Oh!' she cried.

'There. Just two seconds. Keep those eyes closed. Good girl! Mrs Chapman, take it to the laboratory and set it up. We'll join you in a few minutes. Martha? It's all over. You can open your eyes now. It didn't really hurt, did it?'

She gave a small dry sob, then smiled. 'No, it really didn't hurt. Much. Uncle Jon, Father McNulty called the hospital and he's coming to see me to-day. Isn't that nice?'

'Wonderful,' said Jonathan. 'Fine.' Robert saw his face, and turned away again. 'And now,' said Jonathan, 'we'll leave you for a few moments to count all the nice red things in that blood I took from you.'

He rose and the two doctors left the room. Jonathan closed the door slowly and heavily. He said, 'Well, Doctor, what is your on-the-spot diagnosis?'

Robert could not remember when he had last felt so wretched and sad. 'I hope I'm wrong,' he said. 'After all, I know—it—only from textbooks. I never saw a case.'

'Of what?'

Robert hesitated. 'Acute leukaemia. Extremely rare.'

Jonathan was silent. His head was bent.

'Tell me I'm wrong,' Robert pleaded. 'That's a beautiful little girl—'

'Let's look at the slide,' said Jonathan, and they went to the laboratories, not speaking as they walked through the long corridors. In that same silence they soon returned to Martha's room. They heard her giggling as they opened the door. Dr Louis Hedler was sitting near the bed in a comfortable chintz wing-chair, and he had apparently told the child some agreeable joke. He turned his head when he saw the younger doctors, and nodded pleasantly and held out his soft fat hand. He more than ever resembled an amiable toad.

''Morning, Jon,' he said. ''Morning, Dr Morgan. Hear you are joining us on the staff. Fine. Hope you'll be happy with us.' He shook Robert's hand vigorously. 'Now, what's this I hear? You took blood from Martha, with a big knife, she says. Why?' He was still smiling happily, but the huge brown eyes were hard and penetrating.

'Just for fun,' said Jonathan. 'We like to hurt little girls, Louis.'

'I did write down that I thought Martha had anaemia, as well as, ahem, rheumatism. What did your precious slides show?'

'Anaemia.'

'Obvious, obvious! At her age. Very common. Nothing to be alarmed about. It's those joint pains that worry me. And a suspicion about her heart—'

'Uncle Jon said I wasn't very sick,' said the child, with new anxiety at the mention of her heart.

'Of course you're not sick!' cried Dr Hedler, with immense joviality. 'I—or rather, Jon here will prescribe an iron tonic for you and you'll soon be as right as rain! I promise you.' He stood up and patted the child's cheek, but she was looking at Jonathan for confirmation.

'Don't worry, Martha,' he said. 'There isn't anything wrong with your heart.' Dr Hedler frowned. 'Louis,' said Jonathan, 'I've a case down the hall I'd like to discuss with you.'

'One of yours? Don't tell me, Jon, that you give a fig for my opinion!'

'There's always a first time,' said the younger doctor. 'Coming, Bob? Martha, I'll come in again before I leave.'

Jon carefully shut the door behind him, and the three doctors stood alone in the carpeted corridor. 'Well?' said Dr Hedler, with impatience. 'Where is your patient?'

'You've just seen her, Louis. And we just came from the laboratories, remember.'

'Yes, yes, so you said! You and your high-falutin' slides and tests! Anaemia, that's what you said, isn't it?'

'To Martha, yes. To you, no.' He turned to Robert. 'Dr Morgan guessed it at first examination; it was only confirmed by the blood test. Bob, tell Louis what we found.'

'Acute leukaemia,' said Robert.

Dr Hedler's mouth fell open with an audible sound. His eyes popped. He swung to Jonathan. 'Why, you're crazy! Jonathan, you don't believe what a young fella just out of the ranks of interns says, do you?'

'I do. I believed it last night, before the blood test.'

'Crazy, crazy! Never heard anything so preposterous in my life! It's insane. Why, that disease is so rare that hardly any of us see a case for ourselves in a whole lifetime! As rare as an angel in hell!'

'It depends on the kind of angel,' said Jonathan. 'Louis, stop gulping. The child has acute leukaemia. I'd tell you exactly what we saw in the smear but they'd be only words to you. You must take our word for it.'

'You arrogant young pup, with your scientific ideas!' Dr Hedler was scarlet with rage. 'Do you know what you're doing? You're condemning that beautiful little girl to death!'

'Not I,' said Jonathan. 'God did.'

'Blasphemous, too.' Dr Hedler was sweating though the corridor was cool. He regarded Jonathan with hatred. 'No, I won't take your word for it! The child has rheumatic fever—'

'You're not her physician, Louis. I am.'

Dr Hedler breathed heavily. He was incredulous. 'Are you going to tell her parents this—this enormity, this guess of yours?'

'It isn't a guess, Louis. I've seen eight cases over the past ten years. It's becoming more common. Twenty years ago only one doctor in a thousand ever saw a case; thirty years ago only one doctor in five thousand saw one. But the Greeks had a name for it: the White Sickness. Remember Hippocrates? He diagnosed it.'

'I forbid you to tell her parents, Beth and Howard, this terrible thing! If it were possibly true, it would be bad enough. But a mere guess—'

'Not a guess. Louis, she isn't your patient. You can't forbid me to tell the truth to my patient's parents, even if you are

Chief of Staff. And I'm going to tell them, to-day. They must be prepared. The child has only a little while to live, at the best. And there's no treatment, Louis.'

'Cancer of the blood! That's what you mean, isn't it? Cancer, at her age!'

'One child in twenty thousand now has cancer in some form, Louis. Don't you read the medical journals?'

Dr Hedler seemed about to strike him. 'The child has rheumatism, rheumatic fever! I've seen hundreds of cases. I was never wrong once. And I'll tell Howard and Beth that you are a fool, and not to believe you. Leukaemia! Bah!' He slapped his hand against the wall and waddled off, trembling with fury.

'Hambledon's crowning medical glory,' said Jonathan. 'Smiling old Louis.'

'Couldn't we have a medical consultation?' Robert asked with misery. 'Someone from Johns Hopkins?'

Jonathan regarded him narrowly. 'Don't you trust your own diagnosis? And mine?'

'I never saw a case,' said Robert, 'before this.'

'I told you, I've seen eight. Not in this hospital, though, and not in the other hospital in town. In Pittsburgh. In New York. In Boston. In Philadelphia. Martha's case is classic. Well?'

Robert studied his large pink hands. 'There's no cure; there's no treatment. There are remissions—'

'Not for long. And not always. Do you want to lie to her parents, Bob?'

'No. No, of course not. You don't mean it, do you, that I must tell her parents?'

'No. I didn't.' Jonathan smiled with bleak pity at him. 'But I'd like you to be present. Break you in:

'And now for my other cases. I'm leaving them to you, Bob, with my compliments.'

' "The quality of mercy is not strained," except that God never heard that particular saying,' said Jonathan, pushing open another door which led into a suite of rooms cheerfully and expensively furnished. Jonathan put his hand on Robert's arm and said to him in a low voice, 'This is a very interesting case. Old Jonas Witherby, eighty years old, old settler, old money, old mansion, good old bonds and stocks and fine old land. I want your opinion.'

They went together through the sitting-room to the bed-

51

room where, in a Morris rocker, sat an old man with the most tranquil face Robert had ever seen among elderly people. He was small and daintily made, with tiny hands and feet and a noble head richly flowing with white and rippling hair. He had the eyes of a young child, clear and blue and steadfast, a snub nose, a sweetly smiling mouth and pink ears. He sat by the window looking at the sunshine and smiling musingly, and when he turned his long head Robert felt warmth and peace rising in him and something very close to affection.

'Ah, dear Jonathan,' said Mr Witherby, holding out one hand to the older doctor and winking. 'I never see you without pleasure. How are you this glorious day?'

'Just terrible, Jonas,' said Jonathan. 'Everything's just as bad as it can be. By the way, this is my replacement, Dr Robert Morgan.'

The old man clung to Jonathan's hand and smiled merrily at Robert, then became sad. 'How do you do, Doctor? You all seem to get younger all the time. Replacement for Jonathan, eh? You must truly persuade him to change his mind. What will Hambledon do without him?'

'Just jog along as meanly as ever,' said Jonathan. He sat down in another chair, crossed his long legs and put his hands in his pockets and studied Mr Witherby with an ambiguous expression. 'Never mind. We won't repeat the old arguments for Bob's benefit. As he will replace me I am turning you over to him. With your permission, of course.'

'Certainly, certainly, dear boy!' Mr Witherby smiled more radiantly than before and considered Robert with great interest. 'Anyone you recommend—'

Jonathan took Mr Witherby's chart, frowned at it, laid it down. 'Still weak, I see. Still eating like that proverbial bird; I know birds; they eat all the time, all through the damned day. But your nurses note down, "ate breakfast like a bird." Silly old hags. How did you sleep?'

Mrs Witherby sighed. 'Please sit down, Dr Morgan. You will find that chair very comfortable; I like to look at young faces. Well, Jonathan, you know at my age one doesn't sleep very well at all. I think, lying awake all night.'

'And you have plenty to think about.' Jonathan, still sitting near the bowered dresser, looked at Robert. 'Old Jonas here was a widower. Two sons, one fifty-three, one fifty-one. Both married, both deserted by their wives. Bill is in a private madhouse, Donald is a chronic alcoholic. D.T.'s, most of the time. In a private sanitorium which dries him out then looses him again. No daughters. No grandchildren. Wife,' said Jonathan in the bald tone of a clinician, 'committed suicide. Very sad, wouldn't you say?'

Jonathan snapped a pink rosebud from a vase and fixed it in his button hole. He was detached as if no one were in this room but himself. He said, 'Languid, listless, tired, enfeebled, anorexia, vague but disabling pains, sometimes severe headaches though no hypertension, tachycardia frequently, some indications of mucous colitis, occasional râles in the lungs. Otherwise, no overt signs of disease. Well, Bob? Want to examine the specimen?'

Robert silently opened his bag and removed his stethoscope and various other instruments. No doubt, he thought, the sorrowful old man was suffering some psychosomatic ailments due to his unfortunate relatives and his disappointment in them. His examination was thorough. Mr Witherby flaccidly submitted to everything as if nothing meant anything any longer to him. Finally Robert put away his instruments and looked long and earnestly at the old gentleman.

'No overt signs of disease,' he repeated.

Jonathan went to the window, stared out, yawned. 'When's Priscilla due to arrive, to-day?' he asked.

'Prissy?' Mr Witherby smiled his enchanting smile. 'In an hour or two, I think.' Jonathan looked over his shoulder at Robert. 'Priscilla, or Prissy, is old Jonas's second wife. Thirty years old, or a little older. A luscious piece.'

Mr Witherby laughed in delight. 'That she is, my boy, that she is!'

Robert stared. This made Jonathan chuckle. 'A rare old bugger, this Jonas,' he said to Robert, making a rude sound. Robert flushed. Mr Witherby laughed again. 'You mustn't listen to our dear Jonathan,' he said. 'He loves to shock. You must really see Prissy. There's only one girl prettier in all Pennsylvania,' and now he smiled slyly at Jonathan, 'and that's Jennifer Heger whom Jonathan loves to call his niece.'

Well, thought Robert, I suppose you can't blame the old gentleman. He has to have some happiness in his life. Jonathan said, 'Priscilla was the town's most expensive doxy. I assume you know what a doxy is, Bob?'

'Now, now, Jonathan,' said Mr Witherby, not in the least offended. In fact, he laughed again. 'Didn't David, in his old age, have a plump young maiden to sleep with him to warm his old bones?'

'But Prissy hasn't been a maiden since she was sixteen, if not younger. But a fastidious little bitch, always. Never slept with anyone for less than fifty dollars: mostly more,' said Jonathan. 'Look at Bob. He's blushing again.'

Robert stared at him helplessly. 'Well,' said Jonathan, with considerable impatience. 'Where's that nose of yours? Smell anything?'

'What a blackguard you are,' said Mr Witherby, fondly, and watching Robert with renewed interest. 'Here I am, an old man of as many afflictions as Job and Jonathan can do nothing but tease me. I came in here after a collapse—'

'Something odd about that collapse,' said Jonathan, as if meditating. 'At first I thought you were trying to show Prissy that you still had it and almost dropped dead trying. Then I decided that Prissy had fed you a little something so she could slip out for some clean air. Come on, Jonas, which was it?'

'Oh, dear,' said Mr Witherby. 'You are very disturbing and uncouth, Jonathan. You will give Dr Morgan some very peculiar ideas about me.' His ancient yet angelic face beamed on the younger doctor. 'I've known Jonathan since he was born and he was always like this. Very startling and unpredictable and forever trying to shock others with the rudest language. But I know him! A kinder heart never beat, a more gentle soul—'

'Shut up,' said Jonathan. 'Don't be such a sanctimonious scoundrel, Jonas.' He looked at Robert sharply, and frowned. 'Well? Where's that nose?'

What in God's Name does he want me to say? asked Robert with that new anger of his. He's been insulting this gentle old man steadily, and his young wife—Robert lifted his head with a jerk. There were those middle-aged sons, one mad, one a drunkard; there had been a wife, who had taken her life. Robert turned his eyes on Mr Witherby and studied him with more concentration. Then indeed he did smell something and he said to himself, the stench of evil.

He was horrified at the thought. Mr Witherby, as he had done with Jonathan, put his hand on Robert's arm and the muscles in that arm involuntarily stiffened. 'Do I smell badly?' asked Mr Witherby, in a sweet and coaxing tone. 'I was just bathed and powdered like a baby!'

Still clutching Robert's arm he said to Jonathan, 'You've almost persuaded me to contribute to that tuberculosis ward for indigent children, dear boy, at the Friends'. A little more of your refreshing conversation and I'll give you my cheque. And won't stop payment on it!' He laughed joyously.

I must have been mistaken, thought Robert, and stood very still. It was my imagination, and Jonathan's prompting, that made me smell corruption.

'If you do give me that cheque,' said Jonathan, 'it'll be the first decent thing you ever did in your life. You might even get a reprieve and go to purgatory rather than to hell. But you don't believe in either, do you?'

'Jonathan! I'm a Christian! Ask the Reverend Mr Wilson— Oh, Jonathan, you are teasing me again.'

Now they both looked at Robert. Robert said, 'You have— you have, Mr Witherby, some of the usual signs of advanced age—'

The old man actually paled and now he no longer smiled. 'Don't say that to him!' Jonathan exclaimed. 'If there's one thing he hates it is the mere suggestion of mortality. Haven't you noticed that, in the wicked? Call them any names you wish, murderers, liars, thieves, perjurers, traitors, sadists, and they'll forgive you. But remind them that they are about to shuffle off and you've made an enemy for life. And an enemy like old Jonas here is a very formidable thing. He has ways of reaching out, even from his bed, to strangle people.'

Robert heard himself saying, 'But, Mr Witherby, you are remarkably well-preserved, and with care should live—should live—a considerable time longer.'

Mr Witherby's colour returned. 'I intend to do that, Doctor. Indeed. My parents lived far into their nineties. I love life, Doctor. I find it endlessly amusing, endlessly fascinating. I always did. You mustn't listen to Jonathan, who could find thousands of flaws in a saint. I never had any need to injure anyone, for I inherited all my money and have increased it. I've been unfortunate in my family. My poor first wife came of unstable forebears; I was warned. My poor sons inherited her predisposition. But there, I mustn't burden you with my troubles. Jonathan, when can I leave here?'

'To-day. When Prissy comes. That should brighten up her life when you tell her! But, if I were you, I'd buy a mongrel and feed him off your plate before you eat, after this.'

'Oh, Jonathan. You mustn't say such crude things.' He

giggled like a boy. 'Prissy knows my will. I have an autopsy ordered.'

Robert did not know if he was serious. He was bewildered again; yet he retreated a step from the old man.

'Good,' said Jonathan. 'Though if I perform the autopsy and even find cyanide, I'll say "from natural causes." After all, Prissy's had to stand you for three years. She deserves some consideration. Bob?'

'I'd like to talk with you a moment, outside,' said Robert.

'Why, why?' cried Mr Witherby, staring from one to the other. 'Are you trying to hide something from me? Is there something really wrong?' He was nakedly terrified.

'I only wish there were,' said Jonathan. 'Sad to say, there isn't, though it's still a mystery to me why you collapsed. I think I'll warn Prissy not to be too hasty in the future.' He bowed derisively to the old man and followed Robert out of the room. They stood in the corridor. Robert said to him angrily, 'I don't know what all this is about!'

'And you didn't smell anything?'

Robert pressed his lips hard together. 'It may be I am suggestible. I thought I—' He stopped.

'You smelled a stench?'

Robert moved his head with fresh anger. Jonathan said, 'You were quite right, and I'm pleased with you. That is the most contemptible and vicious monster you probably ever met in your life, and I doubt you'll ever meet another as bad. He drove his wife to her death, with his sweet malignance and malice, and he drove one son into madness and the other to the bottle. And I'm willing to bet everything I have that never once in their lives did he ever raise his voice to them or threaten them or speak roughly to them. I bet he never did anything violent in his whole existence nor inspired open fear. Yet, he really frightened his wife to death, and so scared his sons that they ran away from him in the only ways they could. You see, soft and gentle characters are particularly susceptible to the presence of evil. But I'm tough. I know all about him.'

Robert looked involuntarily at the closed door. 'You don't believe in demonic possession, do you?' asked Jonathan. 'Well, I do. There may be many things I don't believe, but I believe in a personal Satan, and old Witherby's one of his best friends. Jonas never swore, to anyone's knowledge; the parsons love him. Children adore him, and so much for that business of "children always know." That mass of flowers in there wasn't sent by hypocrites but by people who really admire the old bastard. But I never go in there without making the sign against the evil eye,' and he smiled and held high his right hand, extended two fingers and thrust them downwards. 'My Catholic training.'

He began to walk down the corridor and Robert had to follow him. Then someone exclaimed, 'Oh, there you are, Jon!' Robert turned and saw three young people approaching with smiles, and outstretched hands. One, he saw, was a plump young priest with a kind and boyish face. One was a pretty woman, fashionably dressed. The third was evidently her husband, a loose-jointed young fellow with a bush of auburn curls and large light eyes.

'How are you, Father McNulty?' said Jonathan, shaking hands briefly with the priest. 'Beth, dear. Howard.' He indicated Robert. 'My replacement, Dr Morgan. Fresh as a daisy, isn't he, and I guarantee that he's just as innocent, too.'

Robert, newly annoyed, shook hands. 'Beth and Howard Best,' said Jonathan. 'Martha's parents.'

Robert was frightened. He looked from one smiling face to the other and he wanted to run away. But Jonathan had firmly gripped his arm. 'Let's go to the waiting-room down the corridor,' said Jonathan. 'I've just seen Martha. I want to tell you about her.'

They all went with him, chattering serenely, and Robert thought of the dying child who was waiting for them. Beth prattled, 'I've been worrying so about Martha, and Howard says I'm ridiculous. I am, aren't I, Jon? When can we take her home?' She smiled back at Robert shyly. 'I hope you'll like Hambledon, Doctor. Such a nice town and we're right up-to-date; I heard you were from Philadelphia. We'll make you welcome, you'll see! But do try to make dear Jon stay, won't you? We simply can't let him go! We love him so much!'

The waiting-room was empty and full of sun and comfortable modern furniture, and Beth sat down and took off her gloves and kept her eyes affectionately on Jonathan, who sat down very close to her. 'Well!' she exclaimed. 'Isn't it a lovely day! We just ran into Father McNulty,' she said to Jonathan. 'He was coming to see Martha, too. Isn't that nice?'

Howard Best patted his wife's shoulder. 'Well, Jon, when can we take our girl home?'

'Just as soon as her fever goes down,' said Jonathan. He was

57

rubbing the thick gold chain that spanned his middle. He looked at the priest. 'I'm glad you're here,' he said.

Howard Best said, 'What? Is there anything wrong—with Martha?'

Beth had stopped smiling. Her colour disappeared. 'Martha? Martha?'

In the mysterious way of the clergy Father McNulty understood. He said to Mrs Best, 'Now, Beth. Let's hear what Jonathan has to say.'

'There's nothing wrong with my girl?' asked Howard Best in a changed voice. 'Why, old Louis Hedler said it was anaemia—'

Robert stood at a distance and again wanted to run and knew he must stay, even though no one noticed him now.

'In a way,' said Jonathan in a gentle voice, 'it is, indeed, anaemia. I took a blood test this morning. I don't know why it wasn't done before.'

'So?' said Howard. 'It's anaemia. That's not very serious, is it?'

'Oh, no, it can't be serious!' said Beth in a voice like a prayer. 'Not our girl!'

Jonathan said, looking into Beth's widened eyes, 'Martha has acute leukaemia, Beth.'

The parents visibly relaxed. They had never heard of the disease. Nor had the priest, it was evident. Now they were hopefully puzzled. 'What's that?' asked Howard. 'One of your new diseases, which your microscopes just discovered?'

'No. It's very old. But very rare,' Jonathan hesitated. 'And there's no cure.'

One of Beth's hands flew to her mouth. 'You mean,' she whispered, 'like consumption?'

'Beth, dear,' said Jonathan, 'we can cure tuberculosis now. Sometimes. I wish to God it was only that. Acute leukaemia— it can't be cured.'

'Do you mean she'll have it all her life, like the effects of infantile paralysis?' asked Howard, sitting down with new stiffness as if he were afraid he would break. 'How do we deal with it? Special tonics? Seaside? Mountains?' He paused. 'What the hell is it, anyway?' and his voice rose.

The priest held Beth's struggling and desperate hand tighter. Jonathan said, 'I'd rather have it myself, I swear to God, than to tell you this, Howard. You see, there's nothing anyone can do. We call it, roughly speaking, cancer of the blood-making organs.'

'Cancer!' screamed Beth, and now she frantically pulled away from the priest and jumped to her feet. Her face was terrible. 'I don't believe it, I don't believe it! Children don't get cancer! It's just old people! Martha doesn't have cancer! I won't believe it—it's wrong, it's cruel of you, Jon! Cruel, cruel, cruel, to say such a thing!'

'But true,' he said, almost inaudibly. Howard stood up and caught his trembling wife to him and she hid her face on his shoulder and shook her head over and over in utter denial, and groaned, 'God, God, God.'

'I never heard of leuk—what do you call it?' said Howard, holding his wife tightly. 'Blood? Cancer? Tumour? Why, Martha has no tumours—it—'

He looked helplessly at the priest, and his young face was ghastly. 'It must be a mistake,' he said. 'Cancer! Martha! It's unheard of in children.'

'No, it isn't,' said Jonathan, and he stood up also and moved nearer the agonised young couple. 'Doctors just don't speak of it, that's all. You see, it is getting much more common now. I've seen eight other cases like Martha's, Howard. Just eight. And they all—'

'Died,' said Howard and there was no expression in his voice.

'Died,' said Jonathan.

Howard held his wife even more tightly. He looked at Jonathan as one who looks at an executioner, with instinctive hatred and despair.

'How long?' he whispered.

'I don't know, Howard. I honestly don't know. Perhaps a few days, perhaps a few weeks, or months. But not more than a year, not more than a year, and only that if she has a temporary remission.'

'I don't believe you!' Howard exclaimed. 'Old Louis Hedler would've told us! He said it was just anaemia! He saw her last night! He'd know it if was—if it was—'

'Howard,' said the priest, and put his hand on the young man's shoulder. But Howard gave him a blind, impersonal glare and shook off that hand. He was panting. Beth had become stiff and still in his arms, and cringing.

'I'll call decent doctors, doctors with experience in this thing, doctors who *know*!' Howard shouted. 'Not young quacks, not a man who—'

'Howard!' said the priest with authority.

'I don't care!' shouted Howard. 'He's lying! I don't know why, but he's lying! He wants to—I don't believe him! We'll take Martha away—to Philadelphia, to competent—one of those clinics—he lies!' He was out of breath. 'He's a rotten—'

'Howard!' said the priest, but again Howard shook him off. He pressed his cheek against his wife. 'Don't cry, darling, don't cry. It's all lies. Martha's all right. She mustn't see you like this. We'll take Martha home, to-day. We'll take her to—' Now his eyes swelled with tears of agony and he looked at Jonathan with the utmost ferocity and loathing. 'How could you say such a thing! To a mother and a father!'

'I wish to God it was I,' said Jonathan. 'I'd give my life, Howard. But it's true. You mustn't hope. It's too true. You must prepare yourselves.'

'Oh, no,' said Beth, with her lips against her husband's neck. 'It's not true. Not Martha. It's just an infection—a bad cold. Martha was never sick a day in her life.'

Jonathan sighed. For the first time he saw Robert. Then he said to the priest, 'Father, you mustn't let them hope. There's no hope. Just help them, that's all, if you can.'

Howard almost screamed, 'He's a murderer, and everybody knows it! That's why he said that—! He wants other people to die, too! He probably makes them die! He—' He strangled. 'I'll kill him,' he gasped. 'I'll surely kill him!'

The priest said to Jonathan, 'Don't mind, Jon. He doesn't know what he's saying, in his pain. Don't mind. You don't, do you?'

'Yes, I do,' said Jonathan. 'I mind like hell. Did you expect me not to?'

'Poor Jon,' said the priest.

The big pretty room, shining with windows and sun, suddenly appeared horrible to Robert. He heard distant laughter in the corridor and, outside, the crunching of wheels over gravel and the sound of lawn-mowers and the call of birds. So beautiful and peaceful, so full of life: he could not bear it. A child was dying, and no one cared out there, and no one knew, and when she was dead it would all go on.

'There's nothing?' the priest was saying.

'Nothing,' said Jonathan, and he walked slowly from the room.

CHAPTER 3

Four nights later, almost at midnight, Father Francis McNulty came to see Jonathan Ferrier. The lights in the big house were out, but the lights in the office were brightly shining. The priest went to the offices, knocked and entered. He found Jonathan sprawled in a chair, more than slightly drunk, with a bottle of whisky on the spattered desk before him. So that's it, thought the young priest sadly, but made himself smile with a glow of his golden eyes. 'Surprised to see me?' he asked, and remarked to himself how inane that was.

Jonathan, who had long ago removed his collar and tie and was now in shirtsleeves, had a rumpled and dishevelled appearance. He scowled drowsily; his eyes were bloodshot. 'Trust the devil to turn up when least expected,' he said. He waved at the bottle. 'Have a drink. There's an extra glass.'

'I think I will,' said the priest. He sat down, poured some whisky into the glass and drank it slowly, attempting to keep Jonathan from seeing his consternation. But Jonathan was not looking at him. He was yawning heavily and glumly. He reached for the bottle. 'Not just yet, Jon,' said the priest. 'I want to talk to you.'

'At this hour of the night?' Jonathan looked blearily at his watch, then snapped the case shut, fumbled for his pocket, could not find it, and let the watch hang. 'Where've you been? Carousing?' He put the bottle down. He tried to focus his eyes. 'What's up?' he asked. 'Somebody died, thank God?'

'Yes.'

'Congratulations.'

'Don't be childish, Jon—'

'If you're going to set up a confessional here, Frank, you can get the hell out. I'm not up to listening to some sad tale.' His voice was slurred and sluggish. 'Nor are you listening to mine.' He became a little excited and his drunkenness appeared to increase. 'Wasn't it you who asked me last December, over and over, if I was "guilty"? Yes, I've not forgotten, you know.'

'I only did my duty, Jon, and you know it. There was always the danger—'

'Of me hanging, in mortal sin. Now, why don't you go home and say your prayers and let me go to bed?'

'I didn't believe you killed Mavis—'

'Well, not after I'd finally convinced you. In the beginning, yes.'

The priest was silent. He said a private mental prayer. He said, 'I want you to forgive somebody. I'd like to tell him—her—to-night, that you did.'

Jonathan forced himself upright, and groaned and snatched at his head. 'Who, for God's sake? And why? And what do I care? Do you mean some pigs have actually become convinced I didn't kill Mavis and have sent you here, at this hour? Can't they fry a little in their consciences until to-morrow?'

'They're waiting to hear, Jon. Right now. By telephone. It is bad enough for them just now. It's worse, thinking of you.'

'Fine. Let them fry. Tell them "no".'

Now he did pour more whisky for himself and gulped it stolidly.

'Jon,' said the priest, 'little Martha Best died three hours ago, at the hospital.'

Jonathan lifted his heavy arms, let them drop on the desk, then dropped his head upon them. He didn't really hear, thought the priest, with compassion. He's fallen asleep. He looked at Jonathan's slack head, at the dark disordered hair, at the side of the sallow cheek, which was as still as wood. Then Jonathan said in a voice that seemed to come from a long way off, 'I didn't know. I haven't seen her for four days. They'd given orders, the Bests, and old swinish Louis Hedler, that I wasn't to go near her. Hadn't I "done enough," lying to them, scaring them to death, trying to make them suffer? That's what they said. Even her nurses were forbidden to tell me anything about her.'

'Yes. I know, Jon. I know. But after the first shock of her death Howard and Beth said to me, "Can he possibly forgive us?" I said I didn't know. And they asked me to come now, not to-morrow. They can't bear waiting. They've got to know.'

'At this time, when Martha's just died? They can think of that now?' He lifted his head and his face was changed and distorted. 'What's the matter with them?'

'They knew this morning that she was dying. It was obvious. But you weren't in the hospital then. They looked for you.'

Jonathan wet his dried and swollen lips. 'So it seems you've got a Mass of the Angels to celebrate.'

'Jonathan, please.'

Jonathan said, 'Don't talk like that to me, in that pained tone of voice! As for Martha, she's well out of it. What does anyone have to live for?'

'You don't know what they're suffering, Jon.'

He stared at the priest in an ugly fashion. 'Let them get their consolations from that old fraud, Louis.'

The priest stood up, sighing. 'So you won't forgive them?'

He waited. But Jon said nothing. However, in a moment he did speak. 'I'm to be the saint, am I, forgiving every son of a bitch who digs into my bowels and turns the knife? Why? Just tell me why?'

'Because, Jon, though you've turned away you are still a Christian. And, I hope, a man.'

Jonathan laughed. 'Words, words.' He waved heavily at the telephone. 'All right. Tell them. Tell them that I grovel before them and beg their forgiveness—' He stopped. 'Hell. Tell them that my heart is broken for them, and then get the hell out of here.'

The priest reached for the telephone and took the receiver from its hook.

'Well, I really don't know, Robert,' said Jane Morgan in her usually discontented voice. 'The rooms aren't very elaborate.'

'But Mother, they are excellently proportioned, and the house isn't that old.'

'I thought we'd live elegantly, and up to our station.'

'We haven't any yet—here.'

'Oh dear, Robert! How can you say that? This wretched little town!'

'It isn't wretched, and you've liked the ladies you have already met and you told me, yourself, that they were very "civil." Most of them have Main Line relatives in Philadelphia.' He stood with his mother in the parlour of the really attractive Georgian house, and, as he had said—prompted by Jonathan Ferrier—the rooms were excellently proportioned, with high moulded ceilings, fine balanced doors, white marble fireplaces and beautiful bright wood floors.

'And the lawns,' he said, 'magnificent old elms, hickories, oaks, and a view of the river from the morning-room and bedroom windows. You won't find any better in Philadelphia at the price.'

Jane Morgan, leaning on her canes, again studied the big room with discontent, her widow's weeds heavy and black this hot day, her white silk and lace cap set firmly on her hair in defiance of 'modern ways.' Her long thin nose twitched; her hard mouth moved with pettish but unspoken thoughts. Her small grey eyes slipped coldly over the sun-shadowed walls, looking for faults and cracks.

'I can't say,' she said, 'that this is a soffiscated town.'

'You mean "sophisticated," Mother.'

'Robert! I'm growing very weary of your impertinent remarks about my use of the Queen's English!'

'It's King's English now, Mother, remember? King Edward.'

The cold little eyes studied him. 'You were never like this in Philadelphia! Something has happened to you here—probably that dreadful Ferrier man. I knew I wouldn't like him and since I've met him my opinions have been confirmed. What a repulsive creature! Haven't you noticed how those thick white ridges spring out around his mouth for no reason at all?'

'That's when he's impatient with people—as he usually is, I admit.'

'Bad temper, that's all. Bad blood. I've been hearing a number of things,' and she nodded significantly and tapped her canes on the bare wooden floor.

'I suppose you have. Hambledon's as bad as Philadelphia for gossip. Now, Mother. We must decide. This house, you can see, isn't far from the Ferriers, and it is very close to the offices I will be renting. I like it; it is cheaper than the other houses you've seen and we are lucky. It would be much higher priced if the lawyers weren't anxious to close an estate.'

'I visualised a more sumptuous home. I can't say I like this home—'

'Mother.' Robert was weary. 'This isn't a "home" yet; we don't live here, yet. So, it is still a house.'

'Home,' repeated Mrs Morgan. She sighed with her discontent. She was really impressed by the house but it was not in her nature to approve of anything. 'Very well,' she said in a grudging voice, 'if it pleases you it'll have to please me, I suppose. But I know I won't sleep well living so close to a murderer—I told the ladies—'

'Mother!' Robert spoke harshly. 'For God's sake, I hope you haven't been calling Jon Ferrier a "murderer"! My God! That's libel. Not here in Hambledon, for God's sake!'

She saw that he was genuinely aghast. She smiled knowingly. 'I do hope you can trust my discretion, Robert. I'm not a fool. And many important people think well of him, and I wouldn't offend them for your sake. Don't take the Almighty's Name in vain; that's blasphemy. I don't like your new manners. But not everyone admires him as you do, and I gathered, from a word here and there—Well, it doesn't matter.'

'Mother, don't lend yourself to gossip here. That would be the one thing that would ruin me forever.'

'Robert, you forget that though I am the mother of a physician I was the wife of one, too. But I can hardly shut my ears and pretend that I don't hear. That would be most impolite.'

'Yes, Mother.' Robert sighed. 'Well, is it settled about this house? I must let the lawyers know this afternoon.'

'I'm not overly pleased with this home,' said Jane, cautiously edging around Jonathan, tapping her canes smartly. 'But I am only your mother, Robert. What pleases you must please me. You mustn't consider me in the slightest.'

Jonathan smiled at Robert with broad innocence. But his black eyes were tired and appeared dissipated. 'Where shall I meet you?'

'At the hospital. St Hilda's?'

'Not this time. The Friends'. My patient isn't rich.'

The Friends' Hospital was strictly utilitarian but thanks to Jonathan it had become what the older doctors said was 'entirely too modern and stark.' Jonathan, it was, who had reformed the somewhat archaic system of teaching nurses and had established a nursing school under rigorous discipline. He had also insisted on halving the wards so that none contained more than twelve patients and he had opened windows, ordered dark brown walls to be painted in more cheerful colours and had commanded clean white linoleum on all the floors. The four operating rooms had come under his critical eye, also. Witnesses to operations, he said, must be gowned, capped and masked to avoid contamination of the air. This was all folly to the Chief of Staff, Dr Humphrey Bedloe, and the others on the staff, but as Jonathan had offered to pay for the modernising of the operating rooms they consented with smiles of indulgence.

However, as in St Hilda's, he had not been successful in his insistence that some of the older surgeons must discard their traditional frock coats and striped trousers and that they should use modern methods of asepsis. The younger ones, trained in better schools, sympathised with him and assured him that time would take care of their elders. 'In the meantime these hacks literally get away with murder,' he had said. 'We should call this place the Morgue.'

When Jonathan came here now he came, he felt, as a stranger, no longer involved. He was not as popular here as he was at St Hilda's, possibly because he and his family had given the private hospital more money. Very often he encountered resistance and sulky hostility and watchful eyes. He ignored it all. He said to Robert now, 'One of these days hospitals will be worse than this. Oh, they'll be cleaner and more modern and very, very big. But they'll be totally indifferent and impersonal. We are already beginning to think of patients as stomachs, livers, colons, uteri, rectums, gall bladders, and what all, and not as people. You can't ignore a man's manhood without making him less than a man. You can't insult his humanity by thinking of him as a mere collection of organs without injuring him spiritually, and even bodily. An ant-hill is a fine place for ants, and collective effort is fine for ants. But man is not an ant.'

They went into one of the large elevators. 'That reminds me,' Jonathan said. 'Here, in Hambledon, we have very lively Fourth of July celebrations. In the square. With a band and flags and howling politicians. You might enjoy seeing how the peasants enjoy themselves.'

'You really hate this place now, don't you?' Robert was quite surly.

'Well, let's put it this way: I don't believe in unrequited love.'

His nonchalance infuriated Robert for some reason. The younger man tugged at his reddish moustache and gave Jonathan a sidelong look. He never saw and talked with Jonathan without feeling heated, disturbed, confused, bewildered, sad or angry. There had been times when he had felt awed and touched; there were more times when he wanted to punch Jonathan. He no sooner felt admiration than he immediately felt rage. Jonathan was much too Protean for him. He was afraid of the day when he would be alone, and in the next moment he could not wait for Jonathan to leave. There was no getting close to Jonathan, no way of approaching him. The slightest effort in that direction was met with sudden coldness or a sardonic remark.

The back of the old man who was operating the elevator had stiffened, and as Jonathan and Robert left the operator he gave Jonathan a look of intense hatred. Robert was not feeling entirely friendly towards Jonathan but he paused a moment to stare with haughty rebuke at the old man, who immediately ducked his head and closed the elevator door. 'What is it?' asked Jonathan, but Robert said nothing.

As they emerged from the elevator they encountered a nurse. 'Oh, Dr Ferrier,' she said. 'The Chief of Staff, Dr Bedloe, is particularly anxious to see you. He said it was most important.'

Jonathan took Robert's arm. 'I can't do any damage now. You've been accepted on the staff. And Bedloe's going to be your particular misery. One of the old diploma-mill hacks.'

Robert recalled Dr Bedloe as a tall and stately middle-aged man with a pink complexion, cold blue eyes and an authoritative manner and an absolutely positive voice. Like so many of his kind he had a thick and flowing mop of white and silken hair, and he was reputed to be very wealthy from his investments in oil wells in Titusville. Jonathan said, as they followed the nurse, 'I'd call Bedloe an anus, except that would be disparaging a very hard-working and long-suffering part of the body, much abused and rarely giving any trouble except to the sedentary. I think I'll just call him a cloaca, which isn't flattering the cloaca, which always serves some purpose, which Bedloe doesn't. Except that he does, in a way, cleanly carry away a lot of the bloody sewage his pet hacks spew up in the operating rooms. He hates my guts.'

The nurse twitched her long white skirts. 'Dr Bedloe,' she began, in her admonishing voice, and then she brightened. 'Oh, here he is now!'

Dr Humphrey Bedloe was indeed bearing down on them like an eagle. 'Jon!' he said. 'I'm glad I caught you! It's very important.'

'Well,' said Jonathan, leaning negligently against the wall, 'what have I done now? You know I don't have but half a dozen patients in this penitentiary these days.' Then he looked at the older man with curiosity. 'What's the matter—Doctor? Having a touch of angina again?'

Dr Bedloe was indeed pale and appeared agitated. He nodded curtly at the nurse, who scuttled away. He bit at the end of his silken white moustache. He glanced warily at Robert. 'I must speak to you alone, Jon. It's of the utmost importance.'

'Speak away,' said Jonathan, not moving. 'Bob here is my replacement. He'll be cleaning up after your butchers, who don't even have a sense of proportion enough to wear the straw hat of an honest butcher. Speak away.'

Dr Bedloe's agitation increased. He gave Robert a quelling look. Only two weeks ago Robert would have obeyed that glance and would have discreetly moved off. Now he stood solidly on his big legs and did not stir. For an instant Dr Bedloe openly and actively disliked him and there was a blue glitter of ominous threat in his eyes.

'It's very private, Jon.'

'Nothing's private. Not to me, any longer.'

Again the older man savagely bit on his moustache. Then he said, 'It's my niece, you know her, Hortense Nolan. You were at her wedding. She married the Nolan boy. Oh, damn it, Jon! I can't stand here like this and inform the whole hospital!'

'If I remember,' said Jonathan, 'you did inform the whole hospital. About me. Even before I was arrested. In fact, you didn't even wait for the indictment before you had me removed from the staff. A very precipitate fella, you. Dear, paternal Humphrey.'

'My God,' said Dr Bedloe, and Robert, with interest, saw actual despair on the man's face. 'Why do you bring that up now? Isn't it over with? I'm thinking of Hortense. I've thought lots of things about you, Jon. Always did. But I never thought you were malicious.'

Now Jonathan was looking intently at him. 'There is something wrong, isn't there? Well, what about Hortense? Pretty girl, if I remember. Lots of red hair and big white teeth. Nineteen? Well?'

'It's—you know, Jon. You know all about it! She was pregnant—'

'Yes. I remember. And I recommended young Harrington to you, when you asked me to deliver her. But young, modern doctors aren't good enough for you and your family, are they? You said old Schaefer would deliver her. That's it, isn't it?'

'Yes.' Dr Bedloe bent his head. 'That's true. He did deliver her, at St Hilda's. Five days ago. A nice baby, a boy.'

'Well?'

'It's this, Jon—'

'Now, don't tell me the girl has puerperal fever, for God's sake!'

'Peritonitis.'

Jonathan lifted himself from the wall and he looked at Dr Bedloe with open hatred and disgust. 'I told you. Old Schaefer isn't fit to deliver a cow. Never washes his hands; it's a principle of his, since asepsis was introduced years ago. He doesn't believe in germs even now, does he? But he's such a benign old bastard and gives the girls such encouragement and pats on their cheeks sweetly before he slaps the chloroform over their noses. Peritonitis, by God! Well, what did you expect?'

'She's dying, Jon. She's like a daughter to me; never had any of my own. And she's dying. They telephoned me from St Hilda's just now. She's—she's been feverish since yesterday, and now to-day—'

'And he infected her, the bloody old swine, with his patting dirty hands. What had he been doing before? An autopsy?'

Dr Bedloe spread out his hands. 'Jon, they think she needs an immediate operation—to save her life. She—she bled a little more than ordinarily after the delivery. Thought she was out of danger. Jon, she's dying.'

Jonathan said in a loud voice, 'An operation? Hysterectomy? At her age?'

All at once Dr Bedloe looked old and stricken and sick. 'It's even worse. The—the baby died last night. A—a brain injury, birth injury, I think. Was doing so well, too, in spite of the high forceps. All at once. She's only nineteen, Jon.'

'Sweet Jesus,' said Jonathan.

Robert Morgan did not even wince. He was too horrified.

'Jon, Louis Hedler said I should call you at once. He said if anyone can save Hortense it is you.'

'Good old Louis,' said Jonathan. He shook his head. 'Look, Humphrey, I'm not going to get into this, not even for little Hortense. It's your dirty work; you're not going to smear me with it. Where's old Schaefer?'

'He never leaves her for a moment. It's—pathetic—'

'I bet it is. She's his goddaughter, isn't she? No, I'm not getting into this filthy mess and then letting you sing it out that it was all my fault. No, Humphrey. I'm sorry, but the mess is in your own lap.'

Dr Bedloe grasped Jon's arm. 'Please, Jon.' His voice broke. 'Don't think of anything else but Hortense. I promise you—'

'Sure you will. Anything as of now. But if Hortense dies, and she probably will, then it'll be all my fault. Wasn't it your wife who spread it around that there was something mysterious about little Martha Best's death? Yes, it was. My mother told me.'

'Jon, I'll be there in the operating room. Half a dozen of us will be there.'

'Fine, fine. In your germy frock coats. No, thank you. I'm sorry about Hortense. But call Harrington, Humphrey, as you should have called him in the beginning.'

Dr Bedloe seemed about to burst into tears. 'I—I thought about that. He refuses.'

'Good for Phil. Look, I'll say a prayer for Hortense, if I can remember who to, but not for me, Humphrey.'

He shook his head and turned away, then caught young Robert's eyes. He stared and said with disgust, 'Oh, not you, too!'

'I'll be there,' said Robert. 'I'll help.'

'You and your pretty little red moustache!' Jonathan regarded him with contempt. 'Let me warn you: never clean up after the hacks. Or try to. After it's too late the hacks will sing, "He did it, he did it!' They never forgive us for having a decent medical education. Come on.'

'Please, Jon,' said Dr Bedloe.

'What more can this stinking town say about me? Just that I murdered Hortense. Bob? Coming? We're going over to St Hilda's.'

Jonathan and Robert arrived at St Hilda's after a fast ride through the town. They had not spoken, though Jonathan had given Robert many a grim and accusatory glance as if all this were the younger man's fault, and as if Robert had forced him into this dangerous situation. But Robert smiled under his moustache. They went at once to the luxurious suite of young Hortense Nolan, and there Jonathan found Dr Emil Schaefer sitting beside the bed of Hortense, who was whining painfully and protesting, while the doctor gently and lovingly urged her to eat 'just a little, dear. This good broth. This dainty piece of chicken, this hot buttered muffin. You must keep up your strength.'

Jonathan walked in, almost running, swept the spoon from the doctor's hand, and lifted the filled and steaming tray and hurled it furiously against the wall with a resounding crash. 'God damn it!' he exclaimed. 'Are you trying to kill the girl? Out, out. I want a conference with all of you.' Dr Shaefer, a short and rosy man with a bald head and a thick grey beard, stared at him as at a mad dog, and rose slowly, his blue eyes blank and staring. Dr Bedloe, who had followed on Jonathan's heels, looked with dismay at the ruins of the 'nourishing lunch,' but said as easily as he could, 'Emil, I called Jon Ferrier—he's used to these things—and we'd like to consult with you.'

'You called this—this—' Dr Schaefer stammered.

'Emil, she's my niece. There are some modern things, you know—'

The fair fat face of Dr Schaefer turned very white. 'If he touches her, then I must leave the case, Bedloe.'

'Louis Hedler had also asked Jon,' said Dr Bedloe, in terror of Jonathan's refusal. 'Please, Emil.'

'On second thought,' said Jonathan, 'I want him here. I want to ask him some questions. I also want those two last-year interns, Moe Abrams and Jed Collins, who've been suffering enough under the hacks. I also want Louis. Go and get them, Humphrey.' He spoke to the Chief of Staff of The Friends as if he were a lackey. 'I won't even look at the girl until you're all here. And you might tell Moe and Jed to bring their notebooks. This is not only for their information but for my own protection.'

His dark lean face was very pale and his black eyes flashed at Dr Bedloe threateningly. Dr Schaefer took out his handkerchief and wiped the sweat from his face and his hands. Jonathan took one step towards him, seized the handkerchief, stared at the elderly man and then at his hands, then threw the handkerchief into his face. 'So you have a cold, have you? And you've been examining her—how many times to-day, you criminal fool? With germ-laden hands?'

'I won't stand this!' said Dr Schaefer. 'I won't bear these insults from a jackanapes, an incompetent, who even bungled—'

'Emil, for God's sake!' cried Dr Bedloe in an agonised voice.

'Deliberately,' added Dr Schaefer, who appeared on the verge of a stroke.

'Never mind him, Humphrey,' said Jonathan. 'Go and get those people. Let him stand there and blubber. He'll have enough to do to answer questions later.'

He pushed his hands into his pockets as if he were sheathing daggers. Does he have to be so violent? Robert asked of himself, then he moved slowly to the fine brass bed and

71

looked down at the young girl there, and he answered his own question: yes, he does!

Hortense Nolan lay high on a bolster and pillows and sheets of the best and softest linen, and it was evident to Robert that she was almost moribund with sepsis. She was so slender and small and young that she appeared to be hardly more than twelve years of age, and her mass of red hair was in strong contrast to the ashen pallor of her little face. It flowed over her pillows like a flag of danger and fell over her panting breast. Her eyes were half-open and sunken in grey pits; their colour was clouded by a glaucous film. Her nostrils were pale and pinched, her lips faintly purple. Her hands were pulling restlessly and aimlessly at the bed-linen, and Robert felt sick and frightened. Her breath was slow yet noisy in the suddenly silent room. But Jonathan would not look at her; he stood at the windows and stared out, while Dr Schaefer pressed his fat back hard against the wall near the door.

Two nurses came in and hurried to the bed. Jonathan said without turning, 'Don't go near that bed or touch that girl!'

The nurses gaped at him, and their fresh-coloured faces hardened with surprise and knowing significance. They turned as one to Dr Schaefer and spoke to him obsequiously, 'Doctor, Mrs Nolan's parents and her husband are outside and wish to see Mrs Nolan.'

'Yes, yes,' said the overwhelmed man. 'Of course. Send them in.'

'No,' said Jonathan. 'If they come in, I go—out. And I won't come back.'

But the nurses only awaited Dr Schaefer's orders, smiling contemptuously, ignoring Jonathan. Dr Schaefer hesitated. His effort to come to a decision turned his plump face scarlet. He looked at Jonathan's back with hate. 'I—we—we are having a consultation,' he said to the nurses. One of them, the older, stepped back in astonishment. 'With Doctor—*Ferrier*?'

'With Dr Ferrier,' said Dr Schaefer. The young women gaped again. They turned their heads slowly and regarded Jonathan at the window. Their astonishment grew immense. 'Please leave,' said Dr Schaefer in a choked voice. The girls flurried from the room, their long white skirts rustling. They could not wait to report this incredible scene to their sisters. Robert could hear their fluting and agitated voices retreating down the hall. Silence entered the room again, except for the anguished breathing of the dying girl, who appeared to be

72

totally unaware of the men in the room, and the broad sunlight of afternoon and the corridor-noises and the soft wind lifting the frilled curtains at the windows. She had sunken into that profound detachment and distance which is the anteroom of death. But Jonathan did not look at her; Robert saw his pale and sallow cheek, the hard jutting of his cheek-bones and jaw, the tensity of his whole body as if he were on the point of losing control of himself.

The door swung open and Dr Hedler, accompanied by Dr Bedloe, and the two young interns, entered hurriedly. 'Jon!' cried Louis Hedler. 'It was good of you to—ah—attend this consultation! Very good!'

Jonathan turned slowly from the window, but he looked at the interns while he replied, 'I want this understood: I came under pressure. My common sense told me to refuse. I came against my will, and because I'm a damned sentimentalist and have a soft heart for young victims of obdurate and medieval old hacks who never heard of Semmelweiss and Lister, and who continue to murder at their will. I came to expose you, as the American Medical Association wants you exposed. I want to rid hospitals of you. That's too much to expect, of course, but time will take care of you.'

'Jon,' said Louis Hedler, 'can't we save these insults for later? Hortense is almost *in extremis*.'

'Louis,' said Jonathan, 'you and Schaefer here, and Bedloe, too, have no right even to treat dogs.' The two interns smiled fleetingly at each other and then with admiration at Jonathan. 'I,' said Jonathan, 'wouldn't permit you to treat me for a first-degree burn.' He pointed to the bed. 'Yet you have probably killed little Hortense here.' He moved to the bed, and regarded the interns with gravity. 'Boys,' he went on, 'I want you to take voluminous notes here. I'll ask my questions slowly so you can take them down. I want you to put down the replies, too.'

'Unethical!' cried Dr Schaefer and looked imploringly at his friends, Louis Hedler and Humphrey Bedloe. But they uneasily avoided his eyes. 'Am I on trial here?'

'Yes. You are, and all the rest with you,' said Jonathan. He opened his bag and drew a chair to the bedside and for the first time gave all his attention to Hortense. He studied her with absolute concentration, leaning forward over her but not touching her. Then he said, 'Fetch a nurse with a hypodermic of 15 mg/cc of morphine, at once.'

'Morphine!' cried Dr Schaefer. 'When she can hardly breathe!'

'Louis,' said Jonathan, not lifting his head.

Dr Hedler hesitated, then rang the bell for a nurse and when she appeared hurriedly gave her the order.

'He will kill her,' said Dr Schaefer in a low and desperate tone. Jonathan glanced at the interns. 'Morphine reduces peristalsis, as you know, among other things. This is a case not only of puerperal fever, but of extensive peritonitis.' Now he began to examine the girl. She moaned feebly. He threw aside the sheets. Then he uttered the foulest oath Robert had ever heard. 'A filthy tampon!' he said. 'A dirty, filthy tampon! What for? To reduce bleeding? Look at it!' and he held the object high up in the air. 'Filled with what our friends here would call "salutary pus"! Or something. When in hell did her bleeding stop, Emil?'

Dr Schaefer despairingly noted that the interns were busily scribbling. 'Until yesterday morning—she bled quite a little. That's why I ordered the tampon.'

The nurse came in with the hypodermic of morphine, and handed it with a disdainful flourish to Jonathan, who deftly injected the fluid into Hortense's arm. She moaned faintly. The nurse, smirking, retreated to the door but stood there. She would have such funny news for the other girls.

Jonathan threw the yellowed tampon on a tray and extended it to the interns. He said, as they looked at it with horror, 'Now, Emil. Did you sew up lacerations?'

'I did.' Dr Schaefer's eyes burned with humiliation and his pallor increased.

'After the high forceps? Yes. And did you sterilise the forceps? No. Did you use modern methods of asepsis on your hands? No. Rubber gloves? No. Boys, you have all this?'

Young Dr Abrams said with portentous solemnity, 'Yes, Doctor.'

'Good. Now, Emil. Were you certain that all the placenta was delivered?'

Dr Schaefer moved heavily against the wall. 'I believe it was. It—appeared so.'

Jonathan pounced on him. 'You "believe it was"! Aren't you sure—Doctor?'

Dr Schaefer spoke in a loud and rapid voice. 'I've delivered thousands—thousands—I ought to know!'

'How many died—Doctor? Of haemorrhage? Of puerperal fever? Of extended peritonitis?'

'I am not compelled to answer that! I will *not*!'

'No,' said Jonathan. 'The Fifth Amendment protects you from self-incrimination. So—we have here a distinct possibility of remnants of the placenta being retained, which in itself would cause all this damage. Moreover, an ominous situation is that the normal discharge has been inhibited, and pus has taken its place.' He looked at Dr Hedler. 'I want an operating room prepared at once.'

Dr Hedler nodded to the nurse and she flurried out, bursting with news.

Jonathan continued to examine Hortense, speaking slowly. He held the chart in his hand and checked it with his examination, nodding at time. 'Tachycardia. Vomiting. Rigidity of the abdomen. You will notice, Dr Abrams and Dr Collins, that I do not do a vaginal examination. The patient has had six such to-day, alone. With dirty hands.'

'I will not—!' began Dr Schaefer, turning wildly to his colleagues.

Now Dr Bedloe looked at him with bitterness. 'Shut up, Emil,' he said.

Jonathan continued. 'Fever of 104° since last night. Violent sepsis. Let us hope to God there is no embolism, too, somewhere.' He examined the drugged girl's small white legs minutely. 'Not yet, at least as far as I can tell.'

Dr Bedloe said, 'A hysterectomy?'

'I don't know. Yet. I find an abscess here, adjacent to the uterus. Extensive peritonitis. Fulminating. Let us hope to God the abscess is walled off! Now, no one shall be admitted to the operating room without complete asepsis, gowns, masks, caps, rubber gloves. You, Dr Schaefer, must not be admitted at all. Your "cold" has helped spread the infection.'

'My patient! How can I know what you will do to her— you young quack?'

Jonathan stood and stared at him with disgust. 'Quack? I? Look in the mirror, Emil. If I save this girl—which I doubt I can—it will be no kudos to you. It will be in spite of you.'

Dr Schaefer spread out his hands to his colleagues. 'Louis! Humphrey! You know what happened! To his wife. You'll let that happen to Hortense?'

Robert did not blame Jonathan for what he did then.

Jonathan walked quickly to Dr Schaefer and struck him savagely across the face. The loud crack seemed to explode the quiet of the room. Dr Schaefer staggered back and put his hand to his cheek. Everyone stood mute and unmoving, and aghast, except for the young interns who regarded their boots demurely.

Dr Schaefer said, 'I'll have you arrested for assault and battery!'

Jonathan said, 'And I'll have you arrested for deliberate malpractice, caused by your ignorance and stupidity and your unfitness even to enter a hospital room. If this girl dies, Emil, as sure as God I'll tell the husband to institute proceedings against you.' He looked at Louis Hedler. 'And against this hospital, for permitting this man to use its facilities and in aiding and abetting him.' His black eyes seemed on fire.

The stretcher arrived for Hortense; she was snoring heavily under the influence of the morphine. Jonathan did not look at the older doctors. He said to Robert and the interns, 'Ready, as soon as possible. With your note-books.'

He shook his head. 'Here is Hortense in an open suite in the maternity section! Do you know how dangerous this is? The infection can spread to the other mothers. She must be isolated, after her return from the operating room—if she survives the operation, which I doubt. Complete isolation. And no one who attends her must attend anyone else. My God!'

But Jonathan had overlooked something very vital. When he entered the sitting-room of the suite he saw there Mr and Mrs Horace Kimberley, the parents of Hortense, and her young husband, Jeffrey Nolan. Dr Schaefer was already talking to the tearful mother, who had flaming hair like her daughter's and was as fat and round as a middle-aged and amiable hen. Her wet eyes were like big bronze coins, and she was fussily dressed in a welter of pink ruffles to her insteps and wore a huge straw hat bending under a burden of great pink roses. Her husband was almost as small, but he was thin and boyish of figure and face and possessed an enormous black moustache. The husband, Jeffrey Nolan, was a serious young man, all pince-nez, light hair, and clean-shaven nervous face, a very rich young man who had inherited 'old' money, which had placed him far above those vulgarians who had just acquired it 'through those dirty oil wells.'

Louis Hedler and Humphrey Bedloe were disagreeably startled, and the latter put his hand on Jonathan's arm. But Jonathan pushed it off and advanced on the four with a cold and angry expression. Dr Schaefer had apparently been talking urgently to the others, and his face was flushed and one cheek was streaked with the crimson of Jonathan's blow. It was Jeffrey Nolan who spoke to Jonathan, while the frantic parents blinked in confusion and fear.

'Hallo, Jon,' he said, and held out his dry and narrow hand. 'What's this I hear? Humphrey called you, is that right? But Dr Schaefer tells us that Hortense is really getting better—'

'Now, wait,' said Jonathan, ignoring Dr Schaefer and speaking to the other three. 'I have to be blunt because there is practically no time. No time. Hortense has what is called puerperal fever, and peritonitis. Please let me finish. Didn't Schaefer tell you that? She needs cleaning out, Jeff, what is called a D&C, dilation and currettage—I don't know yet. The abscess also needs evacuating. Drainage established. I have to do it at once, right now. She's almost *in extremis*, Jeff, do you understand that? She will be dead in less than twenty-four hours, if I don't operate. That's certain.'

'I don't agree!' shouted Dr Schaefer. 'She is definitely improving! She has longer periods out of coma! Her heart sounds are better! She just needs nourishment, for her strength, and good nursing—!'

'Jon?' said the young husband in a voice as dry as his hand. 'She will die, and very soon, unless I perform that operation,' said Jonathan. 'That I can promise you with absolute certainty. Jeff, I didn't want to take this on; I wanted Schaefer to suffer from the butchery he is guilty of, and the incompetence and the scorn of what he calls "modern methods." Young Harrington refused to be involved with this, for excellent reasons. Jeff, say the word and I'll withdraw. It's no mess of mine.'

Dr Schaefer pleaded with the parents. 'Julie, didn't I deliver you of two children and did you suffer?'

'No,' said the weeping mother. 'It was all perfect. Horace, I don't know if we should give the permission. I'm so upset; I can't think.'

Jonathan said, 'Mrs Kimberley, it isn't in your hands to give the decision. It's in Jeff's, the husband's. Well, Jeff?'

Jeffrey looked despairingly at Louis Hedler and Humphrey Bedloe, who had come up to them. 'It's quite true, Jeff,' said

Dr Hedler, and Dr Bedloe nodded silently. 'Oh, God,' muttered the young man. He caught Jonathan by the arm.

'Tell me, Jon! If you operate—will she live?'

'I don't know. As of this minute, I don't think so, Jeff. She has sepsis. She's terribly infected. I won't go into details; you wouldn't understand them, anyway. She will assuredly die without the operation; with it, she has one chance in a thousand. That's all I can promise you. She's far gone.'

' "Far gone"? Jon, can't you give us any hope?'

'Not much. Practically none. I can only do what I can to undo this terrible damage.'

'I forbid it,' said Dr Schaefer, his voice breaking into a huskiness. 'It would be criminal to deprive this young lady of her child-bearing capabilities! That's what he wants to do! It will be murder!'

'If she dies,' said Jonathan to the young husband, 'it will be murder, indeed. But I won't be the one who committed it. I won't remove the uterus if it is possible to let it remain, Jeff. I'll have to see. The choices are desperate, and I know it only too well. Hortense may die, either on the operating table or a few hours later—or she will die without the operation—or she will live, after the operation, unable to bear children in the future. The choices are not mine.'

'There's no other alternative?'

'The very faintest one, that she will live after the operation and be able to bear other children. The very faintest one. I can't give you any hope. It would be cruel to do it. I can only offer you my knowledge and my promise that I will do all I can.'

Dr Schaefer again appealed to the parents. 'Does my experience count for nothing in comparison with this man's "new" and superficial knowledge? Do you want a—' He stopped. But the parents knew what he had almost said.

'I don't know, I don't know!' the mother wailed, clinging to her husband.

Jonathan sighed and looked at his watch. 'Each minute that goes lessens Hortense's chances. Give me your answer, Jeff. It's all in your hands.'

Dr Bedloe put his hand on the mother's shoulder. 'You've heard, Julie. It isn't in your hands. I know Jon Ferrier. Yes,' he added, in a tone of deep shame, 'I know him. I wronged him, Julie. I, too, was afraid of him because he knew more, and I hated him for that reason, too.'

Jonathan's black eyebrows raised themselves in sombre mockery. 'Well, Jeff?'

'I give my permission,' said the young man. 'Where's the damned paper? Hurry, Jon, for God's sake, hurry!'

He signed the paper, the pen shaking in his fingers. 'You have condemned that child to death,' said Dr Schaefer.

'No, you did,' said Jonathan, folding the paper. 'But I'll try to save her from your judgement of execution.'

He looked at Robert who followed him out of the room. In the corridor Jonathan began to race and Robert ran after him. Once in the scrub-room the young men began to wash their hands, over and over, and over and over, while the sceptical nurses stood silently by exchanging meaningful glances. Now Jonathan seemed to relax. 'Old Bedloe's a hack and he's always known it. Now he admits it. That's like the sun rising west. There may be some hope for him. How did I get myself into this, anyway? Hortense isn't my patient.'

'Do you think there is any chance?'

'Who knows? I don't. Will my horses win at Belmont in September? I can answer that as easily as I can answer your question. Didn't they teach you at Johns Hopkins that a doctor never asks, nor answers, such a question? If they didn't, then I will immediately lose respect for them. Come on, another soaping. Seventeen times, remember. Must be something cabalistic about that, don't you think?'

Then Robert knew that he was deliberately relaxing himself, making himself objective, detached, before facing the ordeal in the operating room. Jonathan confirmed this at once by saying, 'The patient has one thing in her favour. She's very young, and youth often confounds physicians.' Hortense Nolan had become 'the patient' to him now and Robert felt an easing of the tension in his own shoulders.

Capped, gloved, gowned and masked, the two doctors entered the operating room, which was brilliantly and blindingly lighted from overhead. It smelled of whitewash and soap and ether and carbolic acid. Dr Bedloe and Dr Hedler and the two interns were already waiting for them, dressed like themselves. It was Dr Bedloe who was administering ether to Hortense Nolan, whose bright hair was wrapped in a towel and who seemed pathetically small and already dead on the operating table. 'That's about the best thing you do, Humphrey,' said Jonathan, his voice muffled behind the mask. 'You learned one thing, anyway. Oxygen ready, too?'

He looked at the nurses, searching for one infringement of the asepsis technique. He looked carefully at the instrument tray, glittering under the lights. 'I assume,' he said, 'that these have been sterilised?'

'Jon,' said Louis Hedler, 'don't you think that's enough levity?'

'Oh, I'm full of jokes,' said Jonathan, nodding to the nurse nearby. 'Solution of carbolic first. That's right, dear. Now, swab the operating field with alcohol, and I hope it's alcohol and somebody hasn't drunk it and substituted water.'

He saw the deadly whiteness of Hortense's cheeks and the gasping sound she made as she inhaled the ether. Her eyes were shut and the lids had the blueness of death on them. 'She's under,' said Dr Bedloe, feeling the girl's pulse. 'I don't dare give her any more, Jon.'

The nurse at the instrument tray laid a scalpel in Jon's gloved hand. This was the moment Robert always dreaded. The actual operations never disturbed him, for he had assisted at many and performed over a score of the simpler ones. But to him, still, the fragile outlining, with the scalpel, on the white flesh, and the thin red wake that followed, made his heart quake with dread. It seemed to him that only a sadist could be so unconcerned at the first violation of the human body; the very delicacy of the first strokes appeared cruel and gloating.

The tension in the operating room increased. Now everyone was silent, but the interns dutifully took notes. Dr Bedloe's forehead had taken on a livid tint, for he was remembering that it was he who had called Jonathan. He watched without a movement; his eyes hardly blinked.

Then Jonathan said, as the instruments clicked in and out of his hand, 'There's one thing certain, now. The infection has spread to the endometrium. And look at this abscess of the uterine wall! Thank God it's walled-off. We hardly ever see that. That's youth, for you, and a good sturdy constitution. We'll evacuate it. We'll put in tubes for drainage. No salpingitis or parametritis, thank God again. How did this child escape that, after old Emil's efforts to kill her? More sponges; counting them, I hope? Tie off this artery, Bob, or are you a statue? Come on, come on, move faster! Where's that Johns Hopkins's technique?'

The minutes moved on. Dr Bedloe said, 'I don't like this,

Jon. Her pulse is weakening. Her pressure is down, 92/110.'
His voice trembled.

'She isn't just having her tonsils out,' said Jonathan. Sweat
was pouring from his forehead. He bent his head aside and
a nurse wiped the uncovered portions of his face. He looked
at the clock ticking ominously away on the wall. Nearly an
hour.

'The blood loss,' said Dr Hedler.

'I know, I know,' said Jon. 'Quick! This spur. Damn you,
Bob, move faster!'

'I think she's going,' said Dr Bedloe.

Jonathan said, 'Look at old Emil's infernal sutures! No
wonder. And, as I suspected, placental remnants. Someone
should cut his throat, and it would give me great pleasure—'

Dr Bedloe started the oxygen. 'How much longer?' he implored. 'I have to try to bring her out, Jon.'

'Go on, then. It's one way or the other.' His hands flew.
He probed and cleaned, sewed. 'Anyway, the uterus is all
right now. Did I ever tell you—?'

The girl on the table uttered a great unconscious groan.
'Good for you, Hortense,' said Jonathan. 'Stay with me,
darling. Bob, you can start tailoring now.'

Robert found his hands shaking. The girl's pulse and heart-
rate and pressure were all increasing, and her belly was beginning to tense. 'Ether!' said Jonathan. 'Not much, but enough
to relax the belly, damn it!'

He watched critically as Robert made his neat stitches.
'Good,' he said. He did not look at his patient. He appeared to
be concentrating on Robert's work. 'I'll have to give her
oxygen again,' said Dr Bedloe.

'All right. Do it. Watch that flap there, Bob. Girls, you
have all the sponges, I hope?'

His hands were bloody, and his clothing. He stood and
watched and only his eyes seemed alive, watching everything,
darting from the girl's face and then to Robert's hands. Hortense groaned again, and the sound was terrible in the silent
room. 'She's still well under,' said Jonathan. 'Don't wet your
trousers, Humphrey. She's still relaxed. Don't give too much
oxygen for a couple of minutes.'

It was two hours before Hortense Nolan was wheeled away
into strict isolation, far from the obstetrical floor, and accom-

panied by nurses who would attend no one else. The four doctors, unaccompanied now by the blatantly admiring interns, went to the sitting-room of Hortense's former suite. The girl's parents and husband were waiting, and they started with simultaneous cries to their feet. 'Where's my child?' exclaimed the mother, staring at them with dread. 'Why didn't you bring her back?' Her hands flew to her mouth. She dared not ask the question.

Jonathan said, 'She's in an isolated room now. She can't come back to this floor. Jeff? Now listen to me, all of you. She has a chance; just a chance. But she won't have even that one miraculous chance if old Emil is permitted in her room, with his own nice little infection and his nice old curious hands. If you let him in, even for a second, I'm off the case. Is that understood, clearly understood?'

Jeffrey Nolan had begun to cry. The parents clutched each other. Jonathan's exhausted eyes smiled at them. 'A chance,' he repeated. 'Just a chance. I wouldn't bet too much on it, but you can hope a little. And, there's another thing. If she lives—I still say, if she lives—she'll have other children, but why anyone would want to inflict life on an innocent soul I don't know. It's one of those unsolved mysteries that always plague me.'

'Jon,' said Dr Bedloe, and took the younger man's hand. 'I can't tell you—'

'Don't,' said Jonathan.

'Jon,' said Dr Hedler, 'Hortense will be under my personal supervision.'

'Oh, God,' said Jonathan. 'Spare us all that, Louis. If any doctor is allowed in here when I'm away, he must be either Moe Abrams or Bob here, or Jed Collins. No one else. Is that understood, too?'

Dr Hedler, who looked like a very pallid toad indeed, smiled painfully. 'All right, Jon. You don't have to insult us. Is it really necessary?'

'Very,' said Jonathan. 'I didn't go through all that to have some hack undo it all. I know you're nice old fellows, but I don't want you in the room with Hortense. Strict asepsis at all times. Me, Abrams, Collins. Yes, and Bob here. He is careful to wash his hands. He's heard all about Lister and Semmelweiss. It might be an excellent idea to read about them some day, Louis.'

'We observe absolute asepsis and sterilisation, Jon, at St Hilda's.'

'Now, that is very lovely. But the fact still remains that in spite of all that men like old Emil have access to the delivery rooms and the obstetrical floor. What do all the precautions mean when one single man can ruin it in a single moment?'

Dr Hedler hesitated. He looked at Dr Bedloe. 'I think,' he said, 'that we'll take away Emil's privileges. Remove him from the staff.'

Jonathan smiled. 'If I've accomplished nothing else to-day thank God I accomplished that. Some poor girls will live rather than die, though what the hell anyone wants to live for I don't know. If there's any whisky or brandy in the house, bring it. Jeff and Julie and Horace need it, or we'll have other patients on our hands.'

Jeffrey followed him to the door and tried to speak. 'Now, now,' said Jonathan. 'Save all your strength for your prayers, Jeff. Remember, the girl is still in the utmost danger. We won't be sure for at least two more days. Pray, Jeff.'

CHAPTER 4

The two young doctors went to see Hortense before leaving the hospital. She was rapidly coming out from the anaesthetic. Jonathan took her pulse, nodded silently to himself. Young Dr Abrams was sitting nearby. 'She opened her eyes once,' he said.

'How's her blood pressure?' Jonathan asked.

'Excellent. Almost normal. I won't leave her, Doctor, until Jed can relieve me. We're going to take turns, as you ordered.'

'And no one must come in, not her husband, not her parents, not another doctor except Dr Morgan, or the intern, until I give the word. And watch those nurses!'

The doctors left the hospital together. 'Aren't we the cock of the walk?' said Robert. 'Who runs this hospital? You?'

'I'd love to. For a couple of months. Old Louis would be the first out on his ass. Poor old swine. I don't envy you taking my place on the staff, Bob. There'll be times when you'll wish I'd absentmindedly used a scalpel on his throat in the operating room.'

The deep purple twilight was all about them on the busy street. Jonathan lighted a cigarette. 'Stinking things,' he said. 'But I don't have the strength just yet to struggle with my pipe. In a way I'm sorry for old bungling Emil.'

'Doctors must always close ranks,' said Robert, lighting his own pipe.

Jonathan laughed. It was a faint and exhausted sound. 'Yes, we must, mustn't we? What if our patients saw us as we are? By the way, have you settled on that house yet?'

Robert paused for just a moment. Then he said with firmness, 'Yes, I have settled on it.'

'Good. They wanted fifteen thousand but I beat them down to ten. For you. Good night. But go in to see Hortense before midnight. This is your first case, Bob.'

The July night was hot and very still. Jonathan rode his horse slowly and wearily homeward. His eyes felt full and aching and his hands were faintly trembling. He had long ago learned to be objective about his cases, but sometimes he could not push them from his mind. He was less certain about Hortense than he had appeared. The chance of her surviving, the chance of the infection having been halted, were very poor. It was now, he thought, in God's hands, as they say. And I wouldn't trust those Hands for a single minute! Not after what I've seen Them really do when He's in the mood.

The streets of the town seemed full of clinging steam. The gas-lamps were haloed with rainbowed rings. Jon could hear the rattle of wheels on cobblestones, the sound of laughter in dark alleys, disembodied voices on porches. He could smell the river, fishy in the heat, and the sweetness of linden trees and the almost anaesthetising fragrance of full-blown roses and the dust on the grass. Footsteps and the clatter of horses' hoofs echoed in the hot night. Doors opened, shut, banged, closed. Somewhere there was a thin singing of a gramophone. The distant shout of a young boy, the cry of a child, the call of an anxious mother in the dark; the giggle of a girl. It was all about him but he felt himself unseen, unheard, unknown. It was as if he were already an apparition visiting old known places, alone and silent. It was well. Soon he would be gone and it would be as if he had never lived. He looked towards the mountains and they were only deeper shadows against a dim sky faintly sparkling with stars. He looked at the houses he passed and saw the yellow light against blinds or caught a glimpse of a small parlour and nondescript furniture, and men in shirt-sleeves reading under lamps or a mother rocking a baby, or children at tables playing dominoes. He, Jonathan Ferrier, saw it all but now it was strange and remote and he had no part in it. He had no home here. He had no one.

Dear Mavis, he thought. I should have killed you, nice and quietly, long ago.

He glanced up the street and saw the dark house where Robert and his mother would live, and between that and his own house he saw his offices, unlighted, silent. He had little more to do there. In fact, he had little more to do with living at all. He thought of the whisky in his offices, and hesitated. Then he went up the long walk to his house, and the shadows of the trees fell over him and these old familiar creatures did not belong to him any longer, either.

Marjorie came through a door at the left of the graceful stairway, and her thin silk dress rustled as she moved. She smiled but her eyes were anxious. 'Dear Jon,' she said, 'I was worried about you. Why, you look so tired.' She glanced down at his hands. She saw they were red and that the skin appeared dry and so she knew he had been operating—a thing he had sworn never to do again in Hambledon. He saw her glance and he said, 'Yes. I did, and I still don't know why. Don't ask me who; I'll tell you later.'

She came to him and kissed him on the cheek and she saw how weary he was. She said, 'I've waited dinner for you, of course. And,' she paused a second, 'and you must have a drink before dinner.'

'Thank you,' he said. 'I'll go upstairs and wash and change.'

'Oh, don't change. Do you know how romantic you look in riding clothes?' She smiled again. 'I never saw another man who looked so in jodhpurs and boots. Just freshen. I'll wait for you in the living-room.' Her smile was still fixed as she watched him go upstairs. He walked heavily and slowly and he did not look back. His dark head was bent. She sighed, tightened her hands together and went out of the hall.

She sat down in the large parlour and never had it seemed so empty before to her and so lonely. She started when some-one took her wrist firmly, and she said, 'Jon! I didn't hear you come in.'

But he was counting her pulse and scowling a little. 'Heat too much for you?' he asked, laying her hand down on the arm of the chair.

'A little. Will you mix me a drink also? There's going to be a storm.'

Jonathan went to a silver tray on a marble table. He poured a large amount of whisky into one glass, added only a little soda, then poured a smaller amount of liquor in the other glass but a considerable quantity of soda. He brought the latter to his mother. Then standing, he drank deeply of his tall crystal glass as if he could not swallow the liquid fast enough. He had almost drained the glass before he took it from his mouth. He smiled down at his mother, then seated himself. Marjorie kept her face carefully bland.

'I cooked the dinner for you to-night, Jon. But I'm afraid it's very heavy on a night like this. Wiener schnitzel; you always liked it.'

'I still do. But you shouldn't have bothered.'

'It's no bother.' She moved restlessly. 'I do hope it'll be nice on the Fourth. Whom shall we invite—it's very late now— for our usual picnic?'

'I've already invited Bob Morgan, and his mother. I know. She's all whalebone, flatus and fraudulent copperplate.'

Marjorie sipped at her glass. 'And I've invited people, too.

Didn't I tell you? Rose and Bert Kitchener, and their daughter, Maude. She's such a nice girl, and so very pretty and talented, and intelligent. Such beautiful eyes and curly auburn hair, and a delightful figure.'

'For Harald?'

'No, dear. Harald left to-day for Philadelphia. What a bad memory I have! Didn't I tell you that he is to have a show in Philadelphia on the fifth? He's already shipped twenty canvases. You know that private and very exclusive gallery on Broad Street? Yes.'

'Yes,' said Jonathan. He stood up and filled his glass again. 'It will cost him a nice penny.'

'He can afford it. And the owner has been advertising for two weeks, and issued invitations and there has been such a wonderful acceptance. It will be very successful.'

'Why didn't you go, too?'

'Oh, I don't know. I've gotten out of the habit of going to Philadelphia. Most of my relatives are dead now, and it makes me feel very sad, and I was a reserved sort of girl and didn't make many friends. Many of them have moved away. I should have gone, I suppose.'

'And you didn't want to leave me alone on the Fourth.'

'Well, dear, it would have been lonely for you.' She looked at him. 'I also invited Jenny.'

'What? Without Harald?'

'Jon. Please don't sneer. It makes you look quite ugly.'

Jonathan said in a mocking voice, 'Childe Harald. I don't understand his impressionistic style, but he may be good at that. He'll shock the hell out of Philadelphia, and so I wish him well. How did you get Jenny away from that island?'

'I just invited her, and she accepted. Poor Jenny.'

'I know. She'd mourn for our Harald. It's a wonder he didn't pack her up and take her with him.'

'Jon, dear. Is it possible that you don't know that Jenny *dislikes* Harald? Are you that blind? You know very well she stays on that island because it is her home, and her father built that house, and she adored him, and she regards Harald as an impudent intruder. She won't let him have it alone. She just sits and stands there, waiting for the day when he won't come back again.'

'Oh, Mother. I don't believe that for a minute. She stays there because of our Harry.'

'You really do believe the gossip of the town? Jon? Oh, no,

you simply can't! You, above all! Jon, Harald wants to marry Jenny. He told me so, himself.'

The glass became very still in Jon's hand, the yellow liquid as quiet as stone. Marjorie watched her son's dark face and heavy brows and hidden eyes with great intentness.

'Harry? He wants to marry Jenny?'

'Yes. He's asked her dozens of times.'

'I don't believe it,' he said. 'I've been there very often, and I've watched her. She stares at him as if she's—hungry. She listens to every word he says as if it came from God. She follows him all around with those big blue eyes of hers. She isn't aware of anyone else when he's around. It's not just the town gossip. I wouldn't consider that for an instant. But I've seen Jenny—looking at Childe Harald. And I'm acutely sensitive to people; I have to be. When he moves near to her she actually trembles. And she waits. She's a woman in love.'

Yes, thought Marjorie. But she said, 'Jenny is only twenty, Jon. And though I don't like to say it, you really don't know much about women, and especially not about young women. In love, Jon? I don't think you could ever detect that!'

The dinner bell chimed softly, and Marjorie rose and Jon with her. Once he staggered a little.

Neither Marjorie nor Jonathan was notable for loquacity even when they felt no strain between them, merely passing pleasant remarks or none at all during the hours they dined together. To-night, as they ate their dinner together and drank their wine, Marjorie and Jonathan were unusually silent even for them. The thunder-storm had burst out from beyond the mountains and was assaulting the small city and the river with fire and great explosions. Mother and son were not aware of it. She saw that Jonathan's exhaustion appeared to be growing. His colour was extremely bad, the sallowness accentuated. He was drinking the good wine not with pleasure but with grim absent-mindedness. He had told her nothing of the operation he had performed not very long ago, nor who had so suffered. That was not unusual: he rarely mentioned his cases. But Marjorie saw that he had totally forgotten who had lain unconscious under his hands that day, and this was indeed unusual for him. He had not touched his dinner, but he was filling his wine glass again, and his face was exceptionally gloomy even for him and exceptionally closed. There was a glaze over his eyes. He was almost drunk. His food was congealing on his plate, and the thunder drummed against the tall and shining glass of the windows and the lightning illuminated them at frequent intervals.

'Damn this storm,' said Jonathan at last in a slurred voice, and he set the wine bottle thumpingly on the table. 'How long has it been going on, anyway? Look at that lightning.'

She started. 'It does seem pretty wild, doesn't it?' she said.

The fresh strawberries and cream and tea had come, and had been partially eaten, and removed, Marjorie observed, though she had not the slightest memory of them. The wine bottle was empty. 'Are you ready to leave?' asked Jonathan. His face was sunken and his eyes were glazed with alcohol, and there was a tremor about his mouth and in his hands.

'Yes, thank you,' said Marjorie. He came to her chair and drew it back for her. He walked to the buffet then, leaving her standing. 'I think,' he said, 'that I'll take a bottle of bourbon upstairs with me. A nightcap. I'm tired.'

The thunderous rain was washing the tall bright windows and the wind was howling in the eaves. Jonathan was laboriously and with considerable careful difficulty fitting a crystal glass over the decanter. He was absorbed in the delicate task. Then, walking with slow caution, and putting each foot down tentatively, he left the dining-room. His mother heard his heavy and uncertain step on the stairs. She listened, during an interval when there was only the rain and the wind. Jonathan had gone into his father's study. She heard the solid bang of the door.

Marjorie wearily climbed the stairs to her own room. She could not face downstairs to-night, the lonely sofas, the empty chairs, the brilliant, lonely furniture, the glittering windows which would reflect nothing but a despairing woman's face.

She could hear Jonathan speaking on the telephone in the study. She paused, then went to the shut door and listened. 'Good, good,' he was saying in the precise voice of drunkenness. 'Don't let anyone in. Little sips of ice water only, or, better, little pieces of ice on her tongue. Don't let anyone in.'

You never did, dear, thought Marjorie. No, you never did. Except for Mavis. He had not forgotten Mavis, and only Marjorie knew that, Mavis the dearly beloved, and the hated.

Jonathan stood drinking in his father's study, drinking slowly and steadily, and he looked about him at the brown, golden and ruddy room, so calm and sedate under the soft lights of lamps. He thought of it as an autumn room, for it was warm and quiet and gleaming, the walls hidden by bookshelves and the books, themselves, chosen, he had suspected even as a child, not for their content so much as for their tawny shining leather and their gilt.

Yes, it was very quiet. It had always been quiet and staid and spacious. Yet, curiously, in spite of the deep leather chairs, the beautifully carved old desk, the bright tables with their little Chinese boxes and ivories, the books, the general air of warmth, the broad mullioned window with its window-seat covered with velvet cushions, there seemed to be no real invitation to rest here, to think, to meditate, to browse, to study. His father had called it his 'retreat,' and had spent most of his leisure here among 'my beloved books, my dearest companions,' yet it did not possess that peculiar atmosphere of repose that distinguishes the true library, the true study, of an intellectual man. In short, it was empty. It was not an abandoned room; it just had never been inhabited.

Jon had known that as a child. But from childhood he had indulged his father in his conceit that this was the throne-room of a dedicated and thoughtful and contemplative man, seeking refuge from a hot and exigent world into the caverns of his own brilliant mind. 'Always I am refreshed,' he would say. 'No matter how weary I am, I come to my retreat and think and muse and give rein to my fancy and let my thoughts soar, and soon peace comes to me and strength to bear the burdens of my life.' What his burdens had been Jonathan never knew, but he implied them, sighing, and would lift a plump white hand exhaustedly for a moment and then let it drop on the arm of his chair. He would then smile pathetically at Jonathan, his big blue eyes misty and wistful.

Jonathan leaned against the oaken door of the library to-night, drinking slowly and steadfastly, and then with the strange clarity of drunkenness he began to smile and he said aloud, 'Dear Papa, you were a terrible but lovable farce, and I always knew all about you. I loved you dearly, and still do, and you were kind. You loved me and I never let you know what I knew about you, because I pitied and protected you from sharp and perceptive Mama even when I was a little kid. Sharp and perceptive Mama. You knew she was on to you. She didn't have the humour and the compassion not to let you know. But I did. And you were grateful, and in a

90

way you'd never understand you taught me a lot about people. You taught me, for one thing, to recognise a bore at once and to avoid him. Never mind, Papa. You were a little man, more ordinary than most, and you were very pretentious, and wouldn't Mama be surprised to know I know all this! She thinks that I thought you an Intellect, and I let her think that because it amuses me and irritates her.

'You were weak and vulnerable, and for some damned reason the weak and the vulnerable get right inside my vest and cuddle up in my viscera. Mama despises them and is impatient with them, and probably with good reason, which leaves me in somewhat of a dilemma. Am I a little weak and vulnerable, too? Was that one bond between us?'

He frowned at the glass in his hand, then took a gulp from it. He muttered a particularly foul word. 'Maybe,' he said. 'I never thought of that before. Well, hell, Papa. Poor old boy. I knew all the time that your insistent kindness and solicitude for others was only your terrified defence against your fellow man. You probably had a faint idea of what people are, and so you tried to fend them off, prevent potential attacks on you with declarations of your belief in mankind, that it really is good, decent, kindly at heart, bulging with the honey of good-will and needing only encouragement to sprout wings. You gave money to every whimpering rogue, thief and lying mendicant who asked your help—so they'd think well of you and praise you for a sensitive and compassionate man. But charitable institutions, and even the Church, rarely got a penny out of you. There, you were parsimonious. Sometimes you mortified me when the priest or the sisters came around. Even though you sent them away with a few coppers or a little silver—poor devils—they thought you were the most benign creature in existence. The funny thing is, you really were. You weren't a hypocrite at all, though I suspect dear Mama always thought you were. You dearly loved yourself, but it was an innocent love, like a child's. God, Papa, you made me ache all over, when I was a kid, myself, and you treated me as if I were your father. Did I like that? Probably. Perhaps that was a bond between us, too.

'I knew when I was still in knickers that you were incapable of dealing, foot to foot, fist to fist, with others. At heart, you were a woman, perhaps even a girl. I don't mean that nastily, Papa. I'm a doctor and I know that every woman has

91

masculine qualities and every man feminine ones; that's our duality. But your feminine qualities were greater than your masculine.

'I think it was your terror of people that made you love harmless things, birds and trees and gardens. They never threatened you. Of what were you afraid, Papa? I don't think you ever knew. I don't think you even had the slightest suspicion. You just didn't want to be hurt. Who does? Unfortunately, all of us can't run away, as you ran away all your life. You did have loving and tender parents, so they never scared the hell out of you. You were born as you were born, with all your trembling genes and your fear. You couldn't help it. But Mama thought you could.'

Jonathan took another big swallow. The glittering surfaces in the room dazzled him. Cautiously he extended a hand and eased himself into a chair. Some whisky spilled on his knee, and he cursed abstractedly.

'Poor Papa,' he said. 'Your parents and your friends protected you. Everybody did. You were so easy to be fond of, with your gentle platitudes and clichés; you never said a word to offend anyone. You couldn't imagine speaking harshly, and I doubt you ever had a mean thought, either. You just weren't bright enough, Papa. The only one who refused to protect and shelter you was dear Mama. I think you came close to hating her, as close as you could hate anyone. You ran away from her. She probably impressed you as a gentle and understanding girl, when you were both young, and here was a new Mama already made to replace the one you had lost. But Mama never really was a Mama, though she bore you two sons. Except, of course, for darling Harald, the apple of her eye.'

There was one last boom of thunder and then the storm retreated and now the rain was steady and swishing against the glass and the wind had died.

'You know,' said John smiling at the chair where his father used to sit 'to receive my child's closest confidences,' 'I don't think you really knew a bad poem from a good one, a stinker of a picture from a fine one. But you tried. I think that's damned touching, and always did. You were sweet and kind. Above all, you were harmless, and that's a damned rare and precious quality in humanity. Harmlessness. I cherished that in you. And I never let you know one single infernal thing about me. I would have scared the dung out of you, and I loved you too much, and had too much tenderness for you, to tell you the truth. You couldn't have stood it. So I invented dear little boyish troubles which you could handle nicely with aphorisms and stroking of my head, and soothing murmurs. It made you happy. You died, thinking kids are innocent lambs, "trailing clouds of glory." That's from your pet poet, Wordsworth, and he makes me ill.'

Jonathan filled his glass solemnly. He toasted his father's empty chair. 'I miss you like hell,' he said, 'I miss your harmlessness. You were the only harmless creature I ever knew. Papa, your health, wherever you are.'

He laughed a little, and sprawled in his chair. 'Papa, if there is anything to immortality, I just know what you are now and what you are doing. You are wandering around the blue and shining halls of heaven with a feather-duster in your hands, and all the angels pat you on the head as they hurry about their business. You are probably about seven years old. God must love you particularly. I bet you never committed a mortal sin in your life. The capital sins were only words to you, weren't they? What did you tell the priests in the Confessional, Papa? Did you have to invent little venial sins? The sins of a child?

'You never knew what Mavis was. You loved her always, didn't you? You didn't live to see us married. You spoke of her as a "dear girl, a treasure, a love." Yes, Papa, she was indeed. Indeed. I'm glad you never knew how many times I came close to killing her. I thought of a thousand ways—'

The glass slipped from his inert hand and dropped to the floor and spilled its contents. He neither knew nor cared. He was fully drunk. He stared blankly before him, but his thoughts were not blank. His exhausted face took on the dark shadow of agony.

Mavis, Mavis, Mavis, he thought. Oh, my God, Mavis! Mavis!

He had been twenty-three years old, two years in medical school when he had first become aware of Mavis Eaton, niece and adopted daughter of Dr Eaton and his wife. Certainly, he had seen the little girl from babyhood, then as a toddler, then a running child shrill and insistent, for she was very spoiled. But so small a child hardly could inspire a boy and a youth with tenderness except in an academic way. So, he had seen her, had absently noted her, had thought her handsome for a child, had idly admired her, but had not been attracted by her pert ways, her open rudeness to her adoring uncle and adopted father, and her loud and unexpected outbursts of somewhat rough laughter. There had been a period when she had been grubby, and Jonathan, even hardly past puberty, had disliked grubbiness. Still later, she had lost her baby teeth, and her hair appeared lank and uncombed, and though he was polite to her in her uncle's house—which he visited often—she appeared to him to have lost the shining and spotless and rounded sweetness of earlier years.

It was on a hot August day that Jonathan Ferrier, twenty-three years old, became aware of Mavis, in her twelfth year. In fact, as he never forgot, it was 12th August, 1888.

He had ridden his bicycle over to Dr Eaton's house, for his horse was being treated for some vague disorder. He was a tall, exceptionally thin, dark young man, with a peculiar grace and elegance about him, and a clever, reticent face which could still become lively among friends. His dark eyes were restless but kind and the corners, even at twenty-three, were wrinkled with the marks of laughter. No one could quite decide whether or not he was handsome, or perhaps even ugly. A very few had seen the thick white ridges spring out about his mouth, so the general consensus, after some time, was that he was 'attractive in a sort of aristocratic way.' The people of Hambledon loved aristocrats, especially those who had made all their money in grosser pursuits than medicine.

Of course, it was said, he could not compare with the rising brother, Harald, who was as gloriously beautiful as a matinee idol, and who already had the girls mad with love for him, and had the 'nicest' disposition.

He wore, on that August day, a suit of light grey wool, a stiff straw hat with a gay red ribbon on it, polished black shoes and a shirt striped in pale blue. His collar was stiff, high and brilliant, and his tie was a devilish scarlet, bought at the university and somewhat shocking to Hambledon. He wore no gloves, and this was unpardonable, and his face and hands were burned dark with the sun, which was vulgar.

He leaned his bicycle against the steps of the high deep veranda of the Eaton house, and was whistling some lively tune whose lyrics would not have been admired in Hambledon. He took off his coarse straw hat and fanned himself briskly and danced a step or two out of sheer youthful exuberance.

He concluded his dance with a flourish, waved his hat high and was about to clap it back on his thick dark hair when he heard a light laugh. Then he saw a young girl moving on a cushioned swing. Seeing that she had attracted his attention, she laughed a little louder and mockingly clapped her hands.

Jonathan coloured with annoyance and dislike, then saw that it was 'only that damned kid, Mavis.' He put his hat on; she was too young for gallantries, and he jumped up the broad brown steps of the veranda. 'Hallo,' he said. 'Doctor home? Almost five, you know.'

'He's home,' said Mavis. 'Hallo, Jon. I haven't seen you for a couple of years.' She paused and smiled. 'You've grown up.'

He stopped at this impertinence from a child, and turned his head and stared at her. 'You haven't,' he said with shortness, then was still. For it was most evident that Mavis had, indeed, approached a quite astonishing measure of maturity, more even than her twelve years should have shown. And she had a look of deep animal happiness.

She leaned back in her swing, smiling, and he was struck by her smile, for it was utterly beguiling. He thought at once: The Laughing Girl, and it pleased him that he had reached, in only a moment or two, a perfect miniature evaluation of Mavis. She was born to laughter, and to laugh, as others are born to grieve or to work or to be intelligent or to be geniuses. It would not be a contrived laughter, or a laughter solely for effect—though it could be that, also, nor a false or artificial mirth, nor a grudging one. Mavis was laughter. It was an integral part of her nature, and she laughed as others merely smiled. She had lost the little irritabilities of young childhood. Now all her innate capacity for finding almost everything amusing, was the strongest characteristic of her nature. And, it was a husky and gleeful laugh, evoking laughter in anyone she encountered. Mavis invariably made things amusing, but her conversation was not scintillating. However, few cared. The fascination of her constant laughter was quite enough.

Jonathan had seen riper figures, for, for all her precociousness Mavis was still only twelve. She was still a child, though she had reached physical maturity. Her hair was tied with a blue ribbon and she wore a blue voile dress with a pink sash, and blue slippers. Childish attire.

It was something else, mysterious and bewitching, that held him there, gawking. It was a quality of absolute bright assurance, of magnificent soft confidence, of healthy amiability and endearing seduction, of enormous vitality, perhaps, of poise. Like many others, Jonathan had tried to describe and understand charm, and had been as defeated as everyone else. Mavis possessed it in overwhelming measure. It did not lie in any particular feature, nor was it caught in her golden mist of hair or in her smallish blue eyes, shining and glowing. There was not the slightest flaw to be seen in Mavis, but Jonathan had seen flawless girls before and had found them intensely dull. He had a confused thought: Was Mavis stupid? He remembered the shrill and grubby child he had avoided through the years, and it seemed incredible to him that that untidy little hoyden had become so gorgeous a young girl. But, was she stupid?

Jonathan, above all things, hated stupidity, and beauty never excused it. He found it the explanation for what was most bestial in humanity.

Mavis, never looking away from him, laughed again. It was a laugh that invited the whole world to an expression of mirth, and Jonathan found himself smiling. He forgot to wonder if Mavis were stupid. He saw that she loved to be alive and expected others to have that love, also.

She approached him nearer, her head a little tilted as she studied him, her squinted eyes a little puzzled at his prolonged stare. Then the puzzled look disappeared, and Mavis understood. Jonathan might be an old man—but he was exactly like the boys she knew and so she was not shy with him. Mavis, in her way, was a very wise girl.

'You've grown up, Mavis,' he said and did not think he was banal.

'Girls usually do,' she said. She had a husky speaking voice also, which trembled always as if the impatient laughter was swelling beneath it and was demanding to be heard. She stood so near him that he could have touched her. And then, a little to his helpless horror he had the most urgent desire to touch her, indeed. He was appalled, for he was a mature man of twenty-three and the girl before him was still almost a child, and he knew that what he was feeling now was a most powerful sexual urge towards her, stronger than any he had known before in his life. She stood before him on the quiet porch, looking up into his eyes and he could not believe that what he saw in her was complete knowledge and that she was amused. Years younger than he, she was incalculably older and more aware, for while the Mavises never appear to grow old they are never young, not even at birth.

'I hope you like what you see, Jon,' she said, and chuckled knowingly.

'You've improved,' he said, and he fought down his desperate desire for her with loathing for himself. He tried for lightness. 'My last memory of you was of a dirty little kid with a runny nose and tousled hair.'

'Really,' she said. 'And do you know what I've always thought about you, Jon? You're dippy.' And again she chuckled.

He found himself chuckling with her, but he still wanted to take her in his arms and kiss her with a man's passion and desire, and he did not know why, for she was only younger but not prettier than so many girls he had known since he had been sixteen years old. He tipped his hat a little mockingly, then went to the door and pulled the bell. The day was hot and there was the raucous shrilling of cicadas in the sun and quiet, and the distant rattle of a wagon's wheels on cobblestones, and the heated swish of trees. They seemed to roar in Jon's ears like a confused cacophony, and for the moments he stood there, resolutely facing the door with its stained-glass windows, he felt the smiling eyes of the girl fixed directly between his shoulders.

'Daddy's in the garden, and it's Mamie's day off,' she informed him, 'and Mama's downtown shopping.'

He heard her light quick step running down the porch stairs, and he was alone, and when he turned he saw the flash of golden hair in the sun and that heart-softening chuckle. He went home. It was not until he was entering his parents' house that he was dismayed, and he stood in the cool and fragrant dusk of the hall and despised himself. His mother came in from the morning room, raising her brows in surprise. 'Why, dear,' she said, 'I thought you had gone to see Martin Eaton. Wasn't he home?'

Jonathan had never learned to lie very well or often, and so he said, 'Yes, he was home.'

Marjorie came nearer him, and she was puzzled, 'Jon, is there something wrong?'

He was impatient. He threw his hat on a chair and it rolled off and he let it lie. Marjorie bent and picked it up and then stood with it in her hands. 'What can be wrong?' he said.

'Well,' said Marjorie, who was a little worried. It had been established that Jon would do his internship under the wing of Martin Eaton's friends, and that Dr Eaton would more than sponsor him in Hambledon. She wondered if Jonathan had quarrelled with him. It was not a fatal matter, but an inconvenient and anxious one. She knew Jonathan's temper, his quick and even murderous rages, his dislike for any quibbling or deviousness, his way of stamping a man a hypocrite under the slightest provocation, and his deadly impatience and intolerance of humbug.

'Come into the morning-room,' she said. 'I have some very icy lemonade and some fresh cake, which I made this afternoon. You look very hot.'

'I want a drink,' he said, and his voice was rude and his manner abrupt. 'And that doesn't mean lemonade.'

Jonathan did not drink regularly, as yet, but when he did it was somewhat disturbing to his mother, for he drank as recklessly as he lived, and always under stress. She said nothing when he went into the dining-room to the liquor cabinet, and she put away his hat then stood in thought for a moment in the hall. She wanted to return to the morning-room but decided that if she did he would not accompany her, but might possibly do so if she waited for him. He came back into the hall with a glass of whisky and soda, and Marjorie noticed the darkness of the drink.

'Where's Childe Harald?' he asked.

'Boating,' she replied. 'He's gone on a picnic to Heart's Ease.' She smiled. 'Let's go into the morning-room, shall we?' and she led the way, her slender figure floating in the light green voile of her dress, her head high. She hoped Jon would follow, and she hoped this ardently, and let out a deep breath when she heard his following if reluctant footsteps.

They sat down together and Marjorie took up her needlework and bent her head over it. There was no use pressing Jon for an explanation, she thought. There had never been any use, even when he had been a child. He talked or did not talk, at his own pleasure.

'Well, since you were so insistent on that damned lemonade, why don't you drink it yourself?' he asked, standing before her.

'Oh. Yes. Of course. Do pour me a glass, dear.'

He poured a glass for her, then stood sipping his own, frowning into the glass. She saw that he was sallow under his tanned face, as if he had had some unpleasant experience. But she merely waited. After a little he sat down, but on the edge of his chair.

'A hot day,' she said. 'Martin doesn't like the heat, does he? I remember when we were children—'

'A long time ago.'

Marjorie smiled. 'Not so long. I was visiting his parents, with my own parents. I was always thin, I remember, and he used to tease me, but then he was a butterball of a boy and that is why the heat affected him so cruelly.' She paused. 'To-day is the hottest day of the summer. Poor Martin must be suffering.'

'Oh, hell, don't beat about the bush,' said Jonathan. 'You want to know if I saw him, and if not why not. I didn't see him, though he was at home. I didn't want to see him.'

'I see,' said Marjorie.

'No, you don't,' said Jonathan. He drank again. He turned the glass restlessly in his hands. He had never confided in his mother but twice in all his life and he did not intend to now. In fact, the very idea staggered him. What would she say if he said to her bluntly, 'I saw young Mavis Eaton, and she's grown into a terrible beauty, and I wanted to drag her away somewhere and tear the clothes off her and rape her, not gently, but brutally and madly'? How did a man explain bewitchment and that awful urge he had never suspected lived in him? His mother, too, was a gentlewoman and she not only would not understand but would rise and leave him with disgust and dread and with his own horror. She would not faint as it was the style for ladies to faint when they were overcome. She would not call for smelling salts and fans. But she would detest him. He had never cared what his mother's private feelings for him were, or her thoughts, or at least he had long ago assured himself he did not care. Yet the thought of her glance of repulsion made him shrink inwardly. And quite right, too, he said to himself. He stood up. 'I want another drink,' he said. Marjorie did not comment. She only hoped he would return. He did not for a considerable time and when he entered the room again she more than suspected that the drink in his hand was his third, not his second.

'Say it,' he said, and sat down. 'You drink too much, Jon, for your age and your health.'

'No,' said Marjorie. 'I promised myself a year ago I'd never say it again. After all, you are not a boy any longer, you are not a youth, either. You are twenty-three years old and so you are a man and your life is your own. And a man must do what he feels he must do.'

'Now, that's a subtle aphorism,' said Jon, in the mocking voice he always used when he felt he must protect himself. ' "A man must do what he feels he must do." Martin Eaton's a sot. Everybody knows it. Is he doing what he feels he must do?'

Marjorie put her sewing in her hands and in her lap and looked at her son long and gravely. Then she said, 'Yes.'

'Yes? Yes, what?'

'Just "yes," Jon. You aren't the only one who can be reticent, you know.'

'I'm reticent about my own affairs—'

'So am I.'

Jon thought about that and was intrigued. Then he said at last, grinning, 'Oh, no! Not you and old Martin Eaton? Before Dad, I suppose?'

'Martin and Flora are very happily married,' said Marjorie, sipping at her own glass. 'It was a very suitable marriage.'

'Imagine!' said Jonathan in a nasty tone. 'He might have been my father!'

'I never considered it seriously,' said his mother, smiling a little. 'It didn't happen back in the dark ages, you know, Jon. We'd known each other from childhood, and I was always fond of Martin. You wouldn't believe it, but I called him Fancy.'

Jonathán laughed. The fearful tension and sickness in him was relaxing under the drink and the soothing voice of his mother. 'Fancy! Old Man Eaton!'

'He's only twenty-five years older than you, Jon, and hardly a patriarch at forty-nine. He told me, when we were very young, that he'd wait until I had grown up, and then—'

Very carefully, Jonathan put down his glass. 'Oh? And how old were you then?'

'Eleven? Yes, I was eleven, or almost.'

'And he—'

'Well, he was older. Sixteen, I think.'

'A man!'

'Almost. We thought a boy of sixteen was a man in those misbegotten days, though now we don't think they are full men until they are twenty-one. It's so absurd. Men to-day are no younger in any way than they were then.'

But Jonathan was drinking again, though more slowly. 'Sixteen,' he said. 'And a big sixteen I should think. Probably had already had a roll or two— I'm sorry, Mother.'

'I'm not very shockable,' said Marjorie. 'Coming down to it, I should think so, about Martin. He was always a lusty boy and a lusty man. That's why I really did almost marry him, though I did not take him seriously. He was like a brother. Now, if he had not been so close to me, and so brotherly all my life, I might have—'

But Jonathan said, 'And you didn't know at eleven, of course.'

'Certainly, I knew! A girl of eleven is really much older than a youth ten years older! It is said that all men are little boys at heart, but it is very doubtful that women were ever little girls. I knew that Martin—what is the delicate phrase?— wished to make love to me, and I thought it very exciting. Children aren't as innocent as you might think, Jon.'

'And you knew, at eleven, that he wanted to seduce you?'

'Yes, I knew he wanted to "seduce" me.' She smiled and her slender face brightened with mirthful remembrance. 'It wasn't moonlight and roses for me, as adults think it is with children. Children are earthy. It is only later that they cover the raw exigencies of nature with a pink gauze of romance and accompany it with poetry and music. Adults are really shrinking souls, but children look at life candidly and see it fully, and are not repelled by smells, nastiness or criminal acts. That is because they have no conscience to confuse things. They are savages, and any aspects of life are always interesting to them, even those we call the dirtiest ones. Well, anyway, Martin didn't seduce me, not even when I was fourteen, fifteen, and so on. By that time he had become romantic and said he loved me.'

'You must have been a fatal woman even at eleven,' said Jonathan.

'You've been reading Marie Corelli,' said Marjorie. 'Let me enlighten you, dear. All women are fatal from the cradle, but some more than most. The rare woman, the very rare woman, is still fatal even when she is ninety or more. But that's a different kind of fatality, thank God. I've seen only two or three women like that, and they were deadly.'

'In what way?'

Marjorie leaned forward and put her elbows on her knees and pretended to consider. But she was thinking more rapidly than before, and she said to herself, Who, for God's sake?

A very young girl? A girl hardly past childhood? Poor Jon. But it may be dangerous.

'In what way?' she repeated thoughtfully. 'A really frightful way, dear. You see, they never loved anyone in their lives. They were incapable of it. They never got over the love affair they had had with themselves in the cradle. And that made them irresistible. Men, especially, adore women incapable of loving anyone but themselves. They feel sure the women have a good reason for all that passionate adoration, and they join the adorers.'

'Narcissistic, you mean?'

'Yes. An excellent word. But those women aren't mentally ill, Jon. You'll find they are unusually healthy and robust and have an atmosphere about them of overpowering zest and long for life, and gusto. Everything is delightful to them, enjoyable; a relish, tang, adventure. They're never openly annoyed. They are always ready for any escapade. And they laugh—always. There's just one thing you must never do to them: you must never bore them. That's the only crime they hold against anyone.'

'The Laughing Girls,' said Jonathan.

'Exactly.' Marjorie smiled, pleased, and nodded. 'The Laughing Girls. And they're the only kind, no matter how beautiful, who don't arouse envy and hatred among other women. They can bewitch women as well as men. They're absolutely female, and that's lethal. Yes. I should say their great charm is that they are entirely female and know it, and exploit it. They all have huge appetites for everything.'

Jon was frowning into his glass. Marjorie studied his bent head. Dear God, she thought, where has he met one? To-day?

'I think you speak as a woman, Mother,' he was saying. 'There must be something else they have—besides laughter and zest—which—arouses—people.'

'True,' said Marjorie. 'I call it diabolism. No, wait. I don't mean they are consciously wicked. They'd be shocked to learn that others think they are, really shocked and hurt. The consciously wicked are a different matter entirely, and one gets on to them easily, you know and avoid them. No, the Laughing Girls, as you have so cleverly called them, have a—well, an innocent diabolism. Like a force of nature. It is themselves. And diabolism—though you have always denied there is such a thing at all—has an awful charm of its own. I've always thought that Lucifer, above all else, must be a most charming angel.'

'Perhaps,' said Jon. He stood up. He appeared irresolute. Is it possible he is going to tell me something? thought Marjorie. He said, 'I think I'll have another drink.'

When he had left the room Marjorie thought with more concentration. Jonathan had left the house in the heat of the day on his bicycle to visit Martin Eaton. He had had time only to arrive there, give or take five minutes or so, and then he had immediately returned. He had not dallied. Half an hour in all. Where could he have met one of his Laughing Girls in that short space of time, especially when he had been on his bicycle practically every moment? He had not mentioned Flora Eaton, so it was probable he had not seen her. He had not seen Martin Eaton. He had gone to the house, found the older doctor home—yet had immediately left without seeing him. Therefore, he had received some kind of a shock almost at once.

He had seen a girl. Marjorie knew the girls of all the best families in Hambledon and she skimmed their faces with her mental eyes. Nice, wholesome girls, some flirts but innocent ones, and none calculated to strike Jonathan so forcibly. Besides, he had known them all his life, these potential wives. Jonathan was stricken; there was no doubt about it. He was under some fierce and devastating spell, for his mother had never seen him drink so steadily before and so much. He was pale; he had the aspect of a man under extreme stress. His hands had trembled a few times. It was someone he had not known before, then. Dear Heaven, not some strumpet of the street! thought Marjorie, then almost, even in her distress, she laughed at herself. Jonathan was not the kind, and where would he have encountered such in half an hour, which had been spent almost entirely on a bicycle?

Her thoughts returned to Martin Eaton. Had there been a young patient in the house, or some distant visiting relative? If so, then the bewitched Jonathan would have inevitably stayed for more bewitchment, and he would not now be so evasive. He would speak. Men do not fly from charmers, on a bicycle. They stay and grovel, thought Marjorie, with some bitterness. They stay and offer their necks for a dainty foot. Even Jonathan would do so. More brilliant men had become victims of the Laughing Girls. They loved to be victims. They dedicated their lives to the victimisation and thought themselves blest. They fly only when they know the object of all that silliness and stupidity is either not for them, or beyond them, or is very dangerous to them—and often they do not flee even then. Very rarely do they flee.

So, it must be a young girl, a very young girl. Who? Slowly Marjorie remembered something that had happened last week. She had been at the Garden Club meeting near the river, and Flora Eaton had brought her adopted daughter with her, though children were invariably forbidden. 'She is really so grown-up and interested,' Flora had apologised. The ladies had not objected, after the first affronted frowns. They had been charmed within moments by Mavis Eaton, who had been so deferential, so beguiling, so lovely, so polite and eager to please. She had laughed so often too, with open delight at everything. Her delight had been something radiant and completely fascinating. And it had not been false and shown for effect. The girl was what she was. A Laughing Girl. Marjorie, of all the women there, had disliked her at once and with unusual intensity.

'What a charmer!' the ladies had twittered when Flora and Mavis had left. 'What an absolute charmer! What she will do to the boys and men when she is older!'

But she was never young, Marjorie had thought. I know her well.

She started now, seeing that Jonathan had returned to the room and was standing before her, drinking again. He was looking a little sick, as if he were remembering in spite of the whisky. Marjorie spoke carefully. 'You say you didn't see Martin Eaton. I'm sorry. I heard last week that he wasn't feeling so well. Flora told me. It was very tiresome of Flora, really, but she had brought little Mavis with her. You remember Mavis, the niece they adopted.'

She knew at once, for his hand quite violently shook for a second, and the whisky splashed on his fingers. He was looking at her fully and the white ridges she always dreaded had sprung up about his mouth. 'What,' he said, 'is wrong with the kid?'

'Wrong? In what way is she wrong?' asked Marjorie, as if surprised.

'I don't mean that, damn it!' He was almost shouting. 'I mean, what have you got against the girl?'

'Jon, please. The windows are all open. I don't understand

you. Why should we be talking about a little girl, a little girl in the eighth grade, I believe? A child? Aren't there more interesting things to talk about than children? I don't remember that they are so very important at all, but rather boring, in fact, and intelligent people—'

'I asked you, Mother, what you have against the girl?'

Marjorie was terribly frightened. She had never known Jonathan to be like this before, even in his reckless childhood. She said, making her voice cold, 'Don't talk to me like that, Jon, and shouting, too! What's the matter with you? Shall we close the subject? Besides, there is something about dinner which I must attend to—' She began to get up.

In spite of her fear she was truly angered when he put his hand against her shoulder and pushed her back into her chair.

'I only asked you a simple, reasonable question,' he said, and there was a hard, thick quality about him which was alien to her. 'Just a simple question.'

'Which I think is too stupid to answer, and far too stupid for an adult to ask. I refuse to talk about a chit. Why should I? Why should you? Are you drunk, Jon? I'm afraid you are. I want to warn you about one thing, my boy. Don't you dare touch me in that manner again. You aren't too old for me not to strike you—hard—very hard—across the face.'

For a moment their eyes held together and Jonathan saw the icy anger in his mother's, and he was ashamed. He put down the drink. 'You're right,' he said. 'I've been drinking too much to-day. You see, I've met one of your Laughing Girls, or mine, I should say.' He tried to smile. 'You must be brave, Mother. I'm not going to be like your Martin Eaton; I'm going to wait for the girl to grow up. But unlike Martin, I'm not going to be put off. I'm going to marry her.'

He was still staring at her. She knew that she must not let him know that she knew of whom he was speaking. She must only pray, if she could, that something would happen— She was suddenly confused and exhausted and ill. Not her Jonathan, not her darling!

She tried to laugh a little before that frightening face. 'Oh, so she's very young? Well.' She paused. 'And you are twenty-three. That makes you a mature man, doesn't it—and she is a little girl. I wouldn't, if I were you, let anyone know—'

'Do you think I am insane?' he demanded.

Probably, as of just now, his mother replied inwardly. Yes, very probably.

'I know what happens to men when they fall in love with children,' he said.

'Oh, Jon.' In spite of herself she winced. 'Please don't say anything else. You'll regret it when you remember, later. Don't say anything else! It's too dangerous.'

'Yes,' he said. 'It's too dangerous. And I can wait.' Later, he wondered why his mother had not been outraged, horrified and shocked to death. Or even amazed.

And he had waited. All that his mother had said that hot August day had meant nothing at all to him. He had never respected her opinion or known her. He had talked to her that day only because his inner extremity had been so great and uncontrollable, and because he had drunk too much. Within a few days, as she never mentioned that talk—assuredly only a rambling affair to her—he was relieved that she had forgotten it. Only fear of himself, of what he was capable of doing, had impelled him to talk so dangerously. But—his mother could not have the slightest idea, and he put her out of his mind. She had no imagination. She was not really very intelligent. And she and old Martin Eaton, by God! Martin had not known what he had escaped. It was unfortunate that his own father had not been so lucky.

That is what Jonathan Ferrier thought that August of his twenty-third year.

He saw Mavis Eaton on every possible occasion during the next five years. and he thought himself exceedingly prudent and subtle at all times. But Mavis had known from the very beginning, and it amused her that this 'old man' was interested in her. She teased him artfully when she encountered him in her uncle's house, or in his gardens, or demurely tormented him. She was not intelligent but she had a primitive wisdom. Her uncle and aunt often spoke of the Ferrier money, and as Martin Eaton was as fond of Jonathan as if the young man had been his son Martin constantly talked of Jonathan's professional future and successes, and even hinted that he might possibly leave Jonathan a part of his estate. When she was fifteen Mavis was already picturing herself as a *grande dame* in Philadelphia or New York, presiding over her successful and famous husband's mansion, for Mavis had no intention of spending her life in little Hambledon. She wanted multitudes of admirers, and craved influence. At sixteen she was more than attracting the casual attention of young men in

New York, where she attended a private school for a year, and at seventeen she knew her great powers, the seduction and fascination of her perpetual merriment, and her beauty.

Very few noticed the smallness of her blue eyes, for they were almost always arched like fringed quarter moons under her golden brows, crinkled and squinted with laughter. There were some women and girls who said she had 'little sly eyes,' but this was accounted as envy. Fewer ever saw the cold and conjecturing gleam of those eyes, for they appeared almost entirely closed at all times, and somewhat sunken in their sockets. Among those who were disturbed by Mavis's eyes, and their secretiveness, was Marjorie Ferrier.

When Mavis was eighteen, Jonathan told his mother and brother abruptly that he was going to marry the girl in the near future.

Marjorie said nothing, for there was nothing to say. But Harald laughed, and said, 'Not Golden Girl! Why, she's a dragon! She'd eat the heart out of you in a year!'

The totally infatuated and adoring Jonathan Ferrier hardly heard. Later, he was to know that the secret of Mavis's charm was her absolute sexuality. It was not overt; paradoxically she was almost incapable of being aroused, herself, almost devoid of sensual passion. She knew that she was irresistible to men, and when she had been fifteen she knew exactly why, and so she had contempt and amused scorn for those she attracted. However, she learned the art of flaunting her sexual attractions in a most delicate way, with rarely a stir in herself. If men were stupid enough to dream that she desired them, more fool they. It had nothing to do with Mavis Eaton's real desires, which she kept hidden.

The Laughing Girls, as Jonathan was to learn much later, have but one love and that is themselves, and but one passion, and that was their enhancement and gain. When Mavis petulantly told him—but with exquisite smiles—that she would not 'dream' of spending her life in Hambledon, Jonathan fatuously promised her that in good time they would move to Philadelphia or New York or wherever she desired. This alarmed Martin Eaton. He had a long talk with Jonathan. 'We need surgeons and physicians of your kind here, Jon,' he said. 'You can't desert us, can you, even for Mavis?'

'She's very young. I'm just humouring her,' said Jonathan. 'Of course, I could have a practice in Philadelphia, too—' It was all in the blissful future, and in the meantime there was

107

Mavis, whose touch and laughter and natural gaiety and beauty almost drove him mad. He could not wait for their marriage. To Marjorie Ferrier, this abasement of her son seemed tragic, for she had expected more intelligence and discernment in Jonathan, and more taste. There was a certain grossness about Mavis, an animal shine and sleekness, which promised many lustful delights. But Marjorie knew that those delights would be an illusion, for the Laughing Girls knew no pleasure but in themselves and their desires, and none of them concerned the happiness and welfare and joy of others. Once Marjorie had said to Harald, 'Mavis, under other circumstances and in a different age, would be the perfect—the perfect—'

'Tart,' said Harald. 'Concubine? Mavis isn't clever enough. Doxy? Perhaps. I think I like tart best.'

'Oh, Harald,' said Marjorie, and smiled sadly, but she knew he was right. 'I really think, concubine. The perfect illusion of the perfect woman.'

'With no personal involvement,' said Harald. He frequently startled his mother with his perceptive comments, and she was startled now, and thought, as she thought very often, that Harald was much cleverer than most people knew. It was out of character, in some way, that he had this worldly shrewdness which Jonathan did not possess at all. (He was to marry Myrtle Heger a little before Jonathan married Mavis Eaton, but no one believed that he loved the woman or that he had married her for anything but her money.)

The marriage of Mavis Eaton to Jonathan Ferrier, on a hot and golden June day, was considered a State-wide Event, and the Governor came, and so did Senator Campion, and, of course, the mayors of several cities. The Eatons and the Ferriers were rich, and Jonathan was already establishing a famous reputation, and his mother came of an 'old family.'

He was never to forget his wedding night.

Jonathan, lying in a drunken sleep now in his father's study, or rather sprawled in a leather chair, remembered that night in his dreaming. His dark and faintly sweating face was contorted, and his head moved uneasily, and even in his sleep he was conscious of a powerful nausea and enormous discomfort. He felt as if he were one ache, mentally and physically, and somewhere there was a loud and furious shrilling as if millions of bees had gone mad.

He pulled himself sluggishly and painfully up from his heavy sleep, saw that it was very early morning, and that the telephone on his father's desk was throbbing unremittingly. Nothing stirred in the house. The low and slanting light of first morning was pulsing through the leaded windows. Cursing, wincing, Jonathan reached out and took up the telephone.

'Oh, Jonathan,' said Father McNulty's voice in relief. 'I hope I didn't wake you, too early. It's almost seven, a quarter to.'

'Don't mind me,' said Jonathan in a slow, thick voice. He swallowed. His throat felt swollen and very dry. 'I'm always awake, like the perfect doctor. Call me in a couple of hours, and perhaps I'll answer then, and perhaps not.' He was not really awake. He blinked and shuddered at the light and his stomach seemed to have a tendency to climb to his chest. 'Good-bye,' he said.

'Jon!' cried the priest. 'Please listen for just a second or two. For God's sake, please listen. This is a matter of life and death—'

'In which I am no longer interested,' said Jonathan. 'Don't you ever sleep?'

'I haven't slept all night,' said the priest. 'I just came home, myself, and I have a Mass at seven. You remember young Francis Campion? I heard you treated him for colitis or something three years ago. Senator Kenton Campion's son.'

Jonathan yawned in agony. His head appeared to be dividing itself slowly and surely into separate sections. 'What about it? I'm not the family doctor. They only called me because their own was away, or something, after he almost killed the boy. Why don't they call him, if the kid's sick again?'

The priest hesitated. 'I think there is a personal reason. Family doctor, you know. There might be some—some embarrassment— You see, young Francis tried to hang himself last night, and only old Tom, one of the servants, heard him and saved his life. Hanged himself with the sash of his dressing-gown—'

'You can be sure,' said Jonathan, with bitterness, 'that there is always some busybody around to take matters into his own damned interfering hands. When a man wants to die, let him die, say I.' He paused, then said with more interest, 'Tried to kill himself? At twenty? I thought he was doing well in that seminary of his, studying for the priesthood. A fine priest

109

he'll make!' Jonathan chuckled, then coughed. 'So, they called you to administer the proper spiritual punishment.'

'Jon, please listen. Tom called me. No one else would. Not the aunt. And the Senator's in Washington, though he is due home to-day for the Fourth of July celebrations. You know the aunt.' The priest coughed in apology. 'No doubt a very estimable lady, but not one to know what to do. So Tom called me. But young Francis would not listen to me at all, and refused to see me. I did stay at his bedside, and he never turned his head in my direction, I stayed until I had to leave, for Mass.'

'A very piteous story,' said Jonathan. 'But has it got anything to do with me? No.'

'I thought—I thought—' the priest stammered, 'that you should see him. No, not for medical attention.'

Jonathan came up from the reddish sick fog in total amazement. 'Are you out of your mind, Father? "Not for medical attention," you say. For what, then?'

'I heard that the boy—trusted—you. Or something, Jon. It's just an inspiration. He needs something. I think you can give it to him.'

'No,' said Jonathan. 'Besides, if I saw him I'd have to report to the police.'

'You saved his life once. I think you could do it again, Jon.'

'Why should I? Let him go and give him your blessing, Father.'

The priest paused. 'You will go, Jon, and immediately?'

'No,' said Jonathan, and hung up. He fell back into the depths of the leather chair. When he had strength enough he would take a cold bath, prepare himself a large cold drink, put a cold cloth on his head and go to bed, and inform his mother that no one, under any circumstances, was to disturb him. Preferably forever. He felt profoundly ill, and knew, after a moment's reflection, that the illness was in his mind as well as in his abused body. Mavis. Was he to be cursed for all the days of his life by remembering her? She was part of his flesh, like an incubus, beautiful Mavis, laughing Mavis, coaxing, teasing Mavis. There were times when he thought he had forgotten her, or that he could live with the memory of her, and then when he was off-guard, or had been drinking too much, the house was full of her footsteps and her laughter, the rustling of her dresses, the sound of her raucous singing. Then the pain returned, as bad as ever.

He pushed himself to his feet, and was dizzy. Why don't I have the courage to die? he asked himself. Why didn't I have the sense to plead guilty and let the State hang me, and so save me the trouble? Then he thought of young Francis Campion, twenty years old, who had tried to take his life a few hours ago. Now, what for, at his age? What could so disillusion a man of twenty to drive him to death, and a budding priest at that? Jonathan leaned on a table and in spite of himself he was interested. He also remembered the boy and how he had saved his life three years ago. That life had been saved almost as much by the boy's will to live as by Jonathan's skill. Yet three years later he had looked for death, the only son of one of the richest men in the State, pampered, indulged, allowed to do what he wished at all times.

Jonathan found himself in his bathroom, naked to the waist, sloshing himself with cold water. He looked at his ravaged face with the bluish growth of beard, and said aloud, 'The hell with it.' He dried himself, dressed in riding clothes. He frowned at his shaking hands. He was all parched leather inside and he craved a drink. He knew he dared not drink water, for it would make him vomit. In complete physical misery, and walking carefully so as not to jar his head too much, he left the room.

Still, no one stirred in the house as yet, though it was almost seven. The house had the dry, aromatic odour of a hot summer morning, compounded of heat, a faint drift of dust, and withering flowers. Jonathan went out into the blaze of the early day, and then to the stables.

He still did not know why he was going to see young Francis Campion, or what he was doing out so early in the day with a fearful hangover and a sense that life had become unbearable. He thought of Father McNulty with angry disfavour. Interfering young idiot! But these priests had the idea that human life was sacred or something, and should be preserved. He, Jonathan Ferrier, wished he could take some of them through the wards where people were dying of cancer, including little children, or wards of venereal disease or tuberculosis, a thousand and one diseases of corruption and agony. Let them see, for themselves, with what respect their God regarded his own creation, that He could bring it so low, far down to the base of screaming animalism, and then abandon it to decay and torture and unspeakable indignities.

Nearly all other houses in Hambledon were 'houses,' but
111

the Campion house was a 'residence,' even to those who possessed a sense of humour. Jonathan was one of the few—and he originated the term—who called the house Pike's Peak because it not only was the highest building on the mountain that overlooked Hambledon but had a curious roof of blue slate which did, indeed, rise to a peak directly in the top-centre of that pile of white stone masonry. Perched on top of that sharp peak reared a weathervane, huge and gilt, which could be seen turning from the streets of the town when the sun shone upon it. It had been built forty years ago by the late Mrs Kenton Campion's father, old Jasper Pike, so again Jonathan had a wry reason for his appellation. Mrs Campion had inherited it together with a great fortune from her father's coal mines, and it was considered Hambledon's only authentic mansion in the grand tradition of mansions, for it had thirty rooms, all immense. The architect had not been decided upon the exact style he wished to produce, so he added a white marble colonnade along the front of the house which was incongruous, surmounted as it was by that soaring peak of glittering blue slate with its slit windows like a tower. Jonathan never glanced up at the mountain without saying, 'Every town has its monstrosity. Hambledon has its Pike's Peak, a nightmare of tasteless luxury, the dream of every vulgarian and illiterate in the world.'

Mrs Kenton Campion had died some fifteen years ago, leaving her politician husband with that one small boy of his, Francis, and all her money. At that time Kenton had been a mere Congressman, but later he had been reappointed by the state legislature, over a period of sixteen years, as a Senator. He was often spoken of as becoming a Governor, and once he had been suggested by enthusiastic—and indebted—friends for second place on the Presidential ticket. However, at that time there had been some unreasonable resentment against wealthy men occupying all the available political positions and though Kenton Campion steadfastly maintained that he was at heart a poor man—had not his grandfather been a journeyman peddler of pots and pans when he came from England?—no one truly believed that he had a poor man's spirit, least of all Jonathan Ferrier who called him the Marzipan Pear, an illusion which Senator Campion only too well understood but correctly believed that few others did. Marzipan, in any shape or form, was practically unknown in Hambledon, which was somewhat unfortunate for Jonathan, considering that the Senator never forgave and never forgot a slight or a gibe.

He had inherited a small fortune, himself, from his grandfather and father, who had managed to buy out a small foundry in Pittsburgh, but it could not compare with the Pike fortune. It was after his marriage to Henrietta Pike—a small and terrified little creature who could not believe that so magnificent a specimen of the masculine persuasion could look at her for an instant—that Kenton's political future became established. He had been kind to Henrietta, and for this she was grateful all her life and so had left him all her money without making any provision for her son, young Francis. A short time after her death, her husband's widowed sister, a flushed woman then thirty-eight and childless, had come to manage the Campion 'residence,' and bring up the motherless boy. She was now fifty-three, a big, massive and handsome woman of awesome stupidity, good-natured in a bucolic way, and, as Jonathan confided to some as irreverent as himself, 'absolutely devoted to all her bodily functions, even the grossest ones. She enjoys them all, tremendously. A bowel movement or the emptying of a bladder is just that to everyone else. But not to Beatrice Offerton! They are delightful daily Events.'

Beatrice loved nothing but her body and her appetites. Francis Campion had grown to young manhood and had made no more impression on Beatrice Offerton than the gardener's puppy. If asked, she would have admitted she was fond of the boy, and so she was when she thought of him—which was seldom—or saw him, but it was a dim far fondness without a touch of maternal concern or tenderness. She was an expert in only one thing: she was a wonderful manager of that bloated mansion on the mountainside, and servants adored her, and she pampered them. They were so necessary to the perfect, warm, flushed and enjoyable functioning of her body. She was ageless. At fifty-three she looked no older than thirty-eight, and the brightness of her colouring and the glowing softness of her hair had not diminished in the least. She attended them with the only passion of which she was capable.

Senator Campion had his young female friends in Philadelphia and Washington, pleasant young creatures who were grateful for the first luxuries of their starveling lives, the first regular meals and handsome clothing and carriages and furs and an occasional jewel. They generally occupied flats in discreet buildings which were filled with their kind, especially in Washington, and were devoted to their benefactors and protectors, who were careful not to leave evidences of their regular occupancy and visits behind them, or any casual note which could be used for blackmail purposes. All messages were written, and carried by clerks, and infrequently telephoned because of 'central,' the telephone exchange full of eavesdropping ears. Senator Campion's little friends rarely occupied the comfortable flat for more than six months, he having a tendency to tire of a current pretty face. But he always sent the girl—none of them over twenty—on their way with a nice thick packet of bills and all the clothes and furs he had bought for them, and the jewel or two, and as they had no means of speaking spitefully to avid newspaper reporters—lacking tangible proof—they remembered him with affection. He was careful, before acquiring them, to have them examined scrupulously by aware physicians, and to have reports of them given to him regularly by the porters in his employ, to be certain that they did not entertain younger and more attractive men in his absence. It was not his intention to acquire any venereal disease.

He was no more envious than the general run of politicians, and was more genial than most, even in that genial profession. He was a rascal, and being intelligent and shrewd, he was a little more of a scoundrel than his colleagues, but this was not accounted against him in Washington, where he was much admired for his wardrobe, his taste in little friends, his grand manners, his appearance, his wit, his reputation for kindliness, his way of knowing the current President intimately, his interesting speeches in the Capitol, his wine cellar and table, and the fact that in a time of ponderous political bores he was never a bore. Nor was he a hypocrite when among close friends, and could always appreciate a bawdy joke on himself as well as the teller.

It was his appearance, and his deep and musical voice, which had made Jonathan Ferrier call him a Marzipan Pear. He was a big man, as tall as Jonathan himself, and massive, as his sister was massive. Like his sister, he had a face larger than life, flushed constantly, and somewhat fat and jowly and with a very fair complexion, and blue eyes and a big, well-formed nose and rich lips. But where Beatrice's face expressed the most profound stupidity his expressed alertness and intelligence. He had her serenity of forehead, and her light chestnut hair—

thick and wavy and tended, without grey—but there was a certain liveliness about him which endeared him to most men and almost all women, a certain gaiety of manner which few recognised as the lightheartedness of the true scoundrel.

There was no man, he would say, but that he could cherish, if permitted, and no man whom he could not understand and with whom he could not sympathise. But there was indeed one, and that one was Jonathan Ferrier, and there was a pleasant mutual hatred between them. 'Please,' the Senator would say, 'for, after all, his father was my dear friend and I always had a sensibility for Marjorie. In fact, I considered marrying her when she became a widow. But Jon is a difficult young man, and then there was that unfortunate affair of Mavis—a lovely girl, I was her godfather. Ah, dear. A little brightness went out of this old world when Mavis—died. A little golden colour, a scent—yes. But if I must admit it, I came at once to Jon's defence. I had many a talk with—' But no one ever knew with whom he had that 'talk,' if any. However, the impression remained that if it had not been for dear Senator Campion's intercession—at some unnamed level—things might not have turned out so agreeably for Jonathan Ferrier. But, was he grateful? Not at all! He never wasted an opportunity to make an unpleasant remark about 'Old Marzipan Pear' and his 'cello notes. A damned smiling fraud and a really incredible rascal. Jonathan thought he knew all about the doings of the Senator, and followed his career avidly. 'You have to admire him, he's so monumental a farce, and such a dangerous one,' Jonathan would say. 'He would sell out his country for a few more oil wells or a trade concession. But then, what politician would not?'

Only Jonathan—and he had no actual proof except his intuition—was aware that the Senator, in spite of his personal wealth, was incredibly greedy and avaricious and that, like his sister, he was incapable of a really tender attachment to anyone but himself.

These were the guardians and the guides and the directors of conscience to the little boy, Francis Campion, a boy somewhat too sensitive, inclined to emotionalism, and with a passionate devotion to and an interest in all that was gently beautiful and harmless, and who, in some unnamed and inexplicable manner, had come to love God and had directed his adolescent years to dreaming of the Beatific Vision and unworldly delights, and had desired, finally, to serve his God for the rest of his life. There had been no pious servant to point the way, nor a friend, nor clergyman, nor a relative. He had found his way himself, in only God knew through what thickets of loneliness and childish despair and silence and friendlessness, through what echoing abysses and frozen fields.

Jonathan had noticed the little boy on the streets of Hambledon, in his father's carriage, accompanied by his queenly aunt, and though he had been but twenty, and even younger at the time, he had been struck by the white hurt of the child's face, the eager, hopeful eyes, the shy ways, the sudden bashful smiles, the grave and gentle politeness. He appeared to need protection, and though Jonathan would have jeered at the idea that he, himself, could never resist wishing to give protection to the helpless, it was indeed that very protectiveness in his nature which had made him remember a not very attractive little boy over the next fifteen years. He saw Francis Campion very seldom, perhaps not more than once a year or so, and he thought of him as a white mouse, with his pale thin face, his dark eyes always seeking, his thin dark hair, his very slight body and nervous small mannerisms. He had the mouth of a girl in his childhood, a little tremulous, always a little parted. It was not until he was seventeen that it became both quiet and firm and resolute and his expression somewhat exalted as if he were acquainted with visions. Jonathan saw him then, when he had treated him for colitis, and he had barely been able to elicit any recital of symptoms from the reserved boy. At the end, however, though Jonathan did not know it, Francis Campion had come to trust him and had wistfully desired to be his friend. At eighteen, Francis went away to his seminary, to the serene acceptance of his aunt and the ire of his father, who had but this one child. 'It is true his mother was a Papist,' he would say to annoyed friends and constituents, 'but I never encouraged him. But then, is it not true that our children, in spite of our best efforts at all times, and our sedulous prayers, often disappoint us? And don't we deserve a little sympathy?' The sympathy was always forthcoming, and the forgiveness, for many had disappointing children of their own. And the Catholics in the State, through the kind offices of one of the Senator's friends, were duly informed that he had a son studying for the priesthood. This did not vex the Senator.

Now Francis Campion, unaccountably home from his seminary, had tried to kill himself last night, in the enormous pile of the 'mansion,' in his lonely room. He had failed, but just barely.

Jonathan thought of him as his horse climbed the steep but well-kept narrow road, and he angrily cursed his vicious head-ache and the young man who was the cause of his early exposure to the heat of the day and this sweltering climb up the mountainside.

Sun broke blindingly on distant hot-houses and clean slated roofs. Above them towered the fantastic roof of 'Pike's Peak,' with its mighty weather-vane fiery under the sky. Stopping to wipe his sweating face and blink the dust from his eyes, Jonathan irately glanced down at Hambledon, swimming in a bluish heat-haze, and at the river which resembled white flame in the sun.

Jonathan was firmly of the belief that because a man never chose to be precipitated into life he possessed the innate prerogative of deciding when he should leave it. If the boy wanted to die, then why should he not die? he repeated to himself. It was his own life; he had not asked for it, but it was now his own.

He reached the iron gates of the Campion house and rode through them to the glistening whiteness of the tall walls and the incongruous pillars and the mounting slate peak. The gardener and his two sons were busy clipping, watering and raking, and they removed their straw hats in greeting to Jonathan, then stared at him curiously. That young priest was here early this morning, and now the doctor, but the house was silent and the doors shut and what was it all about and what did it mean? Not a single maid came out to inform them, though they were certain that one eventually would.

A pretty little maid in black silk uniform and with a frilled white cap and apron met him at the door, and she was rosy with subdued excitement. The madam, she informed Jonathan in a hushed voice, was in the second drawing-room waiting for him, and Jonathan gave the girl his hat and asked her to have a groom take care of his horse. Then dusty and sweating he went through the cool dusk of the great hall and along the marble corridor to the second drawing-room, and he hoped to God that Beatrice Offerton was not hysterical and surrounded by maids ministering to her and holding smelling salts to her nose.

The second drawing-room was as large as a tennis court. Jonathan was astonished to see Beatrice Offerton alone, stand-

117

ing serenely beside a centre table and carefully arranging huge crimson roses fresh from the garden. Jonathan was freshly outraged. He had been told of a tragedy. There was no evidence of it here, though even one so stupid and self-engrossed as Beatrice should at least have shown the merest agitation. He wanted to swear. Though he made no sound, standing on the marble in his riding clothes and with his bag in his wet hand, Beatrice became aware of him, and looked up, vaguely and distantly startled. For a moment she appeared not to recognise him. She stood with the little scissors in one hand and a great red rose in the other, and slowly and methodically blinked at him and her face was absolutely empty. One ponderous thought seemed to be running through what mind she possessed: Can that possibly be Jon Ferrier? If so, why? To-day? Her staring blue eyes were like the eyes of a wax doll.

'Jon? Jon?' she said at last, in her pretty deep voice. 'Oh! It's you, Jon, isn't it?'

'I think so,' said Jon, 'though we could both be dreaming.'

She considered that, and then she slowly smiled. 'How nice,' she said. 'Dear me, you do look warm. Do come into the morning-room in a moment and we'll have some strawberry lemonade and some nice fresh pastry. Or perhaps you'd prefer to wait for luncheon? Kenton is expected on the next train, you know. He is to make the speech on the Fourth of July. He'll be so happy to see you, you are quite a favourite of his and he always said you should be in politics, but Washington is so hot, isn't it, and—'

'I think,' said Jonathan, 'that I was sent for, Beatrice, or am I dreaming that, too?'

Again she was startled, and again she considered placidly. Then at last she put down her scissors. 'Oh, dear,' she said, and smiled that sweet and meaningless smile of hers. 'Such a trial, isn't it? I was sure it would be perfectly all right, if one just forgets these unpleasant things and pretends they never happened, and that—that priest—he did not agree with me. He said you really must come. I didn't truly send for you, Jon dear. I was truly against it. Such a bother and embarrassment, and Francis didn't mean it at all, and I am sure it is an accident and can be explained sensibly, but that priest—'

Jonathan was now totally exasperated. 'Correct me if I am wrong,' he said, 'but I understand that Francis tried to hang himself last night, in his room, and a servant heard the crash

118

of the falling chair, and he ran to Francis's room and rescued him in time. Hanged with the sash of his morning robe, I was told.' He shook the bag at his side. 'Well, what is the truth, anyway?'

Beatrice's flush had paled just a little, and she moistened her full pink lips and looked down at her hands. 'I'm sure it can all be explained,' she murmured. 'So tiresome for Kenton, when he hears. I'm sure Francis did not intend—it was looped over a sconce on the wall, it could have caught there by itself, such things do happen—'

'And it made a nice little noose of itself and just threw itself around Francis's neck while he was climbing a chair—no doubt to polish the candle-sconce at midnight, he disliked dust so much after the austerity of a seminary, and then by some chance he kicked the chair over—and there he was,' said Jonathan.

Beatrice was actually nodding, slowly and massively. 'It could well be,' she said in a blank tone. Then she stared at the roses, wet her lips again, and blinked. She touched a drooping flower. 'I do love roses,' she murmured. 'And so nice that we still have some left. Kenton adores them. They make a room so cosy—so homelike—'

Jonathan, though he had known Beatrice well ever since her arrival in Hambledon over fifteen years ago, was incredulous. He came towards her, really staring at her, his black eyes ablaze. 'Look here, Beatrice,' he said in a brutal voice, 'you don't seem to understand. I'm a doctor. I'm compelled, by law, to report the crime of attempted suicide to the police. Do you understand? To the police. And then the newspapers will get it.'

He had hoped to shock her into some semblance of comprehension and intelligence. At least, he saw that her hands dropped limply to her sides and that she was paling again and that her blue eyes were enormously dilated and fixed with the faintest terror on him. 'Police?' she said. 'The police? No, that is utterly not to be thought of, Jon! What are you saying? What about Kenton? Kenton! The shame. Oh, no, not the police. That terrible, thoughtless boy—The police. You are joking, aren't you, Jon?'

'I'm not joking, so you'd better pay me some attention, Beatrice. You're Francis's aunt, after all, for God's sake! Haven't you any feeling for him at all? Weren't you notified at once, when it happened? What did you do? Why wasn't I called immediately, or at least some other doctor? What did the boy say to you? To the servant? How did Father McNulty come to hear of it, and who called him? Give me some answers, Beatrice!'

Beatrice looked about her vaguely, then seeing the chair near her knee she slowly sat down in it. 'So disturbing,' she murmured. 'And so inconvenient. Kenton will be travelling all over the State, speaking, and it does wear him so. It's not that he can be elected, you know, it's the Governor who appoints him, and if the Governor hears of this, such an upright man and such a Christian, but a little rigid—I do wish they'd pass that Amendment so that Senators can go outright to the people and get elected without the Governor—Poor Kenton.'

'Beatrice,' he said, 'it's the State Legislature which appoints Senators, not the Governor. Never mind. Answer my other questions.'

She ruminated, her head bent, the handkerchief twisting slowly in her hands. 'I don't understand it,' she said at last. 'I didn't understand when Francis came home. I did think he seemed a little tired and worn, by all that study, and I've heard the priests are very harsh to seminarians. But I thought a few days' rest—I don't know, Jon. I confess I never did understand Francis. Such a strange little boy, even when he was a baby. Quite like Henrietta; she was quite hysterical, you know. A weakness in the Pike family—'

Jonathan, leaning against the table now, prayed for patience somewhat blasphemously. But he had to wait until the slow and heavy thoughts could give utterance and answer him.

'Well, dear me. I thought to go to Francis's quarters and ask him the trouble, but then, there was that reticence, and my dislike of prying. I thought it would be all settled when Kenton came home.'

The boy had been alone for more than two days, shut up in his room with God only knew what black and terrible thoughts and what conjectures. And then the final decision.

Now Beatrice was flushing and there was actually a gleam in her blue eyes and the gleam was, incredibly, emotional. 'It was that interfering servant, that Tom! He found Francis, and helped him in that dangerous situation—I suppose it was dangerous, though one never knows, and Francis can be so hysterical at times, and perhaps he intended to be found, knocking that chair over so loudly, it even disturbed me, though I went back to sleep at once. And then Tom was knocking at the door; I think it was about one, then, and I am never at my best before the sun comes up. I couldn't understand what he was saying for quite some minutes; quite breathless and excited. The common people, you know, always so excitable. I suppose I should be grateful, but I am sure that even if Tom hadn't gone—Francis would have come to his senses immediately.'

'And put the chair back under his feet and unfastened the noose,' said Jonathan.

'Yes,' said Beatrice. She sighed. 'Still, one never knows, does one? Tom says—but you can't really believe that class—that he—well rescued—Francis, and then made him breathe again, and bathed his throat with cold water, and put him to bed, and left him for a moment to tell me, and then he said he had called that priest. I'm beginning to think he was insolent—'

'Yes,' said Jonathan. He was smoking now. 'Tom exceeded his authority, not in calling the priest, but in saving Francis's life. Kick him out.'

'Indeed,' said Beatrice. 'I will consult with Kenton about discharging him—' Then she was staring at Jonathan and her eyes were protruding glass. She gulped. 'What are you saying, Jon, that Tom should have let—have let—'

'Francis die. Of course.'

Jonathan thought, 'I bet that keeps her from totally enjoying her lunch, but I doubt it.' He went back into the hall and there encountered Tom. Tom had evidently, and shamelessly, been listening, and Jonathan winked at him.

'You have disturbed the madam,' said Tom, with a grave face.

'So it would seem. I suggest a little soda with her lunch, just before. We can't have Mrs Offerton not relishing her food, can we? A tragedy. Tell me, Tom, why did you send for Father McNulty before dawn? Was Francis asking for him?'

'No, Doctor. I asked him, and he said no. But they used to be such good friends, and Mr Francis had almost committed a mortal sin, and maybe he did commit one, even thinking about it, and I—well, I've known that boy since he was born. I know all about him.'

'I bet you do,' said Jonathan, 'and that makes you a minority of one. Go on. Did Francis talk to the priest when he came?'

'No.' The old man's face became sad and fallen. 'Father McNulty came at once, on his bicycle. It's a hard climb, on a bicycle, even for a young man, and I've often wondered why none of his rich parishioners, or a few of them together, never bought him a horse and a buggy.'

'Don't look at me,' said Jonathan. 'I'm not one of his parishioners. So Francis wouldn't talk to the priest.'

'No, Doctor, he would not. He just lay on his bed with his face turned away and it was kind of like he was dead, not listening, not moving. Father McNulty stayed until it was almost time for Mass, and so he was tired, and hungry, too, and he made me promise not to leave Francis for long, and said he'd call you.'

Jonathan was looking down at his dusty riding boots and was hitting them idly with his crop. 'Hum,' he said, thinking. Tom waited. Then Jonathan said, 'Any idea why he performed this caper, Tom?'

'No, Doctor, I don't, except that the boy's been miserable for over a year. He never told me why, though I asked him.'

'Perhaps he made up his mind, a year ago, that he wasn't cut out to be a priest, but he didn't have the courage to tell his superiors.'

'No, sir,' said Tom, with sudden strong emphasis. 'You don't understand Mr Francis, Doctor. He always had courage for three boys, not just one. He was the bravest little kid I ever saw, Doctor, And a brave man. If he thought he'd made a mistake, he'd have told the Fathers, right out.' He paused. 'I think he did, this time. He didn't say, but I think he did, but he wasn't screwing up his courage for a whole year, Doctor. It was something else.'

Jonathan thought again. 'All right, I'll see the patient.'

They went up the enormous white marble staircase together. He opened the door and, leaving Tom, entered a large and brilliantly shining sitting-room with a fine view of the purpling mountains. But the carpet had been removed from the parquetry floor, and the furniture was small and uncomfortable and plain. Beyond lay a bright bedroom as austere as this, the walls bare except for an enormous crucifix, the furniture nothing at all but a narrow bed, a commode, a chest of drawers, a bare table, and a single chair. The floor was partly covered with a straw rug, suitable for a veranda only, and rough to the foot. The room resembled a cell. This was no new matter. The boy had insisted on such Spartan quarters from earliest youth, as Jonathan, who had been here before, knew quite well. It expressed Francis Campion's personality with fervid force, as if he had revolted against the opulence and luxury of his father's house.

The young man was lying on his bed with the white sheet drawn up under his armpits. He was not looking at the great crucifix which faced him on the wall, but through the uncurtained window at the mountains. Jonathan sat down, and placed his crop and bag beside him. He lit a cigarette leisurely, and began to smoke. He waited. Francis did not move. Jonathan saw this was not obduracy or resentment or sullenness, or even shame. It was pure withdrawal and indifference and lack of curiosity as to who had entered this room.

'It is customary for those who expect to die,' said Jonathan at last, 'that they at least make some provision for others they are leaving, that is, if they are decent. For instance, Francis, you expect to die one way or another, and are planning on it. Yet the one person who really cares about you is to be left destitute, for he will be fired from this miserable job of his, no doubt because he was indiscreet enough to save your life. You don't have one red copper. If you had, and then left it to Tom Simmons, I'd say, "Go, and God speed you, wherever you are going." But what does Tom mean to you, anyway?'

For a minute or two Jonathan was afraid that Francis had not heard him, that he had really removed all his senses from ordinary life, including hearing. Then the long thin head turned slowly on the pillow and Jonathan saw the deathly young face, still and rigid, and he also saw the thick and swollen bruises on the other's neck.

'Tom?' said Francis, speaking with pain.

'Tom. Auntie is going to boot him out, because of you. Seems he was not only worried about your life, which I admit was stupid, but he was more worried about your immortal soul. That's unpardonable. So Auntie, of course, can't forgive him. Perhaps she'll be kind enough to give him a week's pay—how much is it?—in lieu of notice. After all, can't have someone around this place who is human, can you?'

The palest shadow of despair ran like a ripple over Francis's face and he lifted his head briefly from the pillow. 'I won't let them make Tom leave,' he said in a hoarse whisper. 'They can't do that to him, just because—'

'Oh, but they will,' said Jonathan, most cheerfully. 'Now, if he'd been sensible enough to close the door when he saw what you were up to and had gone cosily back to bed, you'd have been found in the morning and some doctor, who's a family friend, could have been induced to sign a certificate saying you had died of "natural causes," and all Tom would have to do, to live comfortably the rest of his life, probably without working, would have been to mention to Papa or Auntie, in private, that he knew what he knew, and what about it? But the world's full of damn' fools, isn't it, including you and me, and especially Tom?'

The young man did not answer. But slowly and with tremendous effort, he began to raise himself up in his bed. Jonathan watched him with no sign of curiosity or interest, and waited until Francis, heaving and gasping, had pushed up his pillows, settled himself upon them in a sitting position, and was looking at him again.

'Damn you,' said Francis Campion, struggling for breath. 'Damn everybody. No one's going to hurt poor old Tom. If—they do—I'll let the whole damned world know why—'

'Good,' said Jonathan. 'You might mention that to Papa and Auntie first, though. Save a lot of trouble. By the way, your father ought to be here in a couple of hours. He's making his usual trumpet speech in Hambledon on the Fourth, and, as usual, you won't be there.'

He wondered if he had lost the youth again, for Francis's face had become expressionless and remote again, as if he were engrossed in unearthly thoughts. Then, to Jonathan's pleasure, Francis began to smile. It was not a bright and gleeful smile, but, as smiles go, it was at least visible, if faintly. 'No,' he said, 'I won't be there.' Then he frowned.

'Unfortunately, I will,' said Jonathan.

Now Francis was looking at him sharply. 'Why did you come, really?'

'That's really none of your infernal business, but, as I said, I don't know myself.'

The quick smile jerked at Francis's mouth again. 'Just your sense of responsibility?'

'Maybe. After all, you did have a bad case of ulcerative colitis when you were seventeen, and I did pull you out of it after the hacks had almost killed you. The Chinese say that if you save a man from death, or suicide, his life is on your neck as long as you live, and he is your personal responsibility. Harsh but realistic people, the Chinese, and very intellectual, and they do have a point. After all, when you interfere with a man's manifest destiny, as ordained by mysterious Entities, then the curse is on you for interfering. So, perhaps I was cursed for saving you when you were seventeen, and Tom is now cursed for saving you, and it is possible that he and I together can work out a deal with the fates.'

A curious darkening touched Francis's overly eloquent eyes, and his white lips hardened. Jonathan watched him without appearing to watch.

'As Auntie says, I don't pry,' he remarked. 'But, as it is a long time ago, just what did give you colitis? I'm not one of those New York and Boston doctors who are listening far too much these days to the Austrian hysteric and Medieval witch doctor, Sigmund Freud, who appears to think that every ailment of the body has its seat in something he calls the unconscious or maybe it's the Id, or perhaps the Superego. Freud has another weird idea, too. He thinks a lot of mental ills, which give rise to physical ills, too, are caused by refraining too much from tossing in the hay with some willing doxy. He hasn't too much respect for what we call Judeo-Christian morality. Can make a man sick in his Id, or something. Now I think that continence, if not carried to the point of absolute absurdity, has a lot to recommend it.'

Francis was listening with that intensity of his which Jonathan had deplored as excessive three years ago.

'So,' said Jonathan, 'what in hell was really troubling you when you were seventeen? Say I'm inquisitive.'

Francis looked away from him, and stared down at his fingers, which he slowly began to flex and unflex. 'You ask me about what ailed me when I was seventeen. It was something that had gone on for a year. Perhaps more. Will it be much of a surprise to you to hear that I adored my father—up to then?'

'Frankly, it would.' Jonathan was more than ever astonished. 'I never admired Daddy.'

'I know,' and again Francis smiled. 'I heard you called him the Marzipan Pear, and even worse. I think I hated you when I was a child, for that. Didn't you also call him a mountebank?'

'Probably. What did Daddy do except be his dear old affectionate self, fully revealed to you at last as human clay? He's too cautious to do anything really heinous, that is, too cautious ever to be found out. Did you find out something?'

'I did,' said Francis, through a tight mouth. 'Several things. It doesn't matter how they happened, how I found out. If

125

they had been the average larcenies and manipulations of a politician, the usual skullduggeries, I'd have finally understood about them, too. There's a hell of a lot of compromising we have to do in living, and coming of age, isn't there? I would have compromised if my father's—crimes—had been just the usual and accepted ones, of a man and a politician, or even if they had been what people call "peculiar," as a way of not mentioning the facts.'

Jonathan listened acutely. He was no longer smiling.

Francis's expression was again grim. 'No, I can't tell you. I thought, when I was seventeen, that it was absolutely necessary for me to tell—well, say important men, men in government. I thought it was a matter of my—country. My country. The country he speaks so roundly and richly about, on the Fourth of July, and Washington's and Lincoln's birthdays, and Decoration Day. The things he has sworn to protect. You see, he never thought I was very intelligent; even when I was sixteen and seventeen, he thought I was a child. So—I heard. I overheard. In his flat, in Washington.'

He stared blankly at the upturned palms of his hands. 'And there was the trouble. My conscience. My country. Above all, my country. Yet, he was my father. What does a person do in that case?'

My God, thought Jonathan, who had a shadowy revelation. Yes, what does a person do in that case? He said, 'I don't know. And so you were torn apart, inside, and you bled inside, and you almost died.'

'You should have let me die,' said Francis, and closed his thin hands.

'You never told him?'

'No. To tell him—I'd have blown apart. I'd have had to do what I was afraid to do. It took me a long time to get over loving him. A very long time. Suppose you had found out something very terrible about your father, Dr Ferrier, something really—monstrous. Something so criminal that in your country's interest it should be revealed, and that if it weren't revealed, he'd go on and on, doing the same thing, and maybe much worse? Would you have—'

'Exposed him?' Jonathan shook his head. 'I don't know. I don't think so.'

Francis sighed. 'Well, there it is. I carried that to the seminary with me, when I was seventeen. And—don't laugh at me now—I prayed. Anyway, I put it out of my mind.'

'You couldn't have been mistaken? You couldn't have been making a mountain out of a molehill? After all, you were hardly more than a kid, and politicians do some very expedient things.'

Francis shook his head. 'Give me some credit. I tried to tell myself that, for over a year. I tried to think he was not doing what other politicians were not doing, only for much more money and that it was a sort of nefarious game with them, only. Like playing dice for high stakes. But men came to that flat in Washington—Senators—others.'

'And he let you stay around to absorb it?'

'No, he wasn't that much of a fool. I kept on visiting him, at times he didn't expect me. I had to know. And I always arrived at night. Finally, he must have suspected something, for when I did arrive, he was always ready for me. My aunt wired him that I was coming. I found that out, too.'

'Christ,' said Jonathan.

'And now I don't know anything. I do know he made a lot of money out of the Spanish-American War. I do know he goes abroad a lot. That's all I will tell you, Dr Ferrier. Except that I've been doing a lot of reading the past three years, a great deal of reading, on a very frightful subject. Have you ever heard of Zaharoff, Doctor?'

'Yes. He's called mysterious and sinister. I've heard his name. Something to do with munitions, isn't that it?'

But Francis did not answer. He leaned back on his pillows in utter exhaustion.

Jonathan said with unusual gentleness, 'Look at it this way: if your father were not doing it, and others with him, there would still be a man in his position to do it. I know that isn't much consolation, and when it comes to affairs like this the individual is pretty impotent, but—'

Francis's eyes were closed. He said in the quietest voice, 'You don't understand, Doctor. I don't care about that any longer. I don't care about anything. I haven't cared about that for nearly a year. I haven't cared about anything for that long, or longer.'

Jonathan was more disturbed than ever. He stood up slowly and went to the bare window and stood and looked out at the long sweep of lawns, the fountains, the arbours and the flowers, and then raised his eyes and looked at the deepening mountains, calm and splendid and remote. Jonathan frowned. The room behind him was too quiet, as if the dead lay there.

127

He said, without turning, 'You say you haven't cared about anything for a long time. You have been in a seminary, studying for the priesthood. Don't you care any longer about —well—let's say God?'

'No,' said the emotionless voice behind him. 'How can I? I no longer believe He exists. Or, if He does, He is not concerned with this fleck of dust on which we live. What faith I have is gone. It took a long time dying. Over a year. It died very slowly, Dr Ferrier. But it did die. I can't be a priest. My faith is dead.'

And that's why you tried to die, too, thought Jonathan, and he thought, What a rotten, disgusting, revolting and sickening world this is, to be sure!

He walked slowly back to the bed and stood beside it, looking down on the spent and suffering young man who lay there. He said, 'If every man who lost his faith, if every man who was an honestly convinced agnostic or atheist, died for it, then there'd be few people left in this world. You can't force yourself to believe, Francis. You learned at your seminary that faith is a gift of God only. I don't think you ever really believed, as a man believes, but only as an infant does. Now you've got a great adventure ahead of you, the search for what God is, and what you are, and the meaning of your life. That should take a whole lifetime, at least.'

'And if I don't find it?'

'The searching will be enough. What could be more important, more worthy of a man? Somehow, though, I think you'll find it.' Jonathan smiled. 'And when you do, tell me about it. I'd like to know, myself.'

Francis could not speak. He watched Jonathan pick up his crop and his bag, and still could not say anything. But when Jonathan reached the door the young man said in a breaking voice, 'I'd like to see Father McNulty—I think I'd like to see him.'

No one was in the corridor when Jonathan entered, spent as he had never been spent even after hours in an operating room. Slowly, he went down the staircase and at the foot old Tom was waiting for him, mutely. Jonathan said, 'I think it'll be all right. I'd like to telephone Father McNulty to come and see Francis at once. He wants to see him.'

'Oh, thank God,' said the old man. He led Jonathan to the

door of the telephone booth, glass enclosed, which stood under the stairway, and Jonathan called the rectory. The priest's elderly aunt, who kept house for him, answered frostily. 'I'm sorry, Doctor, but Father was up all night, and then there were two Masses, and he's just exhausted, and is resting a little before he makes sick calls.'

Jonathan, as usual, lost his temper. 'Miss McNulty,' he said in an elaborately precise tone, 'I too, have been up all night, and I've been working on one of Father's pet cases, at his request, and I haven't eaten to-day and I have to go to the hospital on my rounds. So, kindly call him, if you please.'

Miss McNulty did not bother to reply, but in a minute or two the priest was at the telephone. 'I haven't been thrown out of this house yet,' said Jonathan, 'but I expect to be any moment, because of your and my impudence. The next time a parishioner of yours has a brainstorm and decides to join the great majority, please don't interfere with his sensible decision. And don't call me.'

'Oh, Jon,' said the priest in a stronger voice. 'Then everything is well with Francis? I knew I should ask you, I knew!'

'You did, eh? Let me tell you something, Father. I didn't examine him. I wasn't called by anyone but you. I had no position in that house; I am not their doctor. So, I didn't examine the boy for the reason that if I'd laid a hand on him or looked at his throat I'd then have been the attending physician and I'd then have to report the attempted suicide to the police. But you didn't think of that did you?'

'I knew you could manage it, somehow, Jon.'

'Then you knew something I didn't. All right, he wants you, as soon as possible, and as he is now in a very emotional mood you should come at once before the tears dry and he gets fresh ideas. May I offer some ecclesiastical advice? Don't quote platitudes at him. Don't express any horror about what he tried. Don't, for God's sake, talk about sin. That boy has encountered enough sin in the past few years to keep a whole curia busy. Don't mouth doctrine or dogma. He's heard nothing but that for years, now. No aphorisms. No cant. You'll only make him desperate. Come to him as a friend who really cares about him, and keep your mouth shut as much as possible, and just listen if he talks, and if he doesn't talk, don't talk either. Get the thought through to him, if you can, that you suffer with him as a man suffers with a brother, and that's a platitude, too, for it's the rare brother who cares a damn about his own flesh and blood. Do you understand me?'

'I understand, Jon,' said the priest gently. He hesitated. 'He definitely has left the seminary?'

'Yes, and I think it's a fine idea. Later, you can suggest to him that he take a trip around the world, or something, and go down into those dens of vice you fellers are always talking about, and kick up his heels and sow several fields of wild oats. What are you laughing about?'

'Nothing. Go on, Jon.'

'Let him see something of the world, and the girls, especially. You remember what St Augustine prayed: "Make me chaste, O Lord, but not yet!" That's what Francis needs. Afterwards, he may decide to go back to the seminary, or maybe he won't, but in either case he'll be a man.'

'Like you, Jon. I hope, in any event, he'll be like you.'

'That's a Christian thought. Well, I'm going home now and you get here as fast as you can. On your bicycle. By the way, I thought you ought to know that he's lost something he calls his faith, so don't approach him through that, and don't bring any little holy tokens, either. He's growing up now; in fact, he's just about grown up.'

The priest said, 'God bless—' But Jonathan hung up the receiver. It was stifling in the hot booth. He wiped his exhausted face and hands, opened the door and confronted, with an inner curse, Senator Kenton Campion and Beatrice Offerton. He had hoped to leave the house unnoticed, and there they were, the Senator beaming like a golden sun and extending his hand, and Beatrice standing in the background, her big face still pale and her eyes somewhat reddened.

'Dear boy!' exclaimed the Senator, taking Jonathan's hand in both his plump warm palms, and speaking in his consciously organ tones. 'How good of you to come! I arrived less than an hour ago, and Beatrice has told me how you hurried to us in our—ahem—unnerving situation! How can I thank you? And how fortunate it was you instead of someone else—'

'It was,' said Jonathan. 'Your regular physician would have had to report it to the police, and such things have a stink about them. As it is, I am in a difficult situation, for I am a doctor even if not yours, and Francis was once my patient. But if no one talks, and if you, and Mrs Offerton, look only astonished if there is any mention of it, and if you still have

130

your old hold on the police chief here, perhaps it'll all die down. I take it the servants don't know exactly what happened?'

The Senator was less golden and beaming. He said, 'Only old Tom, and Beatrice is going to discharge him immediately for disturbing the household for—ah—nothing.'

Jonathan wanted to hit him. 'Nothing, eh? Is that all you can say, and promise, about an old man who saved your son's life? I know you don't give a damn about Francis. It's been town-talk for years. But what if Tom hadn't saved him? Do you think your friend, the Governor, who comes up for re-election this fall, or your friends in Washington, would still think you were a mighty fine specimen of a gentleman, or would they ask what kind of a father had a son who committed suicide? Your political career would be over. At the very least the gossips would say that there "must be insanity in the family," and though there's plenty of insanity in Washington these days they just don't want to add to it overtly. Now, what are you going to do about Tom?'

Jonathan, the Senator saw, looked dangerous and ugly, and he was swinging his crop in a very nasty and and rapid way as if he were longing to use it. The Senator coughed. He put his hand, his large white fat hand, on Jonathan's dusty sleeve.

'Now, Jon. I spoke without thinking. Why, old Tom will have my eternal gratitude! Old faithful family retainer, and all that. It was just my natural, paternal agitation—Forgive me, a stricken father. I became quite faint when Beatrice told me.'

'From what I can smell,' said Jonathan, 'several big belts of bourbon revived you.'

The Senator smiled his rich smile. 'And from what I see, several such belts would help you, too, Jon. Do come into my study.'

He said, 'No thanks. I am going home and will try to rest for an hour or so, and then I have hospital calls. I'm glad to see you're so concerned, and crushed, about Francis, but don't grieve too much.'

The florid Senator coloured and his blue eyes had a wicked and malignant gleam for a moment as he stood smiling benignly at Jonathan.

'Certainly, certainly, a dreadful shock. The only son, with such hopes for him, and everything, a fine character, it doesn't seem possible, it must have been what the French call a *crise de nerves*. One doesn't know what is happening to the young people these days. So nervous, so agitated, so restless, so dissatisfied. They fly from place to place, without knowing where they really wish to go. Very unsettling to parents, very disturbing. One does one's best—it truly is discouraging, discouraging. A Christian life, upbringing—it all seems to come to nothing. Duty is rejected, and honour, too, and sobriety, and responsibility, and regard for family name. Well. These are things we must endure in this new century, I suppose.'

'Yes, mustn't we?' said Jonathan. The vast marble hall, full of the blazing shine of the sun, was making his head ache abominably, and he was now sick at his stomach and shaking internally with rage. He had a thought. 'By the way, it was Father McNulty who called me.' To think that this golden son of politics had not even asked how his son will be, and if he is badly injured!

'Ah, yes, yes, yes,' said the Senator, in a crooning voice. 'Very good of the young man, very good. I must remember to send him a little gift.'

'Say five hundred dollars,' said Jonathan. 'That will help towards the horse and buggy he so badly needs. He'll be here soon—on his bicycle—climbing in this heat, and I know, to show your gratitude to him, and perhaps to me, that you'll have your cheque ready.'

The Senator's large rich mouth fell open, and his eyes started. 'Five hundred dollars!' he repeated.

'Little enough to pay for discretion, isn't it?'

The Senator struggled for lofty rectitude. 'I know that the clergy are always discreet. They don't bruit about private matters they encounter. Really, Jon.'

'But I'm not a clergyman, and as a doctor I am supposed to report this.'

'You—' exclaimed the Senator.

'That I am. I'm a bad, mean, contemptible, corrupt, degenerate character, Senator, as no doubt you have always heard in Hambledon, and I have no scruples at all, and you don't strike my heart with the slightest pity. If Father McNulty doesn't inform me joyously soon of your magnificent generosity, then I'm afraid.' He shook his narrow dark head and Mrs Offerton gasped in the background and put her hand on her breast. 'I'm putting myself in a very precarious position by keeping my mouth shut, you will understand.'

'Are you sure,' said the Senator, in a silky voice, 'that you

132

wouldn't prefer the five hundred for yourself, Jon?'

Jonathan stared at him. He half lifted his crop, and the Senator stepped back in horror and indignation. Jonathan dropped the crop. He said, 'I know three Senators in Washington, Kenton, three fine men. Friends of mine. I saved the life of the daughter of one. One word from me, Kenton, and a word to the Governor, and a few more to the State Legislature, and you'll be gracefully, more or less resigning. Do I make myself very, very clear?'

But the Senator was no cringer. He said, 'I regret that I came to your assistance, Jon. I fear that there was more, behind the scenes, shall we say, than appeared at the trial.'

'Indeed, there always is.' Jonathan was smiling. 'As for your "assistance," you are a liar. If you did anything at all, in your discretion, it was your disavowal of knowing the Ferrier family "well." It doesn't matter. I want to advise you about something. Before you begin to stuff yourself with your usual hearty lunch I want you to go upstairs to your son, and say at least five decent words to him, not in reproach or condemnation, but in kindness. He has some faint idea of what you really are, I am sure, though he'd die rather than tell. Be grateful for that. Just a few kind words, if you think you can manage it. And then let him alone.'

Beatrice Offerton spoke for the first time, and in a surprisingly shrill voice.

'How dare you insult the Senator like this, Jonathan Ferrier! And what are you implying about my brother, my good Christian honourable brother?'

'Why don't you ask the Senator yourself, Beatrice?' said Jonathan, and he swung about and went to the door of the hall. The Senator watched him go, and there was no happy complacency on his face now, no sweetness, no affection. The big blue eyes were so narrowed that the colour had disappeared between the short chestnut lashes. Jonathan's footsteps clanged on marble.

Now, there's another enemy, thought Jonathan, waiting for his horse to be brought to him. He did not care in the least.

CHAPTER 5

Jonathan Ferrier and Mavis Eaton had been married in the First Presbyterian Church of Hambledon, in a candlelight ceremony, when Mavis was just past her twentieth birthday.

The big fieldstone church, austere and dark even in the hot bright evening, flared with shadows and candlelight, and the air was stifling and rustled with fans. Those who had been invited to the wedding filled every pew, and the sultry atmosphere became more oppressive with women's scents and the fragrance of banked flowers everywhere. The mayor was present, and Senator Campion and State Senators, and the Governor himself, and other dignitaries, and their wives. It was a gala occasion.

Jon waited with his brother, sweating with embarrassment and expectation, his dark face clenched. He seemed to be frowning. 'Quiet,' Harald whispered, with amusement, and Jon glanced at him irritably, and flushed. Then the organ, and the triumphant voices, rose to the entrance music, and there was Mavis, on her proud uncle's arm, and she was floating down the aisle to her bridegroom.

Jon watched her, stiff and entranced, as she swayed on her uncle's arm and the wedding march made the hot and scented air tremble. He felt both exultance and joy, and he also felt intoxicated. It was not only Mavis's beauty which fired him, which made him breathe heavily. With Mavis he would be carefree, as he had never been carefree, and he would be young, as he had never been young. She would laugh away many of his intensities, and her humour would make him smile, and he would be unburdened. He would, in short, play and be refreshed, and he would even laugh, himself, at some of the things which he now found intolerable.

The reception for hundreds of guests was held on the lawns and among the gardens of Martin Eaton's vast and hideous house. There was champagne and whisky and a magnificent feast. Long hot shadows fell below the trees as the day swung towards evening. Beyond the lawns the river shone like a wide path of blue, and in it stood the silly island, Heart's Ease, and beyond the river and the island rose the violet mountains brilliant with the falling sun.

Mavis was gracious and ebullient, and her loud and husky laughter, so joyous and so abundant, was everywhere, as she moved among the guests and accepted their toasts. They pressed about her stroking her gown, tenderly kissing her cheek, patting her hands. Her sparkling white gown set her apart in all that colour. It was her uncle she chose to walk beside her, and Jonathan and Flora Eaton moving in her train, Flora in lavender taffeta, a colour most unbecoming. Marjorie stood apart, watching and fearing and aching, but outwardly serene in her gown of soft rose silk, her dark hair shaded by her rosy hat of tulle. Her head was aching, and her heart also, and there was a tumult in her ears of congratulations and mirth and merrymaking and happiness. Above all, she heard Mavis's laughter and her sudden whoops of rough glee and it seemed to Marjorie that it was the most insensitive sound she had ever heard, totally crude and distasteful, and even repellant. Marjorie had given the girl a gentle kiss, and then Mavis's eyes, sunken and secret, had opened a little and Marjorie had seen the cold blue gleam, the indifferent yet cunning gleam, as far removed from warm humanity as polar ice.

But no one, except Marjorie, could resist the boisterous laughter of the girl, the gaiety that was indeed coarse. Everyone was as bemused as Jon at the way she would throw back her head, unaffectedly, showing all her big white teeth in her mirth, her eyes crinkling above, her cheeks glowing. Her spirits, always boisterous, enchanted them all, for they held no reticence but were bold and teasing. She slapped admirers on the arm with her white and jewelled fan, and pushed her bouquet gaily into faces, and joked coaxingly, and looked about for fresh admiration and affection. She had none of the shyness of a bride. When Jonathan would push to her side she would stare at him and then grin deliciously.

The bridal couple was to spend the wedding night in the Quaker House, in its most lavish suite, waiting now and filled with flowers. To-morrow they would leave for the races at Saratoga, and then to New York for the balance of the honeymoon.

Japanese lanterns were lit at dusk in the gardens, and there was music over the long lawns, for Martin Eaton had hired the Hambledon German Brass Band for the occasion, with the brass overpowering the violins and the 'cellos. The first dance, on stiff green carpet laid on the grass, was claimed by Martin and he and Mavis whirled together in a sprightly waltz,

Mavis's train over her white kid arm, and her head thrown back so that her big white teeth glowed and glittered in the lantern light, and her veil flew behind her and her full and lovely figure gleamed in its white satin tightness. Next, she danced with her bridegroom, and she kissed the side of his face cheerfully and squeezed his shoulder affectionately in her gloved hand, and grinned up at him. He recalled with happiness that never had he seen Mavis in a 'mood,' or otherwise than her charming, bouncing self, in a cloud of laughter and scent. She was enormously healthy, too, a most desirable trait in a wife, and health had its own enchantment. Her rosy face was damp with heat and exertion, but she did not pause to wipe away the little drops but let them shine on her vibrant skin. Her golden pompadour loosened, and a few ringlets fell from it. Jonathan could feel the soft but vigorous movements of all her muscles, and he thought of the young mares on his farms, silken and fresh and trembling with eager life. He looked down at Mavis and tried to see her eyes, but as usual they were crinkled with mirth and pure animal enjoyment and the awareness of her beauty. Her translucent flesh appeared to palpitate.

At length it was time for the bridal couple to leave for the Quaker House, and Mavis disappeared with her running bridesmaids and her matron of honour and her Aunt Flora, and there were screams of joy from the lighted house when she threw her bouquet from the stairway. The band continued to play and the guests continued to drink and eat and dance and joke and laugh, and this would go on for hours after the newly married pair left. A little later Mavis reappeared, still vibrant but now cool and softly powdered, and dressed in a white silk suit with a flow of exquisite white lace tumbling from her neck down over her bosom, and a broad white straw hat covered with pale blue roses of silk. The hem of her suit just daringly lifted over the arch of her white stockings and hinted of fragile ankles, and she was dazzling and fresh and shining like the moon.

She never stopped smiling for a moment, her great white-toothed smile, and she kept throwing back her head in a boom of laughter and everyone, as usual, was fascinated and forced to laugh helplessly in return. She stood with Jonathan, her hand on his arm, and cajoled and affectionately slapped a cheek here and there, or squeezed a hand, or gave a swift kiss, and she was never still for a single second. She was all beguilement and vitality and gusto, though to some ears her laughter sounded like a screech, and it rose even above the music and the loving babble of the many guests.

The bridal couple drove off in Flora's own victoria and with her coachman, and to the last Mavis waved and laughed and called back to the guests who gave them Godspeed. Jonathan, beside her, thought it was like sitting next to a dynamo, scented and breathing and strongly pulsing. Once on the street, Mavis apparently became aware of him, and she squeezed his arm gleefully, and said with immense cheer, 'Wasn't that a lovely wedding Jon?'

'Yes, darling,' he said, and lifted her hand and kissed it and she looked down on his thick black hair with affection. 'I love you,' she said. Jonathan lifted his head, deeply moved, and suddenly remembered that never before had she said that to him. He pulled her into his arms, in a cloud of rose fragrance, and kissed her lips with passion. She purred against his lips like a big, contented kitten, then drew away. She said, 'I wish we were going to Europe, though, to Paris.'

'I told you, darling, that I have several operations in two weeks.'

'I know.' Her voice was husky and a little hoarse always, but now it was more so. 'Uncle Martin and Aunt Flora have told me what it means to be a doctor's wife.' Then he saw her deep dimples in the flare of the lamps on the street. 'But I'm not going to let you become dull and smell of ether all the time, like Uncle Martin, and never having fun again.'

'Perhaps, next summer, we will go to Europe,' said Jonathan. He was exhausted and exhilarated at the same time, and he thought of his coming night with his wife.

'Um, um,' Mavis crooned, and patted his cheek, and began to hum the wedding march under her breath. 'A lovely wedding,' she said again. 'I'd like to get married every day.'

'Why?' asked Jonathan, with adoring fondness.

'It's such fun,' said Mavis, again gleeful. He did not know why he felt a touch of disappointment. He looked at Mavis's face, glowing beside him, and there was no shyness on it and no nervousness. When he kissed her again she responded absently, and her lips were smiling, and he felt that she was hardly aware of him but was indulging in some delightful thought of her own, far removed from him.

The bridal suite shone resplendently with crystal chandeliers and was heavy with the fragrance of hundreds of flowers.

Mavis had the gift of flattered gratitude, and she went from room to room, exclaiming over the kindness of friends who had sent silver baskets and bowls of rich fruit and bouquets and heaps of little parting gifts. 'Everyone loves me,' she said, and looked at Jonathan eagerly.

'No wonder,' he said. 'And I do, too. Remember?'

But she whirled again through the rooms, singing loudly and laughing over some little note among the gifts. She had thrown her hat on a blue damask love-seat, and her gloves on top of it. Her luggage, and Jonathan's, was in the great bedroom with its enormous brass bed and lace counterpane. He began to tremble. He called to Mavis, 'It's nearly ten, darling, and we must be up at six to catch the Saratoga train at eight in the morning.'

She came running to him, and she grasped his arms and looked up into his face. 'I am hungry!' she declared, with pleasure. She pressed her cheek briefly but strongly against his chin. 'Hungry as a wolf. Getting married did that to me, but I can always eat, anytime.'

'You mean—now?' asked Jonathan. She nodded with that immense good nature of hers, and laughed her exultant laughter. 'Yes, yes,' she said, 'I had hardly a bite at home, just half a plate of creamed chicken and a slice of ham and some rolls and cakes. And,' she continued, with astonished joy and animation, 'I want some more champagne!'

So a little table was brought up to the suite with covered silver dishes, steaming, and a bucket of ice with champagne, and Mavis, still in her white silk suit, hovered over the place-settings lustfully, and smiled and smiled and smiled and made little joking comments to the infatuated waiter. 'Oh, how delicious it all smells!' she exclaimed, sniffing loudly and lifting the silver covers of dishes and then humming with anticipation. Her golden head bobbed emphatically, and she looked at Jonathan, grinning, and he saw the glittering slits of blue between her yellow lashes. He could not help it. He laughed back. He remembered that she was very young and extraordinarily healthy. And innocent. Innocent, above all. He must be patient and tender to one who knew nothing of marriage and what marriage meant. She was a child.

Before Jonathan could seat himself Mavis had already filled a plate with heaping portions of meat and gravy and potatoes and stewed tomatoes, and was purring deeply in her throat with ecstatic enjoyment and appetite. Well, he thought, we'll never have any vapours to contend with at any rate, and thank God my darling is abundantly healthy. He could not touch a bite. He drank champagne with Mavis and watched her eat. She ate daintily, but all at once he had a thought that she was also gross, a thought he squelched immediately. Even while she ate she smiled and purred in her throat in simple animal pleasure. She drank the champagne like water, and looked over the rim, twinkling, at her husband.

'You aren't handsome in the least,' she informed him, and chuckled. 'Not like Harald.'

'Does that matter?' he asked, with indulgence, and worshipped her with his eloquent dark eyes.

'Um, um,' she said. Then she suddenly stood up, raced around the table to him, and kissed him smartly on the top of his head. Before he could seize her, she was back in her chair, and eating again. Part of her hair was tumbling down her back and it caught vivid gilt lights from the chandelier. She motioned to Jonathan to fill her glass again, and she laughed aloud as the bubbles tickled her nose. He had never seen such verve before, and he thought how marvellous life would be with Mavis, how lively and gay, and refreshing, after he came wearily home from the hospital. She would be like a bright effervescent pool of water, fragrant and reviving to exhausted flesh, and the house would ring with her joy of life and her husky merriment. He was so moved at this thought that he could only stare and smile at her with the most touching hope. She would teach him so many things, adventure, new insights, lightness, happiness, peace, and, above all, zest in living. He had forgotten what zest was, but he would learn again.

'I wish,' she said, with a mouth full of ice-cream, 'that we weren't going to live in that old house of your mother's, Jon.'

'I know, dear. You've said that before. But it is my father's house, and mine, and not my mother's, and it is very beautiful.'

'Your mother doesn't like me,' she informed him, and grinned flashingly.

'She loves you, Mavis. Who could help but love you?'

'Well, she doesn't.' Mavis spoke like a malicious child. 'Not that I care. I can get along with anyone, really. She won't disturb me. And I won't disturb her. I don't care a bit about running a house, and perhaps I should be grateful that your mother will continue to do that, and leave me free.'

'For what, love?'

She waved her white hand on which Jonathan's diamond broke in light. 'Why, for so many things! All the parties we'll be giving, and accepting, and lawn fêtes, and dancing, and shopping and being with friends, and teas, and receptions.'

Now she was looking at him with the strangest expression, and her little eyes were sly and calculating and a little cruel. But he did not see the cruelty. He saw only her humour.

'There are more things in life than that, Mavis,' he said, and thought what a child she was.

'I'd like to know what is more pleasant,' she said. 'Um. These lovely little cakes! Marzipan.' She burst out laughing. 'I remember what you called Senator Campion. A Marzipan Pear. Uncle Martin thinks it is precious. Did you know he's afraid of the Senator?'

'No. Is he? And why?'

She chuckled. 'I don't know. Who cares? But he is. And the Senator is such a handsome man, and so kind and happy. I love happy people, don't you?'

'I love you,' said Jonathan.

Mavis threw back her head and began to sing hoarsely. 'Happiness! Happiness! It's a great wide wonderful world, it's a great wide wonderful world, it's a great wide beautiful, wonderful world!'

Teach me how it is, thought Jonathan. Mavis sprang up again and began to whirl about the room, singing, her arms thrown out, her falling golden hair swirling about her, and she was entirely unconscious of her husband's presence. She was staring sunnily at the ceiling and had her own relishing thoughts. She picked up her wide white skirts and he saw the firm and graceful calves and her delicate knees. He got up and tried to take her in his arms, to dance the dance of life with her. But she pushed him off with head-shaking impatience and danced away from him, as if she needed no one but herself for her own joy.

But Jonathan did not know that now, though the faintest coldness touched him as he watched his young wife whirl alone and dance dizzily through the rooms, singing only to herself. He watched her with passion, exulting in her beauty and vigour.

I don't deserve all this, thought the proud young man with rare humility. I don't deserve all this beauty and youth and sheer exultation in living, and all this hope and happiness.

Mavis stopped suddenly, across the room from him, and she shrieked with mirth, bent and clasped her hands between her knees, and shook with her delight and exuberance. She flung back her hair and raced to him, seized him by the shoulders and kissed him heartily. 'Oh, what an old man you are, to be sure!' she cried.

He seized her and held her, vibrating, against his chest. 'Teach me how to be young, Mavis,' he said, his lips in her fresh and scented hair.

But she was moving restlessly in his arms, like a cat. She danced away again. It was hot in the suite and the scent of flowers and food was overpowering. He caught a glimpse of Mavis's face and he was surprised to see that it was no longer smiling, and that she was sullenly pouting even as she danced. Her small eyes, as usual, were hidden in their arched lashes, and she seemed to be thinking furiously.

'Mavis!' he called to her.

She stopped at once, panting, and pushing back her hair. She stared at him.

'What?' she asked, as if disagreeably reminded of his presence.

'It's half past eleven, almost.'

'Oh, who cares?' she cried. 'Are you so old that you can't miss an hour or two of sleep without being ill, or tired, or something? Can't you enjoy anything?'

He was startled. He, as a doctor, was always aware of time and its pressing. He was disturbed. Then he thought, I must get used to this, to having someone near me who isn't harassed all the time, and can enjoy the passing moments and live in the present. I've been so immured, so shut in.

'Yes, I can enjoy, Mavis,' he said in a humble voice. 'But I thought you must be tired, after the wedding and everything.'

'I'm never tired!' Her hoarse voice was emphatic. 'I don't know what it is to be tired! And I hate tired people! I won't have them around me, ever!' She shook her head with such vehemence that her hair flew. 'I detest serious people, such slugs!'

Half alarmed, half pleased, he teased her: 'But I'm a serious person, Mavis.'

Again her eyes shut cunningly. 'Yes, I know,' and then she laughed as at some enormous joke. 'I don't mind you being serious, Jon. It helps you to make such a lot of money, and don't you just adore making lots of money?'

She was only a child, he reminded himself, as yet unaware that women like Mavis are never children.

'Such a lot of money, a lot of money, a lot of money!' sang Mavis, and kicked up one leg like an expert dancer. She whirled on the other. There was something frenzied in her movements.

Then she stopped abruptly, and again stared at Jonathan, and again her gaze was cunning and thoughtful. 'All right, old man,' she said. 'I'll tuck you in your bed so you won't be too tired to make money!'

'But you have a lot of money, yourself, darling,' he said, 'and you are your uncle's heir—'

'Nobody has enough money!' she shouted pettishly, then ran past him into the bedroom, and slammed the door behind her. He sat down, and the air in the suite seemed fetid to him, as well as hot and stinking with the smell of rich food. He stood up and pushed the table out into the corridor. The champagne bottle was empty. He was conscious, all at once, of the need of a drink of whisky, several drinks. He was also, he admitted, very tired, and then he was aware of a kind of hollow emptiness and disorientation. The lights in the parlour of the suite stung his eyes and he got up heavily and turned off all but one lamp. Now there was an odour of gas in the suite. He opened the windows and leaned out and drew in the hot air, burdensome with the smell of heated pavements and brick and dust. The lights of Hambledon winked at him, and he yawned, then rubbed his eyes. He saw the far glitter of the river, and the dull shadow of the mountains against a dark but burning sky full of stars. There was a rumble of thunder somewhere, and a little dusty wind blew over his sweating face.

Then he became aware that he had forgotten he had a bride in those brief seconds. He looked about him, somewhat dazed. He felt no passion any longer. He was too tired.

'All right!' shouted Mavis, from behind the shut door. 'You can come in now, if you want to! I'm finished with the bathroom.'

He went into the bedroom, shamefully aware of the aching in his legs and back. He was only thirty. He felt like an old man.

Mavis had hung up her suit and put away her hat and gloves, and now she stood before him, a pillar of gold and white in her silk nightgown and *peignoir*, her hair hanging long

142

and flowing down her back. She smiled at him, and she was neither nervous nor shy. Her scrubbed face shone rosily and her teeth were like young ivory, big and wet. She was freshly perfumed, and, weary as he was, he thought how tireless she was, how young, how adorably alive and greedy for life, and again he hoped.

When he had bathed and undressed in the bathroom he came out. Mavis had dimmed all but one light in the big hot bedroom, and was lying high on the pillows in the bed, contemplating something mysteriously. She turned her little eyes to him and said, with affection, 'I never saw your hair mussed before, Jon. I like it.' She held out her arms to him like a child eager for a doll.

He lay beside her in the hot darkness. It was some time before he heard her muffled chuckling, and turned towards her and she buried her face in his shoulder, and her young and gorgeous body was under his hands. She was laughing at him, and he was happy. 'What is it, love?' he asked with tenderness. Now she would tease the weariness from him.

'I'm just thinking,' she said. 'Old Betty Grimshaw, one of my bridesmaids. You know. Twenty-five if she's a day, and never a beau! She caught my bouquet, and she almost cried! She'll never get a husband.'

He drew away his hands from her. She lifted her head from his chest and tried to see him in the darkness.

'What's the matter?' she demanded. 'Too tired? Or afraid of hurting me? You needn't be afraid. Aunt Flora told me all about it. It's something a woman has to stand, she said. And Uncle Martin gave me a book. I'm not scared.'

Shallow, mindless, he was thinking with a rush of deadly new despair. There's nothing for me, in her. It's not her fault, the child. The fault was in me, and my fantasies. All my life has been full of fantasies, and I never knew it until now.

Her hair brushed his cheek. 'Poor old boy,' she said, and laughed. 'Well, you go right to sleep. I'm sleepy, too.'

The marriage was not consummated until the second night in Saratoga. Mavis's lack of passion and enjoyment devastated her bridegroom. He told himself that this was new to her, and would pass, and she would eventually respond. He did not know for a long time that Mavis was incapable of responding to anyone but herself, and that if she were ever to feel passion it would not be with him. She had submitted herself to him, not with resignation and frigidity, but with indifference. He

143

had been only her means to a larger and fuller joy of life, away from her uncle's home. He had been only a way to adventure, and the adventure did not include him. He was her 'old man.'

Her easy affection for him lasted nearly a year. She had nothing to give him, and never would have anything. She had nothing to give anyone, except pleasure in her laughter and her verve and teasing. But, being the man he was, that was not enough.

He continued to love her for a long time, from a distance, but a terrible, yearning distance, and did not know when it also became hatred.

Before the hatred finally arrived—though the helpless, hoping love long stayed with him—Jonathan would take Mavis to Philadelphia, Pittsburgh and Boston, and even Chicago and New York with him, for conventions and consultations—and there, as usual, she would charm everyone and awaken envy of him on the part of other physicians. Jonathan could even enjoy her then, and her cheerfulness and her cuddling coyness, and her sudden bursts of affection for him, though he soon learned that that affection was also mocking. Her beauty was like the sun, inciting adoration even on the part of women. When alone with Jonathan she was like a golden kitten, purring, coaxing, promising delights which never materialised, promising hope of understanding where there was no hope, promising subtlety where there was only animal enjoyment of living, promising adventures of the mind where there was only adventures of the senses.

I must not blame her, he would repeatedly tell himself. She is what she is. But what Mavis was he did not entirely know for a considerable time. He had told himself since he was twenty that there was nothing to expect from others and that it was cruel to expect more than they had to give in love and perception. But when he finally realised that Mavis was not only mindless and shallow, except where it concerned her demands and appetites, but avaricious and hard-hearted and callous towards suffering and intolerant of need and loneliness, and greedy beyond measure, he came to hate her while she still fascinated him and continued to make him believe that if he could but penetrate her shining avidity and triviality he would find a pulsing core of gentle humanity and tenderness.

She said to him once, cuddling against him in bed, 'When

are we going to move to Philadelphia and New York, Jon dear?'

He said, 'We are not. What gave you that idea, Mavis?'

She was outraged. 'You can hardly expect me to live in this miserable little town all my life, can you?'

'I am satisfied here.' He was astonished and freshly shaken. 'This is my home, isn't it?'

She became sly. 'Jonnie, Jonnie. Don't you know nearly everyone hates you here? I hate it, for your sake.'

'How can they hate me?' He was surprised. 'I give all I can of myself to my patients and to the city, in charity—'

'That's the reason why,' she replied, and chuckled knowingly. 'People who give everything,' and she held out a giving palm, 'get nothing. People despise them. You've got to take everything you can in this world, and then people will respect you—for your money and your position.' She clutched her hand greedily to her breast, and grimaced happily.

He was both sickened and revolted by her then. It never came to him that Mavis had an animalistic but pragmatic knowledge of mankind, which not all his intelligence could ever acquire, and that she lived on a level of vulgar realism which he had rejected in childhood as unbearable if one was to live. He did not know that Mavis was fearless because she had accepted life for what it was, and men for what they were, and asked no concessions. He did not know that though he was brave he was also expectant and too vulnerable.

Mavis continued, for at least two years, to insist that they leave Hambledon. When he gave her his final refusal she became sullen and withdrew from him, and came to hate him with real and resentful hatred. He loved her, as helplessly as always, and would listen for her laughter in his house and the rustle of her dress, and her quick footstep which never stopped at his door. As far as Mavis was concerned, Jonathan ceased to have meaning and verity for her, and was only a means of supplying her with handsome gowns and jewels and position. She joked with him on occasion, and laughed at him always, but she lived apart in a joyful world of her own which was full of admiration for her, and had nothing but love for her.

Finally, total desolation came to him when he fully realised what Mavis was and would also be, to the very end of her life. It was then that he began to muse on ways of killing her and removing her from the heart of an existence which was becoming intolerable to him. She had betrayed him, he would think, betrayed him in the only way which mattered to a man like himself.

Four months later Mavis was dead, and Jonathan Ferrier was arrested for her murder and the murder of his unborn child, and the house never heard Mavis's laughter again.

When Jonathan Ferrier arrived at St Hilda's he found a harassed Robert Morgan, who glanced at him resentfully. Jonathan, to him, appeared too insouciant and careless, and Robert had no way of understanding that this was the pose Jonathan assumed when matters were too stressful for him or he was too exhausted. Jonathan said, 'Well, how are you managing our mutual patients?' He did not wait for an answer. 'After the Fourth, you know, you will take over my offices and out-patients entirely. I've persuaded old Miss Forster, who used to be my assistant, to come back and help you and she will be there on the fifth. Yes, I'll be around, introducing you. The whole town knows the offices will be open on the specified day. By the way, I hope you won't entangle yourself in the hospital war going on in this town.'

'Hospital war?' asked Robert.

'Between St Hilda's and the Friends'. They are overcrowded now, and desperately need new wings, but still they compete for patients! And denigrate each other. Don't get embroiled in it all. St Hilda's wants the well-paying patients, though it has to take the other kind too, and the Friends' would love the affluent to make up their deficits and charity list, and has a preponderance of the poor. They are constantly puffing up their staff and gilding them. Don't tell me that you haven't heard rumours!'

'Well,' said Robert. He looked into Jonathan's darkly sparkling eye, lit with derision. 'I hate controversies,' said Robert. 'I prefer to compromise.'

He gave Jonathan a brief account of the many patients. 'By the way, a friend of yours is on the third floor, private room. Jefferson Holliday.'

Jonathan sat up. 'Jeff Holliday? I didn't know he was even in town! When did he get back?'

'Two days ago. He said he tried to reach you, but couldn't. Are you his doctor?'

'No. His mother is a fierce hysteric, and likes old Louis
146

Hedler, and he was always a boy who listened to Mama. We went to school together. He was one of the few friends I ever had. Old Jeff Holliday! Wonderful. Fine engineer, went to South America for the past six years, don't know why. But full of "advancing our technical knowledge." An undeclared hero. Or perhaps just in flight from Mama, who hates me as a "bad influence." What seems to be the trouble with him?'

Robert frowned. 'Frankly, I'm puzzled. He has darkish coppery patches on his skin, face, backs of hands, trunk. Roundish. Low fever. Says he gets them with a fever. I didn't try to intrude,' said Robert, quickly. 'But as he was asking for you he was told that I—was taking your place. I went down to see him. Just as a possible friend, and to tell you, but, as you say, Hedler is his doctor. I looked him over, anyway, just in curiosity.'

'Good,' said Jonathan. 'A doctor who loses his curiosity is a dead doctor, even if he tries to continue his practice. Does he seem sick?'

'Well, not very. Just those reddish patches he gets when he has a fever. After the fever goes the patches fade way. There's just one thing I don't understand. He showed me the sites of old patches—they are thickened and a little nodular, but not painful. Now he has a fresh outbreak of patches, and that low fever.'

'How long has this been going on?'

'About a year. He forgot about the first attack, and didn't make much of the second. Had no medical opinion in those South American countries. Thought his trouble was fungus. Was told in New York it was. Some fungus extant in hot damp countries. They gave him an ointment in New York, a fungicide. He was in New York for two weeks, consulting with his firm. When he arrived in Hambledon he had a fresh —rash. Rash is all I can call it. I can't recall seeing anything before like this—defined, symmetrical patches, some as big as a quarter. Probably some semi-tropical disease.'

'Is he in isolation?'

'No.'

'Dear old Louis!' said Jonathan. 'He wouldn't recognise a case of smallpox if he saw it. Not that I think this is smallpox. Let's go down and see Jeff.' He stood up.

'His mother is with him,' said Robert.

Jonathan studied the younger doctor with amusement. 'I see you've encountered Mrs Holliday.'

'Yes.' Robert paused. 'She is putting sulphur compresses on him. She's quite a manager, isn't she?'

'Very rich, too. Big benefactress of St Hilda's. Inherited a lot of money from her unfortunate husband. If she wanted boiled onion compresses here the nurses would be running with hot onion stew and flannels, and old Louis would be beaming and saying, "Yes, indeed, Elsie, yes, indeed, very efficacious." Let's intrude.'

'Should we?' asked Robert.

'We should, indeed. At least, I will.'

They went down to the third floor and to a large and lavish room. The patient, a man Jonathan's age, was sitting comfortably in a chair near the window, while his mother, temporarily, was desisting from the compresses, and sitting opposite. He was a handsome young man, with the broad and vigorous face of an out-doors-man, short and pugnacious of nose, generous of mouth, and lively of grey eye. His thick blond hair curled in damp ringlets over his big head. On seeing Jonathan, he shouted with pleasure. 'Jon! You damned old hound, you! Couldn't get you, though I tried. Jon, it's good to see you again!' He held out his bronzed hand to Jonathan, and stood up. He was apparently bursting with health and vitality, and there was no illness apparent in him except for peculiar roundish and coppery patches on his cheeks and hands and throat, and his partially exposed chest.

The two young men embraced each other awkwardly, with blows on shoulder and arm, and obscenities. They shouted incoherently, in insulting terms, while the prim thin woman nearby, in her early fifties, averted her head and showed the tense white cheek of the born hysteric, and the trembling lower lip. Her hair was grey and untidy under a harsh black straw hat, and she wore the grim black clothing of one who will not defer to weather.

Jonathan, his arm about his exuberant friend, looked down at her. 'How are you, Mrs Holliday?' he asked.

She slowly and reluctantly turned her head to him and her cold light eyes studied him with contemptuous disfavour. 'Very well, Doctor,' she answered. Then she added, 'Dr Hedler is my son's physician, and had him brought here last night. It's all nonsense, of course, but Dr Hedler is so—conscientious. Unlike many other doctors I could name.'

'Good,' said Jonathan. Jefferson Holliday coloured at the

affront to his friend, but Jonathan squeezed his arm. 'Probably nothing but one of those damned semi-tropical diseases, anyway.'

'Disease?' Mrs Holliday's voice became shrill and full of offence. 'My son has no disease! What a thing to say.' She agitatedly pulled at the gloves in her lap, black kid ones. 'Nothing but a scruff. That's what I told Louis. I told him that, I kept telling him that—'

'No doubt,' said Jonathan.

'Sulphur compresses, hot,' said Mrs Holliday. 'Sulphur ointment.' She looked up at her son. 'I really think you should ask for discharge, Jefferson.'

'I intend to.' The young man beamed at Jonathan. 'Sit down. Yes, I've met Dr Morgan. He was kind enough to stop in to see me.' He exuded buoyant well-being and immense cheerfulness 'I'm on six months leave, Jon. You'd never guess! I'm going to be married.'

'No!' said Jonathan. 'What brings on that sad news?'

'Oh, now,' said Jefferson, laughing. 'The daughter of the head of my concern. You'd never guess. An anthropologist, by God! Mad about it. She was with me for some time down in South America. Those Inca ruins, you know. Studying the natives for signs of the old Incas. Thinks she has a clue. Lovely girl.'

'I bet,' said Jonathan, thinking of a hardy, striding woman in short skirts and boots, and with a loud harsh voice.

'You're wrong,' said Jefferson, laughing. He reached to a nearby table—covered with vases of flowers—and took a small framed photograph from it, and held it out to Jonathan. Jonathan saw the picture of a gentle young girl with dark hair, a serious smiling face, soft lips and extraordinarily lovely wide eyes. Her white shirtwaist was open at the neck and showed a throat unusually delicate and slender, with a thin link of pearls about it. 'Elizabeth Cochrane,' said Jefferson with pride. 'She has a quirk. She believes in reincarnation. She thinks she was an Inca princess once.'

'That's a change,' said Jonathan, studying the photograph. 'Usually they think they were Cleopatra or at least Queen Elizabeth.' The photograph impressed him. There was a vulnerable look to the girl which uneasily reminded him of someone, but who that one was he could not immediately remember. 'A nice girl,' he said.

'Marvellous,' said Jefferson, looking fondly at the photograph even when he had put it down. 'After we are married we'll give up all that exploring—at least after a year or so. My work is finished in South America. We've done as much as we can, but now it is up to the people, themselves. I haven't much hope. They lack American bustle and determination. What we value as enterprise they think is ridiculous.'

'Sensible,' said Jonathan. He was looking at the reddish patches on his friend's skin. 'When did you get that affliction?'

'A year ago.'

'Dr Hedler is his doctor!' said Mrs Holliday in a shrill voice and she moved spasmodically on her straight chair as if about to go into a fit. The hot room, in spite of the large opened windows, stank with the odour of sulphur ointment.

'Mama,' said Jefferson.

'I don't care!' cried Mrs Holliday. 'I don't want him saying things—things—'

'Mama,' said Jefferson.

'Never mind,' said Jonathan. 'I'm just curious. Mind if I look at it? Just academically, not as a physician.'

Mrs Holliday sprang to her feet like a wild young girl and plunged her thin black-clad body out of the room in a rush. 'There she goes, after old Louis,' said her son in a rueful tone. 'Can she cause you trouble, Jon?'

'Not more than I already have,' said Jonathan. 'Bob, come over here. We'll look at this together.'

The two doctors bent over the indulgently smiling patient and carefully examined the blotches. One of them was noticeably thickened, and there was a nodule in it. Jonathan pressed. Jefferson winced. 'Hurt? How old is this patch?'

'It's a new one, in place of the old, which disappeared.'

Jonathan felt around the nodule, and pressed the flesh. 'Hurt?'

'No.' The young man frowned. 'In fact, I don't feel anything there.'

Jonathan lifted the eyelids of Jefferson Holliday, stared at the membranes. He examined the nose and throat tissues. His normally darkish-pale face became sallow and tight. He shook his head. He glanced at Robert Morgan. 'Well?' he asked.

'I can't diagnose it,' said young Robert. 'I never saw such a skin disease before. Did you?'

But Jonathan did not answer. A look of sickness settled about his mouth. Then he took out his pocket-knife and gently and carefully scraped the surface of one patch, and noticed that the patient showed no signs of pain. He held out the blade to Robert. 'Go to the laboratory, stain this, and look at it,' he said. To Robert's surprise his hand was trembling a little. 'The stain for tubercles.'

'My God!' exclaimed Jefferson, with great alarm, and pulled away to look up at the face of his friend. 'You don't think I have tuberculosis of the skin, do you, for God's sake! Listen. I don't have a cough. I'm as hearty as a horse.'

'No,' said Jonathan, 'I don't think you have tuberculosis of the skin.' I wish, he thought, that was all you had, Jeff, I wish to God.

'Or cancer?' asked the patient, trying to smile.

'No. What gave you that idea?' Jonathan sat down and stared at the floor. 'Under what conditions did you live in South America?'

'Conditions? Oh, sometimes crude and primitive. Most of the time. We had a camp where Elizabeth and the others stayed, except for occasional explorations. But I had to go often into the interiors, among the natives. Sometimes I slept in their huts, during the rains. Sometimes in the jungles, with what cover we could cut. Machetes. Why? Do you think I have a parasite of some kind?'

'Maybe,' said Jonathan. 'Did you see anyone else with this kind of skin disfigurement?'

The young man frowned. 'Yes, I did. Two or three. A child. A woman. An old man. In fact, I stayed in their hut during the rains for several weeks, before we could get out and back to the river. Why? Do I have something contagious?'

'Perhaps,' said Jonathan. 'Mildly so.'

'My God! Elizabeth!' said Jefferson. His bronzed face paled. 'Do I have something I could give her?'

'I wouldn't worry about that. You aren't married to her, yet.'

Now the young man darkly coloured. 'If you think I've picked up a venereal disease it's possible, between you and me. My God, I can't stand the idea! The woman in the hut: she was young, and wasn't blotched then. After all, Jon, I'm a man— What's that arsenic thing they are using?'

'You're thinking of syphilis,' said Jonathan. 'I don't think you have it, though it's always been endemic among Indians. That's where the white man picked it up in the first place. Let's not worry until we know.'

'What did you do to me, with your pocket-knife?'

'Took a sample of your skin cells.'

A thick hard silence fell in the room. Jefferson was pale again. He kept glancing with dubious fear at his friend. He remembered the old stories of Jonathan Ferrier. 'A fanatic. Always looking for the worst. Everything complicated, nothing simple. One of those new scientists, finding trouble in the mildest things.'

'Microscope?' said the young engineer, trying to control a strange tremor along his nerves. 'Will it show anything?'

'I hope not,' said Jonathan. He looked at the photograph of Elizabeth Cochrane again, and was again sickened.

The broad door swung open and Mrs Holliday returned with white and vindictive triumph, bursting into the room before Louis Hedler. 'Now!' she exclaimed. 'We'll stop all this nonsense!' She breathed loudly and victoriously and went to her son and put her hand on his shoulder. Dr Hedler smiled widely and mechanically at Jonathan and said, 'We're happy about Hortense, Jon. We owe it all to you, of course, and the skilled care she is getting. I talked with old Humphrey this morning— Well, never mind. We're all grateful, Jon, believe me. Never mind. What is this Elsie is telling me? Usurping my patient?' He continued to glow indulgently.

'No,' said Jonathan. 'No usurpation. Just curiosity.'

'Curiosity!' said Mrs Holliday. 'Asking my son questions! It's unethical!'

Dr Hedler put his hand tenderly on her visibly shaking arm. 'Now, Elsie. Let's be calm. Jon is a very talented—yes, indeed—talented, physician, and Jeff is his friend, after all, and doctors do get curious, you know. Nothing wrong, my dear, nothing wrong. In fact, I'm pleased. Always like a new opinion.' He glowed upon Jonathan, though his big, froglike brown eyes showed both suspicion and caution. 'Well, what do you think? Nothing serious, of course. One of those nasty semi-tropical fungi. Isn't it? Some of the patches are already fading. What do you think?'

'I've sent a scraping down to the laboratory,' said Jonathan.

'Scraping? Why? Oh, to show the fungi?' Dr Hedler was relieved. He turned to Mrs Holliday. 'Nothing more serious than fungus, my dear. Like, er, like the blisters one gets on one's feet. Nothing to worry about.'

But Mrs Holliday was staring with large angry malice at Jonathan. 'Look at him! He doesn't agree with you, Louis!

He's thinking up something terrible about my boy! Something terrible. Stop him, Louis!'

'Now, Elsie. How can I stop anyone from thinking?' Dr Hedler's voice was like a sweet ointment. 'Thinking doesn't make a thing so, you know.'

'I believe it does!' said the hysterical woman with passionate emphasis. 'You can do terrible things with your thoughts! I've heard you can even bring death—'

'Let's not be superstitious,' said Louis. 'Here, my dear, sit down. Do stop trembling.'

But Mrs Holliday pulled her chair as far as possible from Jon, and then reached out and took her son's hand, her own cold and sweating. She said to her son, peering desperately into his face, 'You mustn't listen, my darling. you mustn't listen! It's all a lie! You know what this man is, you know what he is!'

'Mama,' said Jefferson.

Her voice rose almost to a scream. 'Jefferson! Tell him to go away! Jefferson, you mustn't listen! You must just laugh at him!' She laughed suddenly and fiercely and looked at Jonathan with ferocious hatred and mad scorn. She tossed her head at him, and bit her lip, and laughed again. 'Louis! Make him go away!'

Louis Hedler was deeply disturbed. He could not upbraid Jonathan, remembering how he had saved the life of little Hortense Nolan only the day before, yet he could not offend Mrs Holliday, to whom the hospital owed so much. He met Jonathan's eye, and saw his hard sympathy, and his plump cheek coloured. He said, 'In a moment, Elsie. We'll just get the laboratory reports.' He said to Jonathan. 'Can you tell me what you were looking for, Jon?'

'I'm not really looking for anything specifically,' said Jonathan. 'I'm just trying to eliminate—something.'

Dr Hedler was relieved. 'What?'

'Let's wait.'

'I was worrying about isolation,' said the older doctor, tentatively.

'And the newspaper men coming, any minute!' said Mrs Holliday, with fierce pride. 'To interview Jefferson! All the wonderful things he's done in South America!'

Jonathan said, 'They can't come in here, until we know.'

'Know what?' asked Dr Hedler. He was newly dismayed. 'You suspect contagion?'

'I'm not contagious!' said Jefferson, aghast. 'Why, I've been with Elizabeth and her father for two weeks in New York, and months in South America! Contagion! My God, Jon, you don't mean—an infection?'

'I don't know,' said Jonathan. 'Here's Bob Morgan. Now we'll know for sure.'

But Robert did not enter the room. He merely stood on the threshold and all the colour was gone from his fresh young face. He mutely gestured to Jonathan, and Jonathan rose easily and said, 'Want to go outside with us, Louis?'

'Why? Why?' screamed Mrs Holliday. She jumped up. 'I won't be cast aside! I want to hear! No one can stop me!'

Jonathan did not look at her. He went to the door, looked back. Louis was taking the trembling woman's arm and bringing her forward. 'Of course, Elsie, you must hear—'

'What about me?' asked Jefferson, with irony. 'I'm only the one most concerned. But don't mind me, lads, don't mind me.'

Jonathan stopped on the threshold. Then he slowly went to the middle of the room. He looked down at his friend. 'You're right, Jeff. You should know, above anyone else. I'm not the kind to keep news of any kind from a patient. Come in, Bob, come in. Let's have a consultation.' Robert Morgan implored him with his eyes, but Jonathan obstinately looked away from him. 'We have a grown and intelligent man here, Bob,' he said. 'A brave man. He should know, no matter what it is.'

'Indeed,' said Louis, lovingly forcing Mrs Holliday back into her chair.

Robert Morgan came into the room, and his look was desperate. He spoke only to Jonathan. 'There's no doubt,' he said. 'I've only seen slides before, but I'm sure.' He paused, and again silently implored Jonathan. 'Hansen's Disease.'

Jonathan spread his legs and took a deep breath. His face was taut and bony. Mrs Holliday looked malevolently from one face to the other, and took her son's hand. 'What! What!' she cried. 'What is that? Hansen's Disease. What is it?' Her glance was again full of hatred, directed at Jonathan. 'What does this stupid, wicked man mean?'

Louis was bewildered. 'Hansen's Disease,' he said slowly. He nodded his head. 'I'm afraid—Jon, you are sure?'

'Bob is. I don't think the laboratory should know—nor anyone else. Do you understand me, Louis?'

The older man was baffled. He turned to Robert. 'Hansen's

Disease. I'm afraid I haven't encountered it before,' he said. 'Something new, tropical?'

'Something as old as hell,' said Jonathan. 'Louis, do you want me to give you the old and ancient name of it?'

'No need at all!' said Louis, with haste. 'One understands. We can't disturb patients, you know, Jon.' He saw Jonathan's face.

'What I'd like to know,' said Jefferson, 'is just what is Hansen's Disease.'

Jonathan said to Louis Hedler, 'I wish you'd persuade Mrs Holliday to go into the waiting-room and have a cup of tea, or something.'

'No!' shrieked Mrs Holliday. 'You are not, I say you are not, going to lie about my boy, to kill him with fear, to lie, to lie, to lie! You bad, wicked man! You—you murderer! Everyone knows what you did to your poor wife, everyone knows what you did to that poor little child, Martha Best, everyone knows—'

'Mama,' said Jefferson.

She turned on him with wild white fire, then stood up and took him in her arms and pressed his face into her meagre breast. Over that tawny head she glared at Jonathan and actually spat at him. 'Go away, murderer!' she cried. 'Go away!

'Oh, I'll take him home, I'll take him home!' groaned the woman. 'Away from murderers! Louis, you'll never see another penny of mine, not another penny!'

Then Jonathan went over to her and took her away from her son, loosening her arms with controlled but steady violence. 'Get away from him,' he said. 'Don't touch him.' He pushed her off, and she staggered a little, and Louis caught her arm.

'I don't understand,' said Louis, jolted. 'It can't be contagious, Jon. Elsie, do stop screaming. Please, my dear. Jon, it can't be that contagious.'

Jonathan looked at him steadily in bitter silence. Then he said, 'Louis, tell me. Do you know what Hansen's Disease is?'

'Certainly.'

'You lie,' said Jonathan. 'I should have known. Take that woman out and put her somewhere, then come back.'

He turned to Jefferson, whose face had become strangely gaunt and still. He put his hand on his friend's shoulder. 'Jeff,' he said. 'Tell your mother to leave, to let you alone for five minutes. Please, Jeff.'

But Mrs Holliday had pulled herself away from Louis and was standing stiffly and hysterically in the centre of the room, her hands clenched in fists at her side, her face thrust forward. 'No one is going to put me out of this room so you can lie and lie, and kill my boy with fear! I am his mother, I'm going to protect him from murderers!'

Jonathan had been through too much the night before, and too much this morning and the woman's repetitious and even gloating epithet had reached him finally. He said to her, with conscious cruelty, 'Very well. I'll tell you the ancient name of what your son has, Mrs Holliday. He has—leprosy.'

'Oh, my God,' whispered young Robert, and turned aside. But no one heard him.

Louis Hedler goggled at Jonathan, and his whole body and face became limp and flaccid. 'Leprosy,' he said in a croaking voice.

'Leprosy?' said Jefferson Holliday. He bent his head and said nothing more.

Then a most terrible scream came from Mrs Holliday. She flew at Jonathan. Her clawed fingers reached for his eyes, his ears, his nose, his mouth. One of them sank into his lip and tore it. She breathed and grasped frenziedly. She fought with him, as he tried to hold her, and to the dazed horror of old Louis Hedler she shouted obscenities he had never heard before. She struggled with Jonathan, and panted. Finally he flung her from him and Robert caught her. But she was beside herself, mad, frightful as a holocaust. At last Robert dragged her from the room and was gone a little while.

'God help us,' said Louis Hedler, and watched Jonathan wipe the blood from his mouth. 'Oh, Jon. It can't be true. Pardon me. I do feel a little ill. I think I'll sit down. Jefferson. We can't be sure—' He started to reach out to take the stricken young man's hand, then shrank, and pushed his chair away.

'I'm sure,' said Jefferson, and his voice was very quiet. 'I should have known. I saw the child—it isn't very rare, down there. Not down there. Not as bad as in Africa and Asia, but bad enough.'

He looked at the photograph on the table, then took it in his hands. He began to cry. 'Elizabeth,' he said. 'Dear Elizabeth.' Then he replaced the photograph and looked at Jonathan.

'What do we do now?' he asked. 'But, first tell me. Is there any danger to Elizabeth?'

'No,' said Jonathan. 'It takes prolonged association, intimate association. Jeff, you have the nodular type. Sometimes it takes a rapid course, sometimes it goes on—for years. The sooner you are treated for it, the better.'

He could not look at his brave friend, but he had heard, for the first time, the hoarseness in his voice and he knew that the disease had invaded his throat. He said, 'I've seen two cases, in New York. It isn't as rare as we like to think, in America. But the old terror of it persists, and perhaps rightly so. Jeff, in Louisiana, there is a sanitorium. You must go there at once. There's an old Indian drug they are using now —chaulmoogra oil. It often arrests the disease. There's no known cure yet, Jeff, but they may find it. You must go quietly. Some way, you'll have to keep your mother quiet. I'm sorry. I lost my head and told her, and that's inexcusable. But there were too many things—I'm sorry. You'll have to silence her, one way or another. You know how people are. There'd be panic in this town, and we can't have it, and hysteria in this hospital. People are ignorant. They don't know that Hansen's Disease is only very mildly contagious, and only after prolonged contact. We can't have panic. Did you ever see a mob?'

'Yes. Often.' Jefferson spoke indifferently, too overcome by his personal tragedy to feel deeply as yet. 'I know what mobs are. I saw them in various parts of South America.' He squeezed his eyelids together. 'What shall I tell Elizabeth?'

'You could tell her the truth. I hear that people can go to Louisiana to be near those who have—what you have—even to see them and visit them. If she cares enough about you.'

'And we can never be married.'

Jon hesitated. 'I've heard of arrested cases. Not many, but a few.'

Jefferson lifted his head. 'No, I can't do that to Elizabeth. I can't ask her to waste her life with me. No. I'll write to her— I'll tell her anything, but the truth. I hope she hates me. It'll help her.'

Jonathan went to him then and put his arm about his friend's shoulders and bent over him. Jefferson laughed a little. 'What should I have? A bell? "Unclean, unclean!" Jon, aren't you afraid?'

157

'I'm afraid of a lot of things,' said Jonathan. 'I'm just beginning to find out. But this isn't one of them.'

'I'm afraid, too,' said Jefferson. 'I'm afraid of this. A leper. Isn't that enough to make you laugh?'

Louis Hedler had recovered his wits. He said, 'Jon, it's not that I'm disputing, but shouldn't we have a consultation, with Philadelphia or New York doctors? It isn't possible to believe—a leper. A leper! What is to become of this hospital when it is known?'

'Have as many consultations as you wish,' said Jonathan. He was surprised by the old man's docility. 'I'm afraid there'll just be confirmations. But let me write to a friend in New York, an expert on tropical diseases. Then we can arrange for Jeff to go to Louisiana, where they are treating scores of these cases. Don't let anyone in this hospital know, Louis, or tell anyone in this town, not even doctors. Just imagine the newspapers!'

'Where shall I go? What shall I do?' asked Jefferson, totally desolate.

'You can go home at once,' said Jonathan. 'Don't be afraid, Jeff, don't be afraid. You can't infect anyone. And wait for us to tell you when to leave. Keep your mother quiet, Jeff. We have a whole town, a whole state, to think about.'

'I've never been able to keep her quiet, yet,' said Jefferson. He lifted his hand and Jonathan took it and held it, and Jefferson began to cry again, deep sobs of complete anguish. He stammered, 'Will I have much pain?'

'Probably,' said Jonathan. 'Nerve pain. For a while. I won't lie to you, Jeff.'

'And I'll be isolated from everyone for ever,' said his friend.

'I tell you, Jeff, they are doing some wonderful things down there. I'm sure they can arrest the disease in you. It hasn't gone far enough to have caused you much permanent damage. There are all kinds of people there, men, women, children, teachers, doctors, former missionaries, people like yourself, from every class and walk in life. I've heard about it. They say it is the most hopeful place in the world. You can do a great deal there for others, Jeff.'

But Jefferson's head had fallen on his chest in incredulous despair.

'Let me write to Elizabeth,' said Jonathan. 'She's an intelligent girl, you say. She has the right to make a choice for herself. Let her decide if she will go down there with you and stay until they have arrested it. It's her life as well as yours.'

'I don't have the right to ask her to make the decision,' said Jefferson, but he lifted his head a little. 'Imagine isolating herself down there, with a—a leper, for God's sake!'

'She still has the right to decide. Give me her address, and I'll send her a telegram at once. That's better than a letter.' He added, 'It isn't the end of the world for you, Jeff. Nothing ever is, until they shovel the dirt on you.' He thought, You're a fine one to talk!

'A telegram to Elizabeth?' said Jefferson, and for the first time there was a little hope in his voice. 'Jon, I'd appreciate that, I honestly would. But what if she doesn't come, or can't stand the thought of me any longer?'

'Then you've lost nothing but a trivial woman, and that isn't a loss at all.'

He suddenly saw Mavis's face clearly but now the internal vision did not bring its usual spasm of anguish. It brought nothing at all but self-disgust and the blank realisation that she had, indeed, been totally worthless and had not deserved all the pain he had suffered.

'You've given me a little hope, Jon. I immediately thought of suicide.'

'Don't be alarmed at that. No intelligent man never thought of it. The world isn't a sweet place. We know that. It's a damned, ugly, painful, wretched place of existence, but we must come to terms with it, somehow.' Something I never did myself, he thought with ruefulness. 'I saw a young man this morning who had lost his faith, all he had in the world, and wanted to die of it. His affliction is worse than yours, Jeff, for now he must find out how to live without the only thing which mattered to him, or find it again.'

'You believe I can rediscover—something?'

'I think we all can,' said Jonathan, and felt surprise.

Dr Hedler had been listening to this with considerable surprise of his own and he stared at Jonathan, who had forgotten he was present. Well, well, thought the older doctor, this boy isn't as harsh and brutal as we have thought, and I, for one, am ashamed that I had thought it, myself.

Before Jonathan left, he said to him in the hall outside, 'Jon, don't leave Hambledon. I know, I know! I've been as bad as everyone else, dear boy, as bad as everyone else, if not worse. Forgive me, if you can.'

'Good old Louis,' said Jonathan, and shook his head and went away.

That evening he sent a telegram to Elizabeth Cochrane, a long and detailed telegram of several pages. He had little hope. Women were not particularly intelligent and though they were emotional, their emotions were superficial, and they were instinctively selfish, and their ability to love was very shallow. At midnight he received Elizabeth's reply:

'I am coming to Hambledon at once to join Jeff, and will go with him to Louisiana. I have sent him a similar telegram. We must work together to give him a reason for living. Thank you, Doctor, and God bless you.'

Well, thought Jonathan. This must be a rare creature, indeed. A rare and unusual creature. How many women would abandon a young and happy life to go into isolation and misery and despair with a man? How many women can love that way?

When he saw Jefferson at his house the next day the young man was almost jubilant. 'I've gained something, Jon. I used to look at Elizabeth and wonder what I had to offer a girl like that! I must be something very special, don't you think?' and he laughed.

'I think we all are,' said Jonathan. 'In a way,' he supplemented, in reluctant qualification.

CHAPTER 6

'You've said that so often before, every Fourth,' said Marjorie, as she worked in the kitchen with the cook, preparing the picnic baskets. ' "Tribal rites. Sentimentalism. Chauvinism." I know them all. Perhaps you are right. But there will be children there, and young people. They have a right to learn to be proud of their country.'

'Mother,' said Jonathan, 'do you think the speeches of the mayor and that damned crafty Campion will inspire the youthful mind and enlarge it and make it proud? As for Campion, he never speaks anything but lies and banalities. I don't know why I'm going with you—under my present circumstances. Just a farewell appearance. Suppose I skip the celebrations to-day?'

'And let me go alone? Harald isn't here, and he never came with us anyway, on the Fourth. Do you want people to pity me, especially that odious Mrs Morgan who is so smug about her boy? And the Kitcheners, and their nice little daughter, Maude?'

'And Jenny,' said Jonathan.

Marjorie bent her head over the bread she was cutting, and she sighed. Dear, stupid Jon, she thought. She said, 'Yes, Jenny. She has given the domestics the day off, and she is all alone, and she was pathetically grateful for my invitation. She has so little pleasure, poor child. That is because she has a grim streak in her. She went to school in Hambledon. But knows no one. Her whole life was a kind of dedication to her father, who never lived on his island after all. She can't get over the sorrow of it—and Harald, to her, as you know, seems the interloper who has no right on the island at all.'

'Not the interloper,' said Jonathan. 'Mother, don't be naïve.'

Now his face was ugly again, and he left the kitchen.

He went to his offices and walked through the hot closed rooms and then stood staring at his files. He no longer hated his dead wife. She had receded into unreality for him. But he hated those who were making it impossible for him to stay in his city, who were driving him out with uttered violence, lies, innuendoes, distrust and malice and hostility. He had asked nothing but to serve them and they had repudiated him. He found a bottle of whisky in a drawer and drank deeply of it, not using a glass.

His telephone rang.

'Dear,' said Marjorie, 'it's time to help me load baskets in the carriage.'

It was so banal that he laughed.

'You are looking very handsome,' said Marjorie as Jonathan helped her to place the picnic baskets in the surrey. 'I like that blue and white striped blazer. But why do men wear such stiff high collars, especially on a hot day like this? And stiff white cuffs and studs and collar-buttons, and that remnant of little thin tie?'

'Why do women wear stiff corsets of whalebone and dresses dragging in the dust? Fashion, woman, fashion.' He took off his straw sailor and wiped his forehead. He eyed his mother approvingly, and she was startled. She could not remember that he had ever admired her before. She wore a slender lawn dress printed in grey and rose and a broad straw hat with soft grey flowers and green leaves bending down its supple circle. Her aristocratic face, so like Jonathan's, was flushed with heat and her hazel eyes were gentle and contemplative as she smiled at him. But there were mauve circles under her eyes and her lips were pale and a little drawn. Jonathan frowned. 'Are you taking that digitalis I gave you?' he asked.

'When I remember. Please don't fuss, dear. Forget you are a doctor, just for to-day. What a lovely day it is. It usually is, for the Fourth.'

He held the reins tightly as he drove the mare down the street, for one had to be watchful of mischievous children who might throw a fire-cracker in the path of a nervous horse. Marjorie was waving to an occasional friend on the walk, and then between the houses they could see the glitter of the river and the green and blue flanks of the mountains.

'So peaceful, so tranquil,' said Marjorie. 'What a lot we have to be thankful for these days! No more wars, just plenty and hope and peace and industry. We are a blessed nation.'

Jonathan turned the horse down the street leading to the square. They could already see the high flags rippling against the sky and could hear the distant hum of the crowd and there was the long booming of a cannon on the lawn of the city hall. This marked the beginning of the yearly festivities. The air was permeated with the smell of powder and a great deal of smoke drifted in the breeze, creating a bright little fog. Now the German Band struck up a Sousa march, and there was a prolonged cheering.

Jonathan tied up the horse near a water trough, and in the shade. The mare snorted anxiously. She was answered by other horses tethered up and down the street. Jonathan patted her again, spoke to her quietly and gave her a cube of sugar. She rolled her eyes at him apprehensively. A policeman strolled up. 'I'll be watching them all, Doctor,' he said, touching his cap to Marjorie. 'No fire-crackers on this street.' He laughed. 'Lots of manure, though.'

Jonathan helped his mother down, and again glanced at her face. It was no longer flushed. She looked increasingly tired. He gathered up the two big baskets and permitted her to carry two smaller ones. They walked along the street towards the square. The houses, on their long silent lawns, were shuttered against the sun on the upper floors, and the big porches were empty. Chinese wind-crystals made a frail music, heard even above the hubbub in the square, their tinkling nostalgic and thin.

'Jon!' said a voice behind them, and Jonathan started and he turned with his mother. Father McNulty, plump and radiant, was at their heels, golden eyes glowing, and young face shining with sweat. He, too, carried a small basket with a blue-checked napkin covering it. He beamed at them. 'It was very kind of you to invite me, Mrs Ferrier,' he said, shaking her hand. His shabby habit had a greenish tint. Then he laughed joyously at Jonathan. 'I have my own horse and buggy now!' he cried. 'Senator Campion insisted. Five hundred dollars! I have only two hundred more to pay. And the Senator is really very generous. He is paying the livery bills.'

'How nice,' said Marjorie. 'Isn't it a lovely day?'

'Marvellous,' said the young priest, wiping the wet forehead under the black hat. 'I haven't very much here, Mrs Ferrier. And my aunt thanks you for the invitation, but she has one of her headaches. Unfortunate. But she baked a very nice chocolate cake.'

'I love chocolate cake,' said Marjorie. 'It will be delicious with the iced tea.' She looked at him fondly. He was such a nice young man, so innocent, so kind. She hoped the Kitcheners would not snub him, nor that frightful Mrs Morgan. There were such unkind things in the press these days about the

'Roman Menace.' That is, in what Jon called 'the yellow press.' Only two weeks ago three newly-arrived Irish labouring families had had the windows of their little shacks broken, here in Hambledon, and filthy things scrawled on their sidewalks. No one had protested, except Jonathan, in an angry letter to the local newspaper, which had not increased his popularity.

Father McNulty ambled along with them, talking with filial deference to Marjorie. 'I like these celebrations,' he said. 'Small cities are much warmer than larger ones, and more personal.'

'That they are,' said Jonathan. 'So much kinder and more brotherly. So much more loving.'

'Now, dear,' said Marjorie.

The square opened before them, its lawns spread with crowded picnic tables, and the whole area alive with shouting and running children. It was far hotter here in spite of the thick trees and the open space in the centre, with its bronze statue of General Sherman flanked with old cannon. The city hall, the pride of Hambledon, stood far back on its green rise of grass, its white Grecian pillars blazing in the sun, its flags flying, and its broad steps, filled with chairs, waiting for the dignitaries. There was a lectern, waiting but empty. Everywhere flags spread to the burning blue sky, and the German Band, in its round wooden stand near General Sherman, was playing with fervent gusto, and boys threw fire-crackers into the air and their parents gossiped at filled tables, and babies shrieked, and young girls sauntered looking at the closed shops, their dresses and hats bright with colour, and young men in blazers and stiff straw hats watched them. The light poured down on the band, turning tuba and trumpet to gold, and the stout uniformed men, with eye-glasses and blond moustaches, puffed so fiercely that their faces were scarlet. Drums thundered, flutes shrilled, children shouted and ran, women called comfortably from tables in the shade. Men laughed hoarsely. They had removed coats and collars, and some were furtively drinking beer from cold bottles beneath great elms. Some even sat on the steps of the First Presbyterian Church, which faced the city hall from across the street, and drank defiantly, and called back and forth to friends fanning themselves at a distance. It was a lively and jubilant sight, full of noise and voices and brazen music and startling colour, bobbing with women's flowered hats, feverish

164

with young faces flashing into the sun and then into shadow. The heat was already pungent with the odour of crushed grass and gunpowder and food and dust and sweating bodies and aromatic leaves.

In places of honour, near the bandstand, sat row upon row of middle-aged men in blue uniforms, the Grand Army of the Republic, the veterans of the Civil War, and behind them sat the young veterans of the Spanish-American war, with their jaunty Rough Rider hats.

'Can you find our table, Jon?' asked Marjorie Ferrier. Father McNulty had taken one of her baskets, and she had not protested.

'I think I see a crow,' said Jonathan, nodding farther down the crowded lawns. 'Yes, it's Mrs Morgan.'

'Now, Jon,' said Marjorie.

'I don't know why I stand this, year after year,' said Jonathan, picking his way among tables, and trying to avoid dishes and glasses on the grass, and little children.

'It's very innocent. And harmless,' said Father McNulty. 'There must be several thousand here. It's very happy.'

Jonathan looked at him sharply. 'I see old Campion has arrived, in all his magnificence. Prepare, as usual, for a mellow ripe speech full of glory. There's Beatrice with him, anticipating goodies. But no Francis.'

'He left last night, for New York,' said the priest. 'He's going to France.'

'Good,' said Jonathan. 'That should be a full education for him.'

'He's going to a monastery in the Alps,' said Father McNulty.

Jonathan stopped abruptly. 'The hell you say,' he said. 'Did you contrive that?'

'Now, dear,' said Marjorie, seeing the darkness on her son's face. 'Oh, here we are. Isn't it nice?'

The Ferrier table was a little apart, in deep shade, and there were fewer children running on the grass. A small silence seemed imposed on the table, an awkwardness. Two men stood up, young Robert Morgan and Mr Alfred Kitchener. Mr Kitchener, and his wife, Sue, were distant relations and they matched each other remarkably in that they both resembled bright rosy baked apples, even to the cinnamon-coloured hair. Both were short and round and sweet and inviting in appearance, with brilliant grey eyes like crystal, dimpled chins and pink cheeks, and both had an air of comfortable innocence, placidity and affection. Their daughter, Maude, twenty-two, was their only child, as small and dimpled and pink as themselves, a trifle plump but endearingly so, and her hair, a vivid auburn, escaped in thick glossy waves and ripples from under her wide gauzy hat. The three had an old-fashioned and contented appearance as if nothing in their lives had ever disturbed them. Mr Kitchener was a prosperous lawyer who never accepted a criminal case. He had cosy offices with five clerks, and an assistant, and had inherited considerable money. Jonathan Ferrier was fond of the three Kitcheners but found them dull if pleasant and soothing company. It was obvious that they were fond of him also, for Alfred Kitchener chuckled at him, shook his hand heartily, Mrs Kitchener smiled happily and Maude gave him an absent grey look, and smiled shyly. Jonathan wondered at that absentness, but soon found the reason. The girl was fascinated by Robert Morgan, and even as she smiled at Jonathan her eyes moved mistily to Robert and stayed there.

Mrs Morgan had the small cold and secret smile of the naturally malicious woman, and it merely became colder as she haughtily acknowledged the newcomers, without a glance, of course, at the priest, whom she ignored even when he was presented to her. Her light eyes examined Jonathan severely, and even with contempt, then withdrew from him to dwell even more severely at the other guest, Jenny Heger.

Jenny, Jonathan saw at once, was dressed as bunchily and as unprettily as always, in a blue and white checked shirt-waist, a heavy blue duck skirt, black-buttoned shoes and a broad black patent-leather belt. Her hat, a big coarse cartwheel of yellow straw, was useful for shading her from the sun but for no other purpose, certainly not to enhance her appearance, with its dusty black ribbon and despondent bow. She sat in stiff silence on her part of the bench after the introduction to Father McNulty, and stared at the table, her hands clenched together in her lap. But nothing could really dim the white lustre of her face, the extraordinary blueness of her eyes, the stern loveliness of her palely coloured mouth, the delicate aquilinity of her nose, and the mass of glistening black hair rolled impatiently under her hat and allowed to droop in a large bun at her nape. Not even the starched wide blue-and-white checked collar of her shirtwaist could hide the slenderness of her long neck, the contour of her superb young shoulders, and the classical lines of her breast. She made pretty little Maude, who had been a belle in Hambledon since she had reached puberty, appear almost common.

Jenny said nothing to him, and he said nothing to her. But Marjorie said, 'Jon, do sit next to Jenny, and I really must sit next to Alfred. I have so many things to say to him.'

Jonathan wanted to say, 'I'd prefer to sit across from Maude,' for the girl always delighted him with her cheerful inanity and soft conversation, and her air that the world was a truly lovable and romantic and exciting place. But Marjorie was already smiling along the table at Mrs Morgan, who bent her head as if being gracious to a lady-in-waiting, and smiling, too, at Mrs Kitchener, who had gently patted the spot next to her for Father McNulty. Unfortunately, he would have Mrs Morgan on his left, and she ostentatiously withdrew to the limit of the bench to accommodate him. Jonathan gave her a hard look and was somewhat surprised to see that Jenny gave her a similar one.

Why doesn't Dr Morgan look at me? Maude Kitchener was thinking. Why does he stare at Jenny Heger that way? She isn't even pretty; quite plain, to be sure. So big, so pale, and so cold. She, Maude, had not believed a single word said about Jenny since she had been almost a child, nor had Sue Kitchener, for there was really nothing wrong to believe. Jenny had always been a retiring girl, turning miserably red if someone spoke to her unexpectedly, and her clothing awful and thick and unstylish, but a wonderful scholar, winning all the prizes at school. Maude, of the gentle heart, had tried to be a friend to that reserved and silent girl, and Jenny had been diffidently grateful at first, but then had seemed to find all social intercourse painful in the extreme, and so had frightened off Maude and some of the other girls who might have been her friends. Poor Jenny. But why was that wonderful young Dr Morgan staring at her so, and ignoring herself?

Mrs Kitchener thought: How lovely it is when dear friends get together like this! Everyone is so happy and at ease, even that poor young Jenny. Sue was so gleeful at this thought that she smiled at her husband, beside her, and pressed his warm plump hand, and was pressed affectionately in return. Lovely, lovely world, sweet world, sweet world, thought Sue.

'We might as well have our dinner now,' said Marjorie, 'before all those awful speeches begin.'

The German Band sprang violently into 'Ta-ra-ra-boom-de-ay!' For the mayor, Emil Schuman, was greeting fresh arrivals on the steps, ladies with big hats and parasols. There was Louis Hedler and Humphrey Bedloe and other members of the staff of the two hospitals, and several clergymen, and Colonel Jeremiah Hadley, late of the Army of the Republic, sixty and grey but tall and stately in his Union blue and medals.

'I've heard,' said Jane Morgan, giving Marjorie her usual cold and knowing look, 'that there is a much more refined gathering to-day in the park near the river, without all this noise and these howling children and the more Vulgar Classes.'

'Yes,' said Marjorie, laying the warm rolls on a silver dish. 'But this is the traditional place, and the traditional celebration. We in Hambledon have been meeting here for this picnic every year, from far back before the Civil War, ever since Hambledon was a village and not a town. And you will notice that Senator Campion is here, and the mayor, and other important people of Hambledon, though I did hear a rumour they are joining the others near the river after the speeches.'

'And no wonder,' said Jane Morgan. 'Such a fearful noise! And that horrible band! Why can't it be quiet even for a minute?'

Last year I was sitting on those stairs, with Mavis, Jonathan was thinking, I was one of the town's honoured 'dignitaries.' To-day I am the pariah, the outcast, the nobody, the despised and the rejected. A man may be innocent until he is proved guilty, but no one seems to have taken that seriously at any time.

The roaring of the crowd, the bursting explosions, the band —all the screaming and singing and laughing—disappeared from his consciousness, and he was again in the courtroom, before the judge and the jury, listening to the prosecuting attorney, seeing the dull averted faces, the harsh and cunning faces, against a background of grimy snow hissing against the dirty windows. He had not been afraid of any of them, and had even smiled grimly at the prosecuting attorney's denunciation of him as a 'ruthless, cruel, bloody-handed murderer of his young and beautiful wife and his unborn child. A calculating, callous murderer! Gentlemen, shall this man go free, and live, with that blameless blood on his hands? Dare you to dismiss him to laugh at you and our Great, Noble, Free American Justice?'

The band crashed into 'Hail, Columbia, Happy Land!' and

the crowd rose in a mass of hot colour and cheered and sang lustily and waved small flags and saluted and lit fresh fire-crackers, and the sun beat down and all the air was heavy with the smell of food and beer and dust and crushed grass and gunpowder.

Jonathan too, stood up. In doing so he accidentally lurched against the rising Jenny at his side, and he instinctively caught her as she stumbled, and his arm was about her waist and her cheek near his lips. They stood like statues, stricken into stillness, and then, very slowly, she looked at him, lifting those enormous blue eyes to his, and turning whiter than before. They could not look away. He felt the girl's body trembling under his hand, and then to his amazement and tremendous emotion, he saw a blaze of light pass over her face and he saw her lips part.

He dropped his hand. He muttered, 'Sorry.' But he, too, was trembling. He looked at her again. Her face was now averted from him. She was looking at the court-house stairs. Jenny, he thought. I must have imagined it. Not Jenny! Not Jenny, his brother's doxy. There was a sick and broken disintegration all through his thoughts and body.

Senator Kenton Campion, in all his florid handsomeness, his chestnut handsomeness, followed the mayor to the lectern, and everyone cheered and clapped, for he was very popular. 'The friend of the People.' The town loved him for his appearance, his money, the little scandals about him, his smiles, his geniality, his repeated stories—and his constant excellent press. He bowed to the crowds, gravely acknowledged the salutes of the veterans, bowed to his fellow dignitaries, lifted his hands like a loving father to still the shouts and the screamed greetings and the flurry of flags, and made his usual chauvinistic speech. Even the clichés and the quotations from Walt Whitman were the same as last year, Jonathan thought.

His voice, big and mellifluous, filled the whole square, and it was rich with emotion.

When at last he finished the people were in an uproar of excitement and jubilation. They roared across the square to shake Campion's hand, and he reached down to seize each eagerly upraised hand and piously to bless it, and to murmur a loving word. Every man whose hand was shaken felt himself honoured and uplifted, though he did not quite know why. He dazedly smiled at his neighbours, clapped neighbours on the shoulder, said, 'Wasn't that a wonderful speech for the Fourth?' And no one said, 'But what did he mean?' It was enough to be part of the sweating and enthusiastic crowd, the crowd beloved of the Senator. It was enough to be shouting with everyone else in a fine hot spirit of brotherhood and zeal.

Trumpets sounded. Applause and cheering and shouting died. Colonel Hadley was approaching the lectern.

He stood silent and tall and thin, and the crowd resumed its clapping, but with less enthusiasm than before. They knew these old soldiers. They had nothing but platitudes to say, unlike the Senator who could really arouse emotion and make a man feel splendid and big and powerful. Besides, the crowd was full of beer and food and cake and lemonade and sluggish with sun and heat and wanted to go home. The dignitaries were whispering together behind the Colonel, and the ladies were impatiently flapping their fans and yawning, and there was some scraping of chairs on the stone.

The mayor introduced the Colonel whom everyone knew. 'Our great hero, in the Civil War,' said the short fat mayor, Emil Schuman. 'He has a few words to say to us on this glorious Fourth. A few words,' he added, glancing imploringly at the Colonel in his uniform. He wiped his glistening forehead, and then his yellow moustache.

People were already leaving many of the tables, gathering up baskets and offspring. The band played louder. The people hesitated, then dropped down at tables of friends, and yawned. But many streamed out of the square, wheeling carts and buggies and trailing little children, who howled strenuously.

The Colonel's voice rose and shook, and he lifted his clenched hand and presented his military platitudes.

There was no applause as he ended. He did not sit down again. He walked down the steps, reached the flagstones, then turned straightly and left the square. The crowd watched him go.

The band struck up 'The Star Spangled Banner,' and everyone sang, and there was a feeling that something portentious had happened and everyone could now go home in this late afternoon and rest, and sit on porches and yawn contentedly, and then put children to bed and brew the coffee for a late supper.

They spoke amiably of the Senator. But few mentioned the Colonel.

'One of your more inspired speeches,' said Dr Louis Hedler to the Senator.

'Thank you, Louis,' said the Senator, as he assisted his sister down the steps, and waited amiably for her to finish a little chat with her friends. He bowed to the lady who was engaging Beatrice's attention. He turned to Louis and his handsome eyes had a peculiar glaze over them, as if they had been covered by glass. 'Louis, may I ask when young Ferrier is leaving Hambledon?'

'Jon?' Louis's froglike face coloured. 'I don't know, Kenton, I don't know. Frankly, Humphrey and I are trying to persuade him to remain. After all, he was ac—'

But the Senator's face had lost all its geniality, and became vindictive and quiet. 'Louis, I want that man out of this town. In fact, I want him out of this State. I have influence in Pittsburgh and Philadelphia. He won't get hospital privileges in any other city. Get him out, Louis.'

Louis had the obstinacy of his Teutonic forebears, and he had never liked the Senator for all they were the dearest of friends. He said, 'He saved little Hortense Nolan's life a few days ago, Kenton, and her parents are the best friends you have in this town. He's saved more people than I like to remember. He is a splendid surgeon and physician, and we need him—'

'Get him out, Louis,' said the Senator, in a soft and deadly voice. 'Is that understood? Out of your hospital, out of Bedloe's. Do you know what he did to my son? He made it impossible for him to continue at his seminary. I objected to the seminary in the first place, but I bowed, like an indulgent father, to the boy's decision. Then this Ferrier almost destroyed him, filled his mind with the most unspeakable things, and the boy has run off to France. I have heard some more about his cases. Didn't little Martha Best die under mysterious circumstances, for instance? And only yesterday my dear and delicate friend, Elsie Holliday was put under sedatives by you, Louis, because your Ferrier drove her son, young Jefferson, out of town, out of his home State, and to some pest-hole near the Gulf of Mexico, after some alleged treatment or diagnosis, which no one else has confirmed and which is probably false.'

Louis's face tightened. 'Now, listen to me, Kenton, you've heard very filthy lies. Little Martha had a very rare disease, cancer of the blood, and it's incurable and Jon diagnosed it

171

at once. My God, man! You can't blame Jon for an Act of God, or nature! I don't know about your boy. I didn't know Jon was his physician—'

'He wasn't. He forced himself, uninvited, uncalled, into my house, and talked alone to my boy, and the next thing I and his dear aunt knew he was off for France and places unknown. Is it ethical to insist on treating a patient against his will, against the will of his family? I thought not. But what about Jefferson Holliday?'

Louis hesitated. 'I can't tell you exactly, but he has something the government designates as a "loathsome and contagious disease." That'll have to satisfy you, Kenton.'

The Senator chuckled, glanced sidelong at his sister, who was still chatting. 'Venereal, eh? Well, young men. What about the new arsenic treatments? Why, Louis, if all the young men who had syphilis or the clap were driven out of the cities we'd have no one left.'

He tapped Louis on the shoulder. 'Get him out, Louis. Is that understood? Come, Beatrice, we'll just have time to drive down to the park and dine with our friends and then see the fireworks at night.'

Louis watched him go, then slowly lit a cigar and walked down the stairs and contemplated the hot litter and silence of the square, now almost deserted. The heated gold of very late afternoon shimmered in the tops of the trees and on store fronts. 'Yes, Kent,' Louis Hedler muttered, 'it's understood. By you, of course. But there are others.'

CHAPTER 7

The ladies of the Ferrier party had discreetly retired, 'for refreshment,' into the interior of the city hall, and the gentlemen also retired for the same purpose into the convenient basement of the First Presbyterian Church. They met again at the table. 'We're practically alone,' said Jonathan, with pleasure.

They idly watched the stout German Band put away its instruments. The hot early evening air was so quiet that those at the table could hear the guttural accents of the musicians. They could hear the dry rustling of the trees and the movements of carriages in streets beyond the park, as the celebrants drove home. Men were clearing away the flags and the chairs on the city hall steps, and the draped banners of red, white and blue, and other men were walking over the grass gathering up the larger litter. No one moved quickly. A man laughed. A distant dog barked. The sun fell lower and lower into a reddening sky. There was a scent of old roses and hay from somewhere, even over the smell of heated stone, and a breath from the river.

'How peaceful it is,' said Marjorie. 'I'm just drugged with sun and air. I'm sure I'll be asleep before we get home. I've enjoyed this day, in spite of the Senator. You must tell me what he said when we get home, Jon.'

'I've forgotten,' her son replied.

'Robert?' said Mrs Morgan. 'I really think we must be getting home. My arthritis, you know.'

Robert stood up. He bowed to Marjorie. 'Mrs Ferrier, it was most kind of you to invite us, most kind. You have done so much to make us happy in our new home. When we have moved into our house I hope you will visit us often.'

'My dear, I've done nothing,' said Marjorie, and her hazel eyes sparkled at him with affection.

Robert stood, and hesitated. He had the strongest yearning that Jenny should look at him, say a word, or simply smile. He could not leave without that. As if she felt his urgent desire she did glance up across the table, for he had moved to help his mother, and she gave him her faint and shrinking smile, then glanced away. It was enough for the young man. He was quite hearty in his last good-byes.

'Such a nice young man, so devoted to his poor mother,' said Sue Kitchener. 'She has led a life of such trials. Quite a martyr. Is he—I mean, has he spoken—'

'If you mean, Sue, is there a girl lurking in the shadows—no,' said Jonathan. 'He's disengaged. I hope he keeps that way.'

'Now, Jon,' said Marjorie, and yawned deeply and richly.

Sue giggled. 'Well, I hope he finds a lovely girl, right here in Hambledon.' She smiled tenderly at her daughter and Maude blushed.

'And I have Benediction,' said Father McNulty, 'not that I expect many visitors to the Blessed Sacrament to-day.'

He rose and made his farewells and trotted off.

'And now I am afraid we must leave, too,' said Sue Kitchener. 'We are having just a light supper—if we can find any room for it—and then we are going down to the river to watch the fireworks in the dark. Are you going, too, Marjorie?'

'I think not,' said Marjorie Ferrier. 'I'm really too tired. Jonathan?'

'Certainly not,' he replied.

'Well, that's too bad. I thought you might like to take Jenny.'

Jonathan was amazed. The very idea was grotesque. The Kitcheners took their leave. Now the last yellow glitter had left the trees and a coolness was rising, and the Ferriers were alone with Jenny, who was sitting in her usual anguished silence with her head bowed and her hands in her lap.

But when Marjorie began to gather dishes and glasses and silver and napkins together, Jenny stood up at once and began to help her, her young hands deft and quick. Jonathan filled the baskets neatly. 'Jenny,' said Marjorie, 'will ride with us to the river. She didn't bring her bicycle to-day.'

'Oh, no, I can walk! ' cried the girl. 'I like to walk! It isn't far!'

'Nonsense. A young girl walking alone on the streets—it's getting quite dark now—and on a holiday, could be misunderstood,' said Marjorie.

'Mother, you're in the twentieth century now,' Jonathan said. 'Young ladies are understood these days, not misunderstood. Isn't that so, Jenny?'

'Don't be unpleasant, Jon,' said Marjorie. 'Jenny, I'll hear no more. You must ride with us, among the baskets, I am afraid. Will your servants have returned by the time you arrive?'

The girl blurted, 'No. I told them they need not come back until the morning. It is a holiday for them, too.'

Marjorie let her hands fall. 'Jenny! You mean to spend the night entirely alone on the island! Why, that's not to be thought of! It's too dangerous. Anyone can row over there and molest you, or rob you. Say no more. You must stay with us to-night.'

'Oh, no!' The cry was purely desperate. 'I'm not afraid, Aunt Marjorie. I'm not afraid, when I am alone.' She looked, in the blue twilight, as if she were about to cry. 'I want to be alone,' she added. 'I didn't mean to say that, Aunt Marjorie, but I did mean it—I mean—'

Jonathan had listened to this with surly amusement. Was she planning a new rendezvous, with Childe Harald away, on that island? She looked distracted enough.

'I won't hear of it,' said Marjorie. 'What if something happened to you?'

'It won't,' said Jenny. 'It never has, before. I've often been alone like this.'

Oh, you have, have you? thought Jonathan, and remembered a recent story, alleged to be directly from one of the servants herself. It was related that the maid had often seen Harald leaving Jenny's bedroom early in the morning, and once or twice had detected Jenny leaving Harald's at dawn. It was a delicious story. There was still another—that Jenny's favours were not Harald's alone, and never had been. The girl was only twenty, yet there was hardly a woman more notorious in Hambledon than she.

There was a desperate resolution about Jenny now, as she pushed aside Marjorie's pleas. 'I really am not afraid. I really like to be alone. I have locks on the doors,' she said. 'Please don't insist, Aunt Marjorie.'

'I'm really too tired to oppose your wilfulness,' Marjorie said with severity. 'And I'm very angry with you, Jenny. Jon will drop me at home, and then will take you to the river. And then,' she said in a clear hard voice, 'he will row you over to the island and inspect every room for you, and the grounds, and then wait until you are locked up. No, Jenny, I won't hear anything more. I'm very tired. I'd like to sleep to-night, and not worry about you. Jon?'

175

He was delighted to make the girl more distracted than she already was. 'It will be a pleasure, dear Jenny,' he said, and gave her a low bow. She looked at him with mute wretchedness and her mouth shook and he was elated.

It was deep twilight when Jonathan let his mother out of the surrey and led her to the house. 'Hurry back,' she whispered, 'I'll go in alone. It would be just like Jenny to get out and run away. Jon, be kind to her, will you? Don't tease her so.'

'Kind? Jenny doesn't want anyone to be kind to her. She's sufficient unto herself, a very haughty and sullen young lady with a mind of her own. At least let me unlock the door for you.'

Marjorie stood in the lighted doorway and watched the surrey drive off. Jenny, apparently, had refused to leave the back seat and still sat crowded among the baskets which Marjorie had forgotten. The surrey clopped through the quiet dark streets. The lamps were already lit, and burned in yellow straightness, for there was no wind. A few voices sounded sleepily from dark porches and there were the creakings of rockers, and an occasional scolding as a woman addressed herself to dilatory children inside the houses.

Jonathan drove in silence, but acutely aware of the girl behind him. He knew that she hated him but he had never cared, until now, to know the reason why. He had seen her in childhood and young girlhood, and then in early womanhood, and it was not until she had been sixteen—and still untouched, he had presumed—that he had sharply noticed her. That had been six months after his marriage to Mavis. Her mother had been alive then, silly Myrtle, and had recently married Harald. No, it had not been that marriage which had changed the girl from a touching young softness to a steely witch, for though it had been evident that she had at first thought her mother had violated the sacred Memories of Daddy, she had regarded Myrtle as a child who must be given what she desired to make her happy and to keep her protected. Jenny had not changed until her mother had died.

Myrtle's death changed Jenny violently. The girl who could speak so gently in her sweet strong voice—when pressed by kind insistence—and could even laugh a little, though she was always so grave, became cold and hard and remote and silent. It was her foolish mother's will, of course, which had changed her. She had probably felt herself betrayed. It was odd, but

176

not so very odd—considering human nature—that money could transform people. Yet, at her early age, she had become Harald's mistress, and not long, if one was to credit reports, after her mother's death. Was it to hold Harald to the island? If he left for more than seven months at a time the money would be hers, but it was possible that it was not only the money she wanted but Childe Harald, too.

Jonathan remembered the first time that Jenny, as an awkward girl approaching womanhood, had become more than a child to him and had invaded his life with Mavis. It had been a spring day and he had visited Myrtle and Harald on the island—they had not long been married—and Jenny, the devoted daughter, was pruning her father's roses.

She had looked up at him, startled, for she had not heard him come, and the sunlight had suddenly struck the contours of her face and made her blue eyes blaze. Knife in hand, still bending, she had turned her head, and the wind lifted her long black hair and blew it about her in a tumbling cloud of deep shadow and sparkling light.

'Hello, Jenny,' he said. 'I thought you were over in Hambledon to-day.'

'No. No, Uncle Jon,' she answered, and for the first time he was conscious of the promise of rich sweetness in her voice. She straightened, and tried to control the tossing masses of her hair. 'I didn't know you were here, either. I—I'm pruning my father's roses.'

He saw her profile now, childlike and softly smiling. She cut expertly. Her lips were parted and he saw her teeth, small and pearly, unlike Mavis's which were so large and so lavishly displayed in her wide laughter, and which just narrowly escaped being called 'buck' or 'horse' teeth.

Jenny, Jonathan had thought, as he stood there easily and smiled at her with his chilled hands in his pockets and his polished boots already muddy. Sweet Jenny. He had forgotten, since his marriage, that there were such girls as Jenny in the world, tender, simple, honest, gentle and diffident, who could be so happy when a dead bush proved it was not dead at all but was importantly and exuberantly alive. Here was no avaricious flirt, no schemer, no liar, no grasping woman with tiny eyes and a huge grinning mouth which could express the utmost in callous cruelty. Jenny's mother was rich, yet Jenny was unaffected and her joy in a rose could never have been known to Mavis.

She stepped back from the rose-bed and her shoe stuck in the mud and she hopped on one foot. Jonathan retrieved the shoe and he never noticed it was several sizes larger than Mavis's dainty slippers. He scraped the mud off on the new green grass, then gallantly insisted on putting it on Jenny's foot again. To support herself, she leaned her hand on his bent back, and all at once a fiery thrill ran through his shoulder and then through his body. For an instant he could not move. Then, his hands shaking, he put the muddy old shoe over the coarse brown stocking and he saw that though the girl's foot was large it was also miraculously slender and beautifully moulded. She was murmuring something but he did not catch her words. He was still stricken by his response to her touch, and now felt the heat in his flesh, and a sudden incredulousness, and a sudden rush of happiness and buoyance. He had never known these before, and he was dazed at his own beatitude.

'Thank you, Uncle Jon,' said Jenny. He stood up, his face darkly flushed. He said, 'I wish you wouldn't call me "Uncle Jon," Jenny. I'm not really your uncle. Call me Jon.'

She studied him seriously. Then in her shyly blunt way she said, 'But, Uncle Jon, you are so much older than I am! I'm only sixteen. It wouldn't be respectful.'

'What's fifteen years between—friends?' he asked, trying for lightness because his breath was coming too fast. 'You call Harald "Harald," and he's only two years younger than I. Come on, Jenny.'

She considered him with that young solemnity of hers. The blueness of her eyes seemed to fill her face, that immaculate face of absolute purity and without any guile at all. And then her expression changed after long moments. It became startled, very frightened and confused, and she turned her face aside and her cheeks were suddenly awash in brilliant scarlet. Without a word she flung herself away from him and ran back to that ridiculous castle.

Jonathan watched her go. He was too involved in his own emotions to wonder why the girl had run like that and why she had coloured so and had been so silent.

He did not see her again that day. But as he lay awake that night with Mavis sleeping blissfully beside him—she had not as yet moved to another room—he could not forget Jenny. Academically, he knew much that was to be known about humanity and human emotions, for he was a doctor, but as young Father McNulty was later to say, he was essentially and amazingly a simple man who could not, as yet, translate his knowledge into personal objectivity. If another man had told him of this experience he would have said, with a broad smile, 'There's nothing mysterious about it. You've fallen in love with that girl, and probably you've fallen in love for the first time, and never mind that you're married.'

His marriage took a change for the worse in the next few days and then he and Mavis had gone to Europe for the summer, on her insistence, and he had agreed in a last desperate hope that he could change Mavis and save the marriage and persuade her to begin a family.

He had not seen Jenny again for nearly a year, and incomprehensibly he only saw her at a distance. In the following years he saw her exactly three times, before her mother's death. He would have jeered to learn that he was a rigidly upright man in his soul, yet for a long time he not only tried to devote himself to Mavis and to change her but he suppressed that day with Jenny in his mind. He had removed himself from his Church, but the moral teachings and doctrines had sunk irrevocably into him. Whenever he remembered Jenny he choked the thought at once and did not know that the heavy sadness he always felt was connected with that spring day in the castle's gardens.

He had not known it until this Fourth of July, 1901, on a peaceful hot day in a peaceful and joyful and busy country. He remembered it now, with all its first poignancy and longing and sharp delirium and passion, and all its sense that something incredibly novel and beautiful had happened to him and had lightened his whole sombre world, had made him young and expectant and unbearably happy, for a few hours at least.

But the girl in the garden and the girl behind him in the surrey were not one and the same any longer. One had been innocent and beloved, and this one was besmirched and unclean. To him, that had been long unpardonable, and worth only his hate. For a second that afternoon, when he had caught Jenny at the table, it was Jenny of the garden again, Jenny of sixteen years, and the look she had given him had recalled that whole day.

The surrey turned towards the river, and down the long street the dark water was glittering and the bulk of the island stood up in it against the sky and the opposite mountains.

'You can let me out here,' said Jenny. Her voice was rough and low.

Jonathan said, 'You heard my mother. I promised her to see you safely home, and on your island, with the doors all locked.' He did not turn to look back at her in the dark. Jenny was crouching on the cushions as if deadly cold, hugging herself with her arms. She was crying silently, great noiseless sobs that shook her body. This was an anguish familiar to her, for it was compounded of grief and despair, of longing and loneliness, of monstrous desolation. Her tears ran down her cheeks without a sound and dropped on the plain blue and white chequers of her shirtwaist. She looked through the watery mist of them at the back of Jonathan's arrogant head and then she closed her eyes and pressed her lips together.

The first flare of the evening fireworks rose in the sky at the left, above the houses and this long street to the river. It flowered like a huge rose in green and red, spreading with a thunderous roar that rolled along the water, breaking into vivid stars against the deepening dark of the sky, in which the ivory curve of the moon was embedded and in which the stars were beginning to tremble and change. Jenny was too absorbed in her misery to see, but Jonathan saw and remembered again the last Fourth of July when he and Mavis were guests of the gay party of dignitaries in the park near the river. Mavis, as usual, had been given the seat of honour and each blaze of the fireworks lit up her luminous face, her smiling face, her constantly tossing golden head, her quick and lively gestures. She had appeared to be enjoying herself, surrounded by love and adulation, and her French perfume had been a cloud of delicious fragrance all over her so that it seemed not to appear extraneous but a part of her smooth and beautiful body and the white lace dress she was wearing. Jonathan's latest gift to her, a necklace of aquamarines and pearls, hung about her throat and seemed to gather colour and warmth from her lucent flesh.

Yet, that night, when they were alone in her dressing-room she had risen to cold and contorted fury. This was not new. Her rages were very frequent when with Jonathan. She had ordered him from her bedroom and dressing-room. But he had stood there, sombre and silent, just staring at her with a kind of incredulity which further outraged her, for she knew by now he still could not reconcile the lovely-lady-among-

180

strangers with the uncontrolled virago who was his wife and who had the most cruel of tongues. He could not reconcile the lady-of-love with this greedy and empty woman. He was always in a state of desperate wonder.

She was sitting at her dressing-table in a peignoir of white lace and satin, with her golden hair streaming over her shoulders and her face as ugly as death, and livid. She screamed at him and beat her fists on the table and her eyes were full of glittering hate.

'You are such a fool! Such a bore, bore, bore! Do you know how boring you are, sitting like a clod among your friends, and not speaking, or, if speaking, making some disagreeable remark! Bore! Bore! Old man, old man, old stupid man! If you weren't so stupid you'd have left this dull and silly town long ago! They can talk about your "brilliance," bah! But I know how stupid you are, how boring, how tedious, how tiresome, with no conversation and no fun. You keep me here, in this horrid town, in this horrid old house, among these horrid people, and all you can say is that it's your "home," and these are your "people," and I'm like to die of ennui and yawn myself into a stupor! What fun is there for me, here—and with you? Tell me! Just tell me!'

He could speak now, slowly and without emotion. 'I'm sorry I bore you. Yes, this is my "home." This is my city. These are my "people." You know it. You've known it from the beginning. I take you to New York and Philadelphia and Boston and Chicago on medical meetings. You know of the offers I've had, in great hospitals and clinics—'

She had listened to him, her furious breaths making her breast lift and fall rapidly, and her rage rising. Again she beat her fists on the table. 'How long do you stay in those wonderful cities? A few days, a week or so, letting famous men flatter you while they are laughing at you out of the other side of their mouths! They know what you are, a small-time, small-town fraud, with no ambition, no imagination. You can't even dance properly. You hardly ever laugh. You're a clod, a farmer, a dullard, a fool! I wish I'd died before I married you!'

'So do I,' he said. Now his voice was heavy and full of thick anger, murderous anger he rarely felt—and then only with Mavis. 'I wish you—or I—had died before we were married. Indeed.'

181

She became silent then, her hands unclenching on the table, and she looked at him and what she saw frightened her and made her turn very white. She half rose. The mirror reflected her pale and fallen mouth. Her tiny blue eyes opened as wide as they could and they were sharp with wary fear. She clutched the edge of the table, and then her pink tongue darted out to wet lips suddenly dry. She blinked, and she watched.

'Do you know how many times I've wanted to kill you, Mavis?' he asked. 'Do you know what I think at night when I can't sleep? I think of ways of killing you. Poison? Cutting your throat? Smothering you? Strangling you? You tempt me all the time, Mavis, you tempt me.'

She knew it was true, and she let out a deep gasp, and then, inch by inch, she moved away from him backwards, her dressing-gown glistening in the lamplight, her hands pressed tightly against her smooth thighs. She began to whisper. 'I—I didn't mean what I said—it's just that I'm so bored here—I'm alone at night—you are out on call, or the hospital. I know you're a doctor—I know—I know. But! I'm young!' Her whisper lifted to a thin and venomous wail, in spite of her fear. 'I'm not an old crone, ready to die. But I'm withering in this house, I'll be old before my time. I'm only twenty-three, but I feel ages, ages. I go out, but it's the same old thing, among the same old people, and the same old talk. No fun—'

'Life isn't "fun",' he said. 'You should know that. You aren't so very young any longer. You knew when you married me that you'd never be able to coax me away from Hambledon. I've given you all I could, bought you everything you wanted, have taken you abroad and to the big cities frequently. That wasn't enough for you.' But nothing would ever be enough for the Mavises of the world, nothing would ever satisfy them, or fill the gaunt lust with which they had been born. 'Fun.' They lived only for that. Some said the Laughing Girls had a tremendous 'lust for life.' But it was an empty and superficial lust, demanding tinsel and endless amusement and endless mirth, and dancing and rich food and wines and money. Above all, money, and adulation and flattery and fawning.

'You won't even give me a child, you trivial, mindless wretch,' Jonathan went on. 'You selfish imitation of a real woman. But then, I should be grateful. What kind of a mother
182

would you make? What kind of a human being would you produce? Yes, I should be grateful.'

He had stared at her with his violent black eyes. 'I should have killed you before this, when I found out what you were. One of these days I may do it. Don't tempt me again.' She saw the hunger to murder her in his face, the pallid shine of his face, the glint of his teeth between his lips, the fire in his eyes. She backed away from him still farther, then suddenly whirled in a rush of gold and white and ran into her bedroom, slamming it in real terror behind her, and locking it. Then she leaned against it and closed her eyes and breathed rapidly, listening for a sound behind the door. But Jonathan went away and she heard his own door close, and all was soft rosy lamplight in her charming bedroom which she had decorated in pink and blue and silver. 'I'll tell Uncle Martin,' she whispered, with vindictiveness. 'I'm not safe here any longer.' She was not afraid now. She was only amazed, horribly offended, aghast that he had dared speak to her like that. She wanted revenge for such an insult to her, Mavis Eaton, who could have married anyone—anyone. It was not to be believed! That wicked old man, that nasty old man, who had betrayed her by marrying her, and who was keeping her a prisoner in this awful dull town which she hated, and where she was not appreciated.

To-night, as he drove Jenny down to the river, Jonathan fully remembered that night when he had wanted to kill his wife, where just a few more words from her would have precipitated him into fearful action. But she had had the cunning of the animal she was, and she had not railed at him again.

The rockets were blossoming in noisy and rainbow profusion in the dark sky, and the river carried the sound of music along the shore and far faint laughter. Ahead, at the end of the street the water moved silently and blackly, and the island stood there, not a single light in any window, not a light on its rising bulk. Jonathan said to the silent girl behind him, 'You didn't have the sense to leave a light burning, did you?'

Jenny did not answer. She knew if she said a word that she would burst out into agonised sobs. But she looked at the fireworks scintillating against the sky, and heard, above the incoherent stammering of her old pain, the voices and the music. Jonathan, for the first time, turned his head and looked over his shoulder. He could barely see the girl as she huddled in the rear, but he caught the outline of her thin body and her face turned to the fireworks. She was only a mute shadow there, but he felt something very odd. He felt a lonely wistfulness in that shadow, a hunger, a silent yearning.

They reached the water edge and Jonathan left the surrey to tie up his horse. Jenny flew swiftly past him down the shallow bank; she was like a moth. In an instant she was in one of the three waiting rowboats. She was actually pulling away after strongly shoving the boat from the shore, when he leapt over the widening black water, half fell into the boat, recovered his balance and raised himself on a knee. 'You damned fool, you stubborn fool,' he said. 'Get over here. Give me those oars.' The broad boat rocked from side to side and some water splashed in and Jonathan swore. He reached for the oars and the girl raised one and its wet side caught silver from the brightening moon. He knew she wanted to hit him, and knew that she would, so he pushed himself to the stern and said, 'All right, I love a show of manliness.'

She rowed with firm young strength, bending and straightening, and the oars were argent, and Jenny's body moved in perfect rhythm and the boat fled over the quiet water. Now, to the east, the bursting fireworks reflected themselves in the river in gaudy splashes of orange and scarlet and gold and blue, infinitely beautiful and weird, exploding into points of falling light. The boat creaked softly, the oars dipped with hardly a sound. A particularly elaborate fireworks display represented an enormous head of President McKinley, important and solid, and loud applause clamoured over the water. Jenny turned her head towards the massive display which was painted on the black sky in fiery colour, and Jonathan saw her face, the smooth white forehead, under the brim of her great ugly hat. It was the face of a child.

When the boat grated at its island landing Jenny did not wait to pull it ashore and tie it. She jumped over the two feet of water, and ran up the bank. Jonathan cursed again, tied up the boat, then searched for the little wooden shelter that held lanterns. By the time he had found one and lit it Jenny was gone, finding her way like an owl in the night. He ran after her, the lantern throwing yellow light all about him, and soon he was on her heels. Immediately she stopped running, but kept several steps ahead of him, moving like a flying shadow in spite of her long skirts. She had already unlocked the door of the castle when he reached it. She

184

turned to him, panting a little. 'That's all that's necessary. Thank you.' Her voice was shaking.

'I'm going to search the damned place, as my mother asked me,' he said. 'Anyone could have rowed over here during the day or even during the last hour. Haven't you any sense at all?'

She blocked the way stubbornly, leaning against the wide bronze doors which caught golden glints from the lantern. Then with a sigh of resignation she went into the hall, her footsteps hard on the black and white marble squares. She lighted a lamp which was waiting on a Spanish commode, and it brightened on the laughable suits of armour against the walnut walls, and threw long shadows up and down the medieval stairway. The stained-glass window on the first landing glimmered into sections of rose and purple, red and yellow.

Jenny turned and faced Jonathan. 'Thank you,' she said. The hall, as usual, smelt musty as if ages had passed here, and the banners hanging along the walls lifted in the light wind which came through the open door. Jenny's face was bleak and still and she stared at Jonathan with formidable bitterness.

'Not yet,' he said. 'I must still search this monstrosity.' He knew his remark would hurt her but he was not prepared for the deep and quivering pain that ran over her face, and he was surprised at the trembling of her mouth. Then she turned and ran up the stairway, her steps clattering and loud, and he called after her. 'When I'm finished, come down and shoot the bolts.' A door banged upstairs and he heard a lock slide. He laughed shortly. He looked about him and found a candelabra and lit the candles on it and held it high, feeling ridiculous. No gaslight here, and, of course, no electricity. This preciousness annoyed him and made him shake his head. He went down a rear passage to the dining-room and glanced in carefully. Everything was deathly silent, and musty and still.

He next went into the vast drawing-room in the towering-wing, and again all was quiet, and the candlelight showed nothing but the Oriental rugs, the green damask of the walls, the tapestry at the windows and the frivolous French furniture all gilt and velvet and silk. He climbed the stairway, careful to keep his footing on the polished wood. Now he was on the second floor and facing a long narrow hall carpeted in Oriental rugs. He knew Harald's studio and went to it and

185

opened the carved wooden door. He could smell paint and turpentine and airlessness, and the candlelight glanced at easels and on canvasses stacked against the wooden walls. He could hear the river gurgling secretly below, and it had a sinister sound. He climbed a much smaller staircase to the third floor where the servants lived and slept, and he examined each quiet room and even the closets and wardrobes. The voice of the river was louder here for some reason, and the explosions that still continued in the park. Jonathan retreated down the stairway and passed the shut doors along the hall, reasonably certain that no intruder lurked there. However, he went back and did open other doors. One of the rooms, very large and exquisitely furnished, was Harald's bedroom where he had slept with his dead wife. He had not bothered to remove certain furbelows and ruffles and pink draperies, and it still possessed a wan feminine air mutely pathetic and lonely. A quick search showed it to be empty. Another search of other rooms verified Jonathan's opinion that no unauthorised person was present. He tried a last door, far down the hall. It was locked. So, this was Jenny's room. The old-fashioned handle was brass and polished; it turned in his hand but the strong door remained shut to him.

He made considerable noise clattering downstairs. He examined the breakfast-room with its plain but beautiful Amish furniture, then he went into the morning-room and wrinkled his nose at the dark oak and chintz. He last came to the library and set the candelabra on a table while he lit two or three oil lamps. This was certainly the gloomiest room of the house, he thought, narrow, cold, and tall, lined with books and furnished in leather sofas and chairs in dull dark blues and blacks and crimsons, and here the air was definitely dank. The lamps flickered on the bearded portraits of Victorian men and prim ladies in their huge golden frames, and they eyed Jonathan with expressions of pure resentment at his intrusion. He opened one of the windows and the long crimson velvet draperies bellied inward into the room.

Where was that stupid girl? Why hadn't she come down, hearing him descend, himself, to lock the doors behind him? He wondered about calling her, then as he did so he heard a quick gasp, and after that, a rustle. He turned quickly and saw Jenny in the doorway, staring at him in the lamplight, unbelieving and alarmed.

She wore nothing but a long nightgown of some light white

cotton with a childish collar of lace, and her hair tumbled down her back and her blue eyes were wide and glittering and her feet were bare.

'I thought,' she said, 'that you had gone!'

Then she looked down at herself and flushed.

The voice of the river seemed to roar into the room like a torrent of tumultuous water, and Jonathan and Jenny stood and looked at each other. 'Jenny,' he said. 'I didn't mean— I was just waiting for you to come down and lock the door after me, as I asked you to.' He heard his own voice, thick and ponderous, and the heat was in his neck and throat again, and the pain was knifing into his temples, and then, with primal instinct, he felt the stab of excruciating desire. It was so intense that he bent a little, and he knew that he had never forgotten this girl at all and had always loved her and wanted her.

'Jenny!' he said. He took a step towards her.

She retreated, and the fright was big in her eyes, and she covered her breasts, in that thin cotton, in the ancient gesture of a startled woman, her arms crossed. Her long thighs drew together stiffly. She had never seemed so beautiful to him, not even in the garden, nor so desirable and beloved, in her present dishevelled state and with the colour leaving her face and her lips parting in embarrassment and shame.

'Jenny,' he said, and took another step towards her. She fell back, and she made a little sound like a faint cry. She began to turn. Then he was upon her, catching her wrists, swinging her around to face him. She tried to resist; he had known she was strong, but she was like a young man in her sudden resilience. She bent backwards to loosen his hands, and he bent over her and tried to kiss her mouth, holding her with violence, but she swung her face from him so that his lips touched only her cheek. She screamed sharply and it was the sound of frantic rage. Again she swung her head and her soft cloud of black hair swept over his face. It fell back. Her exposed white throat gleamed in the lamplight, and he bent over her again and pressed his mouth into its soft warm hollow.

Their bodies cleaved together, Jenny's arching back, Jonathan's following hers. Then Jenny was very still, no longer struggling. He felt the long sweet length of her against his clothing, the pressure of her breasts, the slender rigidity of the wrists he held behind her back. He exclaimed, 'Jenny, sweet

Jenny!' and kissed her again, and he was determined, in the shout of his desire, to have this girl, and to have her at once. She was not resisting now. Her flesh clung to his, languid and weak, and now he found her mouth eagerly and with ruthless demand. He began to groan, to pull her farther into the room, and her stumbling feet followed him. 'Sweet Jenny,' he said, and he let her wrists go and his hand fumbled for her breasts and found one and closed tightly about it. It was like a sun-warmed apple in his hand, and the scent of her flesh was in his nostrils, fresh and maddening and young.

Then she came to wild life. Her hand knocked away the hand that held her breast with a force that amazed him. Then both her hands were on his shoulders and were pushing him away from her. He was so surprised that he fell back from her.

Her eyes were one furious blue blaze of hatred through great tears, and her teeth could be seen, clenched, between her white lips. He came to her again, lust pounding in him, and when he had almost reached her she lifted her hand, swung it in a large circle and struck him viciously across the face. She jumped back and faced him, and her breast rose up and fell in frenzied outrage.

'Murderer!' she shouted. 'Murderer!'

Her voice rang in the library. It was the ugliest sound he had ever heard, and the most terrible. She was no longer afraid, and her hands were clenched at her sides. She trembled with fury.

The strong lash of her hand had made his face burn with throbbing pain, and had rocked him on his heels. It had the effect of increasing his ferocious desire for her, and he also wanted to inflict the same pain on her and subdue her, and conquer her, and lie upon her and take her brutally and at once.

If she had struck him only, and had not thrown that hateful word at him, he might have controlled himself. But he was aroused. His dark face was a dull and heavy red, and his features thickened.

'I'm not good enough for you—is that it?' he said in a slow and malevolent voice. 'It's just for my brother, isn't it?' And he motioned at her loins in a gesture he had never used to any woman before. 'And for a few others, too?'

Jenny's white face flushed with horror, and it quivered visibly. Her mouth opened and she gasped. 'Your brother?'

she said. 'Harald?' She could not believe it. She stared at him. She had not understood at all. And then she understood. She uttered a fierce cry. 'Get out of here! Why, you murderer, you—you—! You filthy monster!'

She turned again and ran from the room, and after a second he ran after her. She ran down the corridor to the hall, and reached the oaken stairway in the murky fluttering of the lamplight. She lifted her nightgown and ran up the stairs like a terrified young animal, and her long white legs flashed in rapid movement. He lunged after her, trying to catch one of her ankles, or a fold of the floating nightgown. But she was faster than he, and her long hair rippled behind her like a banner.

If he had felt lust before it was nothing to what he felt now, this urgent passion and rage, this desire not only to take her but to hurt her violently for the things she had screamed at him. She could hear his hoarse panting behind her, and she ran even faster when she reached the upper hall, and raced for her room, full of dread and fear and hate.

She reached the door of her room and pushed it open and tried to close it. But his hand flung out and held it. They struggled for the door, and Jonathan began to laugh through his teeth, wondering at her strength, and sweating. They battled ridiculously for it, swinging it back and forth, Jenny on the inside pushing it towards the lock, and Jonathan on the threshold, pushing it upon the girl. Her strength continued to astonish him; she thrust her shoulder against the door and almost reached the lock, and he had considerable difficulty in preventing its closure. He could hear her loud and struggling breath, her broken exclamations, but he said nothing now, intent only on winning this battle which was beginning to appear absurd to him. His pride was turbulently affronted that she denied to him what she gave so freely to his brother. 'Don't be so coy, Jenny!' he exclaimed.

He gave an extra heave and the door flung itself back on its hinges and Jenny was also thrown back into the room, which was dimly lighted by only one lamp near her bed. Instantly Jonathan was upon her, seizing one arm. He used his other hand to grasp the neck of her nightgown and to rip it down her body to her knees. Before she could move his hands closed about her slender damp waist and he had pulled her to him and was kissing her mouth in a rapturous storm of desire. She struggled frantically. She tried to kick him with her bare feet and he laughed, and his fingers pressed themselves into the warm flesh of her body, and his mouth held hers, forcing her lips apart. He felt her warm breath in his own mouth and he grunted, 'Jenny! Jenny! Jenny!' His ecstasy was like an agony in his own body. He pushed her backwards towards the bed, and her struggles became even more frenzied. The torn nightgown impeded him, and in one movement he tore it completely from her and she was naked.

He pushed her against the bed, and her knees bent from the pressure, and she fell backwards upon the white narrowness and he fell on top of her, his mouth still holding hers. 'Sweet Jenny,' he whispered, and his knee fumbled at her body, trying to separate her legs.

Then her body arched in one last desperate attempt, and so strong was that effort that he was almost flung from her. He fell beside her on the bed, still half straddling her, and the lamplight struck down on her face, and he saw it.

What he saw was utter and complete terror, unaffected terror, virginal terror. He had seen it but once before in his life, when he had been nineteen, and he never liked to recall that episode and had always felt shame at the memory. It was not to be mistaken for anything else but what it was—the affrighted woman faced with the unknown and recoiling from it and preparing to fight to the death against it.

He held her but did not move, and he looked down into her eyes and saw the awful and shivering fear there and the blue and fainting cloudiness, and he saw her stricken lips and heard the chattering of her teeth. He leaned over her, all desire gone, and with only shame and remorse.

'Jenny,' he said, 'my God, Jenny.'

She looked up into his face and she lay very still and tears began to roll from her widely opened eyes and she uttered a whimpering sound of total defeat. He took the edge of the sheet and pulled it over her nakedness with tender care and shaking hands, then stood up and looked at her as she lay with the sheet under her chin and her eyes now closed, and weeping, her girl's young body outlined under the covering.

Dazed and infuriated with himself, and ashamed beyond anything he had ever felt before, he looked about the room and saw that it resembled a monastic cell in its small and quiet simplicity. The walls were white, the polished floor bare except for one small rug, and there were only a desk, two straight chairs, a painted wardrobe, a table, and one single lamp in the room. There were no ornaments here, no womanish daintiness or ribbons or silks or taffetas, no intense scent of perfume. There was not even a dressing-table with a mirror. In fact, there was no mirror at all. It was the cell of a nun, the bed the narrow hard bed of an ascetic woman.

If Harald had ever occupied that bed he had occupied it alone! That was the foolish and humiliated thought that came to Jonathan as he clumsily rearranged and smoothed his clothing which had been rumpled in his tussle with the girl, and his attempted rape of her. He detested himself. He wanted to take one of Jenny's hands, now so flaccid on the sheet, and kneel beside her and beg her pardon for his animalistic attack on her, which seemed completely monstrous and unbelievable now. How was it possible that he had tried to do this thing? How was it possible for him to have believed the lies about her? Now his hate for himself was mixed with pity for the girl, and abysmal love.

'Jenny,' he said. 'I wouldn't blame you if you never forgave me. No, don't ever forgive me. I'm ashamed, Jenny.' His voice was humble as his voice had never been humble before in all his self-confident and self-assured life. 'Jenny, I wish there was some way I could tell you—but I suppose there isn't.'

He leaned his palms on the bed beside her and stiffened his arms and bent over her. She continued to cry helplessly with her eyes shut. 'Jenny, I want to say just one thing: I love you, darling. I've always loved you, since that day in the garden, when you were sixteen. Think about that, dear, and perhaps you'll be able to forgive me, some day, some time.' But she continued to cry silently, far removed from him.

'Jenny? I really love you, my darling. That's no excuse for what I—well, what I tried to do. Don't be afraid, Jenny. I'm going away now. Watch for my lantern, through your window,' and he glanced at the little bare casement, innocent of any draperies at all. 'Then when you see I've gone, go downstairs and lock the door. Jenny?'

But she did not answer him. She only lay there rigidly, her black hair flung about her in complete disorder. There was a growing bruise near her mouth and when he saw it he hated himself more than ever and he had to hold back to keep from bending and kissing it gently. He wanted to do this with a passion greater than any lust he had felt for her, and he hesitated. Then he straightened up, and went from the room.

191

Jenny heard his footsteps dragging slowly and wearily down the stairs. She heard them echoing in the hall. Then the bronze doors opened, and she could hear him close them behind him. She saw the faint reflection of the lantern on her window, and then she heard him going down the flagged marble of the walk, and finally she could hear him no more.

She sat up in bed, then sprang from it and ran to her casement window and flung it open. She saw the flickering lantern light retreating down the length of the island, twinkling through bushes and trees, dying away into the distance.

She dropped her head on the wide window-sill and burst into anguished little cries. 'Oh, Jon, Jon, Jon! Oh, Jon!' She cried for a long time, until she slipped to the floor, and then pressed her cheek against the stark wall and mourned over and over, 'Jon, Jon.' She was exhausted and desolate. She slept there, crouched in nakedness on the wooden floor, and when she awoke it was a dim and purple dawn.

When Jonathan let himself quietly into his father's house he hoped that his mother had gone to bed, but he was no longer in the soft and silvery hall than he heard her voice from the morning-room. 'Jon? Is that you? I'm in here, having a cup of tea. Do have one with me.'

He cursed silently to himself, and hesitated. Then he went into the dining-room, and by a very dim light he filled a glass full of whisky and soda and carried it into the room where his mother was waiting for him. She looked extremely fatigued, but she smiled at him affectionately. 'Was everything safe on the island?' she asked. Then she uttered a consterned exclamation. 'Jon! What's wrong with your cheek, all puffed and red, and with that long scratch on it?'

Lies were unfamiliar things to him, and so he felt his face and tried to think of one. He finally said, 'Oh, that. I bumped into something in the infernal dark on the island.'

Marjorie stared at him thoughtfully, and then she smiled inwardly. Jenny! She felt a real pang of happiness. Was it really possible that at last he had admitted to himself what she had known of him and Jenny for several years? Her tired hazel eyes began to shine. 'Do sit down, dear, and talk to me for a minute before I go to bed. I just didn't have the strength to move until I had some tea, and a little quiet. What a noisy day, wasn't it?'

He had seated himself reluctantly on a chair in this charming and restful room, but he could not force himself to look at his mother so he examined the contents of his glass and frowned at it. 'Awful day,' he said.

'I do believe,' said Marjorie, 'that your young Robert has what we used to call a crush on Jenny but Jenny is oblivious. Such an innocent girl. She never learned to flirt or be young or gay or light-hearted. Poor child. It was that awful Peter Heger, you know. Wouldn't it be nice if Robert and she— What's the matter, Jon?'

'That's nonsense,' said Jonathan. The little white ridges had come out about his mouth. 'Mother, you know Jenny well. She's often here. Is there anyone?'

Marjorie made her eyes very artless. 'Oh, yes, indeed. There is someone she dearly cares about. Quite a bit older than herself, of course, but eminently suitable. She's loved him a long time. I know you don't like the word "love," Jon, and think it is absurd and that there's no such thing, but only "love" can describe the way Jenny feels about that certain man.'

'What's his name?' asked Jonathan. 'Do I know him?'

'She never mentioned his name, and I never asked, and I only know about it because I am a woman, too, though that, too, will probably surprise you, my dear. But there are certain things a woman can't conceal from another woman, and among them is when she is in love. I know all the signs.'

Jonathan drank half his glass of whisky and soda in one breath. He shook the glass. His black brows drew together. It was unbearable to think of Jenny in love with a stranger. He had tried to take her forcibly to-night, had intolerably insulted and attacked her, had gone away certain he would never be allowed to see her again and knew it was all he deserved.

'It's possible that you're mistaken, Mother. Do you have any idea who he is?'

'Yes.'

He stared at her formidably. 'Who?'

'Why don't you ask Jenny yourself?'

He stood up and began to walk slowly up and down the room. 'If she never told you, she certainly would never tell me. That's ridiculous. Does Harald know?'

'No,' said Marjorie, with slowness. 'He doesn't. As I've told you before he wants to marry Jenny. But you always laughed when I told you.'

Jonathan stopped and looked at her. 'Mother, who has been spreading those disgusting lies about Jenny in Hambledon?'

If Marjorie had had any doubts before she did not have them now and she almost laughed with joy. 'I don't know, Jon.'

'Does Jenny know—about these vicious tales?'

'Jenny?' Marjorie was shocked. She put down her teacup. 'She's never once suspected. You don't know Jenny very well, Jon. She's as simple and innocent as an infant, and it would seem incredible to her that wicked people would make up vile lies about others. She just wouldn't believe it. It would have shaken Jenny to her very heart. She avoids people because her father told her, when she was a child, that she was ugly and unattractive and that no one, except him, of course, could ever love her, and so she must stay at home with him.' Marjorie's pale face coloured, but she looked Jonathan straightly in the eye. 'I'm not a simpering, old-fashioned woman, Jon. I wasn't brought up in a velvet-lined box and put away with Mama's pearls in a dark and secluded place. My father liked the very idea of the "new woman," and what he called "the new candour." Personally, I think he carried it a little far, sometimes.

'Well, I know all about Peter Heger, Jonathan, from the perfectly innocent things Jenny said about him. I think he—'

Jonathan smiled nastily. 'He had incestuous thoughts about our little gosling?'

'I don't think Jenny ever once considered that a man might want her—' She stopped, for Jonathan was looking at her grimly.

'She does now,' he said. 'All right. I must tell you something, before Jenny does, or even if she doesn't you'll wonder why she never wants to come here again. I tried to rape her tonight. Do you understand me?'

Though Marjorie more than suspected that, and was delighted at the thought, she knew that propriety demanded some quite contrary reaction from her. So she sat upright, arranged her features into an outraged expression, and exclaimed, 'Jon! How could you, how dare you, a defenceless young girl alone and unprotected! How terrible, how dreadful, how unbelievable of you!'

He waved his hand wearily. 'Very well, I'm a blackguard, a dog, a despoiler, a stinker, a hound—think them all. I'm all of them. Well. I didn't succeed. Jenny fought me off like a wildcat, like a female cougar. Partly, it was her fault. She called me—something. I think that precipitated the whole thing, though perhaps not. So while we're being so bloody frank, as our English cousins call it, I might as well say that she convinced me that she was what is prissily called a "pure" girl, and that I was particularly loathsome to her anyway. That stopped me. Of course, had I continued the little wrestling match I'd have discovered the whole truth in a minute or two for myself, and that, of course, would have been beyond repair.'

'Yes,' said Marjorie, 'it indeed would have. Women don't like to be taken by force.'

'Like hell they don't,' said Jonathan. 'Mama dear, I'm not a little boy. I've known a considerable number of women. But Jenny wouldn't have liked it, to use an understatement. Did you say you didn't know the name of the man she's in love with?'

'I didn't say.' Marjorie considered what Jonathan had told her and now she felt a trifle disturbed. Would Jenny ever forgive her son? Yes, she would, eventually. She might even look into a mirror and study herself very soon and wonder what there was about her that had aroused Jonathan so and had incited the attack upon her. Once let a woman suspect she has charms that could drive a man to assault her, and she will love him then—if she had never before—for desiring her. Things were progressing very nicely, thought Marjorie. She gave a great yawn, and then regarded her son seriously.

'Jonathan, you have behaved atrociously, as you know, yourself. I don't have to tell you that. If Jenny were not fond of me she might prefer charges against you. This isn't a light matter. Poor Jenny. By the way, what *did* make you lose your head like that?'

'It's not important,' he said. 'Men are always losing their heads over some damned woman, figuratively or literally.' He smiled at her. 'You've called us men "a stupid race." No doubt. Say I lost my head. Jenny's a very beautiful girl, and a very desirable one, and I was having one of my moods to-day, and to-night, and there Jenny was, apparently available, though I don't suppose you understand that.'

'Yes, I do. Still it was an abominable thing. Jenny's only twenty, and a very young twenty, and you are an experienced man of thirty-five, and a widower. You're almost old enough to be Jenny's father. In some cultures you would be.' She paused, and watched him closely. 'I don't suppose, while this joyous caper was going on, that you gave a single thought to Mavis?'

He looked at her blankly. 'Mavis?' He was more blank than ever and Marjorie thought, Thank God, then it is all over. 'What has Mavis to do with it?'

'Nothing, to be sure!' Marjorie almost sang.

He carried a fresh glass of whisky into his bedroom, then went to the window and looked out at the hot and breathless night, so still now that all festivities had ended and the fireworks already forgotten. He craned for a glimpse of the river, which held the island in a watery moat, and he thought of Jenny. Then he thought of Mavis.

He went into her dressing-room and then her bedroom, and lit a lamp and looked at the beauty there and the rosy lamps and pretty furniture. The very ghost of Mavis's perfume floated towards him, but Mavis would never wear it again. He closed the door upon her room as one closes the door on someone who would never wake again.

Now he could think of Jenny. It was possible—though he did not actually believe it—that he would never see her again, or that, if seeing, she would never speak to him. He had done a violent and unpardonable thing to her, but women have rarely held that against a man. He dismissed the thought of her loving someone else as totally inconsequential, and not to be given serious consideration. What did young Jenny know of love, anyway? He would contrive means of putting himself near her. She would not be able to avoid him! He chuckled. Then, after many months—but not too many—she would be forced to take him seriously, she would begin to think about him. How long would it take? A year, perhaps, if he could wait that long.

CHAPTER 8

When Jonathan entered his offices, whistling, the next morning, he found, as he expected, young Robert Morgan already there studying the files which the elderly spinster 'typewriter' had laid before him on Jonathan's desk. Robert stood up, easily flushing as always, and said, 'Good morning. I didn't mean to take over your desk, when you are still here, but the lady placed the files here and—'

'Perfectly all right,' said Jonathan. Robert stared at the court-plaster on his face. He said, 'An accident?'

'Just a romp with an unusually spirited lady last night,' said Jonathan. He appears very lively this morning, thought Robert Morgan. He watched Jonathan as he flipped through the files, and nodded.

'We enjoyed yesterday, mother and I,' said Robert. Jonathan lifted his black eyes quickly to him, and the whites of them were very clear and bluish as if he had slept well. 'You didn't seem to be enjoying yourself much.'

'Well, I wasn't.'

Now Robert's easy colour was rising again, but he affected to be studying a file. 'You didn't seem to like most of the people there. Not even that lovely young lady, Miss Jenny Heger.'

Jonathan, sitting in a comfortable chair which was reserved for patients, stopped in the motion of lighting a cigarette. Then he slowly blew out the match.

'Jenny? My niece-in-law, if you can call her that? What about Jenny?'

His voice had changed so sharply that Robert was startled. 'I mean,' he said, 'that she's exceptionally—well, comely. Any man would be charmed.'

'And I wasn't charmed?'

Robert turned and looked at him. He did not understand that tone, and now Jonathan was regarding him with what could only be cold displeasure. Robert was bewildered.

'I shouldn't have been so personal,' he apologised. 'Excuse me. Now, this Mrs Summers—'

'No, no. Go on. About Jenny.'

'There's nothing to "go on" about, Jon.' He was remem-

197

bering the first time he had seen Jenny, on the island, and he also remembered Jonathan's derisive attitude towards her and his sneering enigmatic remarks. 'Does it offend you that I find Miss Jenny pretty and attractive?'

'Why the hell should it offend me?'

Robert laid down the file very carefully. He stared down at it. He said, in a very precise voice, 'I find Miss Jenny very pretty and attractive. I hope she will let me visit her on that island. I hope she won't find me too repulsive, and that she will let me take her, soon, to a concert or a play. You do have concerts and plays in this town, don't you, or have I flattered it?'

'No flattery. We have a decent little orchestra which calls itself The Symphonic. Or is it the Philharmonic? We don't entirely subsidise it, but almost.' Jonathan had begun to smile, but a trifle disagreeably. 'The members of the German Band you heard yesterday are members of it, and then there are some college boys from Scranton who are quite "gifted," as the ladies say. Sometimes the music is recognisable. They do have courage. And if they are a little heavy on the brasses and the cymbals and the drums—that makes a hearty sound, good for the corpuscles. They're best on Sousa, though, and I defy any orchestra, even yours in Philadelphia, to get more out of "The Star-Spangled Banner" than our boys do. As for plays—we have stock companies condescending to visit us in the summer from New York, with only a third rate cast. And once the great Sarah passed through here and paused for a single performance. Even New York can't beat all this, not to mention Ringling Brothers or Barnum and Bailey in the Spring. That's really a fragrant occasion.'

In spite of his anger Robert was laughing. 'I see this is a very cultured town and not barbarous. I'll enjoy taking Miss Jenny to some of these extravagant events.'

'I hear—what is that delightfully coy expression, so loved by the ladies?—"her heart belongs to another".'

Robert looked at him with quick and open dismay. 'Who?'

And that's what I'd like to know, thought Jonathan. 'Who knows? It's only a rumour. However, that is a very unapproachable as well as an irreproachable young lady. I will leave you to it all, and make my rounds at St Hilda's,' and he went out whistling.

Everything, now, to his eye looked fresh and new and interesting, and those who encountered him at St Hilda's thought that they had never seen him in such good spirits, not even before his marriage to Mavis Eaton. He was actually affable, a very rare thing. He could be heard humming. Near the doctors' lounge room he encountered Dr Louis Hedler. 'Well, Louis,' he said, 'I've been in to see young Hortense Nolan and she's coming along splendidly and in about a year she can start a new baby. But, for God's sake, get that new gynae-cologist, young Harrington for her, or someone like him. What's the matter?' he added.

Dr Hedler was looking very solemn and high-minded. 'Come into the lounge, Jon,' he said. 'No one is there just now. This is private.' He importantly seated himself and regarded Jonathan portentously. Jonathan knew that expression. Louis had something to impart to him which was personally un-pleasant, but which would give Louis pleasure. Too bad, thought Jonathan, that a grateful man can't remain grateful. He sat down and neatly arranged the legs of his trousers, and crossed his knees. 'All right, Louis. What did I do now which has raised the dust on Olympus?'

'You have done nothing "wrong," nothing at all, Jon. You will recall that you made a very loud uproar not long ago about surgeons performing operations when it was more than suspected that they were taking drugs?'

'I do. No man under the influence of heroin or morphine or any other derivative of opium should touch a scalpel under any circumstances, nor should such a man even practise the most innocuous medicine, nor should his diagnosis ever be accepted. We're not running a slaughter-house here, and God knows enough surgeons like that have slaughtered, and in recent history, too.'

'Well, now, Jon. I always did think you were too harsh. You have new-fashioned ideas about the dangers of addiction on the part of doctors. I still don't quite agree. Nothing, so far, has been definitely proved that those drugs are harmful or can impair a man's efficiency. A doctor is under stress most of the time. If he takes something to relax him, there is some evidence that this is not only supportive but beneficial. I'm sure that some doctors are what you call "addicted," and it has been my opinion that they did no harm, and that the unfortunate events in the operating rooms here in St Hilda's, and in the Friends', would have occurred anyway even in the hands of a non-addicted surgeon. But I gave this opinion before, before the Board.'

'I disagree,' said Jonathan, flushing with anger. 'I investigated the last two "unfortunate events" myself. They were uncomplicated and simple operations. The victims—yes, they were victims of men made incompetent by drugs—died needlessly. I am working with a large committee of doctors now, from all over the United States, to have the Federal government proscribe the indiscriminate giving of narcotics by practising physicians to patients, and to bar addicted doctors from surgery or the practice of medicine, until they are cured.'

Louis smiled indulgently. 'I doubt that even politicians would be stupid enough to pass such a law,' he said. 'In my opinion those drugs are no more harmful, nor dangerous, than aspirin or bicarbonate of soda. I never tried them myself, but neither am I addicted to alcohol.' He looked meaningly at Jonathan, who laughed shortly.

'So, it is rumoured around, as well as other rumours, that I am a drunkard, too? Where did that come from? Dear Mavis?'

Louis was shocked. 'Jonathan! How can you speak so contemptuously of that lovely girl who was your unfortunate wife?'

'Come on, now, Louis. Mavis spread that rumour. There was some grounds for it, I admit. But I never enter an operating room if I have had a drink within the past six hours, and I never drink the night before an operation, except for a little beer or a glass of wine. I drink very little at social gatherings, and everyone knows that. So only Mavis could have told it around that I can punish a bottle as well as the next man, if I have no following responsibilities. And you surely aren't insinuating that alcohol—to a man who isn't an alcoholic—is no more dangerous than narcotics?'

'I consider them all narcotics.' Louis was righteously pompous.

'I consider gourmandising addiction, too,' said Jonathan. 'Anything to excess is dangerous. But drugs are in a special class by themselves. They aren't self-limiting. A man who is a gorger at the table does arrive at the place where he can't eat any more, and an alcoholic does drop off into a stupor where he can do no harm. But drugs aren't like that. More demands more, and the appetite increases, and eventually the man dies or goes mad. I'm no humbug, Louis, no self-appointed busybody about my fellow man. I believe in minding my own business. Let a man kill himself with food or women or drink or drugs. That's his own affair. But when he becomes a menace to the innocent who trust him in an operating room, or in his offices, then he has no business there, and it is our business to put him out of business.' He paused. 'A man who is drunk is soon detected by patients, and his practice vanishes. But what layman can tell when his doctor is dangerously ill of drugs, and incompetent?'

Louis said nothing. Jonathan stood up, pushed his hands into his pockets, and began to pace the room. After a few moments he stopped in front of the older doctor. 'Louis, we've had patients here, scores of them, unfortunate men and women addicted to drugs prescribed by their physicians. You've seen some of them, many of them, when we've taken them off the lethal things. Some of them die in convulsions. All of them suffer tortures. We have to institute a slow withdrawal programme, and it isn't permanently successful. The poor devils leave here "cured," and within a few days there they are again in the drug stores, with a new prescription, given to them either by a doctor who refuses to face the truth, or an addicted one. Haven't you been reading the new articles in our very own medical journals?'

Louis moved restlessly. 'There were a lot of warnings about aspirin, too. Adults, and children, have taken over-doses and have died.'

'Louis, for God's sake! Aspirin doesn't cause addiction, nor does the taker of a few tablets, even regularly, need desperately to increase his dose. You can die from an over-dose of any-thing—even water, and you know it. But addiction isn't merely an over-dose. It is a craving, a deadly, destroying appetite, which only more and more will satisfy, until the man is killed, or kills, or loses his mind. Law authorities are reporting, with alarm, that drug addiction is one of the main causes of crime. And then you talk about aspirin!'

Louis took out a fretted-silver cigar case and slowly and carefully lit a cigar, not looking at Jonathan. After the cigar was drawing fully, he said, 'It was you, Jon, who insisted that six of our best surgeons here at St Hilda's, and ten of our best attending physicians, have their privileges revoked. You had all your "facts" and your figures and your quotations. You impressed the Board; you were very passionate. A majority agreed with you. They were removed from staff. Eight of them were my very good friends.'

'I'm sorry about that, Louis, but I only did what I had to do. I liked those men, personally. But their patients' welfare had to come first.'

'You might not have been so virtuous, Jonathan, if you had had, among them, a very dear and valued friend. That would have been a horse of another colour.'

'No, Louis, it would not. Private emotions end where public welfare begins.'

'Good. I'm glad to hear that,' said Louis Hedler. He smiled and Jonathan did not like that smile. Louis stood up. 'I regret I must tell you this. Tom Harper, one of our most talented and respected surgeons, and one of your closest friends—I believe you lent him money during his last two years—is a drug "addict," as you would call him.'

'Tom Harper?' Jonathan was stunned.

'The very same. He had a hard time getting through medical school, didn't he? His father sold the family farm to finance him. The farm was mortgaged, wasn't it, so the sum after the sale wasn't very large. Tom had to work hours after his studies to pay the difference in the fees. His parents died in the most extreme poverty—malnutrition, I think it was. But Tom is one of those dedicated doctors, who could never have been anything else, and his family sacrificed, even to their lives. Still, when he was studying surgery he got married. A nice girl, one of our nurses. She, too, worked to put him through. A desperate situation. He was already thirty-six years old, when they were married, and he was still here, interning. Then they had children—very unfortunate. Four of them. You'd think a doctor would be more—careful. How old is he now? Middle forties? Yes. Unfortunate. Let me give you the facts of his "addiction," Jonathan, and his accidents in the operating room. Perhaps you will wish in your heart to be more tolerant, as I wished to be tolerant about my own close friends.'

Jonathan could not believe it. But the older doctor, with enjoyment and relentlessness, gave him the undeniable and the dreadful facts.

'In here,' said Jonathan to Tom Harper. They went into an examination room with its table and a desk and two chairs, its bright lights and windowless walls covered with white paint, its cabinets of instruments. Dr Harper sat down, and

Jonathan noticed his stiff care. Jonathan closed, then carefully locked, the door. 'What's this?' asked Tom. 'Don't want to be interrupted?'

'That's correct,' said Jonathan. He stood near the door and looked intently and closely at his friend, the long thin body, the unusually slender wrists below the stiff white cuffs and the cheap cuff-links, the shabby but polished boots, the sleaziness of his suit with the long old-fashioned coat at least eight years old. But more than that he saw the bony and yellowish face, the sunken darkness under the clear grey eyes, the clefts about his mouth, and the curious lack of lustre of his light brown hair.

'I'm not going to run around the mulberry bush, Tom,' he said. 'You know I'm on the Board, here. Dear old Louis Hedler has told me he more than suspects you're taking morphine from the supplies, and as doctors have easy access to drugs anyway—there being no law as yet to register drugs and control them—this spells just one thing to me. Tell me if I'm wrong.'

Tom Harper's sallow face had begun to sweat, though the room was not hot. The drops of sweat became larger on his forehead, as if they were tears. He said nothing. Jonathan went to him then, roughly took his chin in his hand, and tilted Tom's face to the ceiling light. He looked down into the eyes and saw the pin-pointed pupils. He looked at Tom's hands, and saw the muscle tremor. Then he angrily seized the other man's arm and pulled up the coat sleeve, tore out the cuff-links of the worn but meticulously starched cuff, rolled up the sleeve—it was darned—and saw the needle-marks. He dropped the lifeless arm. Dr Harper had not offered the slightest resistance. He had become flaccid.

'A week ago,' said Jonathan, watching the other doctor slowly and dreamily pull down his sleeve and fasten his cuff-link, 'you operated on an old man, Finley. Gall-bladder. A nasty, bloody, dangerous. operation, I admit, but you're famous for your cholecystectomies, Tom. You do things I'd hesitate to do, and you do them with flair and success. You haven't lost a patient yet. People come even from Philadelphia for your operations. I've seen you in action. Old Finley had a routine case, calculi, no inflammation, no complications. Field pretty open, I'm told. Yet, you tied off his common duct, Tom, and even when his resultant symptoms were urgently called to your attention you said it was "nothing." And so, he died. It was told me that you were "airy" about the whole matter.'

Dr Harper scrupulously fastened his cuff-link. His head was bent. The drops of sweat were falling down his cheeks now, one by one, and Jonathan thought he could hear them drip.

'Old Finley hasn't been the only one, has he, Tom? Simple operations—not your usual kind—but four patients have died in the past month. Louis insisted on autopsies, unusual around here. He'd been suspecting you for a long time, months. And in every death there were the signs of carelessness, stupidity, incredible clumsiness. Louis doesn't like you, Tom. You're one of "us," and so to be wary of, and guarded against, and watched, and triumphantly found out and disgraced, if possible. But Louis, to give him credit, now won't let a surgeon operate when he suspects he is an addict. Drug addiction among doctors, and surgeons, is common these days and they all say it is "harmless." When they merely bungled, but the patient didn't die, or they managed in spite of the drugs, Louis used to say nothing. He let them go on. But now Louis draws the line. Tom, aren't you going to say anything?'

Dr Harper spoke in a far voice, as if nothing mattered. 'I did my best. I don't know how it happened—I didn't even know about the autopsies. I suspected—yes, I suspected, how it had come about. I warned myself not to operate.' His voice died away as if he were infinitely weary.

'Then why did you?' Jonathan was both enraged and horrified and could hardly control himself. 'You've murdered five innocent people! Yet, you still operate! You're a murderer, Tom. If we didn't close ranks, you'd be up on charges for malpractice at the very least. Tell me, why did you, damn you? Knowing your addiction and unreliability, and the danger, why did you?'

'Are you going to revoke my privileges?' Dr Harper brushed away the falling sweat and then looked stupidly at the back of his hand. 'You won't do that to me, Jon.' He shook his head over and over. 'You won't do that to me.' He began, to Jonathan's awful exasperation and increasing horror, to cry. He bent his head on his chest and stammered, 'No, you won't do that to me, Jon. There's Thelma, and my four children.'

Jonathan sat down in a straight chair and thrust his own

shaking hands violently into his pockets. 'Tom, I am going to do just that. I'm going to prefer charges against you, with Louis, and you'll never operate again, until you can give us all assurances that you've stopped taking the drugs. And you'll never see the inside of another hospital.'

The stricken doctor continued his dry soft weeping as if he had not heard. 'You won't do that to me, Jon. I need the money. I'm forty-six years old. In the past six months I've made five thousand dollars. Five thousand dollars! Four of them went to pay off old debts. I have six operations scheduled. Next week. One hundred dollars apiece—six hundred dollars. A fortune. I must have that money, Jon.' He spoke with quiet and desperate firmness.

'You're not going to make it. You're not going to murder anyone else in this hospital, or anywhere else.' Jon spoke heavily, for his instincts were informing him that rage could not shake this unfortunate man, nor threats, for something far more terrible was destroying him, even more terrible than the morphine he was giving himself. 'Listen to me, Tom, if you can. Try to focus on me. Look at me, damn you, and stop that ridiculous womanish crying! Tom, I'm your friend. I know how hard it's been for you, and Thelma.'

'No,' said Dr Harper. 'You don't know, Jon. Look at me, Jon. I'm dying.'

'I don't believe it!'

'It's true. I have what you call the Beast, Jon. I have gastric cancer.'

'Who told you?' Jonathan's voice was rough because he did not want to believe this monstrous thing.

'Jon, I'm a doctor, too. You know how we are. If we suspect something is wrong with us, or we have a few symptoms, we are the ones who get medical advice last, and besides we're too busy. Then, we know all there is to know, and that makes cowards of us. It isn't ignorance that makes us cowards, contrary to the old saw. It's knowledge. It started several months ago. For a considerable time I'd been having epigastric pain, and I thought, "Oh, if I don't stop taking on so much I'll be developing an ulcer," so I took the usual anti-acids. I began to lose weight, and Thelma said I was working too hard, which I was—all those debts. Then I lost my appetite, and started to vomit—and about three months ago I had that famous coffee ground vomitous. I examined my blood. Anaemia, and then I found occult blood in my stools. The classic picture; nothing vague. My mother died of cancer, you know. Now, I don't sleep very much—except—'

He made an exhausted and vague movement of his thin and trembling hands, and then dropped them on his knee.

'You know the prognosis of that, Jon.'

'Would you mind if I examined you?' Jonathan still did not believe it. Tom Harper silently stood up and removed his clothing. Jonathan was aghast to see his rib cage clearly visible; his legs were only bone covered with a thin layer of muscle and skin. Tom lay down on the examination table, and Jonathan silently examined him for the most part, asking questions only when necessary. Once he said, 'If only to God we had an X-ray machine here in town!'

'What if we had? It would just be interesting to doctors, but not for me, Jon. Well?'

'Get dressed.' Jonathan carefully washed his hands so that he would have something to do, and so calm himself. He wiped his hands on a clean towel then sat down near his friend.

'I suppose you know that it's already metastasised to the liver? And to the supraclavicular lymph nodes and peritoneum?'

'Yes, I know. As a doctor, and as a patient—I know.'

'Why the hell didn't you come to me months ago?'

'To have you tell me the truth?'

'I've seen two rare operations, Tom—resection. I can do it myself. I assisted at one, in New York.'

Tom smiled drearily. 'How long did the patient survive after that?'

'A year longer than he would have done without an operation. But another is still surviving, not in a rare and roaring state of health, but he's still alive.'

'If he were a doctor, would he be able to keep up his practice?'

'No. Frankly, no.'

'You see,' said Tom, 'it would have been worthless to me, even if I had survived. What would I do without medicine? I can't do anything else. And there are my children and my wife. Well. Now you know. I can keep going on morphine, Jon. It keeps the pain down enough. I'll be making enough money to give Thelma a little breathing space. There's five thousand dollars in life insurance—all I could afford. The boys won't have much chance, but at least they're healthy. I've got to go on, Jon. I can't stop.'

Jonathan looked down at his narrow, polished boot. He swung it back and forth, his lips pursed as if whistling. His manner was nonchalantly thoughtful, but he was thinking rapidly. Tom Harper finished dressing. He, too, washed his hands mechanically at the basin, then, sighing, he smoothed his damp hands over his thick brown hair.

'Tom,' said Jonathan, 'you are a country born boy. You lived on your father's farm until you entered medical school. And twelve or fourteen years ago he sold the farm so you could continue? But you know farming. I have four farms. One of them is about two hundred acres. I have a tenant farmer there, in a house by himself. The farm-house is big, with running water, and comfortable and has been renovated. It's very old, but it's a fine house. The farm is stock with some truck. Three hundred head of cattle, Holsteins. My bulls have won a lot of prizes, and my cows, too. The farm's perfectly equipped; it brings me a good income, even after my tenant farmer gets his share, and he gets a very generous share. Excellent man, with a family, and his house isn't far from the main house. A good school two miles away. Highway nearby—less than an hour's drive to Hambledon. A church a mile away. Rolling country.

'I want you to go and live in that farm-house, Tom, and take Thelma—who's a country girl, herself—and your four children. A healthy and tranquil life for all of you. And I guarantee you this, and will sign a contract with you to that effect: Thelma is to occupy that house during her lifetime, unless she marries again, and the children with her until they leave permanently for marriage or career. And the income from the farm, after the tenant farmer's share, goes to you, as long as you live, and to Thelma, as long as she lives, or until she marries again, which I doubt she will do. There'll be no fine print, Tom, but just as I've told you.

'I've seen temporary remissions in what you have, Tom. A life without strain and with peace, and with the knowledge that your children are provided for—Thelma can save from the income for their education—and your wife, too, will prolong your life for a few months, perhaps. You'll have peace of mind, above everything else. And, Tom, I will, within the next few days, arrange that all expenses of the farm be paid by me, and all improvements, even to the seed and fertiliser, new machinery, and everything else. You'll have no extraneous expenses. If Thelma dies prematurely, your children will live there under the same provisions.

'Now, what do you think about that?'

Tom said nothing. He merely looked at Jonathan with tortured stupefaction, his emaciated face working without a sound. His hands knotted together, and then he wrung them over and over.

Jonathan said, 'There's the little village of Russellville down the road, and old Dr Jonas lives there and practises what he can practise. But he is a good man. Occasionally, when you feel well enough, you can help him out—once in a while. No night calls, no deliveries, no operations, of course. Simple diagnosis. You know the farming regions, and people.

'Tom, your addiction to drugs comes from your pain, and I know that only morphine can relieve it. So, take a good supply with you, a very good supply, but use it only when absolutely necessary. For you know as well as I do that as long as it's possible for a cancer patient to function even a little adequately it's best to keep the dosage as low as it can be. Or later—nothing will help the pain, except death. And we want to postpone that as long as we can, for Thelma's sake, and the sake of your children. On the farm, without stress and the necessity to work as a surgeon, you will find that you can keep the dosage pretty low for a long time, and save its real benefits—for the last.'

He stood up. He could not look at his friend's face now; it was too much for him. 'Do you want me to tell Thelma for you, Tom? Will it be better that way? Or shall I go with you now and we'll tell her together? She's a sensible woman, Thelma.'

'Jon,' said Dr Harper, in a very low and rusty voice.

'Yes, Tom?'

'I've got to tell you something, Jon. I can't accept your offer without telling you first, and perhaps after I've told you, you will withdraw it, and I wouldn't blame you.'

Jonathan smiled. 'All right, tell me. It can't be very important.'

Tom threw back his head so that his thin and contorted neck reared out of its high stiff white collar. He stared at the ceiling, and groaned. Then he reached up his hands and covered that straining face and spoke from behind them.

'Jon, weeks before you were arrested—it was accepted that

you had been away. I went to Humphrey Bedloe, and spoke to him in private. I swore that if he repeated what I said to anyone, or called me in before witnesses, I'd deny I ever said it, and I'd deny it on the witness stand. Jon, I told Humphrey Bedloe that I had seen you, right here in Hambledon, on the day your wife told her uncle that she had had that criminal abortion which caused her death.'

Jon stood as if struck in the centre of the room, and, slowly, his face became terrible.

Tom continued, 'Humphrey went to the Sheriff, and told him, but did not give my name. He knew it was his duty. He said only that he had "information." It was on that little "information" that you were arrested, Jon. It doesn't seem possible that in this day and age that would happen, without a sworn statement before the proper authorities, and questioning, but it did. This town hates you, Jon. It's always hated you—that is, the important part of it if not your patients, and even some of them do, also. They wanted to believe the worst of you, Jon. Out of envy, and because you—you have an abrasive way sometimes, and you have no patience with lies and hypocrisies and pretensions, and malice, without which most people could not live a full life. And you let people know what you think, and that's not forgivable.'

He had dropped his hands heavily to his knees again and he inclined his head like a man totally undone and broken, but his eyes looked at Jon unflinchingly and with anguish.

'With what I told Dr Bedloe, and what Martin Eaton did, too, it was enough. Perhaps one without the other wouldn't have carried weight. My weight carried, Jon, it carried weight.'

'What really did you tell Bedloe?'

'I—well, I said that I had seen you not far from your house, as I was in the neighbourhood. I said I had seen you walking along the river bank, deep in thought. You—you had a bag with you, a piece of luggage. And then you walked in the direction of the station. Bedloe didn't doubt me, Jon. He never had reason to doubt me before, and has had no reason to doubt me now. Don't hold it against him, Jon, that he removed you from the staff of the Friends' even before you were indicted. It was my doing.'

Jonathan said with soft wonder, 'You son of a bitch. You son of a bitch.'

He went to the door and unlocked it. Tom said behind him, 'Yes. Yes. I'm much worse than that. You cancelled the five thousand dollars I borrowed from you, Jon. You called it a "gift to medicine," and "a public duty." I tried to think it was only that, Jon; I would not let myself think for a moment that it was the greatest generosity and kindness in the world. I even persuaded myself that you did only what you ought to have done and that in a way I was your benefactor, and not you mine. That's the way people are, Jon, that's the way they are, but I don't think you ever knew that.'

Jonathan's tall back was to Tom Harper. He put his hand on the doorknob, and began to turn it.

Only a few weeks ago, perhaps less, he would have turned it and would have gone out, and that would have been the end of it and there would have been nothing left to do but to make certain that Tom Harper was removed from staff and his patients taken from him. But there had been some dark, and still unknown, uprooting in the deeper places of his mind lately. He stood at the door and faced Tom Harper again.

'Why?' he said. 'Just tell me why. I want to know.'

Tom sighed despairingly. 'Jon, my father sold his farm to help put me through medical school, and there was very little left after the mortgage. Your father bought that farm, Jon, about fourteen years ago. It's yours, now. And you've always been rich, and that was another thing, and you didn't have hundreds of cold black nights going through medical school, when you wondered whether you'd make it or not, and you were hungry, and you couldn't afford to sleep because you had to work outside to make expenses. It wasn't your fault, Jon, that I went through that, and my father, too, but there it was. That is the way people are. I took your five thousand dollars—that's the way people are.'

'Yes, so it is,' said Jonathan. 'I always had a low opinion of humanity and now you've dropped it down another thousand or so fathoms, Harper. I was ten years—more—behind you in age. I didn't know when my father acquired the farms he left me. You have no accusations to throw at anyone, Harper. My father bought that farm, because it was offered for sale, through a county agent. He neither knew nor cared why it was being sold. Why should he have? If it had not been your father's farm it would have been another. My father liked land. I knew nothing about it. My father was the only one who wanted to buy that farm and he paid the money asked.

He wasn't guilty of "exploitation" or deliberate cruelty. But that's what you thought, wasn't it?'

'That's what I made myself think, Jon. I must have been insane, all those years. Thelma thinks you are the most wonderful man in the world, and sometimes I'd say to her, "Sweetheart, if you only knew!" '

'Well, it was a nice boost to your ego! It put you on the level with Jonathan Ferrier, or even made you his superior. The funny thing is that I never considered you "below" me, Harper, and I never considered you inferior! To me, always, you were a fine doctor and surgeon, far above the average. We were at least equals. I was proud to help you—because you were a member of a profession which seems to me to be the most important in the world.

'Now that I've seen some specimens, lately, I'm not convinced. And you've helped, Harper, you've helped.'

'I know, Jon, I know. Say anything you want to me. It isn't half what I deserve.'

The sick man bowed his head on his chest. Jonathan looked at him with the greatest hate and bitterness and thought: He wants me to feel sorry for him, to pat his shoulder, to laugh heartily and say it's nothing, and the farm arrangements will go on!

Then another thought came to him. Tom Harper had had no compulsion but one of conscience to tell him what he had done. He had had only to keep silence—and accept. Yet, in this desperate business he had deliberately risked what could have been the answer to his catastrophic situation. He had sacrificed himself, his wife and children, in order to feel honourable again, and in order to right an injustice.

Jonathan slowly came back into the room. 'Why did you tell me, anyway?'

'I had to—after your offer. Do you think for a moment I could have accepted it, even for Thelma and my children, knowing what I had done to you, out of envy and malice and resentment, when none of it was your fault at all, and you had given nothing to me but kindness?'

'I see,' said Jonathan, and frowned at the floor.

'Men don't reason with their minds,' said Tom Harper. 'They reason with their guts, their emotions. That's why the world is what it is. I took your friendship and all that went with it, but because you are rich, and I was and am poor,

I think I hated you, Jon, while at the same time, I liked and respected you and was your friend. Complicated, isn't it?'

'Not very,' said Jonathan. 'We're a pretty ambiguous race, and all at once I'm beginning, half-way, to believe in the dogma of Original Sin.'

Jonathan said with hard contempt to Tom Harper, 'All right, get off your knees, I've absolved you and you can leave the Confessional. Let's go and talk to Thelma. And if you tell her one word of what you've told me you'll regret it the rest of your life. You're not going to burden Thelma with your crime, so that you can wallow in her forgiveness, too, and perhaps even get her to pity you, for Christ's sake!'

'Jon,' said Tom, 'I swear this to you, and you know I am dying: I would never have let you be convicted. It was in my mind—I must have been crazy—that your arrest would pull you down a notch, as they say, and make you less haughty and proud and arrogant. You weren't those things, I know. I just thought you were. Because, God help me, in your position, that's just what I'd be and so would ten thousand other men.'

'Shut up,' said Jonathan. 'I don't know who's forgiven you. I haven't. I'm going to do what I suggested, but not for you, Harper. If it were you alone you could rot along with your disease, and I'd never give you another thought. But why should your innocent wife and children suffer?' His dark face had flushed with rage and his eyes sparkled.

'You know what this is going to do to me the rest of my life, Jon? It's going to make me do penance, and perhaps some time you can be superhuman enough to forgive me.'

'That will be a long summer day in my dotage, Harper. When you are dead and forgotten, even by me.'

'Did you hear what Jon Ferrier did to that unfortunate Tom Harper his best friend, or almost that—the other day? He forced him to resign his hospital privileges just because Tom took a little morphine occasionally, for Heaven's sake!' This was said by Jonathan's colleagues and 'friends,' with head-shakings and compassionate cluckings. 'But then, Jon was always a vindictive man. I'll never forget the time he refused to testify in behalf of Jim Spaulding, in court, when poor Jim was sued for malpractice by that worthless labourer who had the wrong infected arm taken off. Almost ruined Jim. Jon stood right up there in court and said that Jim should have every damned cent taken away from him in damages—and Jim one of the finest surgeons in the country, and who was that labourer with the foreign name, anyway? Well, that's Jon for you. Glad he'll soon be getting out of this town.'

Later it was rumoured that Jonathan had given Tom Harper a job as a hired hand on one of his farms, and the resentful hatred and envy of Hambledon against Jonathan became more vociferous than ever. Senator Campion was particularly vocal. He marked the incident down in his little black record book and smiled with satisfaction.

CHAPTER 9

When Jonathan came into his office six days later, he was gratified, for Robert Morgan's sake, to find every chair taken in the waiting-room, Robert busy in the examination room, and even a few standees in the hall outside. He went into the office and Robert came in and said, 'We have a rush. Was it always like this?'

'Yes. Nice, isn't it? The news that you are not married and that you are handsome and rich, must have gotten around, for I see quite a number of well-dressed Mamas out there, all, no doubt, equipped with marriageable daughters, and there are two or three young ladies, too.' Jonathan removed his hat and wiped his ridged forehead. 'Four o'clock, and the evening rush hasn't begun.'

Robert picked up a typed card from the polished desk. 'Now, here's a young lady who interests me. A Mrs Edna Beamish. Beautiful, and apparently with money. She insists on seeing only you. Hints she has something quite extraordinary wrong with her.'

'Never heard of her.' Jonathan took the card and read the address. 'Kensington Terraces. That's one of the few places in this town which can really be called an apartment house—unpleasant things, harbingers of the bright new future when men will be living in ant-hills. But this, so far, is a nice and very expensive group of flats—why do they call them "apartments"? Flats. I've been in one. Lavish, surrounded by gardens. Hum. Edna Beamish. Twenty-two years old. Any idea what is wrong with her?'

'No. She looks very well to me, naturally good colour, very pretty and stylish. And with a gay eye. I've told her you are taking no new patients, but she says she has heard so much about you and will see no one else. Take a look at her, anyway. She probably has a fat purse,' and Robert grinned. 'She's worth looking at, and from her manner I gather she wouldn't object too much if I invited her out for a decorous evening.'

Jonathan went into the waiting-room. 'Mrs Beamish?' he asked of the crowd. A lissome young lady rose, dressed in a simple but obviously costly lavender silk dress which sheathed

214

her figure tightly and dropped in a mass of rustling ruffles to the floor. She wore a broad silk lavender hat to match, with pink roses, and her hands were gloved in white and she carried a beruffled parasol the colour of her hat and dress, or gown would more properly describe it, thought Jonathan. She had a very attractive bosom, indeed, on which reposed a long string of amethysts set in gold, and the same gems enhanced her ears.

Her hair was fair and she had a small and mischievous face with large light brown eyes and impressive lashes, and a dimple in a pink cheek. The eyes flashed seductively at Jonathan, roving rapidly from his face to his feet. She sighed and smiled. 'Mrs Beamish,' she murmured.

Jonathan was intrigued. He said, 'I am taking no new patients, Mrs Beamish. You were told that. But Dr Morgan will see you.' He waved to her to precede him and she swept by him in a sweet rustle and embowered in a rich and enticing perfume, which Jonathan appreciated immensely.

Once alone with him in the office she turned, gave him another view of the deep dimple, sighed and smiled. 'Oh, Doctor.' Her voice was light and caressing. 'I'm so sorry, but I just couldn't see anyone but you—after all I have heard.' The fine eyelashes fluttered like moths and threw a dainty shadow on her round cheeks. 'I really couldn't.'

'That's nonsense,' said Jonathan, inspecting the figure again. 'The town is full of good doctors, and Dr Morgan is one of the best. He'll admit it himself.'

She trilled with delight, then coquettishly tapped Jonathan on the arm with her parasol. She shook her head. 'No, only you, Doctor. I heard Dr Morgan isn't married—' She dropped those wonderful eyelashes modestly.

'Oh,' said Jonathan. 'I'm not, either. By the way, I've never had the pleasure of seeing you before.'

'I've lived in Hambledon only a few months,' said the young lady, waving a little gloved hand and so setting the perfume in motion again. 'I have a slight—chest. I was told, in Scranton, that the air here is very good for such things.'

And the chest is very pretty, too, thought Jonathan approvingly. 'That's silly. Of course, Scranton is smokier, but not too much. So, you are from Scranton?'

'Yes. I'm not well known there either, Doctor. You see, I come from a very unimportant working-class family. Poor, but honest. But I married well. A gentleman from—from

Chicago. He was visiting in Scranton, and liked it, and so we were married.'

'But he likes Hambledon better?'

Again she sighed, and the lively face became sorrowful. 'I am a widow, sir.'

'I'm sorry,' said Jonathan. Her sigh was very beguiling.

'A lonely widow,' said Mrs Beamish.

'Oh, I doubt that!' said Jonathan, gallantly. But she shook her head and gave him a sidelong vision of her lashes and tilted nose. A very alluring baggage! Jonathan was beginning to have some idea about the lady and he doubted she was inconsolable, and that she would reject the suggestion of a quiet and private little dinner somewhere, with good wine. He knew just the place, and knew it well.

'It is very hard for a lone woman to become acquainted with genteel people in a strange city,' said Mrs Beamish with a sorrowful but fetching glance. Now Jonathan heard her accent, common and uncultured, but nice for all that. Commonness was not to be despised in a very pretty woman; on the contrary.

'Well,' he said, and looked at the card as if considering. 'If you insist, Mrs Beamish. But I warn you that if your condition demands long treatment I shall have to turn you over to Dr Morgan.'

'What a treasure you are!' she exclaimed. Robert appeared, with his patient, from the inner examination rooms, and seemed surprised, and pleased, to see Mrs Beamish. 'I shall examine Mrs Beamish,' said Jonathan with a grave voice, and winked at Robert 'If you don't mind, Doctor. Then, she is yours.'

'That,' said Robert, 'will be my pleasure.' The girl tittered, but not disagreeably, and gave Robert a flirtatious glance. Jonathan opened the door and let the young lady go in. Robert shook his head at him, and smiled.

'Disrobe, please,' said Jonathan, and removed his coat and put on a white jacket. Mrs Beamish surveyed the immaculate room with its table and its formidable array of cabinets with fearful instruments in them. She seemed a little daunted. 'Disrobe?' she said.

'Well, I can hardly examine you with that dress on, and your corsets, can I?' Jonathan asked with reason. 'I'll go into the other examination room, while you at least take the dress off, and loosen the corsets.'

216

When he returned she looked more fetching than ever, in her white silk and lace petticoats and what was known as a camisole, all white ribbons and embroidery. The bosom did excellently for itself without the whalebone. She had taken off her hat, too, and her hair was very bright and fluffy. Most appealing, thought Jonathan. He sat down near her and took one of her small plump hands. 'Now, tell me what you think is wrong,' he said. 'Chest, again?'

She dropped her eyes. 'Well, no, Doctor. I'm afraid it's female trouble. Inwardly.'

'That's where it usually is,' said Jonathan. 'I've never seen it elsewhere. Now, my dear, I am a doctor, and I'm sure other doctors have examined you before for one thing or another, so shall we put aside the modesty for a few minutes and get down to questions?'

She laughed at him demurely. She answered the questions readily enough. She had a pain in her right side very often, every month. 'Probably just ovulation,' said Jonathan. 'Quite often a little painful.' Oh, but this pain was agonising! It tore her apart. She screamed, really she did. Nothing helped at all. It went on for days. She couldn't sleep or rest or eat. It was frightful. Her face became quite awed and pale.

Ovarian cyst? thought Jonathan. He asked more questions. She became a little vague. Her knowledge of her own anatomy was very sketchy and grotesque. When he said 'ovary' she stared at him blankly. 'You know,' he said in a jocular voice. 'Where the eggs are.'

'Eggs? Doctor, I'm not a hen!'

'Nevertheless, you do lay an egg every month, I assure you,' he said. She looked offended. He gently slapped the white silken thigh and said, 'Now, I'll examine you. Just lie down on this table, please. And here are the stirrups. Put your feet in them.'

'Stirrups?'

'Have you never been examined this way before?' asked Jonathan.

'No. It was always just my chest.'

'We'll examine that, too, after this. Now, just don't be so stiff. Lie down. That's a nice girl. Cover yourself with this little sheet. And up with the feet. I won't hurt you.'

But she looked at the dilating instrument with real terror, half-concealed though it was with a napkin. She pulled her knees together. 'It won't hurt you,' said Jonathan. 'Perhaps a little discomfort, but you're a big girl now, and you've been married.'

His amused voice reassured her, and she endured the extensive examination with only a wince or two. After the first flurry she appeared to lose her modesty and concentrated her attention on the instrument, and didn't mind Jonathan's careful peering.

'All right,' he said after about five minutes, 'you can sit up now.' He carried the instrument away to a basin, to await sterilisation. The girl sat up and arranged the sheet very carefully over her legs. Jonathan came back to her, smiling.

'I have good news for you,' he said, 'though it's sad that your husband is not alive to hear it. You are nearly three months pregnant.'

'Oh!' cried Mrs Beamish, and fell back on the table and began to cry. 'Oh! poor Ernest! Not to have known about it, and he did want a baby so! He died two months ago, Doctor.'

'Unfortunate,' said Jonathan, with real regret, both for the deceased Mr Beamish, and for himself. 'Well, now, you must take the best care of yourself, and rest as much as possible, and be brave, and walk quietly every day. I will give you a little booklet—'

Mrs Beamish suddenly gave vent to peal after peal of tearing and tortured screams, so loud that even those in the waiting-room could hear them. While Jonathan, stunned and motionless, looked at her in absolute amazement, she rolled back and forth on the table, howling.

'Doctor, please, please, please! Oh, Doctor, you are killing me! Oh! Oh!'

There was a loud knock on the door, which Jonathan did not hear, being petrified by the screams, and then Robert rushed in, very agitated. He looked at the convulsed and half-naked girl on the table, and then at Jonathan. 'What the hell?' he asked.

'Hysterical,' Jonathan could manage at last. 'She's a widow, and pregnant. Legitimately, I assume. Here,' he said to Mrs Beamish. 'Stop that!'

'My God, you can hear her on the street,' said Robert, quite shaken.

Jonathan deftly slapped the girl's face and she stopped at once. Tears ran down her cheeks. She looked at Robert imploringly. 'He hurt me terribly, when he did it,' she sobbed. 'Hurt me terribly. I didn't know it would be that bad.'

'Nonsense,' said Jonathan. 'You never let out a whimper. Go on, now. Get dressed.' He said to Robert, 'Just the usual pelvic. A robust piece.'

Robert looked at the girl, frowning. 'I think you'd better leave her to me,' he said. But the girl was hastily dressing, crying quietly and shaking. She did not put on her hat or gloves, but instead she galloped out of the examination room, raising her voice in loud and frenzied sobs, and staggering visibly. She rushed past the astonished spinster at the typewriter, and the aghast and staring patients, and she exclaimed at the door, 'He almost killed me, and he said it wouldn't hurt!' Then she fled outside.

'For God's sake,' said Robert. 'What did all that mean?'

Jonathan shrugged. 'We get all kinds,' he said. 'I just think she's upset, knowing she's pregnant and her husband recently dead. She'll calm down, and be back in a week or so.' He heard a carriage draw up outside, and looked through the window. 'And a very nice vehicle she has there, too,' he said. 'A good pair of mares.'

Robert was uneasy. 'You never saw her before? Where has she been hiding?'

Jonathan explained. 'I still don't like it,' said Robert, perturbed. 'If she goes yelling like that to another doctor, it would hurt your reputation.'

Jonathan laughed. 'Nothing can hurt my reputation any longer,' he said. 'No. She'll be back. If only to look at you.'

But Mrs Beamish never returned, and after a few days the two doctors forgot her entirely. The elderly spinster did not, however, nor the other patients present. It had been very dramatic to people with drab or uneventful lives. Gossip spread through the city.

Marjorie Ferrier read all the newspaper clippings pertaining to her son, Harald's, show in Philadelphia, and she almost cried with gratification and sadness. 'Wonderful, dear,' she said to Harald. 'How very successful! I am glad you were so appreciated, and sold so many. We must send these clippings to the local newspapers.'

'Three thousand dollars,' said Harald. 'Not too bad. But then there were collectors from New York who know the coming trend in painting. By the way, I was offered five thousand for one—five thousand!—but I refused it.'

'But why?'

219

He smiled at her with her own fine hazel eyes. 'I saved it for you. I want you to have it. It was the only portrait, and one of the few I ever did.'

He lifted a large canvas and carefully removed the several burlap coverings, and then exposed it to the vivid July light in the morning-room.

It was a portrait of Jenny Heger. It depicted her in profile against a faintly umbrian interior, like rich but muted sunshine. She wore a dress of bluish-white of no particular style, except that her throat was visible and the top of one smooth shoulder. A small high casement window, mullioned, had been thrown wide open and the girl appeared to be looking out at nothing at all but a bleak and glaring light, a nothingness stark and empty. There was not a shadow, not an outline, of a single thing in that remorseless and almost blinding illumination, at once desolate and haunted. Her expression was brooding and quiet and very still, as if she knew that she was contemplating a barren glow in which nothing would ever move or live. Her black hair had a wild and dishevelled appearance, suggesting that she had thrown it aside in haste when she had run hopefully to this casement, only to let it fall heavily down her back in her devastated realisation. One hand was half-lifted in a gesture intended to smooth that hair, and then she had left it in that lonely gesture, half-way to her cheek. Her mouth was only slightly coloured, and apart in childlike wonderment and sorrow, and the blue of her eyes appeared to shimmer in the abandoned brilliance.

'Oh,' said Marjorie. 'How very beautiful. And—how very terrible. How you have caught poor Jenny! When did she pose for you, dear?'

'She never did. I didn't need her to pose, Mother.'

'No,' said Marjorie, still looking at the portrait, enthralled and deeply moved. 'I suppose you didn't, Harald. No, I suppose you didn't. It is just like Jenny, and conveys so much. I— well, I must confess that I never knew how much you—' She stopped.

'How much I understand and care for Jenny?' Harald's handsome face smiled easily, but his eyes were ambiguous. 'I thought you knew. Anyway, it is yours, Mother, because you are so fond of Jenny, and I want you to have it.'

I will hang it in the drawing-room, thought Marjorie, and then she had a quick and disturbing thought. Jonathan must never see what his brother had painted of Jenny. Marjorie wanted to cry in her sudden wretchedness. She watched Harald place the portrait against the wall of the morning-room, and she saw all his slow and absorbed movements. Then he stood off from the portrait and looked down at it, his head bent as if he had forgotten her. He said, 'I've watched her so often, with that very expression. She's had a miserable life—Jenny. Like a recluse, and she's only twenty. That was Pete's doing. Then Myrtle did not care about Jenny with the strong love Jenny had for her mother. Myrtle was incapable of anything strong in the way of emotion or attachment. She accepted everyone's affection graciously and kindly, and appreciated it, and was fond in return. But love—no. She wasn't very intelligent, but she had gentle ways. I liked her very much. I really did. I tried to get her to do something about Jenny, to send her abroad for her own good, to meet her contemporaries, to force her to dress better, and Myrtle did try, with her soft persuasiveness.'

Harald laughed shortly. 'If she had suggested to Jenny that she hang herself the girl wouldn't have been more horrified! No, she said. She had to stay—to take care of Mama and watch over dear Papa's castle, and his rose gardens. Particularly his rose gardens. I've seen women possessed by men, and jewels, and pleasure, and vice and all the passions, but I never knew anyone possessed by a rose garden before! Did you?'

'No,' said Marjorie, wanting to cry more than ever. 'Perhaps the rose garden means something—someone—to Jenny, who is immeasurably dear to her. She haunts it.'

'Pete, probably,' said Harald. 'What a gross little fat beast he was! And crass about everything but his foolish castle.'

He turned to his mother, and his highly-coloured and appealing face was serious. 'I've asked you before: Isn't there any word you could put in about me to Jenny?'

'No, dear, there isn't, and I've told you that too, before.' Marjorie shook her head and looked at her son with pity. 'Harald, dear, I think you'd better look elsewhere.'

'I don't want anyone but Jenny, Mother. I never will. I'm not very young; I'm thirty-three. That's old enough to know what you want.' He regarded his mother thoughtfully. 'Something just occurred to me. Is there something you haven't told me? You are sure Jenny will never be reconciled to me or consider me.'

Marjorie hesitated. 'Perhaps,' she said, 'there is someone

221

else. Jenny hasn't told me, but there is something—something about her that makes me feel there is, indeed, someone else.'

'That's not possible. Jenny never goes anywhere, never meets anyone, hasn't seen half a dozen men in as many years! And only one or two young men.' Harald smiled confidently. 'It's something else. Pete's memory.'

Marjorie was silent. Harald's light eyebrows dropped over his eyes as he studied his mother, and his suspicions increased. 'Mother, have you any idea?'

'Jenny has never said a word to me.'

'That's not exactly what I asked you, dear. I asked if you have any idea, yourself.'

'I'm not a mind-reader, Harald.'

'No, but you're evading the question.' He smiled at her with affection.

'Harald, I can't conjecture without absolute knowledge. And Jenny has—'

'Never said anything to you. I know. You haven't seen her anywhere, with anyone else, have you?'

Marjorie looked at the portrait. 'She was at the Fourth celebrations with me, and Jon, and Dr Morgan—such a nice boy—and the Kitcheners, and Mrs Morgan.'

'Now, that's a lively gathering if I ever knew one! The Kitcheners are like soft, rolled breasts of chicken cooked in cream, and about as pungent, and Mrs Morgan, I have heard, is a harpy, and young Dr Morgan is very innocuous, with all that boyish charm. Our Jenny, who constantly reads Pascal's *Pensées*, and Molière and Walter Pater, and St Augustine and God knows what else, can't be interested in Dr Morgan.'

'I think he was quite smitten with her,' said Marjorie, glad that one name had not been mentioned by Harald. 'He stared at her as if bewitched all through the meal. He looks like a hearty young man with an excellent appetite, yet he hardly ate a thing, and when he got chocolate icing all over his fingers he quite simply sucked them—and stared at Jenny, enraptured.'

Harald laughed, seeing the picture vividly.

'And how did our Lady of Shalott respond to that?'

'Well, you know how unaffected and unworldly Jenny is, and how little she appreciates her beauty or even knows she has it. She kept blushing. Robert made her uneasy, I am afraid.'

Harald stopped laughing. 'When a man makes a woman

222

uneasy, even if he is sucking chocolate off his fingers, then it is serious. That uneasiness can grow into interest, and interest into something stronger. Has she seen him often before?'

'I really don't know, dear. You know that Jenny comes into town once or twice a week, on that deplorable bicycle when she could have a buggy of her own, or hire a hack, and it's possible she's encountered Robert on the street here and there, or in a shop. He's looking for a special mirror which his mother wants, and some old paintings, preferably of London in a foggy rain. That's Mrs Morgan's taste.'

But Harald was not diverted. He considered. 'He's just the sort of red-gold lamb who could appeal to a woman's cradle instincts. Such men end up with blue ribbons in their hair, eventually, put there by Mama.'

'He's not that soft and weak and unmanly, Harald. He gives the impression of virility and a lot of stubbornness and other masculine qualities. I had invited him because of Maude Kitchener, who was enraptured as much by Robert as he was enraptured by Jenny.'

'And who do you think Jenny was enraptured by?'

The sharp and sudden question affected Marjorie unpleasantly. She said, 'I'm sure I don't know, dear, as I told you before. It is just a—tenuous feeling I have. But, could you really imagine Jenny enraptured by anyone, so that she might be present in person but far off in mind, dreaming?'

'I do indeed,' said Harald, in that same sharp tone. 'I do, indeed! She is just the sort. Now that you mention it I *have* seen her in that absent condition, staring into space almost by the hour.'

Marjorie sighed. 'Do we really have to talk about poor Jenny so much?'

'Mother,' said Harald, 'she is the only thing I ever think of, most of the time.' He sat near his mother and though he had much of Jonathan's appearance of containment and control, just then he gave the impression of urgency. 'I can't keep on just trying to change Jenny's mind about me any longer. I have to bring her to realising—well, that I love her and want her. I've told her dozens of times! It doesn't seem to penetrate her mind, shall we say? That's why I thought you might be able to help me, to put in a word—'

'Harald, I couldn't. You know I never interfere, and I'm absolutely no good at hints or insinuations, and I wouldn't want to offend Jenny by seeming to be minding her own

223

business.' She bit her lip a little. 'It's possible we'll know soon enough, if there is anything to know.'

'And that'll be too late for me. You're hiding something from me, aren't you?'

'You've been home three days, haven't you, Harald? You've seen Jenny. Have you shown her those clippings?'

Now she saw Jonathan clearly in him for the first time, concentrated and annoyed at her attempt to change the subject. 'I've seen her,' he said, in Jonathan's own hard and impatient voice. 'I've talked to her. I might have been talking to a statue, a statue which finds me particularly revolting, if a statue can feel anything. Show her the clippings? She'd throw them in my face! And what in hell did I ever do to her to merit all that hate?'

'Did it ever occur to you, Harald, that a young girl like Jenny might find it a little—well, repulsive—to think of marrying a man who was married to her mother?'

'Not in this case. I told her frankly after Myrtle died that— what is the delicate little euphemism?—we had not lived together as husband or wife, though we manifestly occupied the same bed.'

Marjorie did not know whether to laugh out loud or to express horror. She rounded her eyes at her son. 'Dear me, I didn't know. How—very confusing. Why on earth,' asked Marjorie, 'did you two ever get married in the first place?'

'It was simple,' Harald was smiling now. 'I needed money, and Myrtle needed a flattering, courteous, attentive man with whom to travel and whom to display—and an attractive one whom other women might envy her. She couldn't travel with Jenny. After all, even an unimaginative woman like Myrtle would find Jenny a little rocky to take while travelling, and among company. Myrtle was considerably older even than Pete. She had been nearly forty when Jenny was born. She was one of those nice, inoffensive, agreeable little women, and full of affability, which men like Pete—bustling, offensive, determined little brutes—adore. But after one child—that was enough dallying in love's arms for Myrtle. So, we came to a pleasant arrangement. She loved art, she said. She wanted to be a sponsor for my art. She needed a winsome escort— that was me. And, she liked me and was fond of me, and I liked her and did not find her in the least objectionable. Her will was a shock to me I admit, under the circumstances.'

Marjorie was fascinated. 'And what did Jenny say to all this, when you told her?'

'I think she wanted to kill me, and for the life of me I don't know why? Do you?'

'Surely. She thought you had married her mother for her money.'

'Well, I did. Though it wasn't so bald as all that.'

Mirth glittered in Marjorie's eyes. 'You know, Harald, you may find it incredible, but sometimes you are as single-eyed as Jon. Not very often, for you know a great deal more about people than he does, and they never surprise and stun you, as poor Jon is always stunned. But still, you were a little naïve in telling all this to Jenny.'

'I don't think so. She's the forthright sort, and so I was forthright. And by nature, I'm not at all that blunt, so please don't compare me with Jon. He's like a sledgehammer, and throws himself at everyone he decides isn't being candid and honest enough for him, or just possesses the little ordinary human weaknesses that everyone but himself, of course, possesses. That's why his—trouble—was worse than it was. All he had to do, in court, was to defend himself respectfully, gently, modestly, and sincerely, with an eye to impressing the judge with his blameless sweet nature, and the jury. Instead of that he showed every sign of contempt for them all, as if he thought them below the status of mankind for even daring to believe he had—done that to Mavis. He was outraged at them! He lacks finesse, the ability to slide around rough edges. He lacks diplomacy.'

'Yes, I know,' she said. 'Jon was like that, from babyhood.'

'You can't go around in this world telling the truth,' said Harald. 'It's a very bad, disgraceful habit and deserves all the uppercuts it gets, and all the infamy and hate. Then, he's possessive. Do you know that he thinks you never cared for him in the least and that all your maternal devotion was centred on me?' He laughed at his mother's astonishment.

'Now, really, Harald!'

'Oh, he does. I used to watch him when we were kids, and I used to torment him about it. He wanted everyone and everything centred on himself.'

'Jon never cared about anyone but his father.'

'Don't believe it, Mother. He took good care of dear Papa's tender little sensibilities, but you were the object of his real affections. He thought he didn't have yours, so he decided that you weren't very intelligent in not appreciating the golden salver he was offering, containing his heart's blood, or something. Maybe his head.'

Marjorie was still disbelieving, and she smiled at Harald in denial. 'Perhaps you are as wrong about Jon as he is about you, dear. You two were always incompatible. I think you both try very hard to find something tangible to dislike each other about. It isn't uncommon between brothers, or anyone else.'

Harald stood up. 'When is he leaving Hambledon, with that rasping tongue of his? To afflict some other community?'

'I suppose soon, when young Robert is well-established. But it's a very strange thing. He hasn't talked much about it lately.' And then Marjorie looked at her son with her hazel eyes darkening and becoming deeper and more watchful.

In turn, he lost his amiable look. He went over to the portrait and affected to be studying it, and his voice was careless when he said, 'I wish he'd leave very soon. It would be better for him. Much better. And very much safer, safer above all.'

Marjorie was silent. When Harald turned to her again her face held nothing but pain, and she showed every sign of intense weariness. 'You mean Hambledon has robbed him of purpose?' she said after several moments.

'No,' said Harald. 'I don't mean that at all. I mean Mavis.'

'Where in God's name did you buy that suit?' asked Jonathan on a very warm Saturday late in July. He surveyed Robert, and laughed.

'You provincials,' said Robert. 'I bought it in New York last spring. It is jealousy, my dear man, which suffuses your cheek with yellow, and envy which has jaundiced your eye. Your remark was poltroonish. Consider the fit, the style, the flair.'

'I can't,' said Jonathan. 'I'm partially blinded as it is. What did the morning's patients think of it?'

'Stunned,' said Robert. 'Stunned to awe.'

'I bet,' said Jonathan. Robert's suit was of light weight wool in a gigantic plaid design embracing black, white, a splash of green, a quick run of red thread here and there, and even a shy hint of orange. The long coat was stylishly cut back. With this he wore a high white collar, the points of which were open just below the chin and flared outwards, and he had crowned the whole attire with a lavish silk tie repeating the plaid and fastened with an enormous pearl tie-pin. His pointed boots shone like black coal, and a pair of yellow leather gloves and a pearl-grey fedora completed the costume. He slowly pivoted to allow Jonathan to survey all the glory, and he touched the tips of his red-gold moustache and jauntily struck a pose.

'Who is the lucky young lady who is going to be paralysed by your costume to-day?' Jonathan asked.

Robert carefully pulled on his yellow gloves. It was obvious they had never been worn before. 'Miss Jenny Heger,' he said, giving much attention to the buttons of the gloves and seeming to have a small difficulty with them. 'I wrote to her last week and asked if she would care for a ride along the river, and picnic, in my company.'

'Jenny?' said Jonathan.

'Miss Jenny. I am not on less formal speaking terms with her,' said Robert. 'I received a kind little note in reply, and I must confess I was both pleased and surprised, and she accepted my invitation.'

Jonathan leaned against his desk and crossed his ankles. 'I don't believe it,' he said. 'Jenny has never accepted any young man's invitation before.'

'She accepted mine.' Robert was very relieved that Jonathan had shown no intense interest or annoyance, though why he should do either Robert could not understand. He only knew that any mention of Jenny, heretofore, aroused Jonathan to inexplicable emotion or lascivious remarks. He smiled a little and looked up at Jonathan, who was lighting a cigarette. 'I know she is a very bashful young lady and I will try to gain her confidence.'

Jonathan's eyes surveyed the suit and accessories contemplatively. 'That ought to scare her to death, rather than reassure her,' he said. 'What if there is an emergency at the hospital?'

'Don't you remember?' asked Robert. 'You kindly offered to attend to that for me, seeing that I haven't had a day's leisure since I arrived. And we doctors do need recreation, as you've said yourself, or we'll soon not be worth anything to our patients.'

'Did I say that?' said Jonathan. 'One of my more careless

moments.' He seemed casually amused. 'You'll quite outshine poor Jenny, who doesn't possess, I have heard, one single pretty gown.'

Robert ran his hand over his fine gold watch-chain and took out his watch. He was more and more relieved. He said, 'My mother once remarked that it seemed strange that Miss Jenny did not employ a companion, an older woman, *in loco parentis*, as it were.' What his mother had really said was, 'It is an affront to the morals of the whole community that that young woman is so brazen in her conduct, and so careless of public opinion and the sensibilities of gently-bred young ladies, that she does not have with her some elderly female of impeccable background and position in this city, to protect her from gossip and give her respectability.' Remembering, Robert blushed, and Jonathan saw it.

'Jenny? An elderly female companion?' Jonathan laughed. 'Jenny, I can assure you, can take very good care of herself.'

'But there is, after all, your brother living in the same house with her, and he a young man still, and only the servants.'

'Isn't he protector enough for Jenny?' asked Jonathan.

The term, Robert recalled, was ambiguous. He began to feel a little heat of anger against Jonathan. 'Just what do you mean by protector?' he demanded.

Jonathan said, 'Now, what do you think I mean? Technically, he's her stepfather, the husband of her dead mother. Don't develop an evil mind, Bob.'

'I'm not the one with an evil mind!' said Robert, and felt a hard constriction in his chest. 'I've seen Miss Jenny only a few times since the Fourth of July, on the streets and in the shops, and a more lovely and innocent young lady I have never seen in my life!' He seemed to swell. 'We've talked a little, here and there, and she's very shy and timid and seems afraid and awkward. I—I like Miss Jenny, very much! I do, indeed. Eventually, I hope that she will take me seriously.'

Jonathan whistled. He eyed Robert and not with kindness, and then with a slow thoughtfulness. 'We have progressed, haven't we?'

'I hope so. I fervently hope so!' said Robert, and shook an invisible speck of dust from his hat and prepared to leave. Then he had another thought. 'Why doesn't your brother supplement her income so she can leave the island for a more —a more—protected residence?'

'I hear he did,' said Jonathan. 'But she refused. I told you,

She regards him as an interloper, a criminal blackguard who married her mother for her money—and she is quite right, Harald makes no pretence otherwise, and it was an amiable marriage—and she considers the island hers, as it was her father's, and she stands guard over it. She'll never leave it unless she is first sandbagged and blindfolded by someone, and somehow I can't see you in that role.'

'Hardly,' said Robert. 'But still, if she marries, she may change her mind.'

'My dear noisy-suited friend,' said Jonathan, 'I should not blow up my hopes if I were you. Jenny and my mother are almost as close as mother and daughter, and my mother has hinted to me several times that Jenny's affections are firmly fixed on some mysterious stranger.'

Robert's face actually paled, and Jonathan frowned. 'If that were so, she would not have accepted my invitation,' he said.

'Perhaps the gentleman is unattainable,' said Jonathan.

'Then all the more should she be diverted,' said Robert, and took himself off in his sartorial glory.

Jonathan had not seen Jenny since that evening when he had tried to seduce her somewhat strenuously. He had often rowed over to the island on the pretence of amusing himself by mocking his brother, but when Harald was there—which was infrequent—Jenny appeared to be absent, or at least she made no appearance. Jonathan had idly asked about her once or twice and Harald had shrugged, had remarked that she was 'in town,' or was not feeling very well, or 'God knows, I don't know where she is!' Harald seemed less easy lately, less nonchalant and less smiling, and to be absorbed in some thoughts of his own. He was restless. If one so affable and pleasant could be said to be brooding, then Harald was brooding. In view of what Marjorie had said, this was interesting to Jonathan. He wanted to say, 'Insofar as Jenny is concerned, sweet brother, you might as well give up, and perhaps I should too, though I'm damned if I will until the day I die.'

When she visited Marjorie Jonathan did not know, though he suspected. Marjorie did not mention the girl, except to remark at one time that Jenny was not visiting her as often as usual. This was understandable, considering that she probably feared his unexpected arrival in the house.

There was one thing which had relieved him excessively: It was most evident that Jenny had never told Harald of his brother's attack on her. She could easily have done so. Harald would then, at her insistence, have forbidden Jonathan to come to the island any longer. (It would have been interesting to see if he could summon up a rage or engage in fireworks or threats for the first time in his life!) But, for some strange reason, Jenny had not told him, and this was exciting in itself, nor had she written asking him never to go there any longer, nor had she asked Marjorie to convey the message.

But he had not seen her. The infuriating thing was that Robert Morgan had seen her on the streets and in the shops he was prowling for his mother, and she had actually accepted an innocent invitation from him. The implications of this nagged at Jonathan. He liked Robert immensely; he felt for him the strong brotherly affection he had never felt for his own brother. It annoyed his pride and his opinion of himself that he should, this hot Saturday afternoon, think many uncomplimentary things of his young replacement, and also of Jenny.

He had never, for a moment, doubted that in the wooing of Jenny Heger he would be successful. He loved her, and he had never loved a woman before, as he realised now. He had everything to offer, such as himself and marriage. Not even when pursuing a particularly difficult lady had he hinted marriage as a possibility, nor had he ever called Mavis 'darling' as he had called Jenny.

Now, out of nowhere had come this naïve young Robert Morgan, with his gorgeous raiment and his ability to get Jenny to do what it had been impossible for any man before him to do. What of the man Jenny was alleged to be attached to—unless Marjorie had been entirely mistaken? Could it be—it was impossible!—that Jenny had been detached from that stranger by Robert Morgan. It was absurd. It was not to be thought of for a moment. Jenny was a girl of intelligence; she was unlikely to be attracted to a man of limited imagination. But one never knew about women. They were capable of the most bizarre revulsions and attractions.

The telephone rang.

A high and breathless female voice rushed to Jonathan's ear. 'Jon? Jon! This is Prissy Witherby! Oh, Jon, I'm scared to death!'

'I shouldn't wonder, being married to Jonas,' said Jonathan. 'Anything specific wrong, Prissy?'

'Jon, please come at once! He's out driving to-day—he goes every day. But all at once I can't stand it! I'll lose my mind!'

Jonathan would have smiled indulgently at this from another woman, but Priscilla Witherby, the former doxy, had the commonsense of her calling and the realism, and so hysteria was unlikely. 'What's he up to now, Prissy?'

'I don't know! That's what makes it so frightening, Jon. But it is something, I know. Since he came from the hospital he sits smiling all alone, like a damned satisfied spider, spinning, plotting—Oh, I know I sound fanciful, but you know Jonas.'

'I do. I'll come as soon as I can, Prissy. How long does he stay out, driving?'

'From two to three hours, in this weather. Jack drives him to the park and around.' The girl caught her breath in a sob. 'He's been gone fifteen minutes. That should give us time to talk.'

After he had finished his conversation with Prissy, Jonathan thought about Jonas Witherby, the soft, smiling, loving evil of a man. The gentle-voiced, charitably-speaking, mild, tender-eyed evil. Damn them, these dangerous ones! Jonathan remembered the dead wife, the ruined sons, all the victims of this monstrous corruption, this man who had never been known to speak evil, to see evil, or hear evil, at least overtly—this man who had deceived almost an entire small city into believing in his goodness and kindness and pure-hearted sympathy. If Jonas Witherby were to testify in a court of law against or for a man the judge would inevitably believe him, listening to his affectionate voice, looking at his saintly face, and so would a jury. Jonathan prepared to leave for the Witherby house when he heard the bell ring in the waiting-room. He frowned with annoyance as he went to the door. There were no office hours here on Saturday afternoons except for emergencies and fixed appointments.

Two well-dressed gentlemen in their thirties, strangers to Jonathan, stood in the deserted waiting-room. He said with abruptness, 'I'm sorry. Dr Morgan is not in, and there are no office hours on Saturday afternoons except by appointment.'

One young man spoke, a tall and pleasant man with shrewd light eyes and blond thick hair and a humorous face. 'Dr Ferrier? Thank you. I'm Bill Stokely, from Scranton,' and he gave Jonathan his card. Jonathan looked at it: William Sebastian Stokeley, attorney-at-law. 'And this other gentleman,' said Mr Stokeley, 'is Dr Henderson Small, also of Scranton.' Another card was given Jonathan in identification.

'Well, what can I do for you?' asked Jonathan.

'We'd like to discuss a former patient of yours, Doctor,' said Mr Stokeley, 'and to pay you for her examination. I understand that you never sent her a bill.'

'What was her name?'

'Mrs Edna Beamish.'

Jonathan considered. The name sounded familiar to him, but he could not recall the patient. He shook his head. The two men glanced at each other in satisfaction. 'You may not know,' said Jonathan, 'but I have—had—a large practice, not only in Hambledon but from surrounding villages and townships, and even from Scranton and Philadelphia. And my replacement, Dr Morgan, has been handling most of them. I am merely here, now, to help him establish himself, before I leave the city permanently.'

'Mrs Beamish lived at Kensington Terraces when she visited you, Doctor?'

Jonathan shook his head again then went to the files, opened one and withdrew a card and studied it. Then he laughed. 'Oh, Edna. Yes, I remember now. She was here almost a month ago. Charming young lady. She did not let me complete my examination, and became a little—disturbed— and ran out after creating a scene. She was understandably upset, for I discovered she was at least ten weeks pregnant, and her husband had recently died, and so he would never know his child. I didn't send her a bill because the examination was incomplete.' He looked at the lawyer.

Mr Stokeley said, 'I am here to pay her bill, Doctor. You see, my firm manages her late—husband's—estate. Ernest Beamish. So, she reports all bills to us, and we pay them for her. She is very young and inexperienced herself, and incapable of managing the rather large estate her husband left her. He appointed us executors.' He smiled. 'In fact, we act *in loco parentis* to her. So when she returned to Scranton to live, two weeks ago, she told us that she had consulted you, and that you had sent no bill.'

'Don't bother about a bill,' said Jonathan. 'I expected Mrs Beamish to return for further examination, and possibly prenatal attention, and possibly for obstetrical purposes, at the hands of my replacement. As she did not return, I don't think she or you are obligated to pay any bill, and I certainly won't send one.'

He looked curiously at Dr Henderson Small, a short slender

232

man, very dark and grave and inconspicuous. 'Are you attending Mrs Beamish, Doctor?'

'I did,' said Dr Small in a significant voice.

'Did she run out on you, too?' Jonathan smiled, noting the past tense.

Mr Stokeley intervened. 'Mrs Beamish is—er—a rather difficult girl. I happened to be in town with Dr Small today, and I thought it well to stop in to see you and ask for a bill.'

'No bill,' said Jonathan. He was becoming irritated. The afternoon was hot and fine. He intended to ride out to one of his farms and see how a certain filly was doing, one who was showing all signs of being a remarkable racer. 'If that is all, gentlemen—'

Mr Stokeley said smoothly, 'As I told you, Doctor, we act *in loco parentis* to Mrs Beamish. Obviously she needs continued treatment. Dr Small, here, is not a gynaecologist. He is a general surgeon, and certainly not an obstetrician! He told Edna he has had very little training in obstetrics—I think that is the new science of doctors who deliver babies? Yes. However, she insisted on him examining her, and he discovered a—slight—abnormality.' Mr Stokeley gave Jonathan a genial smile. 'He referred her to an obstetrician in Scranton, but so far she hasn't followed his advice. By the way, did you find any abnormality, Doctor?'

'None,' said Jonathan. 'At least not during the pelvic examination, which was as thorough as I could give, considering the fact that she was squeamish and resistant, not an unusual thing in young ladies under the circumstances.' For the first time he saw that Dr Small was discreetly taking notes in a very abbreviated little black notebook. 'What is this?' he asked.

'Just for reference, Doctor.' Mr Stokeley was very pleasant. 'You see, there is that large estate, and naturally a—er—natural issue would be important, wouldn't it? We feel every responsibility for Edna. Now, Doctor. Would you mind telling Dr Small exactly what your examination showed?'

It was almost two o'clock. It would take at least an hour for Jonathan to ride out to his farm, after seeing Prissy. He glanced at his watch.

'I found no abnormality,' he said, with increasing impatience. He looked at the reserved Dr Small. 'What did you find?'

'No abnormality in the pelvic regions,' said Dr Small. 'But

233

something unimportant in the pancreas. We did want your opinion before sending Mrs Beamish—insist on sending her—to a competent man in Scranton.'

'It isn't necessary,' said Jonathan, more and more impatient. 'I found her approximately ten weeks pregnant, a healthy young white female, widow, with no previous history of disease of any kind. She did complain of "terrible pain" in the lower right quadrant of her abdomen, which she gave as the reason for her coming to me in the first place. This usually occurred during ovulation, a common thing. I examined her for a cystic ovary, and found everything normal. I then examined her for chronic appendicitis, or blind bowel, as the laity call it. Nothing pathological there, either. I intended examination for possible kidney involvement or—'

Dr Small interrupted. 'But insofar as the pelvic examination was concerned, there was no abnormality?'

'None. Didn't you say that was your opinion, too?'

Mr Stokeley gave Dr Small an enigmatic and unfriendly glance, and the doctor said at once, 'I saw no evidence of a natural—a natural—abnormality.'

Jonathan found this ambiguous. He looked intently at Dr Small and said, 'We don't usually speak of "natural abnormalities," Doctor. A contradiction in terms.'

'And of semantics,' said Dr Small.

'Yes. So, what did you mean?'

'Oh,' said Mr Stokeley, 'let's not get into a medical discussion, gentlemen, on this fine day! Our train leaves in half an hour for Scranton.' He held out an expansive palm to Jonathan, and said in a rich but slow and emphatic voice, 'So, you did not receive payment for your examination?'

'I told you, no.' Dr Small quietly wrote that down.

Mr Stokeley grinned and shook his head. 'That Edna! She is always complaining that she never has any pocket-money. Let me be frank, Doctor. She claims she paid you two hundred dollars for your examination! In cash, and not by cheque, on which we usually insist.'

Jonathan laughed. 'Had I completed the examination as I had wished, I'd have sent her a bill for ten, perhaps fifteen, dollars. I'm afraid our little Edna is attempting a little financial wheedling from you. She never paid me a cent and I never sent her a bill. Now, if you will excuse me—'

'Thank you, Doctor, thank you,' said Mr Stokeley, effusively. 'I shall really have to castigate our Edna, I really shall. I suspected it all along. Good day, Doctor.'

The two men left, and Jonathan saw that a station hack awaited them outside. He watched it drive away in the direction of the depot. He forgot the episode at once in his hurry. After all, it was not unusual. Pregnant ladies with money were understandably, and expensively, concerned with their state. He was about to replace the card in the file, then thought about it. Mrs Beamish would not be his or Robert Morgan's patient. He tore up the card and threw it away. He liked to keep his files neat and up to date, and have no dead and useless information in them.

He went off, whistling. He was usually whistling these days. He felt such vitality, lately, such an awareness of life and strength, such a consciousness of joy in living, in spite of all that he had suffered and endured since his marriage.

He had almost reached the street when a uniformed messenger approached him. 'Dr Ferrier?' asked the lad, then touched his cap, gave Jonathan an unstamped but sealed letter, and rode off on his bicycle. Jonathan looked at the writing on the envelope and it was unfamiliar to him, and for some peculiar reason he thought, This is a feigned writing and not the real one of the writer. Perhaps it was the elaborate curlicues, or the change in slanting, or a 't' crossed differently from another 't,' or a baroque circle over an 'i' when following 'i's' were merely dotted with a tiny dash or not dotted at all, which made the writing appear hidden or contrived. Jonathan opened the letter, to discover the same writing inside.

'Murderer!' it shouted. 'If you are not out of this good city by 1st September, at the latest, you will be ridden out on a rail, tarred and feathered! Do you remember the effigy of you which was hung near the courthouse when you were falsely acquitted of the murder of your wife? The next time the rope will hold your neck and not an effigy. Beware! Your crimes are all known.'

Jonathan could not believe it. His first impulse was to laugh, then destroy the letter, for only a madman could have written it. But then he was impressed by a sense of malignancy in the writing more than in the wording, a deep and terrible hatred of him, a personal hatred. He had received hundreds of vicious letters from not only Hambledon but from Philadelphia and Pittsburgh, and even from New York and Boston, when he had been acquitted, and after his initial rage he had begun to laugh at them and destroy them and forget them at once. A sensible man did not give any of his attention to the sly and anonymous wicked ones of the world, or he would go mad himself. He did not brood over the general worthlessness of humanity, its malice, cruelty, depravity, meanness, or he would end being an even greater despiser of his fellows. But this letter caught his attention as none other ever did. Someone in Hambledon had sent it. The messenger service in the city had been paid for this. Jonathan went back to his offices and called the messenger service.

A youthful male voice answered him. This had been a very busy Saturday, it informed Jonathan, with many people coming in and leaving packages and messages, and no record was kept except in cases where a reply was expected. Yes, indeed, sir, he did recall a letter for Dr Jonathan Ferrier! But was it a young lady, or a gentleman, who had brought it in for delivery, and had paid the fee? Jonathan waited and could almost see the avid ear of Central listening in. Confound the girls. They were always eavesdropping on his calls these days, and he must complain about it. The young male voice was obviously ruminating, if one could imagine such a thing. Then it returned with apology. It could not remember at all. It was 'someone' it was sure, but who that one was escaped it entirely, and it was very sorry. It was also sincere. Jonathan hung up. He went back to his private files, opened one and took out his bottle of whisky, and drank a considerable amount. He knew, again, the desire to kill with his own hands. He had not had that desire for a long time, but now it had returned. He stood with the glass in his hand, his elbow leaning on the files, and his face was again stark and hard and pale under its darkness, and his mouth was set and harsh. He drank again. Then he remembered that he had promised to see Priscilla Witherby almost immediately. He put the bottle away and locked the files, and once again left the hot and silent offices.

He went to the livery stable for his horse, and spoke absentmindedly to the groom, who watched him canter away. What was wrong with Doc Ferrier now? He hadn't seen such a look on his face for a long time, and now it was back. It was the face of a man who could not only kill but would enjoy the killing. They called him a tough man in Hambledon, and the groom could well believe it for the first time. No, sir, he wouldn't want to cross Dr Ferrier!

Jonathan tied up his horse before the handsome white brick and stucco house of rich old Jonas Witherby, careful that the animal was in the shade of the great elms. He went up the flagged walk; the stones were coloured rose and faint blue and yellow, in a very artistic pattern. But to-day everything looked malign and hurtful to him, and too sharp in outline and tint and shade. He had often wanted revenge. He wanted it now with a terrible hunger he had never felt before, except for a few times with Mavis. The brilliant white door, with its polished brass knocker, opened for him and he was confronted by Priscilla, who took him at once by the hand and pulled him quickly into the large and pretty hall with its scent of jasmine.

'Jon, dear!' she gasped. (Prissy always gasped, as if unbearably surprised, outraged, delighted, overcome, amazed, startled, or aghast. It was considered very intriguing by her admirers.) 'Oh, Jon, dear, I wondered if you'd forgotten me! I watched by the windows every second!' She was out of breath. She had a dear little voice, like a very young girl's, or a breathless child's. 'Do come into the drawing-room, where it is so nice and cool! I have your favourite whisky. Jon, you get handsomer every time I see you, I swear it! And you should never wear anything but riding-clothes, and boots, and carry a cane!' She burst into tears. 'Jon, I can't bear it, not for a single minute more, not for a single minute!'

She threw her arms about his neck, standing on tiptoe to do so, and kissed him fervently on the lips, and hugged him harder, pressing her face into his neck. He held her by the arms, gently, then put her off. 'All right, Prissy, did the old bastard put arsenic in your coffee?'

Prissy was at least thirty-two and had been a whore since she was fourteen, and a very jolly and appreciative and expensive one. She was a little woman, small even in an age which preferred little women. She was a perfect miniature of a female lovingly formed, a figurine of porcelain, softly but brightly coloured, smooth and glowing with porcelain lights. There was a sleek polish about her which transferred itself by magic to her clothes. She was always *svelte* and clean and perfumed and exquisitely and fashionably dressed.

She owned considerable property in Hambledon, including

237

a lumber business of increasing prosperity, and was known as a very shrewd businesswoman. She was a scandal. The ladies hated her, though since she had married Jonas Witherby she was often invited to the 'best' houses. 'For Jonas's sake,' the hostesses would apologise. 'Dear, darling old Jonas.' They were certain that Jonas was Prissy's victim, though gentlemen held exactly the reverse of that opinion, and wondered often and loud, and resentfully. Had old Jonas gotten 'something' on Prissy? a very few asked each other, including Jonathan. Jonathan was certain he had, though Prissy denied it vigorously. He was very rich, and she had liked him, honestly she had, and she had thought him so good and kind, and after all a girl had to think of her future too, didn't she? Prissy was never the 'legendary prostitute with a heart of gold.'

The drawing-room was most tastefully furnished—by Prissy. She had removed the huge and sullen furniture it had once possessed, and now it reflected Prissy in its small and gay and colourful chairs and settees and really good paintings on the white walls. She led Jonathan to a chair, and, with fresh tears rolling prettily down her cheeks, she poured him a large drink, hesitated, tossed her head, and prepared one for herself. She sat down near him, a delicious china figure, and stared at him hopelessly.

'Come on, Prissy, what's the trouble?' asked Jonathan, after a pull at his crystal glass. 'I have an appointment later in the afternoon.'

'You know Jonas,' said Prissy. 'Ever since he came home from the hospital—Jon, you never did believe that I tried to poison him, did you?'

'No, dear. But I often hoped you'd poison him.'

Prissy giggled abruptly. 'Well, I've thought of it, but I'm not a fool, Jon. You know who they'd first suspect, and maybe with good reason, him with all that money, too. Not that I'd grieve much now if he'd drop dead. But he'll live to be a thousand, Jon! A thousand! He's just that bad—he'd live to spite me.'

'And spite others, too,' said Jonathan.

'Well,' Prissy sighed. 'Jon, I know you won't believe me. But I'm sure now that Jonas was really poisoned. I'm sure he did it to himself. Go on, laugh at me.'

Jonathan shook his head slowly. 'No, dear, I won't laugh. I believe it, myself. Oh, he didn't take enough to kill him, of course, the old devil. But just enough to make him interestingly sick—and make people ask questions. About you.'

'But why, Jon, why?' The girl cried again..

'He wants people to remember his "illness" in the hospital. I hear he talks about it constantly so they won't forget. Then, when he does die there'll be ugly conjectures. Nothing positive will be proved about you—but they'll talk. Perhaps there'll be litigation over his will. Perhaps he's already arranged that. Perhaps there's something rotten about you in that will; it wouldn't surprise me. Perhaps he's left you nothing, saying that he had always "suspected" you tried to kill him before, and that you were thwarted by fast medical attention. To be truthful, his record on admission does say that he "showed all symptoms of poison." But he didn't vomit in the hospital, and so we had no samples, and don't make such a nasty face, Prissy. However, he insisted, the dear innocent loving old man, that he had eaten nothing you hadn't eaten, and that it was surely only "acute indigestion." He actually cried when I questioned him. I wasn't his admitting physician. I was away when he came in.

'But he did need a fella who'd suspect poison after all, and so I did. He didn't want soothing-syrup doctors who wouldn't make good witnesses. He handled it very cleverly. No overt evidence. I saw him forty-eight hours after he had been admitted to the hospital under emergency. He was suffering the aftermath of poison all right, but what kind was not clear. I think, myself, it was arsenic.'

'I still don't understand, Jon, why he should do that!'

'Prissy, dear, like all sanctimonious brotherly-lovers he hates people. I don't know why. There are still some hell-holes in the human psyche that baffle me even now. It could be that the brotherly-lovers are afraid they might be detected in their luxurious hatred and then others wouldn't love them, and they do cherish the regard of others! They know all about themselves, probably, and secretly despise themselves and their only defence against the horror of their whole being is to see the deceived love-light and admiration for them in the eyes of other people. We all have our methods of self-defence against the world. The brotherly-lover probably more than most, for he is a weakling and can't accept what he is, and is afraid that if found out the world would punish him—as it ought to do, by God! He's a menace.'

Prissy had listened with puzzlement. She shook her head.

'It sounds very strange to me, Jon. I've always been decent to others and always thought they'd be decent to me in return. Until I knew Jonas. Why should—what do you call them? —brotherly-lovers enjoy seeing others suffer?'

'Because they are crazy, my dear, absolutely mad. And they're evil. In some cases evil and craziness are the same thing. One breeds the other. Well, you know the history of Jonas's wife, who killed herself, and his wretched sons. They hadn't injured Jonas. But they were handy for his malice. He'd call that "reforming" them. 'You'll notice that it is the haters of humanity who are always trying to reform it. They want to feel superior to the general run of mankind. Besides, they're malevolent to the very heart of them. What did Christ call them in one of His less benign moments? "Hypocrites, liars, sons of the Devil."

'Well, that's what old Jonas is. And so, he wants to make you suffer. I don't think he has anything against you. In fact, I think he likes you in his perverted way, and is very fond of you. But, you are handy. If he can make you totally miserable, then he'll be contented and beam like a rose. It could be that I'm wrong about his will, though such men as Jonas get great satisfaction in thinking what consternation and heartbreak they can cause after death, with their vindictive wills. They brood on it; it makes their days brighter and more serene, contemplating the anxious and disturbed faces of the future, and the protestations, and denials, and the shame. Still, it may not be his will. He knows you have influential friends in Hambledon, including me, who would testify for you and help to overthrow any contemptible will.

'I think his little play-acting with the arsenic was to frighten you, to make you fear the whole city and the whole city to suspect you. Some do, you know. Yes, I see you know that. He knows that you know you didn't poison him, but he loves to see your fear that others might think it. Very good at reading minds, the wicked ones. So, he keeps you in turmoil. He keeps you frightened, and afraid of what he might do next to involve you in scandal or suspicion. They always find out a person's weakest point, and if they can't find one they make one. Yours is your past history, dear, and the dislike the ladies have for you, and their willingness to believe you are a mercenary hussy and a heartless one. So, would not such a woman think of murdering a helpless old man who had loved and "redeemed" her, just for his money? Why, of course.

'So, he's twisting you. He is bruising you mentally. He keeps you simmering with terror. I don't know how he managed to do that with his first wife, but he did it, and so she killed herself to escape him, and his sons escaped him, too, one way or another. Prissy, you won't take my advice, but I'll give it. Pack up and leave at once. Unless, of course, you have the strength of will to pretend a great serenity with him, and if you can make yourself wink at him sometimes and imply that you're on to him and that you're not in the least disturbed.'

'Golly, Jon, I've stood more than three years of that old wretch! Don't you think I deserve something after he's dead? If I left him now I'd get nothing. Though I admit I do get restless, sometimes.' She gave him a pretty and significant smile through her tears. He patted her hand. 'I'm sure you still have—friends,' he said. 'If you can manage it discreetly.'

'Oh, I couldn't. He watches me all the time. If I go shopping, I must give him a detailed account of every damned minute, Jon. And what I bought, and if the clerks were slow. He times me. And Jack drives me, you know, and he gets reports from Jack, too. I know it.'

'He isn't concerned with your fidelity, dear. It's just his little way of making you miserable. I agree you deserve something for enduring him for three years—and he'll probably live forever. You must make up your mind as to whether or not it is worth it, for you.'

'Oh, my God!' exclaimed Prissy, glancing through the window. 'Here he is now, and he's looking at your horse and he knows it is yours!'

'Let's pretend we didn't know he had returned,' said Jonathan. 'That'll be his first disappointment—not to find us romping in your bed, not that he really cares or is capable of romping, too. And let's smile at him sweetly. Then, leave us alone. Perhaps I can put the fear of God into him, though I've noticed that the brotherly-lovers don't believe in God at all.'

Old Jonas Witherby came into the house, elaborately assisted by his coachman who handled him as though he were extremely fragile. But Jonas was vigorous and strong, even if he permitted his servant to pretend that he was not. He came in beaming and rosy, all silken white hair and holy smiles and happy eyes. 'Jon, my boy!' he said, holding out two soft warm hands and taking one of Jonathan's and pressing it

241

tenderly. 'How delightful to see you! But is Prissy ill?' He looked at his wife with enormous concern and affection.

'No, she isn't, and aren't you glad?' said Jonathan. 'I was passing by and I thought I'd drop in and see how you were, and to find out if you were still interested in giving me a cheque for the new tuberculosis hospital we're still plotting about.'

Jonas cackled happily and shook his head as if Jonathan had perpetrated a wonderful joke which was greatly appreciated. He sat down with a rich sigh of pleasure. 'What a marvellous day it is!' he said. 'So comforting to old bones. Prissy, love, would you give me a drink? My usual. Just a little, a very little, whisky, but plenty of cool soda. I see you have both been celebrating in my absence.'

'Yes, we have,' said Jonathan. 'After all, how often do you leave this house?'

Jonas chortled. He pretended, all at once, to be very watchful of Priscilla. 'Sweetheart,' he said, in a very wistful and timid voice, 'is that the whisky you and Jon have been drinking?'

Priscilla looked up with a start and her lovely face became strained. She did not see Jonathan shake his head at her in reproof. 'Yes, it is,' she answered, and her hand trembled as she poured the liquor. Jonathan watched idly. He said, 'You know, Jonas, I wouldn't blame Prissy a bit if she dropped arsenic in it—though, how could she get arsenic? Jonas, I asked you a question.'

The old man was still intent on the pouring liquid, pretending to helpless concern. Then he said, 'Eh?'

'You heard me. You know that arsenic isn't easy to come by, though it is used for insects in gardens. Not the pure stuff, of course, to get the pure stuff you must buy it from a chemist, and sign for it. That's the law. So, how could Prissy get it without throwing suspicion on herself?' Jon sat down and smiled sweetly at the old man. 'Perhaps you could tell us, Jonas?'

The old man's face was cherubic with infantile bewilderment. 'Eh? Another of your jokes, Jon? Really. Very bad taste.'

Jonathan leaned back in his chair and studied the high white ceiling. 'Of course, one could give a story about rats. Or send someone for it—in another town, with a false name and address. Prissy, have you been tampering with Jack, the gardener-coachman?'

'Jon! What are you saying?' Priscilla stood with the bottle in her little hand and regarded Jonathan with terror.

'Just speculating, Prissy. I'm a great speculator. Besides, I'm curious. Jonas, what do you think?'

'I wouldn't poison even a rat,' said Jonas in a sad and trembling voice. He took his glass from Priscilla's hand, gave her a courtly bow of his head in thanks. 'I love all that lives.'

'Oh, I'm sure you do. You have a reputation for that, Jonas. Prissy, would you give me another drink—from that very bottle, dear—and then leave us for a minute? I'm still concerned about Jonas's health and would like to ask him a few questions.'

Priscilla was very pale. Jonathan saw how her hands shook. When she caught his eye he winked at her broadly, and for the first time a little smile appeared on her mouth. Her fingers touched him urgently as he took the glass, and he pressed them deftly in return. Then with a murmur she left the room, walking with tiny grace, her dress flowing behind her. Jonas watched her, allowing Jonathan to see his wide soft smile, his air of indulgent adoration. 'Dear girl,' sighed Jonas. 'How she has brightened my days, and brought new life to an old, helpless body.'

'I bet,' said Jonathan. 'But what does Prissy get out of it?'

'My all,' said Jonas, in a deep tone. 'My all. My worship, my protection, and, at the end, my money.'

'Good. I love precious marriages like this. So rare. Prissy will still be young when you are gathered to your ancestors, Jonas. That should give you happiness, knowing that she can enjoy your money for a long time—though without the delight of your presence, of course.'

A dark and ugly look sparkled in the old man's eyes, and Jonathan saw his spirit, malign and treacherous and lying. Then it hid itself behind benignity again. 'Ah, yes,' he sighed. 'It is really one of the satisfactions of my days, to think of that.'

'I really love you,' said Jon. 'In a naughty world you are a shining light of virtue, Jonas. A light of peace and good-will towards men, blameless, tender, trusting, generous. Innocent, above all. Now that we are alone, Jonas, where did you get that arsenic?'

Jonas regarded him with smiling soft hatred. 'Now, Jon, please don't joke about such serious things.'

'I'm not joking, I assure you. Jonas, stop being so damned sanctimonious. I'm a doctor. Remember? I have only to make a few inquiries here or in other cities in the State, and I'll get the information I need. It will take a little time, and a few descriptions, and a little pressure, but I'll get it. Do you understand?'

Jonas smiled superbly. 'Really, Jon. If anyone bought any arsenic, anywhere—'

'It wasn't Prissy. I've already told that about. What's the matter? Do you feel ill?' Jonathan rose with pretended sudden alarm.

Jonas waved him back. He pulled his linen handkerchief from his pocket and wiped a sagging old face which was no longer pink. 'No, no, there's nothing wrong, Jon. Just a touch of the sun, perhaps.' His breath was now honestly harsh. 'I don't know what you're talking about, Jon. What is all this about arsenic? I wasn't poisoned.'

'So you weren't. I know you'll mention that occasionally. We have you down for acute indigestion with a touch of the liver. I made that emphatic on your chart.' He remained standing. 'Unless, of course you wish it to be known that you tried to poison yourself—you couldn't stand the wickedness in this old world, or something—and so took the arsenic in a moment of noble desperation.'

'I've thought of it!' Jonas's voice was all tremulous and full of dolorous music, 'I have thought of it!'

'Well, we all think of it occasionally. Only the stupid never contemplate suicide. But don't think of it again, Jonas old boy. Try to enjoy life.'

Jonas was much moved. He looked at Jonathan with gratitude. 'Dear boy, what a comfort you are to a poor old soul.'

'Indeed, I am. And I won't mention a word of this conversation, poor old soul, unless it becomes absolutely necessary, which I am sure it will not.'

'It will not, Jon, I give you my word. After all, it would not sound very nice if I mentioned that my doctor hinted I had poisoned myself, would it?'

'Oh, by then I'd have proof,' said Jonathan, with an airy gesture. 'Names, dates, descriptions. You know how people would laugh, don't you?'

Jonas drank slowly and appreciatively from his glass. 'Jon,' he said, wiping his lips, 'I don't think you truly love, do you?'

'Indeed, I don't,' said Jonathan with affability.

Jonas sighed. 'I have devoted my whole life to humanity, nurturing, offering, comforting—'

'Well, you can do that again. Send me five thousand dollars, by cheque to-morrow, for that tuberculosis hospital we have been discussing all this time.'

Their eyes locked together, Jonathan's amused and hard, the old man's vicious.

'Five thousand dollars,' said Jonathan. 'Not made out to me, but to the Hambledon Tuberculosis Hospital. Why, we'll have a plaque on the wall for you, dear heart! "Gift of Jonas Witherby, Founder." In the most prominent place, naturally. Perhaps with a bas-relief of you, with your fine patrician features, smiling your benevolent smile. Isn't that a lovely thought?'

A tear moistened Jonas's eyes as he considered, but the evil light in it did not diminish. He nodded. 'To-morrow, Jon, I give you my word.'

'Good. And let there be no more talk of poisoning, even by innuendo, dear heart.'

Jonathan saluted amiably, and left the room. He met the fearful Prissy in the hall. He whispered, 'Don't worry. I've stopped him. I think.' He kissed her cheek lightly.

After he was gone Jonas, with a very sprightly walk, went up to his bedroom. He gave a number to Central, speaking in his unctuous and loving voice. A few moments later a voice answered him, and he said, 'Kenton? Jonas Witherby here. Yes. When can we have our little talk?'

The still apprehensive Priscilla, not quite reassured by Jonathan, and always nervously suspicious these days, had followed her husband discreetly, and when he had closed his bedroom door she pressed her ear against it, and listened.

Jonathan rode rapidly out of town on horseback to his nearest farm, which began on the outskirts of the city and which was now being managed by Dr Thomas Harper. He took the narrow riding path and road along the river, not only because it was cooler here but because it was the shortest way to his farm. Thelma had written him recently that Tom seemed much improved, 'and able to take short rides every day.'

The island was partly behind him now. A little mist was rising from the water into the heated air, and the island seemed adrift, a faery place, and Jonathan thought of Jenny and Robert Morgan, and chuckled, but not very agreeably. He would have to corner the elusive Jenny very soon, and no more delicate approaches. Women were not responsive to delicacy, for they were robust and hearty creatures under all their flutterings and agitations.

Robert Morgan and Jenny Heger were only a quarter of a mile behind Jonathan. Robert had met the girl at the little dock on the mainland side, though he had wanted to go to the island and row her to the shore. However, when he arrived in his smart new buggy he found her waiting for him, diffidently smiling and silent. He knew nothing of women's clothing, but somehow he immediately guessed that her apparel was new, and he was delighted that she had gone to this trouble for him and cared enough to do so. She wore a frail white shirtwaist all tidily tucked from chin to waist, with frills, here and there, of white lace, and her skirt was of expensive white silk with a black patent-leather belt and a glittering buckle. She wore white stockings and slippers, and her ankles were occasionally visible as the wide skirt flared with her movements. Her head was covered with a new hat of Leghorn, a very pale gold, and heaped with snow roses of silk, and there were actually white gloves on her hands.

Her face was sunburned but she carried no parasol as a 'proper' young lady would have done. The extra colour in her cheeks and on her lips made her appear more vivid than usual. She was 'rosy' or 'dewy,' as his mother called sweating—a euphemism that made Robert laugh—and her upper lip was beaded artlessly with water, and her forehead too. She smelled of lavender soap and sachet. When she strode to Robert's buggy, still not speaking, she walked like an elegant young man, sure and free, not mincing as other girls minced, setting her feet down firmly yet not hard. She climbed in before he could help her. He thought that she wished to avoid his touch but saw at once that she was acting in full simplicity. He climbed in after her, picked up the reins, then smiled down into her eyes and noticed, again, the candour of her face and the dimple in the white chin.

'I brought a really nice lunch,' said Robert. 'The hotel put it up for me. We aren't quite settled, yet, my mother and I, in our new house, so we're still at the hotel. We expect to move into our house on Monday. Well, it's a nice lunch,

I think. Cold chicken and salad and buttered new bread and strawberry shortcake and cheese, and a good bottle of white wine, with goblets. I hope you enjoy it.'

'Yes,' said Jenny. She had naturally accepted the fact of the lunch, unaware that ladies usually prepare the picnic collations. It was the first time she had spoken, but at least she was smiling faintly and shyly at him, and studying him with the frankness of an honest child. Yet, for the first time, he wondered uneasily why she had really accepted his invitation. It was not quite in character for Jenny Heger, the young and frightened recluse about whom such appalling stories were told in the town.

They drove off along the river road. 'A wonderful day,' said Robert. 'I'm so glad you consented to go with me, Miss Jenny.'

She was silent. She was looking at the river as if she were all alone, and at the island. Robert drew the thin buggy cover over her clothing to protect her from the dust and she was not even aware of it.

'I found an admirable spot, when I was visiting patients the other day,' Robert went on. 'Very beautiful, very secluded. And very cool, even in this weather. With a view of the river, too.'

'That's nice,' said Jenny, in her strong clear voice, and then she looked at him with that lovely but uncertain smile. 'It was good of you to invite me, Doctor.'

He hesitated. His kind eyes smiled down at her. His red-gold moustache was very bright in the sun. 'It was my pleasure, Miss Jenny. But I hope it isn't exclusively my pleasure.'

She was unaccustomed to gallantries he saw at once, for she pondered his hint with amusing seriousness. Then she said, 'I like it, too. The only picnics I've ever gone to were those given by Aunt Marjorie. Mrs Ferrier, you know.'

'A charming lady,' said Robert.

'Yes,' said Jenny.

All at once the conversation died, to Robert's disappointment. But it was enough for him that Jenny was beside him, her elbow sometimes touching his sleeve as the buggy rolled over uneven places in the road. She exhaled freshness and youth and innocence. Then Robert knew that he had loved this girl from the very beginning, and he was deeply moved. Because of the dangerous and sudden intensity of his emotions he looked for easiness. He wondered what she liked, this

247

mysterious girl, and what amused her. He had heard she had had a good schooling, and then when she was fifteen her mother had hired a tutor for her for two years to complete that schooling. (There were tales about that also, in Hambledon.) Yet, she had gone nowhere. She had seen nothing of the world. The only point of reference between him, Robert Morgan, and Jenny Heger, was Jonathan Ferrier. But he did not wish to talk about Jonathan, above everything else.

It was Jenny who indirectly approached the subject. He saw that it was awkward, even painful, for her to initiate a subject, so he was not surprised when she stammered, 'Do you like Hambledon, Doctor?'

'Yes, very much. I could have remained in Philadelphia, and I was offered staff positions in New York and Boston, but I wanted a small town. I don't know why, Miss Jenny. But now I know, I think.'

He waited for her to ask for further elucidation, but she did not. She said, 'New York. Boston. Paris. London. Vienna. St Petersburg. I—I think of them often. I'd like to go, I think.'

'Perhaps you will, some day.' He thought with what joy he would take Jenny to those far-off places, and what he would show her. They would explore, for the first time, together.

'Yes,' said Jenny, but there was no conviction in her voice. She waited a moment and then with that painful difficulty she said, 'So, you will remain here.'

'Yes.' (Damn that monosyllable!)

'And Jon—Dr Ferrier—will truly go away?'

'Yes.' (He was falling into a helpless game.)

'Soon?'

'Yes.' (At least she was talking!)

'Where to?' asked Jenny. He was surprised that she was interested in a man she so obviously loathed. However, perhaps she was eager for him to get out of her sight.

'I don't know,' said Robert. (Why weren't they talking about himself, and, best of all, their own future?) 'I don't think, though, that he'll ever come back to Hambledon. Never again. I have a feeling his mother will go with him, too, for it's doubtful he'll ever remarry. The town treated him abominably, as you know.' Now he was curious to know her own reaction to the murder trial. She said nothing. So, he went on, 'How anyone can believe that Jonathan Ferrier killed his wife and —er—child, is beyond credibility.'

Jenny turned and looked at him gravely, and shook her

head. 'Jon never did that, Doctor. Never. He—he couldn't have— he was away at the time. Of course, I once read that anyone is capable of anything. But Jon didn't do that, he didn't do that.'

He was surprised at her mixture of sophistication and ingenuousness. 'I'm glad to hear you say that, Miss Jenny. But you and I make up a minority in this town, you know.'

'Yes.' She paused. 'I didn't think Jon was such a coward.'

'Coward?'

'Running away. He should stay—and fight.'

'I think so, too. But how can you fight cobwebs, even if they are poisonous?'

'I think he should,' said Jenny. Now her face was exceptionally pale under all that sunburn, and he could see the sudden whiteness around her mouth.

'I suppose you do,' he said with sadness. She jerked a little with her own surprise, and then, to his greater amazement she coloured violently and unbecomingly.

'What do you mean?' she demanded.

'The stories,' he said.

'About Jon? I don't believe them in the least!' Her voice was vehement.

Then it came to him that Jenny knew nothing about the tales concerning herself, and he was sad and freshly moved, and filled with the desire to protect her. But, why was her face so red now, and so almost challenging?

'Does Jon ever talk about me?' she asked. Her voice was trembling.

'Jon? Why no. Why should he?'

'Oh.' The colour left her face and she seemed to be relieved.

'He wouldn't talk about his relatives, anyway,' said Robert.

'I'm not his relative!' said Jenny. 'His brother is my step-father—but Jon is no relative of mine!'

She looked at the water and said, 'Isn't it beautiful? The sun on the sails, and the colour of the mountains and the water? I've seen so many paintings of far away places—the Rhine, the downs of Devon, the Seine, the Riviera, and the Orient. But none seems to me so beautiful as here, and I want to spend my life on my island.'

She looked at him with that touching candour of hers and said, 'You know, everyone thinks Papa built the castle for Mama. But he built it for me. It was a secret between us, so that Mama wouldn't feel neglected.' He couldn't tell in what direction her thoughts were flowing, but he was enchanted when she smiled a real smile this time and he saw her small and brilliant teeth. 'Mama and I had secrets, too. She said gentlemen did not appreciate intelligence in ladies and that it was the duty of ladies to play the fool to keep the gentlemen happy. She also said that a man never really forgives a woman for marrying him.' She laughed for the first time and he thought it an endearing and childlike sound. 'Mama deceived Papa, and Harald, and almost everyone else, into believing she was only comfortable and fluffy. But she was really very sharp.'

'I am sure,' said Robert, 'that it would be impossible for a stupid lady to have a daughter like you.'

She blushed and drew away from him a little, and her eyes were suspicious. Then they brightened with anxiety. 'What do you mean?' she asked.

'Why, Miss Jenny, you are the handsomest young lady I have ever seen in my life!' He spoke with deep sincerity, and Jenny watched him closely for a few minutes after he had spoken. Then she was smiling again.

'Do you honestly think so?' she asked, not in flirtation but with a real desire to know. 'That is, as children say, cross your heart and hope to die?'

He lifted his yellow-gloved hands and solemnly crossed his heart and Jenny was openly pleased. 'Why?' she asked, with disturbing directness.

'Didn't you ever look at yourself in a mirror?'

'Yes. Of course. I am very plain.'

He glanced at her with disbelief, but again she was perfectly sincere.

'Who told you that, Miss Jenny?'

'Why, Papa. And he was quite right. They used to call me a great gawk in school. You see, I am so tall and thin, and have big hands and feet—and I don't look well in pretty clothes. I'm not gracious, not charming. I don't know what to do with myself!'

Robert drew up the buggy under the shade of a giant elm, fastened the reins and turned fully and solemnly to the girl, and she instinctively shrank back from him a little. But he did not touch her. He said, 'Jenny, I want to tell you now that I've seen many beautiful girls and women in my life, in big cities over all the eastern part of the country, and there

250

is none who could match you. Did you ever ask yourself why I wished you to come with me to-day? Did you think it was my Christian kindness of heart?' He smiled into her eyes which were widening slowly. 'It was my selfishness. I wanted to be with a lovely woman, a great lady, and that is what you are, Jenny. A great lady.'

She pondered over every word he had said, weighing his truthfulness, his actual meaning, and finding nothing wanting at all. She looked faintly incredulous. She adjusted her hat, smoothed her gloves, bit her lower lip, but never took her eyes from his.

'Has nobody ever told you that before?' he asked.

'No. That is,' and she hesitated, 'two did, but I didn't believe them. I still don't. Oh, yes, Aunt Marjorie told me, too, but she is very kind and so I couldn't believe her. Truly, you don't find me repulsive?'

'Jenny!' He wanted to take this woman, who was still a child in her mind, in his arms and kiss her hard and repeatedly, but he knew that that would frighten and outrage her. He was so sensitive to her by now, so full of the acuteness of love. 'Jenny, you are as repulsive as a rose, as ugly as a young green tree, as hideous as a butterfly! Now, is that sufficient?'

She laughed reluctantly. 'Perhaps to you, and thank you,' she said.

He saw that she trusted him, and he was elated. He said after a moment, 'Who were the "two" who told you what I've told you in honesty?'

Now her blue eyes left him and she looked down at the dust-cover that lay over her knees. 'They don't matter. One was Harald, and the other was Jon.'

'Well, Harald should know. He's an artist, a painter, and they are very perceptive to beauty. And Jon—well, I understand he is quite a connoisseur of women.' He added this delicately, but it was apparent at once that she took his remark on its face, for she nodded.

'Mavis was the prettiest woman I ever saw,' she said. 'She was like the princess in the fairy-tales I read as a child. Rapunzel. The sleeping beauty. Cinderella. Snow White. She was all of them, Mavis. Of course she was a lot older than I was, four years. She was—dazzling. People always stared at her, absolutely hypnotised. I wanted to look at her for hours —but she was never still.'

'You mean, jiggling with her hands and her head, the way the ladies all do now—except you, Jenny? The fashionable jiggling, pretending to animation or something?'

She giggled. She actually giggled. He thought it an adorable sound. 'They do look as if they have palsy, don't they?' she said. 'No, Mavis wasn't like that. It wasn't that she was quiet. On the contrary. She laughed all the time, boisterously. It was the only ugly thing about her, and I thought how it spoiled her appearance. But others seemed to like it!' She shook her head in wonder. 'They always talked about Mavis's laugh, as if it were marvellous. Perhaps I was the one who was wrong. I don't like noisy people.'

'And Mavis was noisy?'

'Well, yes. I know that sounds unkind, but it is the truth. She was noisy. And cuddly. She was always cuddling against people, and laughing that raucous laugh of hers,' and now Jenny's voice rose with honest indignation. 'She would do that with Jon, when they were first married, and I felt sorry for him, for she embarrassed him. But no one else was embarrassed. I think Jon annoyed Mavis.'

'He's too severe, perhaps?'

'I never thought so.' She was again surprised. 'In fact, I began to think him frivolous, light-minded, superficial, since Mavis—died.'

There was no limit to the power she had of astonishing him. 'Jon—frivolous? He seems very bitter to me, and I've heard he was harsh, though I know better. He is the most unhappy man I've ever known. But grim men like Jon always make disastrous marriages and heaven only knows why.'

'Yes,' said Jenny, 'it was disastrous for both of them, Mavis and Jon.'

There are some who would call this gossip, thought Robert Morgan. But Jenny is as guiltless of the intent to gossip as an infant. She speaks whatever comes to her mind without malice or cruelty. Now he was afraid for her. She had no one in the world of her own, no way of protection, no wall against her vulnerability. Her only defence would be marriage, and he was more than ready to offer that defence. But he knew he must not alarm her.

'Jon is bitter because his friends believe he killed Mavis,' said Jenny. 'No one told me, but I know. Otherwise, he is jaunty, if you don't like the word "light-minded." You don't, do you? Oh, he was never afraid of anything. He despises

252

everything, and he was that way before Mavis died. He never took anyone seriously.'

For the first time it came to Robert disagreeably that their only real conversation so far, on this gorgeous day, had been of Jonathan Ferrier. He could not remember that he had instigated this conversation, but he did not like it. He preferred to talk about himself to Jenny, and he wanted to inspire her regard. So far, she had shown no open interest in him, though at least she was now talking and not merely answering 'yes.' That indicated trust, and the young man's heart rose as light as a bird.

Unfortunately, a surrey was approaching them on the narrow road, filled with four young women. They had just come round a bend, and now the air echoed with their gay laughter, their little squeals and their high and girlish voices. The horse trotted along briskly, the fringes on the surrey swayed, and the girls held their hats. Robert cautiously guided his horse to the extreme right of the road to let the equipage pass with its pretty burden. Then, as it was beside him, the driver halted, and he saw the pink dimpled face and auburn hair and sparkling eyes of Maude Kitchener. Her mouth was like a plump rosebud, but it stopped smiling when she saw his companion.

'Oh, Dr Morgan!' she trilled. 'How are you to-day? Oh, and do you know Betty Gibson, Susie Harris, Emiline Wilson? Girls, this is Dr Morgan—the gentleman I have been telling you about—' She stopped and blushed furiously. The girls eyed Robert with animated curiosity and some sly smiles, and it was evident, even to the young man, that perhaps Maude had been somewhat too confiding about him to her friends. In their turn the girls openly admired his magnificent apparel and his face, but when they glanced at Jenny the nasty smirks appeared on their young mouths, and Robert saw that, too. He had taken off his hat, and it lay on his knees.

'A pleasant ride, ladies?' he asked.

'We've been to lunch at Emiline's aunt,' said Maude. Her sweet voice was subdued. She regarded Jenny with trouble. 'How are you, Jenny?'

Jenny had become stiff and remote again. Her nod was jerky. 'Very well, thank you,' she replied, and the stammering note was back in her voice.

The other girls said nothing at all to Jenny but averted their eyes from her and talked in a lively fashion with the young

253

doctor, of whom they had heard so much, particularly from Maude who had hardly stopped talking of him all through lunch. They did not know whether to pity her or to be a little happy that the young man, whom she had hinted was 'much taken' by her and practically ready to propose, had found that unspeakable Jenny Heger more to his liking than Maude Kitchener, at least for this day. But then, everyone knew what that hussy was, and gentlemen will be gentlemen, even such a nice, handsome young man like this.

Robert was not so obtuse that he did not observe the snub given Jenny, and so it was he who put on his hat and lifted the reins and said good-day to the young ladies. He was the one who drove off first. The surrey moved off behind him with less vigour, he thought with some satisfaction. The only nice girl among them had been Maude Kitchener, and he felt warm towards her. Women!

'Really, that creature!' said Emiline Wilson. 'Whatever in the world does he see in her?'

'Guess!' said Susie Harris, with a naughty giggle. Betty Gibson hit her on the shoulder coyly and said, 'Don't be lewd, Susie.'

'If I had any interest in him at all,' said Emiline, in a meaning tone, 'I'd tell him all about her, that I would. It's disgraceful. He probably believes she's respectable. Poor man.'

'He hasn't been here long,' said Maude. Then she added, 'But of course Jenny is respectable! You mustn't be mean, girls. You know as well as I do that it is all lies that people say of Jenny. We went to school with her. If—if Dr Morgan likes her, it's no wonder. She's so very beautiful.'

The girls chorused 'No!' with loyal emphasis, and Maude was pleased.

'This is really a very stupid town,' said Emiline. 'I don't suppose anyone has invited Dr Morgan to dinner, except the Ferriers. Have they?'

All but Maude answered in the negative. She knew that her parents had invited Robert on many occasions, but he had been in the hospitals or on house calls or otherwise engaged. But he had promised to dine with the Kitcheners next Monday, and had expressed his gratitude to Mrs Kitchener. So Maude said, 'He's been so busy, but he is to have dinner at our house on Monday.'

The girls spoke their happy envy of Maude, and they all

began to laugh again. But Maude remembered how Robert had looked at Jenny before they had driven away, and she wanted to cry.

Robert found his promised spot a few minutes later. He turned his buggy up a rambling little side road, and it mounted steeply. Then at the top it was like a small and grassy knoll, with one huge oak in the very centre. Below them was brush and untended shrubbery, behind them was a lonely meadow, and before them lay the river scintillating in blue lights in the sun, and the mountains rising above it like a green barrier. Buttercups and wild daisies and Indian paintbrushes huddled in the thick warm grass, which was not too high though very dense. Robert held up his hand to Jenny and this time she took it to alight, and at the first touch he had had of her Robert was struck as by lightning and turned very pale. It was a moment before he could help Jenny to the step and then down to the grass, where she stood smoothing her white skirt with her gloved hands and looking about her with shy pleasure.

'Do you like it, Jenny?' he asked.

'Oh, it's wonderful,' she said. She took off her hat, and her hair, hastily pinned as usual, began to drop about her face. She tried to restore her attempts at a pompadour but it was useless, so with a shrug she merely shook out her hair and let it fall on her shoulders and down her back.

Now she began to laugh, uncertainly, as she helped Robert anchor the checked tablecloth on the grass, for here it was breezy under the tree. She ran about, finding good stones for anchoring, and brought them back gleefully in both hands. She showed keen interest in the food, laid the plates and the silver and polished the goblets with a napkin. Then she sat down, folding her legs like an Arab and laughed again with pleasure.

'What fun picnics are!' she exclaimed. 'Mama and I used to have them before she—married—Harald, and I was just a child. On the island, of course. We told each other lots of secrets, and the trees were so thick and the rose gardens were unbelievable. The rose gardens,' she added, and her face changed and she was not smiling any longer.

'Beautiful gardens,' said Robert. As the host, he filled Jenny's plate first and she stared down unseeingly at the large portions he had given her. He opened the wine bottle and poured the pale golden liquid into the glasses,

255

'What?' said Jenny, coming back with a start.

'What? Oh, I said your rose gardens are beautiful.'

Jenny picked up a fried chicken leg, eyed it absently, then began to eat it. Her mood appeared to pass. Fresh colour came up under her sunburn. The weight of her black hair fell across her ears, and her lashes gave another spiked shadow on the rose of her cheek. Robert could hardly eat for enchantment and new and deeper contentment. He had loved her for her beauty from the beginning, and for her redoubtable innocence. Now he loved her, besides, for what he had guessed about her, and her simplicity. He lifted his wine glass high, and her blue eyes followed it.

'To you, dear Jenny,' he said.

She picked up her own glass at once, smiled back at him, and said, 'To you, Doctor.' He wished she had shown some coquetry, and that she had called him by his Christian name. But still he was content. He had not dreamed at first that she would be so responsive to him, and so childishly happy in this picnic. He looked at the river which was not so blue as Jenny's eyes. He could smell pine near him, aromatic and exciting, and the grass gave off a hot fragrance sweeter than any manufactured perfume. Jenny was part of it. She was alone in this shining silence with him. There was no one else.

She drank the wine eagerly. 'Oh, this is delicious,' she said. 'I don't like it as a rule, but I do like this. Is it a French wine?'

He gave her the bottle to study its label, and was gratified to see that she was impressed. '1890,' she said. 'Eleven years ago. What a long time!'

'To you, perhaps. You were only nine then, weren't you, Jenny? But I was much older.'

She glanced at his young face and his luxuriant moustache, and then he saw another side of Jenny, subtle and amused. She smiled at him frankly, and shook her head, and the breeze lifted her hair and tossed it. 'You are really very young,' said Jenny, and he did not know whether to be pleased or displeased. 'You believe the world is good, don't you?'

He considered that, then nodded. 'Don't you believe the world is good, too?'

'No, I truly don't. People think I am foolish and ignorant, but I'm not. I listen. I hear. I see. I think. I read. I walk along by myself. I am never lonely—by myself. I watch the birds. Nothing very much surprises me.'

256

For some reason Robert thought of Jonathan Ferrier and did not know why. The thought came from nowhere, and it jolted him.

'No one but a fool would think you foolish and ignorant, Jenny.'

Again she gave him that amused and subtle smile. 'You must chatter all the time, in this world, and be doing something in a rush, or something you call important, or going somewhere very fast, or returning from somewhere just as fast, to be thought clever and sophisticated. But if you are contented with your own self, and don't like confusion and only your own thoughts, and the work you love to do, then you are mad, they say, or you don't like your fellow man, and are even unChristian.'

He had not thought her capable of making such a long statement, but as he saw the flush on her cheek and her empty glass he knew that the wine had taken her shyness from her, and that Jenny was herself with him, and he blinked his eyes rapidly.

He refilled her glass and she watched him with that touching pleasure. 'As for myself,' she said, 'I am content to be a nobody, going nowhere. That's the nice thing about being a nobody: you don't feel you have to go somewhere—and there's no somewhere, really.'

Now her face changed again, and she looked down into the wine glass with sudden melancholy. 'Nowhere,' she repeated. 'Nowhere at all.'

'Oh, come, Jenny. You are young and the world is open to you.'

'No,' she said. 'I'm afraid it opened, once, when I was sixteen, for about three minutes. Three whole minutes. And then it closed again, and that was all there was to it, and all there ever will be.'

'Tell me,' he said, wanting to know more and more about this enigmatic girl.

She shook her head. 'There's nothing to tell. It was all in my imagination.'

She put down her plate from her knee, and quickly drank the wine. In a more worldly woman it would have been a theatrical gesture, for effect. In Jenny it was swift desperation. And again, for apparently no reason, Robert thought of Jonathan Ferrier.

'Jenny,' he said, 'why don't you go away for a while, to see something of what you should see?'

'Oh, I can't, Doctor. I couldn't leave my island. But if Harald ever leaves permanently, which he won't, then I could leave it for a little while myself.'

That sounded strange to Robert, and he frowned. 'You see,' said Jenny, with all earnestness, 'I couldn't leave the island alone to him. Could I?'

'Why not?'

'Well, when I came back it wouldn't be the same to me.'

He was baffled. 'One day, when you are married, you will leave the island and never go back except for a visit.'

'No. I'll never leave the island. And I'll never get married.'

A vague dimness came over the earth for Robert and nothing was very bright any longer. He said, 'You'll change your mind, Jenny, when you find someone who loves you.'

To his horror and concern he saw her eyes fill with tears, and she shook her head. She put the empty wine glass on the cloth and it rolled from her and she watched it.

'Hasn't anyone spoken of—well, love to you, Jenny?'

She only shook her head over and over.

He wanted to say, 'I love you, Jenny, my sweet Jenny. Let me tell you how much I love you.' But he knew it was too soon. He would only alarm her away, send her off into her silences again. There was someone else like that whom he knew. Jonathan Ferrier. The slightest extension of stronger friendship or personal concern given by anyone to him sent him off into one of his cold remarks or a ribald aphorism. He rejected the close touch as much as Jenny feared it and would reject it. Robert did not like the resemblance.

Jenny had taken a long grass in her hand and was pulling it through her fingers. Her head was bent and he could not see her face.

'Won't it be very hard for you to take all Jon's practice, when he has gone?' she asked. 'It's a very large practice, I heard.'

'I hope to do my best,' he said, and heard the stiffness in his own voice.

'Yes,' said Jenny. She wound the grass over her fingers and pulled it hard.

'He may come back from time to time to help me, if he can.'

She looked up so suddenly that he was startled. 'Did he promise you that?'

'No. He didn't. He said that when he left here he was finished with the town forever, and with everyone in it.'

'But you feel he will come back?'

'No, I don't, Jenny. Why should he? He didn't abandon the town. The town abandoned him, and for no good and worthy reason.'

'Did he—recently—say he would never come back?'

'Only this morning.'

Jenny drew a long breath and he heard it. 'But he has his house and his farms.'

'I hear he is looking for a buyer for his farms, except for one. And the house is really his mother's. No, he won't be back. He is leaving before the first of September, he told me a few days ago.'

'Four weeks,' said Jenny.

'Yes.'

He was bored and unaccountably disturbed by the conversation. He let himself lie back on the grass, his arms folded under his head. He did not know why he said, 'Then, again he may take someone with him. A lady calls him up at least once a week and he sounds very pleased to hear her. It isn't a patient, I know. He uses his "personal" voice when he talks to her.'

The sky was suddenly blotted out for him by Jenny's head, bending over him.

'A woman?' she said, and there was deep shadow on her face. 'A woman calls him?'

'Yes. I don't know who she is, Jenny. I do know he calls her "dear".'

'Oh.' Then Jenny said in a flat voice. 'Perhaps he is thinking of marrying her.'

Robert deliberately yawned. 'Who knows? Why don't you lie down, too, Jenny, in this soft thick grass, before we go back?'

She did not hesitate at all. She stretched herself beside him, and he could hear her light breathing, and could see her profile. It was blank and pale. Then she closed her eyes and her head was like a fallen statue's in the grass. He felt the poignancy, the lost and broken abandonment of it. Something had gone wrong in this halcyon day which had begun so vividly and with so much joyful contentment, and he did not know what it was.

He saw her hand near his hip, and he carefully lifted one of his arms from behind his head and let his hand wander to hers, and then over her fingers. He expected her to snatch her hand away, but she did not. Nor did she open her eyes or move. Her fingers were cool under his, but still it was enough for him, at this time, just to hold her hand and to feel again the sweet contentment of his love for her. He wished they needed never to go home, and that they might spend eternity here like this, with the wind blowing over them and the dark green tree arching over them, and the butterflies in the grass, and the faint sound of the lighted river just slightly disturbing the scented air.

He drowsed. He began to have a curious half-dream or fantasy. He thought that he awakened and when he did so Jenny was not there, and it was autumn, and the bronze and red leaves were falling all about him, and the river roared, and he was full of cold desolation for he knew he would never see Jenny again, and that she had gone away forever.

He came awake with a violent start. Jenny indeed was not beside him. But she had gathered up all the dishes and the linen and had put them neatly in the basket, and she was standing, her back to him, looking at the river and winding up her hair.

Her back was to him. He could see the long and slender lines of her figure, the lithe grace of her waist, the fine modelling of her shoulders and arms. She had forgotten him. What she was thinking of he could not remotely guess, but he knew that she was lost in her own dreams, or thoughts, as he had been lost in his. Her hands pinned up her hair now. Her arms dropped to her sides. She sighed, and turned.

'Well,' he said, 'It seems I fell asleep.'

'Yes.'

'It must be late.'

Jenny looked at the watch pinned to her shirtwaist. 'Five o'clock,' she said. Her face was quite still and indifferent, but when he caught her eyes she gave him, again, her shy and diffident smile. 'It's late.'

'Not very.' He hesitated. 'Jenny, will you have dinner with me?'

She replied with haste, 'Oh, I couldn't!'

He did not ask why. He got up, found his coat and put it

on. He brushed himself down. He put on his hat. Jenny watched him, and when he glanced at her she was smiling gently, as one smiles at a child of whom one is fond. 'I want to thank you for a lovely day, Doctor,' she said.

'Jenny, why don't you call me Robert, or Bob?'

'Very well, Robert.' He had never heard his name said before like that, or so it seemed to him. He was quite cheered. They went to the buggy, and found that the horse had eaten all his oats, and they climbed into the vehicle and turned homeward. They were half-way to Hambledon when Robert said, 'You forgot your hat! We'll go back at once.'

'No, no. Please. It doesn't matter at all. It really does not.'

And she means it, thought Robert. Has she accomplished something with the hat, and her new clothes? The thought was very queer to Robert, himself, and yet he could not shake it off. He could hardly speak the rest of the way, and Jenny made no remark. The world was less glowing to Robert now, but he was still resolutely planning to meet Jenny again, and very soon.

'You will go somewhere with me again, Jenny, in the near future?'

'Yes. Oh, yes.'

He was so elated that he wanted to bend towards her and kiss her cheek. But she was looking at the gardens along the way and seemed to be absorbed in them. They arrived at the little dock, hardly more than a plank or two, where the island boats waited. There was only one left. 'Harald must be home,' said Jenny, and she appeared disappointed.

Robert was helping her out of the buggy when they heard the brisk tattoo of horse's hoofs, and there was Jonathan Ferrier on his horse, looking down at them and smiling broadly. He touched his hat with his crop and said, 'How was the picnic?'

'Splendid,' said Robert, and felt less cordial to Jonathan than usual. 'Here, Jenny, take my hand.' She did so, in silence, and Jonathan watched her descend as if her every movement was intensely interesting to him.

'How did you enjoy it, Jenny?' he asked.

Jenny had jumped to the ground, she did not know where to look. As if involuntarily pulled, her eyes rose to look at Jonathan. And then Robert saw the deep and ugly crimson on her face, the heavy tears in her eyes, and her trembling chin. She stood like that, stricken, and she and Jonathan could not look away from each other, and Robert saw it all, and he knew.

Jenny, at last, walked towards the boat and Robert followed her on legs that felt like stone. Yes, he knew. He knew now why Jenny had gone with him. She had gone to hear him, Robert, speak of Jonathan Ferrier, and give all news of him. She could ask him, with openness, things which she could not ask his mother.

'Let me row you over, Jenny,' said Robert and his voice was dull.

'No. Please. I like to row,' said the girl, not looking at him. She jumped into the boat. She still did not look at him. But just as she rowed away she did look once again at Jonathan, and the crimson was still in her face and her mouth was shaking. Robert watched until she was only a dark figure on the gleaming golden water of the evening river. He forgot Jonathan. When he turned Jonathan was still there, on his horse.

'I wouldn't,' said Jonathan, 'take Jenny too seriously, if I were you.' And then he touched Robert lightly but smartly on the shoulder with his crop, and rode off.

The jocular blow stung Robert. Had it really been jocular, or friendly? Robert looked after Jonathan until he had disappeared. Jenny, he thought. Jenny, I'm not going to give up. I don't know what this is all about, Jenny, but he isn't the man for you, nor are you the woman for him. I won't give up, Jenny, I have something more wholesome and something more of life to give you than a dangerous man who will soon have no home of his own. I have youth to give you, and hope, and peace, and some fun and laughter, and travel, and I have all my love and no terrible memories. From those, I will protect you.

CHAPTER 10

Jonathan had just left the operating room at St Hilda's where he had watched Robert Morgan perform an operation, and had assisted. In the corridor he met a fairly new member of the staff of whom he strongly approved, the gynaecologist, young Philip Harrington. 'I'd like to talk to you in private,' Philip said. 'Let's look in the lounge.'

The doctors' lounge was empty, for it was lunch-time, and the two young men sat down in comfortable chairs near the windows. Phil had lumbered to them, and when he turned to Jonathan his usually buoyant and amiable face was disturbed and uneasy.

'Don't tell me,' said Jonathan, 'that you have another girl whom you've knocked up and you can't get rid of her.'

'Be serious for once,' said Phil. 'This concerns you, not me.'

Since his arrest Jonathan had become familiar with a sudden sick dropping in his chest, something which he had never experienced before in his brave life. He lit a cigarette and watched Phil Harrington. 'Well, tell me,' he said.

'I wish to God I could come to you with facts and conversations and "he said" and "they said", and all that, and with dates, but I can't, Jon. I began to suspect something was in the wind when the other fellas would stop talking when I came up on them, because they know I am your friend, and once or twice I heard your name. It's sticky. I keep getting side looks and smirks and questions about how you are these days, as if they don't see you in the hospitals as much as I do.'

'Hum,' said Jonathan.

'It's even more obvious at the Friends',' said Phil. 'I wish to God there was something definite I could tell you, but I think there's some danger in the wind for you, Jon.'

Jonathan thought of the malignant letter which had been delivered to him by messenger. He said, 'I wouldn't worry, Phil. After all, no matter what they say or what evidence they think they have, I can't be tried the second time for the same crime. Double jeopardy. Anyway, I'll be out of here in a few weeks, for ever. That ought to satisfy them.'

'They know you're going, Jon. But this thing has blown up

very recently.' He paused and frowned at his big competent hands. 'It's worse than months ago, if that's possible. There's a kind of elation in the air among the fellas who never liked you. You know them. They were the ones who were almost out of their minds when you were acquitted.'

'I know.' The sick and fallen feeling in Jonathan's chest became stronger. And then with it came a deep and bitter anger and the white folds sprang out about his mouth.

'There's nothing anyone can do to me,' he said. 'I'm financially independent of my profession; I'm a rich man, with sound investments and property. So they can't hurt me in my pocket. They can't injure my reputation, for I haven't any here, and be damned to reputation anyway. They can't take away my patients, because I have sold my practice. So what can they do to me?'

'I hate conjectures,' said Phil.

'Well, what do you "conjecture"?'

'Jon, so help me, I don't know. It's just a feeling I have.' He got up and put his hands in the pockets of his untidy trousers and lumbered heavily up and down for a few moments, and Jonathan thought he would be one of the few people in Hambledon whom he would miss. Phil stopped in front of him and looked down gravely. 'I smell danger,' he said. 'It's the kind of inner smell I get about a patient even before I pick up the scalpel. A feeling that something's wrong though all previous indications have suggested this is going to be a very simple and uneventful operation. I had a young woman last week with what all examinations seemed to show had just a cystic ovary, and the uterus was clean and healthy. But when I took the scalpel and looked down at her unconscious face—a nice healthy-looking face, plump, too—I knew there was something not so pure and pretty going on here. And, by God, I was right. The poor girl had a carcinoma, and the damned thing had spread—way up.'

'So, you think there's something cancerous going on around me.'

'Don't smile, Jon, but that's exactly what I think.'

'And not a single word or hint to prove it.'

Phil sat down, thrust out his legs straight before him, pushed out his big red lip and stared at his boots. A shaft of light touched his thick blond hair, and he looked like a troubled schoolboy, for he had round large features, full of young health and vitality.

'Well, there was just something a couple of days ago. I was passing old Louis's office and he was talking to someone behind the shut door, and he was yelling, and we always try to listen when Louis yells. He was shouting, and I caught your name, but that's about all, except that he did say "don't believe it." If I hadn't been uneasy for some time I wouldn't have thought a thing about it, but I went back down the hall and waited. And then out of Louis's office came a sweet-faced old man with white hair and that scoundrel, Senator Campion. Old Louis just stood on the threshold and glowered at them, and then he slammed the door right on their heels.'

'Good for Louis,' said Jonathan, but his voice was absent. 'And that was all?'

'Thinking back, I heard Louis saying that something was "beamish," and that's one of Lewis Carroll's coined words, isn't it, from *Alice in Wonderland*. Now, beamish means gladsome, if I remember, and smiling, and shining, all at the same time. He was bellowing then, and why was he doing that when things were so "beamish"?'

Jonathan suddenly sat upright. 'Beamish?' he repeated. 'Was he talking about a—a woman? A patient, perhaps of mine?'

Phil shook his head. 'I don't know, Jon. I just know that Louis looked as if he was about to have a stroke, there on the threshold, and Campion was as rosy as could be, and grinning, and the old man—'

'You never met Jonas Witherby, did you?'

'Witherby?' Phil thought. 'Oh. Once. A couple of years ago. And I've seen his photograph in the newspapers when he's been sponsoring something or other, or laying a cornerstone. Yes, by God, it was Witherby!' He paused. 'Now look, Jon, maybe it means nothing at all. Maybe I just thought I'd heard your name from Louis. I've been on tenterhooks about you for the last few weeks.'

'Perhaps,' said Jonathan. He shrugged. 'Don't worry. I'm not going in to old Louis and ask him anything and so get you in trouble. It could be nothing at all.'

'Sure,' said Phil. 'Oh, the last thing Campion said before he had the door slammed on him was, "We'll bring you the depositions first. Thought it was only fair".'

'Well, never trouble trouble until trouble troubles you, as the old saw is,' said Jonathan.

'If it weren't for the smirks I've been getting and your

265

enemies asking about you, I wouldn't be so nervous, Jon. But maybe I've been building up something from nothing. You know how it is in a hospital, among the staff and other doctors. They hear the slightest rumour, mostly without truth behind it, and they spread it all around fast. Never saw such gossips as doctors. They must do it to relieve the strain, or something.'

'But it's worse at the Friends'?' asked Jonathan, thinking of Humphrey Bedloe.

'Yes, thicker, but still just that—feeling. Do you want me to scout around?'

The thought of cumbersome Phil Harrington being subtle and indirect made Jonathan smile. 'Don't bother, Phil. Just keep your ears open, will you? Though damned if I can think of anything they can do to me now.'

'I will, Jon. I will. Don't worry yourself.'

He went back to the offices in a murderous state of mind. He told himself that he was imagining things, but now he recalled that for the last two or three weeks his colleagues had indeed either been avoiding him, or greeting him coolly, or not stopping for chats in the corridors. He had thought that was because he was already no longer one of them, and that he was leaving. He had few real friends among them, very few indeed. Had he intended to remain, he had thought, they would have treated him as always. But he was a departing guest, and they were remaining at home, and what had they in common now? No more hospital gossip, no more attending at operations, no more joint consultations, no more familiar ground.

He had thought that was all. But Philip Harrington had brought him that sullen sinking illness in his guts again. It was his conviction that in his case it would have been better if he had not known. Being forewarned was all very well for the soldier who was staying in his fortress, but it was irrelevant for one who was already marching away with his bastillions to safety. 'The hell with them all,' he thought. 'What can they do to me?'

Then he recalled 'beamish.' Edna Beamish, the rich and hysterical young widow, who had been so anxious to pay her bill, and which he had refused to tender? He thought of the doctor and the lawyer who had visited him. Well, what about it? He had not accepted any money for an incomplete examination. Phil could have been mistaken. He had listened outside

266

a shut door, a dangerous thing, a thick shut door. Possibly Louis had not said 'beamish' at all. Squeamish, perhaps. Campion could make anyone squeamish, and Jonathan now recalled, with a loud laugh, that Louis had not wanted him to be appointed United States Senator, and had so written to the State Legislature, he having a better man in mind. Campion had probably never forgotten, and perhaps was pressing Louis on some matter, and Louis was 'squeamish.' Old Witherby and Campion were great friends. No doubt Campion had taken Witherby along as support. As for Phil hearing Jonathan's name being mentioned it could possibly have been half a dozen 'Johns' and not Jonathan Ferrier at all.

The elderly spinster at the typewriter gave him a telegram when he arrived. Jonathan did not like telegrams on principle. He opened it, and his premonition was confirmed.

'Must inform you with sorrow that my dear husband, Jeffrey Holliday, died last night in the sanatorium in Louisiana. Unsuspected nodules had invaded his throat and though desperate measures were employed he suddenly suffocated. He had been doing well, far better than expected, thank you, Jon. If this accident had not occurred we should have been so happy as always. But we have had these weeks together and they must last me a lifetime. Jeff must be buried here as you know. Pray for him, and for me, too. Elizabeth.'

Jonathan stood with the telegram in his hand and he thought of his friend and the valiant loving woman who had married him, and he felt ill with sadness. Only two days ago he had received a letter from Jeffrey, a buoyant letter full of hope and contentment and the surety that he would be eventually cured.

Jonathan thought of Jeffrey's hysterical mother, Elsie Holliday. He felt pity for her. She had lost everything she had. He did not know that at that very moment she was sitting in Louis Hedler's office, broken with anguish, holding the telegram she had received, and that she was accusing Jonathan of 'having sent my boy to die down in some pest-hole in Louisiana!' If he had known he would not have cared, for his own grief was heavy.

The spinster lady cleared her chaste throat. 'There is a veiled lady waiting for you in your office, Doctor. I told her there were no office hours until six o'clock, but she insisted! Really! Said she was a friend and this was a personal matter.'

Jonathan went into the inner office. A small and fragile

young lady waited for him in a dark blue linen suit and white frilled blouse and dark straw hat over which she had drawn a thick black veil to conceal her face. But he knew her at once.

'Well, Prissy!' he said. 'Take that damned tent from your face, will you? You attract more recognition with it than without it.'

She threw back the veil and he saw the reason for it. Her face was very white and she had given up the paint pots since she had married Jonas Witherby and her eyes were red with sleeplessness and not with tears. He sat down near her and took her black-gloved hand and it was trembling. 'Don't tell me the old bastard accidentally took another dose of arsenic and did himself in! That would be happy news, indeed.'

She tried to smile. Her nice mouth was very pale and dry. 'No. Oh, I wish he was dead! How could I have been such a fool to marry him? Just for money, as if I hadn't enough! That's greed for you, Jon.'

'It's the old desire of women to be respectable, though God knows why they should care so long as they're comfortable and having a fine time of it. Well, what is the matter, Prissy? You aren't ill, are you?'

'No.' She fumbled in her purse, took out a scented handkerchief and pressed it to her mouth. She regarded him with pain. 'It's you, Jon.'

He frowned, and again the weak and plunging sickness hit his middle. 'What's wrong now?'

'Do you remember when you came to see Jonas recently, when I was so afraid of him? Well, after you left he went up to his bedroom and closed the door and I don't know why I should have listened to him telephone. I never did before. He was calling Senator Campion, and he said they should have a talk, a little talk. And then he said, "But we have to make very, very sure, Kent, and build up quite a case, here and there, so Ferrier will be finished once and for all." That's what he said, Jon. "Finished, once and for all, not only in the State but in the whole country, too".' She gave a little dry gasp. Then she took out a little golden case in which she kept her violet-scented Turkish cigarettes, and Jon lit it for her. Even over his anger and consternation he remembered the odour of those cigarettes in Prissy's little house, in her tasteful and gracious parlour where she met her friends, and friends they were.

'Oh, Jon, what did you ever do to the old son of a bitch,
268

that he should try to hurt you? Oh, you've joked with him and made fun of him to his face, but he always laughed and seemed to enjoy it.'

'I don't think he did, Prissy, and I never intended that he should. I let him know that there was one in this town who knew all about his pious lies and sweet mouthings and Christian tolerance and soft pattings-of-arms, and tender voice.' He got up, walked about slowly, then stood behind his desk, staring down blankly at it, then rubbing a little dust with one dark finger. Prissy watched him with acute and loving anxiety. 'A man will forgive you if you catch him in larceny, or even in a great lie, or if you best him in business or undercut him or rob him, or even if you run off with his wife or ravish his daughter. But he'll never forgive you for catching him out in hypocrisy, or calling him a psalm-singing rascal to his face. After all, he's spent a lifetime polishing up his public image as a saint, and garlanding it, and gilding it with a halo, and he washed that image's feet until they are as white as snow and arranged every damned fold in its heavenly toga. From childhood he has practised the saintly voice as sedulously as a singer practises, until every modulation is full of music and prayerful sanctity and as round as an organ note. And then comes along a suicidal idiot like me and knocks the plaster image over and it cracks, and out crawl the black smelly worms of pure iniquity for everyone to see. No, Prissy. A man never forgives that.'

'But Jon, I've known a lot of bad men, and they even enjoyed being told they were bad—'

'But no one who pretended that he had the personal Ear of the Lord, Himself. Old Jonas is a disaster, as I don't need to tell you. He's destroyed more people with his sweetness and light and loving voice and ways than a maniac will do with poison or a gun. And even his victims will tell you, with tremolos, that "Jonas is such a good man, such a saint!" It wasn't his pawing fault that catastrophe happened to you, or you are sick at heart, or undone, or broken, or despairing, or scared out of your wits by menacing shadows. Oh, no. It was really your own fault. Jonas did everything he could to help you. Wasn't he always there, purring and fondling and sighing, and advising? Yes, indeed.'

'I wish there was a way of getting away with murder!' said Prissy through her clenched white teeth. She beat her small knees with her gloved hands. Her large blue eyes flashed.

'So do I. I've thought the law was most unfair about murder,' said Jon. 'Murder is as deep an instinct in the human soul as self-preservation, or sex, and just as valid and perhaps just as healthy. After all, our cave ancestors practised it with fervour and thought nothing of it. Kill or be killed. That still lies under our civilisation, in spite of religion, and those who deny it are cowards afraid to face the truth or ashamed of it. Well, I'm not ashamed of my impulses to murder.'

Jon came back to her and sat down.

'Jon, what do you think the old—scoundrel—is trying to do to you?'

'I don't know, my love. I wish I did.'

'Why don't you go to him and ask?'

'And cause you trouble? No, Prissy. Besides, he'd just give me that darling haunted look of his, his precious innocent look, and be all bewildered and heart-broken. He might even burst into tears! No, Prissy, don't even think of leaving him. He can't live for ever. Even the Devil gets impatient for his own at last and one of these days, soon I hope, you will be a rich and happy widow.'

She was so deeply distressed for him that he made himself smile and he took her hand again. 'Dear Prissy, I can fight my own battles, and what you've told me is not news to me. They can scheme and plot, but they can't hurt me, dear.'

'Truly, Jon?'

'Truly.'

She kissed him, and he kissed her pleasurably in return, and saw her out, veiled again, and Miss Forster stopped her typing and was full of curiosity. Before Jon went back into his office, she said, 'Doctor, I deposited two large cheques in your account three weeks ago, for examinations you gave two ladies last November—before—before—'

'Before my trial, dear. Yes. When did the money come in?'

'Oh, I forgot. They weren't cheques. They were cash. Should I have put it in Dr Morgan's account, seeing he bought your practice?' She looked as if she were about to cry, for she was very devoted to Jonathan.

'Well, no. They were old accounts. How much?'

'One was for fifty dollars, the other for seventy-five.' She consulted her books. 'A Miss Louise Wertner, and a Miss Mary Snowden. I receipted the bills and they took them away. Then I wanted to make a note in their folders, but there were no folders in your files.' She frowned worriedly. 'I know you throw away old cards and folders, Doctor, but you should wait at least three years. You never know.'

'Never know what? We don't have income tax any longer, dear heart, to pay for any war. No use cluttering up your files.' He recalled that he had thrown away Edna Beamish's record, too, and for some reason he felt a vague disquiet.

'Well, anyway,' said Miss Forster, with disapproval. She was very meticulous. 'Do you recall those young women, Doctor?'

'From last November, with this place crowded to the eaves every day? And I also had other things to think about, if you recall. It was a time that could be lightly referred to as "trying".'

'Yes. But you must have seen them often, to have such large bills.'

'They do seem large, don't they? They were typed on my letterhead, were they?'

'Yes, indeed, Doctor. And typed with this very Oliver. The "d" is always crooked. It spoils the look of letters, reports and—'

'Take it up with Dr Morgan and nag him into buying you a fine new Underwood. You deserve it, dear, after all these years with the Oliver.'

She smiled at him dryly, and he went into his office and sat down and began to think. He forgot Miss Forster and her worries. Jonathan went over in his mind what Phil Harrington had told him, and Prissy. Vague, but disagreeable. There was no doubt that his enemies were plotting something, and he could find no area in which he was vulnerable. Then he thought, But who is invulnerable to malice? He shrugged. Now he found an acid pleasure in speculating on what his enemies were up to, including Kenton Campion. They knew that the town was driving him out, or that he could no longer endure living in it. What more did they want? His licence had been restored to him the moment he was acquitted. (They had had no right, the State Medical Society, to insist on its revocation before the conclusion of the case, and he could have caused them some unpleasant moments, or he could have sued for malicious mischief and punitive damages, but he had been only too glad to drop the matter, even though the newspapers had been gleeful enough to print the news of the revocation of his licence in large type, and be damned to the unlawfulness of it.)

Malpractice. Was some unknown former patient, man or woman, about to sue him for malpractice? The procedure, in such a case, was for an attorney to approach a doctor and ask for an out-of-court settlement first, 'to save notoriety and money and fees and costs.' Besides, he could not recall a dissatisfied patient, or one who had complained. 'The hell with the Campions and all the rest of them,' he said aloud.

He thought again of Jeffrey Holliday, and then he wrote out a cheque for Father McNulty, and added a note: 'You knew Jeff, I believe, and he is dead now, and so I am enclosing my cheque for twenty-five dollars as an offering, and hope that you will mention him in your prayers. And, by the way, I have a large old house on Fordham Street, near St Leo's, now empty, and it is yours—for that residence for nuns you are plotting to bring in for your confounded parochial school, if you can raise a bank loan. This is no incitement for you to harass me for further funds.'

The mere writing of that flippant note to a young man of whom he was truly fond, and whom he respected, unaccountably lifted Jonathan's spirits. Now he would really have to corner Jenny and persuade her into a quick marriage, and then leave Hambledon with her.

Softly whistling, he went into his examination rooms, clean and empty and white. There, in the left corner of the second room was one of his big shining cabinets. It was filled with instruments, including the most complex for operations. These had been the gift of his father on the occasion of his entering medical school, and each fine steel instrument was engraved with his name in a flowing script. In those days every surgeon had his own personal instruments, engraved like these, which he carried with him, but since then the majority of hospitals supplied their own for surgeons, a progress towards asepsis in the operating room. Now these glittering instruments, for which his father had proudly paid a considerable fortune—they had silver handles, many of them, and silver sheaths—were unnecessary, including the large morocco leather bag in which they had originally been carried. Jonathan had used them but four times in his surgical practice. They were anachronistic. He had often thought of sending them to some poor priest-physician-surgeon, and now was the time to think of donating the whole expensive outfit to the Missions.

As they were so costly Jonathan kept the key to this cabinet among his other keys. He stood before the cabinet and stared at the brave and shining array. That instrument for opening the skull: its form had not been changed for thousands of years and was almost a replica of the instrument the ancient Egyptians had used. Fine old boys, the ancient practitioners. Modern medicine had hardly improved on them. There was even a high forceps of a sort for difficult births. They had been reinvented again only a few years ago.

Then he noticed a little gap on one shelf. He bent closer. Some instrument was missing. He tested the door; it was locked. But someone had taken an instrument from the cabinet. He went into the other examination room, frowning, wondering if Robert Morgan could have done this, and then he searched the other room, also. It was foolish to suspect Robert. He had high instincts of privacy, and besides, he did not need these particular instruments. The other examination room had a host of ordinary ones for office procedure, though not for major surgery. Jonathan frowned. When was the last time he had opened this cabinet? A year? Two years? Once a year he carefully dusted the instruments himself, because of their value and their association. Had he done that last year? He could not remember.

He stood and frowned and considered, looking at the empty space. Someone had tried to move slender instruments together to conceal the spot, but its impression was on the original white satin which his father had insisted be laid on the glass shelves. A narrow long depression. Now, what was it? Jonathan slowly turned over in his mind all the instruments, counting them, thinking of them. Then he knew. It was a curette.

Why would anyone want a curette, and who had taken it? It was a sharp and chancy instrument, and had to be used with the utmost care or a womb could be punctured when the products of spontaneous abortion, or a miscarriage, had to be removed. Special training was needed for the use of a curette. Only in cases which threatened sepsis did a man use it, or if there was danger of a haemorrhage.

Jonathan minutely examined the depression where the curette had lain, and saw that it was faintly peppered with dust. So, the instrument had been gone a considerable time, and not lately. He went out to Miss Forster and said. 'Has anyone, unauthorised, been in my offices when I wasn't present, or Dr Morgan absent?'

'Why, no, I'd never permit that, Doctor! I believe I know
273

my duties! Of course, there was that veiled lady who claimed to be a friend—'

'No, no, dear. I should think several months ago, at least.'

'Never!' said Miss Forster, with emphasis. 'Why, is something missing, Doctor? After all, there are prowlers—'

'Who had my key, of course, and took only one instrument, and then carefully relocked my cabinet and restored my key.'

Miss Forster seemed ready to cry, so Jonathan patted her shoulder, told her it was probably a mistake, his mistake, and went out for his horse and his ride to his farm.

A grey heat-haze hung over the cities of the valley. No rain had fallen for nearly three weeks and the river was low and tributary streams were dry in their beds, with boulders roundly blazing in the sun. Lawns, browned in town, but on the mountain sides where springs and deep brooks still spurted the grass was green and flowers burned. The island, in the quiet and sinking river, was cooler than the mainland, for the breeze did ruffle the trees and enter the open windows. But the water had a brazen look, molten and still, and seemed to exude heat by itself, though the sky was far and pale blue and burning. The springs that fed the earth kept the grass green and the trees glistening in leaf and the gardens flourishing, but every stone was hot and the little castle seemed to palpitate as if afire inside. Dust ran in little twirls along the paths, and there was a fetid smell from the various ponds. The boats lay on barely wet stones and had to be pushed far out into the water before they floated.

Jenny sat in the library reading, with the shutters half-closed. The large long room, in its duskiness, gave the illusion of coolness, but her flesh stuck to the leather upholstery and her face was damp. She wore a thin brown skirt of linen and a severe shirtwaist, open at the throat, and she had pinned her hair high on her head for coolness and it rose in a large untidy black mound over her pale face. Harald never came into this room, and so to her it was a sort of sanctuary, just as she had small hidden grottoes on the island where she often sat, and about which Harald did not know, he not having much curiosity about the island.

The library door opened, and to Jenny's consternation and anger Harald entered, his handsome face reserved though he smiled affably enough when his eyes met Jenny's vexed ones.

He held a sheaf of papers in his hand. When Jenny jumped up to leave, he said, 'Please give me a moment. This is very important—to you, Jenny. To you. They are legal papers.'

'Consult my lawyers,' said Jenny, closing her notebooks and preparing to leave.

'I already have. And these papers are the result. For God's sake, Jenny, this is most important for you.'

'Nothing you have to say—' said Jenny, but she did not run out. She watched him darkly as he continued to advance into the room.

'It isn't what I "say," Jenny, it is what your lawyers and mine, say.' He sat down near a table. 'Sit down. Please.' His hazel eyes studied her gravely, and they shone with seriousness, and Jenny was reluctantly impressed in spite of herself. She sat down stiffly on the edge of her chair and tightly folded her hands on her knee. She stared rigidly at a point on his broad white forehead, and waited, filled with repulsion and hatred.

Harald picked up the papers and studied them, and did not look at her. 'Jenny, you know I don't like this island. I detest that part of your mother's will which states that I must spend at least seven consecutive months here, or I lose the very nice income from her large estate, which is held in trust for you and which will be yours when I die. My income is thirty thousand dollars a year, sometimes considerably more, depending on the dividends of the investments. That isn't a sum one gives up lightly.'

'You intend to give it up?' Jenny was astounded. 'You mean, you will leave the island—forever?'

'That is entirely up to you, Jenny.'

She could not believe it. The tense lines of her young face relaxed in wonder and tremulous hope. Seeing that, Harald was filled with genuine and very deep pain and sadness. He looked at the papers intently, and rattled them.

'You see, Jenny,' he said, and his voice was very gentle, 'I am establishing myself as quite a famous artist. That doesn't interest you, I know. But I did excellently in Philadelphia. I have five fine orders. I can sell all I produce. But I don't want to stay here, for the place stifles me. I know that hurts you, but it does. When your mother was alive we weren't here a great deal of the time. We travelled. We were free. We had some happy times—'

Jenny made a curious sound, and Harald looked up and saw the dense bitterness on the girl's face and the sudden aliveness of emotion.

'Yes, we did, Jenny. Your mother and I were very happy together, though you choose not to believe it. It was an arrangement—it satisfied us both. An arrangement. I was very fond of your mother. What did you say?' he asked, as again she made that smothered sound.

'Never mind, Harald. I'm not interested in your "happy times" with my mother. Go on with your important business. You said you wished to leave.'

'Yes.' The sadness was like an old sickness in him, and the longing for her was the greatest hunger he had ever known. 'Now, if I leave I forfeit all the income from the estate. I'm prepared to do that, under one condition. I have made out a contract here—a contract with you, ready for your signature. It is true that you are still a minor, but the lawyers will act in your behalf, if you are willing and give your consent. (He knew this was not true.)

'When I permanently leave you will immediately come into the millions left in trust by your mother. I will make it short. If you, when you come into that money, will give me only three hundred thousand dollars of it I will sign away my right to the lifetime income from the estate. A lump sum of three hundred thousand dollars. I will then leave you both the money and the island. Do you understand?'

'Yes.' She was more astounded than ever, and now began to tremble with hope.

Is it hopeless? he thought. Jenny, Jenny, Jenny! He said, 'Do you want to read these two contracts, yours and mine, now?'

'Please.' She extended her hand for them, and he reached towards her and gave them to her. Her hands shook, but she read clearly and steadily. 'I, Jennifer Louise Heger, hereby contract to deliver to Harald Farmington Ferrier, the sum of three hundred thousand dollars, from the estate of my late mother, Myrtle Schiller Heger Ferrier, which will revert to me, when the said Harald Farmington Ferrier gives up all his rights to the income of the estate and departs from the residence on the island called Heart's Ease and never returns. He is to leave me in full possession of the residence and the estate, with no later demands and upon his recorded oath that he had relinquished all rights to said residence and estate forevermore, of his own free will and desire.'

There was considerably more, and Jenny's rapid eye went over it quickly, suspicious of any fraud. Then she read Harald's contract. 'In consideration of the sum of ($300,000) three hundred thousand dollars, from the estate of my late wife, Myrtle Schiller Heger Ferrier, I hereby relinquish all rights to said estate and the residence called Heart's Ease, and will leave said estate and residence and never return—'

Jenny let out a long and audible breath. Her intensely blue eyes shone like cobalt. She almost smiled at Harald.

'To-morrow,' he said, 'you and I will have to go to the lawyers and sign these contracts before witnesses. Are you willing?'

'Yes. Yes!' She spoke with fervour.

He held out his hand for the papers and she gave them to him. Then he sat in silence and looked at her, and her face was soft and young and sternly sweet, and she seemed to be in an ecstatic dream. He watched her for a considerable time. Of what was she thinking, this quiet and enigmatic girl, so young and naïve and unworldly, which made her face shine so brilliantly, and her parted lips acquire a deep rose?

'You will understand that this is a big sacrifice I am making, Jenny?' he said at last. She started. Her eyes stared at him for a moment without recognition.

'Sacrifice?'

'Yes. That money is scarcely ten years' income for me, from your mother's estate. I will be only forty-three—if I choose to spend thirty thousand a year, as I have been doing—when the money is gone. Do you appreciate the sacrifice, Jenny? I am in good health, and could live into my seventies on this island, and my income would come steadily to me, and would probably increase. Hundreds of thousands of dollars, at the very least. Yet, I am willing to give it up—to please you.'

'I—I thought you said this place stifles you—'

He smiled, and his hazel eyes regarded her kindly. 'So it does. But still, I have five free months to go where I will—and receive the income, and security.'

She was confused, and frowned at him, trying to understand.

'You've made it painful for me to stay here, Jenny.'

'Painful?' Now she coloured unbecomingly.

'Yes. Still, one can stand a lot of pain for thirty thousand dollars a year for life. What is ten years' income—and freedom—compared with that?'

'Then—then why are you doing it?'

He laid the papers on a table and looked at them, and his profile was sombre and she had never seen him like that before, and for the first time his handsomeness did not offend her and she was not revolted by his mass of curling ruddy hair. But still she trembled with eagerness never to see him again, never to hear his voice or his footsteps.

He began to speak slowly, still looking at the papers as if reading from them. 'Jenny, I've said you've made it painful for me to live here. You've been ugly and unpleasant and—and almost savage—towards me since your mother died. Before that, you were friendly and even laughed with me. Perhaps you were embittered by her will. In a way I don't blame you. I should have felt the same under the same circumstances. It was an affront to an only child, an only daughter, and your mother loved you dearly, Jenny. I never did understand that will. I wanted Myrtle to change it—'

'I know!' Now her face became dark and furious and pent. 'I know you overheard her telling me, in the hall, that she knew she had done me an injustice and that she was going to change her will! That was only two days before she died!'

He showed no surprise, for he had heard that revelation from his mother months ago. 'Yes, that is quite true, Jenny. And I was glad.'

'Glad!' She jumped to her feet, bent towards him stiffly in hard and violent rage, and spoke through clenched teeth. 'You were so glad that you and your brother plotted together to kill my mother before she could change her will! I heard you both! And he did, he did! That murderer!'

He turned absolutely white. He stood up, very slowly, and confronted her. He tried to speak, wet his lips, then tried again. His voice was queer to his own ringing ears when he said, 'Are you mad, entirely mad? Have you gone out of your mind?' His eyes dilated and became fixed, like amber.

She made a disordered and fierce gesture.

'Do you think I cared about that money? Do you think it was important to me? Do you think I was outraged at my mother's will? It was her money, her money! She could do with it as she wished, as far as I was concerned! It meant nothing to me, nothing at all. But her—her—life—it meant

278

everything to me, and she was killed to prevent her changing her will, and you can lie and lie—what a liar you always were! —and nothing will ever change the truth!'

He looked involuntarily at the shut door, and his pale face was sick and changed. 'Jenny, lower your voice. How can you think that of me, and Jon?' He was trembling himself, now. 'So that was what has been wrong since your mother died. Jenny, Jenny, you are insane. Believe me, I am convinced you are insane.'

'Insane!' She threw back her head so far and with such fury that the muscles in her neck stood out like white ropes. She laughed, and it was a short and awful sound. 'That's all you can say, in your guilt—and you know you are guilty! You and your brother, the doctor!'

He caught one of her stiff arms and held her and when she tried to pull away from him he held her tighter. 'Listen to me, you fool,' he said in a low voice. 'Listen to me instead of your crazy imaginings. Your mother died of a heart attack. She knew she was dying for months, but she didn't want you and me to know, and made my brother pledge his silence. But after she was dead he told me. She was a brave woman. She preferred not to make us unhappy before it was time. A brave woman. She knew she could die any moment, but she said nothing to us. I won't have your insanity hurt her now, Jenny, I won't have it!'

She tried harder to pull away from him, frenzied, and now he let her go and she reeled with the sudden release and had to catch the back of the chair to keep from falling headlong. He stood and looked at her with his set face and it was the face of a stranger to her, cold and rigorous and condemning. In spite of her wild rage and hate she became confusedly quiet.

'I'll have a doctor examine you, Jenny, and have you put away until you are cured of your mad obsession. I mean it, Jenny. But before I do that I want to know how you acquired that twisted idea, for you have a twisted mind, Jenny, a strange and peculiar and inhuman mind.'

'Very well, I'll tell you!' she cried, and now tears ran down her face and her breath caught in her throat. 'It was the night she died. Your brother came here to see her, and then you both went downstairs into the hall, talking, almost whispering, together, and I was frightened about my mother. I knew she was sick, but not very sick. Jon was treating her. He came almost every day. I thought you two were hiding something from me and so I crept down the stairs, you didn't see me, and I heard you both almost whispering together in the hall.'

She stopped, swallowed, gasped. A lifetime of grief and suffering stifled her breath. She put her hand to her throat and choked, and then she moaned.

'Go on,' said Harald, in his brother's own relentless voice.

'I—I didn't hear it all, but enough! I heard him say "—I gave her an injection. Don't give her the digitalis she's been taking. Throw it away. The injection may do it".'

Harald's face became like Jon's, closed and hard and drawn.

'Go on,' he said with quietness.

'She needed that digitalis to keep her alive! But you took it away, and I couldn't find it! And then—and then—two hours later she died—after what he gave her, that injection!'

Jenny put her hands over her face.

He waited. His face was slimy with sweat. When Jenny finally dropped her hands he saw her abysmal pain and despair, but he was not moved.

'Did your mother ask for her digitalis, Jenny?'

'No! But I always gave it to her at night, the last thing, and I couldn't find it, I wanted to ask her, but the—the thing—your brother gave her—it made her drowsy. I think she went into a coma—Oh, God, I don't know! But she never woke up.'

Then Harald shook his head slowly and dazedly and sat down and regarded the floor in silence.

The girl was sobbing now, heaving dry sobs that shook her whole body. She held to the back of a chair and bent her whole body in her anguish. At last the sounds she made penetrated Harald's stupefaction, and he looked at her, and then he was full of pity.

'Jenny, Jenny,' he said. 'That night when Jon came, he found she was practically *in extremis*. He thought of the hospital, but decided she was too ill to be moved. She had been in very bad pain all that day, and she never said a word to us, did she? But I knew she was more ill than usual, and I sent for Jon, and he came. He said there was one last thing he could try, something new. Adrenalin. She was in shock, and dying. Jon stayed with her until she was a little relaxed, but he told me in her bedroom that she could not live, though perhaps there was some small hope. He'd come the next morning. But she died in the night, as you know.'

'You lie, you lie! You wanted her money! That's all you married her for—her money!' But Jenny, of a sudden, looked stunned. 'And—you had her killed! You wanted her to die before she could change her will!'

'Oh, Jenny, you fool. Jenny, do you remember that your mother's—your mother—was taken to the hospital the next morning? You were so broken that you didn't ask why. But I knew. Jon wanted an autopsy. Autopsies are important to doctors. I gave my consent. I was sorry afterwards, thinking of Myrtle's body— But, by God, I am glad now! Glad, how glad I am! Your consent wasn't necessary. The husband makes the decision. Your mother's—heart—it was closely examined by at least five doctors, besides Jon. It was a classic case of what they call myocardial infraction. I think that means a big blood clot. In a way, her heart disease had had nothing to do with it. It could happen to anyone, but it was worse for her, having a weak heart. They wondered how she had survived those hours before Jon arrived. In fact, one of the doctors wrote about it in a medical magazine—with photographs.'

'You lie,' Jenny whispered. It was only a whisper. But a glazed look of horror began to spread over her face.

Harald sighed and shrugged. 'Jenny, the hospital records are there for you to read for yourself. Go to St Hilda's tomorrow, see Dr Louis Hedler, and ask to see the records. As Myrtle's daughter he won't refuse you. Or,' and now he laughed with something close to contempt, 'do you think all the doctors, including Hedler, are in league with Jon and me? Perhaps you think all of Hambledon conspired with Jon to "murder" your mother.'

Jenny collapsed into a chair. She looked at him with huge eyes in a grey face. She could not speak.

'To think,' said Harald, 'that on the basis of a little suspicious and ugly eavesdropping, you could think my brother, a reputable physician, would plot with me to kill your mother! For what? Some of her money? She was fond of me, Jenny. I know she intended to change her will. She meant to give half her estate to me and half to you—with no damnable provision to jail me on this detestable island for seven months of my life, every year. We discussed it, Jenny, before she even mentioned it to you.'

He shook his head over and over, then put his elbows on his knees and dropped his head into his hands.

'It's all Pete's fault,' he said, as if speaking to himself. 'He twisted you, shut you away from life, from people, and I have a disgusting idea why he did it. You were his princess, he said. Your mother told me. You were his darling. He wouldn't ever let you get away into a sane and normal life, for then you'd see things in perspective, see a whole world you had been missing. You'd leave him, eventually, for somebody else, some other man. Are you following me, Jenny, into the sewer that was your father's mind? Don't look at me like that, Jenny. I might be sorry for you, after all your accusations, and I don't want to be sorry yet. I think I want to laugh at you a little, to despise you a little, though I know it isn't your fault. It is your fantasies, the fantasies your father encouraged in you, so you'd never leave him. He built up a world of madness for you, to make you afraid of others, to suspect dragons in every corner, to mistrust everybody. To keep you shut in. For himself.'

He dropped his hands. 'I have some letters your mother wrote to me, when I was in New York before we were married. We were engaged. She wrote that she hoped that the normal life we could bring to you, together, would change and free you, once and for all. I'll give you the letters to-night, Jenny. I never wanted you to see them, but I think you need the punishment.'

He stood up, very weary and shaken. He looked down at the girl whose head had fallen on her breast. He wanted to hold and comfort her, tenderly, without passion. She was suddenly a broken child to him. Jenny, Jenny, he thought. This will pass. You're young, and you'll recover. And then, perhaps, there'll be some hope for me, after the nightmare you've been living.

But Jenny was thinking. Jon, Jon, Jon. How can I ever look at you again, Jon? How dare I look at you? Oh, Jon, can you ever forgive me? I must have been out of my mind. I was willing to believe anything of Harald. But how could I have believed it of you?

That night when she could finally go upstairs, weak and quivering, she found her mother's letters on her table, and she read them all, weeping.

If Jenny did not sleep that night neither did Harald Ferrier to any extent.

His gesture to Jenny concerning her mother's estate was at

least partially sincere. He found the island more and more distasteful, and the months he was compelled to spend here were months he designated to his friends in New York, Boston and Philadelphia as 'my penal servitude.' It was not his modern taste or habits and he found it oppressive. He was restive every moment he spent there, for since early childhood he had despised Hambledon and had dreamed of a more cosmopolitan existence than the slow tide of the town.

But he loved Jenny. At first he was amused at the very idea, and found it novel. Later, experiencing its pains, he found the condition of being in love disturbing yet exciting. He truly wanted the girl, but he wanted her without the island. In offering to return the estate to her, he was also returning the detested island. He had believed that her infuriated and constant antagonism towards him since her mother's death had been due to her anger that she had been treated so indifferently by that mother, for Harald, in spite of his agreeable and casual approach to life, valued money above all else. He could not conceive that others would be uninterested. In giving Jenny her mother's estate he believed that he would have removed both her antagonism and her reason for rejecting him. Like his brother, Jonathan, he had found women always ready for light romances and always susceptible to him. He had no reason, therefore, to believe that Jenny was an exception.

Had she not flown at him like a wild young eagle, all talons and slashing beak and blue fury, his next step after her acceptance of his conditions would have been a gentle reminder that he loved her. He had had it all planned, like a stage scene. Her rush of gratitude and joy over the prospect of receiving all her mother's money, and the island to boot, would have softened her, made her take him seriously, made her think that money was not everything to Harald Ferrier but that she was. No woman could have helped being flattered and touched by such devotion and sacrifice, especially as the obstruction had been removed. In a few days—for Jenny was a thoughtful girl—she would begin to feel kindness for him, and regret that she had treated him so vilely and so unjustly. The future would then be inevitable.

He lay on his bed—or rather, Myrtle's bed—sweltering in the heat which would not relent and stared at the hot stars and the hot moon and did not know whether to curse mildly or laugh. Poor old Jon. It was not enough for him to have been accused of two murders but to-night he had been accused of another, and the last so absurd, so contrived in the mind of that poor silly girl who suspected everyone and everything, that even Jon would find it excruciatingly funny. One of these days, when Jenny and I are married, thought Harald, turning over his hot pillow, I'll tell him about it. He has no sense of humour, only a brutal wit. Still, he should find it funny as well as incredible.

It was not Harald's intention at all to relinquish his dead wife's estate to Jenny, and also resign his rights to the island, if Jenny should remain adamant to his proposal. Should she continue to refuse him, then he would not sign those contracts. His little speech about seeing their mutual lawyers to-morrow had been only to shock her into noticing him, for the first time, as a heroic and sacrificing figure, attractive, benign, loving, devoted. Well, to-morrow was another day. He would pretend utmost hurt over her accusations, and would not let himself forgive her so soon, and so he would take time to 'think' the matter over carefully.

He had indeed been shaken, and cosniderably frightened and alarmed, at Jenny's mad accusations, but not for long. He knew a great deal more about erratic human nature and its irrational storms than did his brother, and nothing much surprised, jolted or bewildered him. So his first consternation was not long in disintegrating, leaving him more and more amused by the moment, and feeling more and more pity for Jenny who had carried this bloody suspicion so long in her naïve mind. Jenny, Jenny, he thought with affection, if I had indeed wanted to do away with your mother I'd have done it with far more finesse and certainly would not have trusted Jon, or dreamed of trusting him, to help me. How little you know of anybody!

Now his usual urbanity and tranquil spirits returned, and he at last fell asleep, reflecting that if Jenny married him or not he would still have the income from her mother's vast estate. But he did not permit himself to think that Jenny would actually reject him. After all, who else wanted her, who would marry a girl with a small income of one hundred dollars a month, with only prospects, it is true, of eventually inheriting a great estate? But those prospects were far in the future, and young men had little faith in the future. They wanted the Now.

With Jenny as his wife he would not only have the one

woman he had ever wanted to marry with any desire and passion and love, but he would have that lovely money as well. They would sell that damned island, or rent it. It meant nothing to Harald, as he drifted off into a peaceful sleep. He had a happy dream that the island had been broken and smashed by a hurricane and he and Jenny, aboard a luxurious liner, watched it drift away in chunks. And laughed.

CHAPTER 11

Robert Morgan walked gloomily through the house his mother and he had bought. It was a beautiful house, of noble proportions, and not afflicted by the Victorian 'wood lace' which Jonathan Ferrier so despised and which he had taught Robert to despise also. But Jane Morgan, who had been born in that very sort of a Victorian house, deemed it beautiful and 'refined' and indicative of 'culture' and taste. So she had brought the heaviest and the ugliest of her inherited furniture to this house in Hambledon, and had hung the darkest and most impenetrable draperies at the windows—which she had also swathed in sombre lace—and the shining floors had been covered from wall to wall with dim carpets. She kept the shutters at least half shut and so a house once radiant with light became dusky and secretive and cold. Every possible corner was crowded with 'antiques' of dubious value and cabinets leaned darkly against pale panelled walls filled with what Jane conceived of as *objets d'art* but which had been made lavishly in factories in Sèvres in imitation of Dresden and Meissen. Marble fireplaces had their mantelpieces draped in dull velvet, red or brown or deep blue, with ponderous fringes, and upon this velvet she had placed fraudulent ormolu clocks, false Staffordshire ware, tall vases corroded with gilt and of weird and depressing shapes, conch shells, little china trays, and crystal holders filled with dried flowers or wisps of pussy-willow.

Even the big mirrors she installed here and there reflected only swart shadows, dejected images, shut and looming doors. The whole effect suggested dinginess, funereal sullenness. It did not seem the same house Robert had bought, airy, bright, clean, the windows glittering, the doors opening on gardens.

After the second night she had spent in the changed house she said to her son, 'Robert, the birds are very disturbing in this town, very disturbing indeed. They awaken me early in the morning and impinge on my nervous state. I have not been able to sleep for more than eight or nine hours a night since we were unfortunate enough to arrive here.'

He said, 'Mother, I don't find the birds disturbing. And, you are not an invalid. It isn't normal to sleep for more than nine or even eight hours.'

'Robert! Have you forgotten that I am indeed an invalid, and have arthritis?'

'None of your joints are swollen.'

'You have not seen my—limbs—or my feet, nor have you felt the pain in my shoulders and my back. I do not understand you, Robert. I have done everything to please you, consented to this little town, to this home which I did not admire from the beginning. There were other homes more suitable—'

'Houses,' said Robert.

Jane raised her voice imperatively. 'I repeat, I do not understand you, Robert! We were discussing the birds. Can we not trap them or at least buy one or two cats to destroy them? How the Almighty could create such noisy creatures, to disturb the peace of humanity, is beyond my comprehension! Once I rather admired them, but do so no longer. They are surely useless—'

'Mother,' said Robert, 'if all the birds in the world disappeared man could not survive more than seven years thereafter. That is a scientific fact. You don't like these beautiful trees either, and I believe you mentioned that you "wondered" why God had made them, too. If trees disappeared from the face of the earth we should soon have only a desert in which we could not live. Rainfall would cease, grass would die, and we'd become a barren world. It is only mankind,' said Robert, in a louder and relishing tone, 'who could disappear totally and never be missed by anything which lives. To tell the truth, he's a worthless creature!'

Jane looked at him narrowly. 'I must say, Robert, that you sound like your dear friend, Dr Ferrier. Blasphemous. Did not the Almighty make man to have dominion over this world and the rule of everything? Then everything else could disappear—and in many cases it would be an improvement—and man would still be triumphantly alive.'

'Not at all,' said Robert. 'He would be dead, and sometimes, during my contacts with my dear fellow man, I think that would be a delightful consummation. Seeing that you are quoting the Bible—again—let me remind you that it states that God made the creatures of the earth, the land and the sea and the sky, and forests and lakes and streams, before He inflicted man on them, and He blessed them first. If He did, indeed, give man "dominion" over these blameless things, then it was not to incontinently destroy them or injure them, but to protect them, for they are beautiful as man is as surely not.'

'Blasphemy!' cried Jane, with horror.

'I have begun to believe,' said Robert, looking again about the large and dreary room which Jane had designated as the parlour, 'that man is the blasphemy by his very existence.'

'That is not Christian, Robert!'

Robert was enjoying himself, 'It may not be Christian, in your sense of the word, Mother, but it is certainly true. The cities are beginning to encroach on the countryside, all over the world. If they were at least beautiful, and if they respected the world, and cherished it and guarded its resources, that would not matter too much, though I dread the thought that there won't be any quiet sanctuaries in the future, and no blessed silences, and only the discordant voices of people. However, I probably won't be here then, and that's one blessing of mortality.

'Incidentally,' said Robert, more and more enjoying himself, and getting revenge for the destruction of his beautiful house, 'I believe the Bible mentions that only man is corrupt, full of sin, vicious, murdering for murder's sake, and practically irredeemable. Not even the serpent or the tiger—and not even the mosquito or house fly—is condemned in such vigorous language. "Man is wicked from his birth and evil from his youth." I don't recall that said about tadpoles or the lowly louse or bed-bug. Just about men.'

Jane had begun to smirk in a peculiar way. 'I see that your friend has really changed your Christian attitude, Robert. But, and how grateful I am for this! he won't be here much longer!'

'True,' said Robert, and it came to him that in spite of what had happened, apparently with such lightness between him and Jonathan, he would miss Jonathan more than he had thought it possible to miss another human being. As he was young and optimistic, he had almost recovered from the shock of that day's encounter, and had seen Jenny a number of times on the island, and she had been shyly kind and had welcomed him with obvious pleasure and trust. He had begun to hope. She had not spoken to him of Jonathan again, and Jonathan had not mentioned her recently.

'A wanderer on the face of the earth. He will be that, Robert.'

'Possibly for a little while. I know that he has had many magnificent offers from New York and Philadelphia and Boston. One hospital even offered to make him Chief of Staff, and another of the surgical division.'

'He will never realise any of them, my dear Robert.'

Robert turned on her quickly. 'What do you mean by that?'

Jane smiled with deep satisfaction. 'I do associate for your sake, Robert, to incline people to you. And during these associations with the ladies in this miserable little town I have heard—hints.'

'Of what?' Now Robert was alarmed and disturbed.

'I am not at liberty to tell you,' said his mother setting her mouth primly. 'Moreover, I am not one to gossip, nor do I permit confidences.'

'Mother, if you have heard of anything concerning Jonathan I insist that you tell me, for he is my friend.'

Jane nodded grimly. 'He is no man's friend, but has set his face against everyone, and so I am most happy that he will indeed be leaving soon, or perhaps he will be forced to leave. That is what I have heard, Robert, and all I have heard, from many indignant ladies, who also hinted that never again will he be permitted to practice anywhere. Certainly—'

'For God's sake!' Robert suddenly shouted. 'What in hell are you talking about? What fool women's gossip have you been listening to?'

His mother rose with slow dignity, lowering her eyes before this violence, and, forgetting her canes for once, marched as if preceded by heralds out of the room, and in silence. Robert seethed, watching her go. He knew his mother. She would tell him nothing. He had deeply offended her. Now she would not speak to him for days except on occasions of deepest necessity, until he would be forced to apologise or she would find her own silence no longer sufferable.

He slammed out of the house into the hot sunlight of the morning, and it was as if he had been delivered from a dank tomb. But his mind was greatly perturbed and anxious. He wondered if he should tell Jonathan. He recalled that Jonathan had lately seemed very light-hearted and pleasant and amiable, and his tongue had been less abrasive. Jonathan, who knew Hambledon, as Robert did not, would surely be aware by this time if some danger had begun to threaten him, some inconceivable danger. He decided not to repeat his mother's malignant gossip. What had she said, really, except to repeat remarks by spiteful women?

His concern for Jonathan, however, removed the last hostility and estrangement he had felt since that day by the river, and his thoughts of him were again brotherly and full of respect. If no one else missed him in Hambledon, he would be missed by Robert Morgan. Perhaps, thought Robert, when he is established somewhere else, he will send for me. I like Hambledon very much. But if Jon asked me to join him, I would.

Senator Kenton Campion got out of his fine Victoria—his sister's—and looked at Dr Martin Eaton's great and monstrously ugly house and thought, that if 'Pike's Peak' was ridiculous for Hambledon, Dr Eaton's house should be razed in the interest of public beauty, after public condemnation. It was no worse, he reflected, than other houses on River Road, and it did have remarkably lovely gardens and linden trees, and had a fine back view of the water, and expansive grounds, but still it was hideous and an insult to an eye that winced at deformities.

He stood on the walk and looked up at the little silly turrets and small absurd towers and the appalling stained-glass hall window that glowered in the very centre of the chestnut-coloured wood facade and seemed to enhance the putrid yellow hue of the shutters and shingles. Ghastly, ghastly, thought the Senator, climbing the stairs to the cool shadows of the deep long porches and pulling the bell. He was almost always good-tempered. The Eaton house increased his feeling of well-being because it was so repulsive, so rich, so pretentious and so without grace. His eyes shone like polished glass. A maid admitted him to the great parlour with all its clutter of china, elks' horns, clocks, vases and dark velvet furniture, and, of course, its shutters pulled against the radiant morning sun. It was dusky here, though not cool, and the Senator felt his way to the centre of the room, considered a deep chair then decided against it. He was too portly to sink himself into that mass.

Flora Eaton came in hastily, in a gardening apron, her thin sallow face damp and her dark hair damper still and dishevelled. She threw aside her gardening gloves and advanced into the room, her dotted cotton dress fluttering about her angular figure. 'Dear, dear Kenton!' she exclaimed. 'How happy I am to see you! How is darling Beatrice? Do forgive my appearance—my sweet-peas, you know, in this weather, and my phlox—not doing well at all—and Martin will be so happy, too, to see you! Iced tea, Kenton, or perhaps,' and her pale lips made a naughty coy moue, 'a little drop of something?'

'A little drop of something, dear Flora,' said the beaming Senator, as he enfolded her thin freckled hands in his warm, fat palms. 'Where is Martin?'

Flora gaspingly informed him that her husband was in his study, as he always was in the morning, but she would summon him and they would have a little cosy chat. Her big, hollow dark eyes rolled meaningly, her big white teeth glittered, her elbows, hands, hips, shoulders, jiggled, and she kept rising and falling on her toes.

'No, no, dear Flora!' cried the jovial Senator. 'I wouldn't take you from your beautiful garden for a moment. I should have called first. I'll go to Martin's study. Dull business, y'know, my dear, dull business, not fit for a lady's ears. I know the way! Don't bother, my dear, don't bother!' He tapped her affectionately on her sharp shoulder, and went off very fast for a gentleman of his girth and size. Flora looked after him languishingly. He was so good, so kind, so sweet, so distinguished. She found her gloves and raced back to her garden, which she was preparing for a tea that afternoon.

The Senator climbed the stairs. Here again all was shuttered and dim, and the shut air smelled of wax and heated varnish and aromatic dust. He passed room after room, with closed doors, until he came to the study on which he knocked quickly. He said, 'Martin? Kent Campion here. Can you see me for a few minutes?'

He heard a creak, a hoarse mutter, then a shuffling which came towards him. The door opened and the tall and shrunken figure of the sick doctor stood on the threshold, staring at him dully. The once fat face was fat no longer; it had sunken in one year. His bald head no longer shone; the skin was yellowed and parched. The once kind blue eyes had faded, and were slitted. Only the big nose and the thick lips remained, ruins among ruins. Martin leaned on two canes, and his left side was almost completely paralysed.

He wore a wool morning coat, for all the heat, and wrinkled trousers, and a collarless shirt striped in white and grey, and braces. He trembled as he stood with the aid of his strong canes. He said, slowly and precisely. 'Good morning, Kent. Come in.' He had regained a good measure of his speech. He shuffled slowly back into the dusky room, which was filled with Mission oak furniture, leather chairs, ugly lamps, and dark blue silk draperies. Here he had held consultations with lesser doctors on important matters concerning an obscure case or a rich patient. Now his precious medical library, which lined the oak walls, was dusty and unused. The rug held no footprints, for few came here any longer. Martin, since his niece's tragic death, had become a recluse, drinking in lonely silence in this room and reading 'light' books and magazines, and thinking, thinking, thinking, his own desolate and anguished thoughts.

The Senator, still beaming, seated himself near the desk and thought, but only for an instant, that he was on dirty business and he wished it was not necessary. However, it indeed was necessary. Besides, in a way, he was doing Martin a favour. No doubt the shattered doctor had been dreaming, for a year, almost, of revenge, and had broken because he could not attain it. His dear friend, Kent Campion, would put it in his hands. So the Senator became cheerful again. 'Yes, yes, Martin, I will indeed have a drink. Thank you.' He watched the crippled man reach for another glass, survey it for dregs, and then fill it with whisky and water. 'Thank you,' repeated the Senator, and leaned forward and took the glass. 'How are you, dear old friend?'

'Waiting for death,' said Martin very slowly.

The Senator laughed heartily. 'Oh, dear me, how morbid you are! But, of course, you are joking. You're a young man yet, Martin. World before you. Two years younger than me. Why aren't you sitting out in the garden, your wonderful gardens? So pleasant in this weather, with cool breezes from the river.'

The doctor had painfully and carefully seated himself. He put aside his canes. He folded his right hand over his paralysed left one, which now resembled a claw. He gazed at the Senator with eyes so sunken and so narrowed that they appeared lifeless and of no colour at all.

'I care for nothing,' he said. He lifted the bottle. When the Senator would have helped him he waved him aside exhaustedly. He filled his glass, added only a dash of water, then put the glass to his lips and drank like a man dying of thirst. The Senator watched him, marvelling that he could drink so much, and not for the first time to-day, either.

He said, with his usual buoyancy, 'Now, Martin, we must pull ourselves together, we really must. For the sake of our—er—friends. Our—er—community. Our—er—loved ones. We Owe it to Ourselves, to Others. We are not Unimportant. We are revered, admired, needed. We—'

'Shut up, Kent,' said the weary voice, and the right hand tilted the bottle over the glass again. 'What do you want? You always want something.'

'Is that kind?' said Kenton Campion, chuckling richly. He drank of his own glass, and tried not to notice the mass of fingerprints on it. 'We've had many a happy hour in this room, dear Martin, many a happy hour. We miss you. We miss those hours. We shall have them again. I promise you that—when all this is forgotten, and—er—consummated.'

One lean broad shoulder rose and fell under the morning coat. But now the dying eyes fixed themselves attentively on the politician. They actually peered in the dusk, and the Senator, perceptive as were all politicians, was aware of a concentration on him, a sudden watchfulness. He pulled his chair closer to the desk. 'I am here to bring you the satisfaction you've been dreaming of for months, Martin, for months. And then a miracle will happen, and your heart will be at peace, and your health restored.'

'Go on,' said the faltering voice, but it had quickened.

'Jonathan Ferrier,' said the Senator.

He expected some show of emotion now, at the sound of that hated name, a quickening, a trembling of the side of the face which was not paralysed, an exclamation, a faint cry, perhaps a clenching of the living hand, an involuntary movement. But nothing of this occurred. Martin Eaton continued to stare at him with those frightening eyes for several long moments, and he said not a word. Finally he stiffly turned his big head, with its glinting yellowish baldness, and he looked at the shuttered windows. He appeared to have forgotten the visitor.

'Jonathan Ferrier,' said the Senator, wondering if Martin's mind had gone also, and if he had forgotten that name.

'I heard you,' said Martin, and still looked at the windows and did not move.

The Senator coughed. 'The man we all still believe killed your niece, and her unborn child.' (What the hell was the matter with him, anyway?)

Martin said in a vague and distant voice, 'They believe that, still?'

'Indeed, indeed, my dear friend! They never believed he was innocent. There are rumours he bought some members of the jury.'

Martin closed his right hand over his left again. He rubbed the dead flesh, slowly, slowly, and did not look at the Senator. His ash-cloured mouth fluttered uncontrollably, and the Senator was pleased, for now he was surely expressing his grief and inconsolable sorrow. Then Martin said, 'He did not buy the jurors. They were honest men.'

The Senator frowned. 'Ah, well, you know rumours, Martin. I never heed them, myself. But who can stop tongues? And —old stories? But we know Ferrier was guilty. You know, too. Didn't you stand up in the courtroom, when the verdict was given, and didn't you cry out, "No! No! No!"'

The fallen chest, once so massive and strong, heaved visibly, and the Senator smiled a little. So, the old hatred still burned there, in spite of the dead and passive face, and the averted head, the hidden eyes.

'Yes,' said Martin. 'I did.'

'So you knew he was guilty.'

There was a long sick silence. Then Martin mumbled, 'He was guilty.'

'Well, then,' said Campion, freshly pleased. 'And now I have some news for you. Do you hear me, Martin? Yes. I hear that Ferrier has decided to remain in Hambledon after all, to destroy and injure at will. To flaunt his crimes in our faces. But we,—shall we say "we" at present?—have decided that this little city must no longer be defamed and shamed by his presence. We—have been working not only to revoke his licence in the whole State, but to revoke it permanently, and everywhere. Who will give him shelter and privileges, when the sovereign Commonwealth of Pennsylvania will no longer permit him to practise, but will drive him out?'

Now the ruined face turned almost quickly to the Senator, and for the first time there was a sharp burning deep within the hollows of the lost eyes, an intense and focused burning. The Senator nodded richly.

'Yes, dear old friend, yes.'

'He is a doctor,' said Martin.

This was not exactly the reply the Senator had expected. 'Well,' he said, waving his hand. 'He soon will not be.' He watched Martin as he lit one of his heavy cigars and then deposited the match in a bronze tray. Martin watched his every movement as if powerfully fascinated. 'With your help, Martin.'

Martin had fixed his gaze on the cigar. The lips were shaking again. The Senator said, 'All you have suffered, in your sorrow, will be avenged. Poor lovely Mavis will be avenged. I promise you that, my friend, I promise you that.'

Then, to the Senator's consternation, the big ruined head began to move negatively from side to side, in denial. 'He is a doctor,' said Martin again.

The Senator wet his lips. 'Yes. But what a doctor! And how he repaid you for the paternal affection you gave him, the patronage, the introductions, the pride, the kindness! He repaid it all with hatred—and the murder of that lovely thing, your heart's joy and delight.'

Now the fiery spark in Martin's eyes dimmed with moisture. 'No,' said Martin.

The Senator took the cigar from his mouth, blew out a cloud of smoke, and said gently, ' "No" what?'

'You shall not have my help,' said Martin.

The Senator raised thick and chestnut eyebrows. 'But Martin, why not?'

The shaking lips firmed and again the slow denial began.

'Come,' said Kenton Campion, and smiled. 'I know it is painful for you, dear friend. I know you do not wish old sorrows to be exhumed again. But you must be brave. Have you forgotten Mavis? Ah, who could forget that vision of beauty and joy and laughter? Not her devoted—uncle. Who adored her. Be brave, Martin. This is the last battle, and Mavis will be avenged.'

'What do you want of me?' asked Martin.

'I will bring witnesses to you, here, Martin, Louis Hedler, Humphrey Bedloe, for your testimony, which you did not give in court. We have long known that you knew something which would have convicted Ferrier, but suppressed it, perhaps because of your old interest—in his mother. Old friendships. A tender heart that had suffered enough. Your heart. Yes, we knew that you deliberately did not testify in a crucial matter, that you kept your silence. I do not want you to keep it any longer, dear friend. I want you to tell your friends of it, to unburden your heart at last, to bring justice to bear on that murderer, finally.'

The reply was a dry whisper. 'Double jeopardy.'

'Yes, I know,' said the Senator with impatience, and again waving his cigar. 'He cannot be tried again for the same crime. But your testimony will convince Hedler, who is proving a little fractious in spite of what he has suffered from Ferrier's hands, to allow us to bring in two prominent members of the State Medical Board from Philadelphia. They already have many—proofs, shall we say?—but yours will be the most convincing of all.'

'Proofs?'

'Oh, not of that crime. But of others. Enough to drive Ferrier out of the country. To the ends of the earth.'

Again the eyes were bits of fire. The slow voice came without intonation: 'What did he do to you, Campion?'

The Senator started, looked with keenness at the broken doctor. His smile became pinched. 'Enough, Martin, quite enough. He did me a great injury. I, too, want revenge. But I will not bother you with my troubles. Yours are sufficient. When shall I bring the witnesses to you?'

Was that a bitter and sardonic smile on Eaton's dying lips? The Senator could not tell. But he did hear the one word, 'No.'

The Senator was angry and astounded and incredulous. There had been such finality in that word, such strength.

' "No," Martin? After all he did to Mavis, and to you, out of cruelty and viciousness and hate?'

'Please go, Campion,' said Martin.

The Senator's eyebrows rose again and stayed there. He studied the end of his glowing cigar. He smiled, reflecting. His big red mouth moved and twisted as if he were thinking of something very delicious.

'You will not help us, Martin?'

'No. No. That is all.'

The Senator sighed. He leaned back in the leather chair and contemplated the ceiling. 'In my profession,' he said, 'it is most necessary to know the secret hearts of people, their thoughts, their emotions, their desires. Mavis was a dear girl. But, she had her faults, her little perplexities, her small defects. Always, Martin, she was shielded by you, upheld by you, devotedly guarded by you. She was dearer to you than anything else in the world, above everything else in the world. You would never hear a word against her, not even from dear Flora, who is a paragon of a woman. Yes, yes, my ears are always open. I never forget anything. To you, Mavis was an angel of light, to be worshipped and honoured, her name kept inviolate. You would have died for Mavis.'

A steady hoarse breathing began to fill the closed and dusty room. 'Yes,' said Martin Eaton, and again the living hand clenched on the dead. 'It is true.'

'Not an ugly word must ever touch Mavis, mar or dim her.'

'No,' said Martin. The breathing was louder and quicker.

The Senator sighed and shook his head. 'Martin, it breaks my heart to say this, then. If you will not help us, I must, in my stern search for justice, bring Mavis's name into public view, to public laughter, speculation. Calumny. And yours, also.'

The great shattered figure behind the desk stirred and shook as if a hand had seized it furiously. The dead lips parted, closed silently. The fallen eyes opened wide and blazed.

So, I have stirred up the wrecked bastard, thought the Senator with pleasure. He continued to shake his head, sighing. 'You know how women gossip, Martin. My wife was the very close friend of your brother's wife, Hilda Eaton. They endlessly confided in each other, and in no one else and in letters. They were like sisters, closer than sisters. My wife was overcome with sorrow when Hilda died. Dear, soft-hearted Henrietta. Dear gentle soul. I comforted her, as any good husband would. And then she told me.'

'What?' the word was a hard rasp.

'That,' said the Senator, with an air of delicacy, 'Mavis was your daughter, not your brother's. That Mavis was the result of—er—adultery. I do not condemn you, dear old friend. But Hilda did resemble Marjorie Ferrier, did she not, and you always—admired—Marjorie Ferrier, and had wanted to marry her. Let us be thankful that your brother died, not knowing, and that you adopted Mavis, you and Flora, and made her your daughter openly, as well as naturally. It was a noble and loving thing, Martin, and I admire you for it. No, no. No one else living, except you and I, know the truth, and the truth is shut behind my lips and will never come forth, unless you force me to it. I will not be denied, Martin.'

Now he looked at the crumbling man with a baleful light in his eyes, and his wide smile was evil.

It was as if all the last strength of Martin Eaton came to him violently. He said, and his voice was almost normal, and loud. 'You have no proof, I will sue you for libel!' The blaze was deep in his eyes, and cold with hate.

'Ah, yes, but I do have proof, Martin. A politician, you will understand, garners all little matters which may be useful to him in the future. It does not matter how trivial. It may be a nugget, later. So, I persuaded Henrietta to write it down for me, in her own handwriting, as a kind of "confession" that she had withheld the truth for so long. Henrietta was a very virtuous soul. She had not been moved that Hilda had been infatuated with you, and that you loved her. There was some sternness in my dear Henrietta's soul. She felt that you had "betrayed" pretty Hilda, had seduced her from her husband's side. Need I elaborate? So I induced Henrietta to write down her own indignation over her beloved friend's fate, and the fact that she had not dared proclaim abroad the true paternity of her child. Henrietta did not blame Hilda. She did not blame the wronged husband. She did not blame Flora. She blamed only you,' and the Senator chuckled indulgently, 'the seducer of the innocent, the breaker of a loving home, the despoiler.' The Senator laughed softly. ' "Thou shalt not commit adultery." To my Henrietta that was a crime above murder, above all the other Commandments. Hilda had not committed adultery, no, not Henrietta's friend! But you had forced yourself upon her. How Henrietta had come to that conclusion is a great mystery, but you know the chaste heart of women,' and he sighed unctuously. 'They cannot believe that a good wife would betray her husband, no, not unless she was "forced".'

He clasped his hands over his silk and patterned waistcoat and looked at the stricken doctor with an air of sadness and benignity. 'Martin, unless you help us, tell us what you know, the name of Mavis will be darkened forever. You do not care about yourself, but you do care about Mavis. It is your choice: the memory of Mavis, or Jonathan Ferrier's punishment.' He sat up in his chair. 'Knowing what you do about him, how can you refuse to help us? How can you deny to Mavis the justice her soul must crave, against her murderer? I cannot believe it! I cannot understand it!' He struck the desk with his meaty fist, in outrage.

The doctor's face was a grey portrait of extreme agony. His mouth had fallen open, and it was twisted, and his teeth could be seen, dimly glimmering in that dusky light. His panting was rough and deep in the room. He stared at the Senator in his extremity of fear and hatred and despair. The Senator stared back, assuming severity and indignation.

Then, very slowly, the live hand opened a drawer and withdrew a piece of white linen, and laid it on the desk. The two men regarded it in silence. Finally, the doctor made a feeble motion towards it, and the Senator reached for it and took it in his hand. It was at once light and metallic within its piece of linen. The Senator unrolled the cloth and found in his hand a curious tool or instrument. He bent forward to examine it more closely. A knife? A curved knife? A medical affair? Then he saw the name in a flowing scroll on the silver handle. Jonathan Ferrier.

'What is it?' he asked. He noticed that the edge was rusty and smeared with an old smear.

'Curette,' said Martin Eaton, as if expiring.

'Curette? What is that?'

'An instrument. Surgery. For emptying a woman's womb.' The breathing was more discordant and shrill.

'Ah!' exclaimed the Senator.

'Mavis's blood. On it,' said Martin Eaton. 'She brought it to me. Gave it to me. Before she died.'

He sank back in his chair and groaned. He rolled his head and his eyes stretched towards the ceiling. 'It was used on her. Her blood. She brought it to me. He—he had put it down. She took it.' He pointed blindly at the cloth, and now the Senator recoiled, The cloth held old rusty stains.

'Good God,' said the Senator in a subdued voice. He had wanted proof, but not one so horrible as this. He rerolled the curette, gingerly. Then he said in a voice of genuine disgust. 'And he used that on that helpless girl, to kill her and his child!' He had not believed it before, but he believed it now, or forced himself to believe it.

The live hand of Dr Eaton darted to the cloth and the instrument and seized it and then thrust it back into the drawer. The drawer was quickly locked. The two men looked at each other, the doctor panting as if he had struggled a long time with something formidable, the Senator with curiosity.

The Senator stood up with an air of satisfaction. 'Thank you, Martin,' he said. 'Please forgive me for pressing you. It was necessary, as I am sure you know now. Very necessary, for Mavis's sake, and yours, and Hambledon's. As soon as the witnesses can come I will let you know, and they will wish to consult you personally.'

'Get out,' said Dr Eaton, and he closed his eyes.

Smiling urbanely the Senator left. He met no one in the lower hall but the maid who respectfully led him to the door.

For many minutes after the Senator's departure Martin Eaton sat in his chair, clenching and unclenching his right hand and staring into space. His heavy breathing subsided, but his mouth remained partly open. He began to look about his gloomy study as if he had never been here before, and was examining everything. Then he said aloud, 'Mavis. Mavis.' Again his eyes filled with moisture. Then he said, 'Jon, Jon.'

He looked at his telephone, and he reached for it, and then he remembered the Senator and he snatched his hand away. But he continued to stare at it for a long time, a very long time, and his sick mind was turbulent.

Then he groaned. 'Hilda. Marjorie. Marjorie!'

Jenny Heger wandered hesitantly on to the terrace where Harald Ferrier was smoking and reading the morning paper. She looked at him with diffidence for some time before he became aware that she was there. Then he glanced up smiling, stood and laid aside his newspaper, and motioned her to a chair in the shining and golden heat of the morning. She shook her head and clasped her hands before her on her rough brown frock.

'I suppose,' she said in a very subdued voice, 'you will never forgive me?'

'Jenny,' he said with the utmost gentleness, 'I never held it against you. I was only sorry that you could think such things of me.' His hazel eyes sparkled largely on her with genuine love. 'But I was a little—hurt. That's why I refused to go with you to our lawyers and sign those contracts. I wanted to think, to get over my hurt.'

Jenny sighed, and peeped at him shyly. 'I've been thinking, too,' she said, in that same uncertain voice. 'Mama wasn't very fair to you, and she realised it. So, I want to do what she should have done, and which she would have done if she had lived. The contract you made out—that wasn't fair. So—so if you want to—we'll go to our lawyers, and we'll divide the estate equally, and then you can—go. I don't know just how large the estate is. I never gave it a thought before. But it must be quite a lot?'

'Yes, Jenny. Several millions of dollars, and still increasing from investments.' He still smiled at her, but he was alert. 'Even divided, it would provide enough income for both of us, a rich income, for the rest of our lives, with the residual estate, still intact, for our own heirs.'

'I'm glad,' said Jenny, with humility. 'And so, you can go. I will stay here, on my father's island, and I will be able to keep it up as he wanted. So we can see our lawyers whenever you want to, Harald.'

He was elated, but he did not let it appear. He said, 'Jenny, I want to talk to you. Please, Jenny, sit down for a minute. It won't take long.'

She was too ashamed of her old prejudices and suspicions to refuse. So she sat on the edge of a wicker chair and coloured a little, and looked at the rushing azure of the smiling river, and waited.

'Jenny,' he said, 'will you listen to me for just a little, without jumping up and running away?'

She looked at him with that directness of hers. 'I've finished with running away,' she said. 'I've been running away all my life, and now it is over.'

'I'm glad,' said Harald. 'There was never any reason for you to run. When I was a child, I used to run, too. It was stupid.'

'Did you?' She smiled at him with interest.

'Yes, I did. I wanted my father to like me, and to like my painting. I thought he was quite wonderful. But I found out he never had any real taste, such as my mother had. He liked stereotyped art, for he had no imagination to judge anything else. So, when I showed him my early attempts he would look pained. He always had a way of looking pained, and very delicate and bruised. He was a silly man. My brother, Jon, never found that out. He thought Papa was the acme of everything, the final resort, and so he didn't like our mother because she was on to Papa herself. Jon doesn't like my paintings because Papa didn't.'

Jenny frowned seriously. 'That doesn't sound like—Jon.'

'Oh, but it's true! Jon hasn't any imagination either.'

Jenny said nothing. She looked down at her hands. Harald laughed gently. 'The only perceptive people in our family, Jenny, are my mother and myself. Jon's idea of something interesting and beautiful is a corpse.' He laughed again. 'He never appreciated Mavis's beauty, for instance, and never understood her at all.'

'There was never anything to understand,' said Jenny with her old bluntness. 'I knew that even when I was very young, four years ago. It was Jon's trouble that he thought she had—had—well, other things that weren't obvious. But she didn't have anything that wasn't obvious. She was what Mavis was.'

Harald was astounded. He was not sure that he liked this acute Jenny.

'What do you mean?' he asked.

Jenny actually became quite animated. 'Mavis was very simple, really. She wanted just what kittens want, food, play, amusement, sleep, fun, a soft place to curl, petting, pampering, and what used to be called "cosseting." Admiration, strokings. And to give nothing in return. And to fight for her luxuries, which she felt were deserved.'

Harald pondered this, narrowing his eyes on this Jenny he had never recognised before. He knew that what she had said was quite true. He only disliked it that Jenny had not been deceived by Mavis.

'Mavis hated anyone who wouldn't indulge her, or who expected anything real and human from her,' Jenny went on.

How true, thought Harald. But how beautiful she was! He said, 'I'm surprised at you, Jenny. You're being uncharitable.'

'No,' said Jenny, with a return to her old earnestness. 'I'm just telling the truth, which Jon found out eventually.'

'How do you know he found that out?'

Jenny looked away. 'I just know.'

'He treated Mavis abominably.'

Jenny swung the profound blue of her eyes to him again. 'How do you know? Did she tell you?'

Harald became immobile in his chair, but his hands tightened on the arms.

'I knew,' said Jenny, 'that you were with her often.'

'How did you know, Jenny?' He was terribly alarmed, and now he sat up.

'I saw both of you along the river at night, talking.'

Harald inhaled slowly and carefully. His fingers twitched on the arms of the chair. Then he said, watching Jenny, 'She had to have someone to confide in. And I was sympathetic.'

'I suppose so,' said Jenny, and one look at her ingenuous face convinced him that there was no danger to him in this girl. 'It was very sad, all around,' said Jenny. 'But I am more sad for Jon.'

Harald took out his scented handkerchief and carefully

wiped his forehead. He said, 'Mavis, though perhaps you won't believe it, had a great interest in art.'

'That's nice,' said Jenny with indifference. She had already dismissed Mavis. 'But you wanted to talk to me about something, didn't you?'

'Yes.' Harald pulled himself out of his fear. It had struck across the sunlit terrace like the shadow of a black and avenging wing but now it was gone. He leaned towards Jenny, his hands clasped between his knees, his smile charming and winsome. Then he became serious.

'Jenny, you never used to believe it when I told you I wanted to marry you.'

She stiffened. Her face became cold and distant.

'Jenny, it usually isn't considered an insult when a man declares his love for a woman!'

'I—I suppose not.' She shifted to the very edge of her chair. 'Don't you believe me?'

It was ludicrous, but she was considering, her thoughts going back to the past. Harald found himself smiling again. Jenny was embarrassed, and the faintest flush rose in her pale smooth cheeks. 'I believe you. Now,' she said. 'I wish you wouldn't talk about it.'

'Why not? It's the most important thing to me, Jenny, and it doesn't concern money.'

'No. No. It doesn't concern money,' said Jenny. Her colour brightened. 'I'm sorry I ever thought that.'

'Well, Jenny? What do you say now?'

She looked at the tangled fingers on her lap, and she was distressed.

'I—I can't think of you like that.'

'Because of your mother?'

'No. It—is something else.'

'Jenny, I've noticed that that young doctor has rowed over here to see you occasionally. Jon's replacement. You aren't taking him seriously, are you?'

'He's very kind!' Jenny was miserable.

'And very puerile.' Harald spoke indulgently.

'You're wrong,' said Jenny, with some heat. 'Kindness doesn't mean you're a fool. I like to talk to him. He doesn't have—hidden—places. He's honest. I like his company. We like the same things.'

'Enough to marry him?'

Jenny said nothing. Her appearance was wretched. Then

when she saw that Harald was waiting, smiling, for her answer, she said, 'I haven't thought of marrying him.'

'Well, that's encouraging. So, Jenny, what is your objection to me?'

'I told you. I can't think of you like that.' She stood up, and looked desperately. 'You mustn't ask me. Never again. I could never marry you, Harald.'

He stood up, too. 'Jenny, would you at least think about it, in justice to me?'

She looked about her as if searching for some hiding place. 'I can't think about it.'

'But there's no one else, Jenny, I understand you. I've loved you for a long time. We could be very happy together.'

'You'll have to excuse me!' cried Jenny, and before he could say anything else she had run off in her old manner. He watched her flying away down the stairs of the terrace into the gardens. He felt some encouragement. At least she had not rejected him outright, and she had shown considerable confusion and distress. That must mean something. A man who disturbed a woman and sent her flying off had a lot in his favour. Moreover she pitied him because she had wronged him in her thoughts, and pity was first cousin to love.

When Howard Best entered the large office of Dr Louis Hedler at St Hilda's Hospital he found not only the doctor there but Father McNulty. They all shook hands, and Howard sat down. He saw that Louis was very grave and that his large froglike eyes gleamed with consternation. Louis said, 'Thanks for coming, Howard. I know it's late; right at dinner time. But I wanted you and Father McNulty here when the hospital isn't teeming as usual, and the corridors rushing, and too much curiosity aroused. This is a very serious and private matter. Private,' he emphasised, looking from one to the other slowly and pointedly.

'You can rely on my discretion,' said the priest, his golden eyes quietly alarmed.

'Yes. And you, Howard?'

'Give me a dollar,' said Howard, smiling. Dr Hedler stared a moment, then took out his billfold, extracted a dollar bill from it and laid it before Howard, who said, 'I am a lawyer. You have just given me a retainer. So anything you say to me, and anything I hear in this room, is completely private and confidential.' His kind boyish face stopped smiling. He put the bill in his pocket and settled his rangy body in the leather chair. He could see the shimmering mountains in the distance, deepening slowly to purple in the evening sky. The weather was still very hot though it was the latter part of August.

'Howard,' said Louis, 'you were Jon Ferrier's lawyer, weren't you?'

'Yes. Here in Hambledon. I was the one who moved for a change of venue, as you know, and it was granted, considering the atmosphere in this town against Jon. And then I got it moved to Philadelphia, and found the best lawyers for Jon there.' His face became as grave as Louis's. 'Why, Louis?'

Dr Hedler looked down at a thick folder on his desk. He sighed. He rubbed his eyes and stared through the windows, and his finger tapped the folder. 'There is one thing,' he said, 'Jon can't be tried for the same alleged crime, can he? Double jeopardy.'

Howard sat up alertly. 'No, he can't. What the hell is this, Louis?'

Louis said, 'But it would ruin Jon, wouldn't it, if fresh evidence were unearthed that he had really "bungled" the abortion on Mavis—perhaps deliberately so—and killed her and his unborn child? It could result in the revocation of his licence to practise anywhere?'

'I suppose so,' said Howard, and now he was as alarmed as the doctor. 'You know more about that part than I do, though. Come on, Louis! Tell me.'

'Let me begin at the beginning,' said Louis, wiping his face with his handkerchief. He lit a cigar and Howard saw that his hands were shaking slightly. He opened the folder and stared at it grimly, nodding his head from time to time. 'It begins with Kent Campion.'

Now the priest sat up very straight in his own chair and both he and Howard fixed their eyes on the doctor.

'Jon,' said Louis, 'made a very bad error when he began to oppose ambitious politicians in Washington a couple of years ago. He joined the Anti-Imperialist League.'

Howard hesitated. He rubbed his long jaw. Then he said, 'I belong to the Anti-Imperialist League, too. I didn't know Jon was a member, though.'

'It seems,' said Louis with a wry smile, 'that not only did he join but he gave thousands of dollars to it, and wrote little anonymous leaflets for it. Campion found out. He's hated Jon

305

ever since. Calls him unAmerican, anti-patriotic, anti-destiny, and such. Even a traitor. Yet I understand that all the League wants is peace at home and abroad, and needed social reforms put into practice, so as to end, justly, the war between labour and capital, assure the soundness of our currency, abolish unjust taxation, advance the cause of the American Negro and the Indians in the West, outlaw child labour, and punish and banish from office all corrupt politicians. I am quoting your League, of course.'

'Those are our objectives,' said Howard, 'and very decent and worthy ones.'

'Yes. But that doesn't help Jon. He made a terrible enemy of the empire-loving Campion and his fellows, though he doesn't know. I also think there is something else—personal. Campion has complained that Jon induced his son to leave his seminary and "flee abroad to some disreputable place where a father cannot reach, comfort and sustain him".'

The priest uttered an exclamation of anger. 'That is most untrue, Doctor! I hope I am not violating a confidence— well, even if I am—but Jon saved young Francis Campion's life! I know where Francis is. He could assure you of the truth, and not lies.'

'Then,' said Louis, 'get him. Bring him back as soon as possible.'

The priest said, 'He is in France. I will cable him to-night.'

Louis sighed. 'At the best, he will be able to return in ten days. Send for him, Father. To-night.'

'I will do even more than that,' said the priest. 'I will explain, in my cable, why it is needed that Francis not only return at once, but that he send me a cable refuting the—er —errors of his father. That should arrive in less than four days after my cable is sent.' His young face was greatly disturbed.

Howard, equally disturbed, said, 'What is all this, Louis? Why is this necessary?'

Louis looked down at the folder. 'I am endeavouring to lay the foundation for what I must tell you.' He folded his arms on his desk, and held Howard's eyes.

'Jon has always been a contentious man, and controversial, in Hambledon, even from boyhood. We all know that. Even worse, he has always been honest.' He gave his guests a rueful glance. 'There were times when I could have smote Jon thankfully. There were times when I accused him of practically

306

everything. He has no tact, no diplomacy. Unfortunately, too, he is usually right, and that's unpardonable, isn't it? You will remember little Martha, Howard?'

'Yes, God forgive me, I do.'

'Do you see him often, Howard?'

'No. I suppose he's forgiven me. He told me so, anyway. But he doesn't forget. He's a relentless man, and won't forgive a wrong. We—Beth and I—kept inviting him to visit us, and he always refused, in his blunt fashion. He informed us he wished to have nothing more to do with Hambledon. Yes, I know he is bitter. My parents do invite Mrs Ferrier, and she accepts our invitations, but when she has dinner guests of her own Jon always has an excuse not to be present. He won't forgive Hambledon—not that I blame him. But what about that new "evidence" you mentioned, Louis? What has it got to do with Jon?'

'To be brief about it, Howard, Campion has declared a vendetta against Jon, all very smooth and righteous, of course, and for the good of the town. The plot has been under way for some time. The Senator, and quite a number of other people—you'd be surprised—not only want to drive Jon out of town but want to deprive him of his licence to practise anywhere. And to subject him to new criminal proceedings.'

'But they can't do that!' cried Howard. 'He can't be tried again for the alleged murders!'

'No. Perhaps not. But he can be tried for performing abortions, can't he?' Louis opened a desk drawer and drew out a slender piece of linen, stained, and laid it on the desk. Then he opened it silently, and the two other men saw a long curved instrument. 'A curette,' said Louis. 'For the scraping of a uterus. It is used for legal—and illegal—purposes. It is a life-saving instrument after a spontaneous abortion, and it is also used by abortionists. Look at it, Howard.'

With horror Howard picked up the instrument, and then he saw the script on the silver handle. 'Jonathan Ferrier!' The priest looked at it, and shrank.

'Yes. I've talked with Martin Eaton, Mavis's uncle, at the Senator's request. I went to Martin's house. He gave me this curette. He said Mavis had brought it to him—after Jon performed the abortion on her. She told him that Jon had insisted on performing the abortion the night before he left for Pittsburgh. He did not want children. She was heart-broken—'

307

Howard looked at him wildly, then ran his freckled hand through his bush of auburn curls. His light eyes bulged. 'Why, that's an infernal lie if I ever heard one! I think old Eaton's lying! Or mistaken—but how could he be? He heard the medical testimony of doctors from this very hospital, Louis, and the testimony of doctors in Pittsburgh, that Jonathan was there two, three days before—' He banged his fist on the desk. 'For Christ's sake, Louis! How could you believe their lies for a moment? Your own surgeons, your own doctors, in this damned hospital, said she had been—aborted—at least forty-eight hours after Jonathan left Hambledon!'

Louis shook his head slowly and painfully. 'I know, I know, Howard. Calm down, if you please. But why did old Martin—old indeed!—he's years younger than I am—lie like that? I have his solemn statement in this folder. He's a doctor, himself. He was here in this hospital with Mavis, and he had admitted, before she died, that Jonathan had been in Pittsburgh for several days. I heard him, myself, while we were trying to save her life. He was distracted. He did say, over and over, when she died, "He's guilty! Guilty as all hell!" Well, we can put that down to his distraught state. The girl must have lied to him—he was alone with her when she died. That's the only explanation.'

Father McNulty spoke in a hushed and shaken voice, 'Nothing in the world, even if he confessed it himself, would convince me that Jon ever had anything to do with that crime, that frightful crime.'

'Nothing in the world, Father,' said Louis, 'would convince me either. I know Jon. I've hated him more often than I've liked him, and wanted to get him off the staff, and do him other mischief when he openly insulted me and called me "Doctor Bogus".' He smiled sadly. 'But I knew him for a good man, even when I wanted to cut his throat myself.' He hesitated. 'The—committee—went to see Dr Humphrey Bedloe of the Friends', too. You know old pompous Humphrey. The committee, I might mention, was composed of Senator Campion, Mr Witherby, and Dr Schaefer—whom Jon called a butcher and a murderer, with some reason—and a few more prominent citizens who have, to put it kindly, encountered Jon before in some of his less benevolent moods, in and out of the hospitals.

'Well, they went to see old Humphrey, and showed him the curette, and he was aghast. He had admitted that he had thrown Jon off the staff, and Board, even before he was tried. He also admitted he had been "hasty" and that he had never really believed in Jon's guilt. Then they showed him the curette, and he almost had a stroke. He then confessed that he knew someone who had told him that he had seen Jon in town the day the abortion had taken place.'

The large froggy eyes moved from one face to another. 'It was on that frail little evidence—though you never knew it, Howard—that Jon was arrested in Hambledon. Humphrey refused to give the name of the man, but when the committee called on him—with this evidence—he blurted out the story. It was Tom Harper.'

Howard glared at him with incredulity. 'Tom Harper, who's dying of cancer, and whom Jon is helping so wonderfully now?'

'The very same,' said Louis, and he told the two men. They looked at him dumbfounded and sick. 'Of course,' said the doctor, 'it isn't possible that it is true. I have my own means of information, and I know they went to Tom. There was a rumour that Jon had been very harsh and cruel to him, had driven him from practice, and then had, even more cruelly, given him a "menial" position as a hired overseer on one of his farms. I see you both know the real story. At any rate, Tom admitted that he had lied to Humphrey, out of envy and resentment of Jon, and he was broken-hearted. They tried to inveigle him into making a false affidavit, I heard. You might as well know. Thelma, his wife, told me. But he absolutely refused, and threatened to go to Jon with the tale.' Louis's sigh was very deep. 'Unfortunately, Tom died at six o'clock this morning, of a massive internal haemorrhage, caused by his disease. So, we only have Thelma's word that Tom had told the committee that he had lied to Humphrey. And the rumour remains of Jon's "cruelty" to that unfortunate man. If Thelma tries to help Jon, it will be brought out, to Jon's injury, that he had given Tom, and her, a contract, most generous—amazingly kind and charitable and generous— assigning the income of the farm to Tom, or to Thelma, for life, and Jon also has paid for their children's education in the future. The committee is already calling that a "bribe to stifle the truth".'

'Dear God,' groaned Howard. 'What kind of people live in this world, anyway?'

Louis was so disturbed that he could not help saying, 'Don't be too hard on humanity, Howard. We—you—are part of it. You will recall the day when Jon told you about your little girl, Martha. I believe you called him a "murderer," yourself. And that was dutifully repeated all over the town.'

The priest looked at Howard compassionately. Howard said, 'I deserved that. I really deserved that. But I wasn't lying, Louis. I thought it was the truth. Or perhaps I did not. Perhaps I was shouting at the threat to Martha, and not really at Jon.'

'We all try to excuse ourselves, myself included,' said Louis Hedler. 'I'm sure this is a familiar story to you, isn't it, Father?'

'Very familiar,' said the priest. 'Even in the Confessional, people will try to defend themselves. And, even on their death-beds, sometimes.' He had suddenly begun to look much older and wearier than usual. Louis took a sheet of paper out of the folder and studied it. 'Yes,' he said, and folded his hands over the sheet.

'I don't know if you know Peter McHenry, Howard, though Father McNulty does.'

'I know the McHenrys,' Howard said.

'Good. Then perhaps you know that Mrs McHenry was in frail health, and had been so for years. Jon examined her, then demanded to examine their child, a little girl of nine, named Elinor, for he was convinced, he said, that Mrs McHenry's illness had a psychological basis and not a physical one. Peter objected to Jon examining his child, or even talking to her, but I think Jon insisted—' He glanced at the priest, who hesitated.

'He didn't exactly insist,' he said. 'You must pardon me. The events of that day are painful to remember. It was all so unjust to Jon, and I was the guilty one who cajoled him into seeing the McHenrys. It is true that Peter objected—at first. Then, if my memory is not failing me entirely, he reluctantly consented.'

'Yes,' said Louis. 'He told Mr McHenry that his child was—psychotic—and that she was the unconscious cause of her mother's illness, though no one, not even the young mother, suspected that. Mr McHenry,' and Louis looked at Howard piercingly, 'was as infuriated as you were, Howard, when Jon told you about Martha. The truth is very hard to accept, isn't it? At any rate,' he continued, when Howard's face darkened with heavy colour, 'they took the child to neurologists in
310

Philadelphia, I believe, and all examining doctors said she was quite normal. Then Mr McHenry came to me shouting against Jon as a trouble-maker, an incompetent and a cruel liar, and demanding his removal from staff and Board. He was accompanied by Senator Campion and Mr Witherby. He said his child had not been Jon's patient at all, and though he had not been called for the child, had insisted on examining her and giving his amateurish opinion—which had caused her parents devastating worry and mental anguish—and acted, in all ways, unethically.'

He lifted the paper on his desk. 'Mr McHenry's affidavit, sworn to three weeks ago.'

Then the priest spoke through pale lips. 'I think Peter will ask for the return of that affidavit, Dr Hedler.'

'Yes?'

'You see,' said the priest, and there were tears in his eyes, 'little Elinor had an episode that even Peter could not overlook. One of the gardener's boys was teasing her one day, the way boys tease little girls, and she picked up a scythe and—well, she tried to kill him with it. When her father, who was nearby, tried to take it from her she turned on him, screaming that he wasn't her father, that he and Matilda had stolen her from her true parents. She was quite—wild. Out of her mind. She struck at him with the scythe, then when he attempted to catch her she raced for the house, shrieking that she was going to kill her false mother. Peter ran after her. They caught her at the door, and she was—in Peter's own words—like a demon. Then she collapsed. When she awakened a few hours later she claimed not to remember the event at all, but Peter says there was something in her eyes, cunning and watchful, which frightened him even more than her violence. He took the child, a few days later, to the psychiatrist in Philadelphia, whom Jon had recommended.' The priest looked down at his shoes. '*Dementia praecox*, as Jon had diagnosed. Paranoid type. The girl is now confined in a private sanatorium.'

'Dreadful,' said Louis. 'The unfortunate parents.' But his voice was a little relieved. He wrote something quickly on the paper. 'Perhaps you can induce Mr McHenry to say he was mistaken in making this affidavit, and to tell the truth.'

'I am sure I can,' said Father McNulty. 'He wrote to Jon, I believe, asking his pardon, but Jon never answered him. You know—Jon,' and he looked at Howard. 'Very unbending. And

311

proud. Peter would have already repudiated that affidavit, Doctor, if he had remembered it. But he's very distraught, just now, and consoling his wife.'

'To be sure, to be sure,' said Louis, but he did not sound too sympathetic. He lifted another paper. 'A similar complaint by Elsie Holliday. She complains that Jon was not the doctor of her son, Jeffrey, but only a friend. However, she swears, Jon forced himself on the case, insisting on diagnosing it. I am not at liberty to tell you what his diagnosis was, but Jeff did die a short time later in a sanatorium in another State, of the disease Jon diagnosed correctly. It still remains, however, that Jon did examine Jeffrey without permission of Jeffrey's physicians, and under the protest of the mother. She claims that Jeffrey did not give Jon permission, either. Of course, it is a technicality, but an unpleasant one, but if the facts are so it does not reflect comfortably on Jon. But hardly enough to cause the revocation of his licence. However, we know the town, and we know Jon's enemies, who insist on repeating the scandals against him, and this is just one more, such as the Harper rumour, and then the accusation spread by Peter McHenry among his associates, before he discovered that Jon was entirely correct. One thing piles on another. It makes for unpleasant reading, in the mass though individually it means little. Cause only for a reprimand, if that.'

'And all that, on top of what Martin Eaton is now swearing, and the curette is a lovely story,' said Howard, making a sick mouth.

'Yes. Yes, indeed. Martin's story, and the evidence of this curette, is very damning, in spite of what we know to be the facts. I wish Tom Harper were alive to repudiate the rumour, which the Senator and old Witherby heartily believe. Or, at least they pretend to. Incidentally, Old Jonas told me—swore to it, in fact—that Jon had accused him, without proof, and on later examination, of trying to commit suicide, and that he had poisoned himself. Jon was not present when Jonas was admitted to the hospital. I think he was out of town. Jon is his family physician, however, and returned a day or two later to take charge of Jonas. Now, it was really very reckless of Jon to tell his patient, later, that he believed him to have attempted suicide. We all know old Jonas. His one terror is of dying. He wants to live forever. I don't know the true story or, what made Jon accuse Jonas of a crime, but that,

312

too, is a sorry tale. It could have serious repercussions, you know, for a physician is supposed to report an attempted suicide. Jon did not. Yet he privately accused Jonas.'

'It smells,' said Howard. 'It smells to high heaven.'

'That is my opinion, too,' said Louis. 'But everyone in Hambledon is certain that old Jonas is a saint, and his word would be taken against Jon, who is not regarded as much of a saint.' Louis smiled briefly. 'I have Jonas's affidavit here. "As a good Christian man, as my friends can all attest, I deeply resent Dr Jonathan Ferrier's accusation to me, that I attempted to kill myself with a dose of arsenic. This is libellous in the extreme. Et cetera et cetera".'

'You know,' said Howard, 'I feel as if I am in a crazy, malignant dream.'

'It has been my experience,' said Dr Hedler, 'that this is a most malignant world.'

Howard was thinking. 'Coming back to that—that curette. Anyone could have taken it from Jon's cabinet. It's in his examination room.' He paused. He suddenly remembered that Jonathan was very careful to keep his precious gift from his father locked away safely.

'But, they will ask, if Mavis visited an unknown abortionist, why did she take the curette with her? He'd have one of his own.'

'Perhaps he asked her to bring Jon's.'

'There is that possibility, yes. But that will hardly be believed, you know. People will ask, "Is Dr Ferrier actually accusing a doctor, an abortionist, of asking for another man's instrument? Aren't abortionists more circumspect than that, or is Ferrier implying that there is a deep-laid plot against him, and that the abortionist deliberately killed Mavis to involve Jon?" That is what they will say, and so no one will believe it. We don't believe that, ourselves, do we?'

Howard shook his head, dismally. 'No, I don't believe it, either. Mavis is dead. I suppose we'll never learn the real story.'

The priest said, 'Murder will out.'

Louis replied, 'I am sorry to disillusion you, Father. It often is concealed for ever.'

Now he was frowning. 'I am approaching the really serious matters, and these cannot be explained, and are totally damning, if true. I have here the affidavit of one Mrs Edna Beamish, of Scranton, formerly of Kensington Terraces, in Hambledon. She alleges that on a certain day—the date is here—Jonathan tried to perform an abortion on her in his offices. She had come to him for that purpose, she swears, because she is a young widow and did not wish to bear a child without a living father. She is very penitent. She claims that she was distracted with grief for her dead husband, and hardly knew what she was doing. However, the pain she suffered in Jonathan's offices caused her to scream so loudly that she was heard not only in the waiting-room but on the street, also. She was in such pain and so terrified that she would not let him proceed, and left. He had demanded two hundred dollars, she swears. She left for her home. Unfortunately—and there is an affidavit from a certain doctor in Scranton to this effect—the injury to her was so extensive—something about the complete dilation of the uterus—that she did in fact abort later. Two days later, in Scranton, while visiting friends. The doctor, who swears in his own affidavit that an attempt had been made to abort the young lady, is a man of high reputation and standing. He was forced to operate on her. She was haemorrhaging. It is doubtful that if she remarries she will ever be able to bear children, the damage, done by the abortionist, was so extensive, and the resultant inflammation so widespread.'

Louis looked at the two appalled men. 'Gentlemen, that was a crime, there is no extenuation. It was a serious crime. The young lady was slightly over three months pregnant. Moreover, we now have affidavits of patients who were in Jon's office that day. The affidavits were reluctantly given, and how Campion and company discovered who those patients are I simply do not know. But they are here—sworn to by simple, honest people of good reputation in Hambledon, who like Jon and only gave these affidavits under pressure. They testify to the young lady's screams and her protestations of agony, and her accusation that Jon was "hurting" her. They have described her dishevelled state and her denunciations as she "fled from his inner rooms."

'The affidavit from Mrs Beamish was sent to Senator Campion, who, as her Senator, was outraged. It seems that he had had a warm acquaintance with the late Mr Ernest Beamish, and esteemed him highly. So Kenton, of course, investigated. The young lady's affidavit, on the face of it, and her doctor's affidavit, then can be considered genuine.'

314

'I don't believe it,' muttered Howard. 'Something smells again. I don't believe it.'

'Knowing Jon, I do not believe it, either,' said Louis.

'I don't believe it,' said the priest, and shuddered.

'Nevertheless,' said Louis, 'there are the hospital affidavits, the attending surgeon's affidavit, and the fact that Mrs Beamish was indeed in Jon's office, and that indeed other patients heard her screams and saw her flee. Moreover, we now have affidavits from Mrs Beamish's husband's executor, and from another doctor in Scranton, that they visited Jon, alleging that there was a bill due him. He pretended, they said, not to recall Mrs Beamish immediately, and then admitted that he did. He told them frankly that she had been three months pregnant, but had "incontinently" run out before he had completed the "examination," and that therefore she owed him nothing.' Louis smiled his wry smile. 'On the face of it, that sounds absurd. No other doctor would have refrained from sending a bill. After all, he did partially examine her. Even if the examination had not been completed, there was still his time, and his good faith in proceeding with an examination she had requested, herself. So, Jon stands damned there, too.'

'But he will have his records of Mrs Beamish,' said Howard Best, the lawyer. 'And no abortionist keeps records of his patients.'

'True. Let us hope he has his records, still. Of course, before a judge and jury, the showing of such a record will not carry much weight, but it still will carry some. Now, let us go on.

'I have here two affidavits from two other young women, a Miss Louise Wertner, seamstress, of Hambledon, and a Miss Mary Snowden, milliner, also of Hambledon. The young ladies —if one can call them such—were indiscreet, indulging in pre-marital experiences, as they admit, themselves, in their affi-davits. One girl is nineteen, the other twenty-one, and in poor circumstances. They had heard, they say, of some "rumours" in connection with Dr Ferrier, and in their extremity had gone to him, and he readily consented to perform the abortions, even to declaring that he detested children and did not blame the girls for wishing to rid themselves of their "burdens".'

The froggy eyes surveyed the two silent men on the other side of the desk, both looking cold and a little shrivelled and despairing.

'The young ladies do not know each other. But one paid

315

fifty dollars for the alleged abortion, the other paid seventy-five. Jonathan had his office clerk send them bills to their homes, one dated 10th November, 1900, the other 21st November, the same year. I have those bills here. They went to his office lately, the clerk recognised the bills, accepted payment of them and receipted them. Would you care to look at them, gentlemen?'

They examined the damning bills, and the receipts. Howard put them down quietly on the desk, clasped his hands together and studied them. Then he said, 'There is no proof that Jon aborted them, as they claim, is there?'

'In a way. They both suffered some slight ill effects a few days later. They went to separate doctors, who, in affidavits I have here, swear that the girls had been pregnant and that a recent abortion had been performed on them. The doctors are reputable. Neither knew that Jon was the "culprit." One of them is on the staff of this hospital, itself. Dr Philip Harrington. I have had Phil in here, told him none of the things in the affidavit, and asked him about Miss Wertner, his patient. He readily stated that indeed the girl had had a recent criminal abortion, that her condition at no time had been serious, but that she had complained of cramps. She stayed one day in the hospital. You both know Philip Harrington. As I already have an affidavit from the other doctor I asked Phil to make one also, and he did so. He says he would like to meet the "criminal" personally, who had killed those embryos and deal with him, himself.'

Howard said in a dull voice, 'Wasn't that indiscreet of Jon, to send the girls bills—if he really did perform the operations?'

'Not in ordinary reasoning. The girls did not have the money. He was sorry for them, or even wished to abort them for some twisted reason or other. Or, he wished to conceal criminal activity and sent them bills for "complete physical examinations," as the bills, themselves, state clearly. There is another thing: the usual fee for examination, conducted for patients who are in such poor circumstances, is usually far smaller than this. The best physicians ask only fifteen dollars, for such examinations take several days, of at least one hour a day. In an office, too. Quite often, under the rule of charging less for the poor, and charging more for the rich, a doctor will charge only a very few dollars.'

'How did it happen, Doctor, that you received those two affidavits?' asked the priest.

'It is the rule, Father, that when a girl goes to a physician and he discovers that she has had a recent abortion, he must report it. Phil reported it to the Board of St Hilda's. The other doctor reported it to the Friends'. This is to protect the attending physician, who must have witnesses during the examinations. It is also the law. It is very necessary to run to earth those despicable creatures, the criminal abortionists, who put the lives of young mothers into terrible jeopardy. The girls often die, you know. The girls were much afraid to report Jon, for fear of legal reprisals, for they are parties to a criminal act. And girls usually know this. They were given assurances that if they did report the name of the abortionist they would be protected and not prosecuted. Still, they returned to their miserable habitations to consider the case. Then they both made affidavits and sent them, one to this hospital, one to the Friends'.'

'And Phil Harrington still does not know?'

'No, Howard. He is a close friend of Jon's. I haven't had the heart to tell him. Yet.'

Howard considered long and deeply. Then he said, 'I don't believe it. Call that an emotional statement if you will, but I don't believe it. My lawyer's instinct tells me that it is a lie they are telling of Jon.'

'I do not believe it, either,' said Louis, and Howard and the priest smiled at him weakly in gratitude. 'But still, there are those receipted bills, there are the affidavits of the doctors. Under other circumstances, Howard, what would you say?'

The young man hesitated. Then he admitted, 'Guilty.'

'So,' Louis sighed.

'Campion does not know of these second and third abortions?'

'Of course not. He knows about Mrs Beamish only.' Louis closed the folder. 'Campion and company are demanding that I call in some members of the State Medical Board to review the "facts." The "facts" he has given me. Now, Howard, as Jon's friend and his former lawyer, what do you suggest I do?'

Howard rubbed his auburn curls wearily, then examined his nails, then scratched his ankle. 'How long is Campion giving you to appeal to the State Medical Board?'

'Ten days.'

'Then you must ask for a longer time. I am going to investigate these serious cases, the Beamish, Wertner and Snowden

317

ones. The other affidavits are only malice and not worthy of consideration. Except for Jon's curette. Eaton swore that Mavis gave it to him and said she had taken it when Jon had laid it down? Yes. I'll try to see Eaton, but he's rabid against Jon. And everyone remembers the Philadelphia papers reporting that he shouted, "No, no!" when the verdict of Not Guilty was brought in. Then he had a stroke. Everyone remembers. They also remember that he had loved Jon like a son, and was delighted when Jon married his niece, Mavis. Men don't turn against such "sons" unless for cause, everyone will say. The cause seems obvious. Or, is it so obvious?'

'I don't understand you, Howard.'

'It is a rule among lawyers to ignore the obvious unless it is written down in black and white as a sworn statement, or a confession. Even then we are suspicious. That's why we scrutinise everything, and that's why we are so often successful in defending a case. The incredible is more often the real explanation.'

'I hope you are not catching at straws,' said Louis. 'Are you going to tell Jon now?'

Howard considered a long time. Then he shook his head. 'No, it would only make him curious and even dangerous. You know Jon. No. I want to have some substantial refutation before I talk to him. And, by God, I am going to get it!' He thrust out his long sharp chin belligerently.

Louis was silent for a few minutes. 'You know,' he said at last, 'I am endangering my position here by telling you any of this, Howard. This is all confidential, you see, as Campion warned me, and he is very powerful on the Board, the only layman. They, too, are preparing the case against Jon. He wants to face Jon with complete iron facts and resolutions, and the State Medical Board members. He wants it all done ruthlessly, like a knife cut.'

'Typical of him, the damned scoundrel,' said Howard with bitterness. 'Such men can't stand honest men, men who oppose them. I'd rather face a tiger than a politician who is after my hide.' He looked at the pale and silent priest. 'Father, what do you think of all this?'

'I think that Jon is surrounded by vicious and vindictive enemies, who will do anything to destroy him, Howard. How he earned those enemies lies in his nature, and in their natures, too.'

'Well, he has friends, too, Father, including Louis here.

318

Louis,' and Howard smiled at him, 'I'd never have thought it of you!'

'Perhaps,' said Louis Hedler, smiling back, but not with much amusement, 'you would have no reason to think that of me even now, Howard, if I were not financially independent! It is very strange and sad, is it not, that the mere matter of economic independence can make a man brave, whereas a man not so fortunate would not be brave at all?'

'Courage is always the price that life demands for granting peace,' said the priest.

'A worthy sentiment, Father, and perhaps true. But if a man jeopardises everything in his life for the sake of the peace of his conscience, he often has reason to regret his nobility. Heroes are lauded in story books, and in history, yet even in history they frequently come to a sad and inglorious end. Later, of course, they are eulogised, but that does them no good at all when they are in their graves.'

'Then only God remembers,' said the priest, and Louis looked embarrassed. He thought he might begin to believe that if Jon were saved from what was planned for him.

CHAPTER 12

To-day, thought Jonathan Ferrier, I will hunt Jenny down if I have to take Hambledon, and the island, apart with my bare hands.

He had not been sleeping well lately, partly because of the heat which did not abate, and the sullen hot days, and partly because as the time approached for his departure from Hambledon he was feeling a strong depression which never lifted. He knew he could not stay in this town under present circumstances, which became worse day by day rather than better, but a heavy sadness had come to live with him which he could not philosophise away nor laugh at in his usual manner. Then, there was the elusive Jenny, and her elusiveness had at first irritated him and then had become a source of impatient anger. He had heard rumours that Robert Morgan was visiting her more and more frequently, in spite of the smart warning he had received from Jonathan, and was even seen at local public gatherings with her, including the circus, of all things. Jonathan was finding it harder and harder to keep from making kindly and derisive remarks to the ingenuous Robert, who no longer spoke of Jenny Heger. It would have to be settled once and for all, Jenny cured of her girlish coyness and plans made for the immediate future.

He had been calling at the island at least three times a week, usually between five and six in the afternoons, and Jenny was always 'not at home,' according to Harald and the servants, or totally invisible and not to be found. Jonathan had thought of writing to her in plain terms, but was afraid that Harald might recognise his handwriting and that was intolerable. Worse, Jenny might refuse to answer.

He decided, early this morning as the sun came up, that he would see, or find, Jenny at noon on the island, before she had time to hide or whatever it was she did when he appeared.

He stood at the bedroom window and looked to the east, hoping for rain. But there was only a brilliant scarlet glittering in the east, sparkling through the long dark fronds of a great willow, and a harsh dusty odour of parching land.

Jonathan cursed as he struggled into clothing already damp

with his own sweat the moment it touched his body. He would make his hospital calls early, overseeing what Robert Morgan had done. He called Robert's house and said with curtness, 'I don't want to be out in this heat more than I have to, Bob, so I am going to the hospitals as much before noon as possible. Will you be there?'

Robert yawned, glanced at his bedside clock, and said, 'For God's sake, it's only a quarter to seven! You don't usually start until nine. Very well. I'll meet you at the hospitals. St Hilda's first?'

'Don't I always?' asked Jonathan, and hung up, feeling again a huge irritation against practically everything and everybody, and waiting for the heavy depression to fall on him again. It did, as he went downstairs to the morning-room, where breakfast was waiting.

Marjorie joined him. 'Aren't you early, Jon?' she asked. She appeared more wan than usual, and thinner.

'I thought I'd make an early start and finish before the worst of the heat,' he said, as he helped her into her chair.

'Is that cold fruit you have been eating?' she asked, looking with mistrust at the remains of the melon.

'Yes, and very good, too. Why should fresh fruit be served only at the end of a meal, and dinner at that? If I don't drop dead of it by to-night then I'll have exploded another fallacy of the hacks, that fresh fruit on an empty stomach can cause the flux, dysentery, colic, colitis, and assorted ills. Never believed it anyway. Have a piece for yourself.'

'It looks inviting,' Marjorie admitted. 'Dear me,' she said, touching her forehead with her handkerchief. 'It is very hot, isn't it? I can't recall it being like this in Hambledon before. When the weather breaks it will be quite violent.'

She told him then that she intended to go to Philadelphia in a few days to visit old friends and distant relatives. 'And perhaps I'll go to Atlantic City, too, for a look at the sea, and some coolness. I've never really got accustomed to living in a landbound town like this.'

Jonathan said, 'When I leave, which will now be very shortly, why don't you return to your home in Philadelphia? After I've done a little wandering, I may settle there, myself.'

Marjorie's lips trembled as she smiled. 'That would be nice, dear. Let me consider it. After all, I've lived here so long, a lifetime, thirty-six years, and I knew it, too, as a child. Still, it never really seemed my home, though I love this house of your father's. It is hard for a woman of my age to be moved easily.'

'Fifty-five or six isn't ancient,' said Jonathan. Now he looked at his mother and saw her pale and dispirited appearance. 'When you are in Philadelphia, why don't you stop in and see Dr Hearndon?'

'I may,' said Marjorie, who had already decided to visit the cardiologist. Her body seemed very thin in its light batiste embroidered shirtwaist and high lace collar which rose to her chin.

'Why don't you women wear sensible clothing in the summer?' asked Jonathan, with some uneasiness. He did not like his mother's colour and her air of lassitude. 'That duck skirt of yours: it looks like iron.'

'And your high stiff collar is even worse,' said Marjorie. 'Well, I hope you won't miss me too much when I am in Philadelphia. Incidentally, Harald is going with me. I do wish Jenny would come too. So lonely on that island, though one hears she has made some new friends.' Marjorie gave her son an artless glance.

'If you mean Bob Morgan,' replied Jonathan, 'he is quite harmless.'

'They have been to dinner several times at the Kitcheners,' said Marjorie. 'Poor little Maude. She is really very smitten with Robert, and he is exactly right for her, though, as men are so very foolish, he probably does not realise that. Yet.'

Jonathan stood up. 'But, I'm sure that Maude, in the old way of women, will soon enlighten him,' he said, and left the room and the house.

He chose his buggy to-day, which would give him some shelter from the probing sun. He drove off through the hazy streets. It was still very early, but from open windows he could hear the unmelodious and—to him—obscene shrilling of the new phonographs and the new popular songs. Edison was truly a genius, and a blessed man to his countrymen, but why he had invented the phonograph was a mystery to Jonathan, who detested popular music and its cheapness. At least three exuberant phonographs were grinding out a particularly detestable song, 'Under the Silvery Moon, I like to spoon—!'

Robert Morgan was not at St Hilda's yet when Jonathan arrived, now in a bad temper. But he met Philip Harrington, whose large good-natured face registered worry. 'What's the matter?' Jonathan asked.

'It's Dr Brinkerman—again.'

'Old Claude? What's he been doing now?'

'Telling everyone I don't know a uterus from a burlap sack But I'm used to that now. You know what he thinks of us younger doctors. A nasty, surly brute, big as a house, and mean as a red-eyed bull, and as arrogant as an ignoramus.'

'I like your metaphors,' said Jonathan. 'But what's the swine—not to mix metaphors—been up to lately?'

'He had a case, a young mother, first baby born at home, as usual, then something went wrong. Child premature; detached placenta. Her own doctor rushed her to the hospital and called Claude, who calls himself "the senior gynaecologist" around here. I and my friends are just butchers, according to him, or in our first year of med. Well, he operated on the girl—to save her life, to quote him—and removed the uterus. Twenty-two years old. Isn't that pretty? While he was at it he also took her ovaries, and that's the prettiest of all. Plunged into old middle-age in her early twenties.'

'Were they diseased?'

'No, of course not. And the uterus could have been saved, with a little skill. But you know Brinkerman. Count de Sade would have loved him. He hates women, and their functions.'

'You were in the operating room with him?'

'Yes. And a couple of others. I tried to intervene. For a minute, there, I thought he would deprive me of my manhood, with his scalpel.'

Jonathan said with disgust, 'Did you tell Louis?'

'Yes, I did. I thought he'd blow up at me, but he has something on his mind these days, or he's coming down with something. Subdued. Abstracted. He only said, "Let's have a little peace here. Claude probably did what was best in his own judgement".'

'Good old Louis,' said Jonathan. 'The Golden Brotherhood hangs together, probably because they know that if they didn't they'd hang separately—with the judge wearing a black cap. I'd like to spring the trap. Well, what is done is done, unfortunately. Don't brood on it.'

'I want your help,' said Philip. 'A tube pregnancy was brought in here this morning. Claude's case. He'll mutilate the girl, as sure as hell, just as he did the other. I can see him licking his chops, right at this minute. He's a great hand at mutilation, Claude.'

'That's because he has a young wife, his second, who could teach Prissy Witherby a few delightful tricks. All other women are proxy for Ethelyn. I've often thought doctors' first practices should be confined to members of their own immediate family, and closest friends, before they went into general practice. That should not only teach them discretion and care, but would help them get rid of secret resentments. A few discreetly murdered wives, for instance, would make a doctor love all other women thereafter, in forgiveness.'

'I wish you'd be serious,' said Philip, and the two young men paused a moment to nod at passing doctors.

'I'm deadly serious. Phil, I can't help you, and you know that. Brinkerman hates me like poison and that's funny because I never had to cross his path except for twice, and that was five years ago. Told him he was unfit.'

'And that should make him love you, or he should have a short memory.'

'That was five years ago. I rarely see him. We don't speak, but we do exchange the most telling glances. We meet socially, here and there, or we used to when I mingled, and we were very, very polite to each other. How could I possibly get into his operating room?'

'You could ask old Louis—for a study.'

'Won't you be there?'

'Yes. But the old bastard scares me to death. He looks at you like approaching Nemesis, if you venture a remark or an opinion. Powerful old bugger. Now, he can't intimidate you.'

'It's all unethical. He'd probably order me out at once.'

'Louis still has the say, in spite of his new preoccupation with some damned problem or other. And Brinkerman's getting a rotten reputation among us younger fellas, and we're spreading the word. That's bad for St Hilda's, and Louis knows that, or he should. Jon, this is a very young woman, only twenty, for God's sake!'

'I don't know how I get into these things,' said Jonathan. He thought of Dr Brinkerman with loathing. He knew more about the older doctor than did Philip Harrington. Yes, a sadist, a lusting hater of women, helplessly infatuated with his gay young wife, and rabid. To him, a man of fifty-two or three, all pretty young women were secret whores, though he was famous for his enchantment with them. He had a way

324

of painfully pinching or squeezing student nurses, then laughing in their grimacing faces and assuring them of his affection for them. They feared and avoided him, running at the sound of his roaring, brawling voice, and his oversized presence. They dreaded encounters with him in the corridors and in quiet places. He had what the girls called 'a dirty mouth,' and dexterously tormenting fingers. He could inflict more torture on a young woman in his examination rooms than any Inquisitor. Yet, for some unknown reason, he had a reputation as a fine doctor and surgeon, to the younger doctors' bafflement. Jonathan believed it was because he was very rich and influential, and a shameless egotist.

Jonathan found Louis Hedler in his office. He was struck, when he entered, by Louis's worried and drawn expression, and his sluggish manner. He was also surprised when Louis, instead of looking apprehensive as usual when Jonathan entered, smiled at him almost paternally. 'Jon, my boy,' he said.

'What's the matter, Louis? Are you sick?'

'Well, no. Sit down, Jon. I'm just—concerned—about a member of the staff.' The bulging brown eyes studied Jonathan with a peculiar expression. 'A fine man, rather young. I'm afraid he's in a little trouble—of his own doing, in a way. Rash. Impetuous. A little indiscreet at times. But I happen to be fond of him.' Louis smiled. 'Personally, he offends me often, but I have to admit he knows what he knows, and in a superior manner. If you had told me,' said Louis, 'a year or two years ago, or even six months ago, that I'd be concerned over him now I'd have laughed tremendously.'

'You're mellowing, Louis. Who's the mellower?'

Louis contemplated him, then smiled enigmatically. 'I don't think you know him, Jon. No, I don't think you know him at all.' He rubbed his lips. 'You never come in here, Jon, without bringing me contention or alarms or worries. Which is it now?'

'Every single one.' He told Louis about Dr Brinkerman and Philip Harrington. He did not know why Louis's face became more and more dismayed as he talked. 'So,' said Jonathan, 'if you have no objection I'd like to be present in the operating room.'

'That's impossible! You know how Claude hates you.'

'Just because we had a difference of opinion? A long time ago? Don't we all have differences of opinion with each other?

I'm not pretending that Claude loves me, but he's surely for-gotten my clash with him.'

On the contrary, thought Louis, very much on the contrary! He said with some malice, 'Jon, wasn't it a few of your bright young lads who insisted that the operating surgeon have the privilege to refuse to have anyone present he did not desire to be there? Yes. In the old days any physician who was inter-ested, and even his friends, could enter an operating room and observe to his heart's content. But not you lads. All for asepsis and no theatre atmosphere.'

Louis smiled at the tight strong face opposite him, and the dark and amused eyes. 'Touché, Louis. And we are right. Who is the young lady, by the way, and who is her family physician who sent her here?'

'Um,' said Louis. He shook his head then said, 'Mrs Jason Hornby. Attending physician, Summers Bayne, friend of yours.'

'Splendid,' said Jonathan, and reached, without permission, for the telephone on the desk and called Dr Bayne and then spoke in his most ingratiating way. 'I'd like to be present, Summers, when Claude Brinkerman operates on your patient to-day, Mrs Jason Hornby, at two o'clock. Oh, ten is it? Even better; I am here at St Hilda's now. You see, Dr Philip Harrington can't be present,' and Jonathan cocked his black eyebrows at Louis and smiled. 'So Phil asked me to be there in his place. There's a little difficulty, Summers. Old Claude doesn't love me as he should. You'll mention that I am there at your request, if he should object? By the way, who picked Brinkerman?' Jonathan listened and frowned. Then he said, 'I quite agree with you. I wouldn't let him clip my dog's nails. Don't worry, Summers. I'll be right there, and you will be, too, and we won't let him do any fancy hemstitching or let him waltz around the vena cava. He does so love that vena cava, and why the Board doesn't throw him out is something per-haps old Louis can tell you.' Jonathan winked at his indignant elder. He replaced the telephone receiver, and said, 'The young lady chose Brinkerman, herself. Insisted, so what can poor Summers do? He was quite relieved when I said I wanted to be present.'

'You're an impertinent rascal, Jon.'

'Oh, I know that. Incidentally, why don't you throw Brinkerman out?'

'Jon, he's an expert surgeon, if a little—radical—at times.

326

He is as bad as you about asepsis. If his judgement, occasionally, fails him, who among us can plead that we are never wrong? If the average layman fully understood into what vulnerable weak hands he was trustfully submitting himself, and to what fallible judgement, we'd have no more hospitals, no more operating rooms.'

'And many people would still be alive instead of rotting peacefully away in some pretty cemeteries. That's just confidential between ourselves, of course.'

'You don't keep that very "confidential" very often, Jon.' Louis was very disturbed. 'I wish I could dissuade you. I have my own reasons for suggesting you not be there. You have enough enemies, Jon, and Brinkerman is a man who cherishes his enemies and never stops until he has cut their throats.'

'We aren't friends, Louis. We never were. But he can't hate me more than he already does.'

Louis was silent, gazing at him, and then he said in an odd voice, 'You are quite right.'

Jonathan went out to inform Philip Harrington that he was 'taking your place. You have an emergency.'

Philip was relieved. 'Mrs Hornby is a nice rich young lady, or Brinkerman wouldn't look at her, and isn't it fortunate for a lot of people that they can't afford some operations? Poverty has done more to save a number of lives than wealth has done, and if that isn't heresy what is it?'

'It's truth,' said Jonathan, and went on his rounds. At half-past nine he was in the scrub-room adjacent to the operating room, and, whistling, was beginning to scrub when Claude Brinkerman came in with a blast like an attacking minotaur. 'What the hell is this, Ferrier, you being my assistant on the Hornby case?'

'Didn't you hear?' asked Jonathan, very mildly. 'Phil has an emergency. He asked me to do him a favour and—'

The hard and flaming face seemed to radiate irrepressible hatred and fury, and the little pale eyes sparked with a murderous glow. Jonathan, who was well aware of their mutual dislike and mistrust, was still surprised at this overwhelming and vehement attack, for the cause of their old disagreements had been trivial. But Brinkerman appeared beside himself as he stood and breathed rage at his junior, clenching and unclenching his huge hands at his sides, his broad chest heaving. Had Jonathan been his deadliest enemy he could not have betrayed more savage irrationality, no more incipient violence.

327

'I won't have you!' shouted Brinkerman. 'I want no mur—'
He stopped, visibly and painfully swallowed. But his rage
grew. 'I won't have you! Is that clear?'

'Summers Bayne asked me,' said Jonathan. 'He has that
right. Or, would you prefer to let Phil Harrington do the job
for you in an hour or two, when his present emergency is
over? This case isn't an on-the-minute emergency, I understand.' He looked at Brinkerman. 'What was it you were
about to call me, Claude?' He shook his wet hands and now
as he looked at the other surgeon there was something in his
eyes that was frightening. Dr Brinkerman looked back at him
and a curious malign flickering ran over his large, coarse
features, and there was a twitching of his long thin mouth.

'Never mind,' he said. His forehead was a purplish red, but
now the colour began to subside. He lowered his voice. 'Ferrier,
I don't like you and I never did. I don't trust you and I never
did.'

'I can repeat those laudable sentiments about you, too,
Brinkerman.'

'You can be of no help to me in that room, Ferrier.'

'But I can be of help, perhaps, to the patient,' said Jonathan, and again their eyes met like boulders meeting.

'Are you questioning my professional competence?'

'Are you questioning mine, Brinkerman?'

The other doctor again raised his voice. 'I don't want you!'
'Summers does. Louis knows, too.'

Dr Brinkerman was suddenly silent. Then he smiled very
slightly. 'Old Louis,' he said, 'may have reason to regret this,
very soon.'

'I want you to know, Brinkerman,' said Jonathan, 'that I
did not exactly force myself into this situation. My presence
was requested.'

'I am aware of that, Ferrier. I shall deal with Summers
Bayne in my own way at my own leisure.'

Jonathan considered this. 'I am not without friends,' he said.

'You would be surprised,' said Brinkerman, and chuckled
hoarsely.

Jonathan frowned. He was remembering what Philip Harrington had told him recently, and the odd way his former
friends were treating him in the hospital corridors and in the
lounge rooms recently. But he made himself smile, knowing
that Brinkerman was watching him closely.

'Very ambiguous,' he said. 'But I have enough friends to

protect Summers, and I am famous for protecting my friends.'
He motioned to one of the nurses who came forward to
powder his drying hands and to help him with his rubber
gloves. 'Moreover, Summers's brother is a State Senator,
close to the Governor, or did you not know that? I also believe that brother is on the Medical Board. If I am wrong,
please correct me.'

Dr Brinkerman had forgotten. He gave Jonathan another
vicious look, but remained silent. The young nurse assisting
Jonathan held her mouth prominently disapproving of him,
and avoided his eyes, and Jonathan again wondered at human
nature, for he knew that Dr Bayne was very popular with the
nurses and Brinkerman's ugly threat against him should have
vexed the girl. Jonathan mentally checked another black mark
against mankind.

The patient was ready when the two surgeons went into the
operating room and Dr Bayne, already scrubbed and masked
and covered, was waiting for them. He gave Jonathan an
inquiring look and Jonathan winked at him. The patient
was under anaesthesia, and all was in readiness. Jonathan
looked at her pretty unconscious face, the face of a child.
Then he looked at Dr Brinkerman who was also studying
those soft and childlike features, and his eyes were lustful and
hungry as a torturer's, and as the sadist's they were.

There was no denying that he was a competent surgeon, and
he made the incision with a preciseness and skill and smooth-
ness that won Jonathan's admiration. It was a routine matter.
The pregnant tube was large and bulging but was not unduly
inflamed nor had it ruptured. The girl was lucky. Dr Brinkerman neatly excised it, and then he said to the watching
interns, ignoring Dr Bayne and Jonathan, 'I will now closely
examine the uterus for deformities, and the other ovary.
I have not yet decided if this one should be removed, and
possibly the uterus.'

The men exchanged troubled glances. But Jonathan said,
'I can see, for myself, that the uterus and both ovaries are in
prime condition, and there is no need for an extensive explora-
tion.'

Dr Brinkerman paused. He turned his head slowly and his
pale eyes glowed with evil fire. 'Am I the surgeon or, are you,
Ferrier?'

'I am your assistant, if you wish to call it that, and I am
also bound by the Oath of Hippocrates, and am a defender of

329

the public weal. Therefore, if you do any damage to this girl's reproductive system I shall do everything I can to prevent you from ever operating on anyone again.'

He spoke clearly and sharply and with assurance, fully aware that he had now done the irrevocable: he had deliberately insulted and defamed the operating surgeon in his own domain, before the faces of witnesses. But to him the young girl on the table, so unaware, so trustful, so helpless, was more to him than any consequences to him, though he knew they could be grave. However, only the strongest threats could stop this sadist, and Jonathan had used them.

'For this alone,' said Brinkerman, in a terrible voice, 'you could have your licence revoked.'

Jonathan laughed. 'I should like to see you try it. I will bring witnesses against you, and be damned to professional ethics and always protecting the bungler or the intentional mutilator. Well? Aren't you going to suture the girl or are you going to permit her to bleed to death?'

He nodded to Dr Bayne, and still watching Brinkerman closely, he went to the tubal pregnancy in its receiving basis and dipped his hand in water and baptised the exposed embryo. Some of the interns smiled indulgently, but at least two looked grave, and Dr Bayne blessed himself. Dr Brinkerman laughed lewdly and made a low indecent remark to the nurse nearest him. But the girl was unexpectedly near tears.

'After your vindictive remarks, Ferrier,' said Dr Brinkerman, 'I have no recourse but to report you to the Board. Moreover, if this patient of mine suffers unfortunate results the blame rests with you, for interfering and overt intimidation.'

Jonathan came back to the table. 'I shall protect myself by watching every move you make, Brinkerman, so you don't do the girl a sly mischief, which I would not put past you. You have a reputation for that.' He looked at Dr Bayne, whose eyes showed his worry and alarm. 'Don't be too concerned, Summers,' he said. 'Just watch the child carefully.'

Everyone was convinced that Dr Brinkerman was about to have a stroke. His hand trembled and shook. Jonathan dared not take the needle from him, for his hand had become contaminated, he believed, even in the presumably sterile water in which he had dipped it. He did not, however, trust the sterilising of very much in the operating room, and so refrained. But he watched every movement of Dr Brinkerman's. The older surgeon had considerable self-control when he wished, and he recovered himself and his awful colour receded, and he completed the stitching without incident. Then he strode, without a word, from the room, viciously stripping the gloves from his hands and banging the door behind him.

'He'd kill you if he could, Jon,' said Dr Bayne, as the interns and nurses tenderly covered the girl closely with the blankets and sheets and wheeled her out. 'That is a very bad man.'

'And a man who should not be permitted to operate on any woman under the age of fifty,' said Jonathan.

'Jon, be careful.'

'In this business, it is a crime to be too careful of a colleague's delicate sensibilities,' said Jonathan. 'I've never covered a man like Brinkerman before and I do not intend to do it now.'

He expected to be called to Louis Hedler's office, but though he remained in the hospital for another hour he received no call. He went down to the river, and to the island.

Jonathan was informed at the door, by old Albert, the servant, that Mr Ferrier was not at home, Doctor, no, I really don't know where he is. Miss Jenny? It was believed that she had gone into Hambledon, though not certain. Would Dr Ferrier like a drink? Dr Ferrier declined, and went away glumly. Where the devil was the girl, if she was on the island? There were all sorts of cool nooks, of course. Then Jonathan remembered that only one boat had been tied up on the opposite bank, in Hambledon. That meant that Harald had left it there before going into the town. Three, including the one Jonathan had used, were now on the island. He began to smile. When Harald arrived across the river he would find no way to get back, unless he signalled and someone saw. Of course, he could be away all day, and even the evening, and by that time Jonathan would have returned to the mainland, and left a boat for him.

So, Jenny was on the island, hidden away as usual. Jonathan began to explore. He knew the island fairly well, for it had intrigued and amused him from the beginning. He toured the island, peering into every hidden grotto, into every trellised arbour. The scent of pine was very fresh here of a sudden, for a slight breeze had risen. After he had searched one side of the island Jonathan, feeling hotter and hotter and more and more irritated, began on the opposite side.

His whistling became a little shriller and now a few birds answered peevishly. The light on the river was blinding and it had a torpid, oily look smeared with metallic blue. Little paths crept down the 'fraudulent' woods, as Jonathan called the stands of expensive, rare trees, but he was grateful for their brief shade as he passed into it and then out of it. He could smell damp earth, rich and carnal, and old fallen leaves, and the rank odour of the few wild flowers permitted to grow here. He saw the tiny artificial bay in which Peter Heger had intended to keep tropical fish. It was covered with algae, another thing which was unusual, and the confined water stank unpleasantly. But a wild duck or two sailed its surface placidly.

He stopped to mop his face, and turned his eyes from the river and the walls and saw a grotto practically hidden by honeysuckle bushes and untended shrubbery. He saw a yellowish movement, quick and alert, beyond the bushes, and then it was still. He had found Jenny. He was certain she had heard him approach, and his whistling. Yet now she crouched on the big stone in the grotto like a hunted thing, avoiding pursuit. This made Jonathan more annoyed than ever.

He pushed through the shrubbery, and lifted aside the wisteria, and saw Jenny indeed crouched on the stone, with books and papers about her, and in a yellow cotton dress as plain as a shift. She looked at him in a white, mute silence and her eyes were very large and blue as a sudden little ray of sunlight touched them. She said nothing in recognition. She merely sat there and regarded him, not with anger or aversion or indignation, but with no expression at all.

'Hallo, Jenny,' he said, and in spite of his annoyance his voice was very gentle, and he was surprised at the emotion that took him at the sight of the girl, and the tender desire for her, and his longing. He stood and looked at her and smiled, and after a moment Jenny turned her head and her mouth trembled. He saw her profile, and it was dearer to him than anything he had known before, and he wanted to put his hands to her face, turn it to him and kiss that mouth and those long black lashes and the slender white throat. 'Jenny,' he said.

He was afraid that she might jump to her feet and run past him, as she had done that Fourth of July, and so he blocked the passage with his tall body, but easily. However, she did not move. Her hands were pressed one on top of the other in her lap, and her face was still averted. But her lashes had begun to blink, as if she were about to burst out crying. Jonathan could see the quick lift of her breast under the plain yellow bodice of the frock, and then its fall.

Very slowly, so as not to frighten her, he let the curtain of wisteria drop and it immediately made a living dusk in the grotto. Jonathan approached Jenny, and again with infinite slowness he sat down on the dark clean earth and hugged his knees and watched her. She did not look at him. He saw her knee near his cheek, and he wanted more than anything else to lean his cheek against it; he could see the coarse threads of the frock and the outline of her long thigh and calf, and then the arched foot in its sturdy slipper.

'I've looked for you for weeks, Jenny,' he said. 'But you've avoided me. I wanted to know that you've forgiven me.'

She spoke as if to the stony earthen wall of the grotto, 'I forgave—you.' Her voice was so quiet that he could hardly hear it.

Then he remembered something he had forgotten concerning that night. When he had thrown Jenny on her bed and then she had fought him off wildly, he had seen her great terror of the unknown about to be thrust upon her so brutally, and with such violence. But with this was another terror: the terror of her own desire to surrender, the weakening of her legs under him, the sudden brief softening of the muscles of her thighs. It was then that she had arched her body in total resistance and had pushed him off, and had broken into tears.

He had been confident in these weeks that he could make Jenny love him. He was startled and overjoyed to know that Jenny had loved him even then as she had fought him off, and had struggled with him. She would not have him as he was then, fighting with her, about to take her by force. And, of course, he thought with indulgence, without benefit of clergy.

'Well,' he said, 'I'm glad you've forgiven me. But, as I told you then, Jenny, my darling, I've loved you for a long time. Didn't you know that?'

'No,' she said.

'And you didn't believe me, that night?'

Her head moved farther from him and she dropped her chin on her shoulder. 'No, I didn't.'

'Do you now?'

She pushed back a heavy fold of her hanging hair and he saw her hand, tanned by the sun, long, elegantly made, like his mother's hands.

'Won't you tell me, Jenny?'

But she pressed her lips tightly together and he thought of a shy but stubborn child, and he smiled again.

'Jenny, I'm going away. I am never coming back.' He could smell the green life about him, and the earth, and the faint scent of the soap Jenny had been using, and the natural warm fragrance of her body and her hair. 'I want you to come with me, Jenny,' he said. 'I love you. I've loved you for years. I want you to marry me. Soon. To-morrow if possible. I want to take you away from Hambledon, where we'll have some peace. I want to show you the whole world. My darling.'

He had never spoken to any woman like this before, nor had he felt this tenderness mixed with desire, and gentleness and even peace.

She said in a voice almost whispering, 'Robert Morgan asked me to marry him, yesterday,' and she raised her hand and childishly wiped away her tears with the back of it. She still would not look at him.

'Bob Morgan?' He almost laughed. 'That boy! Well, I admire his taste if I don't care for his impudence.'

She turned suddenly to him then and her cheeks flared into colour and her blue eyes flashed with anger. He had always suspected Jenny of a deep temper, and he saw it now.

'What impudence, yourself!' she exclaimed. 'I can tell you this, Jon, he's an improvement on the Ferrier men!' Her voice was strong and direct and clear. He was delighted again. He squeezed her foot and very softly he let one of his fingers rise to her slender ankle and caressed it. He felt the flesh start a little under his touch; she did not snatch her foot away as he expected.

'Oh,' he said, 'I have no doubt that almost any man would be an improvement on us. We're a bad lot, as the English would say. Harald's an idiot, and I have the worst disposition in town, as you've probably discovered, yourself. We are no gems on the matrimonial market, and there I agree with you. I wonder how you will endure being my wife. I really pity you.' Now his whole hand was about her ankle. He wondered how much higher he could dare to raise it. It was a delicious thought. Then he was aware that she was very still, and he looked up and saw she had a tremulous, bemused expression, as if all her awareness was directed to the ankle which he held. He watched her closely. Then he leaned his cheek against her knee. It stiffened, jerked, but she did not draw away, and his hand slid upwards to the slim round calf, warm and firm and smooth.

A deep heavy flush swept into the girl's face. She began to cry again, soundlessly. Very slowly, Jon rose to his knees, looked into her face, then took her into his arms, hesitated, and pressed his lips into the hollow of her throat. Her head fell back, helplessly. He felt the sudden bounding of her pulse against his mouth.

'Jenny, Jenny,' he whispered. Her body was young and soft in his arms. He dropped his head and pressed it against her breast. She stirred once, then was still. He felt her rapt and virginal passion. She was not afraid, though she had begun to shiver. The duskiness of the cavelike grotto appeared to enlarge to him, to be filled with unbearable excitement, pleasure and happiness, to be waiting. The quiet was not disturbed except for the distant sound of the cicadas, the faint whispering of the trees, and everything was heightened to the senses, the fragrance of earth and leaves and young flesh.

Jonathan thought, in the intensity of his now rising desire, that there were worse places in which to take a beloved woman who was surrendering. He kissed her bare throat again. His hand fumbled at the buttons on her bodice, little plain white buttons, which he saw as large as plates. He unfastened one, two, three, and then she caught his hand and her own was strong.

'No,' she said. She burst out crying, not cries of fear or protest, but sounds of desolation.

He immediately stopped. He held her gently as before, and then he pulled her head to his shoulder and let her cry. What else had he expected of this inexperienced girl? He was terrified that he had ruined everything, and had confirmed her previous bad opinion of him. 'Jenny, my darling,' he said. 'I'm sorry. But I love you more than my life, Jenny. I won't annoy you again, or disturb you. Until we're married. Jenny?'

'I can't marry you!' she cried, and his shirt was wet with her tears. 'I want to, but I can't!'

'Why not?' He was elated.

'I've done something terrible to you!'

He paused. He laughed a little. He held her more tightly.

'For God's sake, Jenny! What "terrible" thing could you do to me, a child like you?'

She rolled her head despairingly on his shoulder. 'I can't tell you, Jon. Please go away. Forget you ever saw me. Go a long way away.'

At this point an alien voice intruded, full of amusement and contempt.

'I hate to end this touching, pastoral scene,' said Harald Ferrier, at the entrance to the grotto. 'There is nothing so lovely as true love, is there? And what a scene! All the elements of dramatic seduction, immaculate surrender, tremolos in dulcet tones, manly force, blandishments—everything. I should have been a playwright. I'd make my fortune.'

Jenny literally leapt in Jonathan's arms, and he let her go and got to his feet, his furious temper rising, his dark face thick with blood. He saw his brother leaning negligently against the entrance to the grotto, and smiling his broad and amiable smile. Harald winked.

It was that lascivious wink, that indulgent smile, which made Jonathan feel acute embarrassment as well as rage, and a sort of juvenile shame. 'What the hell are you doing here?' he shouted.

Harald raised his ruddy eyebrows and beamed. 'Why,' he said, as if surprised, 'I believe I live here. At least, I thought I did. Didn't I?'

'Spying on us!' shouted Jonathan, feeling foolish.

'Oh, I'm sorry. Perhaps I should have waited for the final scene, but I confess I'm a little too prudish for that. There would have been a final scene?' He looked at Jenny crouched on the stone, her head turned away. 'I'm surprised at you, Jenny,' he said in a mock reproving tone. 'A nice girl like you.' He regarded his brother again in a friendly way and his eyebrows cocked humorously. 'Quite a dog, you, Jon. No girl is safe with you, not even an untouched morsel like Jenny. I really should be very outraged. After all, I am her natural guardian. At the very least you should have observed etiquette and asked for her hand, and not have tried—er—to take it robustly, if I may put it in a euphemious form?'

Jonathan wanted to kill him on the spot. He also hated him. He also felt ridiculous, a little contemptible, and wholly sheepish.

'Button your frock, Jenny, my dear,' said Harald in a paternal tone. 'Quite extreme, the way it is gaping open. You should be more careful when you dress. And do drop the hem of your frock. Young ladies are not supposed, I believe, to expose themselves almost to the thigh—in broad daylight, too. But that happens during a romp, I have heard.'

Jon's fists clenched. The heavy blood was still in his face. Then he looked at his brother's eyes and saw that they were not smiling in the least, and that their usual handsome hazel had turned an ugly, dark brown, and were glinting.

Harald laughed softly. He stared at Jonathan. 'Let's end this comedy, shall we? It distresses me to catch frolickers in an—indiscreet—moment. But, I heard voices, and I was looking for you, Jon. I was told you were still on the island. I was resting in the castle, and it was believed I was in Hambledon. So, I was searching for you. It was not my intention to force my company on you and Jenny. Had you both been talking nicely and politely in a genteel fashion, conversing as is customary when a gentleman calls upon a lady, or perhaps been drinking tea—Jenny, did you forget the teacups?—I should have withdrawn to a distance, made some commotion, called, to let you know of my approach. But there was something in the sounds I heard—scuffling? kissing?—that alarmed me.' He spread out his hands, pleadingly. 'So, what else could I do but to hurry to save Jenny's honour, which was apparently in the direst danger, or rescue her from—what do the ladies call it—"a fate worse than death"? Jenny, you should be very grateful.'

The girl had buttoned her frock and dropped its hem and now sat rigidly and very still on the stone, her hair fallen partly over her face.

'Now that you've had your little moment of fun,' said Jonathan, restraining himself from hitting his brother only by the greatest effort, 'suppose you let us alone.'

'To continue the seduction of an innocent and helpless girl?' Harald recoiled in a parody of horror. He grinned, showing all his large white teeth, and struck himself on the chest dramatically. 'Not I, the protector of my stepdaughter!'

Again, Jonathan saw the ugliness in his brother's eyes above that wide smile and he thought, He hates me as I hate him. Why? Jenny? Yes, it could only be Jenny. He would kill me as easily as I could kill him. Now, this is a pretty situation.

'You don't need to protect Jenny,' said Jonathan. 'We are going to be married, practically immediately.'

'Before or after?' asked Harald.

'Oh, go to hell,' said Jonathan. He looked at Jenny, who was too silent, too stricken. 'Jenny? I'll have my mother invite you to stay with her until we are married. You will come, won't you, Jenny?'

Harald shook his head sadly. 'No, I am afraid she will not, Jon. I truly am afraid not.'

Jonathan ignored him. For some perverse reason he now wanted to laugh, explosively. He wanted to comfort Jenny, too, and make her laugh. 'To-morrow, Jenny?' he asked.

'Ah, no, dear brother,' said Harald, when Jenny did not answer. 'Jenny has her reasons, don't you, my dear? A very upright and valid reason, too. Jenny is all honour, or, at least, she was until about half an hour or so ago. You see, Jon,' said Harald, assuming a mournful air, 'Jenny thought you were a murderer until quite recently, when I enlightened her out of the deep charity of my heart.'

'What!' said Jonathan. 'You're lying, of course.'

'Not at all! Ask Jenny, herself. She believed that you murdered her mother. Tut, tut! All these murders you are accused of! Blackbeard was a tiro in comparison. What a reputation you have! And what a black face you have, Grandpa, all at once.'

Jonathan was looking at him with a daunting expression, but Harald was enjoying himself too much to be overly alarmed. However, he did step back a little. 'Why don't you ask Jenny yourself?'

Jenny was now sitting upright on the stone. She had pushed back her hair. Her face was very white in the green gloom of the grotto.

'Jenny?' said Jonathan, turning from his brother.

'It's quite true,' she said in a muffled voice. 'It was very stupid of me. I—I thought you—and Harald—had conspired together to kill my mother, for her money.' She suddenly put her hands over her face. 'How could I have been so stupid, so ignorant? I thought, that just before she died, that injection you had given her—I didn't know she was already dying, and that you tried to save her.'

'And all this time,' said Harald, in an affectionate voice, 'the poor child believed we were brother-murderers. At least Jenny had not thought so badly of me; she thought I was guilty of only one murder, or the instigator of one. You were the real brute. With your little deadly needle.'

'Christ,' said Jonathan. He stared at the girl with disgust.

Then he said sharply. 'Jenny, you can't have been that big a fool, can you, not even you?'

His tone made her shrink. She could only sit with her covered face and dolorously shake her head. Even when Jonathan picked up his coat and hat and pushed past his brother she did not look up. Harald had lit a cigarette and was smoking it tranquilly. Jonathan stopped a short distance from the grotto and said with harsh contempt, 'So that is why you were always running from me, Jenny, like a whipped mouse! If you hadn't conjured up that wild fancy in your mind, Jenny, would you have let me share your bed with you that night?'

'Oho,' said Harald. 'What a lovely vision arises in my brain! When was "that night," Jenny? Was our Jon too ardent, too pressing? He has no finesse, you know.'

Jonathan raised his hard brown hand and slashed his brother across the face, and Harald fell back against the side of the grotto. Then Jonathan went off, the sound of his enraged departure slashing through the silence for several moments.

Jenny was weeping. Harald smoked and watched her kindly until she could cry no more. She fumbled in her pocket for her handkerchief and blew her nose fiercely like a child. Harald said, 'Nature can be very dramatic and heroic, but she inevitably ends on a ludicrous note. We weep out our hearts, then have to blow our noses, or pay a visit to the water closet. Very banal. Jenny, this isn't such a tragedy as you now think. You've seen Jon at his worst, if that's possible. He never waited for explanations; he never does. He makes up what he considers his mind, and never hears the defence. Think what you've escaped, Jenny.'

She blew her nose and glared at him with anguish and anger.

'I know, my dear. You're blaming me. But I did it for your own good. You see, Jon wasn't treated so unjustly by you, after all. Perhaps you never knew it, but there are some very vile tales going the rounds about you, in Hambledon, and he—'

'About me?' shouted Jenny, springing to her feet. 'Me?'

'You, my sweet. That you are my mistress, and probably the playmate of many other gentlemen, too.'

'Oh, what a filthy liar you are!' Jenny screamed, advancing on him.

'Jenny, compose yourself, pray.' His mocking tone halted her. 'And Jon believed them all, every one. He has made many obscene jokes about you, Jenny, in my company and in the company of others. He has made them, with some slight reservations, to my mother, too. If you don't believe me, ask her. You might ask others also, in Hambledon.'

Jenny's long black lashes, wet and matted, blinked rapidly at him. She was thinking, even while fresh tears ran down her face. She remembered the covert smiles she had been enduring in Hambledon since her mother had died, the avoidances, the snubs. She had always been miserably shy. She had thought that her increased shyness had brought out the half-hidden sneers she had detected in the town, and that her 'plainness' was becoming more and more evident and was arousing hostility. Her father had told her she had no 'graces,' and she had come to think of herself, in her early maturity, as a clodhopper, quite deserving of smirks and indifference. She recalled Jonathan's perverse remarks, too, which she had not understood.

Then on Fourth of July, Jonathan had attacked her in her father's house, where her mother had died, when she was alone and with no defender. She had forgotten what he had said to her in the library, and while he struggled with her in her room, for she had been too guilt-ridden later and too remorseful to remember. Now she recalled, with sick cold horror, his taunt that she was withholding from him what she gave so freely to his brother. She remembered that she had struck him across the face, as he had just struck Harald. How could she have forgotten? How could she have forgotten his manifest contempt for her, his jeers, his laughing accusations that she was 'coy'?

Her face turned scarlet now as she faced the smiling Harald, who was dabbing carefully at his cheek, touching his lips with his handkerchief, then examining it for blood. 'Are you thinking of confirmation, Jenny?' he asked. 'If so, I am glad. If Jon had had any respect for you, he would not have tried to force himself as I gather he did, on "that night," nor would he have attempted to do the very same thing to-day, without me to protect you, and far from the house. He treated you like a trollop, Jenny, a drab, a slut. Surely even you are clever enough to realise that? A gentleman does not try so crudely to seduce a young girl, especially a girl like you, unless he believes her beneath respect. His offers of marriage —Jenny! Had you—er—succumbed to him, let us put it nicely, he would have laughed in your face afterwards.
340

Believe me, I know my brother. He has a bad reputation among women.'

'Jon could think those things about me?' muttered Jenny, in pathetic wonderment.

'Jenny, Jenny, haven't you been listening? Isn't it evident that he did, and still does? Isn't his conduct enough for you?'

'Oh!' cried Jenny, and put her hand to her cheek and turned her devastated face aside in shame and sorrow and bitter loneliness.

'I know this is hard, my sweet,' said Harald, exultant. 'But how much better it is for you to know it now than later, if I had not come to your rescue. Think what you would have endured then. Jon's a bad man, Jenny. He was cruel to his wife, Mavis, and drove her out of his life, though you choose not to believe it. He is ruthless with women, absolutely ruthless. A woman serves but one purpose for him. The female part of the whole damned town adores him, except when it has reason to hate him. Now, isn't that strange? I will forget modesty for a moment and remark that compared with me he has no charm or appearance.'

'I hate you both,' said poor Jenny. 'I despise you both.' Then she flung back her hair and marched to the archway of the grotto. But Harald smiled at her, shaking his head and not moving.

'You don't despise me, sweet Jenny. You despise what I've told you, and is that fair to me? You wronged me terribly in your thoughts, and I've forgiven you, and wasn't that magnanimous? Who else would forgive such an awful accusation so easily, except someone who loves you?'

'Please,' said Jenny, in a broken voice, 'please let me go. I—I can't stand it any longer. Please.'

'Of course,' he said with gentleness, and moved aside and she passed him in a rush and he heard one loud sob from her as she ran towards the castle.

'Dear Jon,' thought Harald. 'One good turn deserves another. I do believe one of my teeth cut the inside of my cheek. At any rate, I think you've seen the last of Jenny, and she of you. Will I invite you to the wedding? I must give that long and serious thought.'

CHAPTER 13

Miss Amelia Forster, at the 'typewriter' Robert Morgan had inherited from Jon Ferrier, regarded Howard Best with horror and disbelief, as he sat opposite her in the deserted waiting-room, for this was Saturday afternoon and Robert Morgan was in the hospitals and Jonathan was not to be found. Howard had called Miss Forster, whom he knew well —his father had been a schoolmate of hers and she was a friend of the family—and asked her if he could consult her in Jonathan's offices. Miss Forster, as the daughter of a minister and a member of the Ladies' Aid, had been accustomed to taking orders all her life and so, though she had had plans for a picnic lunch with her sister's family it never occurred to her to mention that she had a previous engagement. Moreover, Howard's voice had been properly grave and insistent and resembled her father's voice in his sterner moments.

So Howard sat alone with her on this hot and dusty Saturday afternoon, the latter part of August, and gave her a circumspect outline of that section of Louis Hedler's story which intimately concerned the office and herself, and asked that the matter be confidential.

She began to cry silently, her thin white nose turning quite red. She removed her spectacles and wiped her eyes. Her stiff muslin leg-of-mutton sleeves took on a wilting air for a moment or two. Then she briskly patted her grey pompadour and sat up straight and folded her lean hands on her desk. She said in a very quiet voice, 'Howard, you know that is all lies, about Dr Ferrier.'

'Yes, Amelia, I know. But it is going to be very hard to convince others.'

'But to think Dr Ferrier, who is so kind and so good— a little strait-laced, but I like that in gentlemen—so old-fashioned but so *good*, could be the victim of so much *hate*, and *malice* and lies and *cruelty*! To think there could be a plot to take away his licence—'

'And send him to prison,' said Howard.

Amelia gasped. 'What a wicked, *wicked* world!'

'Indeed,' said Howard. 'However, we aren't going to have a discussion about wickedness. Now, please look at these receipted bills, 10th November and 21st November, of last year, made out to Miss Louise Wertner and Miss Mary Snowdon, of this town, respectively, one for fifty dollars, one for seventy-five. Did you receipt these bills a short time ago?'

The spectacles now in place, Miss Forster examined the bills closely and said with firmness, 'Yes, indeed. I remember the young ladies well on that day, rather small, and pale.'

'Did you recognise them at all? From an earlier date?'

'No. But the doctor has a large practice, you know. It is impossible to remember all who come and go within these walls, especially if they are not regular patients. To my own knowledge I never saw these young ladies before they came in to pay their bills, and I accepted the money in cash and receipted these bills.' She rested an angular forefinger on them.

'I see.' Howard pondered with some melancholy. 'And this is your handwriting?'

'Indeed, yes. And the bills were typed on this Oliver, and in my fashion. No one forged those bills, Howard,' and she gave him a faint smile. ' "Complete physical examinations".'

'So these bills were sent out last November, as dated, after Jon examined the girls?'

Miss Forster frowned. 'Why, no, Howard. The girls did not bring bills with them.'

Howard sat up, catching his breath. 'What do you mean, Amelia?'

'They came in, hours apart, and they both said they had forgotten to bring the bills, but the amount was so-and-so, and the bills were dated on those dates. Now, I accepted the money, of course, and I typed out fresh bills, and I receipted them and—'

'Three weeks ago?' shouted Howard and jumped to his feet with a wild expression.

Miss Forster stared at him, somewhat frightened. 'Why, yes,' she stammered. 'I told you so, Howard. Was I wrong to accept the money when they had no bills? It is absolutely senseless to believe that people will come into this office and say they owe the doctor money, and offer it, when they don't owe it at all, and you simply must not—'

'Wait!' Howard was breathlessly elated. He sat down and regarded Miss Forster with a beatific smile. 'Let me understand this clearly. You, to your knowledge, never saw these young ladies before, but they came in a short time ago, told you they owed Jon money, mentioned the amount, and claimed that they had forgotten to bring the bills? But the dates were for last November?'

'Quite correct,' said Miss Forster.

'And three weeks ago—on that very date—you made out new bills?'

'Quite correct.'

'And receipted them, then and there, and accepted the money?'

'To be sure.'

'Then as far as you can recall you never sent out bills for those amounts last November?'

'Not as far as I can recall, but it was so long ago, nearly nine months. When I accepted the money I went for the young ladies' files—to note down the payment, of course, so no new bills would be sent.'

'Darling Amelia! Let me see those files!'

She blinked at him. 'But there weren't any, Howard.'

'There weren't any?' He was incredulous, but deeply smiling.

'No, indeed. It worried me a little, too. I mentioned it to Doctor later, and he wasn't disturbed. You see, he often destroys records which are no longer active. I think it very incorrect, myself, but we'd need a warehouse, considering his practice, and if the bills are paid and the patients do not appear again within six months or a year, he destroys the records and—'

'He often does that?'

'Usually. He says it isn't necessary to keep old obsolete records, because there isn't any income tax any longer—'

Howard was still breathless. He leaned back in his chair and regarded Miss Forster with love. 'So, it wasn't unusual at all not to have a file on those young ladies?'

'No. Though he doesn't throw away files unless they have been paid, of course, or he has decided not to charge the patient—he is so very charitable, you know, Howard, so *feeling*, so pitiful towards the poor—'

'Yes, yes, I understand that. Amelia, if called on, would

344

you swear that these bills, though dated last November by you, on demand, were really made out only three weeks ago, because the patients claimed to have forgotten the original bills, though they knew the amounts?'

'Swear, Howard?' Miss Forster was aghast.

'You know what an affidavit is?'

'Yes. I do know, certainly. No one has ever doubted my word in this town, so—'

'Dear, sweet Amelia. If I make out an affidavit for you, in my office, will you swear to it—all right, don't shake your head—will you affirm that it is true, all these facts you have given me?'

'I will do that, Howard.' Miss Forster looked resolute. 'But I do not understand what this all means, you have given me only a brief sketch of some nefarious plot against Doctor—'

Howard considered her. 'Those young ladies, Amelia, have already made out affidavits to the effect that on those dates last November, Jon aborted them right here, in his examination rooms.'

Miss Forster's thin and colourless mouth fell open and her eyes bulged on Howard, and then a dark crimson rushed over her dry face. She looked away and blinked rapidly.

'I thought you understood, Amelia, when I told you that certain females have alleged that Jon performed upon them—well, what is considered illegal surgery.'

'No. I did not,' said Miss Forster in a stiff voice. 'I thought you meant surgery which should have been performed in a hospital, but Doctor decided to do it here without anaesthetic—that is very wrong, you know, and not to be justified, if true, but—'

'I was talking of something called criminal operations, Amelia.'

Miss Forster stood up, very agitated. 'You must excuse me, Howard. I feel quite ill. I must lie down for a few moments.'

Howard stood up also. He took her arm. 'I'm sorry, Amelia. I understand. But now you see what all this really means. All right, dear, cry if you must, but try to listen. You see the enormity of the dangerous charges against Jon?'

'Yes, yes. But surely no one could be so evil? Those girls— they were pale and poor and very gentle, and talked to me so nicely, and were so apologetic about not bringing the bills, and I thought how well-mannered they were for their station in life, which was obvious.'

Howard smiled at the stilted language. He hugged Miss Forster very gently.

'How is it *possible*, Howard, for such meek little things to be so *wicked*?'

'Well, I've heard that demons often disguise themselves prettily.'.

'I—my father—we didn't believe in demons, Howard.'

'They certainly exist. Never mind. But if it will help you I can almost assure you that those girls did not think of all this by themselves. I think their names were furnished to certain parties. It doesn't matter, dear Amelia. Perhaps some force was exerted on them, or threats, to make them perjure themselves. We may possibly never know.'

She blew her nose, which had become quite swollen, and mutely nodded her head. She still had not grasped in full the extensiveness of the plot to ruin Jonathan Ferrier, though now she could see the dim outline.

'And on Monday, Amelia, you will come to my office to—affirm—that affidavit?'

'Yes. But what excuse shall I give Doctor? I can't lie, Howard, and I have promised you not to tell him of these—matters.'

'You must tell him that you have a matter of business with a lawyer, which will take but a few minutes. After all, my office is only ten minutes' walk from here.'

She clasped her hands tightly together with new agitation. 'Oh, Howard, what a frightful thing to do to Doctor! These people must be punished, punished, punished!'

Then Howard said, 'Do you recall a Mrs Edna Beamish, Amelia?'

She frowned and thought, then nodded. 'Oh, yes, a most hysterical lady.'

She told Howard of what he already knew, and her voice rose indignantly. 'Such a vulgar display! Rushing out with her hat in her hand, and waving her parasol as if demented. Really!'

'She did not appear to be in pain, or hurt?'

Amelia looked at him in astonishment. 'Why, no, not at all. I did hear her scream that Doctor was hurting her, and then Dr Morgan went to the examination rooms—he was across the hall, and I saw him, because I was so alarmed that I opened the door, and I heard their voices, and Doctor was laughing as if at a joke, and Dr Morgan swore a little. I did hear that. And then I hardly reached my desk again— I was truly astounded—when she burst out into this room and screamed at all of us here, the patients and myself that Doctor had hurt her, and I almost laughed, for he has never hurt anyone—'

'You are a jewel, Amelia.' Howard patted her shoulder. 'I will include that in the affidavit, too.' He had another thought. 'Do you know if Jon still keeps the instruments his father gave him?'

'Yes. In a locked cabinet.'

'And no one has the key, but him?'

'No one. Not even Dr Morgan, who would not need them anyway. There is another cabinet, quite complete, in the other examination room, and Dr Morgan has the key to that. Not surgical instruments, however, but just for examination. Our hospitals are modern, you know.'

Howard went into the white and deserted examination room and studied Jonathan's cabinet and saw the expensive instruments on their white and silken beds. He saw where the curette had lain, and he saw the dark pepper of dust in the empty indentation. Who had taken Jonathan's instrument? Who had had access to his keys? The only answer was—his wife. Howard stood, rubbing his chin, staring absently through the glass doors of the cabinet. Mavis. So Mavis had taken the instrument. The question was, why? Mavis had been a stupid young woman. She would not have known the name, or the use, of the curette—unless it had been described to her.

Miss Forster was still waiting for him, for she must lock up the offices.

'Amelia,' he said, 'several people, both men and women, were here in this office on the day Mrs Beamish ran out accusing Jon of hurting her. Some parties have sought them out, and they have—with some reluctance—made affidavits of the affair, as much as they remembered of it. I haven't been able to understand how they found the names of Jon's patients on that day.'

Miss Forster stared, then leaned forward. 'Why, Howard, I think I can tell you that. At least, I do think so. A gentleman, who said he was a police official—I have no doubt but what he was, for he showed me his credentials—said that some lady claimed to have left her purse, containing a considerable amount of money, in this office. I do not recall the particular lady in the least. There were so many on that day. I was told the exact date, and I did get out a few cards, and gave the police officer the names of four or five people. It was the day, I remembered later, when Mrs Beamish was here. The police official said that perhaps a lady had mistakenly picked up the purse, or a gentleman had taken it, believing it was his wife's, and I remember being puzzled, for with the exception of Mrs Beamish on that day there were no absolute strangers waiting to see the doctors, and I *know* that there were no thieves among them! I gave the official a piece of my mind, and I told him—'

'Would you recognise him if you saw him again?'

Miss Forster considered, then shook her head. 'No, I do not think so. A very nondescript little man. Howard, do you think he was a fraud? Do you think he lied to me?'

'I don't think he was a fraud,' said Howard, with grimness. 'But he lied to you. He wanted those names for affidavits against Jon. Of course, he probably told the patients that Mrs Beamish was making some claim against Jon, and he was trying to protect Jon, so would they just please say so and so, about the woman shrieking that Jon had hurt her? They were reluctant, I see now, very clearly, not because they thought they were hurting Jon, but because they have the ordinary citizen's aversion to dealing with the law in any form.' He thought a moment. 'Of course, that is what it was! And all the time I've been thinking something else. Everything, Amelia, is not always exactly what meets the eye.'

Once out in the street he climbed into his trap and sat and thought long and hard. He had considered going to 'the young ladies' who had made affidavits alleging that Jonathan had performed criminal operations on them, but had discarded the idea. They had unseen but powerful friends, of that he had no doubt. There were large and shadowy figures behind them, and they would report to these figures at once.

There is something worthwhile about living in a small city like Hambledon, he thought as he drove away. Almost everyone knew Miss Forster, whose ancestors had helped found this city. She, and her family, were held in the highest respect, and though they were in rather poor circumstances now the word of a Forster would not be challenged. Her brother was minister of his father's church, and had a considerable reputation everywhere. Miss Forster's word—and affidavit—would be accepted in any court of law, and even Campion understood that. Howard considered again. The Senator had claimed no acquaintance with the little seamstress and milliner, nor had they claimed any knowledge of him, but Howard's lawyer's intuition assured him, without the slightest proof, that there must be some connection. Still, he dared not approach them directly or indirectly, for they would run in terror to those who had demanded their perjury.

At the proper moment, however, they would be confronted. Howard had a plan of his own in mind, and it was broadening moment by moment.

Howard Best was well-known to the police in Scranton, and the chief of police was one of his best friends for they had known each other from childhood.

So Howard went to see William Simpson confidentially. 'It's just a little matter,' he said. 'A small claim against Mrs Edna Beamish, who used to live in Scranton. I am doing it as a favour.' Friends though they were, Howard was enough of a lawyer not to be too forthright and honest.

William Simpson laughed. 'Oh, Edna. A girl from across the tracks, as we say. Pretty little trollop. Prettiest little thing who ever picked up her skirts to show off her wares to the highest bidder—on the right side of town.'

Howard laughed too, genially. 'That sort, eh? And all the time I've heard that she was married to a rich man in Scranton, one Ernest Beamish.'

'Well, that's true, too. Old fool, Ernest. Never married in his life, and when he saw Edna he decided he'd found the girl of his dreams. She wasn't cheap, Edna. No common whore. She had style, too, and nice sweet little manners. Almost a lady. She married him when she was eighteen, and had been in business for at least three years before that.'

'Very enterprising,' said Howard, trying to keep the intense interest off his face. 'Have a cigar. Twenty-five cents apiece. What this country needs—'

'Yes, I know. A good five-cent cigar. What's this about a

349

small claim against Edna? Old Ernest left her quite a lot of money when he died two years ago and—'

Howard sat up. 'Two years ago?'

'That's right.' The chief of police chuckled. 'Perhaps Edna kept him too busy.' Now his sharp eye studied Howard thoughtfully. 'Come on. Tell me the truth. Why do you want to know about Edna Beamish?'

Howard was annoyed at himself. But he smiled and waved his hand. 'It is a small matter. She lived in Hambledon, and there's a matter of a confection, some millinery, she forgot to pay for.'

The chief of police pursed up his mouth and gave Howard a sceptical look. 'Now, that's quite a story. Edna never lived in Hambledon in her life, so far as I know, and I keep up with the gossip in this town.'

'Why, that's impossible, Bill. I have the bill of sale right in my office. Thirty-five dollars.'

William Simpson shook his head, and for some reason he began to laugh deeply to himself, and Howard watched eagerly. 'Howard, someone's pulling your leg. I repeat: Edna never lived in Hambledon. Old Ernest Beamish was well-known to me. We played poker together. He never lived in Hambledon, either. They had a nice house in town, very stylish, and they gave fine parties, and I was often there. After Ernest died—'

'Yes?'

But the chief continued to smoke and shake with silent laughter. Then he said, 'That Edna,' in an admiring tone.

'What about her?'

'I thought,' said the chief, 'that your sole concern for our local Jersey Lily was purely on behalf of a millinery claim, and Howard, I'm ashamed of you, a prominent lawyer like you making up a ridiculous little story like that. I thought better of you. Can't you trust an old friend?'

Howard considered him long and steadily. 'I want to know her connection with Senator Campion, one of our unfortunate Commonwealth's two Senators.'

A closed look came over William Simpson's face. He carefully deposited cigar ash in a tray. He said, 'Why didn't you say that in the first place, instead of trying to make me believe that you believed Edna had lived in Hambledon?'

'She did. She lived in a place called Kensington Terraces.

Not for as long as she claimed, however, but for a few weeks. Recently. Very recently.'

The chief said, 'One of the things a political appointee learns very early—if he wants to survive—is not to talk about powerful politicians, that is, repeat gossip about them. But hell, a few people know, and I'll tell you if it goes no farther, Howard.'

Howard hesitated. 'It might have to, Bill. I'll try to keep it as quiet as possible and look for information which will be a result of your information, without revealing the source.'

'I know you lawyers,' said the chief, and looked at Howard with large cold eyes. 'When it comes to a client you'd betray your best friends—for a good fee, of course. You haven't been exactly candid with me, and why should I be candid with you?'

'For no reason except that if I don't hurry and get some information—and not just about our little Edna—a good fine man will find himself unjustly in prison, not to mention the loss of his reputation and profession.'

'Oh. Why didn't you tell me? Has Edna gotten him into some mess?'

'Yes. She had an abortion, a criminal abortion, only a short time ago.'

'Ha!' said the chief, and began to laugh again. 'The Senator won't like that! Little Edna playing house when the master is away. Sneaking away from Washington to kick up her heels in a dead-dog town like Hambledon, at that! Papa won't like it, not at all.'

'I don't suppose he will,' said Howard, pretending to laugh deeply himself, though he felt intense exultation.

'And little Edna found herself with a bun in the oven which didn't belong to the Senator, eh?'

'Maybe it did.'

'I thought,' said the chief, sober again, 'that you were implying that Edna went into the bakery business with that friend of yours in Hambledon?'

'Let me put it this way, Bill. Edna has let drop a few remarks that my friend is—responsible.'

'I can hardly believe that of Edna! She knew how to keep her mouth shut!' The chief's eyes were hard and suspicious again.

'Oh, not that. I mean she is accusing my friend of performing an abortion on her.'

351

'Edna? Doing that openly? The Senator will kill her! He's a Hambledon boy, keeps his reputation all glowing and sweet-smelling. Come on! What is this all about?'

'Just what I've told you. Now, would you advise me,' said Howard, with a great air of earnest artlessness, 'to tell the Senator?'

'My God, no! He'll murder Edna if it ever even got out that he was playing Papa and Mama with her in Washington! She's the latest of his little friends and has lasted the longest, and only a few in Scranton know about it and they know that if the Senator ever caught them scandalising about him they'd land in a pitch pit. Powerful boy, the Senator, and never forgets his friends or his enemies. Look here, Howard, I don't want any part of it!'

'People must know, in Washington.'

'People know a lot of things in Washington. But they don't talk about them.'

Howard stood up, affecting to be disappointed and down-cast. He sighed. 'Very well, Bill, I should have thought about your position before coming here. You have told me nothing and I am not going to ask you anything. I can appreciate your need to be discreet.'

They shook hands, the chief very relieved. It was only when Howard had left that William Simpson began to wonder, sourly, if Howard had been entirely candid in his disavowals, and if he, himself, had not been led up the garden path. In the meantime Howard was considering how best to prove Edna Beamish's liaison with Senator Campion, the fact of her manifest pregnancy by him, and her resorting to an unknown abortionist either in Hambledon or Scranton. He also needed to know why she had appeared in Hambledon and in the offices of Jonathan Ferrier, though he now had a rather clear idea of the circumstances—to his incredulous horror—and the use to which Edna Beamish had been put, and the reason. As a pragmatic lawyer and paradoxically an honest man he had always discounted the conspiratorial theory of both history and human conduct, but now he admitted freely that both were not only possible but probable. In Jonathan Ferrier's case they were actual.

Howard thought of Senator Campion very thoroughly. He knew that the Senator regarded Hambledon, privately, as bucolic and simple-minded. We'll show him how really crude he is, thought Howard, on the train home. What a stinking, amateurish plot he has thought up! However, it had been Howard's experience, amateurs could often display a boldness experienced plotters could well envy, and by their very clumsiness convince.

During the next few hurried days Howard made several other discreet investigations, and was well satisfied as well as infuriated.

Flora Eaton said, 'Howard, it is very sweet and kind of you to call to see poor Martin, but he is very sick, you know, and needs his rest and peace and quiet.'

'Yes, I understand, Flora. But, you see, this is a matter of extreme importance to someone very important to Martin.'

They sat in the huge dim drawing-room of the ugly house near the river, and Flora eyed Howard Best dubiously, plucking at her grey linen skirt and biting her lips. 'Howard, Martin hasn't been at all well since Senator Campion called on him. Visitors seem to disturb him very greatly.'

Howard sat up quickly. 'The Senator was here?'

'Yes, indeed. So concerned over Martin, they are such good friends, you see. But it was too much for Martin, too much stimulation. He quite collapsed after Kenton had left and I had to call the doctor for him, and the doctor said he was not to be disturbed or upset, or even stimulated again. After all, it has not yet been a year—'

'I know, I know! But I think it will do Martin a lot of good to see me, Flora, I really do.'

'Legal business, Howard?'

'In a way. I know Martin has something on his mind, and if he tells me about it it will be a relief to him. Please ask him to see me for five minutes, Flora.'

Still doubtful, she lifted her thin flat figure from the chair and left the room and Howard felt a sense of excitement and elation. So Campion had been here, had he, and had 'disturbed' Martin Eaton? What had he threatened, or said, to make Martin give up that damning instrument to Louis Hedler? This was very interesting, indeed. In spite of the closed shutters and draperies the room was very hot and Howard, restless and more and more excited, wiped his face and his hands and looked impatiently at the door. He could hear the voice of the river, rustling softly in the morning silence, and the whirring of lawn-mowers, and the bark of a dog, and he thought how peaceful the world was, or could be, without mankind.

Flora Eaton returned, uncertain and hesitant. 'I've talked with Martin, Howard. He's been writing and writing and is so exhausted. But when I told him you were here he consented to see you for a few minutes. Howard, please don't stay long, will you? He needs to rest.'

Howard stood up. 'Writing? Is he writing a book?'

Flora simpered, and made a foolish little gesture with her hands, crossing them at the wrists and then fluttering them out. 'I am not at liberty to say, Howard.' The idea had not occurred to her before this but the suggestion intrigued her. 'But I do know it is quite voluminous, and not a letter. Such a secret!'

Howard Best had not seen Martin Eaton for months and even in his preoccupied state he was shocked at the change in a once powerful and robust man with presence. He could smell the acrid closeness in this room, and the higher odour of illness and mortality. Martin was a dying man, shattered, ruined, cavernous of face and appalling of colour. He looked dully at Howard as he advanced across the room towards the desk, and sat there unspeaking like a crumbling Buddha sifting into dust in some lost temple.

Howard was so full of pity that he forgot to smile and did not wait to be asked to sit down. He sat down across from the desk and Martin and he said, 'Forgive me, Martin. I know you are ill. I should not have imposed on you if the matter were not so important and so immediate, and concerned—'

'I know,' said the faint and empty voice. 'You were always Jon Ferrier's closest friend. You moved for a change of venue, and succeeded. You procured the best lawyers in Philadelphia for him.'

Howard studied him, and listened to the voice to catch any echo of animosity or hatred or hostility or contempt. But there was none. The tone was lightless and unaccented and indifferent.

'So,' said Martin, 'I know why you've come. It is about Jon Ferrier.'

'Yes,' said Howard. 'He is in terrible danger, and he is innocent. I know you don't believe that, but it is true.'

Martin Eaton looked down at the desk again, and now Howard saw that there was a sheaf of papers there, closely written upon, neatly stacked. Martin's hand still held a pen.

'I do not know what is truth,' said Martin, 'or what is lies, any longer. I do not know even what is guilt.'

'Martin, surely you know in your heart that Jon did not kill Mavis.'

'You are wrong.' The voice was louder but still indifferent. 'He killed her. I knew his guilt. I've always known it.'

A little chilliness ran over Howard's warm cheeks and hands. He looked at Martin intently. Then he said, 'Guilty of killing her—how?'

For the first time Martin smiled, a dreary, painful smile. 'You lawyers. I made a simple statement which would be accepted by anyone but you. I said Jon Ferrier was guilty of Mavis's death; that should have satisfied you. I don't lie. But, you say "how?"'

Howard's hopes rose. Martin lifted his living hand, which held the pen. 'Kenton Campion has been here, and has told me everything, so it is not necessary for you to tell me the detestable tale of the plot against Jon. I assume Louis Hedler told you. Poor Louis. I know there are other ramifications of this plot, not concerned with me and Mavis. So, spare yourself, Howard.' He looked again at the papers on his desk, and sighed a long and gusty sigh.

'I have written the whole story here, lest it die with me and evil again be done. I am glad you came. I did not know to whom to entrust this story. But, as Jon's friend, I know I can trust you. I have but a few more lines to write, and it is finished. Then you may read it for yourself, and save both you and me from copious explanations and words. I am so weary these days. So—beset.'

Howard felt that this was a momentous time. He sat in silence as the pen painfully scratched its way across the page. He saw it dipped into the ink, saw it write, saw it dipped again. The dead hand lay on the paper, unmoving. The shutters were open here and the hot bright wind entered, fluttering the written pages, stirring the dust, lifting the pages of open books, glittering on the edges of furniture. The large dying face of Martin Eaton was intent, and there was grey sweat on his parched forehead and fallen cheeks.

There was something to be said in favour of a man who was dying with dignity, thought Howard Best, a man who asked for no pity, no sentimentality, no false denial of the truth. Howard had not the slightest doubt that the agonisingly written document he was about to read would right an evil and save a man from complete ignominy and injustice.

Martin laid down the pen and stared at the final paragraphs he had written. He said, 'I have made this out in the form of an affidavit. I had thought of you, to act as the notary, or the witness.' He looked at Howard now, raising his eyes with a conspicuous effort, and what life remained in him shone, for the last time, with indomitable life and determination. 'This has not been easy for me to do. I know this will destroy others. But there comes an hour when a man must do as he must do, and there is nothing else.' He nodded at the papers, spent, and Howard reached to the desk and took them. Martin lay back in his chair and closed his eyes.

The writing was amazingly clear and careful, as if written so there could be no conjecture over a single word. It was small and sharp though sometimes wavering, but every period and comma was there, every large capital.

'I, Martin Joseph Eaton, of River Road, Hambledon, in the Commonwealth of Pennsylvania, make this statement, on this date, 29th August, 1901, of my own free will and desire, and in my own handwriting, which can be verified, in order that Jonathan Ferrier of this town will no longer be the subject of calumny, odium, disgrace and scandal and libel, as he has been since 5th November, 1900. It has been in my power, and in the power of someone else to be named, to have righted this wrong, but I have refrained for reasons I will now set forth.

'The dead are beyond our feeble hatred and our derision, and this I should have known long ago. To protect the name of the dead is not only futile and sentimental—when they have caused misery and despair—but they would not have it so and perhaps do not wish it so. If God is a God of love He is also a God of justice and even of wrath, and so I dare not die until I have written all that must be written on this day.

'My niece, Mavis Alicia Eaton, was not my niece. She was the daughter of my brother's wife, Hilda, Mrs Jerome Eaton.

'In my youth and young manhood I loved Marjorie Farmington, now Mrs Adrian Ferrier of this town. But she married Adrian Ferrier, and I believed that I would care for no other woman. Then my brother, two years my junior, Jerome, met a young lady of considerable family and fortune in Pittsburgh, where he was a teacher of history. Her name was Hilda

Gorham, and she resembled Marjorie Ferrier in a most extra-ordinary way. I did not know her until she had married my brother, for I was in Heidelberg at the time for a year's supplementary study. When I returned and saw Hilda for the first time it was as if my whole life had been renewed, and Hilda told me later that she had loved me instantly. However, she had no reason to divorce my brother, and she was fond of him, and we both decided he must not be hurt, as he was a man of singular innocence and kindness and trust.

'I have no excuse to offer for my love for Hilda and our subsequent actions. Love, I have heard, is its own reason for being. It is also its own terror and suffering. When Mavis was born it was Jerome who held her proudly in his arms and claimed her as his daughter, and not I. He was an unworldly man and was never suspicious, as he ought to have been under the circumstances, on which I will not expound.'

Howard felt greatly moved and full of a sympathetic suffering. He looked up from the pages, but Martin lay back in his chair as if asleep, his face peaceful and resigned.

'My brother and Hilda and Mavis remained in Pittsburgh and I saw them only occasionally. Therefore, I was able to maintain my equanimity and composure, and to sustain Hilda in her silence. I saw the child infrequently also, but loved her with a passionate adoration which should be reserved for the Deity only. I would gladly have given my life for her. When her parents died suddenly, I knew I must take her into my house. I had, in the meantime, married my dear Flora, who will be the one to suffer excessively when this document is made public, as it must be. I needed her devotion and her affection, for I have always been a lonely man. I believe our marriage has been happy and I have given Flora no reason to mistrust me.

'She, too, loved Mavis, who was the most beautiful child I have ever seen, and she happily agreed that we should adopt her as our own, for Flora could bear no children. She treated Mavis with the affection and care of a mother, in all respects. Sufficient.

'To me, at least, Mavis was perfection, not only in appearance but in character and grace. When I held her on my knee and fondled her I could hardly endure my joy and delight and love. As she grew to girlhood and then to womanhood my pride in her became daily stronger, my care closer. All who have seen and known Mavis can testify to her beauty, her winsomeness, her happy laughter, her gaiety, her fascination. This is no mere drivelling of a father, but the truth.'

Again Howard looked at Martin Eaton, but he had not moved. Howard thought, My God, how this will shake this town! It was not a pleasant thought, and Howard hesitated before continuing to read.

'I have always loved young people, especially those of beauty and charm like Mavis, and those of dedication, intelligence and honour, such as Jonathan Ferrier. He was not only my loved Marjorie's son, but he had her character and uprightness, though not her humour and tolerance. From earliest childhood he was somewhat relentless and a stickler for pride, and what he called, as a child, "justice." These are admirable traits, but like all admirable traits they can be carried to excess. I often told him, when he was very young, that he could never expect absolute honour and truth and justice in this world, but I discovered that he did not believe me and I know that he was very angered when he was forced to perceive the reality of evil and malice and cruelty in our midst. There is much that is intolerant in Jonathan, and this has been his burden and aroused much hatred against him—though I confess that he was intolerant against all mendacity, double-dealing, lies, hypocrisy, injustice, hard-heartedness, and sentimentality. I often told him that it was excellent to be against these evils, but that he should soften his expressions when he encountered them, for it is the curse of mankind that it must pretend not to condemn when condemnation—if this were a good world—is necessary. "Truth crushed to earth will rise again," is a pretty aphorism, but it is not valid, and if it does rise then it is a miracle for the ages to stand before, agape.'

Amen, thought Howard, with deep sadness.

'I saw from the beginning that Jonathan would make an excellent physician and so guided him into the noblest profession any man can pursue with the exception of the clergy. He was much intrigued, even as a child, when I told him that once all physicians had been priests, and all priests physicians. The thought fascinated him, and he saw immediately that there was the closest of all relationships in those professions, for a man does not deal with the body successfully unless he considers the soul, nor does he deal with a man's spiritual vices unless he also deals with the body which manifests them.

'I was his mentor. His father did not highly approve of Jonathan's choice of profession, but I will not comment upon Adrian except to say that I wonder to this hour why Marjorie Farmington had married him. Marjorie, however, believed Jonathan would make a splendid physician. We had many quiet discussions about the matter. But Marjorie was also of the opinion that Jonathan must curb, to some extent, his pride, his intolerance, his relentlessness, if he were to live among men with any comfort. I am afraid that neither of us has been very successful with Jonathan in this regard.'

That is putting it very mildly, thought Howard, and for the first time since beginning this sad history he smiled a little.

'I loved Jonathan Ferrier as my son. When he told me, when Mavis was only fifteen, that he wished to marry her in good time I was filled with happiness. The two I loved most dearly in the world would be my children through their marriage. The day of their wedding remains in my memory like a beautiful painting, perfect, without a flaw. I will carry the memory of that day with me into eternity, if there is indeed eternity for us.

'I do not wish those who read this to believe that I was totally insensible to Mavis's faults, as if I were a stupid and blinded man. I knew her to be selfish and even petulant at times, and demanding, but it gave me pleasure to satisfy all her desires far beyond her needs. I knew Jonathan would so treat her, or at least I believed he would. I gave her to him less than giving her in marriage to another man, than in putting her in the arms of a younger father who would protect and guard and love her when I was dead. It was a fatuous error, and I have no explanation for it, and no excuse, though I know it was ridiculous. A husband demands more of his wife than does her father, and he has a clearer eye for her faults and a duller eye for her virtues. But this I did not know until the day of her death.

'All seemed well with that most auspicious marriage for nearly a year, and then I observed that Jonathan appeared distrait at times, and unusually nervous and abstracted. But he was new in his practice and I believed that was the trouble. As for Mavis, she was herself as usual, deeply enjoying life, radiant in the mere act of living, full of laughter and brightness and luminous smiles. If sometimes I thought that she seemed still a little frivolous for a young matron, I remembered her youth and her inexperience. She told me how deeply she loved Jonathan, and I had no way of knowing that this was not the truth—then. Mavis, Mavis.'

Again Howard was almost unbearably touched at those last words, written as if spoken to Martin's deepest self and not to anyone who would read this. The heat in the dusty study increased, the wind was more dazzling, the light sharper. Martin Eaton had not moved a finger. He had withdrawn to some great distance where no one could ever reach him again with pain or despair or longing.

'I am growing weary,' the dying man had written. 'I must be briefer for I may die before this is completed. As the few years of that marriage continued I saw that Jonathan was growing more absorbed in his work and less in his wife, but I judged that to be quite common among doctors, who do not make the most desirable husbands in the world. If they are truly dedicated men—and only dedicated men should practise the holy art of medicine—then they cannot give themselves entirely to their wives and their children. Much of them belongs to their patients, and this must never be denied. Sometimes I told Jonathan that he must not pursue even medicine with such single ardour, but that he should give some thought to Mavis. Invariably he agreed, but I remember, now, that his face would darken and he would quickly change the subject.

'Then, two years before her death Mavis complained to me that Jonathan desired no children. This was on the occasion when I delicately suggested to her that a child, or two or three, would crown her married happiness. I was much disturbed at her answer—that Jonathan wished no family. I hinted about it once or twice to Jonathan himself, but he would put me off with a smile, one of his harsh jokes, or a shrug, or again, with a change of subject.

'I know the truth now—and from Mavis's dying lips—that it was she and not Jonathan who was averse to children. I know that she wished to keep herself uniquely herself, the first-adored of all who knew her. She did not want competition, nor had she any maternal instincts.

'For the last three years of their marriage, Mavis and Jonathan lived apart, and had no conjugal intercourse with each other.'

Howard could not help an exclamation of astonishment, and it was abrupt in that hot and sunny silence. But Martin did not stir. He merely sank lower in his chair, and appeared to dwindle.

'All this I discovered later. In the meantime, and I must confess it, I was feeling the stress of my years and my practice, and I could not forget Hilda, the mother of my daughter. I resorted more and more to whisky for release and comfort. This is well-known in Hambledon. I give this as my excuse for not noticing the signs of disaster in Mavis's marriage until less than two years before her tragic death. Mavis appeared to have become more petulant, more absorbed in her own desires, more impatient, and on a number of occasions she would jibe at Jonathan in the company of others, and before me. I do not, even now, fully know the reason for this raillery of hers, but Jonathan never rebuked her. He remained silent, and for a hasty and imperious man this was remarkable.

'Then, over a year before she died, Mavis told me that Jonathan, on several occasions, had threatened to kill her, and that once he had even taken her by the throat in rage. She exhibited actual terror of him to me, when she told me, and I knew when Mavis lied and knew when she spoke the truth. She really feared him. I said I would speak to him, for I was outraged and appalled, but she implored my silence.'

The stilted, old-fashioned phrases did not jar on Howard's mind as they sometimes had been doing as he read. Now he felt an intense alarm and consternation, and he was afraid. He felt for his pipe and lit it. He puffed a moment or two, and again read those damning words. Then he hurried on with his reading.

'I tried to question Mavis closely. I knew Jonathan's rash temper, his disregard for consequences when he was in a rage. But Mavis was evasive. She was not certain, she said, what it was that so displeased Jonathan, but she thought it was because she was so much younger than he was and much less serious, and that he expected too much of her. I was relieved, God help me. I agreed with her that this was probably the cause of his anger and that time would improve the situation. She assured me that I was probably right, and would speak no more of it. However, I did notice that when she would look at Jonathan it would be with sullenness, defiance, malice, and apprehension.

'Jonathan had made my Mavis unhappy, had brought out

in her those traits which were less pleasing than others, had caused her to fear him and to hate him. She was a light golden bird and he was a hawk, dark and sombre. I see now, as I did not see until Mavis's death, that the marriage had been disastrous not only for Mavis but for Jonathan, and had inevitably been leading to tragedy. But Jonathan was older and wiser, and he was a man. Therefore, I hold him guilty of Mavis's death, and him alone.'

Howard read this over, and over, and his consternation grew.

'Yes, I hold him guilty, though he did not do the deed of which he is still accused. It was not his child which Mavis was carrying. It was his brother's, Harald Ferrier's.'

Oh, my God! thought Howard, with repulsion and incredulousness. He put down the sheets of paper and went to the window and looked out and saw nothing of the beautiful gardens below, or of Flora among the zinnias, or of the shining blue floor of the river beyond. He had a single wild impulse to take those papers and destroy them, and only the quick knowledge that they must remain intact for Jonathan's sake prevented him from acting. He went back to his chair. He lit his pipe again, for it had gone out. The scratch of the match on his sole was like a shot in the silent room, and he started at the sound. But Martin seemed asleep.

'On 30th October, 1900, Jonathan Ferrier was called to Pittsburgh for a consultation, for over the years he had acquired a broad and excellent reputation. He remained there until the afternoon of 5th November, and of this there is no doubt, for so it has been attested to, under oath, by the most eminent men.

'On 3rd November, 1900, Mavis came to me, desperately ill, haemorrhaging. She brought to me the curette of Jonathan, her husband, and told me that he had aborted her on 29th October, for again he had told her he would have no children in his house. As she was obviously almost *in extremis*, I took her to the hospital. Otherwise, I should have hidden this crime, this infamy, in my house. I will not write here of my suffering and despair and hatred and rage. I will only write that Mavis told me that she had been aborted, in Jonathan's own examination room, and by him, on the eve of his departure to Pittsburgh, on 29th October.

'As I sat by her bed in St Hilda's Hospital, with all the help about Mavis which she needed, I swore to her that I would
362

avenge her. I knew that she was dying. She was badly infected. Worse, they detected signs of mutilation, deliberate wounding, as by a savage madman, who hated her. Then it was brought to my attention by competent colleagues whose word could not be challenged, that Mavis's condition plainly showed that she had been aborted no earlier than 1st November. They preferred to believe that it was even later, on 2nd November. The septicaemia, while fulminating and spreading rapidly, was not so advanced as it would have been had the abortion taken place on 29th October. And so I knew that Mavis had lied to me. But in the extremity of the hours I did not admonish her. She was so gravely ill, bleeding slowly to death, and agonised with pain and fever. Her uterus had been perforated in several places. The vagina was lacerated. The abortion, I was told, had been done by an amateur or a fiend.

'Then I knew that Mavis was dying, that it was a matter of less than an hour. She had remained conscious throughout her suffering. I sent strangers from her room. I took her burning hands in mine and said to her, "Before God, Mavis, you must tell me the truth, for you are dying and will soon face your God, and you must not go to Him with a lie on your lips."

'The child was fearfully frightened. She struggled with herself, and then she confessed.

'Jonathan, she said, had long ago rejected her and was not living with her as man and wife. He despised her, upbraided her constantly, called her a fool and mindless. She had wanted only to be happy in her life, to dress prettily, to be adored, to be pampered, to be treated as a lovable child who must not be denied. It was most piteous. Mavis was a woman, almost twenty-four, yet she spoke as one who is only five years old, and as simply. She had often wanted to return to her old home, she said, to the arms of her adopted parents, for she was lonely and unwanted and unneeded and unloved in her husband's house.'

Liar, liar, thought Howard. She still could not refrain from lies even when she was terrified and knew she was dying. She must leave behind her the blameless and luminous memory she had created in her life. All Howard's pity was for the stricken father and the maligned husband of that craven young woman on her dying bed, who must preserve a lie, and would have died with lies, if her father had not so pressed her.

'I listened to Mavis's faint and dying voice, so unlike her

363

exuberant own, and did not fully understand at first. She told me that she had sought love and admiration apart from Jonathan, who withheld them from her. I do not remember clearly! I know she spoke of at least four men, but their names have gone from my recall. I was stunned beyond grief, beyond speech. Mavis pleaded for herself, for her forlorn state, and I could only hold my child in my arms and weep over her, and try to listen to this most important confession.

'Her last lover, the father of her aborted child, was Harald Ferrier. When she discovered her condition Harald decided that she must be aborted, and told her that though he was fond of her he did not love her, and had no intention of asking her to divorce her husband and marry him. Moreover, he said, he was committed to another. He had regarded the liaison with Mavis as "midsummer madness," to quote his own words, and had not believed Mavis was more serious than himself. Their mistake could be rectified. I will not expound on the morals and degeneracy and bestiality of this man's character, a man judged to be amiable, admirable, kind and tolerant in this town, for all his light follies, which are well known. I leave the judgement to God.

'He told Mavis that he had heard of an abortionist, a competent surgeon in high esteem in Hambledon, who obliged unfortunate ladies in Mavis's predicament. This conversation, Mavis told me, was held in the Ferrier house during Marjorie Ferrier's absence, and in the weekly absence of servants. Mavis had sent for him to consult with him. When it was agreed that Mavis must be aborted, Harald Ferrier then called the scoundrel, the murderer, in Mavis's presence. She was afraid, but not heart-broken. She confessed she had been deeply attracted to Harald Ferrier, but had not loved him. The abortionist agreed to the operation, and named the time on the next day or so. Mavis, in her dying state, was not certain which was the date. She only knew that Jonathan had not been in town for at least two days. Approaching death was already confusing her mind.

'Then the abortionist made one demand. He asked that Mavis bring with her Jonathan's own curette, which, he declared, he had once seen in Jonathan's own examination room when they had been friends some years before. (I believe they had some disagreement later which had caused coldness and aversion between them.) I am of the opinion that the abortionist demanded Jonathan's curette in the event that should Mavis suffer some consequences, he would not be held responsible. I refuse to believe that he had asked for the instrument with the deliberate intention of injuring Mavis, or even killing her, in order to involve Jonathan in his wife's subsequent dangerous illness or perhaps death. No, no man can be that vile.'

No? thought Howard, and felt the deepest bitterness of his life. Much was being revealed to him now than ever he had dreamed of, than ever he had feared of his fellows.

'The name of the murderer must be written here. It was Claude Brinkerman.'

No! thought Howard, and then he said aloud, 'Oh, no.' For his own wife, Beth, was now expecting her third child with happiness, and so was almost consoled for the death of the little girl, Martha. She had been delivered of her little son by Jonathan, but since he was leaving Hambledon she had chosen Brinkerman, who had quite the highest reputation for dexterity and skill in obstetrics. If quite a number of his patients appeared to die, it was generally accepted as unfortunate and not the fault of the physicians, and besides women always had mysterious 'inward trouble,' due it was said, to their tight corsets and heavy long skirts.

It was some aghast moments before Howard could continue his reading.

'Mavis knew where Jonathan kept his office keys, which he had not taken with him on his journey to Pittsburgh. She was able to secure the curette, which had been described to her by Jonathan, himself, long before. She then relocked the cabinet and replaced the keys.

'How can I continue this dreadful narrative, recalling everything with so much vividness and torment? Mavis died. That is, perhaps, the only thing that matters to me.

'The hospital had already been aware of Mavis's story that Jonathan had aborted her. She had screamed it over and over, in the presence of attending physicians and nurses, and myself. There were some who knew it could not be true. But Jonathan has many enemies. These were only too eager to believe the awful lie, even though they had been told it was not possible. They spread it through the town. I had sent a telegram to Jonathan the evening before to return, that Mavis was gravely ill and it was feared she was dying. He returned only three hours after her death, on the first train available.

'Why have I not, before this, told Mavis's true story to

others, and to Jonathan? Why did I let him be tried for murder of his wife and unborn child—though he knew the child had not been his, and he had not injured my daughter? Why did I shout, "No, no!" when the verdict of not guilty was brought in by the jury?

'You who have read this, have pity on a father who adored his daughter beyond reason, and even with blasphemy. I believed that Mavis had spoken truly when she said that Jonathan had rejected her, had made her desperately unhappy, had almost driven her from his house. I still believe he had threatened her life. He had made my child wretched and that was unpardonable. In her unhappiness she had sought love illicitly, and if that was wrong it can be pardoned and understood. But she was so joyous, so affectionate. Love was part of her existence. She could not live without it, and the admiration it brought. She wanted only to dance and sing and live, and this was denied her by both her husband and the man who murdered her.

'There was her name to protect, above all else. I vowed to keep clear and untarnished the lovely name she had made for herself not only in Hambledon but in many other places. Her good name was precious to me. No malicious scandal must touch her. No jeering name must dirty her. As she had lived, so she must be in death, loved, admired, remembered for her beauty and her youth, her laughter and her gaiety. The truth, spoken by me, would have condemned her name to infamy forever. What father would bring that upon his daughter?

'Would I have spoken had Jonathan been convicted for murders he had not committed? Before God, I do not know. I think I should have done so, as I write this, for there was the thought of Marjorie Ferrier, the mother of Jonathan, and I frequently confuse her in my mind with Hilda, for I loved them both. I should not have let Marjorie Ferrier's son die—at least I think that now.

'I must repeat: had Jonathan loved my daughter as I loved her, had he been a second father to her, indulging her with affection, as I did, then she would not have strayed, she would not have died. Again, therefore, I hold him not guiltless of her death.

'I have but two things to speak of now. One is for verification, in the event that anyone might challenge a dying man's confession of his guilt and his love. I have written that no

366

one was in the Ferrier house on the day the abortion was arranged except Harald Ferrier and my daughter. There was one other: Marjorie Ferrier. She had intended to be absent that afternoon, and Mavis thought she was alone in the house. But Marjorie, who suffers from a serious heart affliction, had decided to rest. She, too, thought she was alone in the house, but then hearing voices downstairs she came down also, and overheard the conversation between her son, Harald, and Mavis, and the arrangements they were making.

'Marjorie has told me this. She said she was afraid she would collapse in the hall. But she made her way upstairs and then fainted on her bed. Later, a physician was called for her. She did not know what to do. To speak to Mavis would have precipitated fresh tragedy, for Mavis was distraught. She dared not think what a revelation to her husband would have brought about: disgrace. The ejection from Jonathan's house. Marjorie knew that Mavis and Jonathan were no longer husband and wife in the meaning of the word. What if Jonathan learned that his brother was the father of the unborn child? So Marjorie, though the thought of an abortion was unspeakable, decided to remain silent, to let the "culprits," as she called my child and her lover, find their own solution. "For the sake of all," Marjorie said to me after Mavis's death, "I kept my silence. My son Harald is my son also, and though I do not condone, but only condemn his actions, I must think of what would happen to him if Jonathan ever knew. I must think, too, of Jonathan. But," she said to me much later, "if Jonathan had been condemned to death for crimes he did not commit, then I should have come to you and told you you must tell the truth."

'Marjorie does not know all the truth. She came to me after Mavis's death and told me that Mavis had informed her that Jonathan had aborted her in his own examination rooms. Marjorie knew this for a lie. She did not want me to believe such a lie. In the awful months that followed Marjorie came to believe, with intuition, that I, and only I, knew the absolute truth. I denied it. But Marjorie knew. I had never been able to deceive her.

'In a strange way we became conspirators of silence after Jonathan was acquitted. We have thought that best, best for the Ferrier family, best for Mavis's name. But Marjorie is afraid that in some way Jonathan will find out the truth, and that he might kill his brother, not just for betraying him but for the anguish he had caused him, and the silence he had kept in the face of his brother's arrest. Jonathan is a violent man, and this I believe with all my heart. He is an unforgiving one, and implacable. I believe in Marjorie's fears.

'This letter should not have been written but for one reason. It is true that sometimes evil will out but not very often. Senator Kenton Campion came to me recently and told me that he knew that I "knew" the truth about Mavis's death, that Jonathan Ferrier had indeed murdered his wife and child. He demanded the "truth." He wishes to destroy Jonathan for various reasons, and so do others equally malevolent. When I refused to speak, he informed me that he was aware that Mavis was my daughter. To protect Mavis I gave Louis Hedler the curette which she had given to me, and let him believe what he willed. For Mavis is, to me, still the only creature of consequence in the world.

'However, I cannot let Jonathan continue to be condemned. I cannot let him become the victim of powerful malice. I do not know what my sentiments are towards him now. I have been so confused for so long a time. But it is possible I still love him. And I remember that he did not testify to the fact that Mavis's child had not been his. Was he protecting me, or Mavis?

'Humanity is not to be understood, no, not even by mankind itself. We do abominable things in the name of love. We do disastrous things to protect ourselves and others. We permit evil to grow more powerful every day, and make no attempt to halt it. We are afraid. We are cowards. We do not possess the manhood with which we were endowed at birth; we lost it, we always lose it, through compromise, through hope, through lies to ourselves, through commitment to false ideals, through fear, through womanish timidity, through exigency.

'We condemn, we lie, by silence, when we should speak. But for that cowardice we cannot be forgiven.

'I beg Marjorie Ferrier's forgiveness in breaking my silence. She will know at the last that I did it for her son Jonathan, and not out of weakness or present fear of death. But what the results will be I do not know. I no longer care, except for Flora, my wife, who has been my dear companion and friend for many years and who will have to endure living when I am dead. The time has come to exonerate Jonathan Ferrier and protect him from the plot gathering against him. As I forgive him may he forgive me, and may he remember, as I do now, the years when I regarded him as my son.

'(Signed) Martin Joseph Eaton, M.D.'

The stark and blazing silence and heat in the study had increased. Howard could hardly breathe for emotion and physical oppression. He gently laid down the papers, contemplated them for a moment, then said quietly, 'Martin? I have finished.'

The lightless eyes opened sluggishly and looked with a dazed expression upon the younger man. Then Martin groaned as if from deep in his flesh rather than from his throat, and he pulled himself up in his chair with all the effort of his body. 'Yes,' he said. His look, his manner, forbade Howard to remark on the dolorous saga he had read, and Howard thought, with increasing compassion, that Jonathan Ferrier was not the only one in this miserable affair who was proud.

'I wish it notarised,' said Martin. 'I have witnesses here, or you may have your own, for there must be witnesses.'

'Yes,' said Howard. 'I will arrange it all to-morrow.'

Martin shook his monolithic head and for the last time Howard was to remember he smiled. 'You lawyers,' he said again. 'It is always "to-morrow" to you. To-morrow. But it must be to-day. Now. Why does to-morrow always fascinate you so much? "The law's delay—" Call your office. Ask for your seal, and your witnesses. At once.'

He looked imperatively at Howard. 'I may die to-night,' he said, 'then it will all be of no use.'

Why, indeed, not to-day? Howard telephoned his office, and then he sat with Martin and drank some of his whisky, and neither said a word. The papers lay between them like something with a life of its own, palpitating. There were many things Howard wished to say to this dying father. He wished to tell him that he had still been unjust to Jonathan Ferrier in his remarks that Jonathan had been harsh to his young wife and had rejected her. He wished to tell Martin that quite a little clique had known Mavis's true character, and her love affairs, and that a few, if not more, knew her heartlessness, craft and malice and self-absorption. But that would bring no peace to Martin Eaton, but only distress.

Two clerks, one with the seal, arrived in fifteen minutes, sweating with zeal and the heat. Howard did not permit them to read the papers; he merely had Martin initial each page, followed by the initials of the clerks. The clerks were eager to read, but Howard was deft. He needed but their acknowledgment that they had seen Martin sign each page, and then his signature at the end, repeating the one he had already written. Then he asked Martin to raise his right hand and swear that everything he had written in the affidavit had been true, that he had made the affidavit of his own will and desire and had written it in his own hand. This done, Howard put his notary's seal on each page, very carefully. It was not necessary, but he knew Jonathan's enemies.

Martin chuckled as he laid down his pen, and nodded when Howard refilled his glass. 'Campion,' he said in his dry rustle of a voice. He looked into the glass then raised it and stared at Howard directly. 'To justice,' he said, and laughed for the last time in his life.

When Howard arrived at his house he said to his wife, Beth: 'Don't ask me questions, dear, or for explanations. But you must never see Claude Brinkerman again. We must find someone else when you have the baby.'

'Well, really, Howard, he is the best,' Beth replied with surprise and looked at him searchingly. 'I have recommended so many of my friends to him.'

'You must never do that again!' he said with such emphasis that she was quite astonished, and stared at him.

'Why, Howard! You look—distracted. So pale, so concerned, so very, very grave. Is something wrong, dearest?'

'Very wrong, Beth. But you must do as I wish, for I know things you do not know. I've had a terrible three hours. I can't tell you. Just do as I say.'

She continued to stare at him with wifely conjecture. Then she said, 'Very well, Howard, you must have your reasons. I wish I had had your advice before, though. Only last November I sent my little milliner to him—a very talented girl with ribbons and plumes, she made my Christmas hat, and we both liked it so much that I permitted her to display it in her little window for a few days. You liked it, too, remember? Fawn felt, with yellow ribbons and orange plumes, quite becoming, you said— What's the matter, Howard?'

'Beth!' He had jumped to his feet. 'What is your milliner's name?'

'Why—why—how extraordinary you are, Howard, and how peculiar you look! And what does it matter? It's Mary Snowden.'

370

Howard smacked his hands hard together, and clenched his teeth visibly with triumph. 'I thought I'd heard that name before, by God! Beth! Why did you send that girl to Claude Brinkerman last November?'

'For goodness' sake, Howard! What questions you ask! It won't mean anything to you, and it is a little indelicate. She had female trouble.'

'What in hell's that?'

Beth dropped her pretty eyes. 'Inwardly,' she said with a prim purse of her lips.

'Well, for God's sake, Beth, what *is* it? "Inwardly" covers a lot of territory, I can see for myself. Please, Beth, forget you're a lady for a moment. You don't know how deadly serious this is. Let's be frank. Was the girl pregnant?'

'Howard! How can you say such a dreadful thing about a poor, talented, good, hard-working girl! So nice, so—almost— a lady. Well-mannered. Clever. Of course she wasn't pregnant! She isn't married!'

'Darling Beth, I love you. You are a treasure, a true treasure. I wish I could tell you how much you've helped me.' He kissed her. She pushed him gently away so she could examine his face.

'Howard, are you perfectly well?'

'Bully, as Teddy Roosevelt would say. Fine, as he'd also say. Last November, you say it was, when you sent Mary Snowden to Claude Brinkerman?' He paused. 'You would not, by the most remote chance of course, know a Louise Wertner, seamstress, would you?'

'Indeed, I do,' said Beth. 'She is a friend of Mary's. Not so talented, or so original, so I give her only ordinary sewing, alterations on old clothes, mending linen, and such. Why, Howard, she's often come here to use our sewing room, especially in the spring and fall. You must have seen her yourself, once or twice, at the least, a very meek, quiet girl, always keeping her eyes down and moistening her lips, poor thing. Neither girl is exceptionally prosperous, though I do encourage Mary who should be more appreciated—'

'Beth, you did say that these girls know each other? Well?'

'I believe so. Howard, what does it matter with that class? Why are the girls so important to you?'

'Beth, has Louise Wertner ever suffered from female trouble, too?'

'Now, Howard, don't be ridiculous! How is it possible for

me to know? Mary only mentioned it to me last November when I remarked that she looked a little ill.' Beth hesitated. Howard, she thought to herself, had one thing in common with all other husbands: a certain thriftiness. But she had had something on her tender conscience for several months, and so she sighed. 'Howard, I bought four hats from Mary, and the bill wasn't as large as I said. I had Mary "pad" it, as we say. You see, she needed fifty dollars, and so I helped her out. I hope you aren't going to be cross? She did go to see Claude and that was his fee for a slight, a very slight—correction—in his office. Exorbitant, for the Poor, but he does have a reputation. Are you cross?'

'I couldn't be more delighted,' said Howard, with fervour. So the girls did not know each other, did they? 'Buy yourself a dozen hats, my darling, to-morrow. Or, at least one.'

That night Martin Eaton died peacefully in his sleep. There was no autopsy, but his condition was known, and it was his physician's opinion that he had suffered another stroke. Only Howard Best, of all in Hambledon, wondered a little, and with sorrow, and then with relief. All that was Martin Eaton had abandoned this world, which had brought him small comfort, and left him bereft in his final years.

It was not expected that Jonathan Ferrier be present at the funeral services nor be a pall-bearer. Nor, indeed, was he there.

CHAPTER 14

'I am afraid to leave you, Jon,' said Marjorie Ferrier. 'I don't know what has gone wrong, but something most certainly has. Is it Jenny?'

'Sweet Jenny? No.'

'I don't believe you. You have been a different, even a terrible person since the day you told me you were going to see Jenny and arrange—'

'Mama, I don't want to talk about it, if you please. I'm a grown man now, or hasn't it crossed your mind?'

Marjorie looked at him with deep worry as he sat opposite her at the breakfast table. For three days he had eaten almost nothing, but he was drinking again and with gloomier determination than ever before. He had spent his time on his farms, had put up two for sale, had not gone to the hospitals more than once, had seen Robert Morgan but twice, and then only briefly in the offices. But at night she heard him walking up and down in his room. His bedroom furniture was laden with clothing and other things and there was a huge trunk in the hall upstairs which she had used on her honeymoon. His wastebaskets were heaped each morning, filled with torn letters, old records, notebooks. Suitcases and bags stood around the walls, half-filled. There was a growing pile of cast-off clothing in one corner. Marjorie had thought with dreariness, If it weren't that it meant that Jon was definitely leaving I'd be so glad to see all that rubbish cleaned out of drawers, wardrobes, closets and attic at last!

So, he was leaving, and very soon, and there was no more talk of Jenny. Marjorie had written the girl just recently that she was to be in Philadelphia for a week or more, and that as Harald was also leaving it would be safer for Jenny to be in the Ferrier house in Hambledon. So far, Jenny had not replied. A lover's quarrel? It was absurd to think that of either Jonathan, who was nearly thirty-six, or Jenny, whose natural restraint prevented her from overt quarrelling. Then, it must be serious, and Marjorie felt faint and sick when thinking of the matter. Were her hopes, again, to come to nothing? Was this house always to be desolate? She saw it boarded up, shuttered, lost in snow and wind with dark windows, silent, abandoned. Even worse, she saw it inhabited by strangers.

She could not remain here alone. For weeks she had been studying the house with a secret joy and anticipation. There would be the new suite of rooms for Jenny and Jonathan, a new white marble fireplace in their bedroom. There were rooms she had looked at with delight, hearing them filled with the cries and laughter of young children. She had planned a nursery garden, sheltered and fenced, with swings and sand-boxes and wooden horses and dolls. Now it had all vanished like all her foolish hopes, and the house seemed a mournful weight on her spirit and a reproach. To leave it shuttered, bolted and shrouded, would be impossible, for it was a living thing with a personality of its own, serene, calm, soft yet steadfast. Yet, to know it known to strangers, in all its nooks and entries and passageways, and to think of strange eyes peering from the windows, was intolerable.

But even more intolerable was the change, physical and in personality, in her son. In an incredibly short time he had become even more gaunt than when he had been released from prison, more taciturn, shorter of temper and sardonic when forced to speak. He appeared very ill. In the worst years with Mavis he had not seemed so tense and distracted and his eye had not had so hard a glitter of incipient violence. That violence was there, even when he was answering the most commonplace question, or asking such a question. It was like something held in him, but not held strongly enough. There were times when Marjorie stammered when speaking to him, for fear of unloosing that tip-toed savagery.

She had spoken of her worry about him on the day she was to leave for Philadelphia, and he had returned to the old jeering 'Mama.' She did not speak of his drinking, which he had resumed with more recklessness than he had shown even during his marriage, and since the trial. It was a sombre drinking and brought him no relief; rather, it appeared to increase that waiting violence in him. She dared not protest, even in love. She was too afraid.

Marjorie left that afternoon after the first futile effort to reach him. She came down the stairs fastening her white kid gloves slowly, her pale travelling suit trim and slender, her broad hat veiled. The station hack was at the door. Jonathan was walking restlessly up and down in the hall, which was hot in spite of the quiet colouring and space. She said, 'Jon, dear, seeing you are packing I have put something in your room
374

for you, to take with you, something very dear to me which I want you to have.'

'Don't be sentimental, dear,' he said, but he bent and kissed her briefly on the cheek she raised to him.

'I hope for happier news when I return,' she said.

He gave her one of his dark contemptuous smiles. 'News of what?' he said.

She sighed. 'Very well, if you insist on misunderstanding me, Jon. Now, I must go. I wish you were going with me. You seem so—tired. Harald is already in Philadelphia, as I've told you, arranging for a new show near Christmas.'

'Bully for Childe Harald,' he said.

She hesitated. 'Jon, I'm concerned about Jenny alone with the servants. Would you please go over a few times while I'm gone and—'

'No, dear.'

'Oh, for heaven's sake, Jon!' She went rapidly from the hall to the blazing yellow day outside, her head bent. As she climbed in the hack he saw, through the hall window, that she was dabbing at her eyes. He cursed aloud. He knew he ought to have taken her to the station; he knew that at the very least he should have helped her into the hack. But he was filled to the very brim with black hatred and seething violence. He went upstairs to his room, even hotter than on the ground floor, and there, laid enticingly on his bed, was a portrait of Jenny.

He approached the bed slowly, and looked at the lonely and longing face of the young girl his brother had painted, at the lifted, halted hand, at the quiet and desolate eyes. She had run to a window as if to answer a beloved call, or to see a beloved face, and then had found nothing but emptiness and cold bright chaos.

'Jenny,' he said. He sat down near the portrait, on the bed, and looked at it. He touched it gently with his hand. Then he said, 'Jenny, how could you have believed that of me? You believed so fully, didn't you, after knowing me all those years, since you were a child, a little girl? Yet, for no honest reason at all, you were willing to believe the worst, to fancy the worst, out of a sort of innate viciousness, or an insane fantasy. You don't believe the worst of anyone unless you secretly detest them. Love, or even kindness, impels anyone, though adverse evidence is there, to hope, to believe, the best, or to give the benefit of the doubt.'

He did not, even for a moment, while looking at the portrait, think of applying the same argument to himself. He did not remember the lies he had believed of Jenny, the unspeakable calumnies. He did not remember the silence he had kept in the midst of lewd laughter he had heard directed at her. Not once had he defended her, or given her 'the benefit of the doubt.'

So he looked at the portrait at first in sadness and despair, and then the violence boiled out in him. He grasped the portrait and smashed the canvas across his knee. It ripped, tearing the still and painted face. He stood up and threw the ruined painting across the room and it struck the wall and the frame shattered. He could hear himself breathing, fast and noisily, like a satisfied animal. 'I wish I could do that to you, in the flesh, Jenny,' he said. He picked up the bottle of whisky on his chest of drawers and drank it deeply. He was panting heavily running with sweat, his heart roaring, moisture showering down from his forehead into his eyes. He toasted the portrait lying destroyed on the floor. 'Sweet Jenny,' he said. The violence was now out in him, the violence which had been rising for many years, ever since his childhood. He had known it with Mavis, had often known it with his brother and even more often had known it with his colleagues. But it had never been so mad as now.

Becoming drunk, he swayed on the bed. His mind began to heave with disjointed thoughts of grief, hopelessness, discordant crashes of music, rage, murder, longing, fury. He began to laugh loudly, slapping his knees, rolling on the bed in an ecstasy of terrible mirth, rioting in a kind of awful rapture of self-loathing and hate and foaming ridicule.

He found himself lying prone, his hands in his hair, his body shaking with his uncontrollable merriment. He gasped into the pillow, 'All those wasted, stupid, God-damned—years! All those books, the hours, the weeks, the months, the years! A whole smirking procession of them. Gaggles of them, mincing, prancing, dancing. Oh, I'd do a lot, I would, against pain and disease! I would be dedicated, I would, like a priest, raising my holy hands on feverish flesh and calming it and curing it! What a—' He filled the room with shouts of obscenity until even the servants, resting in the noonday heat in their rooms, looked at each other in fright, hearing the shouts piercing up through wood and wall and catching some of the riper expressions. The cooks said to the young maid, 'Cover your ears, do, dear, it isn't nice for a young girl to hear such talk, and if Doctor weren't almost out of his mind—and who can blame him?—he wouldn't yell so.'

'He's drunk again,' said Mary, wiping her damp face with a sheet. 'He's always drunk now.'

'He has his troubles,' said the cook in a dark tone. 'Worse than most. It's all broken out in him, all at once, after almost a year.'

The black and soundless hiatus of drunkenness fell over Jonathan, sprawled, sweating, on his bed. He never remembered those hours of utter, obliterated despair. The sun fell over his body, and he did not feel it. It left his body and touched his feet, lighted the wall for a little, then moved away, its scorching yellow radiance blasting grass and tree as it fell in the west. Eventually a hot and purple dusk succeeded it, then a warm velvety darkness filled with restless stars. Jonathan was unaware of it all, for dreams had come to him, frightful, chaotic, churning, terrifying, vivid with fear and hopelessness. He dreamt once of Jenny. He saw her in a desolation of grey chalkiness, near the side of a slipping mountain the colour of ashes, and she was running down a twisting path which lifted and fell like the coils of a snake. Her black hair blew behind her and her arms were outstretched and her mouth was open on agonised screams. He tried to run to her, to seize her, to hold her, to quiet her, but she was always a pace or two ahead of him, and at last he fell into a pit, without a bottom and without a gleam of light.

He heard a loud and imperative knocking, and someone was shouting, 'Jon. Jon! I know you're in there! Wake up! Answer me!'

'Go away,' he groaned. There was a light in his eyes and it stung them unbearably, and he blinked at the moisture. His head was like a drum, and someone was pounding it with iron sticks. He lifted his hands and held it, afraid that it would burst, and there was a dry and burning sickness in his mouth and in his whole body.

'Jon! Let me in! It's important! Let me in!' Then the voice swore and said, 'Damn it, he's bolted the door!' The door rattled. 'Jon!'

Jonathan could see more clearly now, and what he saw in his dazed state stupefied him. He was in his lighted office, and not the house, and not in his bed. He could not remember coming here. Someone, something, had gone wild here, for the books had been taken from his medical library and torn and thrown all over the floors. Files were open and emptied, the papers scattered. The patient's chair was overturned, and flung aside. His framed diplomas had been ripped from the wall and smashed. The etching his father had given him, a sentimental but moving thing called 'The Doctor,' had not only been wrenched from the wall, its glass shattered, but someone had shredded it. The soft green draperies which Marjorie had ordered had been pulled from the windows and lay in gleaming heaps in the light of the one lamp on the desk.

'For Christ's sake,' Jonathan muttered, looking at this mad destruction, this hatefulness expressed in ruin and violence and vandalism. A sudden turbulence rose in him, and he knew who had done this thing in fury. It had been himself. He did not remember coming here; he did not remember the hours when he had gone berserk, and a terror struck him that he had gone insane in some darkness he could not recall, and he wondered what else he had done.

'Jon!' the voice shouted, and the door rattled more strenuously.

Jonathan pushed himself out of his chair and immediately staggered helplessly. He came up with a crash against a wall, and almost fell. He shook his head to recover. He began to pick his way slowly through the destruction on the floor, the shards of glass, the scattered books, the frames of pictures and diplomas, the overturned furniture, the confetti of paper. He reached the door and was again stupefied that he had locked it beyond the waiting-room, for though it had been there for years he had never shot that bolt before.

It took all his strength to release it, and then the door was flung open and there was Robert Morgan on the threshold. Robert stared at him, and then said in a subdued voice, 'For God's sake.'

'What do you want?' Jon asked, barring the way. But Robert saw over his shoulder and his face became horrified, and his reddish-gold moustache bristled. Slowly, then, he turned to look at Jonathan again, and he said, 'Did you do this?' It was a foolish question, he knew, for now he could smell the rank alcohol. Jonathan's grey and sweating face and disordered black hair and soaked shirt were evidence enough of what had happened in this room. He saw that one of

Jonathan's hands had bled a little; the brownish crust was all over the back in wrinkles.

'My God,' said Robert.

'Pretty, isn't it?' said Jonathan. 'Now, what the hell do you want?'

Robert could not look at him in this state, so he looked down helplessly at his shoes. 'You. Dr Hedler wants to see you in his office. It's very important. At St Hilda's. He must see you at once. He asked me to come for you. He didn't want to use the telephone. All these listening girls at Central. It's most important—Jon. He's waiting for you.'

'Tell Louis to go to hell. You can all go to hell,' said Jonathan. 'What does anything matter to me any longer? Good-bye, Bob. You won't see me again.'

Robert looked up at him quickly, and his blue eyes darkened. 'Oh, yes, I will, if you don't come with me now. I've got my buggy outside. I'll see you, Jon, and very soon—in jail.'

'What?' Jonathan rubbed his hands over his wet face, then stared at his injured hand. 'What are you talking about? Go home, Bob, like a good boy.'

'Worse, prison,' said Robert. 'Can't you hear me? Prison. For a long, long time—unless you help us to help you. There's a warrant right now in the Sheriff's office for your arrest, waiting to be signed right after Labour Day. He's holding it up, at Louis's request.'

'You must be out of your mind,' said Jonathan, with awe.

'No, you are, you crazy idiot!' said Robert. 'Look what you've done here!'

'What's that got to do with—What the hell are you talking about?' shouted Jonathan. 'Sheriff. Warrant! Are you out of your mind?'

'No, you are,' Robert repeated. He was quite pale. 'See here, they are waiting, your friends. There's something you have to know at once. I won't tell you, so stop glaring at me. You must hear for yourself. Can't you clean yourself up in a hurry?' Robert added in pure desperation. He took Jonathan by his arm and shook him. 'Clean up, in the washroom! Now! You've got to come with me!'

Jonathan frowned. He rubbed his throbbing head. He swallowed dryly. He examined his hand again. What had the fool said? Prison. He stared at Robert who had gone to the washroom adjoining and was already running water into the basin. 'I'll mop you up, if you're too helpless to do it yourself,' said

Robert. He came from the washroom with a wet towel and threw it into Jonathan's face. 'You ought to be ashamed,' he said, in a suddenly boyish and broken voice. 'Ashamed.'

It was that tone that finally reached Jonathan. He pressed the wet towel over his face and rubbed the blood from his hands, and he was smiling a little. Then he went into the washroom, and closed the door, and Robert, wincing, heard him being sick. While he waited, Robert took a closer survey of the room, shaking his head. A few months ago he would not have understood, but now he knew too much. He had always known that Jonathan Ferrier was violent by nature, but the violence had remained pressed down for a long time. What had caused it to erupt? Robert sighed. He had a very clear idea. But if it had not been that, it would have been something else. The pent rebellion, for nearly a year, had finally grown too powerful to keep locked up and leashed. A tiger can be kept at bay only so long, and then it must charge.

Jonathan came from the washroom, grey but quiet, combing his dampened hair. He looked very ill, but at least he was as composed as a man like him could be. 'Where's my jacket?' he asked. 'There it is. Look at it. I must have slept in it. And where's my collar and tie?'

'Here,' said Robert, taking them from the desk. 'I suppose you don't remember anything. That's a fine state of affairs, a man of your position getting mad drunk.'

'You must try it sometime, Sunday-school boy,' said Jonathan. 'What did you say? Old Louis wants to see me in his office? At this hour? What time is it, anyway?'

'Nine o'clock. What's wrong with your watch?'

It was dangling by its chain, and the two men looked at it and saw that it was smashed also. 'My grandfather's watch,' said Jonathan, and he detached it from its chain and laid it down on his desk, 'A repeater. Nine o'clock? What is Louis doing there in his office?'

'I told you, he's waiting for you, and that is all I am going to tell you. Have some gratitude, if you can. Come on.' He watched Jonathan fumbling with his collar-button, then went to his aid deftly. He saw Jonathan's eyes close to his, black and whitely polished, in spite of his state, and Jonathan smiled at him almost gently. 'You're a good boy, Bob,' he said. 'I'm getting very fond of you. What's on Louis's mind? Someone done some more slaughtering in the operating room? If so, I don't intend to do anything about it.'

380

'Come on!' said Robert, with a sudden access of impatience. 'You look like a tramp, but it can't be helped.'

As it was half-past nine St Hilda's was quiet but glowing with lights here and there in the hot darkness of the night. In silence, Jonathan and Robert went to Louis Hedler's office, passing only one lone nurse and one intern, who stared after them curiously. Robert opened the door and said, 'Here he is, at last. I found him dead drunk, and I had to pull him together.'

'A canard,' said Jonathan. He stopped. He saw, in the room, not only Louis Hedler at his desk, a fat and foppish frog, but Father McNulty and Howard Best in leather chairs near the desk. 'What is this?' asked Jonathan, slowly.

'Come in, Jon,' said Louis, staring at him with a formidable expression. 'You look very dapper, I must admit. Did Robert pull you out of a trash barrel? Robert, my boy, would you please lock that door behind Jon? We don't want to be disturbed for a while, at least.' He stared at Jonathan again. 'Is whisky always your fortress and strength, Jon? Is that how you answer living?'

'Tell me a better way,' said Jonathan, but he was watching Robert Morgan locking the door. He raised his eyebrows when Robert put the key firmly in his pocket.

'Hallo, Jon,' said Howard Best, rising and coming to him and holding out his hand. They had met occasionally in the last months, but Jonathan had never been cordial and never engaged his friend in conversation any longer. So, his temper rising again, he looked pointedly at the hand and did not take it. Howard dropped it, and colour came into his kind face. 'All right, Jon,' he said. 'You never give up, do you?'

'Why should I? Now tell me what all—'

'No, you never give up,' said Howard. 'A damned proud, bellicose bastard—that's what you are, Jon. An unforgiving— well, I won't call you that name because it would reflect on your mother, whom I respect, which is more than I can say for you. What's the matter with you?' Howard had begun to shout. 'You and your damned choleric pride, your self-righteousness! I admit I was rough with you, I admit it. But, curse it, weren't you ever rough with anybody? Hah! Didn't you ever accuse anybody of something which was false?'

'Yes, he did,' said Robert Morgan, standing beside Louis's desk. 'He's self-righteous, all right. He believed all the lies of the town about Miss Jenny Heger. He told me some of them, and laughed, too. But that's all right for Jonathan Ferrier! What he believes is truth, no matter how much of a disgusting lie it is. He makes all the judgements; no one dares to challenge them.' The young man's face was quiet and resolute, but he looked the astounded Jonathan in the eye.

'I talked with Jenny to-day,' said Robert, and now he turned his head aside. 'I wanted to marry her. She is the loveliest young lady I've ever known. She was—well, she was just distracted. It seems that she thought something unpleasant about Jon, but she didn't tell me what it was. But she did tell me that he had believed vicious tales about her, and had never defended her, and had behaved abominably to her. If—if I were more of a man, I suppose, I'd punch his teeth out, talking and thinking those things about Jenny, as he did.'

Jonathan's face had closed, the muscles rising and standing up on it in hard ridges. He was thinking. Then the sickness he had felt in his office was nothing compared with this. He thought of Jenny and he put his hand to his forehead. He said, 'I think I must sit down, if you don't mind.' He saw an empty chair and went to it, walking very carefully, and he sat down and he looked at the edge of Louis's desk and felt the accusing silence about him. He said, 'Jenny told you all that?'

'Yes, she did. She's a very reticent girl, as you ought to know, and very innocent and restrained. A lovely girl.' Robert's voice shook a little. 'She wouldn't have told me if I hadn't asked her to marry me, for about the tenth time. I saw she was in a very agitated state of mind. She couldn't help herself. She cried. And so she told me. I'd like to know what you did to her, Ferrier.'

Jonathan considered, then he looked up, and he smiled faintly. 'You can punch my teeth out, if you want to, Bob.'

Louis Hedler laughed, and so did the priest who had as yet said nothing, and Jonathan held out his hand to Howard Best frankly and said, 'I don't deserve having you shake hands with me, Howard, but do it anyway.'

'It almost kills me,' said Howard, 'it really almost kills me.' But he took the offered hand. 'And I bet it just about kills you, too, to show a little common charity.'

Father McNulty spoke. 'I think Aristotle, in his *Poetics*, mentions that the hero of a tragedy must be a worthy man,

382

and admirable. He must also have some grave fault of character which is the source of his tragedy. That is you, Jon.'

'Very well, I confess I am a swine, that everything that has happened to me is my fault, my own fault, my most grievous fault, Father—if I remember the Confessional.' Jonathan's face had begun to spark again and temper showed in his eyes. 'I was accused of two murders I never committed, and so that is my fault. I spent months in prison and was tried, and that, too, was my fault. This town believed that I was guilty, and drove me out, and lied about me—and that is my fault. I never wanted anything but good for it—but that is my most grievous fault. For that, of course, for all of it, I can't ever be forgiven. Unpardonable sins.'

'Now, Jon,' said Louis Hedler.

But Father McNulty was regarding Jonathan with stern sadness. 'You are that worthy and admirable man Aristotle spoke of, Jon. But you have a terrible defect of character and soul. You lack charity. You demand perfection of everybody. You have no pity for weak human nature. You despise it—'

'Oh, so I should forgive and kiss and sob over every dog who's licked at my reputation for years, must I, and thank him for the smear? Frank, I never considered you overly intelligent, but I did think that you had some understanding.'

'Thank you.' The young priest's face had flushed and his golden eyes brightened with his own anger. 'No, no one expects you to fawn on your detractors who've done you an awful mischief, and those who falsely accused you of crimes you did not commit. But you have raised up enemies—'

'And that's my fault, too, I suppose.' Jonathan's harsh voice grew louder. 'I only had no patience for lies, for incompetence, for hypocrisy, for pretence. But I should have "charity" for them, I suppose? I should smile at liars, incompetents, hypocrites, pretenders, and tell them they are dear souls?'

'No.' The priest sighed. 'No decent man would expect that. But there is a way of correcting error. There is also another way: using a sledge-hammer. That's your method, Jon.'

'Final, too,' said Jonathan, and he laughed shortly. No one laughed with him.

'One should walk softly in this world,' said Louis Hedler. 'Not stealthily, but softly. You never learned discretion.'

'Is this what I came to hear?' asked Jonathan, rising. 'Then I will go home, if you don't mind.'

Louis went on as if he had not spoken. 'No one expects you to connive at evils, Jon, or even suffer them in silence. But you don't have to accuse a man, before others, of being whatever you think he is, or whatever he really is. If only in self-defence you should have had a little more—call it self-protectiveness, if you will.'

'Thanks for the advice,' said Jonathan. 'Bob, open that door, if you please.'

Robert Morgan ignored him.

Jonathan's expression became furiously irascible. 'Didn't Christ whip the money-changers out of the Temple? If I remember correctly He also addressed some of the men of His day in ungentle terms, such as "liars, hypocrites, sons of the Devil".'

'You are hardly Christ-like,' said the priest.

'But you think I've earned a cross? Such as this running lecture? It seems I came here under false pretences. I heard a rumour of Sheriffs, and prisons.' He glared at Robert. 'To be frank, I've been drunk all day, and your errand boy disturbed me, and that is something I will remember.'

Louis said, 'All this is preliminary to what we must tell you. You've raised up deadly enemies. Some men make friends, others collect foes. It depends on your taste. You tried desperately to make an enemy of me, Jon. You worked at it very hard, very sedulously, with admirable persistence. You concentrated on it.'

Jonathan could not help smiling. 'I'm afraid you are right, Louis. Very well. I apologise. Is that why I was wanted here? To confess my sins, be absolved, and sent lovingly on my way?'

'Not quite. Please let me continue. You worked just as hard to make other enemies, perhaps even harder. Most of them, I will admit, are detestable men. For that reason, alone, you should have avoided them, for your own sake. Or, if you could not avoid them, there were other ways of dealing with them instead of that sledgehammer Father mentioned. Other men have been falsely accused, then cleared, and everyone was happy. But not in your case, Jon. They were disappointed. Why? Perhaps because the majority of men are naturally evil and malicious and they can't bear honest men, and partly because they were antagonised needlessly. Never mind. This is not a meeting to discuss morals or theology. It concerns you, only.'

He glanced at Robert, Howard Best and the priest. 'We who are here are your best friends, Jon. You have no better in the world. There isn't one of us you haven't insulted and derided, either in your usual bad-tempered way, or in pretended indulgence. But, we are more charitable than you. We disregard your nastiness and your impetuousness and your endearing ways, and remember you for a good and dedicated man, suffering the defects of his own virtues, and stumbling blindly through a cave of snakes, absolutely unarmed. For that's what you've always been, Jon. Absolutely unarmed. Helpless against cruelty and malice and calumny. Not even recognising your enemies. Not even stepping warily about them, and watching them. You have our sympathy. Now, if you will draw your chair closer to this desk I will give you something to read. It makes very bad reading, Jon.'

He gave Jonathan a sheaf of papers. 'Affidavits from Jonas Witherby, Mrs Holliday, Peter McHenry. And a few others like them. But after you have read those, you will find much more—interesting—affidavits towards the end. Take your time, my boy, take your time.'

Jonathan looked at Howard Best and frowned. 'Affidavits. I smell a lawyer.'

Jonathan's hands were still trembling from his debauch. He glanced about him suspiciously, then began to read. They watched his tense face. He was reading casually, and the first affidavit was Jonas Witherby's. 'Not only did he accuse me of attempting suicide, but he tried to blackmail me into giving him money for his alleged wing at St Hilda's Hospital for tuberculosis—'

'Why, the old dog,' said Jonathan, and shrugged. 'Poppycock He didn't try to commit suicide. He tried to make it appear that Prissy had poisoned him. What trash.'

Louis Hedler lit a cigar, Howard lit his pipe, Robert lit his, and the priest lit a cigarette. It was quiet now in the big handsome office with the soft lamps burning, and the windows were open and a night wind stirred the draperies. Smoke curled towards the high white ceiling. Jonathan continued to read, muttering under his breath.

Lightning suddenly snaked over the tops of the black mountains, licking them with a forked tongue. The wind rose higher. Now they could hear the thudding of a night train and then its long dolorous wail as it wound through the valley. There were subdued noises in the hospital at this hour, the rolling of a car, suddenly quickened footsteps, the rapid tap of heels, the opening and shutting of a door, an abrupt cry, a wail, a soothing voice. The priest heard them and Howard Best, but the three doctors were accustomed to these sounds and they did not reach their consciousness.

Jonathan, as he read, was becoming paler and paler and his face narrower and narrower as every muscle tightened in it and elongated. In comparison his black lashes and brows and thick black hair became sharp and vivid. They saw him examine the receipted bills given to Louise Wertner and Mary Snowden. He reread their affidavits. He reread Edna Beamish's affidavit. He looked up, cleared his throat, and spoke in a very quiet voice.

'These are all lies,' he said. 'Every one is a lie. I merely gave the Beamish woman a preliminary examination, told her her condition, and then she—' He paused, and looked from one still face to another. 'As for these other women, I don't remember them at all. I don't know why they were sent these bills. I—I never touched them. If I had made a complete examination of them I'd have remembered. The bills—they are exorbitant. I never charge women of that class more than five or ten dollars for a complete examination.'

'They claim abortions,' said Louis Hedler. 'Those are higher.'

Jonathan now fixed all his attention on the other doctor. 'I never performed an abortion in my life. I never used a curette on a woman unless it was absolutely necessary to remove the results of a spontaneous abortion, or to save a life, or for diagnostic purposes. Do you believe me?' He appeared in a state of shock, but now the black eyes were beginning to glint and the livid ridges were appearing about his mouth.

'We believe you,' said Louis Hedler.'If we did not, you'd not be here now. But here is a statement, or affidavit, made to me by Martin Eaton, who died two days ago and was buried to-day. He made it in my presence, and in the presence of others.'

Jonathan's hands were trembling more and more so that the paper rattled. He read Martin Eaton's first affidavit, then reread it, made a slight sound, and reread it again. He put it down and contemplated Louis Hedler and the black spark in his eyes was ferocious.

'Eaton lied,' he said. 'Or it may be, that he believed Mavis, in spite of all the evidence. He was besotted by her. She was always a liar and a humbug and a fraud. She is dead now, and I wish she had died before I ever saw her.' His voice was all the more forbidding because it was so quiet. 'I never used a curette on her, mine or anyone else's. I wish now that I had really killed her.'

Louis, without speaking, opened the drawer of his desk, removed a covering of linen and laid it down before Jonathan. He nodded at it. Jonathan took the cloth and opened it and his curette lay in his hand. He looked at it incredulously. Louis said, 'Martin gave that to me, after he made that affidavit. I must admit he gave it up reluctantly.'

Jonathan held it in his hand. He said, 'I explained some of the instruments to her. She was always curious about everything, but rarely retentive of anything. When I explained its purpose she made a round, imitation frightened mouth, and stretched her eyes. Then she cuddled against me. She was always cuddling against—everybody. That was at least two years before she died.' His low voice was suddenly charged with cold violence and hatred. His mouth opened and he choked. 'I need a drink,' he said.

'Give Jon a drink please, Robert,' said Louis. Robert went to a cabinet and poured a glass of water for Jonathan and brought it to him. He looked at it numbly, as if it were a hemlock cup, then put it on Louis's desk. 'I didn't mean that kind,' he said.

'I suspected not,' said Louis.

Jonathan again examined every face in the room. At last he said, 'Is there anyone here who thinks I am lying?'

'No,' they said. 'No, no, no.'

Louis folded his hands on the sheets of paper. 'Kenton Campion is behind most of this, and this I know. He is the one who insisted that I send for members of the State Medical Board. They will be here Tuesday. They will issue an—order— for you to be present for examination. The sheriff will also be present—with a warrant for your arrest, Jon.'

The ugliest smile stood on Jonathan's face. 'I might have expected it,' he said. 'I have too many enemies, as you remarked yourself, Louis.' He thought. 'Campion. The traitor, the seller-out of his country. It's quite in character for him. Well, it all comes back to Mavis, doesn't it? She was the starting point.'

They felt the ghost of Mavis Eaton in the room, like a raucous and exultant presence, even Robert Morgan who had never seen her, and had only heard descriptions of her. Jonathan repeated, 'I wish I had really killed her. At least I'd have that satisfaction now.'

'Mavis wasn't the starting point,' said Louis Hedler. 'You were, when you were born. Campion, these women, Martin Eaton, all the others who made affidavits against you, would be guiltless of this perjury if they'd never known you. You were the precipitating element, Jon. Now wait,' and Louis held up his hand. 'I am trying to make something clear to you. I am not blaming you for anything. Campion is a scoundrel and I've known it for years. But I've never known him to hate anyone as he hates you, and he is a very sound hater. In a way you should be complimented,' and for the first time Louis smiled.

Jonathan said, 'So they'll have their wish. I'll be tried on the strength of these affidavits, and the evidence of these whores, and that will be the end of me. I should have left months ago.' They saw the sudden shine of his teeth between his parched lips.

Louis nodded to Howard Best, who began to take a thick sheaf of paper from his briefcase. Louis said cheerfully, 'Oh, I don't agree with you, Jon. While you were busy making more enemies and antagonising more people and generally making a nuisance of yourself, your friends, who believe in you, were very busy. Very busy, indeed.'

Howard was smiling broadly. 'I've given up a great deal of my time to you, Jon, and your predicament. Louis called me and Father McNulty in some time ago and showed us those affidavits, and I've been busier than a bee since. Now, read these, and then you may make obeisance to me and perhaps I'll forgive you for slighting me over the past months. Perhaps.'

Jonathan saw their smiling faces. He was still in a state of shock. He took the thick sheaf of papers and began to read. Louis had prudently removed Martin Eaton's dying statement.

There was Peter McHenry's abject apology and new affidavit, which Jonathan hastily read then put aside with bitter contempt. Then he said, 'That poor little kid, Elinor.' He read Amelia Forster's 'affirmation' closely, and he began to smile, and then he smiled exultantly. 'So, that explains the bills! Good old Amelia! I must give her a pension at once. No, we can't spare her. God bless our Amelia. And the affidavits of my other patients: I see that they thought they were "protecting" me from a false claim of injury to the Beamish bitch. There are times when I begin to hope for human nature, that is, when humanity shows itself, which is very rare.'

Then he read Howard Best's affidavit of his interview with William Simpson, chief of police of Scranton, and Jonathan swore in delight, and laughed out loud. 'So, she was Campion's little bed-pillow, was she! I ought to have thought of that, myself. I can see it all. He sent her to me, to involve me, and then to someone else who actually did the abortion. It would be a miracle if we could find that murderer. He might be able to tell me something about Mavis, too.'

'Go on,' said Howard, pleased at the sudden colour in Jonathan's pale face. 'You've only finished the soup of the meal. Wait for the entrées.'

Jonathan read on. Howard had made another affidavit, attesting to the following affidavits of Louise Wertner and Mary Snowden. He mentioned that he had 'persuaded' the young ladies, in the name of justice, to abjure their previous affidavits—which they had made under duress, and to make others which were absolutely true. (Howard neglected to explain, in his own affidavit, that he had visited the girls separately, told them he was an officer of the court—which he was—but which had sounded terrifying to the unsophisticated girls. He promised them immunity from prosecution, or at least amelioration of any punishment for their being parties to the crime of abortion, and seeking out an abortionist, if they would now swear fully and freely to the truth.)

They did not name the abortionist, but explained that they had given the name to Mr Howard Best, to be opened in a courtroom if necessary, for they feared reprisals.

They testified that on separate dates in November, 1900, they had been aborted 'of illegal offspring,' and that they were unmarried. They had paid fifty and seventy-five dollars, respectively. They had thought that the end of it, though each had suffered 'minor inconveniences' afterwards, which were trifling. Then, on 15th July, 1901 the abortionist had called at their residences, had declared that he was 'under investigation' by various unnamed parties for performing criminal operations and that if he were arrested he would not spare their part in seeking him out, imploring him to be party to a crime, and working on his sympathy. 'I,' he had told them,

389

'am a rich man. I may be fined. But you will go to prison for years, and then released only to the streets where you rightfully belong.'

However, related the cowed and terrified girls, the abortionist had promised to use his influence with 'unnamed parties' if they would make affidavits to the effect that Jonathan Ferrier, physician of Hambledon, River Road, Commonwealth of Pennsylvania, had performed 'these criminal acts' upon them, and had extorted enormous fees from them. They were to go to his offices, during his absence—of which they must make sure—and claim to his clerk that they owed those sums of money but had forgotten the bills. They were to ask the clerk to predate the bills—as of the time of the alleged abortions—and then to receipt them. The clerk had followed their instructions 'in all innocence and in good faith, believing the stories told to her.' The affidavits then followed. The girls admitted perjury, begged for mercy and for understanding of their plight and their 'natural terror' before a man who was rich and certainly powerful and who could do them great injury. They also added that when they had delivered their affidavits to Dr Louis Hedler of St Hilda's Hospital, of Hambledon, they each received fifty dollars from the abortionist 'in appreciation of their services.'

A peculiar look had been gathering on Jonathan's face, which no one present had ever seen before and which they did not recognise. It was a look of compassion, and not disgust and anger. It was a look of pity and even sadness. It was almost soft.

'The poor girls,' he said, and stared at the affidavits, his head bent.

They were naturally startled at this and looked at each other with amused raised eyebrows. Jonathan said, 'What can be done about these young things? When the case comes to court —as it must—will the girls go to prison for their part? I don't want that. I refuse to have it.'

Howard chuckled. 'Who said anything about court?'

Then a new and angry light glittered in Jonathan's eyes. 'I demand it! I want full exoneration! I want revenge!'

'You shall have it,' said Louis. 'But now, here is the *pièce de résistance*.' He held Martin Eaton's dying statement in his hand now, or rather a copy, he was afraid to trust the original to the unpredictable Jonathan Ferrier. Louis became very sober. 'Jon, this is a fearful thing I have here—a copy of a very long affidavit. It is a pathetic thing. It is a tragic thing. In a way, it will affect you more than anything else has ever done in your life, I am afraid, even your arrest and trial. I want you to compose yourself. I want you to read this quietly. I want you to display, for this man, some of the pity you have displayed for Louise Wertner and Mary Snowden, who had less reason to injure you than this man. At least, they were under duress, and in fear. This man was under no such. He wrote it in his own hand, to right a wrong. He exposed his soul, and the soul of someone he loved more than anything else on earth—to help you, and for no other purpose. He admits that he wronged you and explains why. Now he has rectified it.'

Jonathan had listened acutely, and his eyes almost disappeared under his frowning brows.

'Jon,' said Louis, 'there is something else in this affidavit which affects you very close to home, and I must ask you in advance to control yourself, and not to go off into one of your wild, uncontrolled violent rages before us, and to promise that you will keep your peace about the matter until everything else is resolved. If you cannot give me this promise I shall not let you read this.'

'I promise.' Jonathan's tone was curt. He was clenching his hands on the arms of his chair.

Louis hesitated. He was very grave. A deep tension rose in the warm room. Lightning flicked at the windows. The hospital was as quiet as death about them.

Louis spoke. 'I have endangered my position by showing you these affidavits, Jon. I have done it out of regard for you, in spite of our past—differences. We have all endangered ourselves, with, perhaps, the exception of Father McNulty, whom I consulted long ago when I first heard of the plot against you. For this is confidential. None of it should have been shown to you, to your lawyer, or anyone else until after the hearing before the State Medical Board. Now you understand the gravity of the situation. You understand how we have jeopardised ourselves. For you to do anything, to say anything, of what you have read, and what you will read, or to name any names, or seek a private revenge on anybody— before the time is ripe—then you will have destroyed us. Have I made this clear, desperately clear?'

'You have,' said Jonathan. He was beginning to sweat again. An awful premonition came to him, but he could not name it. He only knew that when he read that affidavit the world would not be the same to him thereafter.

Louis looked at the others. 'I have shown these things first to Father McNulty and to your friend, Robert Morgan, your replacement. I have consulted them all, and asked their advice, especially Howard's. They said in all fairness—though it is very dangerous—I should show the affidavits to you, for they know your character. They wished you to read what you have read, and now this, so that an interval can pass so you can calm and prepare yourself and think clearly. If you should appear before the State Medical Board members, and your enemies, in a state of passion—as you should if you had not known all this—and with your usual recklessness and fury, you would be exonerated of the alleged crimes, but you would make such a vile impression on the members of the Board that you would be in disgrace for the rest of your life. The State Medical Board does not like physicians who lose their heads, and threaten, and rage. Your reputation would be irretrievably lost. Is that clear, Jon?'

'Louis,' said Jonathan, and he was visibly moved. 'I will do nothing to hurt anyone here. No one will ever know, before Tuesday, or even afterwards, that you have shown me these things beforehand.' He suddenly grinned, for the tension was growing. 'I kiss your hand, Louis.'

'I don't know which is more distasteful, your rages, your sarcasms, or your humour, Jon, if you can call it humour.' But Louis smiled also, and shook his head.

'The best thing, of course,' said Howard, 'would be to gag him right here and tie him up and hide him in that closet until Tuesday, allowing him out, still gagged and tied, for only strictly sanitary purposes.'

'Excruciatingly funny,' said Jonathan. He was white again. 'Now, may I read?'

'With compassion,' said Father McNulty. 'The man was weak, and tragically foolish.'

Jonathan made an unpleasant grimace. 'I never had compassion for such men, Frank,' he said. 'Except for my father. He cured me of sentimentality, because he was the most sentimental of creatures. I see these papers are typewritten, I thought you said they were in the man's own handwriting.'

'The original is,' said Louis. 'But we have a reason, which no doubt you will understand after you've read the affidavit, to keep the original from you as of yet.'

Jonathan frowned at him, but Louis only nodded at the papers, and Jonathan began to read. After a moment, when he saw that this was the last affidavit of Martin Eaton, he uttered a loud and contemptuous curse, and then was still.

They all watched Jonathan, and now no man smoked but sat very stiff and rigidly in his chair. They were like men watching a powerful but unpredictable lion, waiting for a movement of its eyes, a bristling of the mane, a twitch of a muscle, to inform them in which direction he was about to leap. By a flick of his lashes, the tightening of his mouth, the raise of his brows, and by his colour, they knew almost exactly the paragraph he was reading. Amazement, hatred, repulsion, scorn, disbelief, sombre melancholy, fury, even surprise: they saw them all.

They knew when he came to the account of Mavis's death, for every muscle in his body straightened and his mouth became ugly and hard. And, when he uttered one foul expletive, they knew he had come upon his brother's name. It was then that he looked up at them, and yet did not see them. He was looking inward, not outward, and there was an ominous expression about his eyes and mouth. He was too quiet. They watched him tautly, leaning towards him. The silence in the room became unbearable. They wanted him to speak, to swear, even to rave. That would have been more normal than this quietude, this glittering reflectiveness, this pallid lack of emotion.

Then he laid the papers on his knee and lit a cigarette and he smoked a little, still staring blindly at each face, then at the walls, then at the ceiling and the floor. They knew he was not conscious of smoking, and that in himself something very dire was going on, something of so profound an explosion that it could not reach the ear or any other sense. His emotions were beyond human expression, too turbulent for speech. His nostrils were flared as if he were lacking oxygen, and then his eyes narrowed and he picked up the papers again and resumed reading.

I asked for calm, thought Louis Hedler, but I'd prefer raving to this. I'd almost prefer that he'd lose his mind, temporarily, of course.

Then he had finished. Very slowly and carefully he put the papers on Louis's desk and crushed his cigarette in the tray.

He watched the last smoke curl up as if it were of the most intense importance. He finally said, 'You have the original, in his own writing?'

'I have,' said Louis.

'Where is it?'

'In a very safe place.' Then Louis knew he had been very discreet indeed, in having copies made by a trusted clerk and not giving Martin Eaton's affidavit to Jonathan.

'It must be destroyed.' Nothing could have been more indifferent than Jonathan's voice.

'I thought you'd think that,' said Louis. 'But no. I am not going to ask you for your reasons. I suspect them. Your pride. The pride that kept you silent in the courtroom. Jonathan, you are not the first man whose wife betrayed him, nor will you be the last. In a way, you may have saved your life by your silence, for then there was no motive for any alleged crime.'

Jonathan said, 'I was trying to protect that old bugger, Eaton—his dream of Mavis. I remembered how it was between us when I was a kid, and how he helped me all the years of my—— He knew all the time! He knew the truth. Yet, he never said a word except to scream "No! No!" when the verdict came in.'

'Remember,' said Father McNulty, 'he did, in his grief and pain, believe that you were in part guilty of your wife's death. It was insane and twisted thinking, but who has not been guilty of that? Not you, Jon?' The priest smiled sadly. 'I know it will take much understanding on your part to feel pity for that distraught father.'

But Jonathan had relapsed into his profound meditation again, and was lost to them. Robert Morgan was somewhat relieved, being still young and uncomplicated, at Jonathan's apparent control of himself when he had expected madness and terrible rage. But Howard Best and the priest and Louis Hedler knew Jonathan much better, and now they were greatly alarmed and very uneasy and disturbed as they watched the silent man.

'No one else must see Eaton's letter,' said Jonathan, after long minutes.

'Jon,' said Louis Hedler, 'I'm not interested as to your reasons for asking that. I know it is the one thing that can lift the libel and hostility and hate this town feels for you. You must be exonerated from even the suspicion that you injured, killed, Mavis.

'There is another matter,' said Louis, and now the froggy eyes glistened with inner excitement. 'Brinkerman must not only have his licence revoked, but he must be prosecuted for the crime he committed against your wife, and those two other girls. God knows how many others he has maimed, caused to die, or aborted. I know his wife is the apple of his eye, and she is wildly extravagant. This has probably been going on for a long time. He must be exposed and punished, and prevented from other crimes.

'There is also Senator Campion. I have not yet fully planned how to approach him and expose him for instigating this plot against you.'

'His son, Francis, will arrive to-morrow,' said the priest. 'I have sent for him, to help you. But, as it is, his help may not be needed, except as a point against the Senator.'

'By precipitating a crisis,' said Howard Best with satisfaction, but still watching Jonathan uneasily, 'Senator Campion has done you a wonderful turn. You could never have lived with the knowledge that Hambledon, and perhaps the whole state of Pennsylvania, and probably other cities, believed you guilty of your wife's murder. You've been acting, since the trial, like a man without a care in the world, but I know you better, Jonathan. I know that you don't want to leave Hambledon, where you were born—'

Jonathan stood up slowly, and then in a most casual tone he told them what they should do with Hambledon and everyone in it. He expounded on the matter with easy eloquence, as if he were amused. But they saw his eyes. He was only half aware of what he was saying. The inner black turbulence was gathering force in him.

Louis interrupted. 'You have forgotten that there is a clergyman present, Jon.'

'Oh, I've heard all the words before,' said young Father McNulty, whose rosy face now had no colour at all, and though he smiled he looked a little sick. Robert Morgan was tremendously embarrassed and he flushed. Howard Best pretended not to have heard.

'I think,' said Louis, 'that as it is nearly midnight, we should disband.' He looked at Jonathan who had gone to an open window and was looking through it, his hands in his pockets.

'Jon?' said Louis Hedler, and struggled to keep the pity from his voice. 'I want you to think of this: in a month you will recall this night only occasionally. In a year you will not think of it at all. In two years it will be like a bad dream, almost forgotten entirely. You are still young. Your whole life is before you now, cleared, clean, ready.' He hesitated. 'Jon, would you consider becoming chief of surgery here?'

Jonathan said as if he had not heard at all, 'I have things to consider.' He turned. The sallow calm was fixed on his face. He looked at each man separately. 'I suppose I should thank you. Howard, send me a bill.'

'Go to hell,' said Howard Best.

'And Louis,' said Jonathan, 'I haven't any words. I still don't believe it.' He actually smiled.

But Louis, studying him closely, did not smile. 'Jon,' he said. 'You have given us your solemn promise, and you were never a man to go back on your word, for good or evil. You must not do anything—rash—or violent. We have put our own safety in your hands, our own reputations. You have promised.'

'I don't break my word,' said Jonathan. Then it was as if an inner and fierce convulsion ran through him and he shivered, and clenched his fists at his sides, and closed his eyes for a moment. 'I leave Brinkerman and Campion to you, at least for the first attack. I will meet with you here at St Hilda's, in the conference room, at what time, on Tuesday morning?'

Louis exchanged a glance with Howard Best and said smoothly, 'I will let you know the exact time later.'

He stood up. 'I think you can have that drink you wanted now.' He went to a cabinet and brought out a bottle of brandy and several glasses. 'I think we all need this.'

Jonathan said, 'No.'

'I will drive you home,' said Robert Morgan.

But the priest said, 'I'd prefer to do that, Dr Morgan. I want to have a word with Jonathan, probably about Francis.'

To the surprise of everyone Jonathan said nothing more. He had relapsed into his inner dream again. He did not even remember to shake hands with the men who had saved him, and they understood. They shook hands with each other, murmuring in low voices, as if there was a corpse in the room, or something that must not be aroused to some towering and fatal detonation. Then the priest touched Jonathan's arm and they left together, and the others watched them go, thankful that Jonathan was leaving, yet more anxious than ever.

'I don't like it,' said Howard to Louis Hedler.

'Disliking it is putting it very mildly,' said the doctor. 'I've seen Jonathan in some dangerous moods before, but nothing like this.'

The next morning quite early Dr Louis Hedler and Howard Best drove up to 'Pike's Peak,' the Hambledon residence of Senator Kenton Campion. It was cooler as the doctor's carriage carried them higher into the mountains, and here at least there was some blessed greenness and glossy shade. But the sky was still that curious saffron colour, though it was hardly nine o'clock.

'He seemed quite unconcerned when I called him last night, before we saw Jon Ferrier,' said Dr Hedler. 'I told him it was important, that I must see him this morning, and not in my office, and he couldn't have been more indifferent or less curious.'

'He probably thinks you are coming to plead for Jon,' said Howard. 'He threatened you, didn't he?'

'To be sure. Kent is a very unworthy man, and a mean one. It doesn't matter. I am now in full agreement with you, Howard, to handle the affair this way, without publicity, without the newspapers, without the State Medical Board, without witnesses. Say what you care to about Campion, and I will agree with you heartily, but we must also admit that he's very careful of himself and knows when to withdraw and when to attack. We don't want Jon to confront all those people—we agreed on that. He was just about out of his mind last night, and God only knows what he is thinking to-day, and what he is planning. So, for his sake we must spare him, and conclude things quietly. When Campion gets a sniff of the carrion we are preparing for Brinkerman, he'll withdraw so fast you won't see him except for a blink. No scandal for Kent.'

'And he won't have to pay for that stinking plot against Jon! A nice thought.'

'Isn't it? But sometimes, to help the innocent, like Jon, one must let the scoundrel get off scot-free. I hope Jon will appreciate that some day, though I doubt he is in a temper calm enough to agree as of now. In his own way, our Jon can be very vengeful. He won't thank us for this morning's work—yet. Later, he may.'

The town lay below them, already shimmering in heat waves, and the water of the river was brassy. Dr Hedler felt uncomfortable in his formal brown suit, and as he was also stout he began to suffer. He pushed his straw hat far back on his round skull and puffed at his cigar. 'You will be able to cancel that warrant out for Jon, won't you, Howard?'

'It isn't signed yet. Something tells me, as I told you last night, that Campion will hurry to call the Sheriff and ask for cancellation, and to assure him that everything is splendid now. Oh, he'll cover his tracks very ably and very dexterously, you can be sure of that!'

Louis sighed. 'I hate to see such a rascal come out of this without a single wound. I hate, even more, to think of him back in Washington, doing his mischief as usual, serene and unctuous and loved and admired. I may have a talk with the Governor in the near future, a very discreet talk, and show him a few documents. Perhaps the Legislature won't confirm Campion again, or perhaps they'll recall him. But that will bring in the newspapers, and reporters are avidly curious, and Jon may be drawn in. I must think about it.'

'We have to walk very tenderly about Jon,' said Howard. 'If he were a more reasonable man we could discuss things with him, and lay our own plans. I think, I am sure, that it was knowing about his brother—that damned dilettante—that really knocked him off his precarious perch. The other things—he could be induced to look at them fairly calmly, in proportion, eventually.'

'I'm sorry for Marjorie Ferrier, with two such sons,' said Louis. 'Now, she disproves our neat theory that much that happens to one lies in his own nature. Marjorie was always a great lady, a magnificent woman, tolerant, kind, composed, full of fortitude and intelligence. She never interfered with anyone.'

'Perhaps,' said Howard, 'that was the whole damned trouble. Tolerance, I am coming to think, can create as much disaster as intolerance.'

'I wonder what Jon will do now,' said Louis, as they approached the Campion estate.

The slim maid at the door assured them that they were expected, and they went into the shining marble hall and then into the room with the Florentine windows looking out at the gardens and the hot purple and bronze mountains. They found young Francis Campion waiting for them, fatigued and strained but smiling, in his black, habit-like clothing. 'I arrived a little earlier,' he said to them, shyly shaking hands but looking anxiously into their faces. 'How is Dr Ferrier?'

'As bad as can be expected,' said Howard. Francis made a distressed sound. He walked slowly up and down the room, a thin young man with a delicate profile.

'Father McNulty sent me a long cable,' he said. 'And there was a letter from him waiting for me here. I can hardly believe it. It's a frightful story.' He looked at them. 'And true, too?'

'Quite true. And much worse,' said Louis Hedler. 'I don't know how much Father could squeeze into a cable and a letter, but there have been many developments since then, and each one is a little worse than the one before.' He paused. 'As it concerns your father so intimately, perhaps you'd rather not hear our conversation with him, Francis.'

'I am staying,' said the young man with resolution. 'I have some things to say to my father, too. If necessary, I will say them in front of you. I've been a coward. I don't want to injure him, but I must think of my country first. It is possible something can be arranged so my father's name won't be blasted in the newspapers. It is entirely his choice.'

Howard and Louis looked at each other, then Howard smiled and sighed happily. 'You give us pleasure, Francis,' he said, and rubbed his hands together.

They heard measured footsteps approaching, calm, casual footsteps, and Senator Campion entered, beaming, chestnut-coloured, flushed with sleep and food. He was like a large, middle-aged cherub, plump but stately, happy with life and, thought Howard Best, he has probably slept like a lamb and as snugly. Always the politician, he greeted his visitors with hearty amiability, shook hands with them fondly, smiled at them, and studied them with his keen politician's eyes, watchful, hard.

'I see you've already greeted Francis,' he said, and put his hand on his son's thin shoulder. When Francis moved away the Senator did not even glance at him. 'Such a pleasant surprise. Quite unexpected, too. Francis, as this affair my friends have come to consult me about is very private, and needs to be managed discreetly, will you excuse us?'

'No,' said Francis. 'I think this concerns me, too.'

The thick chestnut brows rose, and slowly the Senator turned on his heel and stared at his son. 'You? How could it possibly concern you, my boy?'

'I know it is about Jon Ferrier, and anything about Jon Ferrier now concerns me.' Francis's thin young face firmed and his eyes were no longer shy but direct.

'How do you know it is about Ferrier?' asked the Senator, and he was not as flushed as before.

'We told him,' said Howard quickly.

'Oh, you did.' The Senator's regard swept to Howard and there was a threat in the narrowed look. 'I think that was very imprudent of you, Howard. As this is a legal matter, you have behaved unethically, and I think the Bar Association—'

'I always behave unethically to protect the innocent,' said Howard. 'Don't you, Senator?'

'There is a slight question of the innocence of your client, Howard. Or, is he your client?'

'Yes.'

'How did that happen? How did you, or he, know about this private matter, not a word of which has so far been allowed to go beyond closed doors?'

'Jon heard rumours,' Howard said. 'Just rumours. So, he came to me, on the strength of the rumours.'

'Rumours.' The Senator contemplated Louis for a long moment. 'From an impeccable source, I trust, Howard?'

'Impeccable. Trustworthy. News does get out in a little town like this, Senator. For instance, frightened girls talk. Indiscreet ladies whisper secrets to each other. A colleague catches a breath of scandal, of danger. Another colleague overhears a private conversation, and reports it to the interested party. People make quiet affidavits, and clerks gossip. It arrives at Jon's doorstep, all of it. Nothing very tangible, of course, but enough. So, he comes to me to ask me to protect his interests. Is that sufficient?'

'I think you are lying,' said the Senator, but he still contemplated Louis Hedler.

'Oh, it won't matter in the least in say,' Howard looked at his watch, 'another hour. Then you will be grateful, and not annoyed, that we consulted you. Before we moved.'

'Before you moved,' said the Senator.

'Exactly. We do have a warm spot in our hearts for you, Kent, we really do. So, instead of calling in the newspapers,

400

and getting out warrants of arrest, immediately, and mentioning your involvement, we came to talk to you.'

'I don't know what the hell you are talking about!' exclaimed the Senator, and his look at Louis had turned murderous.

'Well, I do,' said Howard, smiling. 'For instance, I was in Scranton recently, visiting friends, and I discovered that they were close friends of a certain Mrs Edna Beamish, and—you know how people are, Senator—they mentioned that you were, yourself, a very close, a very dear, a very intimate friend of Edna's. Very intimate, indeed.'

The Senator had turned a curious colour. He glanced quickly at his son, who was listening alertly. 'What of it?' asked Kenton Campion. 'I knew her husband well.'

Then Howard, watching him closely for signs of guilt and fear, said, 'You and she also know Dr Claude Brinkerman, don't you?' He had no proof of the involvement of Edna Beamish with the doctor, but he struck this blow deliberately, hoping.

The Senator's face had become the colour and texture of wet lard. But he was not a politician for nothing. He said, 'I know Claude Brinkerman. What of it?'

Howard shrugged. 'I too, know Brinkerman, and all about him. News gets out. To support his wife in the manner to which she was never accustomed, he turned to performing abortions. Now, I have it on excellent authority that Mrs Beamish had occasion to visit Brinkerman, and I also have it on authority that you two are very close to each other—in Washington—and people do talk, as I've reminded you before. I also have it on good authority that Mrs Beamish recently had an abortion, and so there is the whole story.'

The Senator said, and they saw the engorged arteries pulsing in his thick throat, 'Ferrier aborted her in his office, and we have the proof, and the affidavits.'

Howard shook his head kindly. 'No, you don't have any such proof, Senator. But we do have proof that Edna was your little friend, and little friends often get into difficulties, and so they have recourse to the Brinkermans. Er, do you wish me to proceed before your son?'

Francis had been listening closely, white with horror. He turned to his father and said, 'Edna? Edna? That was the woman I saw in your house a year ago in Washington, Father, when I arrived unexpectedly! She was in your bedroom, Father.' Francis's mouth twisted with pain and disgust. 'Edna left very soon after my arrival, rather dishevelled. But I knew all about you, Father, and it did not surprise me. I've known about your little friends since I was sixteen. I never knew the names of the others, but I heard you call her by her name that morning, very early, urging her to get out as fast as possible.'

Howard smiled with glee at Louis Hedler, who had been having somewhat of a bad time for some minutes, and Louis smiled back.

'Filthy, mean, dirty little spy,' said the Senator, with hatred bleak and open on his face as he looked at his son.

'Yes, I was. And I am glad, too. For I learned a great deal about you, Father. Enough to make me want to die very often.'

'I wish you had, I wish you had,' said the Senator. He turned to the others. 'I think we should sit down and have a quiet talk, gentlemen.'

'I think so, too,' said Howard with alacrity. 'After all, there is a lady involved, Mrs Edna Beamish, or Mrs Ernest Beamish, and she has been party to a crime, and she has also perjured herself freely, in making out an affidavit against Jon. Oh, news does get around, and people do peek and read!' Howard smiled affably at the grim Senator. 'Now, if and when little Edna is arrested, and knowing the nature of ladies, especially ladies like little Edna, I doubt if she will suffer in silence. But you know Edna best, don't you, Senator?' He was teeming with elation.

Again the Senator looked at his son, and the loathing he had concealed for years under a paternal amiability was stark on his large face. 'Get out,' he said.

'No,' said Francis. 'I stay. And if you take these gentlemen to your room and lock me out, they will tell me everything afterwards. Won't you, gentlemen?'

'Indeed, yes,' said Howard. 'I must do everything to protect my client, Jon Ferrier. Besides, it will all be in the newspapers shortly, the national newspapers—after all, Francis, your father is a very important man—and you can read it for yourself.'

'Newspapers,' said the Senator and sat down heavily. 'Are you threatening me, Best?'

'I certainly am,' said Howard. 'Don't the newspapers love a juicy little romantic story! Sweet little Edna and Senator Kenton Campion—and an abortionist. Tut, tut. Americans are still very narrow-minded, still, Senator, as you doubtless know.' He sat down and faced the Senator and gleamed happily upon him.

'Let's be finished with lies and start with the truth,' said the Senator. 'Louis, you are responsible for this. You betrayed a trust, put in you by your own medical societies, not to mention betrayal of private matters to this shyster.'

'In a few minutes,' said Howard, without rancour, 'you will be glad that someone put trust in me, and very grateful. Indeed, let us start with the truth. Senator, I have here, in my briefcase, numerous documents. I don't think you will enjoy reading them, but you will find them interesting.'

'I thought you might like to know, Kent,' said Louis, who had regained his confidence, 'that a warrant will be issued for Claude Brinkerman this morning. Men like Brinkerman don't keep their mouths closed. I think he may talk when the facts are presented to him, and then decide to throw himself on the mercy of the court. I've heard he was a close friend of yours, Kent, and not just a casual acquaintance. That is why he induced two young and frightened girls to perjure themselves and accuse Jon Ferrier of performing criminal operations on them. But read for yourself.'

Senator Campion took the papers extended to him by Howard who, with Louis, was perched on a settee of gilt and pink silk, but the Senator looked fixedly at the younger man. The ripe colour of his rich lips had turned purplish at the mention of Claude Brinkerman's name again; his blue eyes had narrowed so that the colour was hardly visible; his jowls quivered for an instant, and a lock of his thick chestnut hair fell over his sweating forehead. Then he began to read, after putting his pince-nez on his large well-formed nose.

He read with the suspicious and scrupulous care of the politician, alert to verbal traps and cunningly-placed phrases, and sometimes he went back to reread a section of a previous page. He was poised and controlled by nature, and he had learned to be more so since he had become a politician. The three men watched him, his son Francis standing near a window, but except for his colour and the sweat on his face he showed no emotion. Somewhere a big clock was ticking, ticking, and a gardener had begun to cut the grass outside, and a fountain splashed, and the cicadas raised their raucous song against the burnished sky.

Then the Senator carefully took off his glasses, let them spring back on the chain which was fastened to his buttonhole, and laid the papers on a nearby ormolu table. He folded his hands on his flowered waistcoat. He looked at Howard Best. 'What has this to do with me?'

Howard was, for a moment, flabbergasted. Then he smiled. 'Everything, Senator. Everything. You surely have not missed Martin Eaton's remarks about you! That alone is very incriminating. You surely understand we know about little Edna, and the abortion procured for her at the hands of Dr Brinkerman. It makes a nice story that you induced Brinkerman to seek out two of his more vulnerable patients to perjure themselves against Jon Ferrier. Then, of course, you and Jonas Witherby were overheard browbeating Louis here, by several of the staff. Oh, there's a lot that has to do with you, Senator! And that is not all. We have much more, which we are keeping for the final event. It would be very silly of us, wouldn't it, for us to tell you what it is?'

Again the Senator's eyes narrowed reflectively on Howard, and Howard knew that he was conjecturing if the lawyer were lying or not. Then Francis spoke. 'There is what I know, also, of what I heard my father saying to his colleagues in his house, when he thought I was asleep, absent for a time, or not in the city. I have already told Jon Ferrier some of it. It would make appalling reading to the American public, and I am ready to give it to them.'

The Senator slowly turned his big chestnut head and looked at his son. There was no fear on his face, not even now, but his large nostrils flared and a most malignant expression passed over his face like the glare of an edge of a knife.

Francis said with sad bitterness, 'I asked Jon, only a few months ago, if I should tell what I had heard and what I knew, and he said if it were his father he would not do it. You owe that to Jon, Father. But now I am ready to tell everything to any newspaper, with names and dates—that you are in an international conspiracy involving munitions, and future wars, for profit and power.'

Louis Hedler sucked in his breath, and Howard stared at the Senator with repulsion, but the Senator looked only at his son.

'You are a liar,' said the Senator with loud, hard precision.

'The invariable reply of a liar to the truth,' said Francis, and he turned away and again stared through the window.

The Senator said to Louis Hedler after a minute, 'Then you did indeed betray all that was confidential to this shyster?'

'Kent,' said Louis, 'you and I are of an age. I am a rich man, as you know. I am economically invulnerable. You cannot hurt me. Complain of me to the State Medical Board? Do you think I care any longer? Compared to what I have saved Jon Ferrier from, my retirement, forced or voluntary, is nothing.'

'I thought you detested him,' said the Senator.

Louis said, 'I detested many of his personal characteristics, and still do. But I know him for a Puritanically righteous man, for all his deserved reputation with the ladies in this town. He is a good man, the best of physicians, an expert surgeon. He has done so much for Hambledon, anonymously, that if the people knew they would rise up and call him blessed.' He paused. 'Just as they will rise up and call you an entirely different name, when they know the facts we have about you.'

The Senator's mouth twitched, but it was not with a smile. He was a redoubtable fighter. 'I know he is hated here. I know I am regarded with, shall we say, admiration, and I am respected. I can fight this thing down, drive Ferrier out of town still, and come up triumphant. Do you doubt it?'

'You've forgotten what I know, Father,' said Francis from the window.

The Senator laughed out loud. 'You! A creature who tried to hang himself only last June! A nincompoop, a defected clerical student! A penniless whimperer! The newspapers wouldn't dare publish what you'd tell them.'

'Now, that is interesting,' said Louis Hedler. 'You leave us no recourse, I, Howard and Francis, but to go to the Governor with this evidence we have shown you, and the more important evidence we have not shown you. I will send a telegram at once to the State Medical Board to delay sending members here until I have seen the Governor.'

'I think,' said Howard, 'that the newspapers will be interested in what Louis and I and Francis, together, have to say, and the Governor's subsequent remarks. I have heard he is not very happy about you any longer, Senator, and you have powerful enemies in Washington. There are ambitious young State Senators with rich and influential families and friends who are itching to replace you, and I am sure that the State Legislature, which appointed you, would listen to them—after the Governor informed them of what we have against you, your lies, your suborning of perjury, your connection with a notorious abortionist, and much more.'

The Senator's face became violent, not in any contortion of feature but more in contour of his cheeks and the swelling at his temples.

'We came to you,' said Louis, 'not for your sake, not to spare you, not to make or beg a bargain. We came for the sake of Jon Ferrier, and his mother, Marjorie, and the memory of Martin Eaton, and even for the sake of those two poor girls induced to put themselves in jeopardy to satisfy your hatred and malice. Perhaps, even, for Mrs Edna Beamish, who will certainly be prosecuted for perjury, at the very least, and I understand that she is not only a rich lady in her own right, and able to procure good lawyers, but is a lady of spirit. When deserted by you, she will think of herself, and she will be indignant. There are many we'd like to spare, and above them all, Jon Ferrier, who has suffered too much as it is. We hope to persuade him not to prosecute his enemies, among them yourself. We can only do that with your co-operation, and I beg you to give it to save a scandal which will rock the whole State.'

'We are even willing to let you return to Washington in peace,' said Howard, 'though it goes against our patriotism. We are willing because of Jon.'

'I never knew he had such friends,' said the Senator with enormous contempt.

'It is unfortunate that you did not know,' said Louis Hedler. 'Had you known you might not have been so sure, and so rash.'

The Senator sat in silence, twiddling his thumbs. He had never been thwarted nor opposed before. He kept swallowing, as if something vile repeatedly rose in his throat.

'You interest me,' he said. 'In the improbable event that I should submit to these falsehoods, this blackmail, how do you propose to handle the situation? I suppose Ferrier has already seen these—concocted papers?'

'Not all,' said Louis, and wondered how much longer he would have to pretend to even more dreadful knowledge than contained in the documents. 'But enough so that last night I was afraid he might come up here and murder you. But he was spent, and he had given us his word that he would do nothing until I gave him permission, or the latter was concluded. Otherwise,' and Louis smiled, 'Jon might really have committed a murder last night. You know how savage he can be, and what a temper he has.'

'And you think you can control such a madman?'

'I think I can,' said Louis, and wished it were true. 'He has not evidence against anyone, except what we hold. He is sensible enough to know that he cannot make accusations without evidence, or at least I will impress that on him.'

'And the evidence?'

'It will go to a very safe place, copies to me, copies to Howard, to be destroyed in the event of our deaths, or to be opened—if necessary. Jon will have no proof.'

The Senator reflected. He looked from one face to the other carefully and they could not tell what he was thinking.

'You have forgotten those three women, Edna and the two girls. Their last true affidavits are a matter of public record?'

'No. Louise Wertner's and Mary Snowden's were made before me, at my behest,' said Howard. 'If we can settle this thing like reasonable gentlemen, if we can agree—then you, Senator, need only inform Mrs Beamish that she must withdraw the complaint, which is the only one of public record, and in the Sheriff's hands. I wish I had known,' said Howard with an affectionate smile, 'and I would have dissuaded Mrs Beamish from the very beginning, with the information I have against her.'

'Then on whose public complaint, to the Sheriff, will Brinkerman be arrested?'

'On Mrs Beamish's. She is responsible, not I. But then she was following orders, was she not? As for the girls' affidavits, they were given to Louis, both sets, I may remark, the ones they falsely made—under orders—and the second true ones, admitting perjury.'

Again the Senator reflected, and he sucked his purplish lips in and out, and began to tap the table with his pince-nez.

'You have only to call your good friend, the Sheriff, who received his support from you, Senator, and ask him, in the kindest way possible, to quash Mrs Beamish's complaint, and to destroy the warrant he has for Jonathan's arrest.'

'And Brinkerman—you say he will be arrested?'

Louis looked at him. 'He will be, unless Mrs Beamish's complaint is withdrawn, unless you ask the Sheriff to overlook

—with a laugh, of course—her indiscreet perjury. I shudder,' said Louis, his face changing, 'to let such a man get away from the punishment he deserves. Yet, for Jon Ferrier's sake I will not let the Sheriff read Martin Eaton's last and true affidavit. What Jon will say to that I do not know. But again, he will have no evidence. I promise you that. We did not even permit him to keep a copy of Martin's affidavit.'

'You have not been entirely frank with me,' said the Senator. 'You threatened and bullied me, implied you had already moved against me and Brinkerman, for effect. Is that fair, or just?'

Howard could not help it. He burst out laughing with genuine mirth and threw back his head. He choked, 'Senator, that remark of yours, about "fair and just" tickles me almost to death, honestly it does!'

'Now, Howard,' said Louis.

Francis came from the window. 'You actually intend not to expose this man as he should be exposed?'

'My dear boy,' said Louis, 'sometimes one has to keep silence to protect others, even if it goes against the grain, even though it leaves bile in one's mouth. Isn't Jon more important to you than your father's ruin?'

'No, he isn't,' said the Senator. 'This white-faced whelp has been trying for years to ruin me, from his own admission.'

With the faintest and most distressful of sounds Francis turned and went quickly from the room and Louis and Howard watched him go with sorrow and sympathy. Then Louis said, 'If that were true, he could have done it before, and not almost died of what he knew about you, Kent. I've known him from childhood, from babyhood. He adored you. What did you do to turn him against you, Kent, your only son?'

The Senator's chestnut brows drew over his eyes and his mouth twitched again. He made no reply.

'Well,' said Howard, 'the Sheriff should be in his office. I believe you have a telephone in the hall below, Senator. May we accompany you, just to listen to your remarks, and have the assurance that no move will be made against Jon?'

'But there is something else,' said Louis, 'and the most important. Howard and I have discussed this thoroughly. Everyone knows that you were a close friend of Adrian Ferrier's and that you have a high regard for Marjorie, and I believe there was a rumour that you steadfastly declared

408

that Jon was not guilty of Mavis's death. How admirable it will seem to the good people of Hambledon—and the national newspapers—when you announce that you personally undertook an investigation of the case and that you are happy to announce that, indeed, Jon was not guilty!'

'No,' said the Senator, with firmness.

Louis sighed. 'Then we will, in spite of everything, have to give a copy of Martin Eaton's last affidavit, which implicates you and Brinkerman, to the Press.'

'God damn you,' said the Senator, in a very soft voice. 'Isn't it enough that I may—may, I remark—ask the Sheriff what you have suggested I ask him?'

'No, it is not nearly enough,' said Howard. 'Don't force our hands into making everything public. At the very least,' he continued with cunning, 'you will be thwarting Jon's explosive demands that it all be made public, for you know he can be wild, and he has suffered a great deal. By saying what we have suggested you say, to the Press, you will be frustrating poor Jon, and it is really very unkind of us to think of it at all.'

'And God damn him, too,' said the Senator, and stood up. He surveyed them. 'I've met scoundrels before in Philadelphia and Washington, but you two bumpkins are the most conscienceless.'

Now Louis laughed as well as Howard. The Senator was not ashamed or embarrassed. After a few moments he laughed himself, briefly and grimly and spread out his hands. 'Let us go downstairs, to the telephone.' He added, 'I think I will return to Washington almost immediately.'

'A very wise thought,' said Howard, as they went down the shining marble stairs together. 'One never knows what Jon Ferrier will do.'

'I suggest,' said Louis Hedler, 'that you warn Brinkerman to give up his extra-curricular activities. As for myself, I will ask him to resign from the staff, and will hint to him as much as possible of what I know. One never knows with a man like Brinkerman, but that is the very least I can do.' He sighed. 'I'm in a very bad predicament. Ferrier would not be so discreet as I, but then he is much younger and he has not had so much experience with mankind.'

CHAPTER 15

Robert Morgan, miserable and apprehensive, came down to breakfast one morning and his mother said with satisfaction, 'We have an invitation to dine with Mr and Mrs Kitchener, Robert.'

'Good.' He looked about the dark, hot dining-room, where the windows were shut as usual against even the slightest breeze or touch of sun. Not that he cared for the sun lately, for he had never experienced such prolonged heat and dryness for so long a time, and there seemed no end to it. Each day the sky became more yellow, as if it were jaundiced, and once or twice a day thick black clouds would gather and darken the earth, but it never rained, and soon the sun would be out again, as fierce as ever. Robert said, 'What did you say, Mother?'

Jane Morgan's grim grey face was simpering. 'I do wish you'd listen, Robert. I merely remarked that Maude Kitchener seems much taken with you.'

Robert thought of Jenny Heger and he felt the usual sick spasm of love and longing and hopelessness. He had not seen her lately. He felt that she would not welcome him on the island at this time, or perhaps never again.

'You haven't touched your toast, Robert,' said Jane. 'I don't know what is wrong with you, lately. You seem so—so concerned with something. I trust everything is going well for you in this little town?'

'Is isn't so little, Mother. Yes, everything is going well for me. I have now taken over all of Jon's practice.' He looked at his cup of cooling coffee but did not lift it. 'I wish he were not going away.'

'He is compelled to,' said Jane Morgan with acid pleasure. Robert looked up, quickly.

'What do you mean by that?'

'Robert, it is town-talk, not that I gossip or listen to gossip. But I do know Mrs Beatrice Offerton quite well now. A very pleasant and comely lady, and so democratic, but yet so appreciative of our better station in Philadelphia. She knows Philadelphia, and we discovered that we have mutual friends. It may surprise you, Robert, that Mrs Offerton has a very low opinion of that detestable man.'

Robert felt that at last he was going to hear something interesting, if he did not press his mother. So he waited. Jane bridled and smirked. 'Indeed,' she said. 'Remember, Robert, that I never liked him, never trusted him and, never believed that he was not guilty of that crime. Mrs Offerton quite agrees with me. She told me, only a week or so ago, or rather, I should say, hinted, that new evidence has arisen proving that he did, indeed, murder his wife.'

Robert smiled, and his mother thought that his smile was extremely odd.

'You don't agree, Robert?'

'Of course not. Doesn't she ever go to Washington with her brother?'

'No.'

'He is there now.' Robert picked up the newspaper by his plate, folded and neat and waiting. Jane had always so placed her father's morning newspaper, and she would never have dreamed, as she did not now, of reading it before 'the gentleman of the house' had first glanced through it. Jane was annoyed that Robert had treated her news so lightly, and then had dismissed it. She studied Robert as he listlessly unfolded the newspaper, and she thought his colour was not so bright as it should be, and that there was a new melancholy on his face. Ah, well, responsibility came hard to the young. He would soon adjust to it. And there was that lovely girl, Maude Kitchener, who was definitely setting her cap for him. Jane started. Robert had suddenly uttered a loud and gleeful exclamation, and he was grinning joyously at the newspaper.

'Dear me, you quite startled me!' said Jane. But Robert was laughing uproariously, and he was handing her the newspaper over the plates, and his blue eyes were dancing.

'Do read, Mother!' he said. 'You will notice that the front-page item of the Hambledon *Daily News*, in a very prominent place, has a Washington date-line. As of yesterday.'

Jane opened her glass-case, put on her glasses, looked at her son suspiciously, then looked at the item he had pointed out to her. It said, 'Senator declares Dr Jonathan Ferrier of Hambledon, Pennsylvania, cleared of all suspicion of his wife's murder last November!'

'Oh!' said Jane, incredulously. She looked at the masthead of the paper, as if suspecting a deception. She peered at the columns below the heading. Her lips, dried and stiff, pursed as if she were about to cry.

'Senator Kenton Campion, senior Senator from the Commonwealth of Pennsylvania, to-day called a conference of reporters in Washington to clear the name of one of his fellow townsmen, Dr Jonathan Ferrier, who was arrested last December for the alleged death of his wife, Mavis Eaton Ferrier, after a criminal abortion. The case will be recalled as having attracted nationwide interest and publicity, due to the prominent position of Dr Ferrier and his wife, and the extraordinary brutality of the crime.

'Because of this, Senator Campion stated to-day, he himself decided that a full investigation must be begun to clear the name of Dr Ferrier. Senator Campion is an old friend of Dr Ferrier and a friend of the family. "Yet this," Senator Campion declared to your reporter, "had no weight in my decision to see justice done and the name of an honourable man and a famous and worthy citizen of my home-town, Hambledon, restored unblemished and honoured once again. Therefore, some months ago I quietly instituted an investigation of my own in behalf of Dr Ferrier, fearless of the truth, and determined only to bring the full facts to public light.

' "The investigation was private and conducted through the most estimable citizens and investigators, professionals in their craft. The investigators were sleepless. Finally they admitted that not a single piece of evidence pointed to Dr Ferrier's guilt.

' "I am *delighted*," said Senator Campion, "by the felicitous conclusion of this sad matter, and the final and complete exoneration of Dr Jonathan Ferrier. The true criminal has not yet been uncovered, but that is not in my hands. I only hope, now, that Dr Ferrier will forgive and forget the unjust and unfair suspicions of his fellow-citizens in Hambledon, and consent to remain in the town and hold his position as a member of the staffs of the two hospitals in Hambledon, and that his unstinted gifts will be as freely given to all of us who live there as they were before his arrest and trial".'

Robert had been watching his mother with a most unfilial malice and enjoyment while she read. Finally she looked up and met Robert's smiling eyes.

She said, 'Oh, that saintly, that charitable, that noble man!'

'Jon, I assume?'

'Robert! I mean Senator Campion. To perjure himself so, to spend so much money, to demean himself, a Senator of his country, to open himself selflessly to gossip and conjecture!'

412

Robert tried to sort this out, and failed. He called for fresh coffee. He appeared rejuvenated. 'I shouldn't suggest, if I were you, Mother, to Mrs Offerton that her brother, the Senator, had "perjured" himself. That's a grave crime. In this case it is a libel.'

Jane was frightened. 'I don't mean it exactly so, Robert! How you always confuse my words! Oh, dear. Now I suppose that frightful man will remain in Hambledon.'

'The unblemished Senator has declared that Jon is blameless and not guilty. What better evidence would you want? A message from Gabriel, in person? I don't know why you call Jon "frightful." You have no reason to think so. You never had. The Senator says not, himself, and if you want to remain on amiable terms with Mrs Offerton you had better declare it abroad that you fully agree with her brother.'

In better humour than he had been for some time Robert went to the offices, where he was greeted by a joyfully tearful Miss Forster, waving her copy of the newspaper at him.

Pennsylvania had been stricken by what the people called 'the yellow drought.' Part of Virginia and Maryland and New York State were also suffering. The newspapers had laid the cause to 'pressure,' which explained nothing, and now they were saying that the underlying cause was 'turbulence' in the Caribbean and 'incipient hurricanes.' One hurricane had already struck the west coast of Florida and another, and a fiercer one, was 'moving up the east coast of the Atlantic.' There were high tides near Cape Hatteras and tides were rapidly rising as far north as Atlantic City. Communities in low-lying sections along the coast were warned of possible danger and asked to remain in readiness for evacuation. No one, of course, took this seriously. The promise of any storm, with rain and resulting coolness, was anticipated with hope.

At sunset Jonathan went out to look at the sky and for the first time he was made uneasy. The enormous sunset, incandescent orange, filled the whole west, and it was sullen and threatening. Even the mountains, dark and rounded, appeared insignificant below that sultry panorama, at once sulphurous and jaundiced, hinting of danger and tempest. The falling sun burned in it, a great red eye, blurred of edge but flaming. The air was pent, hot, still, and the earth was like scorched bread, crumbling and powdery. As Jonathan watched, a great phalanx of black clouds began to boil over the mountains into the vast

413

sea of orange and scarlet, and from them shot blinding bolts of lightning. Then came the long boom of thunder, followed almost immediately by a tremendous flow of wind, and the dry trees rattled with a crisp and tormented sound, and the bronzed grass bent, and a livid shadow ran hastily over the earth.

Jonathan was fascinated by the spectacle, which reflected his stormy thoughts. He walked into his mother's garden, which, as it was on higher land, gave a view of the river. The water was liquid brass and the island stood in it blackly under the sunset and the increasing shadows. Then the rain came, huge plump drops falling with rapid splashing sounds, and the lightning flickered over all the country and the thunder howled hoarsely from the mountains. Jonathan ran inside the house, feeling a primitive exultation, a longing for destruction.

The cook and the maid were already running about, closing windows, struggling with shutters, catching blowing draperies, and moment by moment the house darkened and the storm rushed upon them. Jonathan wanted to shout with exultation, as he helped the two women. He saw their pale and frightened faces in the dimming light. 'Only a storm,' he said, between detonations of thunder.

The wind became heavier and heavier and the rain poured down the windows and gutters and eaves overran, chuckling and gurgling, and the glass rattled in its frames and strong doors shivered. The noise was becoming deafening. It sounded as if dozens of rapid freight trains were roaring overhead. The three in the Ferrier house lighted gas lamps, and the yellow glow and the quiet within only intensified the gigantic tumult outside. It was hard to distinguish between the bellow of the wind and the crash of the thunder. Fiery glares lit up the premature twilight that had fallen on the countryside, immediately followed by explosions of incredible sound. Yet some of the mountains were still outlined against the ochreous light in the west.

Jonathan, standing near a window, could barely see the trees on the lawn, which were bent almost double as if in agony, throwing their leafy arms upwards and about them, contorting themselves in fresh blows of the gale. They twisted, reeled, turned, stretching this way and that, anguished and nebulous shapes in hell. Sometimes they appeared to stagger, shaken to their heart-roots. Then branches were detached with a raging screech and shriek, and saplings were torn up and thrown across the grass. Jonathan went into the lighted kitchen to find his two employees sitting side by side, grasping each other. 'I see we have the hurricane that was promised,' he said. His easy attitude, his lack of fear, reassured them, until another enormous crash of thunder shook the old sturdy house and a flying branch struck a wall like a titanic whip.

'Never saw anything like it,' said the cook.

'It will pass,' said Jonathan. A glare of lightning lit the kitchen, brighter than any artificial light, and the two women saw his face and shrank.

But it did not pass. As the hours went on the storm increased in madness, and the wind quickened and trees fell and the river filled and the sepia land was flooded and ran with water, for the earth could not absorb it. At midnight the storm was worse, if possible. Now, between explosions of thunder, coud be heard the bells and the rumblings of fire-engines, and the sky, in all that rain, turned murky-red here and there. The air did not cool. It became hotter, seemingly, at midnight, especially in the closed house. Jonathan prowled from room to room, listening, exulting, trying to peer through streaming windows. Then a chimney was struck and the two women, in their upper bedrooms, screamed as they heard the tumbling of bricks on the slate roof, and smelled the suddenly pervasive odour of ozone. Jonathan raced up the stairs to the eastern end of the hall and saw the bricks rolling down as the lightning hit them, and he waited for indications of fire. But the house had seen storms before, and the brick walls were impervious. Jonathan called up to the women, 'It's all right. Just a small chimney.'

Another lightning bolt showed him that at least three old giant trees had fallen on the lawn, and the ground was littered with leaves and branches and twigs. The heat was stifling, so Jonathan opened a casement with caution and immediately could smell the sharp electricity in the teeming air.

Jonathan stood at the window and forgot the storm and thought of the island and Jenny alone there with one or two of the servants. It was the first time he had permitted himself to think clearly of Jenny since the day he had left her in the grotto. She had invaded his dreams, but he had known that if he was to 'settle' things for himself in Hambledon he must not let his mind wander to Jenny.

Now he could see the island as he had seen it as a child after such a storm as this, and for the first time since he had left Jenny the rational part of his mind became dominant. He knew he could not see the island from the house now, after midnight, and in the storm, but he went to the east hallway and looked through the window, straining towards the river. He waited for lightning to light up the water, but when it did it only illuminated the rain and made of it a frightful and silvery cataract like a living wall. There seemed hardly a pause between the blasts of thunder. His head was ringing with the constant and infernal noise.

He stood in the quiet room, and it was lit only by lightning and seemed apart from the disaster outside, calm in its lovely furniture, its bevelled Florentine mirrors, its glancing prisms, its pale and panelled walls. There was a faint perfume here of spice and roses and lavender, and the lamplight gleamed on green brocade draperies and polished every piece of glass and silver. He looked about him and thought. 'I shall never know this room again, but I'm afraid I will always remember it.' For the first time an abysmal loneliness came to him, a desolation.

He did not know what to do. To attempt to work in the bursting noise, in this threatened house, was impossible. To try to read, to think, were equally impossible. He began to move through the house, slowly, looking at objects, at vistas, at corners, at hallways, at stairs, as if he were a ghost revisiting a house still dearly beloved. He thought of this, and the mournful delusion was complete, for the light bluish mist was everywhere like a supernatural emanation. He went to his crowded room, heaped with luggage and boxes, and he sat down in a big wing-chair and listened to the storm, which seemed to be lessening. I will think, he said to himself. Instantly, he was asleep, exhausted from the turmoil and hatred and anger and pain of the past days.

When he awoke it was to wan, quiet and watery sunlight, and it was morning. He felt for his watch, then remembered that it was still at the jeweller's, being repaired. He looked at his bedside table and saw that it was half-past nine. He had slept for seven hours. He was cramped and aching, nervously itching. He got up and went to the windows and saw the ruin outside, the dying branches and thick green carpet of tossed leaves, the shattered trees. His mother's gardens were devastated. Every late flower lay flat on the torn earth. The flower-beds, and much of the shrubbery, including the lilac bushes, were smashed. Here, too, trees had fallen, delicate mountain ash, young white birch, a tall blue spruce or two. But, in the quiet sunlight, so frail and uncertain, the birds were singing their last songs of the season, and the sky was a ragged blue. The eye of the storm was over this section of the State, and though the air was clean and washed it held a certain premonition. And everywhere, in low places on the lawns, and in the streets, were deep puddles of sky-blue water.

Beyond the gardens, beyond the lawns and the buildings on the far side, Jonathan could see the river rushing turbulently. It was only his imagination, of course, but it seemed to him that the island, whose western point he could see, had sunk in the water, which had risen very high in the past few hours. Jonathan told himself that it had only now reached its normal level. He wondered if the castle and its trees had been damaged to any extent.

And then, without warning, it seemed incredible that he must leave here without Jenny. He leaned his hands on the sill of the window and let the sense of incredulity wash over him. He knew that he must control himself. There was nothing for Jenny in his coming life, for that life was already dark and bleak and without hope, and he must suffer in it until the end of his life or until—he thought of killing himself. The impulse was so immediate and so urgent that he could not breathe easily for several moments. It came to him it was the only solution. A life without Jenny and his work was not a life at all. It was only a mass of fallen stones, and he could not live in them. He gazed at the island and said aloud, 'Jenny, Jenny.' But he knew himself. He loved Jenny too much to take her and bring her into the ruins with him. For never again would he practise medicine or lift his hand to help any sufferer. He had done with the self-delusion that any man was worth saving, even himself.

What will I do to-day? thought Jonathan. He went outside, and was surprised to find that within an hour the air had turned sultry again, and was still and pent. He was amazingly tired and sluggish. At noon the sky turned brazen again, and the heat was appalling, and puffs of heavy wind were beginning to swirl fallen twigs and leaves in the gutters. At two o'clock the sky was very dark and boiling, and lightning snaked and thunder muttered discontentedly in the mountains. At three the storm broke.

Just as the water began to fall in the semi-darkness Marjorie Ferrier arrived home in a station hack, hurrying towards the house, the driver dashing behind her with her luggage.

Jonathan, after a very light lunch, had felt so weary and numb that he had gone to his room and had fallen across the bed in a state approaching stupefaction. So he did not hear his mother return. He did not hear the preliminary cannonading of the thunder. He slept heavily until five o'clock, to find twilight about him again, and an infernal roaring in the air, and a pressure in the atmosphere like pouring steam. Someone had closed his open window and pulled in the shutters. His face and all of his body was sweating and his mouth was dry and he felt weak and dazed. For a moment he did not know where he was, what was the time of the day, or how it had come about that he was here at all.

He sat up, stunned and blinking, wiping his face, staring about him, listening. Then, after a long time, he got to his feet, bathed in cold water, and sat down to smoke and think. Something had happened to him, but what it was he did not know. He only knew that a sort of quietus had come to him, an area of non-feeling or thinking.

The room steadily darkened as the storm increased but Jonathan did not light his lamps for over an hour. He tried to read, but the storm distracted his very slight attention, and so he confined himself to listening. Abruptly, the rain stopped but the thunder and lightning and wind intensified. There was a knock on his door, then the door opened.

'Jon?' asked Marjorie.

She stood on the theshold, very pale and quiet, her dark hair fluffed about her cheeks as if she had been sleeping. Her mouth was without colour, and her eyes were unusually large and bright in the lamplight, as if she were feverish. She had taken off her travelling suit and wore a calico wrapper printed in grey and blue, and bedroom slippers.

Jonathan sat in his chair and looked silently at his mother and did not move, but the hard muscles sprang out about his mouth and his hands tightened on the arms of his chair. Marjorie gazed at him, and saw that his black brows had met above his eyes and that his eyes were shining like black fire.

'Jon?' she said, again, and moistened her lips. 'I came home, but you were sleeping, and I did not want to disturb you.'

She advanced into the room and the feverish brightness in her eyes had widened, and she began to breathe a little faster as if she were very frightened. She clasped her hands tightly together. She said in a very low voice, 'I know, dear. I read the Philadelphia papers last night. It's all over, Jon, it's all over.'

'Yes,' he said, and stood up. 'It's all over.'

They stared at each other in a silence broken only by the boisterous uproar outside, and the lamps flickered and somewhere a loose shutter crashed against a wall.

'I must talk to you, Jon,' said Marjorie.

'And what will you tell me, Mama? More lies? More sweet evasions? You and old Martin were very clever about the whole thing, weren't you? A giggling little conspiracy of silence.'

A look of deep alarm and suffering ran over Marjorie's face. She sat down near the door as if her last strength had left her. 'Jon,' she whispered. He could see her lips move but could not hear her. So he moved closer so that she would hear everything he said, and his look was so formidable, so totally unknown to her, that she cowered away from him as from a terrible stranger. She could not endure the look on his face and in his eyes.

'Did you believe that swill in the papers?' he asked.

She tried to speak, then coughed and put her trembling hand to her throat. 'I—I felt there was something else,' she said.

'Oh, indeed, Mama, there was a great deal more! But you know a lot of it, don't you? Sufficient to say now that before old Martin died he made out a last affidavit and confession, and he finally told the truth he and you both knew. The truth, Mama.'

She swallowed, and even in her terror her expression questioned him.

'And a lot you didn't know, if that is possible. I won't tell you about that. Perhaps Howard Best will be glad to enlighten you.' His voice, normally harsh, had a sound in it she had never heard before, and her fright rose.

'Where is darling Harald now?' he asked, and loomed over her so urgently that she thought he was about to strike her, and in that abysmal fear she said, quickly, 'He returned yesterday morning, Jon!'

'Oh, yesterday morning.' He looked down at her and smiled. 'So he is there, with Jenny. He has been alone there, with Jenny, for a long time, and you knew what he was from the very beginning, and you did not care in the least for Jenny—

alone with him, a man like him—so long as you could continue to protect him.'

'Oh, Jon, he would never harm Jenny!'

'No more than he harmed Mavis. Is that it?'

'Jon,' she almost groaned, 'if you know everything, as you say, then you must know what Mavis was!'

'She was my wife.'

Marjorie put her hand to her thin cheek as if he had hit her in reality, but she looked up at him and her lips moved soundlessly.

'My wife,' he said. 'A fool, mindless, wanton. Yes, all that, and more. But she was still my wife when he took her, as if she had been a common whore. She was still my wife when she conceived a child by him. She was still my wife when she died of her abortion, and he would still have lived, in all those lies, if it hadn't been for Howard Best.'

Marjorie was too stricken to speak. She could feel the painful lurching of her heart and could hear the thunderous explosions outside and could see, almost blinding her, the steady and fiery lightning.

'My wife,' said Jonathan. 'It was nothing to you that he had done this thing to me, his brother. It was nothing to any of you. It meant even less when I was arrested for a crime that I had never committed, which I could never have brought myself to commit. If I had been hanged for that crime you would still have kept your pretty lips well closed.'

'Oh, Jon!' she cried. 'You cannot believe that! You don't believe that! If there had been any danger to you at all, if you had been convicted, we should have spoken, Martin and I!'

'And that is another lie,' said her son, and his hand lifted as if indeed he would strike her, but now she sat upright and looked him fully in the face. 'It was nothing to you, was it, Mama, that I spent those months in prison, that I spent those weeks in a courtroom before grinning crowds and reporters, and had to listen in silence to the prosecuting attorney accuse me of every stinking thing under the sun, such as murdering my wife and my unborn child? No, it was nothing to you. You let it all happen to me. And when I came back here you still did not speak, either of you, not even to me! You let a whole town malign me and despise me, and drive me out, and call me murderer to my face. Why, Mama?'

Marjorie dropped her head a little. 'We thought you were strong enough to bear it, Jon. We watched and waited and prayed. If there had been any danger— You forget. Harald is also my son, weaker than you, we thought. We thought he— we tried to protect him from you, Jon, and you from knowing. Can't you understand? Won't you try to understand? It was really for you that I kept silent.' Her head bowed lower. 'You are both my sons. By not speaking I thought—I thought I'd saved you both.'

He laughed abruptly. 'And you never dreamed that the truth would come out, did you? It still would not have come out if a very nice little plot hadn't been laid against me by Kent Campion, and various others, including the man who aborted Mavis, and killed her. Suppose that plot had succeeded—tell me, Mama, would you have spoken then?'

She could only stare at him speechlessly, growing paler and paler. She put her hand tightly against her breast.

'A plot to send me to prison, probably for life, for alleged abortions,' said Jonathan. 'That would have been comparatively easy, with my first trial still fresh in people's minds, and the conviction that I was guilty of killing Mavis. Mavis has been the precipitant in this whole vicious mess, from the very beginning, but you helped very efficiently, Mama, very efficiently, and I congratulate you. While I was in prison, no doubt you were very pleased with yourself.'

She got to her feet, staggering a little. 'Jon! You can't believe that! You don't believe it!'

He said, 'There is just one thing I want to know, and tell me the truth this time.' His rage was rising, and was more than Marjorie could stand. 'Did you know that he had seduced Mavis before you heard them both arranging for Mavis to be aborted?'

'Yes,' she said. 'I knew. But I couldn't say anything to Harald, or to Mavis. I was afraid that it would—it would cause something, and that you would know. Always, I was trying to shield you, Jon, to protect you from knowing. I thought it would end, and it had ended, and it would all be over and no one would be hurt.'

He said very gently, 'You were quite successful in a way. No one was hurt, except that Mavis died, and I was tried for murder, and my name blackened all over the country. Harald went his way and everything was lovely, and he lived on Myrtle's money and tried to get Jenny to marry him, and— by God, now I know that all the time he was laughing in my face!'

'Jon, won't you try to believe that it was all done to protect you?'

'And to protect smiling, laughing Harald?'

'Yes! Harald too. He too is my son.'

He looked about the room, and his eye lit on something. 'You can protect him no longer. I am going to find him and I am going to kill him.' He walked across the room to one of his bags and picked up his riding crop which he had thrown there the last time he had used it. Marjorie saw and cried out, and when he was near her again she grasped his arm and looked up into his face, that appalling stranger's face.

'Jon! You must be out of your mind!'

'I think I am,' he said. 'But that doesn't matter, does it? You can thank yourself for that, Mama.'

He flung her off and she fell heavily to her knees. She put up her hands to him like one pleading for her life. 'Jon, think of Jenny!'

'I am the only one who has been thinking of Jenny. Not you. Not Harald. Just myself.'

'Oh, Jon, you believed all those lies about her, you believed them all, and now you can talk about "thinking" about her!'

He paused and looked down into her suddenly flooded eyes. 'I've been doing a lot of thinking, Mama. Who began those lies about Jenny? I made a few inquiries, since you were away. I traced at least two back to Harald. Ah, I see that you knew that, too.'

Marjorie put her hand over her face as she knelt.

'And you let that go on about Jenny, and about me, and you kept your serene silence, and never said a word in defence of anybody!'

He made to step about her and she reached up and grasped the crop in his hand with both of hers. 'Jon, you have a life to live, a future before you, you and Jenny, here or anywhere else. But one reckless thing—Jon, in the Name of God, try to be reasonable, try to think!'

He laughed again and wrenched the crop from her hands. 'I've been thinking, Mama. I've been thinking of thousands of things.'

She tried to grasp his ankle, his leg, but he was quicker than she, and then she saw his face, black and murderous in the flickering lightning, and she quietly lay down on the floor and closed her eyes.

Jonathan ran down the stairs in the thunderous dusk, and

flung open the door and was immediately outside, buffeted by the gale, almost blinded by the lightning. But no rain was falling. He ran through the dark and deserted streets, splashing through deep puddles, sending spray all about him. No lamps were lit. The city lay cowering under the exploding illumination of the storm, and Jonathan was all alone, racing like a madman through the streets, bounding across flooded kerbs, flying towards the river and the little dock. He never remembered that wild flight, for he was conscious of nothing but his savage hunger for vengeance.

The little dock, he found, had been washed away, but one boat was pulled up on the bank. He slid down the bank in a welter of wet and slimy mud and almost fell into the river. He scrambled back up, and got into the boat, panting, drenched, smeared. His feet sank into deep water and he had to turn the boat over on its side to empty it. He found the oars, slippery and cold, and then the rain began again, brightened by lightning, torn by the wind. He pushed the boat into the river, and the river caught it and almost wrenched it from him, for the water was high and roaring and rushing and swirling. He finally struggled into the boat and sat down, and he did not notice that his hands were bleeding, for the boat spun out into the river and swung into circles and fled out into the night.

It was a long time before he could control it, and now he was sweating and shivering in the fresh rain, and the river flared into violence under the lightning and then became a silent and hidden thing in the dark, tumultous as if alive and filled with fury. He fought both the river and the boat. Looking over his shoulder he could see the dusky bulk of the island behind him, lighted swiftly and regularly, its trees tossing, and it was like a struggling ship about to founder. His foot felt for the crop he had thrown into the boat, he clenched his teeth and fought to gain the island in all that wildness and bellowing storm.

The rain dashed into his face, and he gritted his teeth and bent body and oars against the foaming water, and the boat heaved up and down between the waves and fought with the swift current. Strange thoughts ran over his mind, like dreams, like convolutions of nightmares. And then the boat grated on stones, and he had reached the island.

He sat there, huddled and soaking, gasping and trying to get his breath, his bloody hands sliding on the oars. Then he stood up, and jumped to the slippery bank, and pulled the boat up on it and threw the oars beside it. He reached for his crop, fumbling in the flaming dark, and turned and climbed the flooded path. When he had reached the top, his clothing torn by the lashing bushes and trees, he had to halt to stop the labouring of his heart. Then he saw that the island was deep in the river, and the walls of it were hardly a kerb above the swirling water. He stood and looked at it, as it appeared and disappeared in the lightning, and he thought, It will be almost covered by morning. He went on, falling, staggering, fighting, towards the faint light in the distance.

Harald Ferrier was sitting in his study, reading, for no other room in the castle attracted him, nor could he stand any other room and especially not the one he had shared with his dead wife. He wondered how much more the water would rise and if the walls could keep it from the higher land. During the lull in the later afternoon he had gone out to inspect the damage, and had almost been flung headlong several times by the gale. The damage was great. Some of the finest trees had been blown down and battered, and the gardens were completely destroyed. None of the windows in the castle had been broken, because they were all mullioned and deep-set and narrow. But all the walks had disappeared and ran like brooks, and there was water at least a foot deep around the walls of the castle itself, where the earth could not absorb it.

There had been storms over the valley, and the State before, but he could not recall one as bad as this. He congratulated himself he had thought to return yesterday, before it broke, otherwise he would have had to stay in Hambledon, and possibly in his father's house. He winced at the thought. He had never liked that house, had never felt that he was welcome there, but only endured, a stranger tolerated because he was harmless and bothered no one and never interfered, and because he had learned to smile when he was the most miserable and lonely and forgotten. Even though he visited his mother occasionally, he still felt like a guest and never believed that she had ever liked him in spite of her gentle ways and kindness. She had never cared for anyone but his brother, he thought, and his father had never cared for anyone but his older son. It was a beautiful house, but Harald had not found it beautiful and never had thought of it as home.

As he was not vengeful by nature, or reckless, or bitter, he had not felt resentful all those years. He had made his own life. By temperament he was easy and adaptable and tolerant. It would have made him happy to have been loved and not overlooked, but as that happiness had been denied him he had eventually accepted the fact. Now all he desired was Jenny and peace and his painting, and travel and ease and laughter and good wine and food. The world was a brutal place and he had retreated from it, never questioning it, never arguing with it, never fighting it, as Jonathan had always done from earliest childhood. Harald accepted what the world permitted him to accept, and he had no quarrel with it, for life was as it was, and only a fool 'kicked against the pricks.' If he reached for something and the world of men denied it to him, he would search for something else he could have without a struggle. He had reached for women, and for Mavis, but never had pressed them, never had urged them, never had seduced them. They saw his hand and they took it, laughing, and he laughed with them. He had desired only the prettiest women, for he hated flaws and mediocrity, and his affairs had been gay if not very passionate. He told himself that he was—happily—incapable of strong attachments and emotion.

With the exception of Jenny Heger. As no woman he had ever wanted had rejected him, he felt that eventually Jenny would be 'sensible' and accept him, too, in marriage and in a carefree and joyous future. She had hardly spoken to him since that ridiculous encounter in the grotto, but she was not angry with him. She seemed to be suffering and brooding. In time, he would laugh her out of her shyness and her moods and they would take, together, what they would be permitted to take.

The studio was lighted by oil-lamps and they flickered as gusts of wind found their way even around the locked and secure windows. Harald listened to the storm and it seemed to him that it was getting much worse, and he saw the lightning through the windows and shrank, involuntarily, at some of the more boisterous thunderclaps. He tried to take his mind off the storm, and looked with satisfaction at some of his canvases standing against the walls, and his easel, with a fresh canvas waiting. He would do another portrait of Jenny. He would sell this one, as he could have sold the first many times over. He thought of Jenny and stood up and slowly strolled about the studio. Jenny was in the library downstairs, where she always 'lurked,' and he hesitated. He wondered if she was frightened now, and then he decided she was not. She had not been frightened yesterday or last night. He had tried to talk with her at meals, but though she had answered him she gave him the impression that she was hardly aware of him. Only once had she spoken voluntarily to him and that was to ask him when he would take her to their lawyers and conclude their contract.

'Patience, Jenny,' he had said. 'Besides, it is my information that the lawyer most concerned is not in town just now.'

Suddenly he wanted to see Jenny, and it was an aching desire in him. He had the excuse of the storm, and so he lightly ran downstairs—he did everything lightly—and went to the library and pushed open the carved wooden door. There was Jenny, crouched under a lamp, reading, and she looked up at him blankly when he entered.

'I thought perhaps you were afraid,' he said with his genial smile.

'Of what?'

'Well, the storm. It does sound awful, doesn't it?'

She frowned, and listened, then nodded.

'You know there has been a lot of damage?' said Harald, still standing.

'I know. But it can be planted again.' Jenny paused. 'My father's rose-beds have gone.'

'I'm sorry, Jenny.'

She smiled briefly. 'I am, too.'

There was another pause, and then they heard a banging at the hall door, and a shout. They stared at each other, disbelieving. The servants had already retired to their rooms, and Harald said, 'Who in God's name can that be?' He went to the hall and walked down its echoing marble floor and pulled back the bolts on the doors. It swung in on him violently, and he cried out, and Jenny came into the hall also.

If they had been incredulous before they were stunned into speechlessness now, as a battered, drenched, torn and muddy figure staggered into the hall, pouring with water, creating instant puddles on the shining floor, and it was grasping a crop. Its black eyes were quite mad and staring, and all its hair was spiked and upright like a drowned bush.

'For God's sake,' said Harald, and stepped back. 'Jon!'

Jenny stood behind him, frowning and staring, throwing back her hair, her mouth opening in amazement. The light of the tall and flickering lamps, shaped like torches, which decorated the medieval hall along the walls, bent before the wind that roared through the open door. Jonathan looked at his brother and saw no one else, and he reached behind him and closed the door, and then leaned against it, breathing stertoriously. Harald looked at him, still incredulous, and then when he saw Jonathan's face more clearly he stepped back and his ruddy brows drew together over his eyes and much of his high colour disappeared.

'What?' he murmured. He said, with a kind of desperate hurry, 'Is there something wrong with Mother?'

Jonathan did not answer. He lifted the hand that held the crop and wiped his face with the back of it. He was a ghastly colour, and his chest rose and sank with his convulsed breathing. He still leaned against the door, and dark streams ran from his clothing. He had begun to tremble. The thunder detonated against the stone walls of the castle with a hollow roaring.

Jenny stood looking at Jonathan, still hardly believing that it was he. Then she too saw his face, and she gasped, and she saw the crop in his hand. She glanced swiftly at Harald, who was as paralysed as herself.

Then Jonathan said in a hoarse and unrecognisable voice, 'While you were away, I found out the truth.' His dark face was contorted and twisted and his eyes reflected the uncontrolled wrath in him. 'About you and Mavis.'

Harald said something faintly, but dared not look away from his brother. He said to Jenny, 'Jenny, go away, please.'

'No,' said Jenny. She had come closer to Harald and stood almost beside him.

Jonathan did not even see her. He was standing upright now, and he seemed to fill the hall with a dangerous presence, not human, but more like the storm outside.

'You let her die all alone,' said Jonathan. 'You helped her die. You arranged the abortion with Brinkerman. It was your child she was carrying. You killed her.'

Jenny cried out and put her hands to her cheeks.

'Jon,' said Harald. His eyes left Jonathan for an instant, searching for some weapon in the hall. He had an impulse to run and lock a door behind him, but he knew that Jonathan, even in his present state, would be faster and he feared a blow on the back of his head.

'Tell me,' said Jonathan.

'I don't know what you're talking about,' said Harald.

427

'I'm talking about Mavis,' said Jonathan. 'My wife, Mavis. She died because of you. While she was still my wife. It must have been quite a joke to you, laughing all these months to my face and behind my back.'

'No,' said Harald. He had to fight to keep his shaking knees from bending and throwing him to the floor. 'You must be out of your mind.'

Jonathan laughed, throwing back his head, and they saw the shine of his teeth in the wavering lamplight. 'I am,' he said. 'You did that to me. You let me be accused of a crime, and you let me rot away in prison and you let me be tried—for something you did. When I was acquitted, that must have been the worst day of your cursed life!'

'I don't . . .' Harald began.

'Don't lie,' said Jonathan. 'You've lied all your worthless, stupid, useless life, while you danced and sang and smeared canvases. Do you know why I'm here now? I've come to kill you.'

'Jon,' said Jenny, and she stepped between the brothers and faced Jonathan.

He reached out his dripping arm and swept her aside as if she were nothing, and she fell against the stone wall. But she recovered instantly and flew between them again.

'Jon!' she shouted. 'I'm here, Jon!'

He looked at her. 'Yes, Jenny, I see you. Jenny, did you know that he told those lies about you in town, the dirty lies that made you a byword?'

'I don't care!' she still shouted, 'Nothing matters at all, except you and me, Jon!'

'And nothing matters to me but what I came for,' he said. He saw that Harald was backing softly away and he lunged upon him and slashed him across the face with his crop. Harald staggered back and fell on the stairway, and flung up his arms to protect himself. Jenny caught Jonathan's arm with all her strength and clung to it though he tried to throw her off. Her teeth were bared and her dress blew out.

'Help! Help!' Harald screamed from behind his protecting arms. 'Help! Help!' He heard the struggle near him and dared not look. His cries echoed back from the depths of the dark staircase with a frenzied sound. He started to scramble up the stairs, backwards, and then Jonathan was on him again and his left hand was at his throat and the crop, wrenched from Jenny, was raised over his head.

'Don't kill me!' Harald cried, and he flung up his hand and caught the murderous wrist above him and fought to throw off the hand that was clutching at his throat. 'My God, don't kill me! They'll really hang you this time!'

Jenny had recovered again herself. She managed to seize the hand with the crop once more, and now in her fearful strength she brought it to her mouth and bit it. She was like a young tiger, and now Jonathan saw her again, in crazed wonder.

'Let him alone, let him alone!' said Jenny. She tore at the hand that was strangling Harald and Jonathan was so amazed that he released his brother and Harald scrambled up a few stairs. The crop had opened his left cheek and the deep cut was running with blood. He was weak with terror. He had never encountered violence like this before and he knew that it was not sane, and that he would surely die if someone did not help him.

Jonathan was trying to throw Jenny aside, but she clung to him, facing him, her arms about his neck. They fought soundlessly and Jenny was strong as she had never been strong before. She knew that she must not release Jonathan, or he would be gone from her forever. She groaned over and over, trying to reach him, 'Jon, Jon, my darling, my darling. Don't, for my sake, Jon. Jon, come back, Jon, look at me.'

He had caught her hair and pulled her face from his shoulder and her white throat stretched in the lamplight and her head arched back from him. She closed her eyes but still clung to his upper arms, and the lower part of her body was pressed strongly against his. She was crying hopelessly, and repeating his name. She would not let him go, and now he could only look at that vulnerable throat and see her tears.

'Jenny,' he said, and he released her hair and her head fell on his shoulder again and she was sobbing and trembling against him.

'For my sake,' she said, 'for my sake.'

He was spent. He felt as though he would fall and die right there at Jenny's feet. He looked at his quaking brother, bleeding freely, and crouched on the stairway in a huddle of absolute dread and horror, overpowered less by his fear of death than by the total violence he had seen and encountered.

'All right, Jenny,' said Jonathan in an exhausted voice. 'Don't cry like that, Jenny. It's all right, my love, all right.'

'Oh, Jon,' she said, and she raised her head and kissed him fiercely on the mouth.

Harald had pulled himself to his feet with the banister, and was wiping his face with his handkerchief. The sight of blood had always frightened him, and he looked at his own blood and leaned against the banister in a half faint. Jonathan stared up at him from behind Jenny's shoulder.

'You deserve to die,' Jonathan said. 'You deserve to die like the dog you are.'

Harald's collapse had indeed been less from fear than from what he had seen in his brother's eyes. A man who could not compel himself to be moderate and civilised at all times was not a man to him, but a wild beast. So he looked at Jonathan and hatred flashed between the brothers as bare and deadly as a thrown knife.

'I may deserve to die, as you say,' said Harald, in a shaking voice, 'but you are not far from that condition yourself. You must be insane.' He straightened a little on the staircase, not caring any longer for his blood. 'Listen to me, Jon, and if you do it will probably be the first time in your life that you ever listened to anyone.

'Mavis wasn't your wife. She told me that you had rejected her only a year or so after you were married, and put her out of your life and out of your bed. Mavis was Mavis. You knew her as well as I did, and perhaps better. She was silly and greedy and stupid, but she was a woman. You had no right to marry her.' Harald paused, to let a fresh thunderbolt die away, and as they waited they again looked at each other with that hatred.

'You never cared about her,' said Harald. He was livid. 'You only had lust for her. If you'd loved her you'd have been patient and kind. If she wasn't what you thought she was, whose fault was that? Not hers. She never tried to deceive you; she didn't have the brains for that, and if you hadn't been as stupid as she was you'd have known it. The fault was all yours.'

'Go on,' said Jonathan.

Harald's face became grim for the first time in his life. 'I didn't seek Mavis out. She sought me. I'd never have—touched —her, if she had really been your wife. She told me about you, how you had threatened to kill her, the names you had called her, disgusting names. She was sincere, then. There wasn't any real love between us. She never intended to divorce you and marry me, and I never wanted to marry her. It was a sort of—consolation—to Mavis.' He wiped his face again
430

and again sickened when he saw his blood. 'I wasn't the only man.'

'I know,' said Jonathan. Now his arm was about Jenny.

'Then what?' asked Harald, with a weary wave of his hand.

'You let me rot in prison. You let me be tried, and defamed. You let me live the miserable life I've led for nearly a year. And all you had to do was to speak.' Jonathan's voice was rough with his exhaustion and his passionate rage.

'My God,' said Harald. 'Do you honestly think I'd have let you be executed? If you think so, then you must really be insane.'

'Then why didn't you speak in the beginning?'

Harald smiled drearily. 'Because I felt the great Jonathan Ferrier was a stronger man than I was, a less weak man, a man of more resistance. I felt you could bear what you had to bear, and it would mean very little to you. I was sure you wouldn't be convicted, and you were not. So, I let it all go, thinking it was a nine-days' wonder, and would all be forgotten. I hoped you would go away. You hated the town so much, and there were larger fields for you. So what did it matter if I didn't tell anyone the truth? Who was hurt so much? Who was ruined?'

'I was,' said Jonathan.

Now Harald regarded him with astonishment. 'You!' he exclaimed. 'It all meant nothing to you, or very little.'

Jonathan saw that he actually believed this.

'It meant my whole life,' he said. 'The town was everything to me. I gave it everything I had to give.'

'Then you aren't the man I thought you were,' said Harald. He leaned his head against the wall of the staircase and gulped for air. 'You were always our parents' favourite. They lived only for you. I was nothing. So I came to believe that you were indeed superior to me, a stronger man than I was, a more able man, a more resolute and powerful man. But they were just as deceived as I was, and for the first time I'm sorry for them. You gave the town everything you had to give! That's the most maudlin thing I ever heard anyone say, and I'm glad our father is dead, for even he would have been ashamed to hear that.'

He looked at Jonathan below him with even more astonishment. 'Why, you haven't any courage at all! You are only brave, and even an animal can be brave. For the past year I've suspected as much, watching you, but I told myself it was only my imagination. There were times when you were gloomy and looked desperate. I thought it was because your pride had been hurt, for God's sake. And all the time the damned town had broken your heart!' Harald laughed with faint weariness. 'A town like Hambledon, which doesn't deserve to have even a horse doctor!'

Jonathan was silent. He looked into Jenny's fearful eyes and he pressed her to him reassuringly. His exhaustion was growing. He felt utterly drained and broken.

'I wanted you to go away,' said Harald. 'You won't believe me, but I thought it would be best for you, for you should have left years ago. Mavis was right, there. And then I wanted you to leave, because I was afraid you'd find out the truth some day and you'd do exactly what you tried to do to-night. One of us had to go. I couldn't: I was bound to this damned island.'

Jenny spoke now. 'But you can leave, as you said you would.'

Harald looked down at her and smiled. 'Jenny, Jenny,' he said. 'I will go. With you.'

She widened her eyes at him like a child. 'But I never said that. Jon is the only man for me, and he's the only one I've ever wanted.'

Harald's face darkened with pain. 'Jenny, you've seen what he's like. To-night. Do you think, when he's in a rage, that he'd spare you and not hate you? Your life with him would be a hell, and not a refined one at that. Thwart him, defy him, deny him, and he'll be at your throat—as he was at mine.'

'It doesn't matter,' said Jenny. 'I can't help it.'

Harald said, 'I won't let you go with him, Jenny, to-night or any other time. For your sake.'

He had not been brave before, but he was brave for Jenny now. He said to his brother, 'You know what you're like, even better than I do. If you have any feeling for Jenny, let her go.'

He said to Jenny, 'You have heard what he has said. What have you to say, Jenny?'

'You are impossible,' said the girl, and laid her cheek against his shoulder. 'You are the most terrible person I've ever known. If I marry you, I don't think you will ever forgive me.'

Jonathan said, 'Probably not. And then again, possibly yes.'

Harald turned his face away and sat down heavily on the stairs. He folded his arms on his knees and dropped his ruddy

432

head upon them in an attitude of complete surrender and prostration. Jonathan said to Jenny, 'Now find a cloak and shawl, I am taking you home to my mother to-night. The island is unsafe ; the water's rising.' He touched her cheek. 'I think, after all, I really came for you.'

'Yes. Of course,' she said, and went to the stairway. She paused as she reached Harald, and hesitated. She spoke to the back of his head. 'Come away with us, Harald.' Then she ran up the stairs and disappeared into the darkness, to prepare to leave and to advise the servants to leave also.

Jonathan spoke to his brother's bowed head. 'We've both lived in a sort of stupid confusion. I always thought my mother preferred you and I hated both of you for it. I always knew what my father was. If you will remember, I warned you not to take him seriously.'

'I remember,' said Harald in a muffled voice.

'I don't think,' said Jonathan, 'that the Ferrier men have been overly intelligent.'

'Speak for yourself, Jon,' said Harald from the depths of his folded arms.

For the first time Jonathan smiled, and it was a sour smile. He looked at the crop in his hand, then threw it across the hall where it clanged against a suit of armour, rocked it, then fell to the floor.

'I don't think I would have killed you,' Jonathan said to his brother.

Harald raised his head and Jonathan saw that he looked ravaged and depleted. 'Oh,' said Harald, 'I'm sure you would have, if it hadn't been for Jenny.' He touched his cheek and winced at the sight of blood. 'Or would you prefer to call this a love pat?'

Jonathan sat down in an armorial chair, and now there was no sound in the hall but the roaring of wind and water and thunder, as they waited for Jenny. They did not look or speak to each other again. When the lightning flashed it showed only their averted faces.

CHAPTER 16

Robert Morgan came into Marjorie Ferrier's bedroom where she was being attended by two sprightly young nurses from St Hilda's. Marjorie's eyes, even while she lay on the pillows under her, watched only the door, and when Robert came in they questioned him alertly though she could not speak. He said, taking the weak and almost pulseless wrist. 'The river rescue boat went to the island for them, and I've just heard. They are landing on this side. I told you. You had no need to worry, Mrs Ferrier.'

Her white lips formed one word, 'Both?'

He nodded. 'Three, and the two servants. The rescuers signalled five people, so I assume that is all.'

Marjorie's eyes filled with tears, and Robert pressed her wrist and watched her face.

He had been called by the maid who had found Marjorie unconscious on the floor of Jonathan's room. The girl had heard the stormy altercation, then the crash of the front door, and then the silence filled only with the sound of thunder. She had discreetly gone to investigate, and then had hysterically reported to the cook who had immediately called Robert at his house, for he had not gone to the office that day and had been able to visit but one hospital. Robert saw that Marjorie was too ill to be moved, that her ailing heart had suffered an almost fatal shock, and that she would probably die of it very soon. It was Robert who had sent for Father McNulty, and for the nurses, and the priest was now in the morning-room listening anxiously to the storm and waiting news of the people on the island.

It was to Robert that Marjorie had whispered of Jonathan's frenzied rush from the house and what he had threatened to do to his brother, and he saw that if she were not relieved very soon her death could not be delayed. He had done all he could do. He had alerted, through the harbour police, the men who had been busy through twenty-four hours of storm rescuing people from low-lying sections along the river, and from two islands upstream. The police, though harried and sleepless, had agreed to call Robert when the river boat signalled the rescue of those on the island. They had also agreed to furnish the rescued with transportation through the flooding night to the Ferrier house, or any other destination.

'They will be here soon,' said Robert, who was red-eyed from exhaustion. He had worked on the injured and battered for hours after midnight, and it was now approaching midnight again.

Marjorie was too spent to speak. She could only thank Robert with her eyes. She let her lids drop and her head rolled weakly on the pillow. Robert kept his fingers lightly on her pulse, counting and frowning. If she died before her sons arrived, then it would be all Jonathan's fault, and it was all he deserved. Oh, of course the damned fool had his grievances, and they were all severe and grave and deserved retribution, and only a clod would deny the truth. But to have shocked his mother in this fashion, and to have told her what he intended to do, was unpardonable.

Marjorie appeared to sleep. A little clock chimed on the bedside table, a faery chime. They should be here soon. Robert went down to the morning-room.

The young priest was as exhausted as he, for he, too, had been working sleeplessly, consoling the stricken, helping to search for the missing. He looked up as Robert entered, hopefully yet fearfully.

Robert said, 'She's holding her own, but that is all I can say. I wish they'd arrive soon.'

The priest sighed. 'So do I. That Jonathan! I pity him very much. If his mother dies without him seeing her then he will never forgive himself. He can be much harsher on himself than his worst enemy, as he has proved over and over this past year. If his mother dies—he will really be destructive of himself.'

'I can almost wish he would,' said Robert, thinking of the dying woman upstairs. The priest smiled at him sadly, his golden eyes bright in the lamplight.

'No, you don't, Doctor. If Jon is a merciless enemy, he is also a merciful friend, and he has been kind to you as you've admitted, yourself. I heard that, because he liked you from the beginning, he sold you his practice at half of what he was offered by others. Only Jon would do a thing like that, and yet he has the reputation of being a very shrewd man with a dollar.'

Robert raised his eyebrows in scepticism. He sat down. Then he said, after some minutes of thought, 'Perhaps you are right, Father. I saw how he treated many of his patients. The children and the old loved him. He was harsh with malingerers, and joked roughly with others. But the sick respected and trusted him, and I suppose that is most important.'

'It is most important, Doctor. Jon knows how to treat the sick. He never learned how to treat the well. The helpless touch his heart. He is ruthless with his peers.'

They listened to the storm. 'I think it is lessening,' said Robert. He sighed. He wondered how Jonathan would have responded to his own situation: loving a woman who did not want him and who rejected him for someone else. He would probably butcher the man and take the woman by force. I wouldn't, thought Robert, put it beyond him. He thought of Jenny, and sagged wearily in his chair. If she married Jonathan her life was certain to be lively, but hardly restful. But Jenny was a girl of character. She would learn, perhaps, how to outshout Jonathan, and how to control him. Robert had his serious doubts, and his longing for Jenny made him feel weak and bereft.

'I came to Hambledon only a few months before Jon's wife died,' said Father McNulty. 'I never knew the younger Mrs Ferrier, but I saw her about the town in her carriage. She was what the older men, and the poets, call 'a dream of fair women.' I thought how suitable in appearance at any rate, she seemed for Jon, gay and effervescent and beautiful and sparkling. One never knows. If anyone had seemed less threatened by tragedy, it was young Mrs Ferrier.'

'He is going to marry Jenny,' said Robert in a flat tone.

The priest nodded. 'So his mother informed me quite a few weeks ago, before he knew it himself.' He looked keenly at Robert. 'What pleasant people those Kitcheners are, to be sure. And a lovely young lady, Miss Kitchener.'

'Isn't she?' said Robert with indifference. This was the night he and his mother were supposed to dine with the Kitcheners, but the storm had intervened. He suddenly saw Maude's pretty eyes and auburn curls and heard her shy sweet voice. How unlike Jenny she was. Jenny was a storm of blue and black and white, for all her apparent diffidence and restraint. Jenny was strong, but Maude was not strong at all, and suddenly Robert's tender young heart felt gentle towards her. The strong could be formidable and frightening.

The priest cleared his throat. He said, 'I heard to-night, at St Hilda's, that old Mr Witherby died in bed last night.'

'So did I,' said Robert. He smiled suddenly. 'Jon will probably send the widow his felicitations with a basket of the most expensive flowers.'

'Yes. That would be just like him. Jonas must have been a frightful old man, from what I have heard and have known myself.'

'Corrupt,' said Robert. 'He had the appearance of a saint.'

'Whereas Jon looks like a romantic version of the Devil. Did I hear a door open?'

Robert and the priest stood up, went along the corridor to the hall where the chandelier was softly lighted. Three people were already there, drenched and dripping: Jenny, Jonathan and Harald Ferrier, and all were drained and stunned in appearance, and Harald's face was oozing blood from a very bad long wound on his cheek. They stared speechlessly at the priest and Robert, and Jenny took the shawl from her head and aimlessly shook it, and the men shook water from their hands and bare heads.

'What?' asked Jonathan, looking from one to the other.

'Mrs Ferrier,' said Robert. He could not help it, but with Jonathan's own sharp ruthlessness he said, 'She is dying. She's had a bad heart attack.'

He watched Jonathan's black eyes deepen and narrow, and Harald uttered an exclamation and Jenny gave a little cry.

'Something,' said Robert, looking into Jonathan's face intently, 'gave her a severe shock. She was found on the floor of a room upstairs by one of your servants, who called me, about three or more hours ago. I've done what I could for her, but I am afraid that she won't live until morning.'

Jenny gave again a muffled cry and started towards the stairway, but Jonathan caught her by the wrist, and held her. 'Never mind, Jenny,' he said in a peremptory voice. He turned to the priest. 'This is true?'

'I am afraid so, Jon,' said Father McNulty with pity.

'You did this to her!' said Harald to his brother. 'You killed her!' His wound had begun to bleed again, and a few drops fell down over his chin.

'Shut up,' said Jonathan, and he turned to Harald and his expression was so daunting that Harald flinched. Then he turned to Robert. 'Quick! What have you done for her?'

Robert told him. Jonathan listened acutely. He said, 'That is good. And now I will see her myself.'

'I think,' said Robert, 'that she wants to see both her sons, and as soon as possible. She wants to be sure you are—safe. Both of you.' He met Jonathan's eyes straightly. 'And I will take you to her. Perhaps it might be best, though, if you both looked less like derelicts. We don't want her to have another shock, as though you had been dredged up from the bottom of the river.'

'Where, Doctor, we'd now all be if it weren't for you,' said Harald, and he was almost his gallant self again. 'The police told us, and the river men.'

'We'll save our lovely expressions of gratitude for later,' said Jonathan, and he dropped Jenny's wrist as abruptly as he had taken it and was now leaping up the stairway. Harald watched him go and his face was not pleasant. 'Very masterful, my brother, isn't he?' he murmured. 'Full of civilised conduct.'

Jenny sat down on the French velvet sofa against the wall, and put her hands over her face, and Robert wanted to go to her and console her. But Harald was looking at her with naked love and misery, and he said, 'Jenny, dear. Let us have some hope, if we can. You're exhausted, and I think you should go to one of the guest rooms and lie down.'

'We're having coffee and some refreshments in the morning-room,' said Robert, and thought to himself, So here is another one of us! 'Mrs Ferrier is resting. There isn't any immediate emergency, and perhaps you, Mr Ferrier, and Miss Jenny, ought to change clothing and then join us.'

'I'll have to put on one of his damned funeral suits,' said Harald, and tried to make his voice light. He still looked at Jenny. 'We saw that the water was rising too high on the island to delay to pack any luggage. Jenny? Perhaps one of the maids can find something for you to wear.'

The girl was shivering. She dropped her hands and they saw her white and tearless face and her grief. 'Jon will never forgive himself,' she said.

'I hope not,' said Harald. He said to Robert, 'I won't go near him even to ask for some clothing. Would you be kind enough, Doctor?'

Robert now understood the situation. He regarded Harald's wounded cheek. 'That's a bad cut you have there, Mr Ferrier. Let us find a bathroom where I can take care of it at once.' He hesitated. 'A fall, perhaps?'

Jenny stared at Harald icily but Harald said almost gaily, 'No, indeed. A gentle reminder from my brother that here-
438

after I must keep hands off his property. It seems he resented my kindness to his dead wife.'

Jenny said, in her strong clear voice, 'How dare you say that! You knew why he did it!'

Harald gave her a little bow. 'But thanks to you, Jenny, he stopped just short of killing me.' He winked at Robert. 'Call it a small brotherly altercation, if you will.'

Father McNulty said, 'Mr Ferrier, I know you are trying to make light of the situation, but Jon's conduct was hardly— hardly—'

'Civilised,' said Harald.

Jenny said, 'You are deliberately giving Dr Morgan and Father McNulty the wrong impression, Harald! You know how unspeakable your own conduct has been!'

'Appalling, we Ferriers,' said Harald, smiling down into her eyes. 'I should like you to keep that in mind, Jenny.'

'I certainly will,' said Jenny. Then she stood up and walked quickly to the stairway and went upstairs, leaving a pool of dirty river water behind her.

The three men were silent until they heard Jenny in the upper hall, then Harald said, 'If I weren't determined to leave this contemptible little town very soon I'd enjoy the spectacle of this coming marriage between Jenny and my brother. Jenny is no Mavis. In many ways she is a good match for Jon, and I don't mean that pleasantly.'

'He can be murderous,' said Robert, full of apprehension. 'And Miss Jenny is still a young girl and he is much older. But let us find that bathroom. I have my bag in the morning-room and if you will wait a moment I will get it.'

Harald was alone with the priest. He had begun to mop at his face with his wet handkerchief and the priest gave him his own. 'Thank you, Father,' said Harald, with his charming courtesy. 'I'm sorry that you've seen the Ferriers at a disadvantage.'

'I've been seeing them that way for some time,' said the priest, with a faint smile. 'But not at Mass. Or in the Confessional.'

'Oh, we're beyond absolution, I assure you, Father. Quite beyond absolution.'

'Only God knows that, not you.'

Harald smiled at him brightly. Robert came into the hall but stood at the foot of the staircase, and Harald joined him. They went upstairs together, and, with a sigh, the priest went back into the morning-room. The storm was dying. The last cannonading of thunder was echoing from the mountains, and the rain was only a whisper now and the wind only occasionally shook the windows and doors.

They met outside Marjorie's shut door, Jonathan and Harald in dark silk dressing-gowns, and Jenny wrapped in a cotton wrapper that had been found for her. She looked like a tall child with her hair down her back, still wet but gleaming, and the wrapper showed her ankles and part of her legs. She was unconscious of her dishevelled appearance and only looked in mute earnestness at Robert. He said to her gently, 'I will take them in to see Mrs Ferrier, Jenny, and perhaps a little later you can go in.'

Jenny became mutinous, but Jonathan said, 'She needs to be disturbed as little as possible, Jenny, so kindly go downstairs and wait for us.'

Robert opened the door softly and they entered the quiet lamplit room. Marjorie was awake again, and she looked at her sons and her mouth trembled. 'Cain and Abel, Mrs Ferrier,' said Robert, 'but I don't know which is which.'

Jonathan went at once to the bed and took his mother's wrist. What he felt alarmed him and made a line of sweat come out below his black hair. Robert brought his bag to him and Jonathan took out the stethoscope with hands that were very steady. He bent over his mother and listened to her heart, and one of her long fine hands raised itself slowly and rested on his head. But she looked at Harald and smiled tenderly, though her lips winced when she saw the evidences of his wound.

'Adrenalin,' said Jonathan, and Robert prepared the injection and the nurses clustered at the foot of the bed. Then Jonathan did something Robert would not have dared to attempt. He drove the needle into his mother's breast, and she uttered the faintest of gasps, and her eyes shut spasmodically, and a grey shadow ran over her spent face.

Jonathan sat on the edge of the bed. He looked, for the first time, at his mother's face, and held her wrist, and once his eyes shut as if he prayed. Robert doubted it. Harald came to the other side of the bed and took his mother's other hand, and was shocked at the coldness and dampness of it and for the first time since he had been a child he wanted to weep. His own hand was warm. He held Marjorie's hand strongly and comfortingly. He thought that he imagined it, but when he felt a dim returning pressure again he knew he had not. Now tears did come into his eyes, and he slowly knelt beside the bed and then let his forehead rest against it.

'Morphine,' said Jonathan. 'Fifteen milligrammes.' His voice was calm and dispassionate. He looked at no one but his mother.

'I gave her the same just hours ago,' said Robert.

Jonathan repeated the order in the same tone and Robert, flushing at the affront, obeyed. Marjorie had begun to breathe rapidly and again Jonathan listened to her heart, and his colour became more and more deathly. He accepted the needle from Robert without a glance, and thrust it quickly into her limp arm. He said to the nurses, 'Hot-water bottles.'

The nurses scurried for the bottles. Jonathan said nothing, and there was only that murmur in the room now and Marjorie's frantic breathing and the sound of the wind at the long windows.

The nurses returned with the hot bottles in towels, and Jonathan flung aside the blanket and Robert saw her feet, marble white and cold. Jonathan put the bottles against them, then covered his mother's long and slender body again, and resumed his watching. Marjorie began to sigh, over and over, deeply, and move her head.

Then Jonathan spoke. 'Mother? You are going to be all right. Do you hear me, dear? We are here with you. I won't leave you, Mother.'

'Oh, Jon,' she whispered, from the depths of her pain. 'Oh, Harald.'

She removed her wrist from Jonathan's grasp, took his hand, and her other fingers rested on Harald's bent head. Harald said in a muffled voice, 'Forgive me, mother.'

'Oh, my dear,' she said.

'I'm sorry,' said Jonathan. 'Believe me, dear, I'm sorry.'

She smiled then, a beautiful and peaceful smile and opened her eyes and they were clear and tender.

'I'm very happy,' she said. 'I haven't been this happy for years.'

There was the slightest tinge of colour in her mouth now. She closed her eyes and slept.

Robert said, 'You both don't deserve such a mother,' and he turned and walked out of the room.

Then the eyes of the brothers met, tentative, cold, wary. Jon-

athan said, 'I hope you have a scar for the rest of your life.'
But he smiled. It hardly lifted the grim corners of his mouth.

'And I hope that Jenny murders you,' said Harald.

It was midnight when Jonathan went downstairs to the morning-room. Harald and Robert Morgan and Jenny were with Marjorie. Jonathan said to Father McNulty, 'I think there is some reason to hope. Her heart is stronger and she is asleep. I will know better in a few hours. If she rallies, as I think she may, she will have to be in bed for months.'

He let himself drop in a chair and the priest poured a cup of hot coffee for him. Jonathan took it. He seemed to have grown much older and to be on the point of collapsing.

'But it will be a miracle,' he said, as if to himself.

'God frequently grants miracles,' said the priest.

Jonathan's thick black eyebrows twitched.

'Such as saving all of you,' the priest added. 'And preventing a fratricidal murder.'

'Which I still regret,' said Jonathan.

The room was warm and bright and the wind had dropped to a soft mutter.

'I suppose,' said the priest, 'that Hambledon will not lose your talents after all.'

'I haven't thought about it.'

'Of course you have. What will you do about Dr Morgan?'

'When the time comes I will consider it.'

'May I offer you my congratulations on your coming marriage?'

Jonathan looked up quickly. 'Jenny?'

'Who else?'

'Time enough for that.'

'Certainly, I'm very sorry for the young lady.'

Jonathan gave a slight laugh. 'I think, perhaps, in about a week or so.'

They drank in silence. Then the priest said, 'Don't regard what I have to say as a homily. I'm very tired, and I must go home. So, I will be brief. You have always maintained to me that the opinions of others are a matter of total indifference to you. But, on the contrary, you have been exaggeratedly sensitive to them. You did not have the fortitude to defy local opinion, at least in your mind. A man of courage would not have been so extremely disturbed by the hostility he met here,

442

after the trial. He would have understood human nature. He would not have planned to leave the town. He would have presented a calm face to friend and enemy alike, treating both with reason, secure in himself and in his innocence. And finally the town would have come to its senses.'

He waited. Jonathan said nothing. So the priest went on. 'It is ridiculous to demand that others understand us, and know the truth about us. How is that possible? We can only do the best we can, in steady patience, and with inner reserves, knowing that we don't understand others, either.

'Jon, you need to cultivate that serenity and detachment of mind that, while keeping you kindly in touch with your fellow man, will make you less vulnerable to him, and his opinion of you. You have entangled yourself with others entirely too much, both in love and in hate, and that is childish and immature. A sensible man is moderate in all things, and particularly in his dealings with those about him. That takes courage. And that will bring peace of mind.'

Jonathan bent his head, and the priest was encouraged for, he knew that Jonathan was thinking. Then Jonathan said, 'It isn't in my nature to be lukewarm.'

'But you can practise outward restraint and balance and firmness.'

'And get ulcers?'

'And keep out of trouble. Mankind isn't very brave and strong, Jon. We are timid, brave only when in a pack. Individually, man is lonely and lost and weak. He is frightened at the need for courage. It threatens what little security he possesses. And how insecure is man, God help him! He suspects that there are forces outside his little life which are tremendous and terrifying, so he establishes a ritual of magical cant to placate the terror, just as his earlier ancestors did.' He stood up, and looked down gravely at Jonathan. 'A man who trusts in man, who believes man is all, who thinks that man is capable of pulling himself up by his own bootstraps and attaining virtue and perfection all by himself, is to be pitied. His ignorance, his pathetic vanity, must make the angels weep. Worse still, his fellow man will inevitably teach him many rude and painful lessons. So he will abandon his fellow man, or he will grow to hate and despise him. Both are evil.'

Jonathan said, 'Somewhere in the nest of your homily, Frank, there may be an egg of truth. I will give it thought.'

'Give it plenty of thought, Jon,' said the priest.

During the next few days the Ferrier house was filled with flowers and gifts for Marjorie, and letters of happy congratulation to Jonathan because, as they said, 'Our dear Senator, Kenton Campion, has proved, beyond the shadow of a doubt, that you were innocent, as the majority of us believed from the beginning. Don't desert us now. We need you. We've always needed you.'

Only a week before Jonathan would have read those letters with rage and disgust and would have replied to the writers with stinging remarks and contempt. But now he laughed, almost indulgently, after his first angry reactions. 'They believe Campion,' he said to some friends. 'Campion who was always a liar and a mountebank, and they never believed me, though I don't lie. Somewhere there is some irony in the situation, but I never particularly liked the Hogarthian jokes of man or God. That is because, perhaps, I never appreciated slapstick, or burlesque.'

'Now, Jon,' said Louis Hedler. ' "All's well that ends well".'

'Nothing ends well,' said Jonathan. 'I'm a confirmed pessimist.' He eyed Louis with hard and unforgiving cynicism. 'Let me congratulate you, Louis, on a broad comedy. I don't enjoy the spectacle of clowns as advocates. Truth, to me, should have a certain dignity, or am I being naïve again?'

'It depends on the point of view,' said Louis Hedler. 'By the way, am I right in believing that you will accept the post of chief of surgery at St Hilda's?'

'Were you serious?'

'Of course, my boy. Though I am a little apprehensive concerning how you will treat the other surgeons. With somewhat less brutality, I hope?'

'Not if they are in the wrong. The patient comes first.'

'Commendable. The patient must always come first. But it is not always necessary to make a Roman holiday of a surgeon's honest error, is it?'

'Not if he is usually a competent man. But I want no hacks on the staff, Louis.'

Louis sighed. 'You would be surprised how very competent those "hacks" are, sometimes, and how wrong the scientific fellas. But use your judgement, Jon, though I do hope there will be no public burnings.'

Hambledon emotionally forgave Jonathan for the crimes

he had never committed, and so forgave itself, and was prepared to grasp him to its bosom. It took all Louis Hedler's diplomacy to prevent Jonathan from explosive retorts at times, and all Father McNulty's admonitions. 'Humour, humour, Jon,' said the priest. 'If a man lacks a sense of proportion, and inner humour, he is a barbarian. And he must always have some pity, even if he is the wronged one.'

'Compromises!' said Jonathan.

'Life is not nearly as simple as you have always believed, Jon,' said the priest. 'It requires a great deal of courage and fortitude.'

Marjorie was now past the danger point. Harald had diplomatically removed himself from his father's house and had gone to the Quaker Hotel. He could not endure seeing Jenny with his brother. He could not return to the island, for even the lower floor of the castle had been filled with mud and water. His lawyers agreed that his absence from the island, in this emergency, could not be construed as violating the terms of his dead wife's will.

Jenny had told Jonathan of the contract between her and his brother. Jonathan had been pressing her for immediate marriage. Jenny had remarked, firmly, that 'it was less than a year, and would not be decorous.' Then Jonathan, smiling, had said, 'Dear child, you are still a minor, and won't be twenty-one until December. You can't sign any contract at all that would be valid. Didn't anyone tell you? But if you marry me soon, I will be appointed your legal guardian and can make contracts in your name for you.'

Jenny had retorted, 'It is you, Jon, who needs a guardian, not I.'

'Well? What is your decision? Are we going to free Harald from Hambledon and send him on his merry way, or are we going to imprison him until December, when you will come of age? There is another thing. I find it somewhat arduous to be under the same roof with you, my love, and not in your bed. Or will you be kind enough to leave your door open some night soon?'

Jenny blushed. 'Very well. I will marry you on 30th September.' She hesitated. 'What will people think?'

'The hell with what they think, Jenny. We have our own lives to live.'

Jenny assisted the nurses in caring for Marjorie. Marjorie said, 'Dear Jenny, now I will have a daughter soon. I have

445

always felt that you were my daughter. I used to watch you when you were a child and I envied your mother. Do have daughters, Jenny. They are so satisfactory to a mother. While no man ever understood any woman, women do have glimpses of the interior workings of men, and mothers and daughters can laugh together at the unpredictable and irrational doings of husbands and sons and fathers. But we must never let our laughter be obvious. Men are such fragile and sensitive creatures.'

'And so very dangerous,' said Jenny. 'Sometimes I think I shouldn't marry at all.'

'Somebody has to marry them,' said Marjorie. 'Otherwise they'd revert fast enough to the cave.'

Jenny had suggested to Jonathan that the island be a museum, as he had once proposed, with his brutal jesting, that it should be. 'And it will be supported by the Heger money,' said Jenny. 'There are so many treasures there, and it will be a landmark for those people who can never hope to see an authentic castle in Europe. We will add to the treasures, and have guards and guides.' The island no longer had significance for her, nor was it a harbour now as once it was, and she often wondered why that was so.

Jonathan prudently estimated the cost. 'I think a large wing for tuberculosis at St Hilda's, and another wing for the study of cancer at the Friends', would be more practical.'

'I have money enough for it all,' said Jenny, with a large gesture.

'After what Harald takes?'

'Jon, don't be mercenary. We can do it all. What is money for but to be used?'

'Jenny, when you look at me with such innocence you almost convince me.'

'People need medicine for their souls as well as for their bodies, Jon.'

He kissed her ardently. 'Perhaps you will minister to my soul to-night, Jenny?'

'On 30th September,' she said. 'Not a day sooner. I think we should inform Father McNulty.'

Jonathan had long consultations with Robert Morgan. 'I will buy back my practice, Bob. You can then be my associate, if you can bear staying in Hambledon.'

'I don't know,' said young Robert. 'I will sell the practice back to you as you obviously intend to stay here.' His face was wretched.

Jonathan said, 'Bob, you are young, and, as I've quoted to you often enough, "Men have died and worms have eaten them—"'

'"But not for love." Yes, that's a favourite saying of yours, isn't it, and I don't believe you mean a word of it. You went thundering over to that island to kill your brother, I've heard, but if Jenny hadn't been there you wouldn't have gone mad and practically swum over there in the hurricane. You'd have lain in wait for him some place, and perhaps smeared him over the landscape—before a good audience. No doubt to teach others a lesson.'

Jonathan chuckled. 'Perhaps. Still, the story, spread by a few "good" friends, hasn't done my reputation much harm. On the contrary.'

'The populace does love a swashbuckler,' said Robert. 'You are out of date.'

'Oh, I don't know about that,' said Jonathan. 'People are still romantic. When a nation stops being romantic it stops being a nation, or a force in the world. By the way, I hear Maude Kitchener has set her cap for you.'

'You hear too many things,' said Robert, and thought of Jenny, and wondered how he could endure living in Hambledon knowing she was the wife of another man. If Jenny had married him he would have contrived to send his mother back to Philadelphia and have rescued his house, his beautiful house. It was almost worth marrying for, to save its beauty.

'Women are very sinister,' said Jonathan. 'You might be wise to run.'

Robert was annoyed. 'I am not running,' he said. 'Nor are you—any more, I hope. Well, I will stay and be your associate, if you will have me. I only hope we will not end up, some day, murdering each other.'

It was a cool September evening and Father McNulty was in the Confessional at St Leo's Church. He had been there for over two hours, listening with sad compassion to the endless repetition of human error and human sin and human fallibility and human arrogance. He was young, but he felt as old as death and life. He was also getting hungry and cramped.

Someone entered the Confessional and knelt down and the

priest waited. The penitent was silent. Then Father McNulty saw a familiar long dark head through the grille, and then, with growing joy and astonishment, he heard a familiar voice.

'Bless me, Father, for I have sinned—'

The priest sighed. 'And about time,' he said, and prepared to listen. He was sure that the penitent thought he had a remarkable story to tell, but it was as old as man, as old as the very stars.